THE HAWK AND THE DOVE

may the spirits always guide you!

Tom Baker

T O M   B A K E R

PAGE PUBLISHING, INC.
New York, NY

First originally published by Page Publishing, Inc. 2018

ISBN 978-1-64350-509-1 (Paperback)
ISBN 978-1-64350-510-7 (Digital)

Printed in the United States of America

INTRODUCTION

The Hawk and Dove is a series of tales about war and the tremendous human struggle for peace down through the ages. Come sail with the spirits of warriors past, spirits that are bound together by love and challenged by hate. Travel through eleven centuries with these people, these warriors, as they seek a seemingly simple thing—lasting peace. Listen to the spirits as they teach the armed warrior and the warrior for peace that their quests are similar. The great truth being that it takes more courage to stand empty-handed before a foe in pursuit of peace than it does to stand with weapons in hand in pursuit of war. The spirits can teach you this if you will only listen.

The warrior stands bravely in the shield wall facing cold steel while the peace seeker stands defiantly in front of hate with no weapons. Their hearts are linked by their courage and their goals the same, to live and love in peace. Who knows the price of combat better than the warrior? Who will say "No more" when everyone else is crying for blood? Follow the spirits and listen to their tales.

ACKNOWLEDGEMENTS

I started writing this novel over ten years ago in an attempt to tell a story about warriors and how they feel about war, about peace, about love, and all the interactions therein. As a combat veteran, I have seen and done many of the actions in this novel, but it is the feelings, the regrets, and the demons that I want my readers to experience.

I knew very little about writing when I started this novel, but I am married to a "peace hippie" who happens to teach writing and rhetoric. She encouraged me with ways to start writing and trust the process. I started to believe that writing didn't mean getting it right the first, or the second, or even the third time.

My friend Alan Wray, who is also a writer and taught writing and rhetoric, helped and challenged me in revising my writing. I remember his first comment after reading the first complete draft of *The Hawk and the Dove*. "Tom," he asked, "how much more do you want to work on this novel?" Aside from wanting to tell an age-old story about war and the search for peace, I wanted—and needed—to allow my own personal experience in combat guide me and maybe, just maybe, heal me. So, I continued the work.

Many of the thoughts and feelings of the characters in the novel are mine or Marsha Lee's or my buddies from Vietnam. The novel has allowed me to face the demons of my combat experiences, and for us to express our desires for peace. A story of bravery, love, hate, and war poured forth.

A healing was beginning.

CHAPTER 1

The Norsemen

Then the Lord said unto me, "Out of the North an evil shall break forth on all inhabitants of the land."

—Jeremiah 1:14

Dark, angry clouds boiled menacingly above three rough-hued dragon ships creeping along a rugged shoreline chocked with large gray boulders and ancient timber. Jagged streaks of lightning flashed in the indigo sky, and the ensuing rumble shook the earth like the end of time. Another dazzling bolt of charged energy crashed earthward and the snarled, wind-twisted top of a giant mountain oak burst into flames. As the splintered wood popped and hissed, the old tree presented itself as a torch and became its own death pyre.

A huge bear of a man stood like a statue at the stern of the last longboat.

"An omen," he spoke in gruff Danish, staring where the lightning had struck. The comment was directed at no one in particular, for he was alone at the rear of the dragon, but his eyes drifted toward the heavens. More rumblings filled the night sky. He shifted his gaze to watch stoically as sparks from the burning tree joined those from a dozen burning huts, and together, they rushed into the dark void above him.

Leaping flames tinted the water of the bay a wine color and painted the three ships silver and gold as they slowly stole away like thieves in the night. The devastated village of Torosay, on the wind-swept isle of Mull, lay smoldering in their wake. More lightning flashed, and the skies opened up. Torrents of cold rain descended as if the Celtic gods shed tears of sorrow at the sight revealed by Thor's great bolts.

* * * * *

The year was 897, and the world lay deep in the womb of the Dark Ages. It would be another five hundred years before the birth of the Renaissance and the age of Enlightenment. This was a time when, in the minds of many, the old gods still walked the earth, their mystic powers holding sway over mortal men. The light of Christianity had only begun to flicker in the darkness, and words such as *honor*, *mercy*, and *fairness* were uttered only in the tales of the bards.

This rugged mountain land, extending two hundred miles north of Hadrian's Wall, had seen many hard winters since Britanius Augustus led the last remaining Roman troops from this island of Britannia. They had marched down a dusty cobblestoned road toward their waiting ships, their red and white pennants embold-ened by a winged pilum. Large flags, carried proudly by stern-faced legionnaires, flew high over the troops of the mighty XX legion as they marched through the main street of Bath in solemn farewell. The Roman legions, of which the XX (or Valeria Victrix) was one of the oldest and most heralded, had arrived to conquer these isles two hundred years before the birth of Christ. These same mighty legions had fought across Northern Europe for years before being sent to Britannia, the farthest frontier of the Roman Empire. Here, after nearly seven hundred years of hard fighting, they had con-quered most of the island's peoples but not all. Their most recent campaign in the western highlands was an unsuccessful attempt to defeat Dougall mac Lomhoirlle, founder of the mac Dougall clan. It failed for many reasons, but mainly because the legions were short of men because troops were being pulled out and sent home. Rome, the golden city, was in chaos. Invaders from the north threatened her very existence, and the legions were sorely needed there.

Caesar was abandoning the island's people to the ravagers from the frozen north or anyone else who had the cold resolve and sharp weapons to rule them.

* * * * *

A solitary hawk sailed high overhead, its wings occasionally dipping ever so slightly as it rode the blustery winds, which chased the low-hanging clouds past sharp-faced cliffs like silvery hair blowing in the breeze. Through the mist, the hawk's shrill cry echoed across the white-capped waters. This hawk was not concerned about the history of the land far below its wings, nor was it worried about the three dragon ships that sliced through the dark-greenish waters. The ships, whose sails were full of the cold North Sea wind and whose hulls were full of fierce-eyed Norsemen, had just turned the rocky point off the isle of Kerrera. They bore straight for a large village that lay partly shrouded in the fog. The stout wind driving the sails of the dragon ships blew ceaselessly along the coastline of the Gaels. And although it was only midautumn, its biting breath carried the promise of a hard winter. The hawk cried out again as it watched the dark swirling waters of Oban Bay spray a frothy mist that drifted about like a fading dream.

The scene unfolding below the big red-tailed hawk had been repeated many times during the three hundred years since the Roman legions had sailed from this land of Picts and Scotti. It would not end this day.

The Scotti were a Celtic tribe that had come to this part of Britannia from Ireland a thousand years before the Romans arrived. They had lived relatively peacefully with the local inhabitants, the Picts, another Celtic tribe, for hundreds of years. The Picts, so named by the Romans for the paint they wore on their faces during battle, were a fierce people, but they were also farmers, fishermen, and herders. They were sorely unprepared for the savagery of the marauding

Vikings or Norsemen or Danes—the invaders were called by many names.

These Northmen came from the frigid north of Europe, the Scandinavian coastal region, and the windswept islands of Orkney and Shetland. They raided at will along the coast of this area, which lay three hard days of riding north of Hadrian's Wall—a twenty-foot-high, twelve-foot-wide barrier with interspaced barracks and training areas for its defenders. It had been erected across the entire width of Britannia by the Roman legions under the command of Publius Hadrian about a hundred years after the birth of Christ. Similar to the Great Wall of China, its intended purpose was to keep the savage tribes from the north at bay. Like the Great Wall, it only worked when there were troops posted on it. The legions, even when they were still in Britannia, were hard-pressed to help the coastal villages this far north of the wall. Now, with the legions gone, these villages had become easy prey for the Norsemen.

The hawk flew high enough over the ships that it appeared no larger than a sparrow to the few human eyes that cared to look up at it, but its lonesome cry cast an eerie spell over the vast harbor. The Norsemen's ominous-looking ships, with spruce stems carved into large dragon heads that towered twenty feet above the oarsmen, seemed to glide through the rough seas like hungry serpents searching for prey.

Large-framed and rough-featured Norsemen, twenty-two in each ship, pulled hard on their thick oars that extended fifteen feet out of the slots carved in the sides of the ships and seemed to reach effortlessly into the cold waters.

The rowers sat on sturdy spruce benches, four inches thick and six feet long. Four rowers to a bench, five benches aligned each side of the ship. A drummer sat on a narrow bench near the stem. When the winds abandoned the sails or blew in the wrong direction, his job was to keep the rowers pulling together. He beat a small hollowed-out log, tightly covered on both ends with goatskin, in a steady rhythm as they strained to drive the beast through the swish and surge of waves battering the hulls.

In the center of each ship stood a single twenty-five-foot pine mast that held a square-cut sail made of either wool or linen. Long spruce riggings were attached at the top and bottom with hoist lines to raise and lower them. Each sail bore the war band's special emblem, a large bear painted brown like the beasts that roamed the dark spruce forests of Orkney.

The ship commander, who oftentimes used a trusted substitute to steer the ship, usually stood at the stern where he could either observe or personally steer the vessel by means of a rudder or steering oar. This device was a curved piece of laminated oak attached, by means of a swivel, to the aft beam or rudderpost at the rear of the ship. The tail of the rudder extended into the water at least five feet below the keel; the strong oak handle curved on deck and was moved against the swivel to steer the ship. The rudder man, or coxswain as he was later called, was also the navigator when the commander was not available. He was usually chosen not only for his strength, which was needed to handle the big rudder, but also for his knowledge of the seas and ability to navigate by the North Star.

Alongside each rowing bench, on the outside of the ship, hung the mighty battle shields, which were placed there for storage since they were large and cumbersome and took up too much room inside the ship. They also were used as a visual symbol of power meant to strike fear into the hearts of the enemy. The Viking shield was made of seasoned white oak strips covered with leather and bronze or iron. Each man decorated his shield with marks used to record the number of enemies he had killed in battle, some covered with as many as fifty kill marks.

The shiplap framing, a crude but effective method of construction that allowed for expansion and stress, groaned as the ship's bow plowed through the rough surf while the oars dipped and pulled. The hawk cried once more and then swooped out of the cold damp mist that lay over the bay. With its great wings flush to its sides, the hawk tore after a covey of doves that fluttered and cooed above the upper balcony of the newly constructed monastery. This gray-stone and split-log structure stood forty feet high at the cliff's edge and consisted of a main chapel area, sleeping quarters for a dozen monks, a small kitchen area, and library. The front entrance sat two hundred feet beneath the crag of Dunolleigh.

A mile out in the bay, two men stood on the gunwale of the lead dragon ship and peered through the dense fog. Their muscular legs, clothed in buckskin britches, were slightly bent for balance in the choppy seas. The ships had just rounded the rocky point local fishermen called the wet grave, a series of rocky shoals that extended out from the island of Kerrera and created havoc with all but the most wary of the local fishing boats. Leeward of the island, the wind had died back and blew from the east. The big sails, which only a few minutes before had been rattling in the stiff breeze sounding like old women cackling around a winter's fire, were hauled down.

A harsh shout from the older of the two men standing on the gunwale had initiated the sails being struck and the long oars being shoved out to begin a row toward shore. Both men held tightly to the main line that led to the mast as they closely inspected the rough stitching that bound together the thick wool in the sails. It was a long way back to Balfour on Orkney, and they had no extra sail.

The older of the two's defining traits were his barrel chest, hard eyes, and a jagged reddish scar that cut its way across his left cheek, finally disappearing under the huge leather helmet atop his shaggy head, tuffs of reddish-blond hair sticking out all around. The younger man was just as tall, a full head over six feet, but with less girth. His clean-shaven face, bright eyes, and dirty-blond hair chopped square at his muscular shoulders made him stand out from the rest of the crew. He wore his hair pulled back and tied with a leather thong. This Viking's eyes were the color of the sky on a cold winter's day, and they stared out from a face not yet scarred by battle. Both men wore leather trousers, tanned a mottled black, with rough side stitching. The pant legs were tucked into the top of their high boots made from the skins of young seals, waterproof and warm. Over woolen tunics, they wore shirts of light mail, which some called hauberks, made from iron ringlets tightly stitched and overlapping. Over the shirts, they wore cloaks made of bearskin as a symbol of manhood. The poorer men or those of less stature wore cloaks made of deer hides.

The larger, older man was Thorma Morestrong of Orkney, an island that lay several days sailing to the north and was a springboard for the other Viking war bands that lived there. The younger warrior was his son, Thomle. Neither man had the traditional tattoos adorning their arms and necks that most of the other members of the war band had, but both wore gold arm rings, for these were a symbol of power and wealth. This was only Thomle's second raid, and at seventeen years of age, he was trying hard not to let his father see how nervous he was. The rumbling in the young warrior's stomach and the slight tremble in his hand, though, were obvious to his father.

Thorma, a battle-hardened warrior of many raids and many kills, possessed a shield that held over thirty marks. He had gone on his first raid with his father and brother when he was only sixteen. The first village they attacked was small; the ensuing battle brief and one-sided. It was here that Thorma had killed his first man (or boy, as it were), but his father wasn't satisfied. The elder Morestrong had beaten his son that day and on several occasions during his first few raids because he seemed to lack the killer instinct that the old man and his eldest son, Olaf, possessed. After three hard years of raiding and fighting with his enemy as well as his brutal father, Thorma decided to leave home before either he or his father died by the other's hand. He was nineteen. As painful and embarrassing as his father's beatings were, as he grew larger, they became more embarrassing than painful. But there was another reason to leave Orkney. He wanted to see what lay beyond the usual route that his father always took. Since they were small children, he and his friend Erikson the Red had dreamed of sailing away toward the sunset. The time had finally come.

After years of dreaming, the two began to work on a plan to leave. During the stormy spring of his nineteenth year, when the dragon ships couldn't sail because of the twenty-foot waves in the Sea of Ireland, Thorma and Erikson went to work. They were able to persuade a few other young men of the village to help them rebuild a dragon ship that had lain abandoned outside Balfour for several years. The work had been very difficult for the untrained boys, but after much effort, not to mention ridicule from the old boat builders, the ship was ready to carry them to sea.

The young crew members said goodbye to their families—everyone, that is, except Thorma. His mother had died the year before from the fever, and his father could not have cared less that he was leaving. Without so much as a look back, Thorma and his crew sailed and rowed west by northwest, toward the sunset. They sailed out past the great ice fields toward a land the Danes had settled over a hundred years before. The Danes called it Vinland in those days for the succulent grapes that grew wild there.

Unfortunately for the young adventurers, the spring storms stayed late in the northern part of the Great Waters, and they were horrific. The inexperienced crew sailed for many tough days and nights in the open water. They struggled with constant leaks, ripped sails, and broken spar lines; they sailed until their food and fresh water were nearly gone, their dreams of becoming rich heroes fading like their food supply. With spirits as low and dark as the clouds that hovered all about them in the dreary sky, the young Norsemen had almost given up hope. But they had neither the food nor the strength to turn around, so they just plowed on day after hungry day.

One rainy summer evening, the days ever so long this far north, the sun fought to burn through the gloomy gray clouds before it sank into the western waters. The crew was exhausted, sleeping with their heads resting on the oars that lay across their laps. The northwest winds pushed the weary band into a bay, deep and wide, sheltered on both sides by high ridges and tall evergreens. Thorma and Erikson stood at the bow of the dragon ship, their pale gaunt faces expressionless, hollow eyes peering into the mist. Suddenly their hearts quickened with a slender ray of hope as they watched a small village come into view along a boulder-strewn shore. The village seemed to creep out of the fog like a wandering spirit. They rubbed their tired eyes. Yes, it was a village. Which one didn't really matter. Relief began to wash over their faces when they realized that it was indeed a Danish village. The two looked skyward and thanked the gods whom they thought had abandoned them and then awakened the rest of the crew.

Thick grayish smoke curled lazily skyward from stout rock chimneys attached to crude huts built from split logs chinked with mud and thatch. The village was nestled near a rushing stream that spilled its grayish colored water into the sea at the head of the inlet. Thorma, his voice dry, raspy, and not very reassuring, shouted, "Vinland." His forlorn crew struggled out from under the heavy oars and peered at the land they had dreamed of for so many days. To the north of the village, a bold stream drained a fog-shrouded cove that climbed and soon disappeared into the mist beneath a rugged snow-covered peak. A group of about fifty curious men and women dressed in buckskin milled about on the rocky shore, watching as the strangers struck their tattered sails and rowed cautiously toward the shore. A passel of naked children ran among a pack of scrawny dogs, all eager to greet the newcomers.

The village they had sailed into was called Gokstad, one of four that hugged the coast of the big island. It lay on the southeast shore of Vinland, later to be called Greenland, and all its inhabitants were anxious to learn about the newcomers' journey. Any news from back in Orkney and the rest of the world was welcomed.

Thorma and his young friends were treated well by the folks in Gokstad. Even the few native tribes that hunted and fished the woods around Gokstad were friendly, so the newcomers stayed for several months. But a long, brutally cold winter, the worst in years, as well as yet another late spring proved too much for the new arrivals. Most were ready to leave by the coming of summer, even Thorma, who during the long cold winter had taken a pretty blonde-haired girl for his bride. The girl's name was Ulrika Roskilde. She was sixteen, and Thorma thought her the most beautiful girl he had ever seen. But even she couldn't stop him from longing for more adventure and warmer waters. He found the settled life of Vinland far too tame for his adventurous soul. The hunting was good and the people friendly, but he wanted and needed more. The girl's father, Geir Roskilde, the village chief who was quite wealthy by their standards, pleaded many time with Thorma to stay.

"I have no sons, Thorma, and I'm getting too old to make them." The elder Roskilde chuckled though his face was stern. Leaning forward, he threw a small log onto the evening fire before continuing.

"You could soon become the village chief," he grunted. "People like you and will listen to you."

"I don't want to be the damn chief," growled Thorma, remembering all the troubles his father had had back at Balfour on Orkney. "I want to see what lies to the south," he added gruffly and rose from his seat on a large driftwood chunk. He stared into the fire for several minutes before finally tossing a stick into the low flames, spinning and walking away toward his hut, his gait fast and determined.

The young warrior grew increasingly restless as the days became longer. He knew there were riches to be had in the south, his own riches, and he had heard many amazing tales of a land called Britannia. Oftentimes at night, he stood alone on the gravely beach and stared southward; Britannia seemed to be calling him.

Two days after the midsummer solstice festival, Thorma gathered his young wife, a few kindred spirits from his crew, as well as several men from the village, and sailed south to warmer waters. Erikson the Red, Thorma's friend and an adventurous soul himself, stayed behind this time; but in years to come, he would head farther west into the great unknown and into history. For it was he, some say, who first discovered the Americas.

* * * * *

Eagerly but somewhat apprehensively, Thomle stared out from his position at the bow of the dragon. The shoreline was rapidly approaching. He shifted his battle gear, removing his heavy leather helmet to make sure its iron cross straps still tightly held the ringlets that protected his neck and ears. He placed the helmet near the gunwale, close to where his shield hung on an iron hook on the outside of the ship. He reached for his shield, testing the strength of the two straps. One he slid his arm through, and it wrapped around his forearm; the other he gripped in his hand. Without these straps, the shield was almost useless. Thorma noticed his son's nervous movements but said nothing. Without wanting to, he thought back to his first raids and shuddered. *His father*—he stopped himself with an angry shake of his head. That was a lifetime ago, and he was not like his father.

Sea mist blew back past the dragonhead as the ship's bow drove through the swells, the cold mist dripping from their faces and splashing onto their shirts. Thomle's mail hauberk had been a gift from his father just before they left on these raids, and he brushed needlessly at the water while gazing across the harbor at the village that had yet to spot the dragon ships. A large stone-and-timber monastery stood like a sentinel above a cliff on the east side of the village.

"Father, what is that large structure near the cliff? Is it their castle?"

"No, son. That building is a house for their new god." Thorma laughed. "Soon we will show these Christians that our god of war, Odin, is much stronger and smarter. Their god will not save them from the wrath of Odin," he continued as they looked shore-ward. "Remember"—he leaned closer to his son and nearly whispered—"these foolish people hide their gold in that building, and the only guards are usually a dozen or so chanting monks."

Thorma roared with laughter and slapped his son on the back. He continued to chuckle as he rested a large hand on the boy's shoulder and gazed at the village, the Viking war drums pounding their rhythm. Sinew and muscle strained as the rowers grunted in their efforts. Despite the lack of a strong wind, the seas were rough and held no direction. The ship's planking groaned from the pounding.

As the Viking ships approached, another sound began echoing down from the hills. It was deep-throated and carried easily on the cold air. It was the sound of a half-dozen bullhorns being blown high up in the pastures above the village. All the men knew the sound well. For several minutes, Thorma kept his gaze on the village as the bullhorns called their warning. He knew that it was only a matter of time before they would be spotted, but he had hoped they would have gotten a little closer to shore before that occurred.

They stood listening to the horns when yet another sound began to echo overhead. High above them, a lone hawk sailed in and out of the mist, crying fiercely just before it tore from its lofty pattern and sliced through the air toward a covey of fluttering doves near the rocky shore.

"We will be like that hawk to these people," roared Olaf as he pointed a large greasy finger at the hawk that cut through the air as if shot from Odin's bow. All eyes turned toward the hawk as it struck a dove and feathers flew in all directions.

Olaf "the Brute" Morestrong was Thorma's older brother. Although Thorma was in command of the war band, he allowed his brother to be second-in-command for the time being. Thomle was still too young and inexperienced for command. *He needs another year or two*, thought Thorma as he watched his son fidget with his battle gear. Then he glanced at Olaf. *And I don't trust my brother to help mentor him if something were to happen to me.* It was no secret to anybody onboard the ships that Olaf longed for the day when he could be in complete command of the war band and that he blamed his brother for the wait. *Someday*, Olaf thought to himself as he watched his brother with his arm around his son, *someday*. Olaf's huge dim-eyed son, Bork, sat next to his father, and the big man looked at him. *I should have killed both you and your mother when you were born*, Olaf growled to himself as he glared at his only son. The big, overgrown boy simply smiled as he pulled hard on the oar.

High on the grassy ridge, the sharp eyes of the young village boys, who were both tenders of the flock and watchers of the sea, had spotted the dragon ships from their vantage point. When the Vikings had come leeward of the isle of Kerrera and rounded the rocky point, their sails had stood out like a black wolf on a snowy hillside. The boys quickly raced to where the bullhorns lay on a large rock, placed the horns against their mouths, and blew hard. The horns emitted a deep guttural sound that carried far out into the bay. It was the early warning system used by many of the villages up and down the shores of Lorn. The horns, cut from yearling cattle every spring, were used for many things, from drinking urns to the bullhorns. The shaggy mountain cattle that the villagers raised grew massive horns if they weren't dehorned as yearlings. Their coats were long and reddish, not very pretty to look at, but they were hearty beasts and could survive the brutal winters that seemed to last forever in this part of Britannia.

Two to four holes were drilled through the base of the horns, and the sharp tips were cut off. This allowed the wind from small lungs to make a sound that could carry down from the high grass fields to the village below and even out to the approaching ships. The deep-pitched wail of the horns mixed with the heavy pounding of the Viking war drums, and together they created a cacophony of crisis in the skies over Oban.

This particular autumn day had begun much like any other for the young boys of the village; Ein mac Neil was no exception. Ein's father had awakened him well before daylight. The pigs had to be fed and firewood gathered before Ein could eat and then head up through the pasture with the other young boys to watch for the wolves that were killing their sheep. Along with their chores of tending to the sheep, the boys were also tasked with watching for the dreaded dragon ships. The Norsemen had been raiding villages farther north near the Firth of Savern and even out on the island of Mull, so all the people along this part of the coast of Gael were on constant lookout.

Ein mac Neil blew hard on his horn as he watched in frightened fascination as the three ships bore down on his village. He had never seen dragon ships before. At ten years of age, he had no idea of the horrors that the ships carried. He and the other boys had only the late-night whispers of their parents to go by. There was always much fear in their voices when they spoke the name Northmen.

Ein tore his eyes from the dragon ships and glanced around at his friends, watching them lay down their horns after only a few minutes of sounding the alarm. The other boys ran down through the grass fields, spotted here and there with cattle and carpeted with late blooming heather. They passed several of the village women who were already climbing up through the pasture, dragging crying children behind them. Some of the women had large bundles of what they considered valuables on their backs. A little silver, a jeweled brooch, or cooking pot—nothing of value should be left for these marauders from the north. Struggling with their burdens, the women sought safety in the thick woods that lay above the high pastures. Ein, angry and surprised at his friends running away, made up his mind to stay longer when he spotted his own mother and two small sisters hurrying up the trail below him. With his friends gone, Ein blew even harder on the horn, his solitary effort echoing down from the high fields and out toward the fast-approaching dragons.

Thorma stood with one booted foot upon the gunwale and listened to the call of the horns reduced to a single voice. "Row harder," he bellowed angrily as he watched the villagers begin to climb up through the fields to safety. High in the pasture, the lone watcher climbed upon a large rock that they had sprinkled with salt for the cattle. He could see the women of Oban—some still gathering what few meager possessions they could carry, others already herding their children into the forest. The women seemed small, moving as if in slow motion. They scurried in and out of their thatched huts while the Viking drums grew louder. Out of breath and worried about his father, who was somewhere down in the village, Ein finally took the horn from his trembling lips. With one last look at the dragon ships, he ran as fast as he could toward the village.

In the village center, people were running in every direction. Mothers, desperate to find lost children, called their names over and over. Men, and even young boys, searched for something, anything, to fight with. Pigs ran squalling, and chickens flew about in panic as the dragons bore down on the village. One young woman, maybe sixteen years of age, who had been caught up in the general panic, suddenly stopped her desperate flight from the village. Shielding her eyes from the glare, she watched as a hawk flew out of the mist that was just beginning to break its grip on the shoreline. The hawk flashed by several doves that fled in panic. With talons flared, it settled on the large stone balcony of the monastery, its sharp-beaked head turning from side to side as if surveying the tragedy that was about to occur.

Morea mac Craig was the girl's name, and she was the only female child born to a family that had lost four male babies during each one's first year of life. A fifth male child, William, had survived; he was Morea's older brother. Morea had been raised almost entirely by her maternal grandmother, Muire mac Erc, because her mother had died in childbirth. Anne mac Craig drew her last breath, smiling as her only daughter took her first, exhaling a scream.

Morea's father had been a fisherman, and although he worked many long hours, he always found time for his wife and small son. But after his wife's death, he was devastated and suddenly seemed far too busy to worry with the children. As his workdays stretched even longer, he had shown even less interest in the skinny girl child. After all, the child's birth had taken his beloved Anne from him, and he did have the boy, William.

The girl grew, and the rift widened. If he ever knew it, Jamie mac Craig never acknowledged the fact that Morea had gradually become a very powerful healer under her grandmother's tutelage. When the other fishermen bragged, as they often did, about the young girl's skills, the elder mac Craig ignored their praises. He simply couldn't forgive the child for taking his Anne from him.

As Morea grew older, her healing talents grew stronger. Her skills with herbs and folk medicine, sharpened by her grandmother's training, were as effective as any Druidic shaman's. The village of Oban was primarily a fishing village, so there was a constant flow of injured fishermen at Morea's grandmother's hut. By the age of twelve, Morea could stitch up a cut hand, help deliver a breached baby, or even extract a calf that was dead in the womb. As she grew into her teens, she developed another sense that lay dormant in most people. Some would call it a sixth sense; the old ones called it premonition. Morea had the ability to sense happenings. When she was young, it was hearing the cracking of a hatching robin's egg high in the treetops or the sudden appearance of a great stag in the cold moonlight of a frost-covered meadow, silent as a ghost. When she was older, it was a slight tingling of the neck hairs or a need to look over her shoulder in certain situations. Not so much an ability to predict the future as an ability to know or feel things before they happen. It was from that feeling she knew or at least sensed the Norsemen's ships approaching long before the warning calls of the young spotters. She had watched as the sea had become increasingly turbulent, as it would before a mighty tempest, but no storm was in sight. The doves and seagulls fluttered about, restless and unable to settle. A bitter tang had risen in the back of her throat, and her mouth morphed from its usual open smile into a stern glare, saying nothing but revealing everything. Something was about to happen; she could feel it.

Through the years of her early childhood, Morea's grandmother had constantly tried to teach her the importance of observing her natural surroundings very closely.

"It must be a part of your self-education. If it is, then it will lead to your preservation, and you will grow old like me." She would chuckle before turning serious. "Do you understand that, girl?" the old woman would press. Young Morea mac Craig would simply nod.

"Yes, Grandmother, I understand." It all came so easy to her. Through diligent observation, she had learned many things in her sixteen years, but one particular bit of knowledge stuck front and center in her head. She knew that animals were born to prey on one another: like the wolf on the lamb or, as she watched, the hawk on the dove. But she never believed that human beings were meant to kill each other, for to do so was to be an animal.

"You should always respect and nurture life, not take it," was one of her grandmother's favorite sayings. The comment was usually followed by her spitting a mouthful of well-chewed sunflower seeds into a wooden bowl for future use. The odorous concoction was often blended with sassafras bark as a remedy for joint pain.

Morea reluctantly tore her eyes away from the hawk and watched the dragon ships, with their predatory cargo bound for her village. She wondered if these Norsemen were indeed human or just animals in some strange human disguise. She dwelled on that thought until her attention was suddenly drawn back to the hawk, its cry filling the sky. It had flown into the air above the monastery, extended its great wings, and was now slicing through the covey of doves once more, scattering them in all directions.

Surprisingly, the hawk ignored the easy meals that fluttered by and, instead, flared its razor-sharp talons just before settling alongside a nearly solid white dove that was a little larger than the rest. This dove had not flown in fear like the others but had waited as if for a lover.

"My god." Morea uttered the oath and then quickly crossed herself in the manner the monks had shown her and everyone else in the village. "A hawk and a dove as mates. How is it possible?" she cried aloud, her voice trembling. "It must be a sign from the new god the monks have told us about." Morea spoke to the sky but spat in the old way to ward off evil spirits, just in case. The old pagan traditions die hard, if they die at all.

Her mind stayed locked on the hawk and dove as pandemonium swirled around her. Only the urgent shouting of her brother finally broke the spell that the birds held her under.

"Morea, Morea! For God's sake, you must run!" William's voice quivered as he urged his sister to escape to the hills above the village. "Run to the high pastures. I'll find you later," he pleaded, repeating the words that most of the village men were telling their loved ones. The fear in her brother's voice was palpable. Finally, although still reluctant to abandon her village, she turned to run. William, his face pale, watched in anguish as she struggled across the rocky ridge underneath the monastery, heading toward the high grass fields.

With a sigh of relief, William turned his back to his sister and ran toward his father's hut. A bitter and lonely man, the elder mac Craig had drowned that spring in a violent storm just off the cliffs of Dunnllegwn, so the hut was now his son's. William brushed aside the heavy cloth door. His bow hung in the back-right corner of the dimly lit structure, his small quiver of arrows on the wall nearby. He looked around for a moment, searching the dark corners for at least one fond memory, but none came. Shaking his head, he grabbed the bow, threw the arrow sack across his shoulder, and tore out for the center of the village where most of the men, at least the braver of them, had gathered with the few weapons that could be found.

Ten men from the village, one of whom was William, owned and were proficient with the Yew longbow, or war bow as it was sometimes called. In the hands of the right archer, this bow was a deadly weapon. It was the artillery of the era and would remain so for years to come. A dozen or so men were fortunate enough to have found short rusty swords. The ill-kept weapons looked as if they had been hidden under straw mats for years. Some of the older men had

sharpened scythes—the same tool used for mowing wheat or bar-
ley—clutched tightly in their calloused hands. Others carried crude
hoes. The makeshift weapons were poor matches against Danish war
axes. The remaining men, unarmed, stood frozen in place or milled
around the village center, looking out to sea, unsure of what they
would do as the dragon ships neared the shore.

Chaos enveloped the village as the bullhorns fell silent and the
Viking drums grew louder.

* * * * *

Sweat ran from underneath their leather helmets as the rowers
grunted and strained in efforts to pull the long oak oars through
the choppy waters. The three drummers, one on each ship, pounded
goatskin drums in a frenzy of constant rhythm, and together they
drove the dragon-headed ships through the mud, onto the sand
and gravel beach. The great oars hauled inside the ships, the row-
ers-turned-warriors grabbed their heavy bronze shields and scrambled to follow Thorma and Thomle onto the beach. The ships sat
in the shallow waters and listed slightly as if the dragons were finally
able to rest after the long rough swim across the dark waters.

Thorma, Thomle, and the other Norsemen leaped from the
gunwales, the sand crunching loudly underneath their heavy sealskin
boots as they gathered around their leader. Olaf, standing beside his
brother and wanting badly to be the center of attention, shouted
orders to the war band as together they began to beat their sword
handles hard against their shields. The noise intensified as the drummers, who climbed down from the ships, joined in the pounding and
the Norsemen roared like demons.

While the Danish swords hammered against iron-strapped
shields down on the rocky beach, many of the men of Oban, some
who simply dropped their weapons, began to run in fear. For some
time, sixty-eight howling Norsemen continued to beat sword handles
against shields and drank mead from leather-covered gourds. The
savage ritual was intended not only to enflame their battle fever but
also to frighten the enemy. The noise became deafening. And more

men of Oban fled, leaving women and children behind. Such was their fear of the Viking horde.

Finally, when all the mead had been drunk and Thorma felt them sufficiently ready, he shouted a hail to Odin, and the horde broke from the huddle. The air shook as the Norsemen raced, screaming up the incline toward the village, the younger men taking the lead, eager to show their bravery.

"Look, Father, they are running away!" shouted Thomle in youthful excitement as he watched several men throw down their weapons and retreat toward the pastures. Thomle raised his sword high, his heart pounding in his chest as he moved up the beach. Thorma, always levelheaded, cautiously eyed a small group of about twenty brave but foolish village men moving warily toward his throng.

"They're not all running," he grunted as he watched his brother storm past him and charge toward the defenders.

The archers, Oban's only real defense, waited behind as the front group of defenders moved warily to the attack. On William's order, ten iron-tipped shafts flew toward their targets, and ten more were readied.

"Shields!" shouted Thorma when he looked up and saw the iron bees descending on them. As one, the battlewise Norsemen dropped to one knee and covered themselves with bronze-plated shields.

"Damn the archers," grunted Olaf as the next ten arrows slammed into the mass of kneeling warriors. One Norseman collapsed, spitting blood, with an arrow through his neck. Another angrily pulled a bloody shaft from his thigh.

William smiled grudgingly at the archers' handiwork and notched another arrow as the howls of the wounded Norsemen rang in his ears. Encouraged by these cries, the men of Oban redoubled their deadly efforts with the Yew bows. In the heated effort to punish the invaders, however, several of the archers soon ran out of arrows. After only a few minutes, even more quivers lay empty until at last the kneeling horde sensed their chance.

"Now," shouted Thorma, and his war band rose quickly with a bloodthirsty growl. Charging through the reduced swarm of arrows, they closed the hundred or so paces that separated the two groups in a matter of a few heartbeats. As the horde charged forward, they easily decimated the few villagers who ineptly wielded short rusty swords. Quickly brushing aside the front group, the howling Norsemen stormed up the rocky beach. One by one, William's companions slung their bows across their backs, clutched their empty quivers tightly in their sweaty hands, and moved backward. With no more arrows, they wisely turned and ran back up the slope toward the village in search of safety and, possibly, more arrows. Looking around and fearing the inevitable, William and his friend Egbert, who stood a few feet away, released one more volley and nodded at each other. The Norsemen had quickly engulfed the swordsmen of Oban, and both men realized the futility of shooting into the mingled crowd just fifty feet to their front. Reluctantly, they, too, slung their bows across their backs and retreated through the village to fight from the shadows.

With gusto and unrelenting force, the flood of helmeted warriors swept through the band of armed villagers like the Roman legions had swept through the wild unorganized Celtic tribes a thousand years before. Smoke soon enveloped the huts closest to the beach as the faster warriors spread havoc. Flames streaked the filthy sky as an awful wail seemed to creep along the street between the burning huts. Bodies lay everywhere as Thorma slowly walked up the beach. Presuming the man dead, he began to step over the body of a young man whom his brother, Olaf, had just disemboweled. As he looked down, the man's eyes flew open, and he stared up painfully at the big Norseman.

"It is a terrible thing to watch a sword rip open a man's stomach," said Thorma, speaking aloud to the dying villager. The boy, who looked only about fifteen, was desperately trying to keep his bowels from spilling onto the blood-soaked sand. Crying now, he pleaded for mercy. Thorma didn't understand all the words he spoke, but he knew the look. Standing over the prone figure, Thorma's shadow fell across the youth's face like a bad omen. Slowly, he raised his sword, its edge reflecting red from the nearby flames. He hesitated for only a second as the boy tightly closed his eyes. Then he drove the

Death Bringer into the boy's heart. Silence hung damp and heavy for a moment after the boy gave a pitiful grunt, his body twitching in pain. Then he lay still. A ghostly voice from long ago whispered in Thorma's ear, then vanished in a rush of noise and confusion.

Thorma withdrew his sword from the boy's chest, turned, and walked on up the beach as the horde moved in front of him through the village. Men were slaughtered just like the cattle the Norsemen sought to take back to Balfour. But the Norsemen were after more than just cattle. They sought slaves, strong young boys, and especially the girls. They sought the pretty ones for sex slaves, but if the girls weren't pretty, they would become kitchen help. There were plenty of blonde and reddish-haired women back in Balfour, but most women of this village were dark-haired, very exotic to these Norsemen. They also sought the ultimate prizes—gold and silver! Several bags of the precious metals lay hidden in the basement of the monastery, the monks having received these gifts from the poor villagers and out-lying peasants in return for penitence. No one thought it strange (or if they did, they at least held their tongues) that only the monks could speak to this new god, a god who was supposed to be so mer-ciful. They simply gave their meager offerings in hope of a heavenly reward. The Christian monks had come into this land about the same time that the last Roman legions were leaving. The pagan tribes had been very reluctant to change their ways and abandon their old gods. Consequently, many a monk had been sacrificed on a Druid's fire for their efforts to spread Christianity among the Celtic tribes. But even-tually, an impression was made in the pagan land, and Christianity began to spread.

The Oban monks claimed to follow the order of Patrick, a truly good man who had lived and died in Ireland four hundred years earlier. The monks, who had taken the peasants' gold and silver, were the same monks who now lined the balcony of the monastery chant-ing, chanting to their god for help. But their god didn't seem to hear the monks this day. The monks were thrown one by one to their deaths on the rocks far below. The crows and seagulls heard their cries, though, and came quickly to feast on the shattered bodies as smoke and fire spilled from every orifice of the timbered structure.

More huts were put to the torch as the Viking horde continued its rape of the village, and the stench of burning flesh mixed with that of spilled blood, sweat, and fear.

Thomle had gradually slowed his eager rush through the village and was now walking somewhat sullenly through the smoke of this man-made hell. His senses were nearly overwhelmed as his eyes darted from one side of the narrow street to the other. He watched the many burning huts belch reddish flames, spewing forth a foul stench as they burnt. The pungent black smoke was like a living thing as it swirled around dead bodies and crying women, its groping tentacles choking the small children who crawled in the blood of their parents. Blood that ran like a small stream through the center of the village to gradually stain the sand around the dragon ships a dusty red. Sparks flew about like fireflies and stung Thomle's eyes as he trudged toward the far edge of the burning village. Gone was the youthful enthusiasm that had driven him off the ship and up toward the village only an hour earlier, and now tears ran down his cheeks. Most of the tears fell because of the smoke, but some fell because of the smell of death and the cries of the dying tore at his soul.

He had felt something stirring deep within him during the last raid, and it was becoming clearer by the moment. He was not like the others in his band. Killing his first man on the previous raid had sickened him. His war band had struck a small village much like this one a few days before. About an hour into the raid, an old man had rushed at Thomle from behind a burning hut. The old man swung his rusty sword with feeble strength, and Thomle had easily parried the thrust. Then without thinking, Thomle had struck down hard with his sword, splitting the man's head wide open. Blood and gray matter had flown onto his face and dripped from his sword hand. He stared at the blood for a long time before dropping his sword and running into the forest, vomiting in a nearby stream as he tried to wash the blood off his hands, which shook like a sick child's. The old warriors hadn't seen him become sick, so when he finally emerged from the forest, they seemed not to notice his pale face or shaking hands. Instead, they slapped him on the back and praised him for his entrance into the Viking warrior clan. They stood drinking mead and shouting approval while proudly watching him paint his first kill mark on his shield. He was a warrior now, but he was not proud. Ever since that day, he was terribly afraid that his father and his companions would somehow find out how sick the whole affair had made him.

Thomle shook the image of the old man's split skull from his mind as he worked his way through the carnage. Suddenly he stopped and started at one particular burning hut. Strange blue flames were shooting from the doorway when out of the smoke behind the hut, an old man ran at him like the ghost of the man he had killed days before. The farmer charged with a hobbled gait and guttural battle cry. Thomle understood enough of the Celtic tongue to know that he had just been called a pig or maybe a butcher. He wasn't quite sure which, but either one probably fit. The rusty spear the old man clutched in his gnarled hands was aimed at Thomle's chest, but he swept it aside easily with a wave of his much larger sword. The old man's feet slipped as his spear was knocked aside, and he fell to his knees. Out of instinct, Thomle's blade struck downward, but this time he used the flat side of his sword, and the blow was not a killing one. It simply knocked the old man senseless, and he fell to the ground with a groan.

The young warrior knelt down and checked the old man's pulse. Proud of himself for having not killed the farmer, he rose and began to walk away. Suddenly, another figure ran out of the smoke and mist. Roaring like a beast, Olaf plunged his sword into the stomach of the old man who lay unconscious on the ground. The prone figure gave a death rattle and grasped, with both hands, the sword that pinned him to the ground like a skewered pig. Thomle stared in horror. After a few final heartbeats, the hands relaxed and slid down the quivering blade to lie still in the sand. Without thinking, the young Viking pulled his sword and attacked with a shout. His eyes burned with fury, and his sword sought flesh. Only years of battle experience saved Olaf from the same fate as the old farmer. The two swords sang an ancient song, and sparks flew into the air like fireflies. The adversaries—one an old warrior, the other young and untested—glared at each other and began moving in a wide circle. Their swords remained locked in a dance, a dance as old as the sullen hills that lay off in the mist. Muscles strained, and both men's arms shook in their efforts.

"He was just an old farmer," spat Thomle, his blue eyes burning with hate.

"We spare no one except the ones fit for slaves," roared Olaf as spittle mixed with sweat ran down his wild red beard. Thomle could smell his uncle's rancid breath as the big man's eyes darted around, watching closely for some kind of opening. Veins bulged in their forearms, and the two swords stayed locked in their dance while the two warriors moved in slow sideways steps. One slip and the other would pounce like a wolf on its kill.

"I hope Odin saw your great kill, Uncle," hissed Thomle as he stared hard into the cold gray eyes of Olaf Morestrong. The Norsemen's god of war would welcome any fallen warrior into the feasting halls of Valhalla. The dead would be swept up from the battlefield by a beautiful Valkyrie and carried on flaming steeds to begin his death journey.

"I will take whatever fate the gods have in store for me," retorted Olaf defiantly, ever so slowly easing off the pressure on his sword. There was gold to be found in the monastery, and he was wasting his time here with this stupid boy. Cautiously, he lowered his Death Bringer, all the while keeping a watchful eye on his brother's son.

"Your father will be very interested in your efforts to protect an old village man." The big warrior laughed as he carefully backed away into the swirling smoke. His mocking laughter floated in the stench of battle until, at last, he turned and raced toward the monastery.

"He was just an old man, nearly harmless!" shouted Thomle at the top of his lungs. But only the dead lay around him, and they gave no reply. Thomle Morestrong shook his head, and sweat ran from underneath his iron-strapped leather helmet to drip off his chin. He sheathed his sword and walked around the dead farmer. His pace was slow, his boots feeling as heavy as iron balls. He passed more burning huts and crying children, his anger raging like a fire in his soul.

"Is this my fate? Does this make me a great warrior? Will Odin welcome me into the great halls of Valhalla for this?" Thomle shouted the questions into the morning air as he walked on up the hill. His blond hair shook from side to side.

"Surely, there is a better way for our people to get the things we need. Why must it take one man killing another in order to live?" His questions snaked among the shadows that danced in the mist, flames leaping as if in rebuke.

"Do the gods demand this from us?" He stopped amid the carnage and watched as several Norsemen dragged six half-naked girls toward the waiting ships. Their screams sounded like those of dying lambs, blood running from their slit throats. The many village women who were too old for these Norsemen's purposes lay near their huts or huddled with small children as the one-sided battle continued around them. The cries of the dying shook the air as a few villagers continued to bravely fight on. But others simply ran, leaving their wives and children to the mercy of the Vikings, a people who did not know the meaning of the word.

How could you not fight to save your family? Thomle asked himself while he watched two village fighters toss their weapons aside and scramble up the grassy field to safety. The very thought of running, of not fighting back, was disgusting to him and alien to his Viking culture. His mind clouded with doubts as the scene played out around him. But the sight of several village girls, with their dresses pulled up, revealing long white legs as they ran toward the rocky cliffs below the burning monastery, brought a nervous smile to his face. This could be his chance, his first woman. The nagging questions disappeared from his mind, and his heart rate quickened.

Lengthening his stride, Thomle kept his eyes on one girl in particular: a beautiful dark-haired lass who was struggling to keep her footing on the rocky slope. The distance between the young Viking and the Oban girl rapidly decreased, and the thumping in his heart grew stronger, a curious excitement spreading over him. Thomle leaped over a pile of dead limbs, and suddenly, the girl was within his grasp. Reaching out, he caught hold of her smock at the same time as her foot snagged on one of the limbs. Stumbling forward, she fell hard onto her hands and knees. Blinding pain shot up her legs, but she managed to spin as quickly as a cat onto her back. Her hair was being blown fiercely about her face by the gusty winds that had suddenly roared to life. Spitting hair from her mouth, she fought desperately to brush the dark curls from her eyes. Thomle's throat was dry and his breathing rapid as his hand grasped the girl's cloak. He could feel the warm softness of her skin beneath the homespun material of her modest wrap. *Now! Now was his chance!* His world began to slow, and he stared at the long white legs and beautiful iridescent green eyes. The girl glared back in agonizing defiance.

"Why?" The word shot from her lips and slammed into his head like an arrow piercing his skull. She scrambled backward. "Why are you doing this?" The question hissed through clenched teeth stopped him cold in his impending conquest. He stood motionless above her while her heart raced like that of a frightened hare. He saw a solitary tear appear in the corner of one eye, glistening in the sunlight like a small diamond. Thomle had learned the Celtic tongue and some Celtic ways from an old slave his father had brought back from one of his many raids. So he understood what she asked him. He drew back his hand and stared down at her dirt-smeared face. Her reddened cheeks, bloody knees, and disheveled hair couldn't hide the fact that she was beautiful. Her complexion was flawless, her breasts ample, her figure as well-formed as any he'd seen. But it was her demeanor that caused Thomle to hesitate. No tears fell from the eyes that dared to stare up at him, and there was a sullen dignity in her that more closely resembled rebuke than fear. Thomle Morestrong was not prepared for this kind of challenge. Fear, hate, and anger he was ready for, but not what she showed. This young woman had courage, a stoic directness that he in his short life had not experienced.

Morea mac Craig watched as the young Norseman slowly drew back his hand. She could sense his hesitation, so she spoke again, this time a little less harshly: "Why have you killed my people? Why have you raped and carried off our women?" The questions flowing from her like water from a broken pail. "Why have you endangered even the smallest of our children? Why have you destroyed our village? Look what you have done." The last statement hung in the air, heavy and dark like the black smoke that swirled about them. She took a deep breath and fought to control her emotions, her gaze settling on the burning village. She spread her arms out wide, her plea for an answer she knew would never come. Thomle, totally caught off guard, rocked back on his heels and looked around just as she had done. He couldn't understand all the language in her rapidly fired questions, but he knew that he had no answer for any of them. He blinked his eyes in an effort to clear his mind and looked back down at the girl, struggling to adjust from the excitement of a few moments ago to the shock of this unexpected challenge.

Morea and the young Viking stood frozen in place and stared in acrid silence at each other. The smooth bare legs of the village girl lying on the ground in front of him boiled Thomle's blood, but the questions that she had hurled confused and saddened him. A thousand thoughts raced through his mind, and he never saw the huge hulking figure that came tearing out of the smoke and mist. He was struck hard in the back, throwing him to the ground, his head slamming into a jagged rock near the girl's feet. Through the stunning pain of the collision and the rush of blood down his forehead and across his eyes, Thomle saw his uncle's ugly tattooed face. Olaf Morestrong towered over the two prone figures, his grin filled with lust and hatred. Thomle rose painfully to one knee, but his feeble attempt to confront his uncle was useless. Olaf lashed out with his booted foot and kicked his nephew hard alongside his bleeding head. The day exploded into a shower of flashing lights. Then there was only darkness.

* * * * *

Morea, unable to gain her footing, scrambled on her hands and knees across the loose rocks as she sought to escape the beast that lustfully stalked her. Olaf strutted forward like a boar in rut, his lips pulled back over crooked yellow teeth, a sneer framing his ugly mouth. Reaching down with one long rank hand, he ripped Morea's cloak from her struggling body. The old warrior leaned back, hands on his hips, and howled with laughter as she tried to cover herself. Backed up against a large boulder, all Morea could do was glare back at her attacker.

"I'll knock that damn defiant look off your pretty face, wench," growled Olaf in his guttural Danish. The big hand flew down and struck Morea hard across the right cheek, causing stars to dance in her blurred vision and blood to trickle down her chin. *You dare not black out!* her mind screamed, and she shook her head to clear away the tiny lights that appeared before her like torches waved by invisible hands. With one hand desperately clutching what remained of her torn dress, Morea summoned her remaining strength from somewhere in the depths of her being and began to stand up. Her mind was threatening to spin out of control when, nearly hidden in the fierce wind, a low moan or growl emerged from the younger Norseman, and she instinctively turned in his direction. It angered Olaf Morestrong that the girl was more worried about his brother's son than she was about her own safety. He nearly exploded with rage.

"I'll show you what a grown man can do for you, girl, instead of that whelp of a boy," he spat as he cast aside his bearskin cloak and removed his sword belt. Thomle, who was about ten feet behind his uncle, had managed to rise to one knee again and was reaching for his sword as Olaf's hand reached for the girl's torn apron dress. She screamed and cowered just as a dark shadow fell across the big man's head. A haunting cry reverberated off the rocks scattered near the cliff's edge. Morea jerked her head, looking past the Viking's hulking form. A shrieking creature, filled with the wrath of the old gods, flew toward them out of the smoke-filled sky. Olaf, like many in his war band, was fearful of the unknown, and the hair prickled on the back of his neck as he watched the girl's eyes grow wide. The blood of rage pounded in his ears, but he, too, heard the awful cry somewhere above and behind him. Slowly he turned his head to follow the girl's gaze just as the hawk swooped out of the mist. The big raptor drove its eight talons deep into the Viking's eyes, raking them inward with amazing strength and ripping both eyes from their sockets. Screaming out in pain, the Norseman fought to cast off the bird, whose beak continued to tear at his exposed flesh. But just as quickly as it had struck, the hawk was gone, having flown off toward the cliffs.

The damage, though, was already done. For a brief moment, either out of fear or confusion, Olaf fell to his knees, covered the empty sockets of his eyes, and cursed the gods. But the same fear that drove him to his knees forced him back to his feet, and he staggered about, moving ever closer to the cliff's edge with each step. Pain racked his body, and he stumbled in ever-widening circles, spitting blood and howling in his own personal darkness. Morea, working frantically to repair her torn garment, found a woolen string in a side pocket and began threading it through the various rips with trembling fingers. She tried to grasp the reason why the hawk had only attacked the older Norseman. *Was this another sign from the new god? Or was it simply an accident of nature?* Her grandmother would know, but she had no idea. Either way, it had at least delayed her being raped by these beasts. To become their slave was unthinkable.

Just down the hill, Thomle finally managed to struggle to his feet. His head spun in bursts of black flame, and cold hard drops of sweat dotted his forehead. He bent over at the waist, and a rush of nausea accompanied his first step. But he took one after another until he reached the girl, where he collapsed at her feet. Without thinking or worrying about her actions, she knelt down to help the young warrior. Thomle's head thundered as if Thor himself had hit him with his lightning bolt hammer, yet the mournful cries of his uncle quickly cleared the fog from his throbbing head. His uncle's stumbling continued to take the big man dangerously close to the rocky edge of the high craggy promontory, until at last Olaf tripped on a loose rock and plunged over the cliff's edge. Small stones and dirt followed his body down, as did the crows, seagulls, and gray kites. The Norseman cried out as he fell with a pitiful realization that Fate, the one god he feared least, had declared his marauding days were over.

Olaf's body landed with a sickening thud among the same rocks where the monks' bodies lay. The feathered scavengers, who were feeding on the dead Christians, scattered begrudgingly into the air for a short while before cautiously settling back down to feast on the newly arrived pagan flesh. Both Christian and pagan blood ran together, but the birds seemed unable to tell any difference. The pitiful screams of the Norseman, echoing off the hills as he fell, sent shivers up Morea's spine. She sat knee to chin, hugging her legs, the young Norseman barely conscious at her feet. She cringed in fear as the hawk suddenly returned to circle over the dead Viking for a brief moment, forcing the scavengers to scatter from their feeding once more. After a few minutes, the raptor flew up and over the cliff's edge, where she sat with the wounded Thomle. With a final cry of its own, the hawk flew off, sailing high on the stiff winds before at last settling beside the nearly white dove perched in the high oaks just beneath the crag. The dove, although smaller, seemed to somehow calm the great bird as it drew near.

Morea and the young Norseman, who was attempting to sit up, watched for several minutes as the hawk and dove nestled close to each other. At last Thomle spoke. "It seems as if the hawk has not only saved your life but has decided to make peace with the doves—or at least that one," he said as blood trickled down his forehead. His Gaelic was rusty, and his head hurt too much to think straight, but he continued as best he could.

"The old people of my village used to tell us young boys that if we died a brave death in battle, we might come back in the next life as a mighty bird of prey like that one." He nodded slightly toward the hawk perched quietly high in the oak. Morea couldn't quite believe her ears as she listened, somewhat shocked, to the young Norseman. He spoke as if nothing had happened here, and it made her angry. She could understand his knowledge of her language but not his seeming disregard for the pain and suffering they had caused. Her young mind struggled further. Only moments ago, this Norseman had been intent on raping her, or it appeared that way! But maybe not—she could only hope. Maybe he was somehow ... different? *God, how strange all this is*, she thought and then immediately crossed herself for the sudden sacrilege. *Was her attraction to this boy clouding her judgment, or was it something else?*

Thomle noticed the odd Christian gesture and stopped talking. The two young people sat and awkwardly gazed at each other for a long minute. Morea was the first to break the silence.

"You're still bleeding," she said, her healing instinct taking over. She bent over and tore a dangling strip of cloth from her homespun dress. Realizing, though, that she was revealing her thigh, she hurried to cover the bare skin. Glancing up, she was surprised at how the young Viking blushed and looked away. She hastened to finish tearing the strip loose from her dress and then gently wrapped it around Thomle's head. Gradually, the bleeding stopped.

"Thank you," he said as he touched his head and grimaced. After a few minutes, he used his sword as a crutch and tried to stand again, but he quickly turned pale and slumped forward. Morea made an unsuccessful attempt to catch him as he fell, only barely grabbing his shoulder, which forced his head to land in her lap and his body to sprawl on the rocks.

A thousand angry hornets buzzed in his head as he squeezed his eyes shut, but after a minute, they slowly fluttered open when the girl gently shook him. So shallow was his breathing; she was afraid he had died. His eyes gradually focused, and he looked into her soft green eyes, which were the color of winter ivy. His breath faltered, but he managed to whisper, "You're beautiful." His heart began to race, and a strange feeling gripped his stomach. Morea blushed but held the boy's gaze.

"My name is Morea." *Why am I telling this boy anything?* She fussed at herself before she went on. "I don't know many words in your language, but you seem to know our Gaelic tongue. How is that?" she asked, the heat rising from her blushing face as he continued to gaze at her.

"Morea." Thomle seemed to ignore her question and simply repeated the girl's name with a slight nod, his vision blurring from the effort. "My name is Thomle," he finally said with a silly grin on his face.

"Thomle," repeated Morea, trying hard not to smile back. His name rolled easily off her tongue.

The young Norseman, his forehead crinkled in thought, began to explain his knowledge of her Celtic language. "My father was—is—a raider. He brought an older slave woman back from one of his earlier raids. She came from a village far north and east of your land, but she was Scotti. Her job was to help my mother in all manners of things, which included raising me." He stopped, seeming to replay a certain scene in his mind before he went on.

"The old woman grew to like me and tried to teach me the Gaelic language, but for some reason, it was very difficult for me." He laughed slightly as he remembered his punishment for many a bad lesson, gently shaking his throbbing head. "The old woman would slap me over the head every time I made a mistake. Consequently, I got slapped many times," he tried to joke.

Irritated with his manner, Morea said, "Tell me, Northman, did this old woman have a name?"

It was Thomle's turn to blush. "I am sorry, her name was Grectik," he answered.

"It means 'pretty flower,' if you didn't know," said Morea. She started to say more but was stopped by the sound of angry voices riding the winds.

"Thomle, Thomle, where in thunder are you? Olaf, Olaf, where are you?" Several fur-clad Norsemen called the names repeatedly as they walked along the cliff's edge, searching. Their shouts carried above the roar of the wind, and it sounded like ghosts wailing in the Netherlands, calling lost companions. "Thomleeee, Olaaaaf."

"They're searching for me and my uncle," declared Thomle as he listened and then painfully rose from his prone position. Morea had to help him to his feet, but once standing, he seemed steady enough. He stood still and scanned the surrounding hillside for a place to hide the girl. The search party was getting closer; only one small knoll now separated the two groups. Morea quickly recognized the urgency of the situation and led the Norseman toward a small cave that she and the other village children used to play in when she was younger.

"Hurry," urged Thomle when he realized where she was heading. The two raced hand in hand toward the cave.

"Once you are safe, I will answer their calling," he said. As they rushed along, he stumbled woozily over several small rocks and dead tree limbs in his frantic climb to get Morea to the safety of the cave. Tugging on the girl's hand, he encouraged her to move quickly as the angry voices grew closer.

The hawk and dove also seemed to sense the danger in the moment, for they sprang from their perch near the monastery and flew toward a clump of windblown oaks that dotted the ridge above the grazing fields. Morea glanced back over her shoulder and saw the pair fly away. She stopped and stared, which forced Thomle to do the same. They watched the strange but beautiful birds as they glided on the stiff winds. A special bond was slowly forming between the maiden and the Norseman that neither one could explain, yet it was there. Something softer than a whisper passed between them while they held hands just outside the cave, watching the hawk and dove sail toward the high ridge. The winds howled about them, and uncertainty tugged at their cloaks. Little did they know that they had seen a glimpse of their future riding the harsh winds of Oban.

Their shadows danced an eerie waltz on the floor as they crept into the cavernous hole. Thomle reluctantly released her hand and turned her toward him. "Morea, you need to stay in this cave until I come back. I'm going to try to divert the search party away from here." Morea, her stomach a nervous wreck, looked deep into the eyes that held her gaze. She desperately searched his icy-blue orbs for some glimmer of hope, some truth to confirm her instincts. Sensing her hesitation, Thomle added, "And I will come back." He had taken only a few steps toward the cave's entrance when she called his name softly but urgently.

"Thomle." He stopped and looked back. "Please hurry," she whispered, reaching out to touch his arm. Magical heat shot through his veins. He looked where she had touched him—it still tingled— then into her eyes, but made no reply. He simply nodded and left with the warmth of her touch lingering on his arm.

The Norsemen's search party stood staring over the cliff's edge as Thomle hobbled back across the small knoll that separated the two groups. Heads together, the six men argued heatedly about how the great Olaf Morestrong could have fallen to his death. Thomle's mind was racing in an effort to establish a plausible story when he spotted Erik Swineson among the group. Swineson was a dangerously bitter and ugly man. His face was covered with tattoos, placed there in a hopeless attempt to hide smallpox scars from his youth. No one cared much for Erik Swineson except for Thomle's uncle, and Olaf only tolerated him because he could always use the scar-faced man to do his dirty work. The search group turned in unison when Thomle walked up behind them, Erik quickly stepping forward in an effort to show his importance.

"Where have you been?" growled Swineson. Thomle, who was several inches taller, glared down at the man.

"I don't answer to you, Swineson," was all he said before walking over to the cliff's edge and staring down at Olaf's shattered body. The crows and seagulls had been busy. The search party moved up slowly behind Thomle, following his gaze. Sensing the shift of position by Erik's men, Thomle spun around angrily, his hand dropping down to grip his sword. The quick move, borne out of caution, caused Erik to stop and tentatively step backward, his companions doing likewise under Thomle's withering stare.

"Lest you forget, Swineson, I am Thomle, son of Thorma. Who are you to ask me any questions?" Swineson, realizing he had overstepped his authority, rushed to make amends.

"We thought you might be wounded … or even dead like your uncle," stammered Swineson as the others nodded in agreement. They were well aware of the hatred between Olaf and his nephew, but they also knew that Olaf, their protector, was now dead. So they had best listen to their leader's son. "We were just worried about you," said Erik contritely, his head bent down in mock humility.

"Huh," grunted Thomle as he began to form the story about the hawk in his mind. *A little of the truth won't hurt and could be a good thing*, he thought to himself. But before he could tell the story of the killer hawk, Erik started beating his sword against his shield and shouting.

"We will kill all who remain in this nest of vipers as vengeance for Olaf's death."

The others eagerly joined in the chant. "Kill them all!" they shouted. Thomle slowly shook his head and turned back to face Swineson.

"Thorma will decide who else will die in this village," spat Thomle, his blue eyes smoldering. "When I tell you how this happened"—he pointed toward the blotted form of his uncle—"then you will know why we must leave this accursed place, and quickly."

Realizing he had their full attention, he began to recount the tale of the hawk's attack. He told them how the hawk had torn Olaf's eyes from their sockets, which was true, and how Olaf's screams had driven the hawk into a frenzy.

"I managed to survive only because I ran. Otherwise, the creature would have killed me too." He looked skyward as if he was still worried about the demon hawk returning, and six pairs of worried eyes followed his gaze. Knowing that most members of his father's war band were extremely superstitious, he exaggerated the size and fury of the hawk as he spun the tale. Erik's group nervously looked around, lowering their swords and beginning to shuffle their feet.

Swineson made one more attempt to take control. "We must avenge Olaf's death!" he shouted as his group looked from him to Thomle and back. Thomle, who loomed over the shorter man, hissed.

"Look around you, fool. Don't you think we have avenged many deaths? In order to prevent any of these foul spirits"—he spat toward the cliff—"from sailing back to Balfour with us, we should leave now." The plan, which had begun as a desperate idea, was fully formed in his mind now. It was a plan he hoped could protect the girl.

On the other side of the nearest ridge, Thorma was sullenly making his way down from the burning monastery with two young girls tied to his waist by a length of braided rope. He was angry and more than a little worried about his men having thrown the monks to their deaths. Beating them would have been sufficient to strike fear in the hearts of the survivors. It had been his brother's idea to kill them, and Thorma had been too late to stop them. *Why take the chance of angering their god further?* growled Thorma to himself as he searched for his son. He hadn't seen Olaf for a while either, but he could not have cared less about finding his brother. Thorma turned a small ridge and soon spotted his son standing with a group of his warriors just ahead. The boy was gesturing wildly with his hands as the men looked into the sky. When he got closer, he could tell by his son's body language that he was angry. *Not only that stance, but the way he moves his arms is just like his mother,* thought Thorma, smiling briefly at the memory. But then he spotted trouble. Erik Swineson, a man who nobody, except his brother, liked or trusted, stood beside Thomle. Swineson and Olaf were, oddly, much alike, reasoned Thorma. Maybe that was why they seemed to get along. The tension in the group was obvious, but Thorma couldn't hear any of what was being said, so he placed his right hand on his sword grip as a precaution. The group of men didn't notice him walk up even though he had two half-naked girls in tow, their wrists rubbed raw by the ropes.

"What are you gaping at like old women at a freak show?" Thorma bellowed the insult when he was about ten feet away. Everyone, with the exception of his son, jumped when he shouted. Thomle was the only one who had reached for his sword and turned to the challenge. *Good,* thought Thorma as he brushed past Swineson, ignoring a rash of explanations. He walked to the cliff's edge and peered down.

"Huh" was all he said as he watched the seagulls and kites circle what was left of his brother's face. "Thomle, do you want to tell me what happened here?" he asked, turning his back on the cliff's edge and slowly walking toward his son. No one said a word, and he stared into his son's eyes.

"Well," he pressed further, not breaking eye contact. The boy refused to flinch under his father's gaze, but his mind raced for an answer.

"I'll tell you," interjected Swineson for the second time, but he was cut short by a large hand thrust in his face.

"I want to hear it from Thomle," said Thorma with venom in his voice. Thomle glanced around for some place that he could talk to his father in private; finally, he nodded toward a clump of large boulders about fifty yards away. The older man understood.

"Erik, take four men and retrieve Olaf's body before the damn crows carry it away. Take it back to the ships," he added matter-of-factly and turned to follow his son. Both men walked across the boulder-strewn slope in silence. The mist had partly cleared, but the smoke from the burning village still swirled about in patches. Thorma began to speak before the pair reached the clump of boulders.

"I never liked the bastard very much anyway," he growled. "He was a brutal man, just like our father. They both had this strange need to inflict pain, and they enjoyed killing." Thorma shook his big bearded head in sad remembrance. Kneeling down, he tied the end of the braided rope to a large rock.

"So what did happen to my brother?" asked Thorma as he put his hand behind his back and stood up with a grimace. His lower back had been hurting him for several days. *I'm getting older*, he moaned to himself. Thomle watched his father struggle with the pain as he began retelling the story of the hawk attacking Olaf. Once again, he left out the part about the girl. Thorma stood listening to his son's tale when suddenly the hair on the back of his neck began to tingle. The old warrior believed strongly in instinct, that belief having saved his life several times, and right now his instincts were screaming. Someone or something was watching him. Years of combat had sharpened his senses, and he could feel … something. He fought the urge to look around as his son talked. Thomle finally grew silent, having finished his tale, and only then did his father glance around. Seeing nothing out of the ordinary, he looked up into the smoky haze. There, high overhead, the mysterious hawk floated effortlessly on the cold wind currents. Thorma put a hand up to shield his eyes from the sun that had finally burned through the smoke and mist. The glare caused his eyes to water, but he could tell that something was flying alongside the hawk. It was a … what?

"A damn dove." Thorma spat, hoping to ward off any bad spirits that were surely accompanying this bizarre scene. *My old eyes must be playing tricks on me*, he mused to himself. *That could not be a hawk and a dove together!*

Thomle had watched his father closely while he retold the hawk story, or at least his version of it. He hated to lie to his father. But really, he wasn't lying; he just wasn't telling the whole story … yet. When he had finished his tale, he noticed his father glance around and then look up into the scattering mist. He followed his father's gaze, and his young eyes saw what his father couldn't believe was there, the hawk and the dove flying side by side. The old warrior shuffled his boots and looked out to sea. After a moment, he turned back to his son and grunted.

"My brother was always quite jealous of me." He made a noise more like a scoff than a laugh, his big right foot kicking carelessly at a nearby stick. "Olaf could never understand why the men would willingly follow me but not him." He paused again to gather his thoughts.

"It's really quite simple, I think. You can be hard, very hard, if you have to be, but you must be fair. Treat everyone the same and never ask your men to do anything that you wouldn't do," he went on. "And you must learn that, son. Do you understand what I'm saying?" He asked the question in an almost pleading tone that Thomle had very seldom heard from his father. Thorma watched his son cast his gaze onto the sand, clearly mulling over what he had just been told.

"Yes, Father, I think I do understand," said Thomle, bringing his gaze back up. "It is not as simple as it sounds, but I have watched you with the men, and I believe I understand."

Thorma stood with his big arms folded across his chest, silently looking out to sea as if some further explanation lay there. Thomle had expected more hard questions about Olaf's death, but instead, his father only stared at the windblown surf. Finally, after several awkward minutes, Thorma turned back and took a hard look at his son's bandaged head. Then, without saying another word, he retrieved the two slave girls and trudged down the slope. The girls struggled to keep their balance on the rocks as their new master dragged them barefooted toward the ships. Their tattered smocks blew in the stiff breeze, revealing far more young skin than was proper, but the girls were beyond caring.

He knows there is more to this story than I have told, thought Thomle, *but he will wait for a better time to ask*. The young Norseman watched his father walk through the center of the village with the girls, trudging through clouds of smoke and stepping over dead bodies, women and children wailing all around them.

* * * * *

The sight of the young women being dragged away by his father jerked Thomle back to the moment, and his thoughts went to the girl hiding in the cave. Turning, he walked intently toward the place where he'd left her, the hawk's cry echoing across the cliffs as he went. The walk soon became a jog, then a mad dash, as he neared the cave's entrance. The sun was a red orb straight overhead. When Thomle entered the mouth of the cave, its limestone walls reflected the sunlight back into his eyes; and for a brief moment, he was blinded.

"Morea, Morea," he called as he staggered forward with his hands held out in front of him. Fear began clawing at his stomach as he called her name over and over. Only silence and the howling wind answered him. Slowly, his eyes began to adjust to the low light, and at last, he noticed movement in the back of the cave.

"Morea," he called again and was finally rewarded with her soft but shaky voice calling back.

"Thomle, is that you?" she asked cautiously.

"Yes, yes," he answered eagerly as the young village girl stepped out from the shadows. Thomle fought the urge to rush as he stepped over and around scattered rocks closing the distance between them. Morea found herself thrilled to see the relief in the young man's eyes when he drew near.

"I was afraid you wouldn't come back," she whispered, standing close to him—so close, in fact, he could smell the lavender in her hair.

"I told you I would come back," he said hoarsely, for some reason having trouble speaking. After an awkward minute, he spoke again, this time in a whisper. "Please, sit with me," he said, brushing invisible dirt from a large boulder before sitting down. He half-feared that some outside force, some spirit, would steal the moment from him as she joined him, their legs briefly touching, Morea smoothing the wrinkles in her homespun dress. The scent of her was stronger now that they sat together, the lavender accompanied by something else he couldn't quite recognize. His mind threatened to spin out of control as an image of the hawk and dove flashed through his brain.

Morea felt the warmth of a blush spread across her cheeks as she realized the boy was simply sitting there, staring at her, a slight grin on his face. She dropped her eyes, and her hands fretted with a rough edge of her torn dress. She fought for control of her senses. *Think, girl, think*, her mind cried.

"I must learn more of your language if we are going to talk with each other," she stammered, trying hard not to look into his blue eyes, for she felt that she would lose her way under their power. Both young people sat in silence for a while, their legs still touching ever so slightly. The heat of a spark at the point of contact.

"I will try to teach you our Danish tongue, if you like." His smile was contagious as she also broke into a big grin.

"What are you smiling at?" Her tongue slid over her straight white teeth as she tried to keep from laughing.

"It's the way you use your hands when you speak," he answered in youthful innocence. "In my culture, we are taught to keep one hand free," he added without thinking.

A dark cloud seemed to pass over her face. "Yes, I know," she interrupted much more harshly than she intended, the sting apparent in her voice. "You must be able to reach your sword." The excited air of the moment, like that from a blacksmith's bellows, seemed to rush away from them in escape from the small cave. Her remark hung heavy in the damp air, but she refused to be sorry for the words she had spoken. They were the truth. She watched as Thomle's shoulders sagged and his leg moved away from hers, leaving a cold void where the heat had been only moments before. She looked at him.

"I'm sorry if the truth is difficult for you, Norseman, but your culture is violent." She sighed. Her shoulders sagged, and a chill swept over her. The young warrior and the young healer thought hard for common ground, but none appeared.

Heavy, dark shadows chased away the light as the sun sank ever so slowly toward the sea. After a time, Thomle worked, albeit halfheartedly, to teach Morea some of his language. Even though their conservation was strained and the awkwardness brought on by Morea's comment still ever-present, he was amazed at how fast the girl learned. For some reason, Morea didn't want to tell this Norseman that her grandmother had known the Danish language quite well and had taught it to her from an early age. She had never asked her grandmother how she had learned to speak Danish, and she herself hadn't spoken it in years.

The light in the cave gradually dimmed, and a cold mist drew down from the surrounding heights, cleansing the stench of death from the air for a short while. The semidarkness that gripped the inside of the cave unnerved Morea, and Thomle could sense her unease. Suggesting they move to the cave's opening, he led her toward the entrance. Together, they watched the last streaks of light peek through the mist and cast a fiery glow on the waters of the bay. Jagged curtains of red clouds emerged like steam from the horizon as the orb disappeared behind the hills of Mull. A stiff wind ruffled Morea's hair and kissed her cheeks as it rushed down from the north, carrying a chill with its breath and a promise of coming winter. They stood side by side, but their shoulders dared not touch, not now, not just yet. Morea began to shiver and made a feeble attempt to wrap the torn dress around her bare shoulders. Thomle watched her for a moment before he removed his bearskin and draped it over her.

"This will help keep the cold off," he said, placing the heavy cloak around her trembling frame.

"Thank you," she answered as the boy's body heat, trapped in the fur, warmed her.

Her spirits rose briefly, and she glowed from his warmth until several mournful cries rode the winds up from the village center like lost souls. Her mind was forced back to the carnage. Tears began to roll down her cheeks. Her face became impassive; her sight turned inward. On the one hand, she should hate this Norseman for all he and his war band had done to her village. On the other hand, her young heart sang when he smiled at her. Thomle saw the girl's tears and longed to comfort her, but he somehow knew that the silence that hung around them was the best medicine for now.

They sat enveloped in the silence, their shoulders still not quite touching, and watched the beauty of the sunset, almost but not quite able to forget the horrors of the day. Morea, heartsick and confused, finally summoned the courage to ask her initial question again, as the sound of wailing continued to rise on the air from the smoldering village.

"Thomle, I have to know, to try to understand why your people raid and kill my people. Why must you take that which is not yours? Why?" She sobbed the question, her face buried in her hands, her shoulders shaking once more under the great cloak. The element of romance in this dangerous encounter was fading like the sunbeams that shimmered in their last dance over the cold waters of Oban Bay. Thomle sat ramrod straight as his Viking pride fought against his young heart. The ache in his head began to grow into a pounding throb as he pondered her questions. He stared straight ahead but could feel the girl's shaking body close beside him.

His heart ached as much as his head while his mind sought answers that would not come. After his first raid and his subsequent first kill, Thomle knew that he wasn't like the others, and part of him was glad to recognize this. But there was another part of him. An ancient part that was his heritage, a part that he instinctively sought to fulfill but also despised. Like Morea, he, too, wondered why his people had to cause so much pain and why there wasn't a better way to obtain the many things they needed. Thomle looked to the darkening sky but found no comfort there, no answers to the many questions tormenting his soul. He gazed at Morea, repressing his desire to reach out to her. He knew of nothing he could say or do that could change the damage done here in this place called Oban—a place of the doves.

Morea continued to weep softly beside him, and the stars burned tiny holes in the dark expanse of the night sky. Gradually, a plan began to form in the young Viking's mind as he looked down at the smoldering embers of the decimated village. *It wouldn't make up for everything, but it would help*, he thought. *And maybe it would create a new beginning.* He rose stolidly from the ground beside the girl and, without a word, began to walk toward the village. Morea, slightly startled by his sudden departure, could only stare at his back as he walked away. Her hand seemed to move in slow motion as she reached out for him.

"Thomle," she cried and leaped to her feet, running after him. He turned at the sound of her voice and watched as she approached, her face streaked with tears, but soft and so beautiful. They stood, separated by mere inches, and looked into each other's eyes, both unsure of exactly what to say. Her heart raced, and his chest rose and fell with a noticeably faster rhythm. Finally, he spoke.

"I know no words in my language or yours that can undo what has been done here today. Nor can I stop the hurt in your heart. But I do have a plan that I think can help." He wanted to say more, to reach out to her, but he didn't. Instead, he turned and walked slowly into the twilight and into a new chapter in his young life.

"Thomle … Thomle." His name rode the haunting winds as she called it over and over.

* * * * *

He walked across the barren rocks as his name followed him like a Valkyrie siren, then across the grassy slope and into what was left of the village. He saw several huts still ablaze, but most were simply smoking heaps of destroyed hopes and dreams. Charred bodies of those who just a few days before had laughed and sang were scattered here and there. The village dogs fought over things he didn't want to know about, and women wept over their fallen mates or lost children. Thomle watched with new eyes as a host of warriors led cattle and sheep down past the burning monastery toward where his father waited to check and record them. The animals were loaded on one ship, while the various other plunder, as well as the slaves, were loaded on another. Thorma himself always kept the gold.

The young Norseman stood very still in the midst of this man-made hell. More slaves—mostly girls but some boys and older women—were marched past him toward the ships. As if drunk, he turned slowly in a circle. He was simply seeing things as they really were for the first time, and it was a dizzying experience. With a newly cultivated anger, he walked up behind his father. Staring at the big man's back, Thomle was about to speak when his father's voice suddenly boomed.

"Where is the cloak I had made for you?" The question came without Thorma even turning around. Somewhat startled, Thomle hesitated.

"I want to talk to you … alone," he muttered, cursing himself for his lack of courage as he glanced around to see if any of the warriors had heard his demand. They were all busy and didn't seem to have noticed, but Thorma detected the sharp tone of his son's voice and slowly turned to face him. He raised his eyes from the tally pad until they met his son's. He stared at the boy for a long time but said nothing. Finally, he nodded toward an area a short distance from the ships where a small stream flowed out of a cleared field and joined the sea. Thorma stooped to tie his now shivering slave girls to a large piece of driftwood and watched his son walk away.

"Damn, how much he reminds me of myself years ago," Thorma whispered to the girls before he tossed his cloak around them. They could only stare back wide-eyed as the big man straightened his sore knees and followed his son. Smoke and fog drifted by in swirling clumps, and Thomle stood watching an ocean cod swimming in a clear pool. Silence hung heavy in the rancid air as father and son turned their gaze far out into the dark sea.

Thorma speculated about his son's urgent request. *Was it another kill, or maybe his first woman?* He smiled at that thought and laughed out loud despite himself, oblivious to the rage on his son's face. Finally, glancing over, he recognized the glare coming from those blue eyes. *His mother's eyes,* thought Thorma, and stopped laughing. Thomle's rage wasn't so much directed at his father as it was at himself—for not knowing what to say or even why he needed to say it.

"Damn!" he groaned and tried again to organize his thoughts.

"Well, speak, boy," roared Thorma, his son's internal struggle showing on his young face. "What's so important that it enrages you so, and where is your bearskin cloak?" Thomle hesitated, remembering where he had left his cloak. He didn't answer; he wasn't even sure if his father expected an answer.

The young Norseman took a deep breath and prepared to speak, but the first words had not left his mouth before the hawk and dove sailed low over their heads. *Why now?* he asked himself as he watched the birds circle the Viking horde. The dim reflection from the remaining fires in the village cast an eerie glow in the eyes of the hawk, and its cry echoed into the dark night. Bork, Olaf's dim-witted son, stood nearby and he too saw the birds flying overhead. Seeing his father's killer, he fumbled in his quiver for an arrow. The big man, who was much better with a battle-ax than a Viking bow, clumsily notched the arrow and began to take aim at the hawk. Just as he released the string, he was struck hard on his right side and knocked to his knees by a charging Thomle, who, for reasons he could never understand, rushed past his startled father to attack Bork. The arrow left Bork's bow and flew just off its mark, sailing between the hawk and the dove before splashing harmlessly into the sea.

The hawk's excited cry reverberated loudly over the stunned group of Viking warriors who stared slack-jawed into the dark night. Bork regained his footing and was reaching for his sword when he felt the cold tip of another blade prick the skin on his neck.

"Enough!" roared Thorma, who had anticipated his nephew's reaction. When Bork stood, the old warrior had to look up at the giant of a boy, but Thorma's hard stare caused his dull eyes to drop and glance around for support. There was none. Thorma knew that his brother's son wasn't a bad young man; he had just been raised by a cruel one.

"Bork, take a few men and build a large fire. It looks as if it is going to be a long night," instructed Thorma. His nephew hesitated, and Thorma asked again, this time more forcefully.

"Go. We'll talk later," he said, softening his voice noticeably. With his large shoulders slumped, the young Bork grabbed two reluctant men and stomped off toward a large pile of driftwood about fifty yards from the ships.

A storm was building far out beyond the horizon, and lightning flashed angrily in the dark sky. The wind was like a cold breath that amplified an inner dread both Thorma and Thomle felt as each anticipated returning to their conversation. Both men remained lost in their separate thoughts as Bork and his group started a large blaze before easing away toward another pile of wood to build a second fire. Grave matters seemed to ride on the air, and all the signs were bad. The men could feel it and were restless.

Thorma stepped closer to the first blaze as he watched his crew move away and his eyes turned toward the black sea. Like the hawk's, the old warrior's eyes reflected the flames. Thomle placed his shield with its one red kill mark against a drift log awaiting its turn on the fire and lay back against it. He was tired, and his head had begun to hurt again. His father spoke first.

"I was a young a man, younger than you, when I went on my first raid with my father." He spat at the sad memory. "I made my first kill on that raid, just as you did a few days ago." Thomle started to reply, but Thorma raised his big hand. "Let me finish," he said in a low voice that Thomle hardly recognized. "I saw a lot of slaughter on those early raids. My father, my brother, they liked to inflict pain, but my heart ached from all the senseless killing. I … I hurt in my soul for all the pain I have seen … and caused."

There was a long awkward pause. The driftwood fire roared toward the heavens, sparks dancing like summer fireflies. Thomle sat silently. Slowly Thorma turned from his spot near the fire and walked over to look down at his son.

"I guess you never thought you would hear that from your father, huh?" He laughed a little as he took off his helmet and scratched his head. Thomle felt the time was right to speak, and he nearly jumped from his seat against the log.

"Then why must we do this?" He pointed toward the smoldering huts, some still aglow. Thorma closed his pale-gray eyes and ran his hand through his bushy reddish-brown hair.

"Because we have always taken what we wanted, what we thought we needed. Always," he answered in a tired voice, the volume trailing off like wind escaping a sail.

"But why?" pressed Thomle, parroting Morea's question that still pounded in his head. Thorma gave a snort of a laugh.

"I asked myself that same question many years ago." He sighed. "I still have no answer." The old warrior turned back to look again at the rumbling sea as if searching for an answer that might surface like a fish chasing after a fly. With his back still turned to his son, he continued, "You are very lucky, Thomle. If I had asked my father that question, he would have beat me senseless. You never knew him, but my father was a hard, tyrannical man, just like my brother—maybe worse." Thorma looked over at the burial pyre being built for Olaf.

A fire to start him on his journey to Valhalla. Will I have such a fire to start my journey? he wondered. Olaf's huge shield lay by his side, and his sword had been placed across his chest. His body lay on top of the pyre. *Odin expects a warrior to come armed to the great feasting hall of Valhalla*, thought Thorma, his mind wandering.

* * * * *

Father and son sat watching the sparks from the fire race into the dark sky as Morea, who had grown weary of the cave, crept cautiously from its entrance. She stopped just outside the cave and looked toward the two large fires in the distance. *Thomle must be down there*, she thought before taking a deep breath and heading in the direction of the blazes. Partly hidden by the bearskin cloak, she seemed to float through the ruins of her village like a ghost, walking past sobbing widows who seemed too distraught to notice her. She floated along the way; a dream slips through the sleeping mind just before it awakes until at last she stood in the shadows only a few yards from where Thorma and Thomle gazed into the heart of the fire. Kneeling, she settled in among several large boulders, pulling the bearskin tightly around her to stave off the chill. Surrounded by the sounds of the night, Morea listened to the young Viking and his father.

Thomle's mind filled with a thousand questions he wanted to ask his father even as he worried about the girl whom he thought was back at the cave. Moving from the opposite side of the blaze, Thorma cleared his throat and began to speak again. Out of respect, Thomle stayed his many questions and remained silent. The old warrior knelt down between the fire and the log that his son sat on, the fire to his back. He had found a long stick and was drawing lines in the sand as he spoke.

"I fought many battles alongside my father and my brother. For reasons I will never understand, the pain they inflicted made them drunk with power, and they seemed to enjoy the killing." He stabbed the stick angrily into the sand as if remembering a particular episode.

"I was as good as either of them with the sword or ax, but I never liked killing." The big man looked over at his son. "I was never able to feel what Olaf must have felt. He and my father often walked the berserker's way in battle, but I always tried to keep my head. My father cursed me in front of Olaf many times for making so few kills, but he also saw that I could outsmart the enemy, which is what wins close battles. My father finally came to understand that. I hope that you will understand that someday too, Thomle."

Thorma rose to pace in the sand, his boots soon obliterating the lines he had drawn. They must have meant something when he drew them, but now, looking down, he couldn't remember what it was. Thomle watched his father pace and nodded.

"Yes, Father, I do understand." Thorma glanced at his son and then went on.

"Almost anyone"—he drew his sword and looked down its edge—"can thrust a sword or swing a battle-axe, but to keep your head in battle when men are dying and there is chaos all around you, that is rare. That is the only reason my father, although reluctantly, made me chief of our band. Not because he liked me best—he liked Olaf much more—but because I could think in battle." He spat. "Olaf never accepted that." He laughed. "Never."

Thorma Morestrong was a battle-hardened warrior who could kill when he had to, but deep inside, he was still that young confused man who cried as he watched the life bleed from the body of his first kill. Thorma had been sixteen at the time. A mere boy, he had plunged his sword into the stomach of another boy about his same age. In addition to all the blood, tears had flowed from the eyes of the young Pict warrior, not so much from the pain of the wound that shredded his bowels, which was terrible, but from the pain of knowing that his young life was finished. His hopes and dreams were spilling onto the ground at his feet. The boy sank to his knees and cried for his mother.

"I still hear that boy's cries late at night. Sometimes I'm asleep, but sometimes I'm wide awake," moaned Thorma. "My father"—he paused and swallowed back something—"my mighty father found me vomiting near a small stream after watching the boy die while I held his hand. The great leader of our band, the man who sired me, beat me with the flat of his sword until I was unconscious." Thorma shook his head and looked into the dark void overhead.

After a few long, silent minutes, he rose from his stiff knee and stood looking into the fire. Thomle didn't know what to say. Neither his father nor his mother had ever told him these tales. The fact that his father, his chief, this warrior leader, had ever had doubts about what they were doing shocked the young Norseman. His mind raced, and he tried to organize his thoughts, hoping his questions would help this sad situation they were caught in. He wanted to show respect to his father, but he also needed to make sure that the crew knew he still respected the warrior traditions that were such a part of their Viking culture.

Thomle rose stiffly himself, his body still sore from the day's events. He looked over at their band of sleeping Norsemen whose lumped forms lay near the second fire some fifty feet away. Only a few guards on the slave ship remained awake. Thorma watched his son rise slowly and walk toward him, the bloodstained strip of cloth still wrapped around his head. As the leader of the war band, Thorma needed to look his son in the eye for what appeared to be a formal talk. The eyes would tell the truth when the tongue could not. The son spoke; the father listened.

"Father, is there not some way to obtain the things our people need, some way to barter or trade or negotiate without killing and taking?" The night sounds seemed to hush as the words poured from Thomle, almost as if someone else were doing the talking. Thorma listened out of respect for his son, but his mind screamed *no*. The very idea of bartering for goods was alien to him and his culture.

From where she crouched in the shadows, Morea herself was listening carefully to these words. She had been able to understand most of what Thomle was saying to his father, and she was thrilled. "Maybe," she whispered, "just maybe."

Thorma stood with his arms crossed on his chest, somewhat surprised at himself that he was not becoming angry. His son called into question the very core of their society, their way of life. But the words Thomle spoke, the questions he was raising, were the same questions Thorma himself had hidden away deep inside—buried, unanswered in the back of his mind.

* * * * *

The ideas and questions were flowing from the young warrior as if a dam had burst, and the water was words spilling forth. Pausing for a moment, Thomle cocked his head to the side and listened to the night. A dove had begun calling from a nearby scrub oak at the edge of the beach as the dark night fought with the first pale rays of dawn. The dingy gray fog quivered in the predawn light, and the cooing of the dove rode along the breeze from the sea—a strange serenity coming over the two men. Thomle shuddered in the quiet chill, gripped by an unusual stillness. The three-quarter moon hanging low in the sky had become blood red as it played hide-and-seek behind the dark clouds. Thorma's instincts suddenly came alive, and the hair stood up on the back of his neck. His big head turned slowly from side to side, and he sniffed the air like his ancestors had millennia before. He could feel it—something was astir, but he couldn't tell what.

The young Viking looked toward the sea where the fog blocked his view of the ships except for their serpent heads that bobbed in the surf. Thorma was watching his son; he started to ask again about the missing bearskin cloak when he saw movement out of the corner of his eye.

"Lo, the gods walk." He gasped and reached for his sword. Out of the swirling fog, an apparition rose and glided over the rocks toward them. Large and hairy, it moved slowly as if hunting for a meal. *Or maybe a soul*, thought Thorma as blood drained from his face. His big, calloused hand found the sword hilt, and he grasped it tightly, all the while his mind urged him to run. Oddly, as the apparition drew nearer, the dove's call grew more urgent. Then suddenly, the hawk's cry shook the damp air.

Morea was literally shaking with fear. Her decision to approach the pair of Norsemen seemed foolish now as she grew nearer and could see Thomle's father reach for his sword. But still she walked forward. The mist parted, and the light from the dying embers cast eerie shadows that danced on the rocky beach in front of her. She was driven forward by the hope she had heard in Thomle's voice even as she recognized the great internal struggles that both he and his father faced. They may indeed kill her, but she couldn't lose this chance to speak to them together. It was time to confront these men who had caused so much pain and destruction in her village. The calls of the hawk and dove encouraged her, and she took the final few steps without fear.

"Damnation," growled Thorma as he spat to ward off the evil spirits that must be accompanying this beast. He withdrew his sword from its sheath just as Thomle grabbed his wrist.

"Are you crazy, or are you just trying to get us killed?" bellowed Thorma, attempting to shake his son's grasp. "It will take both of us to kill this thing," he growled as cold sweat rolled down his brow. Spinning around, Thorma faced his son, who he was afraid had come under the creature's spell. "Damn you, let go of my arm," he cursed.

"No, Father!" shouted Thomle, having recognized his bearskin cloak. He struggled with his father as Morea drew closer. "It's the girl from the village," he said with a strange look on his face.

"What damn girl?" shouted Thorma, confused.

"The one I never told you about," confessed Thomle.

Thomle knew it wasn't a spirit that approached them, yet both he and his father stepped back when Morea walked out of the mist, shed the bearskin cloak, and stood before them. Seeing it was indeed a mere girl, Thorma relaxed only slightly, still gripping the sword hard. He spat again just in case they both had been bewitched. The two men dwarfed the girl, and the scene was almost comical, but no one, except maybe the gods, laughed.

Morea's heart pounded so loudly she was sure Thomle and his father could hear it, but it was too late to turn back now. Not quite sure how to begin, she looked past the two men toward the second fire and the warriors sleeping around it. She spotted the two soon-to-be slave girls clutching each other in the cold mist. Someone had thrown a bearskin cloak across their shoulders. *Could it have been Thomle's father?* she wondered and briefly glanced in his direction.

She recognized the girls from her small village. Looking around, she realized it had just become much smaller.

Summoning her last bit of courage, she turned toward the two men in front of her, totally unaware of how strange a figure she struck. Her shadow extending huge and dark behind her for thirty feet, her every move reflected against the rocks. Thomle wanted to say something, but no words came as the fire seemed to dance on the girl's dark hair, and her bare shoulders glistened in the early morning mist. Thorma nearly tripped over a stick of wood as he moved back even further when she spoke.

"Why?" she nearly whispered the word. "Why have you come to our peaceful village? We have done you no wrong, caused you no harm." She paused for a second, letting the question sink in. Speaking slowly in the Northmen's tongue, her grandmother's lessons flooding back into her memory, she continued, "You have killed and plundered, you have raped and destroyed, and I ask you, Why?" Struggling to keep her emotions in check, her lips quivered ever so slightly as she waited for an answer. None came.

Fear and anger battled for possession of her mind, but after a few heartbeats, the air of confidence she had been projecting began to escape from her. Trying hard to keep her hands from trembling, she managed to straighten her back and stare into the eyes of Thorma Morestrong. She would stand her ground even if it cost her life; her questions demanded an answer.

Thorma glared back at her. He wasn't frightened anymore, but the damned wench had thrown him off guard, and her gaze was cutting deep into his soul like a sharp knife. He had seen this look before, but mostly from men. He had to think. He had to stay calm. After a long minute, he spoke, looking at his son.

"So we must speak to a mere peasant, a girl at that. I should tie her by her wrists and put her with my other slaves." It was all he could manage to say, the bluster trailing off as Morea's eyes bored into him.

Her stare never wavered, and its effect was palpable. The big man reached down and slowly pulled his sword from its bloody scabbard. The sword, its flat surface reflecting fire, was nearly as long as the girl was tall, and it trembled ever so slightly from his anger. He knew he could hide behind this piece of steel, for he had no answers to her damn questions.

Taking one menacing step toward the girl and then another, he expected her to run, but she never moved. She simply stared straight into him. The hawk was crying out overhead as Thorma's grip tightened on the sword handle. In a flash, Thomle's hand shot out and grabbed his father's wrist. Thorma, caught off guard, jerked back hard. When his arm still wasn't free, he turned a threatening gaze toward his son. The world stood deathly still for a long, slow heartbeat. Father and son stared into each other's eyes. Neither blinked.

"No!" shouted Morea, and she stepped toward them, her hand lightly touching Thomle's. "Hasn't enough blood been shed already?" she cried, her voice soft but full of intent. Sinews bulging in their sword arms, the warriors stood on the edge of a deadly void. A sad place where men had found themselves for untold years. It formed a line that, once crossed, allowed for no return. The hawk grew silent, but the dove echoed Morea's plea.

"Please ..." She looked them in the eyes. "No more blood, not from you two!" Thomle's grip on his father's arm lessened, and the act was rewarded by the sound of a sword sliding back into its sheath.

"So this is what happened to your cloak," growled Thorma, though his voice held little of the tension of a few moments ago.

"Yes, Father," said Thomle, an embarrassed grin spreading across his face. Both men had backed away from the deadly edge, and now Thomle, taking a deep breath, began explaining the complete story of what had happened to Olaf. Thorma barely listened to his son for he was nearly spellbound by the girl, her courage greatly impressing him. When Thomle finished speaking, Thorma just shook his big head.

"I have no answers to your questions, girl," he grunted, seemingly unconcerned about the new details of his brother's death. "My son and I have just now been asking ourselves these same questions. The truth is ... the life of a Norseman is hard, and our ways are hard." He slammed his big fist against his chest, causing the chain mail to rattle. "We are a hard people!" he nearly shouted. Thomle watched the girl jump when his father beat his chest, her slight frame beginning to shiver. He reached down to retrieve his cloak and moved to place it back upon her shoulders. But her small hand waved it away.

"No, Thomle. I am cold, but I must finish that which I have started before I can ever feel warm again." Walking with her head down, she moved to the edge of the dying embers and gazed into their mesmerizing depths. Standing there for a long moment, she gathered her thoughts before slowly turning to face the two warriors again. Tears flowed down her dirty cheeks despite her best efforts to prevent them from doing so. In the distance, the crew had begun stirring. Some, upon waking, had started walking toward where their chief stood. To get a better look at what was happening, the Norsemen fanned out to form a wide semicircle. *It is now or never,* she thought. She straightened her dirty smock, brushed the tears from her cheeks, lifted her trembling chin, and looked Thorma in the eye. As she began to speak, the Danish language rolled off her tongue to the amazement of this fierce band of Norsemen.

"My people have always lived a simple life here near the sea. We fish, and we tend the few meager crops that will grow in this rocky soil." She kicked the dirt under her feet for emphasis. "We raise our sheep and cattle, and we pray to the new god, whom the monks tell us is caring and loving. We bother no one. All we ask is to live in peace and watch our children grow up with full bellies and happy hearts. Then you come." She paused and looked into the hardened faces staring back at her. "You come with your dragon ships and your battle-axes. You kill our men and turn our small children into slaves. You rape and carry away our young women. You burn our huts. And all we can do is stand and watch, hoping that you do not come back." She paused and wiped away a lone tear.

"But you do come back. You always come back. You come back because we are easy pickings and because you—you Vikings— must have been born without hearts. For if you had hearts, surely, the cries of children would break them, as they do ours." Her voice had grown louder, nearly shouting this last comment, but now she simply sighed, her shoulders drooping as if she had finished a long journey. Tears once again formed around the corners of her tired eyes, but she willed them back. "No more tears," she whispered to herself, and none fell. Silence wrapped the beach and all who stood there in a blanket as heavy as the damp fog rising from the sea. Time slowed, and even the waves from the cold North Sea, waves that had rolled relentlessly past a thousand lonely isles on their way to lap the beaches of Oban, seemed reluctant to come ashore. The Viking horde, some with mouths agape, stared at the young strange woman as if they expected more. And she was happy to oblige because her words flowed freely now.

"We would be willing to give you many of the crops and cattle you take from us. We could trade our goods for the furs you carry on your backs. But instead, you take and keep on taking. That which we work hard for and that which we hold dear, you take from us without a second thought. Surely," her voice almost broke, "the death and pain you cause is carried somewhere in your being. The cries of our young heard, if not by your ears, then in your very souls. We ask that you spare us this pain, and we will give you much of what you need. Please, no more killing and no more raping. Leave us in peace. And somehow we will repay you for the act."

Dozens of booted feet shuffled in the sand as everyone waited, especially Thorma. No woman had ever spoken to him so forcefully, not even his mother. But what really struck him hard was that no one had ever before come so close to saying the things he had kept hidden in the depths of his heart for so many years. He remained silent; they all were silent because nobody knew how to reply to this young woman who stood, alone, in front of them.

* * * * *

Thomle stood off to the side, gazing, awestruck at Morea, while Thorma, who had just reached to take his helmet off, was wondering if maybe a better way of life truly could exist—each man mesmerized in his own way when suddenly a savage roar erupted just behind them. With the quickness of a large cat and experience born from years of combat, Thorma spun with his sword in his hand.

"No!" he shouted at his attacker, and his sword shot up from reflex to block a vicious blow from his nephew Bork. Sparks flew as their swords sought flesh and danced the ancient dance of death in the early morning light. Thomle was a second slower to react, but he understood the roar of mutiny growing among a section of their crew, and he turned with a roar of his own. Quickly parrying a thrust aimed at the girl by Erik Swineson, Thomle gently pushed Morea aside and jumped into the fight. Death rode once more on sharp swords and bared talons.

Several of the crew members were indeed in mutiny; the remainder stood back, awaiting the outcome—just the latest manifestation of an age-old struggle. Their allegiance lay with the warrior with the strongest arm and the quickest sword. It was no surprise to Thorma that the mutineers were spurred on by Erik Swineson, who now led a chant of "Kill the girl, kill the girl," and rushed forward. Thomle struck down his assailant and moved swiftly toward the pock-faced Swineson just as the hawk dove out of the mist, striking Erik's face the same way it had done Olaf's. Erik was luckier than Olaf, though. He turned his head slightly as Thomle approached, and that saved his eyes. Instead, the sharp talons tore flesh from his cheek and jaw, and the wounded Viking fell to his knees, clutching his torn face.

The attack lasted only a few seconds before the hawk flew off toward the high oaks as Thorma's voice boomed in the morning air.

"I am still your chief, and I alone say who dies and who lives." Father and son stood shoulder to shoulder in front of the girl, their swords held high and ready, reflecting morning light toward the others. Sweat rolled down the combatants' cheeks, and the air burned their lungs. All the men waited.

"That damned bird ruined my face," cried Swineson as blood ran through his clenched fingers. Tears mixed with blood and sweat as he spat curses at the gods, rocking back and forth on his knees. Bork looked around at his small band of mutineers. All stood with heads down, either from shame or fear or both. He slowly lowered his sword and faced his uncle.

Thorma, sensing the change of mood, stepped forward. "I am your leader!" he shouted, challenging each man by looking him in the eye. "I am your leader!" he shouted again, gruffer this time, demanding a response.

"Yes, you are our leader!" they shouted back in unison. Thomle relaxed his stance slightly and turned toward Morea, the dove once more cooing nearby. His heart raced. She smiled faintly, still very scared, but relieved he was so near.

"Thank you," she mouthed in Danish, which made him smile. Morea was struggling with the need to say more, and her heart sorely wanted to believe that this young Viking was indeed different from the rest. *Words, words!* her mind screamed. She so terribly needed the right words, words that would help these men understand the reality her people faced. She felt that Thomle and his father were good men, but glancing around at the burnt-out huts and the savage warriors who lurked around the dying fire, she had few illusions. Morea mac Craig knew that this confrontation would be the most important of her life. In fact, her life might very well depend on it.

Thorma kept one eye on Erik's band and the other on his son and the girl. He sensed that she was not through speaking. He just hoped that he and Thomle could keep the crew at bay long enough for her to finish. Morea took one last look into Thomle's eyes and walked tentatively up to Thorma.

"My lord," she began, her heart beating as loud as the Viking war drums.

"We could work for you—not as slaves but as partners in an endeavor. You could give us protection from other raiders, and we could share our crops and livestock with you. Some of our young men could even go with you as apprentices to learn new trades. Our young women would not go, for they would not be safe." Her eyes never wavered as she spoke.

Thomle listened to Morea but kept his eyes on the mutinous warriors. Every so often, his gaze would drift back to the young girl—his father towering over her as she spoke to him. The wind had picked up and was blowing her hair, which she brushed out of her eyes. *What is this feeling I get every time I look at her?* Thomle asked himself, puzzled. All eyes were on the pretty young woman who stood defiantly in front of their leader. Sword in hand, Thorma stood in a battle stance, ready for another attack, but he was listening. As part of his mind pondered what she said, another part marveled at her courage. This girl was far braver and wiser than most of the men in her village. Overhead, the dove cooed, and the hawk cried out as she spoke. *Maybe it is a sign from their god, for surely, this girl controls these birds*, thought Thorma. He spat to ward off the spirits even if they were friendly.

Morea paused when the big Norseman spat, an ancient custom that her people still practiced as well. *Oh, please let some of what I say find its mark in his heart*, she pleaded to whatever god was listening. Thorma wasn't as superstitious as most of his band, but something made the hairs on his neck tingle. It was not her ability to speak their language that amazed him the most, but the way that her god seemed to protect her. The great hawk circling overhead in the dawn's early mist was proof of that. The Viking horde stood mesmerized. Several dared to look up at the hawk, wondering whether she truly controlled this bird.

Thorma wanted to give Morea the answers she deserved, but a struggle raged inside him. *If I go with my heart and say we will try this agreement, I know what my men will say*, he thought to himself. *And what about the village elders back at Balfour? They always want more— more slaves, more cattle. Where does it stop?*

"Damn," he groaned. Thomle watched his father, knowing he was struggling. He saw Morea standing, seemingly alone, hoping the violence that had consumed her village for generations could finally come to an end.

Two separate events occurred simultaneously just as Thorma was about to speak. First, the few remaining men of the village began walking as a group toward the beach where the Vikings were gathered. Second, the group of mutinous Norsemen had regained their composure and still led by Erik Swineson, who had wrapped his wounds, seemed to be plotting another strike. The hawk had flown over to where the dove was perched high on a white oak limb, and both watched as the drama unfolded below. Thomle was facing Morea and saw the approaching villagers behind her. What he didn't see, having focused on the girl, were the mutineers behind him.

"Why would your people be coming down here?" Thomle asked. "Have they not seen it is useless to fight us?" He moved his hand down to the hilt of his sword.

Morea jerked her head around and stared up the beach. "I don't think they want to fight anymore, Thomle." She placed her hand on his sword hand. "I'll go see." She had not missed the trepidation in the young Viking's voice, so she started running up the rocky beach toward the solemn-faced villagers, her brother among them.

Neither she nor Thomle noticed the group led by Swineson start to spread out around them. Thorma, though, being an old warrior, had sensed the shift of bodies and spun to meet them. The girl ran toward her brother just as the trap closed. Thomle, still unaware of the mutineers' movements, had drown his sword in case the villagers attacked. Father and son, once again, stood back-to-back and ready to fight, though each faced a different challenge. The sun had finally burnt through the morning mist, and beams of light bounced off the two swords held aloft. The screaming mob behind him caused Thomle to abandon his front; he spun just in time to see an arrow strike his father in the shoulder. The big man grunted and shook off his son's look of concern. The light mail hauberk had done its job. The arrow hadn't struck bone, but blood poured from the wound when Thorma reached up and ripped the shaft out of his left shoulder. The big sword continued to swing in his right arm as blood dripped onto the sand.

Bork avoided Thorma and went after his cousin instead. Thomle saw a blur of movement out of the corner of his right eye and turned just in time to dodge Bork's mighty thrust aimed straight for his head. The boy had been watching his father rip the arrow out of his shoulder, and it nearly cost him his life.

"Damn, boy, watch yourself!" shouted Thorma when he saw how close Bork's thrust came to skewing his son. Recovering quickly, Thomle spun and drove his sword toward the attacker; skill and youth guided the blade, and it quickly found flesh. It sang the song of a thousand ages as it sliced through the air and struck Bork's thick neck. Blood and bone sprayed into the air and onto Thomle's sword hand as Bork's lifeless body fell to the ground, jerked a few times, and lay still.

The Vikings' killing blood was on the rise now, and only cold steel would stop them. Swineson, shouting encouragements from the rear, drove his small band forward as the hawk rose from its perch. The bird of prey circled high overhead, the echoes of its shill cry joining the clash of swords below. "I, Thorma, demand you stop this mutiny. You men have sworn an oath to me on your sword." Thorma bellowed the demand even though he knew it was useless. An arrow flashed by his head as if in answer.

Morea, out of breath, raced up to her brother and the village elders as they stood watching the Norsemen fight among themselves.

"You must go back. Please go back," she pleaded between breaths.

"Back to where, Morea?" cried her brother. "No place is safe from them." He pointed toward the Norsemen. "Our only chance is to attack while they are distracted."

"It won't work. The only real chance you have is if Thomle and his father can win the battle, but I'm afraid they won't survive this mutiny," she cried.

"What are you talking about?" her brother asked, his eyes darting back and forth between the Vikings' battle and several elders who had dropped their weapons and begun fleeing back up the beach through the destroyed village. But most of them stayed to listen as Morea desperately tried to explain what was happening down on the beach.

Erik Swineson, thinking himself smarter than the fallen Bork, was still leading his group from the rear, shouting threats and encouragements from the back of the mass of fighters while Thorma's sword worked its savage trade. Erik fetched his bow, knowing it was a great weapon to use from a distance. He had only gotten two clear shots at Thorma, but one of those had found its mark. Now, however, he turned his eyes skyward, taking aim at the hawk as it circled overhead. Fearing he would anger the gods who seemed to control the bird, his arm that held the bow trembled ever so slightly. But finally, he let loose the arrow. It sailed at a brisk pace through the early morning air and struck the hawk's left wing. The giant bird gave a mournful cry and fell toward a clump of heather near where Morea stood with her brother and the other villagers. The girl glanced up and watched in horror as it fell from the sky. Never hesitating, she turned from the group and rushed to where the hawk had fallen, her brother pleading uselessly for her to stay.

Erik Swineson smiled. But the smile was painful, given the damage done to his face, and it quickly became a grimace. "So much for your god and his birds." He spat and started tracking Thorma with his next arrow. The sweat that rolled down his forehead stung his eyes as he looked for an open shot at his leader. Father and son were fighting like madmen. Three bloody bodies lay sprawled at their feet, but Thorma's blows were beginning to weaken. Feeling the impact of the loss of blood, the warrior's movements were slow and uncertain, his feet unsteady. Finally, the big man stumbled, and Erik, seeing it happen, let loose another arrow that flew seeking its prey. It was the small platelets in his mail jargon that saved Thorma's life. The arrow tip of polished iron had crumpled when it struck them, though it managed to penetrate the flesh about an inch. Sadly for Thorma, it was in his good shoulder, the mighty right arm that wielded the deadly sword, the Bringer of Death. His left arm now hung mostly limp, still seeping blood onto the already deeply stained sand.

Thomle was battling for his life with two opponents but watched out of the corner of his eye as his father was hit with another arrow. Throwing caution to the wind, he broke from his fight with the mutineers and quickly pulled the shaft from Thorma's right shoulder. The big man roared in defiance and raised his injured arm, yet his whole body was stiff, and he was barely able to stand. Thomle was reluctant to leave his father's side but finally moved off to his right, barely dodging a slashing sword from another assailant as he did so. With an angry growl, he resumed his fight.

From a crouched position, Thorma Morestrong miraculously parried several vicious blows from his nearest adversary, but he knew in his heart that to finish the fight, to even survive, he had to attack and attack now! With a mighty oath to Odin and a prayer to Valhalla, Thorma rose to his full height and swung his mighty sword with his last bit of strength. His blade glistened in the morning light, driving the mutineers back as he desperately searched for the leader of the rebellion, Erik Swineson.

Thomle fought his two adversaries on the fringe of the battle area, and although he had seen the arrow strike the hawk, he was in no position to offer help. He circled slowly to his left so he could observe his father, and it took him only a second to see that the old man was weakening from his wounds. His mind screamed *Help him*, but Thomle was fully occupied with the two men that stalked him—like wolves after a dying calf. He could not help. Not yet. He was younger and stronger than the two mutineers he faced, but they were more experienced, having survived many battles. It made the fight a draw. Thomle had always moved better to his left, so he continued in that direction until suddenly he saw a flash of movement out of the corner of his right eye. He half turned in that direction, fearing a third adversary. What he saw was a young villager, with hair and eyes just like Morea's, swinging a large wooden staff at one of his opponents. A well-used Yew bow was strapped across his back; why he wasn't using it instead of the staff, Thomle couldn't understand. But the staff worked. It struck one of the mutineers near the base of the skull, and the unsuspecting Norseman went down without knowing what had hit him. The downed fighter's companion saw the odds change in a heartbeat and slowly backed away as Thomle's sword rained several crushing blows against his shield.

Thorma, with blood dripping from his left arm and his right shoulder throbbing with every stroke, fought his way through the remaining mutineers until at last only one man stood between him and Erik Swineson. That man wanted to run; Thorma could see it in his eyes. But the grizzled old warrior saw that there was no escape and was forced to stand and fight. He lost a hand to one of Thorma's vicious strokes a minute later. The sword fell, still clutched in the severed hand, and the man stood there in a daze, looking down at it for a second as if it was all a bad dream. When blood began shooting from his wound, though, reality quickly set in. In shock, he bent over, picked up the sword still clutched in his fallen hand, and walked with a drunken stagger toward the ships. At last, Thorma, with his great chest heaving from his efforts, faced the leader of the mutiny.

Erik Swineson watched the last of his fellow mutineers throw down their weapons, cursing them as they stepped back out of the way. "You cowardly scum, I'll take care of this dog myself, then I will deal with you." He spat and shook his sweaty head from side to side. His eyes were slits of hatred as he began circling the tired old warrior like a wolf would circle an old stag in their death match. Eric, sensing weakness, made a few short thrusts at his leader to test his reaction. Thorma, his sword arm dragging, stumbled slightly as he moved to dodge Swineson's blade. Blood ran down his arm as he struggled to block an overhand attack. The remaining warriors stood back and waited. Erik's confidence grew as he played the deadly cat-and-mouse game. *I can kill him now*, thought Swineson. *He's too weak to block my strokes.* A wicked smile crept across his scarred face. Thorma, appearing exhausted, dropped to one knee after blocking a powerful thrust. *I have to fool him into thinking I'm nearly finished*, thought Thorma as he struggled to his feet. Wearily, he broke out of his fighter's stance and leaned heavily on his sword, staggering slightly as he exaggerated his breathing in a ruse to confuse his smiling adversary. Erik, watching closely with his weasel-like eyes, took the bait and moved in for the kill. But his savage downward stroke missed, and the big man, despite his wounds, moved quickly. Roaring like a beast, Thorma sidestepped and swung his sword down as Swineson attempted to regain his balance from his missed stroke. The sword called Death Bringer, the sword of Thorma Morestrong, drove through the mail armor of the startled Erik Swineson, down into his lung, ripping apart his pounding heart. Swineson died with a look of bewilderment on his face; his eyes glazed over as he sank to his knees before pitching forward onto the bloody sand. Jerking his sword from the dead body, Thorma slowly turned to face the last remaining mutineers. Although barely able to stand, he was determined to finish this fight.

* * * * *

67

Father and son once again stood side-by-side facing their foes, who having seen Erik's death were now begging for mercy. But Thorma and Thomle were in no mood for mercy. Caught up in the carnage and what the old warriors called the berserker's way, they advanced on the kneeling men. Only the sudden appearance of the grayish dove stopped the two fighters. The dove flew from her perch in the scrub oak and sailed between the two groups, landing on a broken spear shaft sticking out of the rocky beach. The bloody spear had been driven into the sand. Who put it there was anybody's guess; later, no one could remember.

The sound of heavy breathing and painful moans mingled with the cooing of the dove as both groups cautiously eyed each other. The sudden arrival of the dove caused the warriors to hesitate.

"Surely, the gods are speaking through this bird," whispered Thorma as he and everyone else watched Morea walk down the beach to where the dove sat atop the spear shaft.

"It is time to stop this needless killing!" she shouted, looking out at the fighters. Only a few of the tired and battered men held her gaze. *The great Odin would laugh*, thought Thorma, *at the sight of this young girl and a small dove standing amongst all this death and carnage.* Thorma shook his head, but he didn't laugh.

Morea's voice was stern, and for the moment, it held sway over the battle. The weary combatants listened intently, especially the surviving mutineers. Some hoped for more words, some just expected more death. *What now?* she asked herself as her breathing became fast and shallow. Her forehead wrinkled in concentration. And her anger grew with each breath.

"It is time to stop, do you hear me? Stop the killing, even if it is one another you're after. We want only to be left alone. Go somewhere else to act like fools and barbarians. Even the poor dove cries for peace."

The survivors of the mutinous group remained on their knees as they looked fleetingly from Thorma and his son to the girl, who strangely enough might become their salvation. With a flutter of small wings, the dove flew from its perch and sailed in the direction of the fallen hawk, its wings beating fiercely.

Silence once more ruled, everyone eyeing each other, until at last Thorma's booming voice rang out.

"It is time for a council." He limped down to the dying fire, its heat no longer needed, for the sun had finally burnt its way through the smoke and mist. It now bore down on the battered Norsemen like an unforgiving god. The bloodied band of fighters hobbled behind Thorma. Thomle followed, keeping a close eye on the mutineers, hoping the fight had finally gone out of them. Thomle walked slowly. Like his father, his body had been battered in the mayhem. As he trudged along, he glanced over and saw Morea standing off to the side near the village elders; beside her was the young man who had swung the wooden staff so well. Cautiously, he walked away from the mutineers and limped up to where they stood. Morea, not completely sure of Thomle's intentions, stepped between her brother and the battered Norseman.

"This is my brother," she said, pleadingly looking up at Thomle's sweat-streaked and bloody face.

"I only want to thank him, Morea, not fight him," replied Thomle. He stared into the other man's eyes before he spoke. William, although shorter, returned the gaze. *That is good*, thought Thomle as he searched for the right words.

"I thank you. You may have saved my life," said Thomle in his rough Celtic tongue. Morea's brother nodded in acknowledgment.

"My name is William, Northman, and my sister told me about you while she was tending to the hawk's wound. She said you may have saved her life; I thanked you the only way I knew how." William wasn't sure if he should trust this overgrown boy or not, but his sister, who stood by his side, seemed to. He decided he would hold his opinion for later. William looked over at his sister before he went on. "She learned the art of healing from our grandmother," he explained, proud of his sister's talents. "She has always liked helping animals." William stopped in midsentence, fearing he had insulted Thomle, but the fear was groundless. *They aren't listening to me*, he growled to himself, watching his sister ogle the Norseman.

"I know," replied Thomle as he looked down at Morea's blushing face.

The sound of feathered wings beating the ground startled all three of the young people as the hawk and the dove flew from beneath the bushes where the hawk had fallen. The hawk's cry seemed defiant. It soared skyward while the trio watched in awe. Morea was the first to speak.

"I was frightened by the hawk at first, especially after what it did to your uncle and the scar-faced one," she said before turning her attention back to Thomle.

"Strangely, when I knelt to attend its injury, it seemed to understand that I only wanted to help. I hope I did. The small wrap I placed on its wing shouldn't hurt its mobility. Luckily, the arrow passed through the wing without doing much damage."

"All this surely means something. It has to," said Thomle and then paused. "But I have no idea what." They watched the birds for another minute before Morea's brother turned and silently walked up toward the few elders who hadn't run away. Thomle and Morea were watching her brother when Thorma shouted from down the beach.

"Damn the gods. I want everybody over here—now. Thomle, bring the remaining elders and the bird girl. I want Erik's band here too."

The shouting had worn down the badly weakened Thorma, and he dropped to one knee, leaning on his sword. Morea gasped when she saw him nearly fall and rushed to his side. Checking his wounds, she began dressing them as best she could. Erik's band, what was left of them, stood off to the side. They were hesitant to meet with Thorma because they weren't quite sure what their leader had in store for them. After a lot of soul-searching and a quick look around, Johan, one of Erik's mutineers, finally stepped forward. He had a rag tied around his bloody head, and he limped from a sword cut to his thigh.

"What do you intend to do with us, Thorma?" he asked with his head down. Thorma waved the girl away and pushed himself up to a standing position with his sword. He glared at the man.

"I should kill the lot of you," he growled and grasped his sword handle tightly. He felt the tension building, though, and tried to calm himself. After a second, he went on. "But we are already shorthanded, so you will live—at least for a while." When Johan nodded and backed away, Thorma breathed a little easier.

The groups of mutineers and villagers stood in the damp sand by the lead ship and waited for the girl to tend to Thorma's wounds. As she did so, he tried to gather his thoughts. The sun was rising high, and a raw miserable day was breaking as the tide surged in. It would soon be time to leave, thought Thorma as he knelt back down to allow the girl to tend to his shoulders. When Morea finished, he had to thrust his sword deep into the sand once again and push himself up off his one knee. Thorma stood a little shakily, but after a few minutes of uneasy silence, he glared out at the expectant faces; everyone was waiting. He spat.

"I have decided to leave this place called Oban." He paused to let that piece of news sink in. "We will free the slaves and return half of the sheep and cattle, but"—he thought for a minute—"we will keep the gold." A low moan escaped the entire crew, which quickly prompted a withering stare from the old warrior.

"I want no more of this accursed place, nor should you. It is obviously a place where the gods protect the birds and the birds protect some of the people." He paused and looked down at Morea, who was busy making an herbal bandage for his other shoulder wound. She paid him no attention, and he briefly wondered where she had gotten the herbs so quickly, but it was a fleeting thought, for he had much more important things to worry about. Looking out over his warriors, he cleared his throat and went on.

"I have never seen a dove settle with a hawk before, and I believe it is a sign from the gods, possibly Odin, or maybe the new Christian god. I don't know, but when a hawk intervenes in man's affairs, it is time for us to pay attention. We will leave now. Johan, have your band throw the bodies of our"—he fought for the words—"companions on the fire. We will at least give them that." The mutinous Norsemen in particular were greatly relieved that their friends would be able to start their journeys to the feasting halls of Valhalla with a burial pyre. Without it, their spirits might lose the way and wander for eternity in the underworld.

71

While Thorma explained his reasons for leaving Oban, Thomle turned and looked into Morea's soft green eyes. She walked over to stand beside him. The morning sunlight danced on her unruly black curls, which were now held back with two combs made of polished shells. A single wayward strand of hair blew across her face, and her eyes shone with a cautious happiness. Just down the beach, Johan and several others built up the fires for the burial pyre. When Thorma finished his explanation, he immediately began directing the release of the slaves, starting with his two. The two girls trembled with fear when he walked up and stood over them, the bearskin cloak offering scant protection for their near nakedness. But when his big calloused hands began untying their bonds, the trembling stopped. They stood rubbing their sore wrists for a moment before cautiously backing away from their captor. When it was clear they were truly free, they offered a slight smile and ran toward what remained of the village.

Thorma and William were busy unloading the sheep and cattle, so Thomle decided to take Morea back to the spot where they had their first encounter. The girl clung tightly to the young Norseman's arm as they walked. Thorma glanced up from his task and watched them and smiled; it was the first time in a long while.

Morea rested her head on Thomle's arm and thought back over the events of the last day. She was surprised by the array of different feelings coming up—her fondness (maybe love) for Thomle, her brother's courageous actions—but it was the gruff old warrior Thorma who surprised her the most, for it was he who altered the whole situation. She knew that his actions weren't based fully in fear of the gods but also in the fact that underneath that rough exterior, Thorma was a decent man. Then a new thought surfaced, and it overshadowed all others. It was the knowledge that she might never see this young Norseman ever again. A terrible internal struggle racked her body, and she began to cry.

The sun was climbing toward its zenith, and the shadows were steadily fading in the east, along the hills of Loarn. Seagulls cried out and played on the strong winds, while kites searched the shore for a meal. Red and silver beams of light gave off very little warmth as they fanned out across the bay, bathing everything in a shimmering coat of brilliance. The autumn breezes that blew off the dark waters of Oban Bay spoke most loudly of the winter to come. The young would-be lovers stood side-by-side, their hips touching ever so lightly. They looked out toward the small island of Kerrera that lay in the center of the bay. Beyond that lay the rugged Isle of Mull, its dark form totally dominating the far horizon. As he stood next to her, his nostrils seemed to be on fire, her scent of lavender and balsam filling the air around him.

"Morea," he spoke her name softly as he turned her toward him, "I have had this odd thought swirling in my head ... or my heart, I don't know, but it has been there for several hours now. It's a strange, almost overpowering feeling." He took a deep breath and looked into the misty sky. "It's as if ... I have known you for a very long time. Maybe in a different time or some other place, but we have met before." The wind, as usual, blew the loose dark strands of hair all about her face while she looked up at the young Norseman. She never took her eyes off his face as she reached once again into her tattered cloak, hoping to find a string or cord with which she could tame the unruly strands. She was not surprised by his remark because, strangely, it echoed how she felt as she looked into his tired eyes.

"Thomle, I, too, feel as if I have known you from a long time ago ... or that we have somehow been together before." She struggled in her effort to find the right words. "I don't understand it either, and it frightens me a little," she said softly as she shook her head, biting her lower lip. Thomle placed a finger under her chin and gently raised it until she was looking into his eyes again.

"I need to tell you ... or maybe I should ask you something," he whispered. She held her breath, preparing for the worst. Sensing her tension, Thomle smiled, and she let her breath out slowly when he did. "I will return, here, to this place called Oban." He paused, afraid that he had spoken too quickly. "That is if you would want me to come back," he added, struggling for the words in her Gaelic tongue.

"Oh, Thomle," she cried as more tears ran down her already moist cheeks. "I will pray to our new god every night that you will come back to me." She stepped closer to him and put her head against his chest. He wrapped his arms around her and placed his head on top of hers.

"There is no body of water or mountain or man that can keep me away," he whispered as he looked past her shoulder at the smoldering ruins of the village and viewed the destruction they had caused.

He closed his eyes for a second and made a promise to himself before raising her chin once more and kissing her on the lips, a long and gentle kiss. Time seemed to stop as their bodies pressed tightly together and swayed to an unheard rhythm. The only thing that mattered in their world was the touching of their lips and the feeling of their bodies pressed against each other. After what might have been several minutes, their lips finally parted.

"I will wait for you, Thomle, no matter how long it takes for you to return," she said, choking back a sob. Thomle kissed the top of her head. Then without risking more words, he turned to go. He walked slowly back down toward the dragon ships, the same ships that had brought him here what seemed a lifetime ago. Morea hugged herself against the cold wind and watched him walk away, a slight limp in his left leg, the cloth strip from her dress still wrapped around his head. She knew in her heart that he was different from the others. The war band that had caused so much pain was taking him away, but she also knew that she was in love with the Norseman named Thomle.

When he neared the ships, Thomle stopped in front of Morea's brother, who had been watching him limp down the rocky shore. William had just finished helping Thorma with the release of the remaining slaves and livestock and now stood off to the side as the Norsemen, prepared to leave. Thomle wasn't quite sure what to say, but he knew he must say something. Walking up to the shorter man, his eyes went directly to the Yew bow that was strapped across his chest. *A hell of a weapon*, thought Thomle, and he had to drag his mind back to the business at hand. He coughed.

"William, I'm not sure how to express my"—he struggled for the right word—"sorrow for what we have done here. But I hope to return and somehow make amends." He looked around sadly. "I would also like your approval for something else. After we sail to

Balfour, I intend to come back to see your sister. I want to marry her." He glanced up to where Morea stood watching them from the windy ridge, and his heart did that strange flutter. Looking back at William, he went on. "I'm hoping to convince our elders to allow me to come back and help rebuild your village. Maybe even implement some of your sister's ideas." The shorter Pict looked the Norseman in the eye. Neither man said a word. Finally, William spoke.

"I will think about giving my approval for you marrying my sister, Norseman. And rest assured, I will look after her. That I can promise you." The two young men looked deep into each other's eyes once again, searching for the truth; then both nodded.

Thomle turned and limped up the plank onto the dragon ship, and William walked back toward what remained of his village. All three war ships listed slightly, but the tide was rushing in, and it would not be long before the dragonheads would stand upright and the long oars would push the boats out into deep water.

"Put your backs into those poles, you dogs!" shouted Thorma as the Viking drums began to hammer out their rhythm and the greenish water boiled under the ships. Soon the dragons began to slide on their bellies, inch by inch, deeper into the surf. Sweat rolled, and muscled arms strained until at last, with a mighty surge, the dragon ships rode upon the incoming tide.

* * * * *

Thomle stood alone at the bow of the lead ship as his father shouted orders to the crew from the comfort of a cushioned seat that had been prepared for him by one of his men. The old warrior raised a stiff arm and stretched his wounded shoulders; he had to admit they felt better after the girl had put the herbal bandages on him. Thomle swept his gaze over the destruction on the shore. The monastery continued to belch smoke from the crumbled timbers in its lower level, while a flock of kites flew among the rocks below, picking at the remains of the monks thrown from the stone balcony. Some huts still smoldered, their previous occupants sitting nearby and staring dejectedly into the ashes. It looked to Thomle as though all the bodies had been recovered. At least there were none visible. Their souls already on their respective journeys—either to Valhalla or to the Christian heaven.

The young Norseman replayed the events of the last two days as the ships passed by the cliffs of Lorn, barely visible in the misty distance. Despite all the bloodshed on both sides, Thomle knew that the dark-haired girl with the piercing green eyes had captured his heart. He also knew that her challenging questions would stay burned in his memory. For reasons he couldn't yet understand, the war hawk and the dove settling together signaled something important to him and the girl, something like an ancient totem that pulled them toward each other. But then he supposed mortal men weren't supposed to understand the ways of the gods. Whatever his fate, he would accept it like a Norseman.

The ships quickly picked up speed through the strenuous efforts of the rowers, but the sails lay limp on the lateral beams. They wouldn't be of any use until they reached the windward side of the grave and the backside of the low green island of Kerrera. Thomle climbed atop the gunwale, reached high into the chilly air, and waved a farewell to Morea, who with tears in her eyes waved back at the Norseman.

The ship's hulls protested in great shudders as the dragons sliced through four-foot swells and the increasingly choppy waters of Oban Bay nearing the rocky point. Thomle watched the village gradually disappear into the fog, the curtains slowly closing on this tragedy. Finally, the ships turned windward of the island; the winds of the North Sea filled the woolen sails and began driving the ships northward along the coastline of the Gaels.

Thorma, after having harassed the crew as much as he felt necessary, joined Thomle at the bow of the ship. He was still angry at some of his men, the ones who had simply stood by and watched the fight, refusing to interfere with the mutiny. It may have been an old tradition, but it angered him nonetheless. He rubbed and stretched his right shoulder and watched his son stare at the shore. Ocean spray shot over the gunwale and sparkled in the wind, dancing on the beams of fading light.

"Forget the girl. Forget this damn place," he growled, trying to be heard over the cackle of the sails. The boy's gaze never turned from the treacherous shoreline that lay a scant five hundred yards to the east. He was fighting the currents with the rudder but managed to reply without shouting.

"Can you forget her or this place, Father?" Thorma cast a frustrated glance his way and then shook his big bushy head, ignoring the melancholy question. He turned back to his already frightened crew and bellowed like an angry bull, "Pull those damn oars if you ever want to see your home again. Pull!" The oars, however, had long ago been pulled in and were resting at the feet of the confused Norsemen.

A few minutes later, father and son glanced skyward when they heard the hawk's lonesome cry echo off the Argyll cliffs like a farewell. They had just completed the turn to the windward side of the long finger of land, named after Fergus and Angus Loarn, which protected Oban Bay. Thomle's dark mood matched the cold gray skies as the stiff winds drove them north along the coast. The weather having turned progressively fouler, Thomle stayed at the steering oar, fighting the angry waters that took him farther and farther from the dark-haired Morea.

Night had fallen quickly, and it was as black as the coal that fired in their braziers. The roar of the surf kept everyone on edge.

"Keep her in sight of land, Thomle!" shouted Thorma as he handed his son a tankard of warm mead. "But watch out for those damned shoals. They extend out further than you think."

Thomle could hear the surf crashing on the jagged shoreline. He wasn't sure what his fate was, but he knew he didn't want to die in this desolate place, not now that he had found Morea. So he tightened his grip on the big piece of oak as the rain began to pour from the heavens. It seemed the gods were angry at the weary men. Lightning flashed in unrelenting fury, quickly followed by Thor's hammer striking hard against the earth. The air shook, and the men pulled their cloaks tightly about them.

It was close to daylight before the storm lifted and the waters calmed somewhat. But as the sun rose over the dark peaks to the east, a thick fog crawled out of the depths and covered the ships in a soupy gray mist. Thorma ordered the sails struck, and the crews worked quickly to bring them down while he checked closely for any needed repairs. The rowers begrudgingly shoved the long oars out once more and allowed them to drink of the cold deep waters. The fog lay over the sea like a death shroud. All day long, the oars dipped and pulled in the greenish water as they plowed blindly through the fog, guided only by the sound of the now gentler surf. Thorma periodically stood on the bow of the creeping dragon and shouted, "Odin, Odin," testing the distance to the shore and their gods' willingness to help them. Late in the day, the sun briefly burned through the fog, glowing fiery red across the horizon as the great orb sank like a blacksmith's heated sword tip beneath the mirrored surface. Tired backs ached and muscled arms burned as the blackness once again wrapped around them.

Thomle's eyes grew weary just past the witching hour of the second day, and he was about to call for his friend Günter to relieve him when he saw an eerie-looking beast slowly emerge out of the mist. The strange beast's head stared down from thirty feet high and then disappeared into the fog. This ship was larger than any he had ever seen before, and he watched in awe as it slipped through the dark night searching for … what?

"Father," called Thomle in a harsh whisper. Hearing his son, Thorma moved quickly toward the stern, where Thomle and now Günter stood. Thomle watched a shiver run through his father. The old warrior cursed the gods for this luck because he recognized the ship or ships since another dragon, this one not quite as large, appeared less than fifty feet behind the first. The beasts belonged to a man Thorma knew well, a brute of a man named Sigrid "the Dog" Hurok. Hurok got his nickname from the manner in which he howled after he made a kill. His crew was reputed to be just as menacing. Thorma had no fear of the man or his crew—hell, he feared no man—but he knew his crew was outnumbered. He waited. Maybe they would pass on by.

The ships approached each other silently, emerging out of the fog like a gathering of great serpents preparing to mate. Thorma turned to his crew and, with a slight nod, told them to be ready for anything. Thomle had heard his father speak of the man called the

Dog, and he, too, prepared himself. He stood rigid on the stoop, a small platform just behind the bow that was usually the drummer's place. The fog swirled around his feet, and the light from the torches made his eyes shine red. Thorma soon realized that they had been spotted. To not hail the other ships might be perceived as fear, so he shouted.

"Ho, you old sea dog, how are the pickings for you these days?" Sigrid Hurok was not a cautious man, but his senses told him that something was just not right here. He knew Thorma Morestrong and his crazy brother. *They bear watching*, he thought and threw a line to the stern-looking young man on Thorma's ship, ignoring the greeting.

"Where are your slaves, Thorma of Orkney?" asked Hurok after they had tied the ships together. Hurok's beady gray eyes surveyed the ship in one glance. *They are undermanned*, he thought, laughing to himself. *Something has happened to them, but what?* Thorma handed his guest a tankard of mead, giving himself a minute to think before he replied.

"We let them go to appease the gods that protect the accursed village called Oban," answered Thorma after taking a long drink of lukewarm liquor.

"The gods," spat Hurok in a voice as cold as the dark waters that surrounded their ships. Even when they boasted otherwise, all Norsemen feared the gods with their awesome powers, like Neptune, god of the sea. The Dog was no exception. Hurok drained his tankard and called for a new one from his own ship.

"Bring three mugs, Haarde. These men need the taste of a good drink." The old Pict slave, who still wore the traditional iron ring around his neck, hurried to the rear of the huge longboat. Thomle, who immediately disliked Hurok, slowly moved his hand to rest on the hilt of his sword as a precaution. Born out of years of fighting, Hurok watched the young man's movement out the corner of his eye and wondered about the overgrown boy.

Hurok was a brute of a man, about the same height as Thorma but wider at the shoulders and with more girth around the middle. He had a large reddish scar much like the one Thorma bore, but the

Dog's scar ran across his forehead and down what remained of his right ear. The old wound was a gift from a brave but foolish Pict, who had objected to Sigrid's treatment of the man's wife and young daughter. Now all three lay in a common grave on the Isle of Mann.

Thorma watched Hurok's eyes take notice of Thomle's movements. He knew his son would feel a threat to Morea from this man standing beside him who had raped and killed all along on the west coast of Argyle. Thorma wasn't sure what Thomle would do or when he would do it, but he knew the boy would do something—that was for certain. Tension gripped the ship with icy tentacles.

In an effort to buy some time, Thorma jested, "The girls were all too skinny in Oban, and they were as ugly as your first wife, Sigrid." Thorma's guest smiled with his mouth, but his eyes never lost their cold stare. The tension was broken only for a moment when Hurok's old slave brought the three tankards of rich steamy ale and handed them to the men.

"I took this ale from a village up the coast a way. They won't need it anymore." He laughed, the implication clear. "It's a very good brew," Hurok said and took another pull from his tankard. Ale ran out the sides of his mouth and down his matted beard. Thomle also took a long drink, but he did so with his left hand while his right never left his sword handle. This battle posturing remained apparent to Hurok.

Both crews stood cautiously watching their leaders as Thorma tried to lighten the mood by talking to Sigrid about old times. Wondering what would happen next, the crew members didn't drink or even begin to relax. Hurok could smell trouble, but he just wasn't sure where it would come from. His crew outnumbered Thorma Morestrong's even with his additional ship. It was something else, though, that bothered Hurok, something he could almost sense. But what? He glanced around, attempting to not seem obvious. Then it came to him. Trouble brewed in his cold, hard stare. *That boy must be his son. They look too much alike not to be*, thought Hurok, taking a slow drink of ale. Without words, the boy's stare told him that the speed of youth could kill him before he could even draw his sword.

Hurok did not fear death, but he was in no hurry to make the journey to Valhalla. He would have to be cautious.

"Tell me again about the birds that protect this village. What did you call it? Oban?" asked Hurok, ale dripping through his tangled beard while he drained the last of the tankard.

"The natives call it *oh-bn*, and it is a horrid place. I have never seen anything like it." Thorma began to retell the tale of the great hawk and its mate.

Sigrid Hurok spat several times while Thorma recounted their battle. The threat of foul spirits bothered him immensely, and it showed. The big man drank more ale and listened. He had known Thorma of Orkney for many years, and he knew him to be fearless in battle. But he also knew him to be wise, very wise. Much wiser than his fool of a brother Olaf or his bastard father. Something had been left out of this story, something important.

"I don't know about magic birds, but I do know that you will have the devil to pay when you get back to Balfour without any slaves." The Dog roared with laughter as he took yet another tankard of ale from his slave.

"Maybe," said Thorma as he watched Hurok drink. The Dog had always gotten mean and angry when he drank too much, and he was well on his way to that point. It was at that moment, maybe from the effects of the mead, that Hurok made a mistake, a fatal mistake as it turned out.

With a tankard of ale in his hand and his blood beginning to boil, Hurok loudly announced, "I think I will take my ships to see this place that caused the great Thorma of Orkney to free his slaves. Unloose the ropes," he commanded and drank the last of his ale, tossing the empty tankard at his slave. Sigrid Hurok had briefly turned his attention away from the boy standing beside him, and then he heard the savage roar. It was the last thing that Hurok ever heard.

Thomle had been worried from the beginning that Hurok would take his crew to Oban, and when the big man drunkenly announced his plan to go there, he had to act. With a roar that chilled even his father's heart, the youth drew and swung his sword in one swift motion. Sigrid Hurok only had time to half-turn toward the sound and had just begun to reach for his sword when the blade hit him. The big man's fingers never had a chance to curl around the grip before Thomle's blade sliced through his thick neck. The fingers twitched eerily as the Dog's head tumbled from his shoulders in a spray of crimson mist and rolled over the railing into the cold North Sea. The bloody head, with sightless eyes wide open, sank into the dark waters where it would soon become a feast for the crabs. The stunned silence was broken by Thomle's angry challenge to the now leaderless crew of Sigrid Hurok.

"Do not go near the village of Oban, ever!" He growled the command and stared each man in the eye. "If you dare, I will hunt you down and send you to hell just like this scum." He reached down and grabbed the headless corpse, throwing it over the side for the bottom feeders of the sea.

Thorma and his crew drew their weapons and braced for the attack they were sure would come, but it didn't. Instead, a large red-headed warrior wearing shiny mail stepped forward out of the stern of the ship.

"Sigrid Hurok was my uncle," said the redhead, looking at Thomle with green eyes as dead cold as his uncle's, "but he was a cruel and hard man, a man we all despised." A couple of heads nodded in agreement. "We will not go to the village called Oban. Instead, we will go home. It has been a long hard voyage." With that said, he turned, cast off the lines that had bound the two beasts together, and as the ships drifted apart, walked proudly toward the bow of the ship. A slight smile flickered cross his lips for a second and then was gone as he settled into the spot that had previously belonged to his uncle.

Thorma's chest rose and fell as he took several deep breaths. He had been ready for battle but not for what had just happened. He had to calm down a little. Staring into the damp fog as it swallowed the departing dragon ships, he thought about what to do next.

Thorma knew he should talk to his son, but he wasn't sure how to begin. His mind raced as he walked over to where Thomle sat on the gunwale.

"I never liked that son of a bitch either," he said, sitting down beside Thomle and slapping him on the back. "But you can't go around killing everybody I don't like." He laughed for a minute before turning serious. "Thomle, I have to ask you. Did you kill that bastard to protect us or that girl back in Oban?"

"Both," Thomle replied without hesitation. He wiped his bloody sword across the rag he had taken from his head before sliding it back into its sheath. "I believe Hurok planned to attack us. He knew we were short-handed. All he had to do was look around. I was also afraid they would raid the village after they were finished with us. I merely cut off the head of the snake in hopes that the body would die."

Thorma stared down at the frothy waters. "The head definitely is a crab feast, but the body"—he looked far out to sea—"is still alive and I'm afraid is still dangerous." He stretched his injured shoulder and winched. The old warrior sat on the stoop, pondered the dark sky, and gnawed on a hunk of lamb someone had handed him. He offered part of it to Thomle, who refused. The image of Hurok's head rolling off the gunwale and into the sea was still fresh in his mind.

"I have no remorse for killing that ... man," said the young Norseman after a long silence. "At least Morea and the village will be safe for a while."

Thorma looked over at his son. "Until another snake comes along. Can you kill them all?" he asked as he closely examined the bone of the lamb chop before tossing it over the side. Thomle didn't answer his father; instead, he stood in silence and stared into the night. A light breeze began to ruffle the rigging lines.

"Hoist the damned sails and let the North Wind take us away from this place!" shouted Thorma, walking back through his crew, kicking a few sleeping men into action. Wearily, the crew scrambled to set the sails before the fickle breeze decided to hold its breath. Thomle's mind wandered back to Oban and the pretty dark-haired girl who was getting further away every hour. The breast of the beast hammered through the swells, and its ribs shuddered as the winds drove them northward. Thorma's mind, however, was set on Balfour on Orkney and what they called home. He moved through the rows of resting oarsmen, some glancing up fearfully, as he walked to the bow just under the dragonhead and stared out into the great void.

Thorma wondered what his wife would say about all that had happened to them in the last couple of days. Ulrika had died five years before, trying, for the third time, to give him another son. He missed her so. He missed her council—hell, he missed everything about her. Unlike his father, he had never taken any concubines. He had loved Ulrika from the first time he laid eyes on her, standing near her father many years ago. And he still did. Thorma shook his head in a vain attempt to purge her memory, and his mind reluctantly drifted to the elders of Balfour. Hurok had been right about one thing: he would have hell to pay back on Orkney. The elders would want slaves for the families of the slain warriors; hell, they would even want slaves for the mutinous ones. Everyone would want to know how Olaf had been killed. *Do I tell them the truth that he was attacked by a damn hawk?* He groaned and raised his eyes to the sky in search of some kind of an answer.

The winds stayed strong, and the tired rowers slept with their heads lying on the long oars. The woolen sails popped and cackled as the beasts fought their way through the moderate swells. It was not a bad night for sailing, except for the dark mood that had returned with the pitch-black skies. It dampened their souls like the icy sea mist that soaked through their cloaks, chilling their bodies to the bone.

Time passed. Thomle, who still manned the steering oar, had been thinking about the girl. He broke the heavy silence that had settled over them as his father stirred in a restless sleep.

"Father," Thomle nearly shouted. Thorma jumped when he heard his son's voice.

"What," he answered, rubbing his eyes. Thomle seemed not to notice his father's gruffness.

"The ideas that Morea talked about—the desire to work things out without killing and taking ..." The boy paused for a second. "Do you think they could work?"

Thomle watched his father rest his shaggy bearded head in his big hands. Thorma replayed the scene of the girl Morea standing in front of them, the determination in her voice, and the directness of her stare. He thought about his own feelings as a young man, the raids with their killing, and the sorrow that they sowed. Finally, he rose and looked at his son.

"I just do not know, son. I would be willing to try to negotiate for all the things that we need or think we need." He shook his head. "But the men want women and gold. Hell, some of them like killing as much as Olaf did. They think it gives them power. So to answer your question, I'm not sure our people are ready for these new ideas. Maybe a few of us, but certainly not all." The big man paused before he went on. "Thomle, you know that Balfour's elders are all hardened warriors who cling to the old ways, especially Thodora, the leader. They would never tolerate a movement away from the traditions."

"I know that, Father, but I still believe we should at least try to talk to them," Thomle eagerly replied. "If you allow me to, I would speak before the council," he went on.

Thorma groaned. "Maybe, Thomle. Maybe," he said. "Let me think on it some more. First, we must make it home alive. The body of the snake is still out there somewhere." His gaze returned to the vast emptiness they sailed into. "My instincts tell me that somewhere out there in that fog, Sigrid Hurok's crew is still a danger to us."

* * * * *

Two more days passed, and the cold wind driving them home became fickle once more, abandoning them to the fog creeping back over the sea. The driver's drum lay silent; the only sounds to be heard were the dipping of the oars and an occasional moan from a tired rower.

"I want every mother's son to be ready," bellowed Thorma as he strained to see through the thick fog that lay about the ship like a damp cloth. "Keep your weapons at hand." It was an order that he didn't need to speak aloud because the dense fog had put everyone on edge. They were ready, but for what, they weren't sure.

The witching hour was long past, and Thomle had returned to the rudder after a short break. He searched wearily for a safe cove to anchor in. They were all tired and much in need of rest. The young Norsemen kept the ship a steady arrow's shot from the rocky shore.

The surf beat a gentle rhythm. Just before dawn, he sensed something stirring at the head of the cove they had rowed into, but the damp fog pressing down around muffled all sound. He cocked his head from side to side, but he heard nothing out of the ordinary. All he knew was that something was happening up ahead, and he strained to detect what it was. Damp gray emptiness lay in front of them as the beasts crawled along the shoreline.

"Gunter, come here. I may need you on the rudder!" shouted Thomle, wrapping the holding rope around the well-worn handle of the steering oar. Once the rope was in place, he climbed onto the gunwale and sniffed the air. A faint but distinct odor drifted on the wind. His nostrils had detected what his ears could not, the unmistakable scent of burning thatch. The rancid smell soon enveloped the ships like an invisible glove.

"Man the rudder, Gunter," shouted Thomle as he ran up the center of the ship between the benches toward the bow where Thorma stood with his head cocked to the side, listening. The old warrior already knew in his heart what was happening at the head of the cove as the beast swam stealthily on. They rowed slowly, the skeletal limbs of the vegetation along the shore reaching out as if in protest of their passing. They rowed until up ahead a faint reddish glow began to pierce the dense curtain of swirling gray fog. Both men immediately knew—a village being raided. As they neared the shore, they could make out ghostly figures running about and hear screams of the dying.

"The body of the snake," grunted Thorma as the outline of two dragon ships emerged before them.

"The Dog's crew is destroying the village, probably as revenge for doing nothing when you killed Hurok," he continued, staring helplessly at the ongoing struggle.

"So all their rage is being unleashed on this poor village," Thomle cried through clenched teeth. He gripped the main line until his knuckles turned white. Thorma watched knowingly as the reddish flames streaked the filthy skies. He was thinking about what to do next when a mournful oath and a loud war cry of "Odin, Odin" pierced the morning air. Thomle, having leaped from the gunwale into the chest-deep surf with his sword held high, was churning up out of the water like an angry sea monster. As the boy raced across the beach toward where Hurok's crew was gathering prisoners, Thorma saw the mask of death on his son's face.

Hurok's overconfident crew had unwisely left no guards on the ships or even on the beach. The shore was deserted as Thomle rushed to stop the slaughter. He charged into the tail end of a group of surprised warriors, who were herding several women toward a small cave to the east of the village. The frightened women had their hands tied securely to a rope that was wrapped around the waist of a burly Norseman. Several small children cried pitifully as they stumbled along beside their mothers. The women were trying hard to keep their scant clothes about them, having been rousted from their huts by the screaming Norsemen in the middle of the night. The children, who clung to their mothers' legs, were totally naked and shivering from the cold as they stared at the uncaring Norsemen and trudged beside their mothers.

Thomle raced up behind the closest group and swung his sword with blinding speed. It tore into the neck of the nearest Viking, who made a gurgling sound, grabbed at the wound, and staggered sideways. He was dead before he hit the ground. The next two died nearly as fast, their weapons never having left their scabbards. Thomle's sword dripped with their blood as he hacked and sliced his way through more of the surprised warriors. Three older men who were in front of the procession turned at the sound of battle. What they saw was a ghostly figure running toward them. Dropping the braided rope that held the women, they hastily drew their swords.

Thomle seemed to float in and out of the fog as he ran forward. He was a thing, a creature of the night, and he wore death on his face. At his shoulder flew a great war hawk. Both had eyes that reflected flames from the burning huts. The ghostly warrior attacked anyone that resembled a Norseman. Screaming an ancient oath, he struck a crushing blow that split the shield and severed the arm of the nearest man, who fell screaming onto the sand. The remaining two stunned and frightened warriors looked at each other and then ran for their lives. They ran as hard as they could into the dark forest, heedless of the brush. It was better to be eaten by wolves than to face this mad man with his hawk. Somehow, they thought, as they stumbled through the heather in their escape, they had angered the gods, and the great Odin had sent this fiendish warrior down upon them.

As more Norsemen disappeared into the forest, a long wavering wail drifted on a falling note high in the mountains. Sheep on board the ships heard the ancient cries and careened around in a desperate attempt to escape. The howling pack of wolves moved down through the forest, and Thomle paused for a moment to catch his breath and listen. He glanced to his right at the group of women who had been heading for the cave, and they, in turn, looked back at him with fear and surprise on their faces. Struggling to untie their hands, rope burns evident on their wrists, they whispered among themselves, unsure of what was happening. They were shocked to see one Norseman killing another, seemingly for their sake. Yet they still feared him as much as any other Norseman. The real fear though, a superstitious dread, was generated by the large hawk that flew slightly above and behind this Norseman as he had stormed ashore in a rage. While Thomle leaned on his sword, the hawk rose into the air and flew in pursuit of the men that had sought refuge in the forest, its cry echoing over the burning village and blending with the howls of the approaching wolves.

Thomle was fully aware of the stares from the villagers, but he ignored them. His eyes were locked on the new leader of this band of killers. His name was Jorge Hanson, and he was enjoying his new role as leader of the Dog's war band, strutting in front of four partly naked young women as he dragged them along with a rope. He was oblivious to what was happening behind him, thinking only of the pleasures that his captives would provide him. Thomle gritted his teeth and sprinted through the smoke, pumping his powerful legs hard. He tore up the sandy slope through the center of the small village, only fifty yards separating him and Hanson.

Bjorn Jorge Hanson marched his captives toward a large stone and thatch hut that lay at the back of the village with smug satisfaction. The terrified cries of his men snapped Hanson out of his revelry, and he turned just as two of them ran past him with crazed looks on their weathered faces.

"Have you gone mad?" he shouted as he staggered sideways, nearly knocked down by the fleeing men. They ran into the forest, looking back as if a demon was chasing them. Jorge Hanson squinted his eyes as he peered through the smoke. Suddenly, the wind picked up, and the smoke seemed to swirl around a lone figure—a figure that the gods must have sent down to earth to help him. The Norseman started to smile, but the smile quickly faded when he looked closer and saw the rage in the eyes of the warrior charging at him. He knew then that it wasn't help he was looking at but death. Death in the form of the young man who killed Hurok was coming hard.

The light from the burning huts collided with the fog and smoke, giving everything a strange shimmering appearance, including the hawk that had just returned from deep in the forest and was soaring through the foul air, coming in and out of sight. Thomle gripped his sword with both hands. Fire seemed to dance off its edge as he moved steadily up the slope. Jorge Hanson stood very still as if he were under a spell, a slight glimmer of fear registering in his cold eyes for a second and then gone. While Hanson pondered what fate had sent him, Thomle held Morea in his mind. *Why do these men kill innocent people to satisfy their own greed? Why must women and children always suffer at the hands of such men?*

Thomle had changed. He no longer thought of himself as a pillager but as a protector—yes, a protector. With that strange but wonderful thought in his mind, he entered into battle with Bjorn Jorge Hanson.

Old men would tell the tale for a hundred years, around a thousand campfires, of how Thomle Morestrong walked the berserker's way, where rage is king and the only reward is blood. The sword in Thomle's hand was like a living thing, and it weaved an intricate pattern in the air as he swung it fiercely, knowing he now fought for something new, something good. He didn't have a word for it yet. But the feeling was there just the same, and it gave him an edge.

Jorge Hanson was taller than Thomle, and he stood on higher ground, but this gave Thomle little pause. Purpose drove him and enabled his blows to land with crushing force. The two adversaries circled to the left, then stepping high, they cautiously moved over and around dead tree limbs and small rocks, ever watchful for an opening. They moved in widening circles, and their strokes became more savage. The iron rang loudly as the grunts of battle mingled with the cries of children and the sobs of mothers who watched the two warriors fight. Jorge Hanson, thinking the boy inexperienced, remembered an old ruse that had worked for him several times in past battles. The big man faked a stumble that quickly drew Thomle into a trap, and he surged forward to take advantage of the misstep. The more experienced Norseman with the shiny mail jargon smiled to himself and leaped to the side. For a moment, the gods held their breath as Hanson's sword drove swiftly down toward Thomle's leg.

Only the speed of youth saved the boy. His sword dropped down like a flash of lightning to parry the blow that was aimed for his thigh. Sparks flew when Jorge Hanson's sword, denied the taste of flesh that it sought, struck Thomle's blade near the handle. Each man drew back into a fighter's position, knees bent, sword held with the handle eye level. Intense rage erupted in Thomle's heart, and it was guided by the knowledge that he was fighting for something other than himself. He was now fighting for Morea and for her ideals.

Blow after blow rained down on Jorge Hanson's shield until at last the big Dane began to tire. With desperation in his eyes, Hanson staggered backward, for real this time, his booted foot tripping over a limb, nearly causing him to go down. Although he caught himself, the stumble enabled Thomle to bear down even harder. With a final stroke, he broke Jorge Hanson's sword at the hilt as Hanson made a desperate attempt to parry the blow. Muscles bulged in Thomle's arms as his blade continued its destructive path, tearing through the shiny bronze mail and into the flesh of the big man's shoulder.

The blood-soaked Norseman sank to one knee, exhausted and unable to raise his arm. He looked up at Thomle and waited for the killing blow. Sweat rolled from under Thomle's helmet, stinging his eyes as he stared down at his enemy. A heartbeat passed and then another; his muscles tightened. Slowly, he raised his sword to deliver the expected blow. A hundred pairs of eyes watched the young

THE HAWK AND THE DOVE

Norseman prepare to add to his slaughter, but the sword never fell. It was stopped in midstroke by two things simultaneously: the call of a dove floating out of the darkness and a voice calling his name. Thorma, who was still recovering from his earlier wounds, hobbled up behind his son while the fog of battle rolled through the boy's mind. The sword, still held high, shook slightly in Thomle's hand.

The world was full of smoke from the burning huts, and pale tendrils of the early morning fog had crept up from the sea. The combination of fire and mist cast a bizarre reflection on the walls of the few huts that had escaped the torch. The haunting call of the dove, seemingly louder than the hawk's cry, mixed with his father's voice. Together, they held the moment. Gradually, Thomle backed away from the berserker's abyss. Thorma quickly glanced around at the villagers who were huddled nearby. *They're afraid of all of us, and they're not sure of what is happening*, thought Thorma as he tried to talk his son down. The old warrior knew that in the heat of battle a single calm voice could be heard above the many screaming in anger. So in such a voice, he continued. Where it came from, Thorma had no idea.

"Son, one more death will not help our situation. And maybe, just maybe, a show of mercy will calm the fear that now holds this place by the throat. Remember, we are still outnumbered by Hanson's men," he added. "They wait just out of sight"—he glanced toward the forest—"to see what you will do."

The bloody sword shook in his grip, but ever so slowly, Thomle lowered the Death Bringer. Almost everyone in the crowd let out a breath that had been held in quiet anticipation. Sweat dripped on the hilt of his sword, and Thomle bent forward at the waist, his head resting on the back of his wrist, which gripped the sword. After a minute, he slowly straightened and stood silent, his face impassive, his sight turned inward. Suddenly, with a guttural shout, Thomle raised the sword and, with the veins on his neck bulging, drove it deep into the sand, next to Jorge Hanson's chest.

* * * * *

Morea stood just outside her hut, shivering in the cold night air. The hour was late, but she was wide awake, having been driven from her bed by a loud mournful shout that had pierced her sleep-draped mind. It had been Thomle's shout, she was sure of it. She had thrown back the meager covers, jumped from her straw mat, and run to the makeshift door of the freshly thatched small hut, her thin nightdress clinging tightly to her body. With her heart pounding from anticipation, she pulled back the cloth door and listened, scanning the dark waters of the bay. But there was no dragon ship. She realized it must have been a dream, but how very real the shout had been, its echo still pounding in her head, ripping at her heart.

She pulled the threadbare gown about her shoulders while the night sounds rode the chill air, a lonesome dog barking far off in the hills and somewhere in the village a small child whimpering in its sleep. A pale light spilled through the doorway of a nearby hut, a solitary candle flickering in the window opening. Morea stood in the damp silence and looked longingly out into the bay. There was only the empty sea.

"God," she moaned, quickly crossing herself at the oath.

"I'm sure it was Thomle calling out. It couldn't have been the wailing of a ghost, it was so real," she whispered. The stars gazed down uncaringly. Morea took a deep breath and leaned back against the wall of the hut. She could hear the crickets chirping their last calls before the coming winter would silence them. A hoot owl called to its mate high above the grassy pastures that stretched out behind the village toward the crag of Dun Olleigh. But there was no young Norseman, no Thomle.

Morea had tried very hard to keep herself busy ever since Thomle had left; around what remained of the village, there was plenty of work to be done. And being a healer, there was a constant flow of wounded to attend. The pitiful orphaned children also needed care, so the days passed quickly. It was the nights that were so long. At night, alone in her hut, she could feel the young Norseman's strong arms around her, his lips on hers. Yes, it was the nights that lasted forever.

"Please, come back to me, Thomle," she cried to the heavens as she glanced across at the ruins of Dunollic Castle, which lay on the Isle of Kerrera just across the way. Reluctantly she stepped back inside her hut and lay down on the cold, lonely mat. She cried herself back to sleep while a light frost sparkled under the full moon, its crystals dancing on the thatched roofs as morning approached.

Dawn broke raw the next morning, and Morea was awakened before the sun had peeked over top of the Crag A'Bharrain to the east. A young mother had brought her three-year-old daughter, Sarah, to have Morea look at a painful rash the child had developed. The mother hoped that perhaps the young healer could apply an herbal wrap to the child's festering leg. Morea quickly concocted a salve made from elderberries and dried heath blossoms that her grandmother had often used for such rashes. The salve, she had said, was also good for minor cuts and burns. Morea explained all this as the anxious mother watched from the doorway. The little girl, who had great curls of flaming red hair, sat on the table and watched attentively as Morea began to spread the salve on her leg. The child's lower lip quivered slightly, but she never cried; she simply stared through the red curls at the young healer.

Morea finished wrapping the child's leg and was putting the extra salve in a small container when the little girl finally spoke.

"Thank you," she said and slid off the table before walking over to her mother and hiding behind her skirt. Smiling back, Morea reached out and wiped a tiny tear from the corner of the child's eye as it threatened to fall. The mother reached down, lifted the child onto her hip, and started to leave. But she stopped when the little girl whispered in her ear. Reddening a little, she reached into her tattered smock and carefully pulled out six brown eggs, which she handed to Morea as payment for the salve. Then with an embarrassed nod, she turned and quickly left. The child squirmed around in her mother's arms and called out as they walked away.

"I gathered those eggs all by myself!" she shouted before burying her head in her mother's shoulder, giggling. Morea smiled as she watched them disappear among the clutter of half-repaired huts.

"Someday Thomle and I will have a little girl like that." Morea whispered the words and blushed at their meaning.

Ever since Thomle and the dragon ships had sailed away, Morea had often scanned the sky for the hawk and dove. Once again, she found herself looking up into the pale blue heavens but to no avail. The hawk and dove seemed to have abandoned her. Unfortunately, there was one person who had not abandoned her, Angus mac Dougall. Angus was the eldest son of Fergus mac Dougall, earl of Dalriade, a wilderness realm of streams, forest, rocks, barren heath, and high mountain meadows. It was a rugged land that stretched from Hadrian's Wall in the south along the Argyll coast and ran north into the wilderness of the western highland. Many small villages dotted this harsh landscape, including Oban itself. Angus mac Dougall was noted for many things, including his horsemanship, his ability with a sword, and his lechery. He lusted after all the pretty lassies in his father's lands, but he was especially fond of the dark-haired Morea mac Craig. Bordering on obsession with her beautifully fair skin and flawless complexion, he constantly sought her attention.

During his frequent and usually unannounced trips to Oban, he always tried to impress her, if not with his father's fine horseflesh, which had been shipped over from Gaul, then with his clothes, which were made of the finest linen, silk, and tanned leather. Today, Angus mac Dougall rode his father's big bay stallion named Eagle Wing, whose mane hung long and glittered with dozens of bronze platelets woven into it. Angus let the fiery horse prance through the charred remains of the village center as several children ran along behind, hoping for a handout that never came. The young noble's retinue of troops followed close behind, riding the much smaller mountain ponies and shouting at the dogs that barked and nipped at their heels. Mothers and older sisters scurried about after dirty-faced children as the procession rode past people much too tired to even look up from their tasks. Winter was on its way, and there was a lot of work to do in preparation for its coming. They had no time for the tomfoolery of the local gentry. Morea had figured that word of the Viking raid would soon reach the earl and that his son would be eager to ride to Oban from their castle at mac Arium to check out the damage. So she was not surprised by mac Dougall's arrival. Sadly, she knew that many of the Dalriade hierarchy were as mean and greedy as any Viking, and the villagers expected very little in the way of help from them.

"Is there no hope, no peace for our people?" She moaned the words in a whisper and looked skyward but found no answer there. She watched angrily as the boor of a youth pompously rode through her village without bothering to speak to anyone or acknowledge their sorrow.

"These are his people. You would think he would care about their plight, but he obviously doesn't," she grumbled and looked desperately out to sea. The agony of anticipation ripped through her like a sharp knife as she grew impatient for Thomle's return.

* * * * *

But Thomle was far from being ready to return. In fact, at that exact moment, he wasn't even sure of where he was or what was happening around him. Sweat flew from under his helmet like water dripping from a mallard's back, and he shook his head in an attempt to clear his eyes and his mind. He looked around a little bewildered. Bjorn Jorge Hanson lay on the ground at his feet; the man's broken sword lay nearby. He vaguely remembered the reason for that, but his own sword had been driven into the ground next to Jorge Hanson's chest and he had no memory of having done that. Reaching down, he pulled the weapon out of the sand and inspected it closely, as if making sure it was his own, then staggered over to where his father was standing. The rest of the crew stood off to the side and watched. Wiping the blood and sand from the sword onto his leather breeches, he walked across the maze of footprints from the earlier fight, struggling to piece together what had happened. He remembered becoming angry as he watched the raid unfold from the ship, he remembered storming ashore, but after that, his brain was drawing a blank. There were only fleeting flashes of memory from the fight with Jorge Hanson. Resheathing his sword, Thomle noticed the eyes of the villagers staring at him with a mixture of fear and puzzlement.

Thomle slowed down, then stopped walking altogether before he reached his father. Glancing around, he turned in a full circle, his eyes finally settling on his own crew. They were staring at him in amazement. It was only then that he began to realize what he had just done.

"I have never seen anything quite like what happened here," said Thorma, his old voice full of solemn awe. Thorma had closed the small gap that separated them and now stood beside his son. Together, they watched the villagers mill about, whispering among themselves in low anguished tones. After a couple of minutes, Thorma turned to his son.

"They are unsure whether to be afraid or rejoice, just look at them," he said.

"I only meant to help them," whispered Thomle as he watched the frightened people huddle into several small groups.

"*I* know that," answered the old warrior, "but *they*"—he nodded at the villagers—"they aren't so sure." In an effort to explain further, he went on. "They have just seen you walk the berserker's way. It has scared them. Hell, it scared me. I thought maybe you were possessed. You will need to talk to them, reassure them that you mean them no harm."

Thomle's head began to throb again as he listened to his father. A nauseous pain went spinning through his skull, and he struggled with what to say to these people. He turned another full circle as the scared, dirty faces cautiously watched him. Children peeked at him from behind their mothers' skirts as tired old men leaned on broken swords and broken hoes. They waited. Thomle's mind was racing in all directions when suddenly he heard a welcome sound.

High in the smoke-filled sky, the hawk and dove glided in and out of the silently shivering mist. The sea breeze began to stir. He wondered for a moment how the pair had gotten there, but his father's voice brought him back to the present.

"Thomle, Thomle, go speak to them." The sounds reverberated in Thomle's aching brain. He took a couple of tentative steps toward the frightened villagers, coughed to clear his throat, and then began to speak in his broken Gaelic.

"I mean you no harm." He paused to let that fact sink in. "I only want to help you, to keep you from a fate that I have seen far too often." He stumbled through the Celtic brogan and was angry with himself for not listening more carefully to the old slave woman.

The only sounds other than Thomle's voice were the pop and hiss of the few remaining fires that burned in the lower part of the village and the dove that cooed as it flew beside the hawk. The great hawk was silent. Tired feet shuffled in the sand as the survivors waited for more words, more reassurances. When after an awkward minute or two none came, a young mother stepped forward. She carried a small girl child dressed in a filthy homespun shift; the child hugged tightly to her bosom.

"We thank you, lord, for what you have just done here tonight." She looked around at a few nodding heads. "But we do not understand why one Norseman would fight another Norseman—for us—unless you want us as slaves for yourselves."

Thomle reached up and, with tired hands, took the leather and iron helmet from his sweat-soaked head, his blond hair falling lank to his shoulders. He would try once more to explain the reasons for his actions as sweat began to run down his forehead.

"I want no slaves." He nearly shouted the words, and the startled villagers stepped back at his sudden anger. He saw their reaction and was saddened. *If only Morea were here*, he moaned to himself.

"I want nothing that belongs to you." He watched the fear dance in their eyes and almost whispered as he repeated, "I want nothing that belongs to you." He was tired, bone-tired, but the memory of the Celtic language was coming back to him, and he pressed on. The words began to flow more easily.

"I want only ..." He paused again and looked toward the golden sunrise as he rephrased his words.

"I *need* to help you," he corrected. Moisture glistened in the corners of his blue eyes. The village survivors saw and whispered among themselves.

Thorma didn't say a word as his son spoke. He simply stood off to the side and wondered what his Ulrika would say about all this. He almost smiled at the thought because he knew she would be proud, though why, he wasn't quite sure. The big man turned his vision out to sea while the sun burned away the light frost that soon began to drip from the treetops like cooling rain. It fell down on the warriors as sunbeams danced on the incoming waves lapping at the sandy beach. The entire crew—mutineers and loyal fighters alike—listened as Thomle tried to reassure the villagers that he meant them no harm. Amazingly, they began to believe him, or at least it appeared that way to Thorma. The survivors from the brutal raid seemed to understand what Thomle was offering them. *I wish to the gods that I could understand*, mused Thorma to himself as he tried to imagine what his son was saying. The one thing he knew for sure was that his son really needed to help these people, for whatever reason.

Thorma looked to the sky again. *He's just like you, Ulrika. Sometimes I couldn't understand you either.* He chuckled to himself. Thorma turned his attention back to his son because he wasn't exactly sure how they—he had to smile at that thought—were going to help these people. Thomle paused again in his speech. As he did, the group of villagers parted, and an old man, with a rough laurel walking stick to aid him, limped forward. Thomle's mind immediately flashed to the old man he had tried to spare back in Oban. The old man, gray, thin, and tough as boiled leather, stopped two steps away. *A fighter's move*, thought Thomle, smiling to himself. The old man looked up at him with eyes the color of rich soil.

The contrast between the young Viking with steam rising off his sweat-soaked body and the old man, who wore a ragged homespun cloak that hung loosely from his stooped shoulders and defiantly clutched his staff, was striking. Thomle looked the old man in the eyes, eyes that held no fear. And soon the man began to speak in a gravelly voice, which sounded like a rusty hinge being pried open.

"They"—he pointed at the still prone Bjorn Jorge Hanson—"have killed most of our young men. We are all that are left." He waved his arms around and looked out at his companions. "They even butchered our sheep and cattle for sport. We will starve this winter."

Thomle responded without hesitation. "We will help you salvage the meat from these animals before it spoils, and we will tan the hides from the butchered livestock so that you will have them for warmth. We will help rebuild your huts before winter comes." Thomle looked over at his father who, surprisingly, had already begun directing his stunned crew toward their new tasks.

"Go get the scum who did all this!" Thorma shouted at several of his men. "They're hiding in the forest behind the sheds. I believe most of the fight is gone from them now." He talked as he strode to where Jorge Hanson lay in the sand.

"And as for you," he growled down at the prone figure. "Go help them. And remember, if you or any of your crew cause more trouble, I will come after you with the hawk." Jorge Hanson struggled to his feet, brushed sand from his leather britches despite his wounded shoulder, and shuffled off toward his men, who were slowly emerging from the dark forest. He didn't want to anger the hawk or the old man, so he instructed his men to do as they were told. Thorma had to turn away to hide the smile on his face, but as he did, he ran straight into one of his own men, a man who had been with him for many years. The bearded and scarred warrior looked at Thorma with a confused expression on his face but didn't say anything. He just shuffled his feet and glanced around, unsure of what to do.

"Well, Thorfin, don't just stand there. Take three men and start salvaging the meat. Begin with the sheep since they spoil the quickest," he bellowed. Thorfin started to protest, but the determined look on his leader's face gave him pause. "Go, friend. It's a new day for us," said Thorma, who turned and began walking toward the edge of the forest. More of Jorge Hanson's men were coming out of the brush where the howls of wolves and the cries of trapped men mingled in the darkness.

Both crews scurried in all directions as Thorma stomped through the village, shouting orders. Borne out of years of habit, he was constantly aware of his surroundings; this situation was no exception. He glanced cautiously over at the closest knot of village men and was relieved to see his son standing with them. He started walking that way.

When the grizzled old warrior walked up and stood by his side, Thomle, without taking his eyes off the laboring crews, whispered, "Thank you."

"I just hope you know what you're doing," he replied, a smile forming in the corners of his mouth.

Hours later, the sun had become a huge orange ball as it sank into what appeared to be a boiling sea, the red clouds rising from the horizon like steam. The last of the salvaged meat lay on drying racks over a smoking fire, and the hides were stretched and scraped, ready for salt and urine. The high ridges turned dark with the lengthening shadows.

"They will still need to find cattle and sheep for the spring to restart their herds," said Thorma, sitting down beside his son and leaning back against a young sapling. He closed his eyes and rubbed his sore shoulder, sleep nipping at his eyelids until the silence forced him to glance over at his son. Thomle had slowly turned his head toward his father, who by now was wide-eyed and staring at him.

"Hellfire and damnation. Odin be damned. I knew you would ask that," moaned the old warrior as he took off his helmet and sat it by his side.

"I haven't asked for a thing … yet." Thomle smiled, also leaning back and stretching his tired body.

"No, you haven't … yet," mocked Thorma, just before he shouted for his crew to come over to where they sat.

One by one, the tired and grungy men gathered around Thorma and his son who were now standing looking out at the ships.

"These people can probably make it through the winter now that we have helped them with the slaughtered animals, but when spring comes, they will hurt, if not starve, without more livestock," said Thorma as he looked at his men trying to gauge their mood. They were all tired from the long day's work, but there was something else. They almost seemed pleased with themselves. *I wonder how they will take this next part*, he worried.

"We are going to release the livestock that Jorge Hanson's crew took from their last raid"—he paused to look over at Thomle—"and we are going to release the remaining livestock that we took from

Oban." The crew stood for a moment in stunned silence and then slowly, without a single grumble, sullenly walked down to the sleeping dragons to obey Thorma's orders. He and Thomle watched the men walk toward the ships.

"That surprised me," said Thorma, who took a chunk of lamb from a very fat village woman and began to chew on it.

"Maybe you were wrong about our people," replied Thomle as he too took a piece of hot meat from the same smiling lady.

"Maybe" was the only word that came from Thorma as he chewed and pondered the reaction of his men.

Thorma gnawed on the roasted mutton and worried about his crew. He had been fooled once; it wouldn't happen again. As he sat there, an idea sprang into his mind. He shouted, "Gandalf!" in the direction of the departing crew. Gandalf was Thorma's master navigator as well as an old friend. A little older than Thorma, he was of medium height and wore a nearly solid white bearskin cloak. Gandalf had been with Thorma since they left Vinland years before. He turned from the crew when he heard his name called and walked back to stand in front of his friend and leader.

"Gandalf, what is the mood of the crew?" asked Thorma as he watched his men begin unloading the cattle.

"Their mood?" asked the old navigator, unsure of the question.

"Yes, their damn mood. How angry, how disappointed are they with what we are doing?" Thorma's temper began to rise from having to repeat the question; he hated having to repeat himself. His old friend knew that and regretted his hesitation. He scratched his grayish beard and thought for a minute.

"Well, they're not happy, if that is what you are asking. But they are also trying hard to understand what you and Thomle are doing." Thorma shook his head.

"Hell, I'm not even sure what we are doing." He growled the comment over his shoulder as he stomped off toward the group of surviving elders, leaving his friend staring after him.

The old men stood off to the side with a look of utter surprise on their faces, as the Norsemen, followed by several small boys from the village, drove the sheep and cattle off the ships and up the slope toward the newly repaired cattle pens.

"This will help you next spring," announced Thorma in his broken Celtic.

"We thank you, my lord. We thank you very much," stammered one of the old men as he looked on in amazement. Thorma, who was unsure of exactly what to say to the man, simply turned and walked back to where his son stood watching some small boys play. The boys were too young to help with the cattle, yet they fought each other with sticks like little warriors.

"Every little boy wants to be a warrior. Why, I'm not sure," stated Thomle, half to himself, as he turned to his father.

"Do you want to be a farmer now?" he asked, a little bemused.

"Maybe," answered Thomle. "Maybe."

After a few minutes of watching the little boys fight their mock battle, Thorma went on. "Are you pleased?" He grunted the question. Thomle watched their crew and the boys who were big enough to help herd the last of the cattle into the pens at the back of the village.

"Aren't you?" Thomle returned the question with a smile and then put his arm around his father's broad shoulders.

"Huh," growled the old warrior. A simple grunt now seemed to be his usual reply to his son's slightly irritating questions. By now, the sun had entirely disappeared beneath the sea, but fiery streaks of light burst through the dark gray clouds that hung low on the horizon like fire arrows shooting in the heavens.

Two days later, the echo of the hawk's cry caused every eye in the village to turn skyward as it sailed with the dove from the elm trees above the village and circled the dragon ships being rowed out into the small bay. The shadows that had darkened the vale fled from the fiery dawn like bats from a cave. It was time to head north again. Thomle's mind returned to Morea as he watched the winged pair sail on the high wind currents. He hoped that she would be pleased with what he—no, what *they* had done here at this village called Inverness. Thorma stood near the stern, and he too watched the birds. But his mind was on what he would say once they got back to Balfour and how he would protect his son from the wrath that he knew was sure to come from the elders.

* * * * *

Morea had not slept well since hearing what she thought was Thomle's cry in the middle of the night. Her days remained busy though, helping the sick and wounded while the coming winter bore on everyone's mind. That fact alone demanded her best efforts, but her nights—her nights were cold and long and ever so lonely. Her brother, William, tried often to make her laugh, but even his crazy antics couldn't shake her melancholy. One chilly afternoon, the seemingly unending parade of those in need had slowed down, and she had stepped, however briefly, outside her hut. The ground beneath her feet was bathed in a pale light that spilled out in front of her when she pulled back the cloth door. Her mind was on the young Norseman as she gazed far out to sea. At first, she didn't hear her brother's shouts, but finally, his anguished calls snapped her out of her reverie. She turned her back to the empty sea and watched her brother as he ran down through the upper pasture shouting, the few surviving cattle fleeing before him in every direction.

Morea waited patiently, hands on hips, as her brother jumped the small creek and ran up to her.

"There is a large group of riders coming hard from the northeast. It can only be the mac Dougall clan," he managed to say, bending over with his hands on his knees, trying to catch his breath. She watched him struggle to get air and asked dismissively.

"And what, pray tell, makes this visit any more dangerous than the others?" She had asked the question calmly, but her gaze drifted toward the high hills as she waited for an answer.

"The young lord, the one who is always flirting with you, has brought his cavalry and their war dogs," explained William anxiously. He glanced back over his shoulder toward the northeast where several riders now appeared on the ridge. Morea had not taken her eyes off the high crag as they talked, and she now saw Angus mac Dougall riding smugly at the front of his retinue.

"Go busy yourself, William. I will be all right." She nearly whispered the words, and when he hesitated, she spoke louder. "Go." He finally left. Walking quickly back inside her hut, she rummaged through an old battered chest that had belonged to her mother. She needed to change her dress, for the one she wore was a little too tight for mac Dougall's prying eyes.

Angus Augusta mac Dougall, whose father claimed to be of Roman descent and had therefore added the name Augusta to his eldest son's, rode his black stallion in front of the cavalry, all twenty of them. His cavalry wore their full battle gear, carried lances as well as crossbows, and rode smaller shaggy mountain ponies. Behind the ponies walked the war dogs and their handlers. These dogs were a mix of elkhounds and the long-haired wolf hounds. They stood about three feet high at the shoulders and pulled fiercely on the ropes that had been braided from leather and hemp and bound them about the neck. The twenty riders responded fairly impressively to a trumpet call, and the young lord smiled as his men spread out in a long line as they approached the village, an obvious and enjoyable show of force. The cavalry's crossbows were strapped onto the sides of their rough saddles, and their spears were held tight against the stirrups with the points straight up. Red and white pennants stitched with the mac Dougall emblem flew at the lance tips.

Angus mac Dougall had formulated a plan for the village of Oban while sipping warm ale at his father's main fortress, though he hadn't bothered to discuss it with his father. The plan was twofold. The first part was simply to make an impression on the survivors of the raid, which included the pretty wench Morea mac Craig. The second part was a threat: if they paid their taxes and shared their harvests, as they should, they would have protection from the Norsemen. *If not* ... He smiled at the thought.

Morea had slipped on a heavier cloak as well as a larger dress, cumbersome and much too warm, but anything was better than the ogling of the young lord. She made one last check of herself, took a deep breath, and stepped out of the hut. She intended to make a proper curtsy and smile, but she had to jump back almost at once—mac Dougall's horse stood nearly at her front door. He stared down at her, his gaze piercing the many layers of homespun. After a couple of minutes of strained silence, he spoke.

"Good afternoon, Morea." He bowed deeply from the saddle.

"Good afternoon to you, my lord," she replied and attempted a curtsy, for which there was no room. He liked her discomfort and even thought he saw a glimmer of fear in her eyes, which aroused him to discomfort.

"I have heard rumors"—he paused to watch her facial expression—"that you practically ran the Norsemen's raiding party off all by yourself." He sniggered but stared down hard from the saddle, waiting for an answer. The big black horse stepped backward and pawed at the ground.

"Not hardly, my lord. I merely … talked to them," she answered with her head bowed.

"Well, it must have been a very persuasive talk, from what I have heard." He paused again, wanting her to know that he had ears in her village. "They released the prisoners, all of them, as well as part of the livestock. I have never heard of that being done before. And left you alive." Mac Dougall scoffed, the stallion all the while becoming almost too much for him to handle.

Morea had to move quickly to the side to keep from being stomped on by the sweaty beast, and mac Dougall was once again pleased to see what he interpreted as fear in the pretty girl's eyes. She knew full well that she needed to be very careful with her words.

"My lord, the Norsemen seemed to have been a very superstitious lot. The mere sight of a hawk and a dove together was enough to cause them to run away in fear," she explained in a cautious tone. He looked around at what remained of the village before he returned his gaze to her and growled.

"I doubt those Vikings fear much of anything, much less some tame birds." His eyes narrowed almost into a squint.

"Perhaps you are right, my lord. Perhaps they just decided to be merciful," replied Morea, who knew she had made a mistake with her choice of words, but it was too late. Mac Dougall's mouth twisted into a snarl.

"I doubt that even more, wench!" he shouted. "I'll show them no mercy either when I catch them, which I will, mark my word." He had yet to fight any Norsemen and was somewhat frightened by them, but he wouldn't let this damn girl see that. Jerking hard on the reins, he shouted for his men to follow him and tried to urge the horse back up the slope. But the big stallion was high-strung and fought to gain control over its rider. It reared up, hooves pawing the air, and the unexpected move nearly threw the young lord off. Catching himself on the saddle horn, he leaned forward in an attempt to bring the nervous horse down. Finally, after a brief struggle with the reins, he was able to calm the stallion, even showing what seemed to be tenderness toward the beast. With a wicked grin, he gently patted its neck and talked soothingly in its ear as the horse's nostrils flared.

"You see, Morea, horses are like a lot of things. You just have to know how to stroke them in order to get them to do what you want." He smiled lustfully as he patted the lathered neck.

The young healer had to look away to keep from laughing in his face. After a minute, she managed to look back with a serious expression, and he, obviously having forgotten about calling his troops, casually asked a question.

"Have you heard anything about a Norse war band that seems to have helped protect a village north of here? The village called Inverness?" He continued to pat the horse's neck, all the while leaning down close to Morea, waiting for an answer. When none came, he went on.

"My spies say that one group of Norsemen"—he spat the name—"was attacking the village when another war band stepped in and not only stopped the onslaught but forced the raiders to repair the damage already done to the village." A mocking laugh escaped his throat, but he watched her eyes closely for anything she might accidentally reveal.

Morea dropped her head. She feared the shifty young mac Dougall would see the excitement in her eyes. The news had to be about Thomle. *It just had to be*, she told herself, her heart pounding wildly in her chest. She had heard the story from a traveling vendor just last evening as they sat around a fire, looking at the wares they were unable to afford. She was afraid to believe it last night, but now it must be true. Why else would Angus mac Dougall mention it? *Thomle is the only one who would fight to protect a village*, her mind cried excitedly. Composing herself as best she could, she replied.

"My lord, I heard a rumor, just last evening in fact, about two Viking war bands fighting each other over a village, but I thought it was only a traveler's tale." She forced a smile. He looked at her for several seconds, pleased with her smile. However, he had been told by some of the paid eyes in the village that she had been very friendly with one of the Norsemen. The very thought made Angus mac Dougall crazy with anger. *She will be my woman and no one else—or at least until I'm done with her*. He laughed out loud at the thought. Morea knew she treaded on very thin ice, but she couldn't resist.

"My lord," she said softly, "the Vikings seem to lust after all women, but especially the ones they cannot have." She bowed slightly in his direction.

Angus mac Dougall once again jerked the reins of the fiery stallion and spurred him hard in the flanks as he raced off toward the ridge. He was smiling as he drove the horse hard across the field, his Cavalry trying to keep up. Morea stood in the lengthening shadows and watched horse and rider gallop off through the pasture—in search of what, she didn't know.

The shadows were long, and the last of the sun's rays were streaking across the surrounding hills when Morea decided to take a walk down toward the rocky shore where she and Thomle had their first encounter. It was warm, unusually warm for late autumn, and she took off her heavy outer cloak as the blackened monastery loomed in the distance like a bad omen. She folded it across her arm and closed her eyes, replaying the events of that day in her mind.

"I was so scared and confused, and so was Thomle," she spoke to the breeze that kissed her cheek and ruffled her unruly hair. She needed him badly and somehow knew he needed her as well. Was it even possible that the young Viking could understand the ideas she had spoken of and that he could come to believe in them? As she stood looking out at the sea, its white-capped waves rocking the small fishing boats that had cast their nets off the rocky point jutting from the Isle of Kerrera, she realized that she didn't know the answer. Her mind could not escape the horror and devastation of the raid, yet it struggled mightily to embrace her heart's certainty—that, yes, it did understand. At last, she turned away from the rocky cliff and, with one last look over her shoulder, headed back to her hut. There was supper to cook, and even though she felt little hunger, she knew she had to keep her strength up, if only for the sake of those who needed her help.

The once-gentle breeze turned stiff, and she draped the heavy cloak around her shoulders as she moved down the rocky path. The darkened shadow of the monastery loomed ominously in front of her when suddenly the soft cooing of a dove rode toward her on the wind. It slowed the pace of her walking but quickened that of her heart. She searched the shadows that had fallen over the charred remains of the Christian god's home for what she felt was her friend.

"And where have you been for the last several days, young lady?" she spoke soothingly to the dove perched on one of the monastery's rock pillars when suddenly the hawk appeared out of nowhere and flew close over her head. Morea watched the odd pair with envy as they finally settled together on a windswept oak that clung to the cliff face above her. *My hawk, my Thomle, will soon return to me,* she told herself. Blushing at the thought, she hurried on across the rocky slope with Crag Dunolleigh looking down mysteriously from the distance.

* * * * *

Thomle wasn't headed back to Oban just yet, though. He was manning the rudder of the lead dragon ship that was traveling due north away from Inverness, still aimed for Balfour on Orkney. They were now in a race with the weather. The late autumn storms, with their gale force winds and twenty-foot swells, were on their way. And when they hit, maneuvering the small ships in the North Sea would be nearly impossible for a few months. Thomle looked up at the North Star and shifted the rudder until the dragonhead lined up with the one steady light in the otherwise shifting night sky.

"Guide us home, Polaris," he asked the navigator's friend. The other stars in the Great Bear constellation shining brightly in the cold night, a shooting star streaked out of the east and raced across the horizon.

"A good sign," he said loudly, accidentally waking his father, who had just lain down to rest. Thorma jerked up and looked around. Everything seemed in order, so he pulled his bearskin cloak tightly around his battered shoulders and closed his eyes again, drifting back into a troubled sleep filled with hawks and doves and mutineers.

Thomle gripped the rough-hued steering oar in both hands, his hip placed tightly against the rudder stem. The wooden handle had been worn slick by calloused hands sliding across its surface for months on end. His mind pondered on the girl Morea. He liked her very much. Hell, he loved her as far as his young mind could determine love. And the way her Celtic name rolled off his tongue seemed perfect. He wanted to take her as his wife, and he wanted to live in peace.

He struggled with the idea of peace without the need for a sword, but he was intrigued by the thought, nonetheless. *It seems that someone is always going to try to take the things you have, and without a sword, how could you stop them? If I had not had a sword at Inverness, I wouldn't have been able to help those villagers. So what do you do? You must be ready to fight in order to protect your family. Would this be breaking with peace or merely preserving it?* He had so many questions and so few answers, but one thing was now certain. He had to talk to the elders when they got back to Balfour. He would try as best he could to convince them that there was a better way just like Morea said.

Several hours later, the dark night still gripped them, and Thorma, having woken from a dream-filled sleep, sat with his back pressed against the single main mast that towered high above his head. He studied the groaning mast made of yellow pine, which because of overuse was becoming harder to find back in Balfour. The great seemingly endless pine forest that had, at one time, stretched for miles along glacier-carved ridges now resembled the hair left on a mangy animal, spotted and patchy. Ship builders had to search far and wide for the tall stout trees they knew could withstand the strong winds of the high North Sea. The woolen sails with their brown bear emblem cackled, as the cold wind drove them up the coast.

Thorma drank tepid mead from his favorite pewter cup and, for the thousandth time, studied the ancient symbols that were carved into its well-worn sides. He had no idea what they meant and, try as he might, couldn't even remember which raid it had been taken on. But he liked to imagine the artist taking pride in the mug he had made. *Another sign of getting old*, mused the leader of the war band, the warm mead soothing his dry throat. He looked over and watched his son fight with the big rudder that was guiding them through the pounding seas.

His big head shook from side to side as he stiffly rose from his seated position, refilled his mug, fetched another tankard for Thomle, and walked back through the rows of sleeping oarsmen. He wanted to be near his son, knowing that he had no rudder to help guide him through the rough seas of love. *How do I tell him that, Ulrika?* He looked up into the troubled sky.

Suddenly, a rogue wave slammed viciously into the side of their ship, and Thorma nearly dropped both tankards. Regaining his balance and shaking spilled liquor from his hand, he angrily kicked a stray boot to the side as several groggy men scurried out of his way. Still ill as a hornet, he walked up to his son and offered him one of the tankards, but the boy shook his head.

"I need a clear head, Father. There is a storm brewing in the west, and it could get difficult this far from shore." Thorma looked out to sea and watched the lightning flash, then set the extra tankard down near Thomle and placed one booted foot onto a bench beside his son.

"I think we need to talk, son," he said after a long pull on his mead. Thomle wasn't sure what his father wanted to talk about, so he just looked at him and didn't say anything. The big man stroked his beard and thought. "Thomle, the way of a Viking is cruel and difficult sometimes"—he paused, searching for the right words—"but it is our way, the only way to live that we understand." He cursed himself for not being able to explain it any better and turned to stare into the overcast night. The rumbling of the coming tempest hammered his ears, as the black clouds rushed by like a stampede.

"It's coming!" shouted Thomle, the black hand of god shaking the longboat. Thorma grabbed the closest guide rope and braced against the gunwale, while Thomle dug his shoulder into the big oak rudder and fought with the minions of Neptune as the seas began to swirl about the dragon ship. The frothy waves crashed over the gunwale and sprayed them with frigid seawater; the ship groaned from the pounding as if its very soul was being ripped apart.

The crew hunkered down, covering their heads with their fur cloaks that weren't waterproof, but close because of all the bear fat that had been rubbed into them through the years. They put their fate in the hands of the gods as the water ran off their backs, and they waited for the deluge they knew was coming. Except the hard rain never came, only the cold fierce winds that hammered them briefly and then were gone like a fickle lover. After a few tense minutes, Thomle relaxed his grip on the rudder and began to speak.

"Father ..." He never finished the sentence. His whole body shook as the rudder slammed against his chest from another rogue wave. Fighting with all his strength, he kept the longboat headed straight into the wind, as another and then another wave crashed over the bow before, finally, it was over. Catching his breath, Thomle went on.

"I know I will probably anger the elders back at Balfour, but that can't be helped. I fully intend to talk to them. I must at least try to explain what's in my heart!" The old warrior scratched the edge of his scar and stared into his mead that by now had grown cold and lacking taste. He nodded without looking up.

"I know, son, I know," he whispered, pouring the cold brew over the side. It was all he could think of to say. Any great thoughts having departed from his mind.

* * * * *

A couple of days later, Morea was walking behind two roan-colored cows and their young calves as they made their way down from the high pasture; it was a cold and blustery day. The cows, their coats long and shaggy, had bags that hung full and low for the calves that chased after them in a constant search for supper. It took harsh and frequent poking with a sharp-pointed laurel staff to drive the older cows along and keep them from stopping to munch on the small clumps of wiregrass still green in the high pasture. The climb up the steep slope in search of the cattle had been difficult for Morea, who was weary to begin with after another long restless night, sleep simply refusing to come until deep into the morning. She shuffled slowly along the well-worn trail until she spotted a large rock and decided to sit down for a while. The flat piece of granite, where the young spotters usually salted the cattle, looked inviting, the cattle having licked it clean. She sat down and smiled despite her weariness, as the young calves butted heads and ran about much like children would play. *Ah, to be so carefree*, she thought.

The calves had been born during the raid, their mothers hiding from the Norsemen in the high forest to give birth. They were still so young, and she knew they would have a hard time making it through the brutal winter.

"I will need to build you a proper shelter soon," she said to the calves, who were now contently suckling, their tails slapping back and forth. She leaned back, the cold from the rock seeping through her wool dress and forming chill bumps on her stomach. She pulled her wrap tightly around her shoulders and closed her eyes for a second, her back gradually warming the piece of dark granite. The nymph named Napper whispered, "Sleep," as she tiptoed around her tired mind.

Much later, a sharp noise thrashed about her dream, and she jumped awake. A stiff breeze blew against her bare legs, and she looked around groggily. The two cows and their calves had wandered over near the forest's edge, but they seemed all right. *What is wrong?* She saw the smoke before she heard the shouts of the old men, who were trying to gather the young boys scattered throughout the village.

"My god," she cried as she stared down at the chaotic scene unfolding in her village. "Not more Vikings." In her hurry to climb from atop the rock, she forgot to cross herself for her oath. She glanced once more at the cattle and decided they were better off where they were before running to another rocky ledge and staring down at the village. Neither Thomle nor his father would return in anger; she was sure of that. It must be another group of Norsemen or … the mac Dougall clan, yes!

"The cursed mac Dougalls," she cried and quickly saw proof that her hunch was right. Several horsemen were scattering startled people as they rode though the center of the mostly unrepaired village. They seemed to be searching for someone … but who? Her anger rose. Then she saw the all-too-familiar figure of Angus mac Dougall riding his black stallion not just up to but inside her small hut.

"God have mercy," she cried, this time remembering to cross herself. "He's looking for me!"

Her hand flew to her mouth as she spun in a dazed circle, trying to figure out what to do next. She threw her walking stick away and nearly tripped as she ran back up through the pasture toward the dark forest. Angry shouts from mac Dougall's men reached her ears despite the blood that pounded there. She had been spotted by one of the retinue, and now the race was on. Forsaking modesty, she lifted the helm of her simple dress in hopes of gaining speed and ran like the devil was after her, which it was. As a young child, she had outrun all the boys in the village; it had been quite a point of contention as the proud youths vied for her affection or, at least, a smile from her pretty face. But today the stakes were much higher. It was possibly a race for her life, and she ran accordingly. Her breath came in gasps as she struggled up the steep trail that the cattle had carved out of the dense heather. If only she could make it to the forest. The timber was much too thick with underbrush for the horses, and maybe there she could hide from Angus mac Dougall's henchmen.

The closest village in the direction she ran was Inverness, the one Thomle had supposedly helped, and she knew the general direction to be north along Loch Linnhe for about sixty miles. She and her brother had made that journey once before as children. They had ridden with their grandmother on a small horse-drawn cart; it had been an adventure then, but this trip would be very different. The angry shouts grew louder, and she dared to look back over her shoulder. When she did, she tripped on a limb and fell. The heather had torn her dress and scratched her legs, but otherwise, she seemed all right. Scrambling to her feet, she dusted herself off and resumed her run. When she did, she quickly realized that her right sandal strap was broken. Kicking it away, she ran on with one bare foot for about twenty paces before striking a sharp root in the trail and tearing a gash in the bottom of her unprotected foot. Bleeding and almost overcome with panic, she limped on until she saw a large black horse out of the corner of her eye; she knew it was Angus mac Dougall. Panic forced her back into a slow, painful run.

The stallion wasn't accustomed to running on such steep ground; his coat was white with lather, and his nostrils flared as steam blew from between the bits clamped tightly in his mouth. Mac Dougall laughed and spurred the tired animal in its bloody flanks, forcing it to the left and driving Morea off the trail. The horse's hooves threw clumps of grass into the air as it bore down on the scared girl. The young lord had a lewd grin on his face as he drew closer to the comely wench whose firm legs were shiny with sweat and bare from the midthigh down. *She will be mine soon*, thought mac Dougall, pressing his horse on. He was just about to cut her off from the thick woods that he knew could be her salvation. Another thirty feet was all he needed, but suddenly, out of the gray mist that hung like sheep's wool near the ridgetop, a shrill cry sounded. A second later, eight razor-sharp talons struck Angus mac Dougall like the wrath of God.

The barbed claws ripped bloody flesh from the face of the young lord, and he hit the ground with a loud grunt. All thoughts of pursuit vanished as the heir apparent came crashing from his horse, his hands tightly clutching his torn face. The horse continued running toward the edge of the forest, the bridle reins dragging the ground around his front hooves. Angus mac Dougall thrashed in the underbrush and cried for help. As quickly as it had begun, the attack stopped. But the hawk remained close, circling low over the wounded lord, who slashed the air with his short sword. Blood and sweat dripped onto his hands, and he lost his grip on the only weapon he had. Frightened and in pain, mac Dougall curled up into a fetal position near a decaying stump and mumbled curses on every creature imaginable until he heard the great wings flapping above him. With a shudder, he began crawling down the hill on his hands and knees, his desperate cries for help drowned by the hawk's fierce call. With the battle over, the huge raptor headed for a stand of oaks just up the ridge. On its way, it passed low over Morea, who had stopped running and was looking back in shock at her antagonist withering in pain, her eyes darting from the wounded lord to the hawk and back again.

As she stood there in the cold fading light, unsure of what to do next, a single reddish feather floated gently down from the heavens, and Morea watched it land softly at her feet like a peace offering. She stared at it through several rapid heartbeats, somewhat afraid to touch the thing, but finally, she summoned the courage to stoop and pick it up. It felt soft and warm in her hand, and her breathing quickened for some unknown reason. Then she heard a pitiful moan escape the torn mouth of Angus mac Dougall, and for a brief moment, she contemplated going back to help the wounded man. Her need to survive, though, quickly overrode her natural inclination to help, so she clutched the feather tightly in her hand and ran.

Even with the injured foot, she ran as fast as she was able deeper and deeper into the dark, threatening woods. The cries of the injured mac Dougall slowly faded as Morea struggled through the thick brush, her heavy breathing the only sound, cold damp mist closing in on all sides. The ancient forest, with giant beech and hickory trees four feet in diameter blocking out the sun, seemed to absorb every sound, while fear pushed her beyond the point of exhaustion. She stumbled several times in her rush to get farther away from her pursuers until at last she collapsed on the bank of a small stream laden with moss-covered rocks. She lay there on her back for a while, listening. Finally, satisfied she was safe at least for the moment, Morea crawled on her hands and knees to the water's edge where she painfully lowered her scratched, sweaty face into the cold water and drank deeply. Water ran down her chin to drip between her heaving breasts. After drinking her fill, she lay back cautiously and listened once again for any sound of mac Dougall's henchmen.

A deep stillness prevailed in the glen, much like a Druid's sacred grove, broken only occasionally by the lonesome call of a kite. It was as if the forest had sucked up every living thing, and together, they all held their breath and listened with her. Surrounded by silence, she wearily sat back in the damp leaves and wept. Her body shook with sobs until sleep finally rescued her, and she drifted into chaotic dreams of Vikings, wild horses, and fierce hawks.

She woke with a shudder many hours later, soaked to the bone and shivering from the cold. Her mind spun rapidly as she took stock of her surroundings. Covered in mud and filth, she reached down into the water and attempted to wash some of the dirt from her legs and arms. The cold water chilled her more but helped to soothe the many scratches that covered her legs. The throbbing in her injured foot had eased slightly, and she elevated it while she sat in the leaves and pondered her situation.

"I can't go back. The mac Dougall clan will blame me for what happened to their young lord," she spoke aloud to the forest, bile rising in the back of her throat from the thought of what Angus mac Dougall tried to do. She wondered about the strangeness of the hawk. *Why is this hawk constantly protecting me? Is it really the new god, or is it the old gods showing mankind that they still have power?* For these questions and many more that ran amok in her half-dazed mind, she had no answer.

Thirty minutes later, after an aborted attempt to clean herself, she half crawled and half limped away from the stream toward a large rock that had a ledge extending out far enough to form a small cave-like shelter. She lay down once more, stretching out underneath the overhanging rock and raking dry leaves over herself to create a camouflaged blanket of warmth. A warm breeze that belied the cold night began to stir over the vale, and it gradually chased the gray mist into the high mountains above her. A full harvest moon rose over the rocky crag called Ben Cruachan, and it played hide-and-seek behind wispy clouds that floated by. The night sounds soon erupted into a cacophony, filling the air as millions of insects sang in their last chorus of the season. Her weary eyes closed like curtains at the end of a long play; her thoughts wandered like thousands of other lovers in the past. *What is my would-be lover doing at this exact moment? Is Thomle looking at this very same moon? Is he thinking of me?* Morea's mind raced across fields of worry, just as her feet had raced through the grass fields earlier that day.

What do the gods, any god, want with me? She only wanted peace and to have children and raise a family. She felt the blood rush to her face with that thought, and she smiled. Then the feeling of Thomle's arms around her returned, and her breathing became more rapid. She shook the lustful thoughts from her mind, focusing instead on the story of the Norsemen saving the village of Inverness, to which she was headed. *It had to have been Thomle and his crew. What had changed them? Was it truly a desire for peace, or was it something different guiding them? If so, is it guiding me as well?*

"Oh, Thomle, help me," she cried aloud. A thousand heartbeats later, sleep gently pushed her anxious thoughts into a place where they could rest, and so did she.

Flashes of sunlight fought their way through the thick canopy of trees that sat atop the near ridge and slowly the dark cove was filled with slivers of gold and red and silver. Swarms of flies and other insects danced through soft clouds of ragweed pollen as the few birds that had not gone south chirped in the high treetops. Morea forced her eyes open and looked around. Painfully stretching her battered body, she happily realized, although stiff and sore, nothing seemed broken.

A slight rustling sound in her bed of dry leaves got her attention, and she quickly raked them from her dress. A small chipmunk poked its head out of the leaves, crinkled its nose as it sniffed the air, and then quickly scurried across her feet. It sprinted toward and then along a fallen beech tree before disappearing into a well-worn hole just below a large fork. She managed a small chuckle at the little rodent as she crawled out from under the rock outcropping. Once standing, she stretched like an old cat, groaned, and glanced skyward. The air was cool and numerous cottony clouds churned across the pale blue sky in their eastward journey. She knew the autumn winds would become more blustery by midday, and she would have to move quickly in order to stay warm. But her injured foot demanded immediate attention. She limped over to the nearby creek, where she plopped down on a moss-covered rock and tore a long strip from her already tattered and much-too-skimpy dress.

With her behind soaking wet but her foot somewhat wrapped, she drank more water and then trudged off, with the help of a stick, in what she thought was the general direction of Inverness. By noon, she had passed high above the Falls of Lora as the mists raced up through the shadow-filled crags. She could hear the roar of the falls from the ridge where she struggled along. Hunger pangs had attacked her stomach down in the afternoon, and she was nearly doubled over as she limped along searching for berries or nuts that the squirrels had missed. Ever weary of the mac Dougall clan, Morea ate small sassafras roots and a few acorns, not much remained in what the animals had passed over.

On the second day of her journey, a freezing dawn leaked into the eastern sky. Morea looked down on a secluded homestead where smoke rolled out of a short rock chimney. A scrawny cock sat atop a battered gate and attempted to announce the new day, its harem of hens already working in the lean-to shed. Morea climbed down out of the forest despite the fierce barking of two mangy dogs held at bay by a length of braided rope. She was able to find a few eggs that had not been gathered, as well as some half-rotten potatoes and to sneak away with them. She felt bad about the theft, but at least the hunger pangs would ease for a short while.

In late afternoon of the fourth day of her trek, Morea climbed wearily up a steep knoll; she thought it was called Stab Diomh but wasn't sure. The knoll was covered with heather and laurel, which forced her to stoop and sometimes crawl on her hands and knees as she made her way up the slope. Finally, reaching the top, she stopped to catch her breath. She stretched her aching back and climbed upon a large rock ledge that offered a view of the country in front of her.

"Oh my," she cried as tears began to rush from her bloodshot eyes. She danced a one-footed jig, watching several wisps of smoke curl lazily up through a cold fog that covered the head of a large rugged inlet below her. A bay, wide and deep, stone-lined and sheltered by a high craggy promontory lay before her. While she stood watching, the wind picked up, and the fog, which looked like a sea of pearly water as it spread out along the inlet, dissipated. It revealed waters that reflected bluish green in the pale sunlight and a rude settlement of mud and thatch huts.

"It has to be Inverness," she cried as she fell to her knees in the wiregrass and began to eat the last handful of nuts and shriveled muscatel grapes that she clutched tightly in her hand.

A few minutes later, she struggled down the main ridge that luckily ran in the direction of the village. A slender spark of hope stirred in her heart as she moved forward. Rugged high country pastureland lay just in front of her, the grass already turning brown with the season. The thought of getting out of the dreadful heather quickened her pace, and receiving one last slap in the face from a laurel bush, she broke out of the thicket where the going became easier. The grassy fields extended as far down the mountain as she could see. Walking along a rutted cattle trail, just below a wide gap in the ridge, she found a small springhead that offered a chance not only to quench her thirst but also to wash some of the dirt off her tired, aching body. She dropped to her knees and looked down into the pool of water; the reflection that stared back at her was of a person that she didn't recognize. Her eyes were sunken back in her head and as red as any of the village drunks', her hair wild and unwashed like some animal of the forest.

"I'm a mess," she moaned and began washing herself, starting with her face. The water stung the cuts on her arms and legs, but gradually the dirt turned loose and washed down to stain the clear pool a dusty brown.

When she had washed as much of the filth off her body as she could, she sat beside the pool of water and gazed at the smoke that curled up from the small cluster of buildings at the head of the cove. She so hoped that this was the village Thomle had helped, but even if it wasn't, maybe she could at least rest and get something more to eat than acorns. As she fought with the tangles in her hair, clouds of worry began to fill her mind again. Frustrated, at last, with her efforts to deal with the mess on top of her head, she grudgingly left the pool of water and started walking down the trail. It led down through a grass field that was spotted with wind-stunted beech and pin oaks. She felt pretty sure that the trail would lead to the smoke and, hopefully, to safety.

As if in contradicting response to her hopes, a long wavering howl came snaking down from the forest like the wail of a lost soul. In a moment, the howl was repeated by another more distant voice that made a long ululating reply.

"Wolves," she cried aloud. Battered and bruised, she limped through the knee-high grass, the security of the forest, even with its wolves, far behind her; only the unknown lay ahead. The trail twisted and turned its way down through the pasture until at last she could see a rock wall and a broken wooden gate about half a mile ahead. As she drew closer, she saw two old men just to the right of the gate. They sat on the low moss-covered wall, smoking briar pipes. A couple of long-haired sheepdogs stood at their feet, ears perked up and pointing toward the howls that drifted down from deep in the forest. Rumbling growls escaped from their throats.

But the dogs' demeanor suddenly changed when they either smelt or saw Morea long before their masters did. They bounded up the trail, eager to give their greetings. Running up and wagging their bushy tails excitedly, they began sniffing places, in their eagerness, no one had ever sniffed before. They seemed to love her as she patted their heads, tolerating the sniffing, and wondered whether the two men would help her or send her on her way with a thrashing from their walking sticks.

Unconsciously, she tried once more to untangle her matted hair as she walked toward the dogs' masters. The old men, despite their failing eyesight, finally spotted her, noticing she was mumbling under her breath. Cautiously, they eased off the rock wall and stood leaning on long wooden staffs as the breeze ruffled the few remaining leaves on the beech trees around them. Morea, tired and frightened, forced a smile and limped up to the men who watched her approach. Their faces were unreadable masks to the young healer. She need not have worried, though. They may have been old men, but they were men. And when she walked up and smiled, the two herders smiled back. Making a sad attempt at clearing her throat, she finally spoke.

"Hello, my name is Morea, and I need your help." She managed to get the words out just before tears began to run down her cheeks, burning her parched lips.

"We can see that, Morea," answered the taller of the two men, calling their dogs away from her. The dogs obediently walked over and sat by their masters' feet, but their tails continued to wag a greeting.

"My name is Caleb, and my friend here is Robert. We live in the village just down this trail." The old man named Caleb pointed down the trail as if she wouldn't understand him. Morea hobbled over and leaned on the rock wall before asking with a long sigh.

"Is this Inverness?" The two men exchanged a side glance.

"Why, yes it is, child," answered Robert. "Or at least what's left of it," he continued. "But come, we can talk later. Please let us help you down the trail. Take my walking stick. You seem to have hurt your foot."

Morea was far too tired to begin an explanation of her injury or the fact that she had left her own stick up on the mountain. She simply took the staff that Robert handed her, and all three limped down the trail with the dogs following close behind. The trail eventually flattened out some, and the walking became a little easier for Morea, but she noticed that Robert had begun to limp worse than ever. After watching him almost fall attempting to cross a fallen tree, she handed his staff back to him. Sheepishly, he smiled at her and took it. The trail left the pasture and ran down beside a small stream that gurgled along in a profusion of small rapids. Huge gray boulders were scattered among tall maples that lined the trail on its way down the mountain. After a few more twists and turns, they emerged out of the forest into a well-tended clearing where, on the edge of the field near the creek, stood two recently built cattle pins made of split logs; beyond that lay the village. As they walked down a lane where charred thatch was piled in several stinking heaps, the trio was greeted by a swarm of curious children and a few idle adults.

In the town center, they were met by a half-dozen women, most with small children. Morea was offered a cup of water, which she drank eagerly until it ran down her chin and dripped onto her tattered dress. Smiling at the woman who had given her the cup, she managed to say, "Thank you," before collapsing onto the ground.

* * * * *

Later that evening, Morea awoke in a freshly thatched hut, the sweet odor of recently cut straw hanging heavy in the air. A newly tanned sheep pelt lay over her, and she could feel the sheep's wool all over her body, *all* over it. She was totally naked and much cleaner.

"Oh god," she moaned, highly embarrassed, and franticly looked around for her clothes. She saw the usual herbs of ginseng, witch hazel, and cloves hanging from the poles supporting the roof and a blackened cooking pot suspended over a rock hearth, but there were no clothes. A low crackling fire filled the stone fire pit, and its smoke curled up through the vent hole in the roof.

"I'm afraid we had to burn your clothes, young lady, all of them," said a voice from the back corner of the dimly lit hut. A slim-faced woman with long reddish hair stepped out from behind a wool screen, which served as a room divider, carrying a small thumb-sucking child who straddled her hip and rested her head on her bosom.

"They were pretty filthy," admitted Morea as the heat from her blushing cheeks spread over her body, "but they were all I had." The woman laughed softly.

"They were so wet and covered with mud, they would hardly burn," she continued, laughing as she walked back into the shadows where she searched through a large wooden chest in the corner of her hut.

"What will I wear?" asked Morea in near panic as she pulled the sheep skin up to her chin and then looked down at her exposed toes.

"You are about my size," answered the woman as she continued to dig through the chest. "At least until I had this little thing." She poked the girl in the belly and was rewarded with a burst of giggles. "Ah, this should fit," she announced, walking back over to where Morea lay and handing her a light-brown dress made from rough stitched wool. It was coarse but clean. Turning serious, the young mother looked at Morea.

"My name is Mary, and if I may say so, you look as if you have traveled a very difficult path, maybe with the devil himself chasing you." Morea looked down at her feet and fought back the tears that threatened to fall again.

"I have," she managed to say, but then paused. Struggling to keep from crying, she changed the subject. Although pretty sure of the answer, Morea asked, "What happened to your village?" The woman named Mary looked down at Morea for a long time. Finally, she replied.

"I'll tell you all about that later, but first, let's get you dressed and fed." Mary walked over and spoke briefly with a shorter, stout built woman who stood at the hut's entrance. The woman handed her a bundle of undergarments, which had been given by another lady of the village, and turned to leave. Mary, in turn, handed the garments to Morea and stood quietly waiting, her hands on her hips. Morea slid from under the sheepskin and slipped on the much too large linen pantaloons. Then she put on the dress, threw a woolen smock over it, and gingerly stepped toward the front of the hut. Her injured foot was still tender, but the village healer Muire, whose name she had found out from Mary, had rewrapped it very well. Mary held back the cloth that served as a door and waited for Morea, who was looking down at her newly bandaged foot.

When she realized Mary was waiting for her, she whispered, "I'm sorry," and stepped out into the fading light. To her surprise, the entire village, what was left of it, was standing or sitting around a large fire that had been built just outside the hut. The fire pit, ringed with large rocks, showed signs of many fires. *It must be the social center for the village*, thought Morea as she limped forward.

She ate as if she had not seen food in days, which was not all that far from the truth. Then her stomach ached from fullness. Mary, with her daughter standing by her side watching, had managed to untangle her hair enough for Morea to brush it out and tie it into a bun that sat on top of her head like a hen's egg, adorned with a blue-colored scarf. The older man who called himself Caleb walked up to her and gently led her to a bench that had been placed near the fire.

"Please sit, and tell us of yourself and your journey. We don't get many visitors here." He paused and glanced out into the bay before he then added, "At least the kind that we prefer."

"He means the pretty kind." Caleb's friend Robert laughed, and almost everyone joined in the harmless banter of the two old friends. When the laughter had died down, Morea cleared her throat and began to tell the now silent crowd about herself, her escape from Oban, and Angus mac Dougall. As she talked, she couldn't help but notice the small number of fighting age men. *Just like Oban,* she thought to herself. For some reason, she decided to leave out the part about Thomle and his father. *Wait,* her mind told her. She smiled when the young boys and even some of the young girls shyly crowded around her as she spoke. Any bits of news from the outside world, not to mention strangers in general, were exciting and rare.

The villagers listened intently as Morea told her story of escaping from the mac Dougalls and her consequent journey. Mary watched Morea's eyes as she spoke and felt there was more to the story than she was telling just now. *That's all right, I would be cautious myself,* she thought. When Morea had finished recounting the escape, Mary decided it was time to tell her about the young Viking and his father, who had rescued their village from the war band. For some reason, she wanted to tell the story before the girl asked, which Mary felt she certainly would.

"Now, let me tell you about the Norsemen who came to ravage our village and the other war band that saved us," announced Mary, picking up her daughter and placing her in her lap.

"Yes, please, I want to hear the whole story. Word of the raid reached Oban several days ago, and we"—she hesitated—"we were concerned," explained Morea excitedly.

So Mary began telling the story of the Norsemen screaming ashore in the middle of the night. Morea's heart pounded in her chest, and tears rolled down her cheeks while she listened. Near the end of her tale, Mary was about to name the Norseman that had stormed ashore and saved them when Morea unexpectedly burst out.

"His name was Thomle, wasn't it?" Mary nodded her head in reply.

"Yes, his name was Thomle, and his father's name was …"

"Thorma," added Morea.

"So it seems you have met them also." Mary laughed. "Tell us about them," she spread her arms out in an invitation for Morea to continue. Morea blushed and took a deep breath before telling the complete story of Thomle and Thorma's actions at Oban. When she finished, Mary and the survivors of the raid sat silent for a moment until Mary said, "There is one thing that I feel you should hear."

"Oh god! Is Thomle hurt?" gasped Morea.

"No, no, he was not hurt, but …" Morea held her breath when Mary seemed reluctant to go on. "But …" She dragged the word out before continuing, "The young Norseman spoke of a need—those were his exact words—a need to help us. Those are very powerful and strange words coming from a Viking." Mary finished with a weary smile. All eyes were on Morea now as she searched for the right explanation of her connection to the two Norsemen.

"Before I tell you the story behind Thomle and myself, I need to know where they went after they left here," said Morea.

"The young Viking spoke of going back to his village of Balfour and speaking to the elders there. He said he wanted to convince them that there was a better way for them to survive, a way to live in peace instead of war. Again, these are very strange words for Vikings indeed."

The blazing fire had been reduced to glowing embers, and the harvest moon had sunk low on the horizon when Morea finished telling the folks of Inverness how she and Thomle had talked and shared ideas.

"Those are not strange words coming from Thomle, but words of wisdom much greater than a man his age should have. I believe they come from his heart," said Morea, who sighed and folded her hands into her lap.

"I do too," added Mary. The crippled old warrior, who had dared to tell Thomle of their needs, nodded in agreement.

"I believe he meant every word he said," the old man went on. "He appeared to be a very determined young man." Morea smiled and nodded.

"Thomle and his father have changed, or maybe they were never like the other Norsemen. I don't know, but I do know that they are different now." Morea paused, biting her lip as she stared into the embers.

"The older one named Thorma was not so sure that the elders back in Balfour on Orkney would listen to his son, though," continued the old warrior, "but still I wish them well." Mary rose as if to turn in for the night, but as she started to walk past Morea, she looked down and spoke.

"I fear they will only be scoffed at when they get back to Balfour. Most Norsemen are not ready for these new ideas, nor are they are ready for peace." She shook her head. "They may never be."

With that final comment hanging in the air, Mary turned and walked wearily toward her hut, her child asleep in her arms. One by one, the other villagers followed Mary to their huts. Some said goodnight, but most just smiled as they walked past. At last, Morea sat alone with her thoughts. She pulled a second woolen wrap, which someone had given her, tightly around her shoulders and stared mournfully at the fire.

"Thomle can do it. I know he can," she whispered to the embers. Her eyes grew heavy, so the very tired and very worried Morea mac Craig rose stiffly from the bench and limped to her hut. As she walked, she looked to the heavens and wondered aloud, "Why is such a simple thing as peace so very hard to obtain? If people can love—and even Norsemen love, the mac Dougalls love—then why is peace so difficult?" The night gave her no answer as she ducked into her cold silent hut.

* * * * *

Two hundred miles north, in a place where the Shetlands lay on the misty horizon two degrees east of the North Star, Thorma stood at the bow of his ship and watched for the torches that marked the dock as the dragon ships were rowed into the foggy bay where his ancestors rested, the bay of Balfour on Orkney.

"Frey will be tested soon," he spoke to the fog as the ships neared the torchlit pier where they would tie up. Frey was the Scandinavian god of fate, and most Norsemen believed he controlled their destiny. But there would be more tested than fate before the week was out—the very hearts and souls of the Morestrong men would be at risk.

Several dozen tired and anxious faces peered through the thick fog as Thorma, bellowing instructions to the rowers, guided the ships toward the sturdy timber wharf where they stood. These were the extended families of Thorma's crew, and they expected great excitement from their returning warriors, who had been gone many months. Instead, they were greeted by a somber, battered bunch of men. There were no slaves, at least that the onlookers could see. And most noticeable was the absence of sheep and cattle. The waiting men, women, and small children stood quietly on the back edge of the wharf, some shaking their heads at the empty boats, others whispering nervously to each other. They may not have understood what had happened, but all would agree it was going to be a long, hungry winter.

Two cold and very hectic days later, anger filled the high council meeting hall. Toward the back, several men were shouting and slamming their tankards angrily on the scarred pine tables. Others were simply listening, stern-faced but quiet. Helmets, placed peacefully on the huge tables at the beginning of the meeting, rattled noisily, adding to the commotion. Mead dripped from the tables' edges. They were discussing Thomle's new ideas, and it wasn't going well. Most heads were shaking in disgust. Erickson Throdora, the leading elder, stood before the crowd and berated Thorma for his failure to bring back anything, not even slaves for the families of the slain warriors.

"Worst of all," he shouted from the raised platform, "is Thorma Morestrong's failure to bring back any cattle for our village. We may go hungry this winter. We eat meat just like the damn Picts at Inverness do." The crowd roared its approval as the fire blazed in the center pit and the torches mounted along the blackened walls spewed oily flames. The meeting hall was a huge structure, fifty feet wide and a hundred feet long. It was made of oak posts and beams that towered thirty feet into the air. The walls were made from hewed spruce logs and were eight inches thick. The roof, constructed from oak shakes covered with thatch, contained a center hole through which the smoke from the fire could escape.

Erickson Throdora, along with the other six elders, stood on an elevated stand in the front of the great hall. He was a striking figure with his long white hair chopped at the shoulders and tied back with a rawhide thong. A jagged scar, courtesy of a Saxon battle-ax, ran across his cheek and down his neck; tattoos and crude kill marks covered his left arm. His battle shield, which leaned against the table in front of him, held thirty-seven kill marks, and he was proud of each one. His big right arm, also covered in tattoos and scars, was raised high into the air. He lowered it and pointed at Thomle, who stood before him.

"These scars are the signs of a warrior, a man who takes what he needs and brings back slaves and cattle, not tales of birds and peace. Peace is when our enemies are dead and their wives and children our slaves. When"—he paused and looked around for effect—"they wait on us and lie in our beds, that is peace," he thundered above the pounding of clay tankards on the tabletops.

Thorma stood a few feet back from the center table and watched his son closely; he wasn't sure how Thomle would react to the ranting of Erikson Throdora. Thorma, who had always found Throdora's tales of battles and kills somewhat dubious, had seen him belittle men in the council hall before, many times. Most just lowered their heads and walked out of the place, but he didn't think his son would slink away. Thomle, who stood a foot taller than the old warrior, kept his arms folded across his chest, his pale blue eyes blazing as he listened to the foul words of Throdora. Thorma watched his son's temper boil, while Throdora ranted on, shouting at the top of his lungs until Thomle finally turned his back to him and looked out at the crowd.

A gasp rose from the crowd at the obvious insult. Everyone in the hall waited for the blades to be drawn and swift retribution delivered. Thomle knew what he had done, but he was well beyond caring. He looked out at the crowd of warriors, some of whom had put on their helmets in anticipation of a fight. Most of them where nodding and shouting in agreement with Throdora, but not all. A small few seemed supportive of this dissent, and Thomle took courage from that.

Steeling himself for action, he took a deep breath in an effort to control himself and turned slowly back to look down at Throdora, who was red-faced and glaring.

"Enough, old man. We have heard enough of your exploits and your"—he paused—"words." The statement was barked with the fury of a badger, and it brought a hush to the already startled crowd. They waited for some sort of violent reaction, but none came. The old warrior's eyes blazed, and his body tensed, but there was something in Thomle's stance that told him not to reach for his sword.

The two men stood mere inches apart, and Thomle could see the scar that ran across Throdora's face twitch, but still the old man didn't reach for his sword, although it was well within his grasp. Their mutual hatred became increasingly palpable. At last Thomle spoke again.

"We came back here to offer our people a chance for peace with our neighbors and a way to obtain the things that we need without killing. But you," he spat the words at the red-faced old warrior, "can only rant of more killing and more taking. There is a better way out there." He pointed toward the south. "One without pain and sorrow. And I'm going to find it." Thomle took a threatening step toward Throdora, who surprisingly responded by shakily moving backward. The veins stood out in his neck, but he still didn't dare move toward his sword. Thomle turned to face the other elders, his glare turning to a half smile as Throdora stepped back. Then he spun and walked down through the crowd.

The closely packed warriors were angry, but with some shoving and elbowing, they managed to find room to step aside as Thomle brushed past them on his way toward the doors at the entrance of the hall. He stopped when his hands touched the large iron handles, and he slowly turned to look back at the room full of hostile faces.

"Anyone that wants to come with me"—he glanced at his father, who was walking out through the crowd toward him—"with us," he added and looked the crowd over again, "will be welcomed."

"If you wish to come, be prepared to leave with the tide." Thorma's deep voice boomed as he joined his son at the door and shot a glance back at the elders. Both men watched the crowd for a second as the sound of shuffling and cursing rose from its center. Six helmeted warriors with mail jargon gleaming in the torchlight moved out of the crowd, then three more rose to join them, and finally one lone individual shoved his way to stand at the great doors. Ten men longed for a better way despite the uncertainty. The remaining Norsemen, who had neither the courage nor the desire to leave, shouted in protest but offered no resistance as the men stared back.

Thorma turned and pushed on the huge doors of the meeting hall, but he needed help from a few of their new companions to open them. A North Sea tempest had arisen outside, and the howling wind accompanied by blinding snow shook the doors and then rushed into the council hall to attack the torches as Thorma led his son and their new crew out into the cold.

"Relight the damn torches!" bellowed Throdora. Several men quickly grabbed lighted logs and ran to relight the hissing oil-fired torches.

"Let the fools leave and good riddance!" shouted another elder before sitting down and drinking hard from his tankard of mead. Relief was etched on his weathered face, relief that the young Thomle hadn't attacked them in his anger and sent them on their journey to Valhalla.

The ten warriors who were, like Thorma and his son, in search of peace and a better life, followed them out into the snowstorm.

"Do you really think we will be able to leave on the morning tide?" Thomle had to shout the question in order to be heard above the roar of the wind as they trudged down the cobblestoned street away from the meeting hall.

"If we don't, we may have to fight our way out of here by tomorrow night," answered Thorma, who had begun pulling the hood of his cloak up over his head but stopped. The ten men who had risked everything and walked out of the hall now stood as a group, awaiting some sort of instruction from their new leaders. Thorma cursed himself for being so damn distracted. Throwing back his hood, he looked each man in the eye, a couple of them he knew while the rest were new to him.

"I sincerely thank you for joining us, but if it's answers you're looking for, we have none. Rather than promises of wealth, we seek something intangible, a new beginning. We will leave, if not in the morning, as soon as the weather allows. Go home now and prepare your things." That was all he could think of to say and the crew seemed to accept it; they simply nodded, turned down the narrow street, and soon disappeared into the swirling snow. The tempest seemed to howl in protest, or maybe in agreement, with the chaos of the last few hours. Either way, the die was cast. Fate would lead the way. Thomle and his father watched solemnly as the ten men walked away.

"Do you know any of them?" asked Thomle, the snow piling up about their feet.

"Only two," answered Thorma, "but they look like warriors, and they did make a tough choice. Besides, we can't row that damn ship back to Oban by ourselves." The old warrior looked up into the white blowing mess. "The old shaman, Fialkoff, used to be able to predict the weather many years ago. Who knows, maybe he still can. You should go see him," Thorma said as he shrugged his snow-covered shoulders.

"I don't much believe in soothsayers, Father. But if you think it would help, I'll go." Thomle growled the reply and started down the narrow street to find the weather prophet.

"You had better take him some of that good ale we took from the dog's crew, Thomle. Years ago, the more Fialkoff drank, the better he could see the future." Laughing, Thorma finally pulled his hood over his head and trudged down a separate street toward where the ships were docked. If there was any chance of leaving in the morning, he needed to make a few repairs on the boat they would take, or there could be problems out at sea. They sure as hell didn't need that.

A couple of hours later, after searching several dimly lit smoky taverns, Thomle finally found the old shaman in a dingy log building called the Boer's Head. It was a two-story structure made of split logs with a tavern downstairs and four rooms upstairs for weary travelers or for the serving wenches who worked the bar and sold their bodies. It sat on the outskirts of town and had the reputation for trouble, but tonight, the only people in the building were the old man, the tavern owner, and one serving wench. She tried hard to entice Thomle into more than just drink, but she gave up and busied herself behind the filthy counter when he ignored her.

Thomle handed the old man a goat bladder full of good ale, despite much grumbling from the tavern owner.

"I make no damn money from your free ale, boy," he spat, but said no more when Thomle tossed him a small gold coin. He bit down on the coin, which proved to be real gold, and quickly stuffed it into his pocket. Besides, he didn't want to anger the overgrown young man. Thomle simply ignored his grumbling, pulled up a chair, and sat listening to the future.

Unfortunately, even with the help of the good ale, Fialkoff couldn't see the future very well that evening. He felt that the storm would blow out that night, a little after midnight. Despite his prediction, the storm lasted two more days. Throdora had sent word through one of the other elders that he wanted to speak to Thorma— alone. But the summons was ignored, and on the morning of the third day, as the tide rolled in, Thorma, Thomle, and the ten men who had followed them out of the meeting hall gathered around the dragon ship in the predawn light. Eight of the ten men had brought wives. Three of the wives gathered their small children about them like mother hens, and another two of the younger women were pregnant. That left three women who could help with the rowing. *Not much of a crew*, thought Thorma as he shook his head and watched the eastern horizon turn red.

"Beware the red morning sky," he moaned to the gulls that paid him no attention while eagerly searching the shoreline for breakfast.

Like a similar farewell many years before, no Balfour villagers turned out to see them off. *Which is not surprising*, thought Thorma as he looked over his small band. With one last glance down the pier, he started to shout for the women and children to load but stopped when he saw a lone figure slowly walking across the wharf. The man, judging from the size of the cloak, was a fairly large fellow. Whoever the man was, he had his cloak hood pulled up around his face. It was solid white.

Thorma watched the man as he grew nearer and suddenly recognized the cloak. It belonged to his old friend Gandalf, who had sailed with him since the early days. The old man threw back the hood as he approached.

"Going south again, old friend?" he asked, shaking snow from the white cloak.

"Not like the first time, Gandalf. Things have changed now, but as always, you are welcome to come along," answered Thorma. He watched his old friend smile slightly and shake his head.

"Too many cold winters have battered these old bones, Thorma, but thank you for inviting me." He paused. "There was a time ..." He never finished the statement; he didn't have to. Gandalf watched the last of the crew board the dragon ship and then turned his eyes to look deep into Thorma's.

"I came down here to tell you that I and several others agree with you and Thomle. There should be a better way, and we hope you find it."

Thorma nodded at his friend. There was no need for more words. Gandalf reached out a big tattooed arm and grasped Thorma in a farewell embrace, then turned and walked back up the pier. The old man flipped the hood up over his head as the cold wind blew across the harbor and soon disappeared in the swirling white powder.

Thorma watched his friend walk away, and a feeling of contentment about their journey began to grow inside him. As the lines were untied from the wharf, he stepped up onto the gunwale and looked over the ship. Thomle had erected a shelter for the children during the storm. He had stretched several old sails across the bow of the ship and tied them to the gunwale. It wasn't perfect, but if the morning red skies meant anything, they were going to need it—and soon. Thorma glanced once more at the red clouds on the horizon and stepped onto the dragon. The three wives without children slid in beside their husbands on the spruce benches and, with faces of stoic determination, prepared to row just like the men. That gave him thirteen rowers: six on each side and one to relieve any tired soul who needed rest—and they all would, long before they reached Oban.

The small children laughed and played among the few possessions their families could bring along. The tide was rolling in, and the serpent head slowly turned southwest as the rowers pulled with all their might. The voyage began. They were in search of a new home, a new idea, and a place to raise their children in peace.

* * * * *

The days passed slowly for Morea. Her heart was somewhere north in the hands of a young Viking, her mind on what might be happening back at Oban, and her body here at Inverness. She was working hard to make a place for herself in this partly destroyed village with its gracious and kind people who had taken her in with open arms. She liked them, and they in turn liked her. Additionally, they were in great need Morea's healing skills.

But she also was sad because deep down she knew it was only a matter of time before the mac Dougall clan would find her. Just like in Oban, there were people here who would sell information to the highest bidder, and she feared that the mac Dougalls, when they did find her, would seek revenge on her new friends.

"Why must there always be fear and hate and pain in our lives?" she shouted the question at the cattle she herded toward the lower pasture and better shelter from the coming winter. The wiregrass had long ago turned brown and provided little nutrition to the livestock still roaming high on the hillside. A weary and somber Morea continued her lecture to the cattle, which she had begun to recognize as a herd originally taken from Oban.

"People are not inherently evil. There is generally much good ... if only it were allowed to grow without pain and hate filling every void in their hearts." The cattle would probably have agreed had they understood, but instead, they just looked at her with their big brown eyes and walked on down the hill. With her words still ringing in the autumn mist, she followed behind them, thinking about the young man she hoped would soon return to her. *Come home, my hawk.*

* * * * *

Thomle stood at the steering oar and stared out at the dreary gray sea, mesmerized by the rolling swells' perpetual journey under the ship and out the other side. He was bone-tired from manning the rudder for twelve straight hours while the late autumn storms battered their ship unmercifully. It had been like this for several days. His arms ached from the effort, and his eyes were heavy from lack of sleep, but he asked no one to relieve him. His mind constantly drifted back to the council meeting and his unsuccessful attempt at talking to the elders. He knew that Throdora's ranting had hurt his father, not to mention the embarrassment he must have felt as his son stood nearly helpless in front of the council. Replaying it in his mind made his blood boil with anger.

Now they had to leave their old home for good. Thomle gripped the heavy oak rudder so tightly that his knuckles turned white, and despite the cold temperature, sweat ran down his brow. He watched his father at the front of the ship as he talked to the small children, reassuring them, making them laugh, despite the fact they were terrified by the rough seas.

My father may be a big burly man, but he has a good heart, thought Thomle, and he was proud of his father—especially proud of his willingness to support him on this journey to find what he hoped would be a new beginning. Everyone on board the battered old dragon ship, even the children, carried with them a unique sense of hope.

As the cold winds blew them back toward Inverness, Thomle shouted in an effort to be heard over the cackle of the sails. "Father, I'm proud to be the son of Thorma of Orkney." Thorma pretended not to hear his son, but he did hear and smiled to himself.

The late evening had been extremely blustery, but the winds became calmer as dawn lightened the skies and Thomle's tired eyes were able to spot the rugged tree-lined shores of the Gaels that would lead them to the village of Inverness. He gradually eased his grip on the rudder and shouted for Sedgwick, a warrior who was new to them but seemed a trustworthy man, to take the rudder. Thomle went forward and watched the cove come into view as the morning turned white with frost. His father patted each child on the head and moved to stand beside his son. By the time they had entered the cove, the sails had emptied of the wind that brought them south. The rowers, as exhausted as they were, extended the long oars to start rowing once again. The beast hesitated for a moment as if it were too tired to go on, but with a hard effort, the rowers pulled the dragon the last few hundred yards into the small harbor of Inverness.

Thomle watched from the bow of the ship, one booted foot resting on the gunwale and a big hand grasping the main line that supported the mast. Unsure who these Vikings were and fearing the worst, villagers ran from their huts and began herding their children toward the hills. A few of the Norsemen's children, eager to watch, came up to stand beside Thomle, all this so new and exciting to them.

"They are afraid of us," one of the older children said, watching the flight from the village.

"You shouldn't blame them," said Thomle. "This village has been hurt before by people like us." The child didn't answer; he just watched the panic on shore continue to spread.

Suddenly, out of the early morning sky, the cries of the hawk and the dove echoed over the bay like a welcoming voice to the weary voyagers.

"Look, Father, the great hawk and its mate!" shouted Thomle, and the children all looked skyward. The hawk and dove circled overhead, their wings almost touching as they sailed in the still air above the ship. Some of the villagers noticed the birds as well and began to slow their rush to the high pasture. After a few more minutes of uncertainty, they stopped their dash up the mountain and eased back toward the center of the village. Ever since Morea had arrived in their village, it seemed as if the hawk and dove were always around waiting for something, or maybe someone, to appear. They needed to wait no longer. The young Norseman and his father, the two men who saved their village, had returned.

Morea, who was near the top of the upper fields, heard the hawk's cry echoing from the inlet below. She was used to the call, but after several minutes, she glanced down and saw the lone dragon crawling through the inlet toward the village. The wind had died down on the water that now lay like a gilded thread winding toward the head of the cove, and Morea watched the oars reach and pull, driving the beast through the harbor. The ship's wake spanned out behind it like the ripples behind a swan swimming on a lake. Her young eyes quickly recognized the occupants of the dragon ship.

Shouting "Thomle!" over and over, she ran excitedly past the startled cattle that bellowed and then trotted after her down through the pasture. Her heart sang as she tore through the village center. Hiking up her dress, she ran out into the surf. Thomle watched eagerly as Morea ran into the sea and waved like a drowning person. Despite the cold, he tossed off his cloak and leaped up onto the gunwale, waving back.

"Don't jump in here, son, for you will surely drown." Thorma laughed as he and the rest of the crew watched Thomle's antics. The young Norseman waved and shouted Morea's name over and over, while the rowers worked hard to reunite the young couple. As the ship bore down on the beach where she stood, Morea could hear her name being carried on the wind.

At last, the breast of the dragon slid up onto the sandy beach, and Thomle was finally able to leap from the gunwale. He nearly tripped when his boots stuck in the wet sand, and Morea had to rush forward to catch him. Then they both fell laughing into the cold water. Struggling out of the surf, he grabbed her up in his arms and twirled her around and around, and falling again, they just lay in the water and kissed.

"That should cool them off!" shouted Thorma, and the crew howled in laughter as they watched the young soon-to-be lovers' passionate embrace.

Later that evening, everyone sat around a large rough-hewn table that had been set up near the fire pit just in front of Morea's hut. After several hours of drinking and telling tall tales, Thorma banged the table with his clay tankard. The tankard, which always seemed to be empty, wasn't this time, and frothy mead ran out the top to spill onto the table. He waved his arms in a vain attempt to get everyone's attention but finally had to resort to shouting in order to be heard over the clatter. The crowd hushed, and everyone stared at the big man. A little unsteady, he staggered to his feet to speak.

"We will sail for Oban on the next tide, which for you, Sedgwick, means at daylight." Sedgwick took the kidding goodheartedly, his wife and two small kids laughing and poking him in the side. Thorma smiled at his jest, while someone refilled his tankard with fresh mead. Satisfied, he sat back down. Sedgwick, Thorma knew, was a good man, but he always seemed reluctant to crawl out of bed early.

The music gradually died down, and people started drifting away from the fire, which by now was reduced to glowing embers. Thorma, a half-empty tankard in hand, staggered away from the revelers. It had been over five weeks since they had sailed from Oban, and this was the first time he had been able to relax. He knew his head would hurt like hell in the morning, but he felt that his present enjoyment was worth the future pain. Thomle and Morea were the last two people left at the table, empty tankards and food scraps strewn everywhere. A mangy old sheepdog sniffed cautiously under the table as two small kittens fought playfully over a discarded hunk of lamb.

Morea, who had spent much of the afternoon retelling the story of what had happened at Oban, was a little tipsy from the mead, her first ever. She had become teary-eyed when she tried to explain to her new friends their reason for leaving Inverness—how the mac Dougall clan would probably be looking for her because of what happened to young lord Angus and how she didn't want the village of Inverness to suffer on her behalf. Further, she explained, she was determined to return to Oban. Only there would she and Thomle be able to have a life, to live in peace, with Thorma and his crew of warriors to help keep them safe. These mostly young men, with their wives and little blond-headed children, shared her dream of a peaceful place, a place where they could raise a family.

When, earlier that day, Morea had watched the Norsemen's children and the Scotti children playing easily together, she had turned to Thomle and giggled. "I hope we have children just like those."

"Maybe we should start right now," Thomle had whispered as he ran his hand under her dress and along her thigh. At the time, she had slapped his hand gently, pointing to Mary and Thorma, who stood by watching. Now, however, they were alone, and his hand traveled along the same path, this time meeting no resistance.

"Let's go down to the beach," Thomle said, his voice thick with lust, blood boiling in his veins. Morea smiled nervously and took his hand even though her heart pounded like a captured rabbit and fear tore at her stomach.

They walked slowly down to the beach, hand in hand. After laying his cloak on the sand beside them, Thomle gently took her into his arms. The soft sound of her breathing mixed with the gentle rustle of her dress as it slid off her shoulders and pooled at her feet. Thomle inhaled with a gasp and devoured her with his eyes in the pale moonlight. She lay down upon his cloak, and after he hastily removed his leather britches and wool shirt, she pulled the young Viking down beside her. He gasped again when she eagerly reached for his manhood and guided it into her. Then it was her turn to gasp, as they explored the uncharted parts of each other's bodies. Their breathing became increasingly heavy, riding the crest of wave after wave of pleasure. Resting in the valleys to kiss and caress, only to ride the high waves once again, the young lovers at last slept the deep gentle sleep of contentment. From behind drifting clouds, the pale autumn moon smiled down on them. The hawk and dove circled overhead, their shadows floating over the sleeping couple as if standing guard.

Early in the morning, Thorma splashed his face with water from a wooden basin, which he then passed on to Sedgwick as they all went through the Norseman's sobering-up ritual, which might have seemed somewhat disgusting to outsiders. Thorma had been right. His head did hurt early that morning, and it still hurt as he walked down to the beach, searching for his son and the girl. He figured they might try to steal away from the crowd. After all, that is what he and Ulrika had done years ago. The sand pipers were dancing at the surf's edge, looking for breakfast, while the gulls squawked angrily overhead. He soon spotted Thomle's bearskin cloak near the water's edge and, despite his headache, laughed out loud. The cloak looked like a beached whale, a small but hairy beached whale, and he couldn't resist walking up and giving it a playful kick. The skin shook like a mating walrus and then exploded, as two naked, giggling figures cast it aside and raced hand in hand toward the cold surf. Diving in, they quickly washed sand and remnants of their lovemaking off each other before emerging with a shiver.

"God, to be young again ..." groaned Thorma as he turned his back on the naked couple and struggled up the beach, hoping the throbbing in his head would soon subside.

Another raw freezing dawn greeted them, but within a couple of hours, Thorma had gathered his small crew and told the folks of Inverness goodbye. As usual, Thomle stood on the railing of the ship, but this time, Morea stood by his side as the rowers pulled them out into the main channel where the wind could fill the sails. They were leaving yet another harbor on their way back to Oban. As it blew them south, the wind of the North Sea was soon spitting snow, which quickly covered the deck as well as the rowers who tried unsuccessfully to hide under their cloaks. The young lovers created quite a contrast with Thomle's blond hair swirling around below his helmet and Morea's long dark hair blowing wildly behind her weaving an intricate pattern. They were warmed by love and the hope that at last they would be able to live a life of peace, watching their children grow up happy and loved.

* * * * *

For three hard days, they fought a wind that was near hurricane force blowing wildly out of the east, forcing the oarsmen to drive the beast into the pounding swells. Frozen seawater sprayed over the bow, coating the ship and everybody on board except the children. The first night out, fierce gusts had ripped their woolen sail to shreds that they repaired in the shelter of a small cove, which Thorma had found seemingly out of blind luck. Two days later, the exhausted, seasick crew finally arrived in the bay of Oban. The wind had died down to a stout breeze as they came leeward of the rocky point off the Isle of Kerrera. With the treacherous shoals now lying in their wake, Thorma had ordered the tattered sails struck. The tired but determined rowers would take them on in. Morea eased closer to Thomle and put her arms around his waist as the village came into view. It was a cold, cloudy day, and a snow-laden mist lay across the rugged cliffs of Argyll that towered up from the beach. Thomle stared stolidly ahead while Morea, racked with fear, saw the unrepaired huts stare back at her like black holes burnt into the white beach. Above the village, the monastery lay in a crumbled heap that begged for attention.

Thorma noticed his son and the girl standing at the bow and felt that he should be with them, so he shouted for Sedgwick to man the rudder. When the new man, who Thorma thought was making a good seaman, had a firm hold on the steering oar, he walked forward. Standing beside Thomle, he placed his hand on Morea's shoulder, and together, they watched the villagers repeat the scene of Inverness, taking flight when they saw the dragon ship enter the harbor.

This time, no warning horns blew from the high meadows, but a feeling of confusion seemed to grip the village. Thorma wasn't surprised when he saw two helmeted men sprint down from a short hill, leap onto staked mounts, and ride out of the village, driving their ponies hard up through the pastures. Both riders paused when they finally reached the ridgetop, turned in their saddles, and gazed back at the ship as it headed for the beach.

"Those two riders are probably mac Dougall's men, and I'm sure they aim to warn him of our arrival," stated Thomle flatly. His face was red from the bitter cold, but his blue eyes blazed with fire, and the veins bulged in his arms as he squeezed the main line.

"Let them come," answered Thorma, stepping away from the gunwale and walking back to the rudder.

"Maybe we can talk to them, explain what really happened," suggested Morea, though her voice lacked conviction.

"Maybe ..." replied Thomle, who wanted to say more but figured it was best to simply hold his tongue for now. "Maybe," he repeated.

The village grew closer until at last Morea shouted, "Look!" and pointed excitedly toward shore, grateful for a chance to change the subject. She could see her brother, William, waving to them from the beach. From where they stood on the gunwale of the ship, William had recognized his sister and the big Norseman and had attempted to calm the anxious villagers. As they neared the shore, William broke away from the crowd and ran down to the water's edge, waving at his sister as he went. *I doubt she has any idea that everyone feared her dead*, thought William while the hawk and dove flew overhead. The villagers remained understandably cautious, milling around in the sand, unsure whether to wave or run.

The two riders' mounts pranced nervously on the ridgetop as the men leaned across their saddles and spoke briefly to each other. The horses were eager to press on down the hillside, as if they knew the danger posed by the Norsemen, who were coming ashore. The riders, just as ready to leave as the horses were, took one last glance at the ship before disappearing down the back side of the ridge as the beast slid onto the sand of Oban. Thorma and his son shared knowing glances and once again prepared to step onto the beach of this troubled village. The riders fled northwest toward Castle Dunollic as fast as their mounts would carry them. They knew the trail well, for they had ridden it many times in the last month. The mac Dougall clan had been waiting for this day when the dragon would return, and now it was back.

Most of the villagers danced about and hugged Morea with joy. Some even smiled at Thorma as they welcomed the new arrivals. Morea talked a mile a minute while Thomle, standing by her side, simply smiled and nodded.

"We feared you were dead," cried William as he swung his sister in the air. After several minutes of rejoicing, though, he turned serious. Sitting her down, he took her by the shoulders.

"The mac Dougalls have put a price on your head, girl, and they have had men posted here in the village, watching for your return."

William's face was somber. "The two rats just now rode away." He glanced toward the ridge, but the riders were already gone from sight. Morea dropped her head onto her brother's shoulder and quietly wept.

"We saw them leave," she said, wiping her eyes.

"Well, William, we will just have to make sure they don't get her pretty head," said Thomle as he offered his hand and pulled Morea to her feet. Smiling weakly, she allowed him to take her in his arms and hug her close. The three of them talked for a while until more of the villagers drifted over and pressed her for yet another explanation of her ordeal. Thomle, eager to escape hearing the tale once again, searched for somewhere to go.

"I'll be right back," he whispered as he bent down and kissed the top of her head. Having spotted the crew struggling to drag the longboat up onto the beach, he headed down to where his father was directing the efforts. They had tied four long braided ropes to the iron hooks on either side of the bow just beside the dragonhead. With four men pulling on each rope, they still didn't have the boat where Thorma wanted it until Thomle added his strength. Finally, with a lot of groaning and sweating, they dragged the ship up onto the stony beach. When Thorma was satisfied, he shouted, "That's good," and everyone gladly released the lines, collapsing onto the ground. After catching his breath, Thomle looked over at his father.

"How can we possibly fight the mac Dougalls with so few warriors?" Thorma knelt down by his son and looked out over the village.

"We will just have to make warriors out of all of them, even the little ones," answered Thorma, studying the crowd that still celebrated Morea's return. Thomle turned and looked questioningly at him.

"I have a plan" was all the old warrior said.

Morea was recounting her escape from Angus mac Dougall for what seemed like the hundredth time when she noticed Thorma near the center of the village walking toward one of the village elders whose name was Jaime mac Kee. The big Norseman pulled the older man aside and spoke to him. She wondered briefly what Thorma wanted with the old man, but she continued telling her story. *I'll find out soon enough*, she thought to herself.

Thorma led the old man, who didn't appear to be very nervous, over to a small clump of bushes to talk with him in private. Another elder had revealed that Jamie was once a warrior and had ridden with the senior mac Dougall years before. Thorma regretted his meager knowledge of the Celtic tongue, but he needed information.

"Old man, do you have any idea how many men the mac Dougalls will send against us?" He wasn't sure he had used the right words, but the old man seemed to ponder the question, which hopefully meant he was at least close.

"My name is Jaime mac Kee," said the old man in the Norse tongue, which surprised Thorma to the extent that it must have shown on his face. "I may not look like much now, but at one time I was a lieutenant with Dougall mac Lomhoirlle. Years ago we rode against the Saxons at the Firth of Savern."

"And who won that battle, old man?" asked Thorma, who already knew the answer. Jaime mac Kee straightened his shoulders a little and stood taller before he answered.

"We drove the bastards into the sea. We killed old Bluetooth himself and many of his men. Then we put their heads on poles near the town."

"Good," said Thorma as he nodded at the old man. "We will do the same thing to the damn mac Dougalls when they come, but first, I need to know this. How many men will they send?" The old man scratched his head and thought for a minute.

"I can tell you that the captain of their cavalry is a wise old fighter named John Holmes, and he will send at least fifty horsemen. He would send more, but the plague has taken many of his men."

"Huh, and how many foot soldiers will this great warrior send?" asked Thorma with disdain. He didn't respect any fighters until he had seen them in action.

The old man finally seemed a little nervous as the big Norseman glared down at him.

"My lord," he stammered.

"Don't call me a damn lord," hissed Thorma before he caught himself. He realized he had better be more civil to these people, especially if he was going to teach them to fight.

"I'm sorry, Jamie. It's just that we don't have much time, and I need to learn all that you know if we are going to defeat these bastards," said Thorma in a more contrite tone. "I have come here to help you, so please, how many infantry and how long will it take them to get here?" The old man thought for a minute before he answered.

"They will send at least a hundred infantry, but it will take the high lord of the mac Dougalls three or four days to get them ready and two days more to march here."

"I thank you for that information. Now come, we have much to do. And know also, Jamie, that I will need your advice and leadership for the next several days." Jamie mac Kee smiled as the big man put his arm around his shoulder and led him toward the blackened monastery.

Thomle had returned to where Morea was talking to her brother and a few other young men of the village. She took his hand when he drew near.

"What is your father talking to Jaime mac Kee about?" she asked, watching Thorma lead the old man toward the monastery.

"My father says he has a plan. That's all I know," answered Thomle, who decided to seize the opportunity to escape once again from the group that had formed around them. He kissed Morea and headed toward the monastery, leaving her to wonder what was going on. She didn't have to wait very long for the answer that came within an hour. Thorma and Thomle came back down with determined looks on their faces, joining her and William as they sat in the sand, eating from a steaming bowl.

Thomle's stomach growled when he caught a whiff of the stew, and he suddenly realized he hadn't eaten in several hours. He peeked suspiciously into the big iron pot where fish and mutton stew simmered over a hickory fire, having been prepared earlier by several of the village women. Morea dipped out a huge bowl and handed it to him. Cautiously, he tasted the first spoonful and then proceeded to shovel in the rest, working the wooden spoon furiously.

Thorma ignored the food and walked over to William. "We have only three or at best four days to prepare for the return of the mac Dougalls and a hell of a lot of work to do in that short time." With that announcement made, he walked over to a small table, grabbed a hunk of lamb along with some hard bread, and flopped down in the dirt to eat it.

William stared blankly at the old warrior, then glanced over at Thomle as if to say, *How?* But he didn't ask out loud. His sister, though, was shocked, and she asked what no one else would.

"What do you mean? Our people? How will you make them warriors in just four days or even a hundred days for that matter?" She looked first at Thomle and then at his father for an answer.

"Then we will turn your fishermen into warriors in three days." Thomle smiled, shrugging his shoulders before he resumed digging into the bowl of stew. "Didn't the son of your god rise from the dead in three days and even feed a multitude with only four fish?" Thomle asked, with a mouthful of food. Morea ignored his question.

"These people are farmers and fishermen," she cried, "not warriors!" Thomle glanced up from his stew.

"Do you have a better idea?" he asked between bites. When Morea gave no answer, Thomle searched hard for what he hoped were the right words. "In order for us to work for peace, we must first stay alive. They will learn to fight." He finished sopping up the last of the stew with a piece of hard bread, his cheeks bulged out like a chipmunk's as he handed Morea the empty bowl and went to help his father get the village ready for battle. She was still angry but couldn't help but laugh at his silliness. *So different from our first meeting*, she thought.

If a crow were to fly in a straight line, which despite the myth they seldom do, it could fly the thirty-five miles that separated Castle Dunollic from Oban in the light of one day. The troops gathering under the watchful eye of Dougall Lommoile would be hard-pressed to cover this winding cart path partially built by the Romans in two days.

Dougall stood on a balcony jutting out from the main house supported by two huge oak pillars. Castle Dunollic sat on a narrow piece of land that extended into Loch Lamach for several hundred feet. Only fifty feet wide where it joined the shore, it was two hundred feet wide at the back where the main part of the stone structure sat. Dougall and his father had picked the spot for their home when Dougall was ten years old. *Forty years, where have they gone?* he lamented.

The last eighteen months had been hard on the old man. His wife and many of his men had died from the pox epidemic that had swept the region. His younger son had been killed down south, fighting an outlaw clan that was stealing cattle. Now it was just him, the castle, and his eldest son who was ... what? Arrogant? Or plain crazy? He didn't know.

A long time ago, things were different, thought the Lord of the Realm as his eyes swept over the scene below him. His trusty captain, John Holmes, an Anglo whom he raised from a boy, controlled most of the army matters, while his son, Angus Augustus mac Dougall, strutted from village to village, showing his importance and chasing young women. Angus sat atop his charger, shouting orders that were hard to understand and generally confusing. His mouth was misshapen, and one eye was completely gone, covered by a black patch. The boy, for he still acted like a boy, had been attacked by, of all things, a hawk—his family crest.

"That should tell me something," the elder mac Dougall growled to the shadows as he walked down from the balcony and prepared to address the troops. Angus fiddled with his reins and fumed as he awaited his father's talk. Revenge, revenge was what he wanted, not talk. He wanted to destroy the cursed village of Oban and all its people. The fact that a war band of Norsemen had, for some reason, decided to settle there was of secondary concern to the heir apparent.

"We fought the Saxons, John. We have fought our own clans. Now we fight the Northmen. When will it end?" questioned Dougall as he walked past Holmes and patted his shoulder.

"There is more to this story than we know, sire," lamented Holmes as they walked up to the waiting troops.

"I know, John, I know," sighed Dougall as he climbed the small platform to address his men.

Hatred filled Angus mac Dougall's one good eye as he watched his father and Holmes chat while they approached the men. His men. "My damn men," he cursed under his breath. The big stallion pranced nervously sensing the tension of its rider.

* * * * *

Back in Oban, Norsemen sweated alongside Scotti as Thorma drove them to near exhaustion, the fact that they only had three or four days never far from his mind. Sedgwick, who had been a woodsman before he had become a warrior, quickly amazed everyone with his skill with the big war ax. The first morning, he had led several men, including his eldest son, into the forest to cut trees for the palisade of timbers needed for the barrier to be built at the front of the monastery. Soon the sound of rhythmic ax blows rang through the forest, and birds nodded on their perches, crooning like old women while tree after tree hit the ground. The women and young boys dug ditches through the fields across the front of the monastery using rough spades, hoes, and buckets. The blonde brides of the Norsemen sang songs of the Valkyries as they worked alongside the dark-haired women of the village, who sang their Celtic hymns. The ditches were filled with sharp-pointed sticks to stop or slow the cavalry, and clay pots were filled with whale oil.

The children worked as tirelessly as the adults in the trenches, especially one young boy named Ein mac Neil. As Ein drove the sharp sticks into the soft ground of the newly dug ditches, he began to form a plan in his mind for how he could help even more. Thomle and a couple of the Norse warriors showed the few remaining men of the village, those who were strong enough, how to handle the Viking battle-axes and the heavy swords. He and his fellow Norsemen had to shake their heads in disgust at the pitiful efforts of the Scotti when it came to handling swords, but the ash spears were another thing. The spears were very much like the farming implements these men used daily, and they wielded them with much greater skill. But it was the bows the men of the village could be proudest of. The Yew bow was the best in the world. It was the artillery of the era, and William and several of his friends who had survived the earlier raid were deadly accurate with them. It was far superior to the Viking bow, which was made from sapling white oak. Although effective up to a point, the Viking bow was not nearly as powerful as the weapon made from the stout Yew trees, which grew well here in the highlands and south through Britannia. Thorma had already taken notice of the abundance of Yew trees around Oban.

"It is a damn good thing we have the dozen archers," he grunted as they heaved the last of the timbers up onto the palisade that shielded part of the monastery. It was to be their last defense. The huge main gate had been repaired and large vats of oil stood ready to be pulled up onto the stone balcony where they would be heated and poured down onto the attackers.

"Archers, with their longbows and an occasional long stake, are the only thing that can break a cavalry charge," he continued, tying a knot in the rope that would be used to open the large gate, the only entrance to the monastery.

"What about the shield wall, Father? You always said it was a terrible weapon," asked Thomle as he pulled the first clay vat up from below.

"Against other infantry, the shield wall works well, provided your heart is strong and your body is even stronger. But a horse charge will break most shield walls," continued Thorma, stretching his sore back and shoulder. "Then there is only slaughter."

* * * * *

Three days full of sweat and hard work later, Morea sat with her back against the short wall that rose above the stone balcony of the monastery. She gazed forlornly over the pastures toward the rocky cliffs. Thomle and William stood off to her side, discussing the differences between the Danish bow and the more lethal Yew bow. Both men spoke in low hushed tones, grave concern etched upon their tired faces. Morea herself was sick with worry as she ran all available options through her somewhat confused mind. She had seen enough killing and the sorrow that it reaped. One particular idea kept returning to her mind as she looked up at her lover.

"Thomle." But he didn't hear. "Thomle," she called again, and he turned his head toward her. "I'm afraid," she moaned softly. Thomle broke off his discussion with William and moved near where Morea sat. He knelt and then slid down beside her.

"I'll always protect you. You should know that," he said as he pulled her close to him. With her eyes full of tears, she took a deep breath and went on.

"I'm not so much afraid for myself, Thomle, but for my village, my people. The mac Dougalls will punish them to get to me, I just know it." She looked up toward the heavens for some sort of guidance but found none there. "Maybe, if I surrendered to them. If I tell them it was all my fault—the hawk, everything—then maybe, they would leave the villagers and your people alone." Tears rolled down her cheeks, and she turned her head to the side to keep her brother from seeing her crying. Why she worried about that right now, she didn't know.

"Morea." Thomle rose on one knee and gently pulled her chin up so he could look into her eyes. "The mac Dougall clan wants more than just you. They want to show every village and every hamlet in their fiefdom just how strong they are. I think they also want revenge for what we did, not just here but at Inverness as well. We made them look weak in the eyes of their people. Sacrificing yourself would not stop them. Only a sharp sword and a strong heart will." He stood and walked along the balcony to look out at the hills to the east toward Crag a Bharrain, with its dark granite dome. The young warrior was angry with himself for not being able to give his woman more peace of mind.

"Why must we always have to fight for what should be so simple, the right to live in peace?" She wept as she spoke the words, but this time, she didn't bother to hide them from her brother. After a while, her battle-clad young lover walked back to stand beside her.

"I can't answer that, Morea, but I do know that these people ..." He pointed to all the men, women, and children who continued working though the sun had set long ago. "These people have courage. Much more courage than I ever thought. And they have something else too." She looked at him, and he took her hand. "These people have a true desire to help you, and they need for you to be strong for their sake." William walked over and knelt beside her, wiping the tears from her eyes.

All three were quiet for a long time as they looked out at the villagers embedding the final stakes in the ditches' rocky soil. Thomle turned his gaze far out to sea as if searching for something lost long ago. After several minutes, he began to speak again, slowly at first, a little unsure of his words.

"I'm afraid that as simple as living in peace with one another sounds …" He turned and looked into the soft teary eyes of the woman he hoped to soon marry. "It's not. To control the desire that some men have to suppress, to take unfair advantage, to reap the fruits of others' labors to fulfill their own needs, good men and women will face a continuous struggle." He paused for a second and then went on, this time a little faster, his voice a little sharper.

"We can and will begin here in this village, this place of the doves, to create a spark of hope that people can stand together and stop tyranny. We can and should stop the wanton destruction of that which people have worked so hard to build."

Morea and her brother were stunned. Morea's hand went to her mouth to stop a sob because the man who had just spoken those words was her man, the man she hoped would father her children. William simply couldn't believe those words came from a Norseman. It still seemed strange to him, very strange, for a Viking to speak of peace. Thomle saw their surprised looks and couldn't control the reddening in his cheeks.

"Oh my god, Thomle," cried Morea. She jumped up and hugged the blushing young Viking. "You have spoken the words that are in my heart, the words that I myself can't speak." She buried her face in his shoulder.

"I'm not nearly the barbarian you think I am." He laughed and hugged her tight against his chest.

William leaned his head back against the cold stone and watched his sister being hugged by a man who should be his mortal enemy but was instead his new friend. He didn't quite understand this Viking, but he liked him, and perhaps most importantly, he trusted him. William couldn't help but smile at the irony of it all. As his thoughts returned to the many problems they faced, however, his smile slowly faded.

"I hate to throw water on you two, but I fear the morning will bring a need for action, not words," he said with a somber tone.

"I think you are right, Pict," said Thomle with a hint of a smile on his stern face. Both men raised their tankards and drank the last bit of lukewarm mead in a toast to each other. Morea could only shake her head in confusion. Her heart was glad, though, that her brother and Thomle were becoming friends. The alternative was horrible to think about.

One of the first orders of battle that Thorma thought most important was to reestablish the warning system that the villagers had used to send alert of the Norsemen's arrival. This time, the boys and girls were stationed farther along the ridge. They used the same bullhorns, for everyone was familiar with the sound and it carried a long way. Thomle, who was constantly amazed by their steadfast courage, positioned the children along the rugged ridgeline. Calling them his watchers, which they liked, Thomle stationed the children every quarter of a mile, all the way to the Crag of Dunolleigh, two miles away. They were instructed to listen for the calls from the east where the oldest boys were keeping watch near the high gap. When the mac Dougall clan was spotted, the oldest boys' horns were to start the chain of events. Now, on the morning of the fourth day, they could only wait, while the fog hung like snow, freezing on the treetops above the pastures.

A few large fires blazed under iron pots full of spicy fish stew with strips of mutton, while several smaller fires were used to prepare the morning brew. To the east, the sun rose over the dark hills, its beams dancing along the tree limbs. Thorma knelt by a crackling fire and sampled the mutton, tender strips of meat firm and succulent from the salt and spices that had been added through the night. He watched his warriors, who appeared anxious, sharpening their weapons. *We're all a little nervous,* he thought and then jumped slightly, turning toward the hills when the first faint call echoed down from the high crag. The call floated in the cold morning air and pierced the fog-wrapped silence, yet it had not entirely faded when the next call rolled from the ancient forest. It was followed by the next and then the next. Soon, the last horn sounded from the lower pasture just out of sight in a clump of oaks, and everyone was spurred into action.

Thorma choked down a piece of hard black bread that a friendly village woman had baked for them the previous night. Unconsciously, he rubbed his sore stiff shoulders while he stared toward the hills. The bullhorn calls were once again progressing down the ridge, across the pastures, and on toward to the village. It was just according to plan: two calls, two minutes apart, if you had time. The big man smiled to himself. The children had done their part, and now it was time for the adults to do theirs. He reached for the Death Bringer, a sword he had made with his own hands years before. He checked its edge as the villagers stirred around him. High above, the hawk's haunting call joined the cacophony of the village's preparation for battle.

Sweat rolling down her face, her heart pounded rapidly in her chest, Morea worked alongside several other women on the partially repaired balcony of the monastery. They were heating the jars of oil that could be poured down on the attackers, should they get this far. While Morea struggled with one of the long oak poles used to feed the heating fire, she heard the soft cooing of a dove and glanced up as the bullhorn calls finally ended. She looked around several times before finally spotting it perched on the stone wall high above. Her heart, which had been working as hard as her hands, slowed slightly as she listened to the soothing call.

"I hope we are both still alive when this is over," she whispered to the dove. After dragging another log over to the fire, she wiped the sweat from her face with her apron and leaned back against the cool stone wall. *If we can just stay alive, maybe peace is possible, at least on some level,* she thought to herself. *But is peace at the point of the sword really peace?* She pondered the question. *Thomle would think so, but I am not so sure. Maybe it is only some sort of beginning.* With that thought running through her mind, she stretched her aching back before trudging off after more firewood.

Everyone—Norseman, Scotti, adult, and child—now stood on the balcony or the stone walls surrounding it. All eyes were on the last of the young watchers as they raced down through the fields. Several of mac Dougall's horsemen were riding hard to catch them, clods of turf flying from their horses' hoofs in pursuit of the boys who were literally running for their lives. Only the newly dug ditches with their sharp stakes saved them. Leaping into the ditches and dodging the stakes, they scurried out the other side while the horsemen pulled their mounts up short. Standing tall in their stirrups, they watched the children run through the gate just before it closed with a loud bang. Their horses pranced about and snorted as the riders begrudgingly turned in their saddles, looking back up the ridge for instructions from their captain.

High on the ridge, Captain Holmes sat stolidly on his gray gelding and slowly shook his head. He could almost feel the rebuke he would receive from the young mac Dougall for not catching at least one of the damn children.

Inside the door of the monastery, the tired and dirty-faced young boys fell near the feet of Thomle and William. Huffing and puffing in sweat-soaked clothes, they stared up at the two men, hoping for some kind of praise.

"Well done, boys, well done," bragged Thomle as William reached down and ruffled the hair of the smaller of the two red-headed boys who, although exhausted, smiled back.

"Go on now. It's our time to work," continued Thomle. "Find Sedgwick's wife. She could probably use your help!" he shouted, and the two tufts of red hair disappeared around the corner.

A few minutes later, Thorma's long strides brought him over to his son, who had climbed back up on the balcony and was standing beside Morea and her brother.

"How many of the bastards did you see?" he asked, looking out at the eastern hills.

"I only saw ten, Father, but you can bet they didn't show their entire lot," answered Thomle as he, too, stared toward the east. "They will probably wait for the main attack before they show their full force," he continued.

"Huh," grunted Thorma, watching the horizon. "I don't fear the horsemen as much as I fear the archers. We don't have enough shields for every fighter," he moaned, "and the cursed fire arrows will wreak havoc on this thatch." He reached up and pulled a handful of the dry thatch from the roof of the monastery and tossed it into the air.

* * * * *

"Oh my god!"

The fearful cry caused Thorma and a couple other Norsemen to jerk their heads around. They looked down the line of villagers to where several were pointing toward the hills. Thorma followed their gaze across the high ridge until he saw what had elicited the cry. Horseman after horseman began to appear, as if by magic, along the ridge east of the cliff Crag of Dunolleigh. At least seventy-five horsemen formed a massive line and moved slowly down through the high pasture. Twice that number of infantry, carrying ash spears with their blue and scarlet pennants flying in the breeze trailed them. Thirty snarling war dogs pulling hard on the braided ropes that bound them, their handlers struggling to keep the big dogs at bay, followed these troops closely.

On the balcony, all was silent, the children staring wide-eyed at the spectacle unfolding in front of them. A cold fire began to burn in the eyes of the Norsemen, who watched stoically as their enemy fanned out in front of them. The veins on Thomle's thick arms bulged, and the raspy grating sound of swords being pulled from their scabbards filled the air. From down the wall, a solitary male voice broke the silence, chanting an ancient Viking ode to death.

One by one, the other Norsemen joined the chant until all the warriors were singing the old battle oath, an ode to Valhalla:

> Lo, there do I see my father
> Lo, there do I see my mother, my sisters,
> and my brothers
> Lo, there do I see the line of my people back
> to the beginning
> Lo, they do call me
> They bid me take my place on Asgard in the
> halls of Valhalla
> Where the brave may live forever!

They repeated this ode three times, each time singing louder until, at last, they seemed to be shouting a challenge to their attackers. The villagers, most of whom professed to be Christian, started their own chant. They sang the twenty-third Psalm as the pagan Norsemen chanted their ode:

> Yea, though I walk through the valley of the
> shadow of death
> I will fear no evil for thou art with me
> Thy rod and thy staff, comfort me
> Thou preparest a table before me in the
> presence of mine enemies
> Thou annointest my head with oil and my
> cup runneth over
> Surely, goodness and mercy shall follow me
> all the days of my life
> I will dwell in the house of the Lord forever.

The Norsemen snarled, and the Christians crossed themselves as the sound of the mac Dougall's war drums reverberated off the hills around them.

"We go to war now!" shouted Thorma, who resheathed his sword and began directing his fighters.

Off in the shadows of the high wall, Morea whispered to the spirit, "We fight for peace," as she stared out at Angus mac Dougall leading his army toward her.

As organized chaos rolled through the monastery, Thomle walked up to his father as he growled, "What we need is some kind of advantage." Thorma and his son watched the prancing cavalry led by Angus mac Dougall, and the advantage they sought was actually right in front of them riding a fiery black stallion with battle armor gleaming in the pale sunlight—the arrogant lord himself.

Angus mac Dougall rode his nervous stallion to the edge of the ditches and sat watching his enemy atop the wall of the monastery. An occasional arrow launched from the wall would sail, as if in slow motion, toward him. As good as the Yew bow was, he was just out of the archers' range, and he knew it. Standing as tall as possible in his stirrups, he looked out into the bay where the dragon ship sat. It had been rowed back out into the harbor and was anchored there, just in case. He tried to smile, but it resembled a snarl because of the scars that crossed his face and hadn't yet completely healed.

His one good eye watered profusely, irritated by the stiff breeze blowing off the bay and distorting his vision as he tried to spot the witch and her lover on the wall. A leather patch covered the sightless eye. Mac Dougall's head suddenly jerked up as the lone cry of the big raptor echoed across the field. He searched the sky until he finally spotted his nemesis, gripping the reins so tightly his knuckles turned white.

Part of Angus mac Dougall's mind fled from reality. He moaned loudly and struggled with the big stallion as he fought to stay in the saddle. The horse reared up frightened when mac Dougall began shouting obscenities at the hawk and shaking his fist in the air. In mac Dougall's tormented mind, there had never been a bird such as the one that now flew just above him. Yes, he had hunted with his father's royal falcons many times, but they would be no match for this hawk, this demon bird. "I'll kill you. Damn you to hell!" he screamed, drooling from the corner of his twisted mouth. "And I will kill everyone in this accursed village, this nest of yours," he spat.

The lord continued shaking his fist in the air as if he were trying to strike a ghost, or at least it appeared that way to the captain of the mac Dougall's cavalry, John Holmes who back on the ridge sat atop his gray gelding and sadly shook his head. John Holmes was a crusty but wise old warrior who had fought by the side of the elder mac Dougall for many years. Dougall mac Lomhoirlle owed his life to Holmes after an incident that occurred in the south during the great battle of Lindisfarne against the hated Saxons. He had always been proud to be part of the mac Dougall clan—until now.

After a few tortured minutes of fierce shouting and sword swiping, the fog in the mind of Angus mac Dougall slowly began to clear. The hawk had flown out over the bay where it was soon joined by the dove, and both sailed about in silence. An exhausted mac Dougall dropped his chin to his chest and sullenly glanced around as his stunned escorts stared at him as if he had the plague. Angrily, he jerked the reins on the big stallion and spurred its already bloody flanks toward the ridge. Riding hard, he reached the ridgetop, where Holmes and his lieutenants anxiously anticipated his word to advance. Reining in the sweaty stallion, he growled without a nod of recognition.

"Well, Captain, what is your plan of attack?" His angry voice dripped with sarcasm while his stallion nervously pranced. Angus mac Dougall glared down at his men while Holmes formulated a plan.

"My lord ..." Holmes hated it when he had to call this boy *lord*. "I believe that we should advance the archers first and show these Norsemen scum the power of the Yew bow." He paused for a second, expecting a snide reply, but when none came, he went on. "We can then ignite the thatch of the monastery with a few well-placed fire arrows. I believe at that point we should wait a few minutes for the fire to catch and panic to set in. Then we send in the infantry. The cavalry can naturally chase down any ... survivors." He made the last remark as if incidental. *That's what your father would do, you pompous ass*, thought Holmes as he stared back and waited for the young lord's reaction. Holmes's smaller horse was jittery around the stallion and it side-stepped in circles while mac Dougall thought about the plan.

As they waited, a servant ran up and knelt beside the stallion. When mac Dougall finally acknowledged the kneeling man, he dismounted and handed the reins to the servant, who then stood with his head down awaiting instructions.

"Rub him down quickly. He will soon have much work to do," commanded mac Dougall, who began pacing back and forth in the short grass of the overgrazed pasture. The pacing went on for several minutes, but it was all a ruse. He had no intention of going along with his captain's plan, sure that he had a better one in mind. At last, he turned to Holmes and smiled.

"No, Captain Holmes, I don't like your plan. I think I have a better one—one that will show this village and all the others up and down the shores of Lorn just who is in control." He walked up to the obviously agitated Holmes, who had dismounted from his gelding and was patting the horse's neck.

"I believe you give far too much credit to these people, Captain. They are farmers, and they are cowards. My plan will be quicker and much more painful for them," he added with a laugh. Holmes's head was down as he listened, but he slowly raised it before raising a question.

"And what exactly is your plan, my lord?" His tone was a little too sarcastic. The young lord spun around with hate in his one good eye and glared at his captain.

"Be very careful, Captain Holmes. You have my father's ear for now, but he will not live forever." Venom dripped from his scarred lips as he spoke. Holmes held his tongue and let the assertion go unchallenged.

"Sorry, my lord" was all he could utter.

"I want to kill these bastards," spat mac Dougall, "not chase them around. We will charge the cavalry straight up to the gate and pull it down. Then I will lead the troops into their nest and kill everyone. If we miss any, the infantry can deal with them." He waved his hand as if a few lives were inconsequential. "We will set an example for all the other villages"—he paused—"but there is one exception." He smiled a wicked smile.

"What's that, my lord?" asked Holmes, equal parts disdain and trepidation in his voice.

"The young maiden who seems to control the birds and her Norseman lover. I want them alive. Hurt is all right, but alive."

Captain Holmes, the old warrior who had stood in shield walls fighting the Saxon hordes, heard his mind scream. *No!* He knew the young lord's plan was crazy. It would put his cavalry in a very difficult and vulnerable position under the balcony of the monastery, especially until the gate was breached.

"My lord, if they have prepared boiling oil, which from the many small fires on the monastery's balcony it seems they have, my men will suffer greatly, needlessly," Holmes pleaded. Mac Dougall's head snapped up.

"Your men, *your* men?" Spit drooled from the corner of his mouth, and a dangerous stare blazed in his eye. "Captain, I want you to take *my* men, do you understand? *My* men. And prepare them for this damn battle." He turned and stomped off where his servant was rubbing the black stallion with a woolen cloth.

"At least someone is listening to me," mac Dougall growled. He stood just to the side, watching the slave expertly rub the horse but soon grew impatient with his slowness and kicked the old man in the ribs.

"Enough, old man. It's a horse, not a damn wench." He snatched the reins, and the servant scurried away, holding his side. Strangely, mac Dougall felt better after kicking the fool, and he mounted the stallion with a smile. But as he rode toward his troops, he heard the hawk's cry once again in the distance. Cautiously, he scanned the sky.

Thorma stood alone on the far end of the balcony as the final preparations for the defense of Oban continued. He was expecting the archers, the dreaded archers, to move forward. He knew they would work their deadly trade well before the cavalry would attack the gate, and he worried about their effectiveness.

"Damn," he swore to himself. Thorma started to shout for Thomle to join him, but then he hesitated, watching the far ridgeline. He noticed what appeared to be an argument between the fancy young lord and his old captain. Both men stood off to the side, away from their troops, and it was obvious that the young mac Dougall was unhappy about something. He stomped about, waving his arms and shouting, when suddenly Holmes dropped his head and walked away toward his cavalry, who sat on their mounts a short distance away.

* * * * *

Thorma was a bit confused as he watched Holmes start gathering his lieutenants. "I'll be damned," he cried when he realized what was happening. Smiling, he watched the cavalry begin to form for a charge.

"Thomle, William! Bring the other archers and come here quickly!" he shouted excitedly, never taking his eyes off the ridge. Now he understood the apparent anger in the old cavalry officer. The fool was going for the gate first.

Thomle ran to his father with William and the other archers close on his heels, their bows clutched tightly in their hands.

"Thank the gods for young dumb lords," said Thorma, turning his gaze from the cavalry back to the confused faces in front of him. "No archers, the fool is going for the gate *first*. This is the advantage we needed." Thomle and the others began to see what was happening, and menacing grins spread across their faces as they watched the cavalry move into position.

"I want half of the jars taken to a spot straight above the gate, and I want the archers on the wall above me," commanded Thorma.

William was still hesitant, though. He looked at mac Dougall's cavalry preparing to charge, at the other archers already climbing on top of the wall, and then at the big Norseman himself. "We only have the twelve archers and myself, Thorma," he said, concern etched on his charcoal-painted face as he stared at the mac Dougalls. He was badly in need of some kind of reassurance.

"Well, William, you will just have to do the very best that you can," said Thorma, placing his hand on the shorter man's shoulder. "You're all that we have." William swallowed, nodded, and turned to make the climb to his position high on the wall. Thorma watched for a moment as the agile young man climbed the stone steps, then put his hand to his mouth and shouted with a laugh, "There will be plenty of targets, Pict, so shoot as many as you want." William climbed on, shaking his head and laughing to himself. Thomle had started calling him Pict in a joking manner, and he sort of liked it.

Inside the monastery, Thomle was torn. He knew he should go to his fighting position on the front wall above the gate, but he didn't want to leave Morea's side. Her position was inside the great walls behind a low stone barricade, the last defense for the children. He hesitated.

"You must go, Thomle. I will be all right," she whispered in his ear as he stared at the cavalry, preparing their columns.

"I love you," he said. Then he turned and pulled her into his arms, kissing her urgently, their lips trying to reassure their hearts.

"I love you, too, Thomle. And I want to have your children, so be very careful." She closed her eyes, and he held her tightly. With a sigh of recognition, he turned to leave, and as he did, he looked down at the children. Dane and Scotti children huddled together in fear. Fear was a mask they wore on their dirty round faces, and silence was their partner as they sat against the stone wall of the monastery and waited.

"Thomle!" Thorma's voice echoed from above, and finally, the young Norseman ran toward the front wall. Thorma stood staring over the edge of the balcony, watching Angus mac Dougall lead his cavalry down the slope in a slow canter. When the slope became less steep, he increased the pace to a trot for a hundred paces. Then as if by a silent command, they broke into a full charge. Clumps of grass flew high into the air behind the horses, their pace increased, and the first line neared the ditches.

Angus mac Dougall's heart was pounding in his chest. He spurred the fiery stallion, and the pace quickened for everybody behind him. The very walls of the monastery seemed to shake from the thundering hooves that bore down on the defenders of Oban.

"Steady, son, steady," cautioned Thorma, watching Thomle reach for his sword. As the thundering noise increased and the cavalry drew nearer, a few of the villagers threw down their weapons and fled from the wall in fear. Jaime mac Kee, who stood several feet down the wall from Thorma, reached out a hand and started to stop the fleeing men, but he paused.

"Let them go, Jaime!" Thorma shouted as he watched the men run. "They would be useless anyway," he said disgustedly and returned his gaze to the front.

Out in the field, mac Dougall raised his thin saber, a recent gift from his father, as he neared the first ditch. "How I love the thrill of a charge!" he shouted to the wind, his knees pressed hard against the saddle, his good eye straining to see the width of the ditch the bastards had dug.

The ground shook when the lead horses approached the first obstacle. Dirt trickled down the freshly cut bank and piled at the feet of a small form rising from the rear of the ditch with a small bow in his hand. Skinny arms struggled to pull back the catgut string and release an arrow. Miraculously, it went true. The arrow didn't sink very deep into the horse's flank, but it was enough to cause it to falter in the jump, sending horse and rider crashing into the pit of sharpened stakes. Somehow the rider missed the stakes, but the horse wasn't so lucky. Two stakes pierced its chest and stomach, and its bowels spewed onto the ground, steam rising from the exposed entrails. The frightened horse thrashed madly in its death throes, while the dazed rider crawled out of the ditch and staggered across the field. He never saw the young boy who was hidden in the shadows, and neither did Angus mac Dougall, whose horse easily cleared the width of the ditch. The small archer crouched back down and readied himself under the lip of the bank.

The lead riders, having cleared the ditches, concentrated on the gate of the monastery, bearing down on their target. Thorma stood in the open, calmly cautioning the archers. "Steady, boys, steady." The partly repaired balcony shook from the charge that threatened to envelop them.

"Now!" Thorma finally shouted, and thirteen arrows soared into the air, quickly followed by thirteen more. The first arrow shot from William's Yew bow flew as straight as if Odin himself was guiding it. He had spotted his sister's tormentor when the big stallion leaped the last ditch and raced across the ever-shrinking stretch of pasture separating them. Mac Dougall held his saber straight out to the front. His knees hugged the saddle, and he leaned forward at the waist in a hurry to reach his enemy. The air was alive with the feathered projectiles, and arrow after arrow flew past him to bury itself in the ground. Mac Dougall began to think himself invincible and sensed that victory was within his grasp until suddenly an arrow slammed hard into his horse's neck, passing almost all the way through so that the arrowhead stuck out just in front of the young lord's face. For a second, he stared in disbelief at the bloody iron tip before the horse fell screaming to the ground, mac Dougall landing with a thud some ways off.

More arrows flew, and more horsemen went down, but enough managed to reach the area in front of the gate to form a small protective curtain for the three riders who carried the ropes they would use to pull the huge gate down. Men and horses screamed alike as the sky turned dark with arrows, but one rider was able to jump from his mount and attach a rope to the large iron straps on the gate before being struck by an arrow that drove through muscle to hit bone. Screaming in pain, he fell to the ground before he could reach his horse. More ropes were needed to apply enough force to pull the gate down, so two more riders leaped from their horses and ran for the gate, ropes in hand. Men were dying, and horses were screaming, but several more men had managed to attach their ropes to the gate.

"Where is the damn oil?" cursed Thomle, leaping down onto the balcony from his post on the wall above. He was hoping to help toss the oil over the side where it would be ignited when he heard the Celtic shouts echo against the walls.

"Go! Go!" Three horses strained hard against the ropes that had been hastily attached to the large gate, and suddenly a low groan rose from the iron hinges. Thorma's wounded shoulder was preventing him from tossing the clay pots of oil with much success, so Thomle rushed and grabbed the other side of the huge vat. Both men were straining to heave it over the side when a spear flew through the air and tore into Thomle's shoulder with a sickening thud. Pain shot through his whole body as the spear tip ripped through his armor's mail ringlets and cut into flesh. Thorma managed to help his wounded son finish throwing the pot over the wall where it landed near the gate with a loud crack. The thick, smelly oil spread over the churned ground, saturating booted feet and shod hooves alike. Thomle, moaning, staggered sideways and leaned hard against the cold stone wall.

"More vats. We need more of these damn vats over the wall," shouted Thorma while he moved to help his son. The nearest two villagers looked at each other tentatively, but finally overcame their fear, they grabbed a clay vat and heaved it over the stone ledge.

The short javelin-like spear that struck Thomle had been thrown by a somewhat dazed but smiling Angus mac Dougall.

"Die, you bastard!" he shouted triumphantly when he saw the lance strike home. Thomle slowly sank from sight, and mac Dougall commenced to strut around like a grouse in season below the monastery wall, all the while giving orders to his men.

Thomle groaned heavily and sank to his knees, then onto his haunches, before slowly leaning back against the wall.

"Damn," he growled and reached up to hold the spear with one hand. Blood trickled down between his fingers, but he couldn't find the strength to pull out the shaft. Thorma, who was shouting orders to the men heaving the pots over the wall, walked over and knelt to examine his son's injury.

"Huh, no broken bones, son. You will live," he grunted and grasped the short spear with both hands. It came out with a sucking sound, and Thorma looked the shaft over to make sure nothing had broken off inside the wound. Satisfied it was relatively clean, he broke the slender piece of ash and tossed it over the wall.

"Thanks," moaned Thomle as he closed his eyes, his chin dropping to his chest.

A few seconds later, he jumped when Jaime mac Kee forced some dried moss under the hauberk and ringlets of his armor to stop the bleeding. When mac Kee was satisfied with his efforts, he helped the groggy warrior to his feet.

"Are you okay?" he asked, watching Thomle's face turn even more pale when he stood to walk with a slight stagger toward his father.

"I'm all right," he answered without looking back.

The battle raged below in the field, and Thomle cautiously moved to the edge of the wall, looked over the iron railing, but then suddenly ducking back. An iron shaft fired from a crossbow flew past his ear and disappeared up into the smoke. Thorma glanced over at his son with a sheepish grin on his face.

"Close, huh?"

Thomle just stared back, wide-eyed. Angry with himself for being careless, he glanced around for a second time before running to the vats of oil and dragging another jar to the wall's edge. It took both him and Thorma to wrestle it over the side, where it crashed just in front of the gate, the smell of whale oil wafting up.

"Good throw, you two. It almost hit someone!" shouted William from high up on the wall as he notched another arrow and let it fly.

"Hey, Pict, shoot a fire arrow into the damn oil, if you think you can hit it!" shouted Thorma as he and Thomle stood back to watch. William held the arrow, its tip wrapped tightly with oil-soaked linen so that one of his fellow archers could light it. When it was ablaze, he shot the flaming arrow into the oil-soaked earth. His aim was rewarded with a loud swoosh when the oil ignited. Reddish-orange flames hissed and popped as they quickly spread toward the three horses straining on the ropes attached to the gate. While the big door moaned and bulged on it hinges, the horses screamed as the flames spread close enough to lick at their hooves. Their riders lashed out at their front withers with the ends of their reins in an effort to escape the flames. Suddenly, as if being torn from the very soul of the building, the sound of wood and metal ripping apart rose like a bad omen from beneath the stone wall.

* * * * *

The frightened horses tore across the churned earth with their riders hugging their necks and the ropes dragging the shattered gate behind them. A triumphant cheer rose from the group of mac Dougall's warriors who lined the ridge high above the battlefield. Angus mac Dougall heard the massive gate slam onto the ground and spun around just in time to see the frightened horses bearing down on him. He leaped out of the way as the horses sped past with wild eyes bulging and nostrils flared. Brushing himself off, he stood and glared into the gaping hole where the gate once stood. A wicked smile spread across his scarred face.

"Now we can attack them in their nest," he howled like a madman and ran toward the hole with his sword held high. An insane creature, Angus mac Dougall raced across the field toward what he felt was sure victory. A dark shadow floated eerily across his path. The blood that had been boiling in his veins with the lust of vengeance a moment before now turned to ice in an instant.

Spittle dripped from his torn lips and his fist shot into the air.

"Damn you! Go back to your witch and her lover!" he shouted, the smell of burnt grass filling his nostrils. The thin saber swept through the air as he swore savage oaths at the circling hawk. His cries drifted back to the ridge where the remaining cavalry as well as all the infantry stood and waited.

"The damn fool," growled Holmes, who sat on his gelding and watched the crazy antics of the heir apparent unfold before him. "Let's go see if we can save his royal arse from his own stupidity." With Holmes in the lead, the reserve cavalry moved forward at a canter, and the infantry jogged behind. The young drummers unhooked their drums and hurried to keep up.

Along with the hawk's, another shadow fell across the scorched earth in front of the breached gate, though at first mac Dougall didn't notice it. He was busy slashing the air above him, as if he might actually reach the demon creature tormenting him from a safe distance. The hawk circled above the ranting noble, but the more immediate threat was lower down.

With a swarm of arrows, William and the other archers had driven the bulk of the cavalry back from the walls of the monastery, and now the two sides glared at each other from a distance. All the mac Dougall clan could do was pace their mounts and stay just out of range of the powerful Yew bows.

Moving stolidly through the cloud of smoke at the gate, blood running down his arm, Thomle paused in the smoke-filled archway and watched Angus mac Dougall. With a resolved sigh, he walked slowly forward. Suddenly a primal part of mac Dougall's brain sent a message. *Danger, danger.* He turned in the direction of the smoking hole. Sweat burned his good eye, and he wiped his hand across his brow in an effort to recognize what he sensed was coming toward him. A dark figure clad in a large bearskin cloak carried a sword nearly as tall as an ordinary man, and it stalked him like a scene from a nightmare. The lord stood mesmerized as Thomle, with one bloody hand, shed the cloak and stepped out of the shadows.

"It is time for you to die, Angus mac Dougall!" shouted Thomle, and he moved forward across the scorched ground. A low moan escaped mac Dougall's throat before he could stop it. He was looking death square in the face and knew it.

"You're dead," he whispered as he realized who was walking toward him. "I killed you with my spear," he sputtered, confused.

"No, mac Dougall. I'm not dead, but you soon will be," answered Thomle, his voice dry as the dead wood in the forest.

While Thomle stalked mac Dougall, another sound began to rise over the clamor. It was a soft sound, like silk sliding through a maiden's fingers. The dove's call drifted eerily across the battlefield, growing louder and louder until the creaking of saddle leather and rattling of sabers couldn't block it out. The dove, whose call soon held the battlefield in a strange and awed silence, suddenly lifted from its perch on the east wall of the monastery. It flew up to join the hawk that sailed in and out of the smoke a hundred feet above the field. The hawk turned silent when the dove joined it. Mac Dougall's men glanced around nervously, unsure of what to do. The reserve cavalry slowed to a full stop, the riders spellbound in their saddles staring into the sky. Even Holmes wasn't sure what to do next. He leaned forward in his saddle, watching first the birds and then the battlefield.

The veteran warriors from both sides took time to catch their breath, but even they couldn't escape the power of the dove's call. Mesmerized, they listened as yet another sound joined the soft cooing of the dove. This sound seemed to float on the smoke-filled air, emanating from the far corner of the monastery. A woman's voice, like that of the mythical sirens of long ago, rose into the air and blended with the dove's call. Together, they wove a tapestry of sound magical and powerful. The voices—one human, one bird—swept across the field while anguished warriors sucked air in preparation for combat.

"Enough," the human voice cried, echoing off the high stone walls. "Enough pain, enough hate, enough killing." The voice drifted through the smoke like a wandering spirit, weaving among the combatants. "All we want is to live in peace. Is that so much to ask?"

The question hung in the air, like a separate living being. On the edge of the field, a shimmering image slowly transformed into the body of a beautiful female. The woman walked out from the shadows and stood alone between the two groups of fighters. Only the snorting of horses and the creak of leather competed with her voice, as riders stood in their stirrups to get a better look at her.

Angus mac Dougall stood frozen in his tracks, his head cocked to the side. The swirling smoke and sweat that ran into his good eye blurred his vision, but he found what he was looking for—the girl.

"You!" he screamed, and the dark part of his mind took over his being once again. His twisted logic told him that if he could kill this girl, this witch who obviously controlled the birds, then he could still win the day. His father would finally be proud of him, and he could deal with that arrogant Captain Holmes, a man he both hated and envied. With speed that surprised all the Norsemen, Angus Augustus mac Dougall, heir apparent of the Dalriada realm, raced toward the girl with the sun reflecting coldly off his raised sword.

Thomle was about thirty paces from mac Dougall when the man screamed and started running toward Morea, who stood on a small knoll about two hundred feet away. Having left his spear leaning against a wall near the gate, and now with only his sword for a weapon, Thomle knew in his heart that he could not catch the man in time. He anxiously glanced at Morea, who stood like a spirit in the middle of the battlefield, her thin woolen dress blowing about her in the stiff wind. Thorma, still on the balcony, bellowed at the archers.

"Kill the bastard! Shoot, shoot!"

William was also watching and had already notched his arrow. When Thorma shouted, his first arrow was already on its way.

Thomle's heart ached, and fear drove him forward. His legs pumped hard as he tore across the pasture, but the distance separating him from mac Dougall was just too great. He watched helplessly as arrow after arrow, shot from the high wall above the balcony, missed its mark.

I am invincible, thought mac Dougall as the arrows rained down all around but none found its mark. *I'm almost there, almost ...* A smile began to form on his twisted face. He could practically feel his saber slicing through the witch's neck and his fingers tingled with the anticipated pleasure.

The labored breathing of the Norseman, who was just behind him, reached mac Dougall's ears, but he didn't care. He knew the big man was close, but he would be too late. His good eye blazed with renewed hate as he watched the dove fly down from beside the hawk and settle on the girl's shoulder.

"I'll kill them both," he growled to the heavens and raised his saber for the killing blow.

"Peace. All we want is to be left in peace," spoke Morea, watching her killer bear down on her.

Her mournful cry for peace would be the last words that Angus mac Dougall ever heard, for a lone arrow, shot from a small Yew bow held by scrawny arms, sailed across the field. It flew straight, as if mighty Odin had directed it, and sliced into the neck of the heir to Dunolleigh Castle. The iron-tipped arrow drove him sideways, a stunned look on his scarred face. The arrow severed the jugular vein and snapped the spinal cord as the shiny sword, a gift from a wiser man, dropped from his limp hand onto the damp ground at Morea's feet. Angus Augustus mac Dougall was dead before he hit the ground at the feet of the woman he would never have.

Morea, who had stood frozen in place as her tormentor bore down on her, staggered backward. As the dove flew from her shoulder and joined the hawk circling close by, the sound of fluttering wings startled her. Thomle, just five steps behind, ran up and grabbed her gently before she sank to the ground. With his chest heaving from the chase, he wrapped his arms around her, and they clung to each other while tears of relief ran down both their faces. Thomle had closed his eyes with his back turned to the mac Dougall clan when he heard his father calling his name. Like at Inverness, it drifted into his tired mind like a voice in a dream, but he couldn't react to it. It was the sound of horses that caused him to spin around with his sword grasped in his uninjured hand. He stood braced for battle, looking up into the gray eyes of the grizzled old warrior, John Holmes.

The two adversaries locked eyes, and the young Norseman gripped his sword tightly, the pain in his left shoulder forgotten for the moment. Thomle glanced around at the grim faces of the mac Dougall warriors staring back at him and steeled himself for the worst. He didn't want to die, but he was prepared to die—this day in this field, for what he knew was right. Holmes sensed it. The two men held each other's stares as more riders arrived to completely encircle the couple who stood over their dead leader's body. Horses snorted and pawed the ground. Everyone waited. Thomle dared not look to see where his father and the others were, but John Holmes did. He saw the archers standing ready, along the high wall of the monastery, with their arrows notched. He saw the small group of Norsemen gathered at the hole where the gate once stood, their huge battle-axes ready. *Everyone seemed ready to die this day—and for what?*

Thomle's eyes suddenly dropped from Holmes's to a struggling bundle that lay across the man's saddle. He hadn't noticed until now, but Holmes had a child draped across his saddle. The boy was fighting to be released. Holmes, too, had forgotten the boy for the moment, and he looked down seemingly surprised that he was there. After a second, his eyes shifted back to Thomle.

"This bow"—he tossed a small bow onto the ground—"is much too dangerous for a young boy to play with," Holmes said, then finally let the youth slide off his saddle and sprawl onto the ground.

"And you should help him with his dagger work too." Holmes grimaced and threw a small dagger into the mud at the boy's feet. Blood dripped from beneath his coat sleeve as he gazed down at the boy. Thomle motioned for the young Ein McNeil to get behind him, and the boy scrambled across the ground on all fours until he suddenly realized he had not retrieved his weapons. Starting back after them, he was stopped by Thomle's big hand.

"Let them be," he grunted. Then looking Holmes in the eyes, Thomle said, "We only want to live in peace." Morea's words seemed to hang in the air, but the fire of battle still ran strong through Thomle's veins as he stood waiting for a reply. When none was quick to come, he took a deep breath and went on.

"We want to raise our children and our cattle and our crops—in peace." He paused again, a little frustrated. Holmes turned in his saddle and looked at his men but still remained silent. Thomle continued. "We will pay your taxes, if they are not excessive. We just want to be left alone. Is that so hard for you to understand?" It was as close to a plea as Thomle would go.

John Holmes listened to the young Norseman, and while he listened, his gaze again drifted to the balcony of the monastery, the archers still standing ready with their bows. Another big Norseman was walking through the smoke that swirled around the hole where the gate once stood. *He looks much like the young man standing in front of me*, thought Holmes, taking in the whole scene in front of him. Behind the older Norse warrior, spread out in a battle line, stood the Viking fighters now joined by their families. Even the women held battle-axes in their hands.

Holmes turned in his saddle once more, looking at the remainder of his cavalry and the infantry that stood behind them. *They, too, seemed ready—but for what? War? Death? Glory?* He slowly took off his helmet, looked down at the body of his young lord, and spoke.

"This," he said at last, pointing down at the body of Angus mac Dougall, "has caused far too much pain across this land. Sadly, he never learned what his father always seemed to know." Seconds ticked by as Holmes stared down at the body in silence.

"And what is that?" Thomle finally asked, growing impatient at the man for not going on.

A hint of a smile crossed Holmes's face as he looked up from the still body and stared into Morea's eyes.

"That you cannot govern people with an iron fist and an empty heart." Tears rolled down Morea's cheeks at Holmes's words, and she nodded her head in agreement. Holmes then looked back at Thomle.

"I will take the boy's body back to his father." He paused again as he instructed his men to load the body on one of the high-wheeled carts. "And I'm quite sure that His Lordship will want to talk with you," he added. Thomle simply nodded. He had no fear of meeting with Lord mac Dougall.

"But understand, Fergus mac Dougall is a much wiser man than his son ever was," said Holmes, who was no fool himself. The old warrior knew he would have a hard time explaining the boy's death to his father, though the elder mac Dougall had watched his son make an enemy of all whom he met and all whom they ruled. *Maybe now there could be peace, at least for a while*, he thought as he looked at the Viking and his woman.

"I hope that you mean what you say, Northman, or I'm afraid that we will be back." Holmes put his leather helmet back on, turned his horse, and fell in behind the cart carrying Angus mac Dougall, heir to the Dalriada throne, back home.

Thomle finally dared to look around. Thorma was standing halfway between him and the other Norsemen, weapon in hand, waiting. The villagers of Oban had now come up to line the balcony just below the archers. Everyone waited. Some held their breath, some tightly clutched their weapons, and some cried.

Thomle felt he should say more, wanting to somehow convince this man who seemed to hold everyone's fate in his hands that they would be true to their word. Holmes had to turn in his saddle to look back when Thomle began to speak.

"Captain Holmes!" Thomle shouted, having heard the old man addressed that way. "Maybe peace is a fleeting thing, like trying to catch a promise. It's a thing that we savor when we have it in our hands yet a thing that we defend to the death when someone tries to take it from us. We can only hope that you allow us to savor it—this thing called peace." Thomle watched the remaining cavalry horses prance nervously in front of the wagon that carried the body, and everyone waited for Holmes's reply.

"We, too, want this thing called peace, Northman. Let's hope, this time, it will prevail for a while." Holmes started to ride on but stopped to look back at Thomle and Morea once more. "Just know that it will be no small matter for either of us." With that said, he drove his heels into his horse's flanks and rode to the front of the column as they climbed up through the high pasture.

A soft cleansing snow descended from the heights and fell lightly on the field, and high overhead the dove's call drifted in the wind that circled the battlefield. The hawk simply sailed alongside the dove and watched the events unfold beneath its wings. As they walked from the battlefield, Thomle put his arm around Morea, dragging his sword behind them. The sword tip cut a furrow in the soil like a plow as they walked, side by side, back to the village called Oban—a place of the doves.

After a few minutes, the hawk and dove drifted southward while the sun set in the west behind red clouds. They flew into the high snow-covered mountains. For a number of years, peace did reign along the shores of Lorn. But the quest for peace is an ever-renewed task, calling forth brave men and women in every generation. The idea is simple, the faithful execution complex. The spirits can attest to that, as we shall see.

CHAPTER 2

Failed Diplomacy

War is a mere continuation of politics by other means.
— Carl Von Clausewitz

A long, roughly staggered line of weary men sat atop half-starved horses whose coats glistened with white lathery sweat. The bleary-eyed horse soldiers, or Cazodores, were God-fearing men, and they crossed themselves as they stared across the low valley, their mounts nibbling in vain at the short wire grass that covered the ground. These remnants of the once mighty Portuguese Cavalry had been trying for months to drive the cursed French from their land, but all their efforts had failed. Their scarlet uniforms hung in tattered disarray like a scarecrow's mantel; their battered and tarnished sabers rested unsheathed across their saddle horns. There were a few of these men, a handful, who leaned forward and soothingly patted the necks of their mounts, speaking softly as if to a young woman. The horses were as tired as their riders, neither having eaten nor slept much in two days, and they pawed the ground nervously in anticipation of the imminent battle—knowing what was to come. Most of the war-weary Cazodores would have preferred to simply turn their mounts and gone home, but they couldn't. They were a proud people, and there was still much fighting and dying to do in this rocky valley. Their captain, a quiet bespeckled father of four, sat on his mount and, with his binoculars, looked across the field at the enemy. It was plain to see that his meager force was greatly outnumbered, but it really didn't matter; they had to delay the French so that the remnants of the Portuguese Army and their British allies could regroup. He looked at his shaking hands, gripped the reins tighter, and then glanced at his troops. They would simply fight to the last man.

The last bugler pressed an old horn to his chapped lips, sounding the sharp but familiar notes of "La Advance," causing the troopers to begin a slow canter. Less than a hundred yards had passed beneath the horses' hooves when another blast echoed through the valley of Almeida, and the canter became a trot. To the left and slightly behind the grim-faced captain, a young Cazodore officer by the name of Feirra leaned forward in his saddle. Sweat rolled out from beneath his once-polished helmet as his sword arm extended along his horse's neck, both horse and rider anticipating the next call. It came a few heartbeats later. A clouded image of his beautiful dark-haired wife and young son flashed through his mind as he dug his heels into the mare. The last eighty horsemen of the 10th Battalion, all that remained of the Portuguese cavalry, broke into a full charge. They had numbered near a thousand when Napoleon's horde had first crossed the border a year earlier.

Across the way, the French commander sat atop his well-fed horse and smiled.

"Un bon!" he shouted to his aide and kicked his gelding in the ribs, shooting forward to meet the challenge. Eighty against two hundred and fifty wasn't much of a challenge, but the French colonel was ready to be done with this rabble. Besides, a fiery-eyed young peasant girl awaited him back at his tent, and he thought of her as his sword sliced down. "Viva la Emperor!"

* * * * *

The dark ages, with their darkest of times, have faded into the shadowy mist of history. The old gods and their mystic Druids have disappeared just like the ancient groves that once hid their most sacred rituals. The year is 1810, and there is a bright star of enlightenment guiding scholars and artists to supposedly new understandings of the world. The ancient spirits are mostly silent now, and most of the world bows to Rome and the newest of the gods that shines his light from the cross. However, men continue to kill, maim, and conquer in the name of this new god, and so some things never seem to change. Strong men and women who possess good hearts and minds must step forward and be counted regardless of the god they fear. And the old gods, if they still exist, probably smile out from their hiding places as the spirits of warriors past once again try to protect the brave and the innocent.

* * * * *

Harsh winds descended from the snow-covered mountains, chasing the low-hanging clouds across a tortured landscape—a hard, battered land surrounding this high plateau, a plateau that forms the southern foothills of the Serra de Estrela. Several icy peaks had punched their way six thousand feet into the aqua-colored sky, looking down on the inhabitants of this rugged land. The high ribs of the plateau stretch along the entire northwestern coast of the Iberian Peninsula, separating Spain from Portugal. Ruled by the Moors for hundreds of years, it could be considered a pious land.

A chill rode the blustery autumn winds that carried a hint of the brutal winter yet to come and mist-filled shadows swept across the jagged black lumps of volcanic stone. Swirling leaves danced on long stems high in the Eucalyptus trees, donning bright streaks of yellow and gold as fall drained the sap from the limbs. Blackthorn and sumac, tough plants that dotted the parched landscape, had already turned a fiery crimson as they awaited the first bite of frost.

In the rolling hills a few miles east of the Rio Tagus, a sweaty young ensign struggled through the thick underbrush that threatened to rip the clothes from his back. This man was not worried about the beauty of the terrain, nor was he concerned about the brilliant fall colors or even, some would say, the fate of his soul. He and his company of green-jacketed skirmishers were simply trying to stay alive. Do their job for the king, mind you, but stay alive. These men, some who were born in and then, years later, pulled from the sewers of the British Isles, searched for the French picket lines that guarded the front and flanks of Marshal Soult's advancing army. Theirs was not an easy task.

Imperial General Pierre Soult, the pride of France and Napoleon's most successful general, was driving his mighty army south out of Spain. Only a small British force, along with a handful of survivors from the defeated Portuguese army, stood in his way. The ensign looking for Frenchmen on the ground, probably right in front of him, remained totally unaware of the hawk sailing high above his head. The hawk's wings dipped every few seconds as it rode the stiff breezes that roared down from the high peaks towering over the countryside.

Ensign John McKinney of His Majesty's Scottish Highlanders, a much-decorated infantry battalion, hailed from Oban, a sleepy little port city in west central Scotland, which with a population of two thousand souls could hardly even be called a city. Oban was considered by some, including His Majesty King George, to be the gateway to the isles. A marvelous place, but not where John McKinney wanted to live out his life.

McKinney's parents owned and operated a fairly successful shipping business in Oban. As would be expected, he was an important part of that business. The younger McKinney had sailed the North Sea since he was a child. It was only natural then, when John told his father that he wanted to see more of the world, that the old man expected him to join the Navy. The elder McKinney was shocked when he learned that his son intended to join the Army instead. Ein McKinney, John's father, was a salty old sea dog who had sailed alongside the British fleet from India to the rebellious colonies for thirty years. Through those difficult years, he had made friends with several high-ranking people in the Admiralty, and he felt that they could help his son if he were to join the Navy, but he knew very few men in the Army he could turn to.

The elder McKinney made several long-winded attempts to persuade his son to join the Admiralty, but his efforts were all in vain. The old man's major argument was that his son's seafaring skills far surpassed his horsemanship—plus, at least according to the elder McKinney, his son knew very little about land tactics. But John had repeatedly explained to his father that he had had enough of sailing the cold North Sea. He wanted to feel the ground under his feet for a while. So with a tearful farewell from his mother and a hearty hand-shake from his father, John McKinney climbed aboard a southbound train and never looked back.

"Boy, have I felt the ground under my feet," moaned McKinney, evidently out loud, for he quickly heard, "What was that you said, sir?" The question came from Sergeant Mike Malone, McKinney's crusty old top sergeant.

"Nothing, Sergeant, I'm just talking to myself," replied McKinney, a little embarrassed.

"That's not a good thing for the boys to hear, sir." Sergeant Malone laughed as he prepared to step over a fallen log.

"You let me worry about the men, and you worry about finding the damn crapauds," retorted McKinney, with a hint of a grin on his young but sea-weathered face.

The two men, who now ran the company of skirmishers because their captain had been wounded several weeks back and had thus far not been replaced, enjoyed a rare combination of friendship and respect. Although it enabled them to joke with each other on many levels, it had a downside for McKinney. The close friendship between him and Sergeant Malone brought constant ridicule from his peers. None of the other officers in McKinney's battalion could understand how he could allow this camaraderie to go on. But after some shared reflection and a cup or two of rum, they would agree among themselves that he was only a lowly ensign and a commoner to boot, so what else could you expect? Deep down, though, most of his fellow officers were simply jealous of the respect that McKinney's men gave him. It was because of this jealousy that most of his fellow officers never allowed him to forget his lowly status as an ensign. Their constant scorn for McKinney and his tactics somehow made them feel better about themselves, if only because it allowed them to ignore their own inadequacies. The purchase of rank in the military was a common practice at the time, and John's parents were able to help him to some extent. The lowly rank was within their means, and so that is where he began his career; any further promotion for John McKinney would have to be earned with rifle and sword.

McKinney's skirmishers were the eyes and ears of Arthur Wellesley's army. The red-coated regulars, called the scum of the isles by some because of their tainted past, were the bulwark of Wellesley's bid to stop Napoleon's generals. Napoleon's army, led by Marshal Soult, had conquered all of Spain and was now driving hard to take Portugal. Soult, in his eagerness to entrap the British, was pushing his army relentlessly toward the city of Alhendra. The port was an important stepping stone to the capital city and very heart of Portugal, and its capture would relieve his overstretched supply lines. General Arthur Wellesley, who had become the latest Duke of Wellington because of his father's death, had been fighting a running battle with Soult in hopes of buying time for the Portuguese Army to regroup after their defeat at Oporto in the valley of Almeida. That horrific loss had been a demoralizing blow to the proud army of General Terras. Since the war had begun, much English blood had been spilled alongside that of the Portuguese, especially at the battle of Oporto. It was now time for the French, or the frogs as the British liked to call them, to do the heavier bleeding. Tasked with finding the lead elements of the French drive to Alhendra, McKinney and his skirmishers sought out the line of pickets protecting the French Army's front and flanks.

John McKinney had served in His Majesty's Army for five years and had been in Spain and Portugal for over a year. For the last three days, he and his skirmishers were consistently pounded by the frog's pickets. The French had finally figured out that their slower-firing muskets were not a good match for the slightly faster and much more accurate Baker rifles. The French muskets were accurate for only fifty to sixty yards, whereas the British Baker rifle, with its grooved or rifled bore, could pick your teeth at one hundred yards. The French may have been arrogant, but they proved capable of adapting when necessary. For instance, the commanders of the French pickets learned to keep their troops hidden in the thick brush until McKinney's men were right on top of them, and only then would they begin firing. A mass of lead would fly and men would fall to the ground screaming; others simply dropped to the ground and started shooting at phantoms. A .51-caliber musket ball can do terrible things to a man's body at close range; knowing this, McKinney struggled to get the job done while keeping his men alive along the way.

"A hell of a way to fight a war," he growled to the uncaring sky.

Knowing that good officers had to lead from the front, McKinney never asked his men to do anything that he wouldn't do. Strangely, this approach caused him to be rebuffed by his superiors on many occasions. But it was the only way he knew to lead, the way his father had taught him from an early age on their sailing ships. During that time, young McKinney's jobs had ranged from cleaning the piss pots to climbing the high riggings. The old salts respected him for that, as did his father.

The respect his men conferred on McKinney, despite his lowly position, made many of his peers jealous and, for the most part, prevented him from forming close bonds with them. There was one officer, though, with whom McKinney had become good friends and shared a rare mutual respect. Samuel Ewart had been a damn fine sergeant in McKinney's 1st Highlanders Battalion, and in the bloody battle of Corunna, Sergeant Ewart had almost singlehandedly fought his way through a dozen dragoons to capture the ultimate prize, a French staff eagle. The eagle was the color standard of a French infantry battalion. Wellesley had been so impressed with Ewart's action that he had given him a direct field promotion, much to the chagrin of the other officers. Ironically, Samuel Ewart was a far better sergeant than an officer. Barely able to read, he struggled with the many written commands. Still, McKinney knew that he could count on Ewart when the lead began to fly.

"We are both sort of outcasts in our own army," thought McKinney out loud. "That's why our bond is so strong."

"Did you say something?" asked Sergeant Malone with a slight smile as they fought their way through the underbrush.

"Watch the damn front. That's what I said, Sergeant, and that's where the frogs are," growled McKinney, a little troubled by his recent habit of talking out loud to himself.

"Yes, sir, eyes to the front." Malone laughed as he tripped on a vine and almost fell.

The skirmishers' movement had been slowed by the thick brush, but after a lot of painful effort, they were finally getting close to their objective—an overgrown and abandoned grass field that lay just above a small town. According to McKinney's map, the town was called Leira. It was a dusty little place where he suspected the people warmed neither to the French nor the English. *They are probably just hardworking people who have seen enough war and simply want to be left alone*, thought McKinney, who was walking point. He dropped to one knee at the edge of the field and signaled for the lead platoon to low crawl up the small knoll to where he was. While he waited for them, he took out his field glass and scanned the sleepy little town.

The remaining two platoons, his company was one platoon under strengthened, waited at the base of the hill, hidden in the brush. Knowing their forces were one platoon short of full strength, the fear of a French ambush weighed heavily on everyone's mind as they lay in the grass and studied the town. McKinney and Sergeant Malone, who seemed always by his side, crawled through the tall wet grass in order to get a better look at their path of advance. It was supposed to be the rainy season on the peninsula, but the heavy rains were late this year, and McKinney and his skirmishers were thankful for it—misery being a constant companion in cold wet conditions, not to mention the fact that damp powder will not fire. McKinney parted the tall grass in front of him with the barrel of his rifle and looked down on the town from just below the top of the knoll. He pulled out his field glass again and uncovered the lens. The glass had been a gift from his father, handed to him as he boarded the train for London five years before.

"Can you see the frog pickets sneaking back into the town like bloody rats?" hissed Malone with a sneer on his ruddy face as he watched without the aid of a field glass.

"Yeah," replied McKinney, lowering the glass, "but the bastards may still have an ambush set somewhere. Maybe in that gulley over there," he whispered and nodded off to their right.

Everyone lay very still, lost in their own thoughts, while McKinney pondered the situation, his brow deeply furrowed. Finally, he turned toward Malone.

"Sergeant Malone, we can't take the whole company into that town. We would be too easily spotted. Go back and pick seven men to go with us. Then send the others back to Colonel O'Shounessey. He may need them pretty soon anyway. Have Second Sergeant Talley inform the colonel that we are going into the town to look around."

Malone crawled backward for a few feet, his rifle dragging along the ground; then he rose and hurried to where the 1st Platoon lay in the thick brush. He picked his seven men and put Talley in charge of taking the rest of the skirmishers back to friendly lines. Talley was busy forming his men in order to move them out when Malone remembered what Ensign McKinney had told him to do.

"Damn," he cursed and quickly pulled Talley aside, explaining what he was to tell O'Shounessey once back in camp. Malone waited until the last green jacket disappeared into the brush before heading back to the knoll. McKinney, nearly hidden in the tall grass, was studying the lay of the land. *If we could just make it to the gulley without being seen, then the going would be much safer,* he reasoned to himself. The other option would be to crawl all the way to the village through the high grass, where the risk of being spotted was far greater and with no apparent escape route.

"The problem with the first plan," worried McKinney under his breath as he scanned the terrain, "is the two hundred yards of fairly low grass and open field we would have to cross before reaching the gulley's edge. And what if the frogs have set an ambush somewhere along the gulley?"

"I'd say more like one hundred and fifty yards," interjected Malone, who had crawled up quietly behind the young ensign and who now smiled mischievously when his friend jumped at the sound of his voice.

"Damn your Irish hide," growled McKinney, sliding the field glass back into its oilskin case.

"Sorry, sir. I didn't mean to startle the ensign, sir," said Malone with a smile.

"Like hell you didn't," countered McKinney, who glanced once more at the distance to the gulley and reluctantly agreed with the one hundred and fifty yards.

"But you may be right about the distance, Sergeant."

"Thank you, sir," said Malone, his green eyes beaming.

"I told Sergeant Talley to inform Patrick"—he paused—"Colonel O'Shounessey that we were going into the town and that there might be a wee bit of trouble while we have a look-see around." His Irish accent was as thick as a pint of Guinness.

Sergeant Mike Malone and Colonel Patrick O'Shounessey were both Irish and had actually grown up in the same small town, Delaney in County York. They had been friends for years, and due to old habits, sometimes Sergeant Malone would accidentally use the colonel's Christian name even though he knew that Ensign McKinney didn't like for him to do it.

"Colonel O'Shounessey would want us to press on, Sergeant, so let's do just that. I will take the point, and you take the rear. We badly need to know what the frogs are up to."

McKinney had always stressed to Malone, who felt somewhat demoted, that walking rear guard was almost as important and dangerous as walking point. Quite often, whole columns would be picked off from the rear, simply because everyone was facing the other direction. With the big Irishman watching his back, McKinney could concentrate on what was in front of them.

As McKinney led the men down toward the gulley in a low crawl, he became aware of something circling overhead. Its shadow would pass over the tall grass in front of him from time to time.

The damn buzzards think I'm dead, he mused, this time to himself. But when he turned on his side and looked up, he had to smile. It was a hawk that circled high above, its cry echoing across the fields and ridges as the mist blew under its wings. The hawk's glossy brown feathers that turned reddish near its tail fluffed out as it sailed on the cold wind currents. When he was young, McKinney's mother had told him many times that the hawks were his ancestors and that someday they would come back to protect him. He had always scoffed at the tale but had been strangely aware of hawks around him all his life. His father had often told the children stories of warriors who died in battle returning as hawks to guard the next generation. *Damn Scottish superstition*, his mind growled.

His father also believed their family had Viking blood in their veins. *With their large frames and reddish blond hair, maybe that part of the tale is true*, McKinney admitted to himself.

"But your temper, son," his father would jest, "that comes from the Scottish side, your mother's side. We Vikings are a peaceful bunch." He would laugh and duck as John's mother slapped his arm in mock protest.

They still lacked about a hundred yards reaching the gulley when suddenly the sound of a musket shot rang out from the edge of the field they crawled through. Everybody froze. McKinney's mind quickly snapped back to the present.

"What would a single shot mean?" he asked, this time not to himself but to Malone who was just two feet behind him. Malone shrugged his big shoulders and stared at the musket smoke as it rose into the air like a genie escaping from a bottle. They both knew the French were a seasoned veteran army. They had been fighting all over Europe and North Africa for years, going back to the days when Napoleon was a mere general instead of the god his soldiers had come to perceive him as. Since to make a careless mistake and expose an ambush could get you flogged, the odds were that the shot was not a mistake. So what was it?

McKinney and his green jackets, as they were sometimes called due to the color of their field jackets, lay frozen to the earth, halfway to the gulley. They were in the dead center of the field. The sound of bugles soon drifted in from the west, and it told them that the lead element of the French Cavalry was fast approaching. The main force probably wouldn't be far behind.

"This town is about to see one hell of a battle," whispered Malone as they all tried to become smaller and disappear into the grass.

McKinney nodded solemnly as he scanned the roads leading to Leira with his field glass. Then with a grunt, he slowly began to inch forward on his belly. His men followed in two-foot intervals, their Baker rifles held tight against their hips. The skirmishers were about thirty yards from the gulley when the lead element of the French Cavalry, a company of Dragoons, finally trotted down one of the two roads leading into town. Dust swirled along the road as they came into view. With their flags and pennants flying from brass and wood guidons, close to fifty riders pranced their mounts into the field John McKinney and his men were lying. In rhythm with the bugle call, the Dragoons smartly formed columns of twos as if part of some fancy parade. The horses came within about forty yards of the hidden skirmishers, who held their breath, clutched their rifles, and shrank into the ground even further. After a few slow minutes, the crapauds, as the British fondly called them, were apparently satisfied with their show and performed two column lefts before heading back to the main street of Leira. All nine skirmishers exhaled slowly and tried to relax their taut muscles as the adrenaline drained from their bodies.

"That was too damn close," whispered a breathless McKinney.

"Thank God for the tall grass and green jackets," added Malone, nervously brushing grass from his field jacket.

The question about the single shot was answered a few minutes later when a lone Dragoon officer rode back to the edge of the field and fired his musket up into the air. He was obviously shooting at the hawk that sailed peacefully overhead, oblivious to the firing.

"For the life of me, I can't understand why the frogs hate hawks so much and yet admire eagles," said Malone with a genuine look of confusion.

"Well, that hawk is safe enough. Those damn muskets are only accurate for maybe fifty yards," McKinney replied with a smirk on his face.

Gnats and flies buzzed all around the sweaty men as they crawled the last few yards to the gulley.

"Hell, the crapauds should be able to smell us," growled someone toward the middle of the small line.

"Quiet," hissed Malone as they sneaked through the grass. But the big Irishman turned his head and sniffed his armpit nonetheless. He crinkled his nose and nearly sneezed from the foul scent before crawling on.

Fifty feet in front of him, Ensign McKinney slid stealthily over the edge of the bank and down into the gulley after carefully looking for any sign of an ambush or snakes. He hated snakes nearly as much as he hated the French. His eyes darting from side to side, McKinney crept forward very carefully, always wary of some sign of trouble, but he saw none. When the last man had eased over the edge into the gulley, he pulled Sergeant Malone aside.

"We'll be a little shorthanded for this scouting probe, but we need to send a messenger back to Colonel O'Shounessey. He needs to know about the frog cavalry coming to town," whispered McKinney. He thought for a minute as he looked over the small group of skirmishers huddled in the shadows. "Send Private Woodard," he ordered when his eyes fell on the slight-framed soldier.

The two men locked eyes for a brief second, and Malone nodded his understanding. Quickly dropping into a crouch, he went over to where Woodard knelt. Malone understood the wisdom in choosing Woodard as the messenger because he was not only the youngest of the group but also the smallest. If it came to hand-to-hand fighting, and it probably would, size usually did matter.

* * * * *

Colonel Patrick O'Shounessey was sitting in his big white tent, a farewell gift from his wife just before he sailed for Portugal, looking over a stack of maps, when his aide, Captain William Queen, tapped on the wall of the tent.

"Yes," boomed the Irishman.

"Sir, you have a messenger from Ensign McKinney."

"Send him in, Captain," replied O'Shounessey as he laid the maps aside and turned toward the front of the tent.

Woodard hardly needed to stoop under the flap of the tent as he entered and snapped to attention.

"Well, Private, what is our Ensign McKinney up to today?" asked O'Shounessey, propping one long leg up on his desk as he awaited the answer.

Woodard crisply reported what Sergeant Malone had instructed him to say. His Lancaster accent made his words difficult to understand, but O'Shounessey listened politely. When he was finished, the young private relaxed his stance a little while the colonel stared up at an enormous brown and red spider on the ceiling of the tent. After a few minutes of solemn contemplation, O'Shounessey looked again at Woodard, who snapped back to rigid attention.

"Very good, Private," he said and started to dismiss the boy when he noticed his slight stature. "Have you eaten today, soldier?" he asked.

"No, sir, not since this morning, sir. And I only had a biscuit then." The boy looked down, a little embarrassed.

"Captain!" shouted O'Shounessey. "See to it that Private Woodard gets some proper food."

"Yes, sir," came the rapid reply from outside the tent.

With their business taken care of, Woodard knew that he had been dismissed. He did a sloppy about-face on the trampled grass of the tent and left O'Shounessey to study his maps and think about McKinney's report, which he did.

"So what are you up to, Le Marshal Soult?" O'Shounessey inspected the maps on his desk like a chessboard, intent on outwitting his opponent. He smiled at the thought of the arrogant French riding into the fields where John McKinney lay close enough to touch them.

"Now we know that you sent your lead cavalry to Leira as a show, but where are you going with your main force, where indeed?" He tapped the tabletop with the fingers of his left hand as the index finger of his right followed the road leading out of Leira. In his heavy Irish accent, Colonel O'Shounessey shouted, "Captain Queen, send a messenger to Lord Wellington. Inform His Lordship that Marshal Soult is on the move. Sadly, we are just not sure where he is going …

yet." He made the last comment almost as an afterthought and as he heard Queen's footsteps fading away, the colonel shouted, "And give him my compliments, of course!"

* * * * *

Arthur Wellesley, the latest duke of Wellington, leaned back in a large overstuffed chair he believed to be the design of Louis XV and thought of his home back in Westchester. He wanted to focus on making plans for several additions to the main house on the vast estate grounds his father had left him, but instead, he was being forced to listen to the pompous-ass ambassador from Spain explain why the English must leave Portugal—and why, of course, the French should stay. Wellesley had been listening to Ambassador Jiminez rant and rave for over an hour, and his patience was wearing thin. Upon his arrival at Wellesley's headquarters, under a flag of truce, Jiminez had explained that he was there on behalf of the emperor of Spain, who just happened to be Napoleon Bonaparte's brother, Joseph.

"We can only bring peace to this peninsula, sir," the raspy voice droned on, "if the British leave. These poor wretched people need our help so ... badly." The last few words spilled from his mouth as if they hurt his lips. Wellesley watched the fat jowls droop into a frown. *He either truly believes his own malarkey, or he is an extremely good actor*, mused the Brit as the Spaniard pondered his next words.

"In order for the Portuguese to obtain that help, you and your troops must sail back to England ... immediately. I am sure, sir, that a man of your stature can appreciate our position." With that last comment hanging in the air, the very much overweight ambassador sighed, took a large sip of brandy, which had been generously supplied by his host, and leaned back in his chair—seemingly oblivious to the hostility that threatened to explode at any moment.

"This is not a very good brandy, senor." He sighed, waiting for some sort of reply from Arthur Wellesley. Forced to dab his forehead constantly with a silk handkerchief, Jimenez was somewhat embarrassed that sweat rolled from beneath his powdered wig even though the day was cool and no fire burned in the great fireplace. He held the glass up to the light in order to inspect the dark contents once again.

"But I thank you for it anyway," he added after some hesitation. Putting the glass to his lips, he drank the last swallow before gently placing it on the table near his chair.

Fuming with disgust and barely able to resist the urge to run his ceremonial sword straight through the arrogant bastard, Wellesley rose somewhat stiffly from his chair. *Damned gout*, he cursed to himself before speaking.

"Sir, what would make me most happy would be for you and your entourage to"—he paused as he fought with his anger—"leave my office." Literally on the verge of biting his tongue, he was able to finish the comment in a more respectful tone than he had first planned. Limping slightly, he walked briskly past the startled ambassador, who squirmed uneasily in his chair, and opened the big double doors. Wellesley stood off to the side, so there would be no mistaking his intent.

"Frankly, sir, I have listened to your arrogant poppycock long enough." A general in the Army, Arthur Wellesley, had a penetrating stare, and he used his most famous negotiating tool with the ambassador, who either out of fear or ignorance of the infamous temper of the man who glared at him remained seated. With his heart racing, Jimenez quickly dropped his eyes from Wellesley's withering stare and glanced around at his underlings in search of support. His aides simply gazed down at the floor and shuffled their feet. The ambassador, quickly realizing he was on his own, didn't know what to do. The duke's stare had made many a general shake in his boots, and Jimenez now understood why.

"Well, I ... I have never ..." he finally stammered as more sweat ran down his forehead and dripped off his chubby chin. Without help from his staff, he was finished, and he knew it. With an indigent "Huh," he rose off his considerable arse and stomped toward the doors. When Jimenez reached them, he turned to face Wellesley and started to say more, but he stopped when he saw the anger in the Englishman's eyes and his hand on the hilt of the ceremonial sword. Whatever he intended to say was quickly forgotten. With another "Huh," the ambassador, followed by his six minor dignitaries, marched past the duke and down the stairway, the big doors slamming loudly behind them.

"Major!" shouted Wellesley as he walked back to his desk. Major Ricardo Lopez was an aide to His Lordship, working as a liaison between the Portuguese and the British. The desk that Wellesley stood behind was in front of a large window overlooking the bustling seaport. The house they used for their headquarters was owned by the mayor of Alhendra, Senor Paulo Rivera. Mayor Rivera, however, had suddenly decided to sail to England when the French forces headed in the direction of his town.

"Major," Wellesley spoke more softly this time. He stood looking over the many ships in the harbor, his hands clasped behind his back. He knew Major Lopez would be standing at stiff attention behind him, directly in front of his desk.

"There must be thirty ships unloading war material," said Wellesley as his anger slowly subsided. He had always admired the hardworking sailors of Admiral Nelson's navy, and today was no exception.

"There are thirty-two ships, sir," interjected Major Lopez after quickly glancing at the harbormaster's shipping list.

"Major," continued Wellesley as if he hadn't heard Lopez, "I tried, though not very successfully, to explain to Ambassador Jimenez that we British would be happy to leave Portugal if only the French would do likewise. His explanation of why we shouldn't help you Portuguese made me so angry that I could have run him through." He reached down and touched the dress sword he had strapped on for the occasion.

"You know, Major, nearly all wars are started due to a lack of proper diplomacy, and that lard-assed Ambassador Jimenez is a perfect example of why diplomacy usually fails." The old warrior shook his wigged head.

"Lord Wellington, sir ..." Major Lopez searched for the proper words. "All or at least most of us Portuguese only want peace. It is Napoleon Bonaparte who desires to rule all of Europe. You English are the only real hope that we have." Lopez remained stiffly at attention as he spoke.

"I thank you for your conjecture, Major," grunted Wellesley, who was still perplexed over the attitude of the fat Spaniard. "Diplomats think they are the only ones who want peace or understand how to obtain it. My Lord, Major, who more than a soldier understands the pain, suffering, and total brutality of war? We don't want war. It is they"—he pointed to Jimenez, who was being pushed unceremoniously into his carriage by two servants—"who thrust it upon us."

Lopez made no reply, for he felt none was needed. Wellesley stood in silence for a long time gazing out into the harbor, his mind on a thousand matters. He suddenly caught movement out of the corner of his eye and turned toward the North, where he saw a large hawk circling high over the ships. It was sailing in a tight circle, and surprisingly, by its side was a grayish-white dove.

"How wonderfully strange," he whispered, "to see a hawk and a dove flying together."

Lopez moved around the desk to where he, too, could see out the window to the north. "Like the lion and the lamb lying together," he answered as he crossed himself and gazed at the odd pair.

Both men turned their sights inward and became lost in their own thoughts as the war material, the lifeblood of Portugal, flowed from ship to wharf on harried barges.

* * * * *

Several miles away, John McKinney led his small band of green jackets cautiously down the steep gulley one step at a time. Although the French were never very eager to crawl into the thickest brush, the hill people from the town of Badajoz, who had sided with the French, had no problem with it. These local banditos knew every gulley and hiding place in the whole area and their short, curved knives could cut your throat before you even had a chance to yell. Twenty yards shy of the spot where a small stream entered the gulley, McKinney brought his group to a halt. Taking out his field glass once again, he followed the stream as it ran toward the center of the town along the south side of several dusty whitewashed buildings. There, the buildings formed a narrow street that angled sharply to the left before running toward the main part of town. McKinney and Sergeant Malone studied the space between themselves and the nearest of the stucco buildings.

"What do you think, Sergeant?" McKinney whispered.

"I don't smell the bastards, sir. And usually I can, if they are near," replied Malone.

"Your nose is hardly ever wrong, so let's go. I'll take point, you bring up the rear," ordered McKinney, who began a cautious climb out of the gulley. Once on level ground, he sprinted in a crouch across the open space.

Running low and hard, McKinney was about halfway across the opening when a young French dragoon rounded the corner of the building he and his crew were heading for. Both men froze in surprise, the hardened warrior and the fresh-faced boy soldier. McKinney was very good with a knife, but the twenty feet that separated him from the young sentry was just too far. They did not dare risk a shot, so McKinney did what any prudent man would do in a similar situation: he turned and ran, his skirmishers close behind him. *Any second now,* he thought, a shot would fire, and he would feel a .51 caliber musket ball slam into his back. But the shot never came. Only the sound of boots scurrying through the dirt could be heard, as first McKinney and then the rest of his band rounded the corner of the nearest building.

When Sergeant Malone ran past him, McKinney growled, "Some damn nose you have."

Malone could only shrug as he sped by. McKinney hastily signaled for the others to continue running as the young sentry, who still had not fired a shot, pursued them with his weapon at port arms. McKinney's heart pounded in his chest as he waited in the deepening shadows and listened to the approaching footsteps. Ready or not, it was time. Three seconds later, the young dragoon came around the corner of the building running hard, straight into McKinney's dagger. The blade plunged deep into the boy's neck, the force of the collision knocking both him and McKinney to the ground. They fought briefly as blood sprayed into the air. Though his vision was blurred, McKinney could see that the sentry was indeed a mere boy, aged sixteen at best. The boy's dark-brown eyes grew wide with shock, staring briefly up at McKinney and then blinking unsteadily while his blood pooled in the street. Seconds later, his body shuddered several times and then lay still. McKinney reached down, pulled out his knife, and gently closed the youth's eyes.

"Damn," he groaned as his head filled with the sound of the dying boy's last breath. He closed his own eyes and wiped the blood from his dagger on the boy's pant leg. "Too damn young to die."

Malone walked over and placed a calloused hand on his friend's shoulder. "The Grim Reaper doesn't care how young or old they are," he whispered. "He just wants his souls."

"I guess," McKinney answered gruffly. His mourning quickly over, he scanned the area for a place to hide the body.

Spotting what he thought would be a suitable place, he dragged the dead sentry behind a shed and covered his body, as best he could, with some scraps of lumber.

"I sometimes wish I wasn't so damn good at my job," lamented McKinney, shaking his head. Malone didn't answer; he knew his friend needed no reply. These demons haunt every soldier, especially after what might have been an unnecessary kill. Malone just hoped his friend would be able to snap out of it. This type of mood could get you killed! He waited. And after a few minutes, McKinney was ready.

"The frogs will miss this boy before long; we need to find some place to hide, and quickly," he announced in his stern, business-as-usual tone. The sun began to fade, drawing a cool mist down from the rugged heights, the dead sentry forgotten, for the moment, like all the rest.

McKinney spotted a small apartment door off to their left, just across the narrow dirt street, and directed his band toward it. All eight men scurried across the road, kicking up dust from under their boots. When they reached the other side, they pressed their backs against the stuccoed wall like a row of condemned men. Malone, as usual, brought up the tail end of the band. He looked anxiously down the line of soldiers and hardly breathed. They stood with their backs pressed hard against the wall and waited. It was almost comical, but no one laughed.

McKinney, who was closest to the filthy but ornate apartment door, carefully reached down for the cast iron knob. It turned easily enough, but the door squeaked ever so slightly as he pushed it open and entered a poorly-lit foyer. His men stacked up closely behind him as he allowed his eyes to adjust to the dim light. Sergeant Malone, still last in line, was partly exposed in the street and didn't like his position one bit. He eyes fervently darted up and down the dirt road, and he prayed to his patron saint, Patrick, that no one would come along and sound the alarm while his arse was plastered against a stupid wall. McKinney looked back at the expectant faces of his men, placed his finger to his lips, and once again slid his blood-encrusted dagger out of its sheath. He eased down the narrow hall toward the sound of a female voice singing softly.

A shaft of pale light sneaked past a once-white door that stood partially open at the end of the hall. This was where the singing came from, a lullaby that McKinney could almost recognize from his childhood. He placed his free hand on the door, eased it open, and stepped through; luckily, it did not squeak. While his eyes adjusted to the new light, he scanned the room ever so slowly. Blinking several times, he tried hard to clear his vision before stepping forward. Just to his right, next to a stone fireplace blackened from a thousand fires, sat a very pretty young woman holding a small child; light from the fire illuminated her curly red hair. The child, a little boy about fifteen months old with his own head of curly hair, stirred uneasily as he slept in her lap. He guessed the woman's age to be about twenty or twenty-one, and she looked as if she had a mix of blood other than Portuguese. *English*, he thought, *or maybe French.*

The eight nervous skirmishers pushed cautiously into the room, driven by Malone, who was tired of being stuck out in the street. They stood staring at the woman who simply looked up at them with big brown eyes. Surprisingly, she showed little fear, simply putting her finger to her lips and saying, "Shh," before humming a few more notes of the lullaby. Finally, satisfied that the child was asleep, she rose and placed him in a beautiful oak crib beside the fireplace. The small blaze popped and hissed inside the cavernous firebox. The woman placed a well-worn woolen blanket over the baby and turned to face her intruders. She and the dirty-faced British soldiers stared at each other until at last McKinney broke the silence.

"Madam, I hope you speak English," he whispered, "because my Portuguese is terrible at best."

He was tiptoeing toward her as he spoke, having placed the knife back into its sheath. The woman's doe eyes stared back as he walked up. *She's either stupid, which I doubt, or she knows not to fear English soldiers*, mused McKinney to himself as he tried to read her body language. Unlike the French, who rape and pillage at will, the English troops were under strict orders to leave the civilians alone or else face the lash or even death.

"I'm terribly sorry about sneaking into your home like this," he continued, "but we are having some difficulties outside." He took another step closer.

"I imagine you are, sir," the woman spoke in slightly accented English, which came as a relief to McKinney and must have shown on his face. The young woman still displayed no sign of fear. The calmness in her voice surprised him, and he took half a step back. She couldn't resist a slight smile.

"My name is Elizabeth Feirra, and I am fully aware of the French scum that have crawled into our village." She paused, and a lump appeared in her throat before she went on. "My husband is ..." She stopped. "My husband was Lieutenant Enrico Feirra, and he rode with the Portuguese 10th Battalion Cavalry, a Cazadore." She caught herself and choked back a sob. "He was killed at Almeida."

Sergeant Malone looked down for a second and grimaced before he stepped forward; the mention of Almeida brought back painful memories.

"Ma'am, I, too, fought at Almeida. It was a hell of a fight."

The woman looked at him for a long minute.

"Aren't all battles, Sergeant?" Malone didn't think she wanted or needed an answer, so he just stepped back into the shadows. The woman continued, this time with her head down.

"I'm sorry you had to fight there, Sergeant. A lot of good soldiers and civilians died." A solitary tear escaped from the corner of her left eye and fell onto the floor. "I hate war," she added before growing quiet. McKinney looked at the small damp spot in the dust before he replied.

"No more than the men who fight them, ma'am," added McKinney in a low strained voice, his eyes scanning the dimly lit room. An iron post bed, a table, three chairs, and a battered chest of drawers hutch were all the furnishings except for the baby's crib.

"Perhaps," she replied as she looked at the weary faces. "But the current problem"—she forced her mind away from her husband's death—"is that there are several hundred French soldiers in our village, senor, and even some of their dogs." McKinney gave her a puzzled look. "Their dogs, the rebels from Badajoz," she explained as if to a child. McKinney and Malone looked at each other and then nodded. "The French will soon be searching for rooms for their officers. You all must hide." There was a slight quiver in her voice.

Courageous and beautiful, thought McKinney. "Maybe we should just leave," he whispered.

"There is no time," she interjected anxiously. As if on cue, the sound of soldiers banging on doors could be heard from down the street.

"Quickly," she pleaded. "There is an old cellar under the floor. The door is under the rug."

The banging drew nearer, but McKinney and Sergeant Malone hesitated. The very thought of being trapped like rats in a cellar, with no way out, shook even these two hardened soldiers.

"Please hurry, please," she begged. "They will kill me and my baby if they find you here."

Finally, with more than a little trepidation, McKinney led his small band down the steps, while Elizabeth held the trap door open. As they went down into the cellar, he made a mental note that the steps never squeaked. When they reached the bottom and the woman had lowered the door, they were shrouded in darkness and damp, stale air; panic began to clutch at their stomachs. The musty smell of dirt and things old invaded their nostrils. Only the scantest fragments of light reached their lair through the cracks in the floor. The sound of shouting officers and crying civilians drifted down to them. The French provosts were forcing their way into home after home, and in some cases, they were having their way with the women, as could be heard by their pitiful screams.

"I can't tell if they have found the dead sentry yet or not," whispered McKinney. He clung to the hope that they wouldn't miss the boy for a while. After all, desertions were not uncommon, especially among the French Army's young recruits. With their hearts racing, the confined men strained to hear what was happening in the street above.

A large calloused hand grabbed McKinney's shoulder. "Listen." Loud knocking vibrated throughout Elizabeth Feirra's house as French voices shouted, "Madame, we are using your house to accommodate Captain Louis LaFloure and his two lieutenants. Please open the door."

Blood drained from her face, leaving her features pale and gaunt as she stood just back from the door and listened. Closing her eyes, she took a deep breath and suddenly realized that her hair and clothes were a mess.

"Madame, must we kick the door down?" shouted the irritated provost. Hurriedly, she straightened her hair, smoothed her crumpled cotton dress as best she could, and reached a trembling hand for the doorknob. Opening it ever so slowly, she found herself staring at her new houseguests. Captain LaFloure stood in a bad attempt at attention, his blue trousers and jacket, the standard dress of the Voltiguers or light infantry, were filthy. His lieutenants were in a similar state of disarray. The provost, who was busy making notes on his roster sheet, wore white trousers with a white shoulder belt across the blue jacket. Elizabeth could tell Captain LaFloure was quite drunk, as were his two aides. The provost smiled dutifully, did a slight bow, clicked his heels, and trudged off toward the next house with his remaining group of officers in tow. The drunken voices of the Frenchmen drifted down to where McKinney and his men crouched in the dark like cornered rats.

"They're drunk," hissed McKinney as he turned his good ear toward the door in hope of catching the conversation from upstairs.

Elizabeth tried hard to quiet the soldiers as they staggered down the short hall and into the area where the child slept, but her efforts were wasted, and the baby soon began to cry.

"Prepare us some food, wench. No, get us more wine. Yes, both, and shut that damn baby up." The drunken LaFloure shouted his demands as he plopped down on one of the three chairs and began to pull off his boots.

"Yes, more wine," parroted the two lieutenants, who staggered around in search of a place to sit. They were soon mimicking their captain, pulling their boots off, and leaning back in the wicker-backed chairs that groaned from the misuse.

McKinney and his men could hear Elizabeth trying to shush the baby, but to no avail. Her frantic tones were being drowned out by the drunken shouts of the emperor's finest. McKinney had begun inching up the stairs, ever cautious of a creaking board, when Sergeant Malone's big hand grabbed his arm.

"Wait until they're asleep, then we will kill the bastards," he whispered, venom dripping from his every word.

"We may not be able to wait that long," growled McKinney, but he slowly eased back down to the bottom of the steps where he kept listening, his blood boiling.

The French officers continued to press their demands for more wine, and everyone held their breath as they heard Elizabeth's footsteps nearing the trap door.

"Madame, what is in that cellar?" Lieutenant Pierre Dupree asked drunkenly, grabbing Elizabeth's arm and spinning her around toward him. He tried to focus his bloodshot eyes enough to gaze down her bodice, but he was unsteady on his feet and only managed to stagger into her, forcing her to hold him up.

"Sir, that … that is my wine cellar," she stammered. "I have only wine down there"—her mind spun—"and of course, rats, very big rats, monsieur."

"Rats," spat Dupree. "I hate fucking rats." And with that, he staggered back to collapse into a chair near the fire, leaving Elizabeth to raise the trap door and ease down the steps.

McKinney's eyes blinked rapidly as the flood of light washed into the cellar. He watched as she hiked her skirt and carefully made her way down, unable to see well in the dim light. McKinney's biggest fear was that she would trip and the French scum would look down into the hole to see what happened, but she didn't. Keeping a close eye on the top of the steps, half expecting one of the crapauds to appear there, he handed her two bottles of wine from out of the dark corner they had crept into.

"Please help me," she pleaded, clutching the wine bottles to her breasts. "I'm afraid that they will hurt my baby."

McKinney grabbed her shoulders, pulled her to him, and whispered into her ear, "We're all dead if we don't wait a little while longer. Encourage them to drink all this wine." He handed her the third and last bottle. "Then figure out a way to distract them so we can sneak up out of this hole and cut their throats."

"How can I distract them?" she cried, looking at him with big saucer eyes. McKinney quickly placed his hand over her mouth and growled in a low whisper.

"You're a woman for God's sake. You'll think of something." He led her back to the steps where he forced a smile and squeezed her arm. "It will be all right," he said and then disappeared back into the shadows.

"God help us," she moaned as she climbed back up the steps, turning back for a brief moment before closing the door.

Darkness engulfed the cellar once more, and Elizabeth, gathering her thoughts, walked back toward the drunken French officers.

Thankfully, the baby managed to go back to sleep, and Elizabeth finished preparing what scant food she had: beans, a few potatoes, and hard bread. Her hands shook noticeably as she carried three plates over to the small wooden table where the men sat. They passed around the last bottle of wine as the two lieutenants laughed loudly at their captain's jokes.

Out of squinty, bloodshot eyes, LaFloure glanced briefly at the food and then at the dark-haired woman as she set down the plates. A wicked grin crept across his face, and he rubbed the stubble on his chin as he gazed at her ample breasts.

"I see what I want to eat." He laughed, draining the wine from the bottle he held in his hand.

With burgundy-colored wine running down his chin, he slammed the empty bottle down on the table and made an awkward attempt to stand. Although his mind was somewhat ready, his feet were unwilling. One socked foot shot out from under him, and he collapsed back into the chair, which groaned in protest. Angrily, he shoved the food off the table, the tin plate clattering loudly on the wooden floor. He watched it wobble for a second, seemingly surprised that his supper had spilled out.

"Fuck," he cursed loudly, kicking the plate across the room. Then he grabbed Elizabeth's arm and dragged her toward him. She flung herself back out of fear and disgust, managing to momentarily break free from his grip. Her mind spun. She thought for a second about simply running from her house, but she couldn't because of the baby. She dared a glance at the rug that hid the trap door and fought briefly with the urge to shout for help, all the while slowly backing away from her attacker who rose shakily to his feet.

LaFloure was drunk, but his right hand was still fast like a snake. It shot out again, locking onto her wrist. This time, he jerked her up against him and ground his manhood into her thigh.

"You will love this, bitch," he hissed into her ear and began pulling her toward the small brass bed that sat in the corner near the fireplace.

"No, please, no! Let me go!" As she pleaded with LaFloure, Elizabeth reluctantly allowed herself to be directed toward the bed and away from the trap door.

Lieutenant Bourgeois was leaning heavily against the fireplace, so fully engrossed in watching his captain strip the dress off the red-haired Portuguese wench that he never heard the door to the cellar rise nor the rug slide down and pool at the hinged base. His eyes were fixated on the woman, whose left breast was already exposed when

LaFloure suddenly tired of the struggle and slapped her hard across the face. She fell on the bed, sobbing as the sharp pain pierced her cheek.

While the tragedy played out near the bed, the trapdoor was laid down atop the woolen rug and McKinney peeked out at the scene, just as Elizabeth was slapped. The muscles in his neck and shoulders tightened, and his eyes filled with hate as he watched the woman sob into her torn dress. Like any combat veteran, he looked around and surveyed the scene before contemplating his next move. He saw that Lieutenant Dupree had passed out in the wicker-backed chair just five feet from the trap door. The other French scum was watching his captain oblivious to anything else. Sergeant Malone, who had crept up the stairs to stand beside McKinney, nodded toward the passed-out lieutenant, and both men understood the gesture. McKinney, moving like a cat, crawled up out of the cellar and eased toward the swaying Lieutenant Bourgeois, who remained totally mesmerized by the attempted rape in front of him. Sliding in behind Bourgeois, McKinney shared a quick nod with Malone, and the big Irishman prepared to drag his knife across the throat of the unlucky Lieutenant Dupree. Both men nodded again. With his right hand, McKinney drove his dagger hard into the lower back of the French officer. His left hand clamped across the man's mouth as air mixed with blood exploded from between the Frenchman's clinched teeth. Ten feet away, Malone pressed down hard on his knife as he pulled it across soft flesh. The razor-sharp blade cut through jugular and windpipe like so much butter, and the job was done. Dupree's eyes flew open, and he reached desperately for his throat as a wet gurgling sound escaped the wound, but it was far too late. His body jerked like a fish out of water as Malone held him down in the chair. A bloody mist sprayed into the air, and after a few more frantic heartbeats, the Frenchman lay still. Malone silently lowered the limp form to the floor and moved to help McKinney. Dupree died without knowing who killed him or why.

McKinney wasn't as lucky in his efforts with Bourgeois; the blade had missed the man's kidney and lodged tightly in the thick cartilage surrounding the ribcage. He struggled in a bizarre dance with the Frenchman as he heaved backward in an awkward attempt to withdraw the knife. His hand slipped from the lieutenant's mouth, and blood spewed forth, the Frenchman choking and gasping for breath. But the knife remained firmly lodged. Their dance of death drove them forward until they reached the edge of the bed, where LaFloure was still busy trying to rip the remainder of Elizabeth's dress off her body.

In a last-ditch effort, McKinney pushed hard on the Frenchman's back as he pulled with all his might on the dagger. A sickening scraping sound accompanied their separation. McKinney staggered back slightly when the knife slid out and Lieutenant Bourgeois slumped forward, falling alongside the lusting Captain LaFloure, who realized with a start that something was very wrong.

Elizabeth, fighting for her life, was only partly aware of what was happening until she saw the dying lieutenant sprawled on the bed. Glancing up, she quickly released the top of her dress in an attempt to distract LaFloure. The dress fell to her waist in several tattered pieces, and LaFloure smiled wickedly at her nakedness. She forced a smile herself and grabbed the French captain around the waist, pulling him toward her in an attempt to delay his reaction to the disruption, but she was unsuccessful. Even through the fog of his drunkenness and the lust of the moment, LaFloure recognized danger. He slapped her hard across the cheek once more, breaking her grasp, and then reached for his pistol. Stunned, Elizabeth flew back against the headboard, her head spinning and blood dripping from her split lip onto her exposed breasts.

Even though LaFloure was quite drunk and even though his trousers were down around his knees, he still somehow managed to pull his pistol from its holster. Spinning toward McKinney, who was crouched at the foot of the bed ready to leap, he aimed the straight bore single-shot Gerent pistol at McKinney's chest. McKinney came out of the crouch and stood rigid, frozen in time. His pounding heart actually began to slow down. He didn't see his life pass in front of his eyes, as some say happens just before you die, but he did figure his fighting days were over. He stared stoically into the looming black hole and held his breath, awaiting the inevitable.

Suddenly, a look of both pain and confusion spread across LaFloure's weathered face; he lurched forward, then jerked backward and sideways as a knife thrown by Sergeant Malone sliced into his heart. The tip of Malone's knife almost touched the tip of a second knife that Elizabeth thrust into the Frenchman's back. LaFloure fell, quite dead, upon the body of Lieutenant Bourgeois. The baby slept on.

A hard, cold silence gripped the combatants while the sound of the crackling fire and heavy breathing enveloped the room. The remaining skirmishers began to cautiously emerge from the cellar, their rifles held at the ready. Soon they all stood motionless at the top of the cellar steps and looked down at the dead Frenchmen. Soft sighs from the sleeping child stood in stark contrast to the horror of the last few minutes. Malone stooped down and searched through the pockets of the dead Frenchmen while McKinney leaned against the fireplace, trying to collect his thoughts. Elizabeth sat on the edge of the bed and sobbed softly as she worked in vain to salvage her torn dress.

A loud crashing sound, like the coming of the Grim Reaper, filled the room, and the front door suddenly burst open. The rest of the skirmishers, who had just emerged from the cellar, swung their rifles toward what they expected to be a French infantry assault. But instead of a mass of Voltigeurs, another drunken French officer staggered through the door and down the narrow hallway. This one was a colonel of the cavalry. His dark blue trousers, as well as his boots, were new but filthy, his blue jacket unbuttoned and sprinkled with mud. In his right hand was a bottle of cognac, but only a swig or two of the smoky brew remained. Although he was quite drunk, it didn't take this officer but a few heartbeats to understand what he had walked in on. He stared at his dead friend, Captain LaFloure, with a dazed and angry grimace on his face. McKinney, who was stone-cold sober, was quick in his reaction to this new threat.

Growling, "Another damn drunk Frenchman," and fearing the problems that several Baker rifle shots would present, he leaped at the stunned cavalryman with his dagger. Death rode the sharp edge of the blade as McKinney went for the throat.

Running toward the startled men, Elizabeth screamed, "No, please, no more," her trembling hands reaching out in a desperate attempt to stop another killing. In the commotion and loud shouting, her son woke, looked around in confusion for a second before his lower lip began to quiver slightly and a wailing rose from his lungs. Elizabeth glanced down at her crying child and then back at McKinney, who stood frozen in his death thrust.

"My husband's death has been avenged with the killing of these swine," she said, pointing to the three corpses. "Let this"—she searched her mind for a word—"bastard live. Please, no more killing."

The stunned Frenchman stared wide-eyed at McKinney, whose dagger had stopped less than an inch from his neck. Adrenaline pumped hard through McKinney's body, but he managed to take a deep breath and lower his dagger. He glared at the Frenchman and was about to instruct Malone to gag him, when he stopped, turned his head to the side, and listened intently to some sound that for the moment only he seemed to hear. Concerned, everyone in the room stared at McKinney as they attempted to detect whatever it was that he was straining to hear.

"What in the bloody hell is the matter, sir?" asked Sergeant Malone, who himself could hear nothing out of the ordinary.

"Do you not hear that?" fumed an agitated McKinney.

"Hear what?" Malone shot back with nervous anger in his voice.

"That damn dove," shouted McKinney. "Tell me you don't hear that bloody dove cooing."

Everyone in the small band let out a sigh of relief; they had feared that maybe some attack was about to ensue. Now they simply exchanged less worried glances, growing quiet to listen to the dove. Even the French colonel turned his head so he too could hear.

"Okay, sir, it's a bloody dove. There are thousands of the damn things around," grunted Malone, his face full of confusion. "What's so important about it?" McKinney just stared at him; he wasn't going to attempt to explain the irony.

The dove, perched high on a sill just outside the front door, continued its call. The sound floated eerily in the night air as occasional sobs and drunken shouts offered a bizarre backdrop.

Elizabeth coughed lightly before she spoke: "My mother used to call them peace doves." A smile spread across her battered face, and she thought about her childhood as she walked over to her child's crib. The sound of tiny wings beating the air announced the dove's exit and an end to its serenade.

"So did my mother," said McKinney as he ignored Malone and turned to watch the woman sink to her knees beside the crib.

"No more killing, please, no more," she pleaded with a voice as soft as the departed dove's while attempting to sooth her child's crying.

Tears that she had courageously held back for the last hour burst forth and began to run down her swollen cheeks, stinging her split lip. She sang an old lullaby as she patted the child's back. McKinney watched her as he struggled to recall the childhood tune, but no answer came, and he was forced to shake his head in order to clear his mind. The futile search for the name of the tune was replaced by more puzzling questions. *How could she ask for mercy for this French scum after all that she has been through?* He glanced around the room and realized that everyone was looking at him now, even the French colonel, who had sobered up very quickly. Sober but not very steady on his feet, the Frenchman leaned against the doorframe to keep from falling flat on his face. The eager young skirmishers were expecting, even hoping for, some sort of swift retribution on the Frenchman. McKinney's hand shook from wanting to deliver it, but the Elizabeth's words of mercy still rang in his ear.

Standing near the doorway, Malone's mind raced in an effort to figure out how to extract their little group from the situation they were in.

"Sir"—he coughed—"the colonel would make a fine prisoner for our Colonel O'Shounessey. Don't you think?" He was eager to get out of town, even if it meant taking the crapaud along.

McKinney looked at his friend and then at the Frenchman. "All right, Sergeant Malone, but if that damn crapaud so much as coughs,

I'll cut his throat"—he paused—"and yours. Tie his hands and gag him. We need to get the hell out of here, now!"

Sergeant Malone tied the colonel's hands with some rough cord from his pack, and then turned him around in order to look straight into his bloodshot eyes.

"I want your word as an officer and a gentleman"—Malone spat the words—"that you will remain silent." He paused to look over at McKinney. "If you don't make a sound, you may live. If you dare to cry out for help, that man"—Malone nodded at McKinney—"will cut your throat … slowly. Do you understand?"

The Frenchman cleared his throat. "Yes, Sergeant, I fully understand, and I give you my word as a French officer that I will raise no alarm." The colonel stood at attention as he spoke, then clicked his heels together sharply and attempted a slight smile. Malone glared at the man and spat at his feet before he shoved him toward the door.

"Crawford, you and Koons hide the bodies in the cellar. Clean the floor as best you can." McKinney paused. "And do it quickly," he ordered. Standing off to the side, he pondered what to do with the woman and her child. After a few minutes, he walked over to where she knelt.

"You know the French will find these bodies sooner or later. You can't stay here." He spoke in a low voice, afraid he would wake the child, who had finally gone back to sleep but stirred slightly.

"I have nowhere to go," she stated flatly, fighting back more tears. "They"—she nodded toward the French colonel—"killed both my father and my husband. My mother died two years ago from the pox." She looked down and shook her head before going on. "My father was English. My mother was Portuguese. He met her in Lisbon while he was serving in your navy. My father became a cloth merchant after he left the navy and spent a great deal of time in Spain. He got caught up in that terrible evacuation from Madrid and was shot because he was English. Can you believe that? For simply being an Englishman. God, how can men be so cruel?"

"Not all men are that cruel, ma'am, even during war. And this damn war will end someday. All wars do," answered McKinney, watching the dead Frenchmen being dragged unceremoniously down the steps of the cellar, their heads banging with a thud on each step. *The rats will feast tonight,* he thought as he brought his eyes back to the woman.

"What will you do when this war ends, Mr. McKinney?" asked Elizabeth, looking into his blue eyes, hoping to get a glimpse of the man inside.

"I'm not sure, ma'am. Find another war, I suppose. It's the only thing I seem to be good at anymore," he replied, a little unsure of where the conversation was going.

She stared at him for several seconds before she spoke. "I doubt that very much," she whispered and blushed when she said it.

McKinney glanced around the room at his men. "I think there will always be a need for men like me, mainly because there will always be men like them," he said, nodding at the French colonel. "Men who want to take that which is not theirs." He looked at the blood stains on the floor "Those men must be stopped." He turned his gaze toward her battered face. "Men like me and those boys"—he nodded at his group of green jackets—"we try to stop them."

Without hesitating, Elizabeth asked, "Why?" She was intrigued by this rugged man who had invaded her house and, by doing so, probably saved her life.

"Every man has his own reasons, ma'am; some men join for the sixpence and a rum that the king pays us each day, some join to see the world or stay out of jail, and some join because they think it is the right thing to do."

"What is your reason, Ensign McKinney?" She nearly whispered the question.

Before McKinney could answer, Sergeant Malone shouted from the door where he and the French officer stood: "Sir, we best be moving before the frogs miss their friends."

McKinney looked down at her. "I'm not really sure anymore," he said. Elizabeth smiled slightly and turned her back to him as she anticipated their leaving. He stood as if his feet were frozen to the floor and looked at the back of her tattered dress, red welts running across her shoulders. Malone shuffled his feet in the doorway, but he knew better than to rush his friend, even as the seconds ticked by.

"I can't leave you here," McKinney whispered, having made up his mind about what to do. "Gather what things we can carry and come with us." He turned, walked to the front door, and stared out into the night, his mind going over the immediate problem of getting back across the street without being seen.

Less than five minutes later, Elizabeth stood in the middle of the small room, ready to go. She wore a dark-blue cotton shift, riding boots, and a brightly colored woolen scarf upon her head. She had a small black bag in one hand, stuffed with personal items and two changes of clothes for her son; she carried the child in the other.

"That's it?" McKinney asked, looking down at the bag.

"That's it," she replied simply, already starting for the door. Halfway across the room, she stopped and looked back as if she had forgotten something, then spun and walked out the door.

"Sergeant Malone, I'll take point. You take rear," growled McKinney in a low whisper as he moved toward the door, the rest of the group filing out of the apartment behind him.

"Yes, sir," replied Malone, a sly smile forming on his ruddy face as he fell in behind the last man out the door. Their shadows, long and sinister, danced on the nearby stucco walls as the band raced back across the narrow street. The oil-burning street lamps, their light muted by filthy globes, shed just enough light to guide their departure. Far off in the night, a lone dog barked at unseen intruders, and a few drunken voices escaped from behind closed doors. Otherwise, the night was quiet.

* * * * *

McKinney, ever wary of more sentries, led the skirmishers back across the dirt street. Once across, they melted into the shadows and headed for the gulley. McKinney was also worried that the baby would start crying and was surprised when he looked over and saw the child was not only wide awake but seemingly enjoying the journey.

Going back up the gulley was terribly slow and much more difficult than the trip down. The gulley floor was strewn with fist-sized rocks, and the blindfolded Frenchman seemed to trip on every one of them. The blindfold had been McKinney's idea; he didn't trust many officers, especially the French, but it was becoming painfully apparent that something needed to change. At one point, the colonel stumbled on a rocky tangle of debris, and both he and the corporal guiding him fell with a loud clatter.

"Bloody hell," growled McKinney as he watched two of his men help the obviously shaken Frenchman to his feet. "Sergeant Malone, take that blindfold off the bastard, and if he stumbles one more time, kill him."

"Yes, sir," replied Malone, walking toward the Frenchman. Elizabeth shifted her son in her arms so that his back was to the colonel. She glanced anxiously at McKinney and then at Sergeant Malone, who was reaching for the blindfold.

"You wouldn't," she whispered, shock and disbelief in her voice.

McKinney stepped over beside her and placed a finger over her lips; he mouthed the word *watch*. Malone spun the colonel around by the shoulder and jerked the blindfold off. Blinking several times to clear his vision, the Frenchman looked up at the big Irishman and then over at McKinney. Their eyes locked for a second, and McKinney knew the man had heard his order. Nodding curtly, the Frenchman simply turned and followed Corporal Hartman, his handler, up the gulley. He never stumbled again.

To the east, a large silver orb rose slowly over the Sierra Los Padres, casting long shadows out into the field that McKinney's band needed to cross.

"We'll stay in the shadows along the edge of the fields as best we can," whispered McKinney as he and Sergeant Malone struggled up the gulley's steep slope.

"Yes, sir," replied Malone. Having moved from his rearguard position, he relayed the order down the line: "Stay in the shadows once we reach the fields," the words a near hiss in his gruff Irish accent.

Twenty minutes later, the last man having crawled up out of the gulley, they took a break in the cool of the shadows. Far below, a heavy damp fog had crept out of the nearby creek, hiding most of the lights in the village. A few dogs barked at alley cats that prowled the night, but otherwise, the night remained peaceful. As they sat in hushed conservation, a dark shape floated across the overgrown field in front of Elizabeth, and she glanced skyward in curiosity.

"What kind of bird is that, Mr. McKinney?" asked Elizabeth after failing to identify the source of the shadow.

Both McKinney and Malone followed her gaze toward the great hawk as it floated above the field just to their west. The three-quarter moon was shining bright, causing the few stars that were out to pale in comparison.

"That's one of my ancestors," answered McKinney, only half joking. "At least that's what my father believes …" his voice trailing off with a tone more serious than he had intended.

After a couple of awkward minutes in which Elizabeth made no reply to his jest, McKinney found himself oddly disappointed and a little sad. His mother, who thought he was bad for it anyway, would have called it sulking when he was young. Regardless, the feeling was real. *Maybe I'm just depressed*, he thought. Tearing his eyes away from the hawk, he began to carefully wipe the dew off his Baker rifle with an oily rag that he kept in his rucksack. The silence dampened his mood even more, and after a few swipes with the oilcloth, he grunted.

"Let's move out," he said, shouldering his rifle. Despite his aching foot, he stepped out in a determined gait, causing the entire group to double time in order to catch up.

"It's a hawk, ma'am," Malone said, answering the nearly forgotten question as he shouldered his pack and walked to the rear of the column.

His foul mood festering, McKinney led the group along the edge of the shadows that jutted out irregularly across the moonlit field just to their right. Adding to his discomfort, a painful blister began to form on his right foot, and he cursed his new boots as he stomped through the knee-high grass and weeds. Grumbling to himself, he glanced up where the hawk sailed across the face of the moon that had crawled halfway through the sky. "A little easier for you, ol' boy," he whispered and limped toward the crest of the nearest hill, the last one separating them from the British picket lines.

"Sergeant Malone," McKinney called out sharply.

"Sir," responded Malone, who was still the last man in the strung-out line of green jackets.

"Send Private McClure out as flank scout. We don't want to be shot by our own pickets now, do we?"

"No, we don't, sir, and yes, sir, I'll send McClure hunting," replied Malone crisply, troubled by his friend's dark mood. He walked down the line, looking at the tired, dirty faces of his skirmishers as he searched for McClure, who stood quietly in line and never let on that he was aware of being searched for. When Malone finally did spot him, he pulled the tall, lanky Welshman aside.

"Hiding were you, Private?" he asked.

"No, Sergeant, I was merely waiting," came the reply in a heavy Celtic accent.

"Huh," grunted Malone before turning serious. "Well, Mr. McKinney wants you to walk out on our left flank, say, about a hundred feet." The Welshman turned to move out through the brush, but Malone grabbed his arm.

"And, McClure." Malone looked past the private into the dark shadows.

"Yes, Sergeant," McClure followed his gaze.

"Walk careful. The boys on picket may be a little trigger-happy tonight, with the frogs being this close and all."

"I'll be like a mouse, Sergeant," whispered McClure as he eased out of line heading toward the south and soon disappearing in the thick brush like a stag slipping into a thicket.

He walked out about a hundred feet and turned parallel to the skirmishers' path. His hunting skills, honed as a youth back in the hill country of Wales, served him well as he moved soundlessly through the dark woods.

McKinney's mind drifted to the young sentry he had killed back in the village. He just couldn't shake the image of the boy's gaze as his life spilled out onto the ground. Deep in that dark memory, he jumped slightly when Elizabeth whispered just inches from his ear.

"John, what will become of me when we reach your camp?" The question, alongside the scent of her hair, floated on the air as they trudged down the sloping ridge through more thick underbrush. He was still a little miffed at her, but her nearness gave him pause. He cleared his throat, taking time to think.

"A-hum"—he coughed—"since your father was English, I'm sure Lord Wellington will give you and the baby free passage to England. After that ..." McKinney shrugged, his voice tapering off. His eyes fixed straight ahead, he waited for her voice near his ear again, but when several minutes passed with no response, he saddened again. It was her fear of rejection that kept her silent, but he had no way of knowing that. *Snap out of this shit*, his mind shouted. In the past, his best method of pulling his mind out of a sad hole was to focus on the business at hand, so that was what he did. They were nearing an overgrown thicket of scrub Cork trees and Cistaceae shrubs, and he slowed their pace, peering into the brush, ever cautious of being shot by his own men.

He was staring at the horizon, trying to identify a bizarre shadow, when something touched his shoulder. He spun around quickly and bumped Elizabeth with his rifle. She was staring at him, her big brown eyes revealing a depth of emotion.

"I would like to stay with you, John McKinney, at least for a while," she whispered, her face reddening slightly. Uttering these bold words made her nervous but not ashamed. *I have the boy to think about as well as myself, and besides, he seems like a good man*, she thought. Thankful that the moon had crept behind a row of dark clouds, shadowing her face, she waited for his answer.

Ensign John McKinney, battle-hardened soldier, was a little shocked by her request. He stopped and looked back at her for a long time, as if for the first time. The moon peeked out for just a moment; its silver beams danced in her hair and brightened her sparkling eyes. As the seconds passed slowly, she started to become afraid that he would say *no*. And this time, it was her heart that sank.

After what seemed an eternity to her but was in fact only a few seconds, McKinney began to reply.

"I ... I ..." he stammered, unable to form any distinguishable words.

She watched his mouth attempt to form words, but no sound came out.

"Are you all right?" she asked, looking into his eyes with a mischievous little smile on her face.

After another long pause, he took a deep breath.

"Yes, I'm bloody all right. And yes, you can stay with me, if you wish," he added with a cough, turning back to the front in an attempt to hide his smile.

She watched him walk on ahead into the brush. *He seems so shy*, she thought. Then hugging her son close to her bosom, she followed behind the obviously flustered Ensign McKinney. They came to yet another small clearing, and she glanced up at the harvest moon before they stumbled back into the brush. She almost laughed when she saw the hawk, which seemed to be following them, joined by a small bird—a dove of all things. *A good sign*, she thought and watched the birds sail through the air, their wing tips almost touching. No one else seemed to notice, and she made no mention of it. As she walked along, Elizabeth began to realize how pleasantly surprised she was by this soldier, this man who seemed so brave and hard yet so reserved in matters of life. She liked that about him.

McKinney was just beginning to step over a log that had fallen from atop a small rock outcropping when a very proper Lancaster's voice shouted, "Halt, who goes there?"

He froze midstride, his heart pounding in his chest. He knew that the picket line was close, but he hadn't seen or heard them before just now!

"It's Ensign McKinney. I have a prisoner for Colonel O'Shounessey," he managed to say in a stern commander's voice. "And where the bloody hell is McClure?" he cursed under his breath before shouting, "Send someone to get the colonel. And try not to shoot any of us. We're coming through your lines."

"Yes, sir!" shouted the sentry. "Please advance to be recognized."

McKinney began to step forward and realized that he had been holding his foot up like some kind of damn hunting dog. Grumbling to himself, he marched out of the brush while Malone kept the rest of the group hidden, just in case. As McKinney moved forward, the old warrior intuition, a sense of unease, wrapped around him; something wasn't right. He had not heard anyone leaving to get Colonel O'Shounessey. Plus, he could see the sentries through the remaining brush, and they were fidgeting like nervous cats. He stepped cautiously to the picket line, a low wall of logs about three feet high and a foot thick. He quickly saw why the pickets were acting strangely. Woods-born and trained, Malcolm McClure had not only guarded their flank but had somehow gotten behind the sentries and sneaked up to surprise them. McClure stood with a large grin on his face, his Baker rifle pointed at the three angry and embarrassed sentries.

"Private McClure, I believe that you can lower your rifle now," ordered McKinney. He was trying hard not to smile but failing miserably, which embarrassed the sentries even more.

"Yes, sir," replied McClure. Stepping back, he shouldered his rifle and stood at attention.

"Damn green jackets," cursed one of the sentries. "You think you are so good."

"We are, Private," growled Malone as he brought the rest of the group out of the brush and marched them up to the line.

Walking past the smirking sentries, they headed toward the main camp and Colonel O'Shounessey's headquarters. Word of their arrival spread faster than McKinney's band could move, and Colonel O'Shounessey soon met them on the outskirts of the British encampment.

"Well, Ensign McKinney, what have we got here?" O'Shounessey quizzed as he eyed the French colonel with interest.

"Sir, this is ..." McKinney never finished his introduction. The snapping of heels was quickly followed by the nasal voice of the French colonel introducing himself.

"Sir, allow me to present myself. I'm Colonel Alexis Benoit of the Emperor's twelfth Battalion, under le General Soult." The heel snapped again as both McKinney and O'Shounessey stared at him.

"I see," said O'Shounessey, looking the man up and down. "Well, Colonel, please allow me to introduce myself. I'm Colonel

Patrick O'Shounessey of His Majesty's 1st Highlanders, and this is my aide, Captain Queen." Queen stepped forward and awkwardly bent at the waist. "Please allow Captain Queen to escort you back to my headquarters. We can chat there later," stated O'Shounessey, trying hard to hide a smirk.

"Certainly," said Benoit, and he followed Captain Queen through the British camp.

O'Shounessey watched the Frenchman walk away. "Damn arrogant French," he growled.

McKinney watched the colonel walk away, too, having temporally forgotten the woman he brought along until she walked up to stand by his side. Elizabeth smiled, rendering McKinney nearly speechless until he could gather himself. O'Shounessey seemed content staring out through the camp, and finally McKinney had to cough in order to get his attention.

"Colonel O'Shounessey, sir. This is Senora Elizabeth Feirra. It was her home that we were able to hide in. Without her help, sir, we would probably still be trapped back in Leira." Remembering their conservation at her house, he added, "Sir, her father was English. He was shot by the crapauds when they took Madrid. Her husband was Portuguese, a lieutenant in the cavalry. He was killed at the battle of Almeida."

O'Shounessey pondered the information before he bowed.

"My condolence on your husband's death as well as your father's, madam. But it's my pleasure to meet you, Mrs. Feirra." He took her hand and kissed it. "Our accommodations are quite meager, but you are welcome to use my tent until we can find better arrangements." Elizabeth nodded and quickly glanced up at McKinney for help.

McKinney coughed again. "Sir, Mrs. Feirra will be staying with me."

"Oh, I see," said O'Shounessey with a twinkle in his eye. He had liked the young ensign for several years, so he was pleased for McKinney even if the woman would only stay for a short while.

"Well, in that case, let me thank you again for your help, Mrs. Feirra. If there isn't anything else I can do for you, I will go see what information Colonel Benoit has for me. Goodnight." He bowed again and marched off.

McKinney and Elizabeth stood side by side, their hips touching ever so slightly as they watched O'Shounessey march toward his tent. McKinney could feel the heat from her body through his trousers; it was like a warm fire calling him closer. As they stood together, the wind began to stir, and the moon was able to escape from behind the dark swirling clouds once again, its silvery light, causing O'Shounessey's shadow to float eerily tall out in from of him. Like a man on stilts, it moved through the long rows of dirty white tents.

O'Shounessey's mind was moving as fast as his feet. He knew that the French supply lines were stretched way too thin in their drive south, and that meant the frogs badly needed to take the port city of Alhondra for their resupply. Soult's decision to attack through the village of Leira was well suited for his cavalry, for which Colonel Alexis Benoit was a battalion commander. O'Shounessey needed to know everything that Benoit knew.

Malone was dead tired, and for some bloody reason, his head hurt like hell. With his head down to ease the throbbing, he led the skirmishers toward their tents, leaving McKinney and the woman alone. Without saying a word, McKinney slid his arm around Elizabeth's waist, pulled her tight, and walked the exhausted woman and her baby toward his tent. Passing through the army camp at rest, McKinney listened to the old familiar sounds of horses stomping and sentries walking their posts. These simple things were constants in his life now, but he worried that they wouldn't bring Elizabeth the same contentment. With a barely audible grunt that Elizabeth didn't seem to notice, he pushed the worrying thoughts to the back of his mind and watched the horizon turn a pale orange in the eastern hills. Daylight wasn't far off, and the cooks were already beginning to stir when he and Elizabeth finally reached his tent.

He paused before pulling back the tent flap, hoping she wouldn't mind the odd-smelling combination of sweat and gun oil permeated the air. As she entered, she showed no sign of concern, not even a slight crinkling of the nose. She just bent her head slightly and entered his home. He was close behind, very close. Walking over to a lone canvas cot that sat stuffed into the far left corner of the tent, she laid her son on two army blankets stacked there.

"We named him Sterling, after my father," she told him. And he agreed that it was a proper English name.

"This is not much of a bedroom," McKinney whispered as she lay the child down.

"I have slept in worse," she replied softly, patting the boy on the back. "The Portuguese Army was not very good to its junior officers."

McKinney's breath caught in his throat as she rose from her knees and walked up to him. Standing up on her toes, she kissed him softly on the lips.

"I ... I ..." he stammered.

"Shhh," she whispered and slowly removed her woolen cloak. Then she slipped out of her cotton dress, one of only two she had brought with her. The sound of cloth sliding over skin was like music to his ears.

The moon peered from behind dark angry clouds casting a yellowish glow through the tent onto Elizabeth's soft olive skin. She smiled and carefully stepped out of the dress that crumpled at her feet. Bathed in the pale light, goose bumps forming over her body, she waited, heart pounding, for John McKinney to take her into his arms. He stepped forward, shedding his own clothes, and eagerly pulled her toward him.

Breath exploded from Elizabeth's trembling lips as she became lost in the heat of the moment, their naked bodies touching in intimate passion. She moaned softly while McKinney rained wet kisses on her neck and then down to her swollen breasts. Her mouth opened to accept McKinney's searching tongue and the fires, too long repressed, exploded in wave after wave of pleasure that pounded their flesh. The special ingredients needed for young lovers, lust and passion, found their expression again and again until at last they lay exhausted and slept. Elizabeth's hand fell lightly to rest on the blanket that covered her child, and all seemed at peace in the world for a while.

But three miles away the French generals plotted.

* * * * *

An hour later, McKinney was awakened from a troubled sleep by the stirring of the army camp. The cooks shouted orders to the servants while sergeants cursed at soldiers who refused to crawl from under their warm blankets. He lay there taking in all the old familiar sounds along with a new one, the soft breathing of a young woman beside him. He turned on his side so he could look at her and watched her one exposed breast slowly rise and fall. The early morning light dancing on her reddish-brown hair tossed wildly about her sleeping face stirred his desire but also something much deeper. He reached out and touched the soft skin of her arm, and she stirred slightly. McKinney had never felt this way in all of his twenty-five years. Sure, he had been with his share of eager young lassies back in Oban, but this woman was different, quite different. *Is it love?* he wondered. *If it isn't, then it has to be damn close.* Reluctantly, he eased off the cot and gathered his clothes, deciding to dress outside so that he wouldn't wake Elizabeth or the baby.

Stepping quietly out onto the grass that surprisingly was covered with a light frost, he looked around at the British war machine. Hundreds of tents stretched in several straight rows, and together, they completely covered the small field in front of him. Just as many horses were tied to their picket lines as they waited for their day of work to begin. To his left, the battered old camp chair he had lugged around for two years sat askew near the fire pit. Dirty white smoke curled up from the damp ashes as he walked toward the chair, his footprints lingering in the wet grass. Once near the chair, he proceeded to hop about like a one-legged man in a sack race until he managed to get his trousers on. Somewhat angry at his dance in the frost, he sat down and struggled to pull his boots on over his wet socks. He got his right foot in first, the blister still sore and hurting like hell. McKinney stomped down carefully in order to check the fit before pulling the left boot on. Looking up into the early morning sky, he was surprised to see a hawk—*maybe the hawk from last night*—gliding through the air with a dove by its side. The pair flew high above the camp, the lonesome echo of the hawk's cry floating off toward the nearby hills. McKinney turned toward the tent where Elizabeth slept, holding his gaze for a brief moment. When he looked skyward once more, the hawk and dove were nowhere to be seen.

Once he was properly dressed, McKinney made his way toward Colonel O'Shounessey's headquarters as the chaos of the camp's morning ritual raged around him. His mind was still focused on Elizabeth. She had touched a part of him that no other woman had ever touched, and it was shocking. *Could this be the right woman for me? Could this be love?* These thoughts crept slowly through his mind, which sorely needed some rejuvenation. *The Army has been my mistress for several years now. Is there even room for a woman, any woman, in my life? Plus, this woman is a young widow with a small child.*

"I'll be damned, I just don't know." He mumbled the statement aloud just before walking into a long dark shadow.

"And that you might be, if you don't watch where you're walking." A very bemused Sergeant Malone chuckled. He took a step back and stood grinning as McKinney nearly plowed straight over him. "Begging the ensign's pardon, but it does seem as if you had a very good time last night." When McKinney's face turned beet red, Malone laughed so hard that he spilled half the contents of the two cups he carried, and tea dripped off his fingers onto the damp ground.

"Shut your dirty Irish mouth, and give me one of those cups," he growled. Malone handed him the cup, shook more dark liquid from his hand, and watched his friend take a sip of the brew. He suppressed a laugh when McKinney frowned and proceeded to spit a mouthful of the bitter substance onto the ground.

"It truly is bad-tasting tea, sir, if indeed that's really what it is." Chuckling, Malone did a sharp about-face, tightly clutching the small cup in his hand and proceeding briskly toward the battalion mess hall with a huge grin on his face. McKinney stomped off in the direction of O'Shounessey's tent.

Colonel Patrick O'Shounessey sat with his back to the front flap of his headquarters-sized tent; one trouser suspender lay across his broad shoulder, the other having fallen down by his waist. He turned in his chair and waited when his orderly announced Ensign McKinney's arrival. McKinney removed his floppy hat before stooping slightly and entering the tent. Once inside, he came to a sharp attention. Neither man saluted.

"John, please have a seat." O'Shounessey motioned toward a ragged old camp chair that sat somewhat askew against the main tent pole. McKinney sat down with his back ramrod straight. "Relax, John. We have a lot to go over." O'Shounessey laughed and handed the ensign a cup of steaming hot tea his orderly had prepared. McKinney carefully sipped the brownish liquid and was delighted by the warmth as well as the fine flavor. *The privilege of rank*, he thought, but he knew better than to say it out loud.

O'Shounessey sipped gingerly from his cup for a second before he began explaining, without any more fanfare, the trove of information obtained from the captured French colonel.

"Your French colonel was extremely eager to impress us with his knowledge of Soult's intentions, and with just how important he is to Napoleon's entire war efforts," said O'Shounessey with a smirk on his close shaven face. He paused and looked McKinney in the eye.

"He explained, in great detail as a matter of fact, the battle plans for Leira."

"He did indeed?" quizzed McKinney, raising his eyebrows.

"According to your colonel, Marshall Soult plans to simply brush us aside with the help of their far superior artillery, long before Lord Wellington can send any reinforcements. After we are disposed of, they can drive unmolested toward the coast." O'Shounessey stared out into space for a brief moment before looking back at his ensign, who was gazing into his cup of tea as if the answer to their problems would be revealed there.

"Now, John, our work truly begins." O'Shounessey offered the comment offhandedly as he reached for his stack of maps. Humming an old Irish tune, he began flipping through the hand-drawn topographic renderings. McKinney's stomach began rumbling, and he had to fight the urge to rub his empty belly.

"I'm thankful the frog colonel was useful to you, sir." McKinney spoke a little louder than normal, hoping to drown out the noise coming from his stomach. "We took quite a risk in order to bring him back," he added. O'Shounessey, who seemed not to have heard the comment as he continued searching through the huge stack of rough drafting paper, never replied. McKinney fell silent and sipped his tea, content with replaying the events of the previous day in his mind.

Finally, O'Shounessey grunted, "Aha," and pulled a lone map from the bottom of the stack he had searched through. "Yes, I thought as much," he growled, more to himself than to McKinney and turned toward his ensign with map in hand. McKinney wasn't sure if he was talking about the risks they had incurred or simply referring to the map, so he said nothing. O'Shounessey's blue eyes bore hard into him.

"John, his information is and will be very helpful, but only if we are ready for the bastards when they decide to attack." He paused to let that thought sink in. "We need to find their main force and with it their artillery," O'Shounessey stated this critical fact quite simply. "I doubt very much that our friend General Soult has split his strength ..." He pondered his own comment for a second, then continued, "Maybe, but it wouldn't make sense, and it doesn't really matter." His hand waved in the air dismissively. "We still need, very badly, to locate their bloody artillery." O'Shounessey stood and walked around the shaky table a couple of times before turning back to McKinney.

"If I were a betting man, which I'm not ..." His gambling was in fact notorious throughout the battalion and McKinney forced himself not to smile. "I'd bet you a case of good Irish whiskey to a guinea that the damn frogs won't put their big guns out in the open. They will attempt to hide them until the last minute, and I think ... It's just my hunch, mind you, but I think they would hide them somewhere above these fields." He spread the map out on an old table that wobbled badly under the added weight. The table he had carried through a dozen years of fighting in two continents was in dire need of attention, like new legs, but it was better than nothing.

With his big index finger, he stabbed at a round knoll just north of the village of Leira. The knoll had no name.

"I need for you and your skirmishers to search the woods around this knoll. Find those bloody guns, John. Destroy them before they destroy us."

McKinney stood and stretched his creaky knees before walking with a slight limp closer to the map. O'Shounessey saw the limp but pretended not to notice.

"As you can see, this knoll dominates all the surrounding fields. If Soult could clear us off these fields—and I'm sure that is where Wellesley will want to fight—then his cavalry could hit our flanks and roll through our lines before heading for Oporto." McKinney bent over and looked closely at the drawing; the fields O'Shounessey spoke of were the same fields he and his men had crawled through the day before.

"Sir, is this a proper map?" McKinney asked as he tried to decipher the crumpled hand-drawn sketch. Like most infantrymen, he did not fully trust the maps that were prepared by the engineers. Far too many of them would create their drawings from the safety of a distant ridge or even back at their tents, instead of risking the chance of getting shot out in the field.

"I believe this one is fairly accurate," said O'Shounessey, showing his poker face. McKinney looked up at his boss. "I mapped it myself," he explained, deadpanning.

O'Shounessey had at one time been an engineer under General Cornwallis, having served in that capacity during the American rebellion. "I also like to lead from the front, Mr. McKinney." A sly smile spread across the colonel's ruddy face.

"That you do, sir," answered McKinney, a little embarrassed.

A somewhat awkward silence prevailed for a minute or two before O'Shounessey, satisfied with the mild rebuke, cleared his throat and went on.

"John, if the frogs are able to get their guns on that high ground, I'm afraid that the king's boys will pay one hell of a butcher's bill."

223

"I understand, sir," answered McKinney as both men returned to their seats. "If the French have their artillery on or about that hill"—he paused—"we'll find it."

"I know you will, John," said O'Shounessey, taking on a serious tone. He liked the young ensign, and he knew that if anybody could find the frogs, it was McKinney and his skirmishers.

"Is there anything you need?" O'Shounessey asked without taking his eyes off the map.

McKinney thought for a minute. "Sir, I would like to have Ensign Ewart's company in reserve, just in case we get into some kind of trouble out there."

"John, I have already thought of that. We will have Ewart's company ready to go, should you need them. We're also assigning a battery of twelve pounders to support you, but ..." *He's not going to like this,* thought O'Shounessey. "It has to be Exler's battery."

McKinney frowned. "Why Exler's, sir?"

O'Shounessey knew the bad blood between Exler and McKinney went way back, something about money and a bar wench back in England. "I know you don't trust Exler, but ..."

"He's a bloody cheat and a drunk, sir!" McKinney shot back a little too sharply for someone of his rank. And he knew it as soon as the words came out of his mouth.

O'Shounessey's Irish temper flared. "Ensign McKinney." McKinney stood and quickly came to attention while O'Shounessey continued, "The assault will begin at precisely 0500. You and your skirmishers must find and stop those guns. That is all!"

O'Shounessey turned back to his maps in an apparent dismissal. "Yes, sir," replied McKinney contritely before giving a sharp salute and proceeding to leave.

"And how are the young woman and her child?" asked O'Shounessey in a less stern voice as he flipped through the maps. The question caught McKinney by surprise as he was almost out of the tent.

"Ah, very well, sir. They are both doing very well. Thank you for asking," he stammered, his face beginning to redden. McKinney stood there a second but quickly realized there wouldn't be any more questions. He ducked under the tent flap and disappeared into the morning.

"Good for you, John McKinney, good for you," O'Shounessey muttered to himself looking up from the maps and smiling as McKinney's back disappeared under the tent flap.

McKinney's mood remained sour as he made his way back to the skirmishers' company area, the army around him noisily continuing to prepare for the business of war. He was walking stolidly between the many rows of tents when Sergeant Malone suddenly appeared seemingly out of nowhere with another cup of tea. Malone started to speak, but when he saw his friend was wearing his now-familiar war face, he handed over the cup in silence.

"Why is the tea you get always lukewarm?" growled McKinney, tasting the tepid brew while continuing to walk.

"And a good morning to you, too, sir." Malone revealed a momentary smile before falling smartly into step with McKinney. Guessing that the meeting with O'Shounessey had been a serious one, Malone made a further attempt to lighten the mood: "What surprises did old Patrick have for us today, sir?"

"Damn it, Sergeant. His rank is colonel, and you will address him as such," growled McKinney, tasting the tea one final time before pouring it onto the ground.

As they walked, Malone thought about possible reasons behind McKinney's sourness. He knew Patrick O'Shounessey well, very well. Once they reached the skirmishers' company area and both men stopped, Malone spoke again: "Sir, Colonel O'Shounessey likes you, and he likes the job that we do for him. I only hope he doesn't like us to death."

"I worry about that myself sometimes, Sergeant," said McKinney as he plopped down into his camp chair. Looking up at his friend, who remained standing, he parroted O'Shounessey's words from earlier: "Sit down, Sergeant. We have a lot to go over." Malone wiped the dirt from an unused fire log and sat near McKinney, who unfolded a smaller duplicate of the map on O'Shounessey's desk.

McKinney laid out a simple plan that he had been working through his mind all morning. It called for a full-company scouting mission that would envelop the wooded high ground above Leira. They would start at sunset with the entire company of skirmishers and head back over the fields to the high knob.

It was close to three o'clock when they finalized the plan. Malone went to the supply depot to draw the necessary equipment for the night search, and McKinney headed for his tent. He had high hopes of finding Elizabeth and the baby there, but the tent was empty except for her scent lingering in the air around his cot.

"I'll be damned," he moaned, a little surprised at how his heart sank when he thought about the possibility she had already left. "Maybe she really is gone," he mumbled to the empty tent as he sat on the cot and began taking his boots off. *And why wouldn't she leave your sorry ass? You have nothing to offer her except this stinking tent*, he brooded. Leaning back and closing his eyes, he was desperately in need of sleep. But his mind refused to rest.

He had told Malone to have the men ready to move out at 1800 hours, which would give them an hour and a half of daylight. It was just enough time to use a little misdirection to confuse the frogs' spies. In this region, Spanish gold could buy many things, including information. The French would know straightaway if a company-sized group left camp. *If only Elizabeth* … "Well, ol' sod, you can stop that thought," he growled to the empty tent. *At least I can get some shut-eye*, his mind reasoned. Grabbing his pillow, he angrily stuffed it under his head, but sleep wouldn't come. Her scent still lingered everywhere, especially on the pillow, and Elizabeth danced naked through his mind.

He had finally drifted off into a fitful sleep, dreaming of sailing the North Sea, when he suddenly jerked wide awake. He felt, rather than heard, movement outside. And the flap of his tent was slowly being pulled back. He braced himself for Malone's deep Irish voice, but his nose caught the faint though distinctly feminine scent of lavender from freshly washed hair.

"God, I hope that's not Sergeant Malone I smell." He laughed. Playing along with her little game, he kept his eyes closed and was soon rewarded with the soft rustle of clothes falling to the ground, followed by footsteps alongside his cot. He willed his eyes to stay shut, but they sprang open in eager anticipation. McKinney saw the tips of light downy hair on a perfectly sculpted stomach, small dimples of stretch marks visible along her hips. The soft fuzz ran down to a dark sensuous mound that quivered slightly as she stood next to his cot, her long, light brown legs slightly parted.

"Well, it's definitely not Sergeant Malone, thank God." He laughed.

"I do hope I look and smell better than your Sergeant Malone." Elizabeth giggled as she spread her legs even more, her hands on her hips.

With his heart pounding in his chest, McKinney asked, "Where is the baby?" In the excitement of the moment, he couldn't remember the child's name.

"My son's name is Sterling. Say that for me, please," she demanded, taking a step back from the cot.

"Sterling, your son's name is Sterling." He uttered the name as his blood boiled.

"That's better," she whispered and stepped closer to him. "I left Sterling with Corporal Worley's wife; she said she would watch him for a while." McKinney fought the urge to sit up, grab her around the waist, and pull her down to him. "I thought it would give us a chance to"—she hesitated as a smile spread across McKinney's handsome face—"talk," she added, laughing as McKinney, who couldn't resist any longer, reached for her and began lavishing kisses on her stomach. "I said talk." She giggled in protest.

"So talk. My mouth is too busy to talk." McKinney mumbled the words, his hands roaming over her thighs.

"You devil, how can I talk when you are devouring me?" She fell down onto the cot and began to return his frantic kisses. Neither one talked for a while.

As the light faded and the horizon glowed red above the sierras, Elizabeth lay with her head resting on McKinney's chest.

"I truly hope that you aren't married, John McKinney, because I never got around to asking you before now. Actually ..." She bit her lower lip and continued, "I was afraid to ask." She whispered the words and gently ran her fingers across a rough scar on his left shoulder. McKinney, who had almost dozed off for a second, rose up on his elbow and smiled at her.

"Well, I'm sorry, but I must confess. I have not one but two wives." He made the announcement with a straight face and an amazing amount of sincerity. It was a little too much, though, because Elizabeth's shoulders sagged, and she began to sob. He reached for her, but she shrugged him off.

"Why would you not tell me, John? Why?" She sobbed. McKinney dropped his head and cursed himself under his breath.

"Oh god, Elizabeth, I'm sorry. It's an old saying, an army joke. I'm married to His Majesty's Army and its life of adventure. I should have known that you wouldn't understand my meaning." He pulled her to him, and this time, she didn't object. Rocking her like a child, he kissed her dampened eyes.

"Oh." She sniffed as he held her tight.

"I'm so sorry I upset you," he whispered into her ear.

"Oh, it's the damn war, John McKinney." She sobbed. "Or maybe all wars. I don't know. I'm just afraid that I will lose you too. I have lost so much already."

Their eyes met and then their lips. "You won't lose me, I promise," he said, wiping salty tears from her face.

"Do you tell all your women that?" She laughed and lightly blew her nose on a handkerchief he had given her. When she had finished, she handed the handkerchief back and thanked him. Expecting at least some sort of response, she glanced up at him. He had grown quiet and was staring at the roof of the tent or maybe a thousand miles past; she couldn't tell. "John, did you not hear what I asked?" she persisted, only half kidding.

McKinney cocked his head to the side in an obvious attempt to hear something. *But what?* Elizabeth wondered. She reached out and touched his arm, wanting to ask him if everything was all right, but he jerked back from her touch. For the duration of several heartbeats, he stared at her in silence, rubbing the spot where her fingers had been. The spot was burning as if a torch had been held there. He looked at his arm, then at her, but the feeling was suddenly gone, the fire vanishing like a dream.

"Can you hear the dove?" he asked in a quiet tone, still rubbing his arm. Her worries had eased a little, and she cocked her head to the side, listening intently just as he was.

After a second she exclaimed excitedly, "Yes, yes," and together, they absorbed the soft melody.

After several moments, he turned her chin toward him and whispered, "Earlier today, I saw a hawk, and flying with it was a dove. They were together as if they were mates." He shook his head, still not believing what he had seen.

"Well, maybe they are mates, John. Last night, as we neared the sentries, I saw them also."

"It's so very odd," he uttered the words almost to himself.

"Maybe they're like us, John. Maybe the war has touched them and pulled them together," she interjected.

"Maybe." McKinney was about to say he felt as if he had been slapped hard instead of simply touched by this damn war, but he knew she had been hurt as much, if not more than he had. So he held his tongue and simply pulled her tightly into his arms. Their lips met, and their passion rose again like a wildfire until it was doused in an instant by the booming voice of Sergeant Malone.

"The men are ready, sir" was all he said. And luckily for him, McKinney couldn't see the huge grin on his face as he walked away from the tent.

"Damn," cursed McKinney. Elizabeth giggled and pulled her dress down over her head. "I'll be right there, Sergeant!" he shouted and reached for his boots. Elizabeth watched him for a minute before reaching out and tenderly touching his arm once more. This time there was no burn.

"Come back to me, John McKinney. Please come back to me." He kissed her on the forehead and stepped out into a misty rain that had just begun to fall.

* * * * *

A waning moon hung low and pale. Dark clouds rushed by in a northeasterly direction, eerily stretching the skirmishers' shadows as they marched across the open fields of the camp. One hundred twenty men adjusted their packs, shouldered their rifles, and moved past dozens of cooking fires that sizzled and popped from the occasional raindrop falling from the passing clouds.

"I would say it is perfect weather for our little excursion, Mr. McKinney!" exclaimed Malone as he pulled his floppy hat down over his bushy red hair and watched the skirmishers march into the night.

"It's a bloody fact, Sergeant. The frogs will suffer in this weather. Hopefully, their pickets will stay hunkered down." McKinney pulled his own hat down on his close-cropped hair and trudged after his men. The rain, which was picking up, ran down over his shoulders and a huge black cloud hid the face of the night goddess as twilight rushed into darkness.

"Keep your powder dry, gentlemen!" shouted Malone, perhaps unnecessarily. "Keep it dry or we die" was one of the skirmishers' rules of war, and they literally lived or died by it. McKinney, in consultation with O'Shounessey, had decided to wait until dark to begin their search. They both agreed that the sight of a company-sized patrol would too easily alert the frogs to their intent even if they used misdirection.

The British knew the French suffered badly in wet weather because of their overcoats, which looked very proper but weren't at all waterproof. McKinney felt confident the French lines would be lightly guarded due to the weather, but he moved with caution anyway, *eyes wide open*—another rule of war for the skirmishers. Leading his men back across the pastures they had traversed two days before, McKinney took care to hug the edge of the woods line. They slid down into and splashed across the gulley they had previously used for cover. It had been relatively easygoing the first time, but tonight this washed-out area carried a foot-deep stream of water and crossing was extremely difficult. Instead of turning downstream as they had done before, they turned up toward the wooded knoll above them in the mist. It was around that knoll, which through the swirling clouds resembled a weathered skull, where Colonel O'Shounessey believed the French artillery was hidden. A hundred twenty pairs of eyes stared into the darkness, and that many pairs of ears listened intently for any telltale sounds of wood being chopped. But all they heard was the *drip-drip-drip* of the rain. The gun crews would have to clear trees and underbrush before setting up the twelve-pounders to ply their deadly trade. So why was there no sound except the god of war pissing on them?

The green-jacketed skirmishers worked their way cautiously through the thick underbrush, limestone outcroppings scattered in front of them. McKinney soon stopped the column once more, rubbed sweat from his eyes, and peered into the darkness while rain dripped off his service hat. The unusual-looking hats were worn proudly by all the skirmishers and had become a badge of distinction for them, much like the Green Berets would later separate the Special Forces from the regular Army. The floppy hats did indeed draw significant disdain from the other officers in the battalion, men who preferred the standard issue shakos, but Colonel O'Shounessey backed the wearing of them. He knew from experience that the hats were very functional in weather such as his skirmishers faced tonight, and they were also a source of pride for the men who met more up-close danger than the regular troops did. So the floppy hats stayed.

Having just passed through a terrible thicket of cork and laurel, Sergeant Malone reached out with a scratched, bloody arm and tapped McKinney's shoulder.

"The men need a break, sir," he grunted as he leaned back on a small oak sapling. They had been pushing hard for the past couple of hours, desperate to find the frogs, but to no avail. McKinney, reluctant to slow down, finally relented after watching several men nearly drop in place.

"Okay, Sergeant. Let them take … ten." There was no time to waste.

Shedding his pack, McKinney glanced up toward the top of the knoll that loomed dark and foreboding in front of them. As he stared up the hill, the lady of the night peeked out from behind quick flowing curtains.

"In another time and another place, you would be pretty," whispered McKinney, who sat on a wet rock, chewing on a piece of cold beef jerky, "but not tonight." He watched as Malone walked up beside him, his gruff voice breaking the silence.

"We should have found the bloody crapauds' picket lines by now," he grumbled before biting off a large chew of tobacco from an even larger cut that had been shipped in from the ex-colonies. McKinney watched his friend with a look of disgust on his face. The big Irishman ignored the glare and stuffed the remainder of the tobacco back into his pack.

"That's a nasty habit, Sergeant," growled McKinney, reaching for his canteen.

"That it is, sir, that it is," answered Malone, unconcerned.

After several moments had passed, McKinney rose from the rock and slid his pack onto his back. "You're right, Sergeant," he said.

"And what might I be right about, sir?" asked Malone, having forgotten what they were talking about.

"That we should have found their pickets by now ... unless ..." He paused and glanced up through the drizzle before continuing, "Unless there is some kind of field on the back side of that damn knoll and O'Shounessey never saw it." He pointed toward the knoll, which became briefly visible up ahead. "The damn frogs wouldn't have to chop down a single tree, not a single damn tree," McKinney continued, the old anger growing in the pit of his stomach.

"You may be right, sir, but I can smell the bastards. They're close."

"Your damn nose nearly got me killed back in Leira, remember?"

"Well, I can still smell them. They're out there somewhere," answered Malone indignantly, shifting his pack. McKinney did the same and grimaced as water ran down his neck.

"Let's move them out," he growled and once again strained to see through the wet branches slapping against his face.

After several minutes of practically crawling through a rough patch of laurel, McKinney looked around at his men, who were spread out in small clumps across a hundred yards. He quickly realized that he could easily lose half of them in the brush as the dark clouds squeezed out any light.

"Sergeant Malone," barked McKinney in a hoarse whisper.

"Sir," came the crisp reply.

"Pass the word to form on us. We will advance in single file. It won't be as efficient, but maybe we won't lose anybody in this damn thick brush."

The company had been moving forward in line, and it took a few minutes for everyone to form into single fill column. While the men eased back to where McKinney and Malone stood, a voice groaned in pain: "Oh, bloody hell." A green running briar had torn through cloth and found flesh.

"Keep it quiet, you bloody fool," hissed Malone as he herded the men into single file. When they were ready, McKinney led them up toward the fog-shrouded knoll. He would reform them into line when they were ready to begin the assault, which if his hunch were right would be just before first light.

Meanwhile, a little over twelve hundred yards away, back in the British artillery park, Lieutenant William Exler sat atop his horse in the drizzling rain. He was a tall, gaunt-looking man with scars on his face from a childhood brush with smallpox. His nose had become bulbous from far too much rum, and his hands sometimes shook like an old man's when he needed a drink, which was most of the time. Why he hadn't been drummed out of the service for his excessive drinking was anyone's guess. He was not highborn, but his family did have money from a small textile business. He was raised in the dirty industrial city of Liverpool in southwest England, where his father, sensing him a danger to the family wealth, had eagerly paid for his commission into the Army. The day William came of age, he had been shipped out—hopefully, thought the elder Exler, far enough away to keep him out of the family business. William Exler had become a fairly competent artillery officer, and he knew the workings of the gun crew better than most, but his incessant drinking held him back. At thirty, he was fairly old for a mere lieutenant, having been passed over for promotion several times.

This morning like most mornings, he had woken up angry. First, because he was out in this god-awful weather and second because his head was pounding from too much cheap rum the night before.

"Bring those goddamned guns around, you bastards!" His cursing was almost as legendary as his drinking. He shouted loudly from atop his nervous gelding, which pawed the muddy ground in an attempt to rid itself of the nuisance that sat atop its back.

"We have to get this damn battery setup, and quickly—I say quickly, damn you!" He lashed out at the nearest mule handler who was pulling hard on a team of harnessed mules. The private, who had been struggling to stand in the ankle-deep mud, slipped and fell, further soaking his already chilled body.

There were six guns in his battery and each battery needed twelve mules, two to a team. The six teams of mules were then attached to the caissons that carried the big guns, forming Exler's battery. The British cataloged their artillery pieces by the weight of their rounds, from five-pounders up to the twelve-pounders that Exler commanded. These twelve-pounders could fire up to a mile, if the loaders did their job properly.

Exler knew it would speed things up if he would only get down off his horse and help the section chief prepare the firing site, but this morning he preferred to shout and curse instead. As the guns were slowly pulled into place, Exler's gray horse began spinning in small circles, and he was having a difficult time keeping him under control. O'Shounessey's orders were to have the battery in place and ready to support the skirmishers with cover fire at 0500 and then to stand prepared should McKinney or possibly Ewart need additional help. Exler had stared off into space as O'Shounessey laid out his orders, his mind more on the rum in his saddlebags than anything else. *After all*, he thought to himself, *I've fired hundreds of support missions before. Why is this one any different?* Now he sat in the cold drizzle, trying to remember exactly what the damn Irishman had told him.

"Well, maybe they won't need us after the initial support firing anyway," he said aloud into his horse's ear, stroking its neck in an attempt to calm it down.

Grudgingly, Exler finally dismounted and tied the reins to the nearest caisson before pulling out the map O'Shounessey had given him from its oilskin case. He halfheartedly attempted to spread it out on a table that was tucked under a shelter half. His section chief,

Sergeant Buchanan, had quickly cobbled the protected work area when the rains became heavy. Buchanan had hoped to get at least a thank-you, but he didn't. The wind was stiff out of the west, and it prevented Exler from properly spreading the map out flat.

"Hellfire," he cursed, bending over in a vain attempt to accurately plot the distance to and elevation of the knoll that Ensign McKinney and his skirmishers were to assault. The wind tore fiercely at the corners of the damp paper and Exler gave up.

"What the hell," he moaned and rolled the map back up, jamming it into its case and shoving it and the table further under the shelter half. By now, his head was really throbbing, and he was pissed at the world. Glancing around angrily, he saw that his crews were busy with the final setup of the guns.

"It's about bloody time!" he shouted into the wind before walking over to the gelding that stood head down in the rain. Sliding his trembling hand down into the saddlebag, he felt glass and pulled the bottle out gently.

"Ah," he said, smiling, "the nectar of the gods," as he took a long drink of the smoky liquid. Closing his eyes, Exler savored the burn going down his throat, waited a second, and took another pull before sliding the precious container back into his saddlebag. The pounding in his head soon lessened, so he walked back to the shelter half and pulled out a worn writing pad. Licking the tip of a stubby pencil he carried in his pocket, Exler wrote down some figures he guessed were the correct elevations needed for the support fire mission.

A couple hundred yards away, O'Shounessey stood at the head of another small table that had been placed in the corner of his tent; it was covered with maps as usual. All his company commanders, with the exception of McKinney, stood at ease on the other side of the table. They made small talk as they waited for their commander to start the briefing. One of the maps that decorated the wobbly table was spread out with weights sitting on each corner. It was an exact copy of the one McKinney carried in his pack as well as the one Exler had been struggling to read. O'Shounessey scanned the map for a few minutes and then looked up into the eager young faces of his company commanders.

God, they're all so damn young, he thought to himself before clearing his throat:

"Gentlemen …" Their chatting stopped abruptly, and all eyes turned toward him. "As we speak, Ensign McKinney and his skirmishers are advancing on this knoll." He pointed to the high ground on the map, and their eyes closely followed his finger. "His job, gentlemen, is to silence the French artillery, which I believe sits somewhere on or around that knoll. The outcome of our assault will depend on his success." He looked out at his men; *they already know that, you can see it in their eyes,* he reasoned to himself. "The main thrust of our assault will be just to the south of the village of Leira through these fields." Again, his finger lightly touched the map.

"God forbid, if they don't stop that artillery," moaned Lieutenant Lawson, a slightly pudgy young man from Worcester who would have the lead company, "the bloody frogs will hammer our right flank." He made the statement without taking his eyes off the map.

"I'm well aware of that fact, thank you, Mr. Lawson," said O'Shounessey in an effort to sound upbeat. "I have complete faith in Ensign McKinney and his boys, as should you all."

The young commanders glanced around at each other and then down at the map once more. They had faith in McKinney and his skirmishers, all right; they just didn't want to have his job. Each man's gut tightened just a little as O'Shounessey continued, "The main assault will commence at precisely 0500 with a thirty-minute artillery barrage from all ten of our batteries, and then …" He attempted a smile before continuing, "You boys will have the chance to earn your sixpence and a rum." He paused for a second, but when no one laughed at his attempt at humor, he cleared his throat and went on.

"Ensign Ewart, you will hold your company in reserve, either for Ensign McKinney or to support the main assault." He looked at his commanders once again; he could feel their eagerness as well as their trepidation. *It's always the same,* he realized, thinking back over his many years of service, back to when he was young, eager, and only a little fearful. Just like these young men. *How many of them will survive tomorrow's battle?* He couldn't help but wonder at the inevitable before straightening his tired, aching back and looking each of them in the eye.

"If there are no more questions"—and there weren't—"then that is all. Good luck and Godspeed."

Silently, everyone filed out of his tent, leaving O'Shounessey to stare down at his maps. "Everything depends on you, Mr. McKinney. You must take that knoll and stop their artillery from slaughtering our boys!" He slammed his fist down hard on the stack of maps, and the table shook like plum pudding. A small bottle of indigo ink tipped over, and ink slowly dripped off the edge of the table, making a dark-black puddle in the grass that lay flattened from foot traffic. O'Shounessey's aide, Captain Queen, felt his gut tighten just a little more as he listened from outside the tent.

The skirmishers broke out of the worst of the laurel a few hundred feet below the high knoll, and McKinney stood in the foggy predawn drizzle, looking uphill. He felt like a bloody drowning rat as he watched Sergeant Malone pull the men out of single file and form them back into line for the assault up the black void that lay in front of them.

"What if all this is for nothing?" He shook his head and moaned to the damp, dark night. "What if the damn frogs' artillery is sitting on another knoll, maybe that smaller one to the south of Leira? Damnation," he growled. Cocking his head to the side, he strained his good ear in the faint hope of gleaning some sign of the French, but all he could hear was the steady *drip-drip-drip* of the cold rain as it ran off everything around him, everything in his world.

It took some shoving and cursing, but Malone soon had his boys ready to advance in line. He walked up to McKinney and announced, "They're ready, sir."

"All right, Sergeant, you know the drill. I'll take them up the hill, and you talk to them." It was a routine they had used in the bitter retreat from Spain and many times since. McKinney would lead the assault, and Malone would encourage the men as they moved along.

"Forward" was the only command necessary. When McKinney stepped out, one hundred nineteen men quickly did likewise. They were willing to follow him anywhere, never faltering. *It is a heavy burden, their obedience*, thought McKinney as he ducked under a low tree limb that blocked his way. Malone walked just behind the advancing line of troops and talked to each man.

"Follow Mr. McKinney, boys. Let's go earn our pay and get a little dab of glory along the way. Step out quickly now. Keep your eyes open. The damn frogs are out there someplace, and we need to find them. Don't fire until you are sure of your target." He repeated himself often as he moved down the line, but it kept the company working like a well-oiled machine. He was proud of his boys, and they trusted both him and McKinney unconditionally.

As they moved forward, McKinney reached down into his pocket and pulled out his watch. It was a gift his father had given him a few days before he left Oban. The beautiful Hamilton said it was five minutes past four. He admired the inside of the gold-plated cover, which was illuminated in the dark. An image of a ship, the newest in his father's fleet, was etched onto its surface. She was called the *Viking*, but her 190-foot length and her triple sails were a far cry from the old dragon ships of his ancestors. He put the watch carefully back into his pocket, knowing if he dropped it here, he would probably never find it. McKinney pulled his floppy hat down tightly onto his head and, limping slightly from his blistered foot, painfully trudged through the laurel.

"Damn boots," he growled. After more or less crawling through the brush for another fifty yards or so, he reluctantly motioned for Sergeant Malone to take the lead. Stopping near an old lightning-scarred chestnut oak, he went over the map in his mind one more time as the men struggled past him. They were good men, these skirmishers, at least most of them. And he cursed himself for having to put them in this situation.

Out of the dark mist came Malone's voice. "They're close, sir," he announced and laughed to himself when the young ensign jumped slightly.

"Sure they are," replied McKinney, looking around.

A minute later, 120 heads snapped around as several musket shots rang out near the center of the advancing skirmish line.

"Hold your fire, boys," shouted Malone. "Wait until you have a target." Both he and McKinney dropped into a crouch as they quickened their pace up the hill. They were about a hundred yards from the crest of the hill when more shots rang out, and this time, men fell screaming to the ground. A grizzled old corporal by the name of Haney was advancing next in line to McKinney; he grunted and sank to his knees. The back of the man's head was spewing blood and gray matter, but his body stayed in the kneeling position as if praying to the god of war. The assault line pressed forward, and another man went down with a musket ball in his right shoulder.

"Keep moving, boys!" shouted McKinney, who had just recently picked up Malone's habit of calling the men "boys." As the firing intensified, McKinney began to get a feel for how the frogs had set up their picket line. They were definitely trying to protect something near the knoll, but was it their artillery? He hoped to hell it was!

A little less than a mile away, by the way a crow or artillery shell flies, Lieutenant Exler stood in the rain and attempted to adjust the elevation lever on a Smithfield howitzer. His hands shook, and he cursed the weather as rain dripped into his eyes. He blinked several times and wiped the backside of his right sleeve across his eyes while he cranked the knob. Three turns past 10 percent, that should get him dead on top of the knoll. Then back off one turn, or what should be fifty yards. *That*, he thought, *should keep a safety zone between the skirmishers and the damn French.*

"If there are any damn frogs at all on the damn hill," he growled. "Cut the bloody fuses a little short, Private Bryson. That will give them an air burst, and in that thick woods, we will need one to be effective," he explained to the young fusilier.

Sergeant Humes, the battery section chief and a veteran artilleryman, had watched Exler adjust the guns and was worried he had set the wrong elevation. But he kept his fears to himself. If there was one thing he had learned through his years of service to His Majesty, it was that officers were always right, always. Private Bryson, the fusilier, was a young eager Welshman, and he cut the cordite fuses just like Exler had told him, a little short.

McKinney grabbed Sergeant Malone's arm just as they were stepping over the trunk of a small pine tree that had fallen years before. The trunk was mostly rotten, but the jagged limbs were still strong enough to scratch their legs and rip at their necessary gear.

"Sergeant Malone!" shouted McKinney.

"Sir," came the rain-muffled reply.

"I'm going to take the 1st platoon out of line and maneuver them around to hit the back of this damn knoll." McKinney's voice was barely louder than the musket fire around them. "You continue the frontal assault; hopefully, we'll meet up top." Just then, a musket ball snapped a low-hanging limb from the tree they stood next to, only a couple feet from their heads.

"Or up yonder," groaned Malone as both men ducked down into a low crouch.

McKinney knelt on one knee and reached into his pocket, pulling out the Hamilton again. It was 0425. He replaced the watch, patted it for reassurance, and moved down the line until he found Corporal Buchanan, who was acting sergeant of the 1st platoon. Grabbing him by the arm, he shouted, "You and your platoon are coming with me!" Without any further explanation, the 1st platoon separated from the assault line and started around the knoll. They moved quickly, almost at a jog, and so far hadn't drawn any fire. McKinney could tell from the heavy firing on the main assault line that Sergeant Malone and his boys were earning their pay. He could also detect the Baker rifles' rate of firing pick up as the fight went on. *There must be plenty of targets*, he thought as he rushed through the brush.

The predawn light enabled them to see where they were going, but it also created shadows that spooked even the older troops. In their guts, they also knew that the dawn light would help the frogs pick out their targets, which were the boys in green. The faint cries of the wounded drifted to his ears as McKinney, who was slightly in front of Corporal Buchanan, led the 1st platoon Highlanders up the backside of the knoll on the double. He was straining to see through the brush when suddenly, up ahead, what appeared to be an old field or a clearing materialized out of the mist. It was about a hundred feet in front of them. A wicked grin began to spread across McKinney's face.

"I was bloody right," he grunted and slowed their mad dash around the hill. "Gather on me, boys," he said, motioning for them to be as quiet as possible. Glancing over at Buchanan, who was gasping for air, he asked, "Are you all right, Corporal?" Then he slapped the man on the back, fearing he was choking on something.

After another gulp of air came the muffled reply. "Yes, sir, I'm …" He took another deep breath before continuing: "Just a little short of breath." McKinney had his war face on, and he stared down at the man with a mixture of anger and concern etched on his face.

"Smoking, you know," coughed Buchanan, whose ragged breathing had slowed slightly. The members of the 1st platoon anxiously shuffled their feet and crowded around McKinney as the battle for the knoll continued to rage off to their left.

The young skirmishers were eager—ready for orders to assault the damn French, who were slamming their friends with hot lead. Swift and painful retribution was the only thing on their minds. McKinney looked at each man with stern gray eyes, and each man nodded back in agreement; they knew the command that was coming.

"Fix bayonets!" McKinney shouted, his Scottish accent drilling the word *bayonets* while a look of pure hate spread across his face. They all wore their war faces now. The sound of cold steel sliding into place echoed through the wet morning air, and McKinney turned them toward the enemy. It is at this point in battle when a man's gut churns and his bladder grows weak. He shouts whatever war cry can escape his parched throat and somehow musters the courage to choke back the fear that threatens to chase him from the field. Then he runs straight ahead, right into hell itself if need be. And that's what the 1st platoon of the 1st Highlanders did.

The French artillerymen were making the last adjustments on the ten-pound field pieces as their infantry fought with the skirmishers to their front. A dapper young French captain was directing his section chiefs to light the lanyards for the big guns when McKinney and his men broke out of the brush not a hundred feet behind them. Screaming like banshees, the British skirmishers charged the surprised French artillerymen from across the small field. The gun crews barely had time to turn around before the cold English steel ran through them. McKinney veered off to his right and headed for the French captain, who was frantically shouting new orders to his crew. The mustached Frenchman watched McKinney charge toward him across the last few feet separating the men, and he quickly drew his saber. McKinney easily parried the feeble thrust of the thin-bladed sword and then slammed the butt of his rifle under the man's chin. He felt the jawbone shatter from the blow, but the Frenchman somehow managed to stay on his feet. Spitting blood and broken teeth, the man backed up against the nearest field piece and stared defiantly at his attacker. McKinney didn't understand the obscenities that spewed from the crapaud's broken mouth, nor did he care what was said; he simply lunged forward and mercilessly drove his bayonet hard into the Frenchman's belly. Blood and vomit gushed from the man's mouth as he screamed and fell to his knees. McKinney put his boot on the man's bloody chest and shoved with a savage grunt. The blade ripped out with a sickening wet sound and the Frenchman fell at McKinney's feet. Feeling he had spent too much time dispatching this one man, McKinney spun around and searched through the mayhem for another target.

Many of the French fought to their last breath. Others simply ran, and a few dropped to their knees begging for mercy. For those few, it was a mistake. Mercy was a forgotten word for these Englishmen. The slender steel of the 1st Highlanders bayonets ran red as the men tore through the pitiful resistance of the artillery crews.

Fifty yards away just down the hill, the French infantrymen were totally committed to the fight in front of them, having never heard the commotion to their rear. Hunkered down behind their wooden barricades, they forced Sergeant Malone and his boys to pay a hell of a price for each foot of their advance. Eighteen Englishmen lay dead in the thick underbrush behind Malone, and four more were down with wounds. The rest fought on.

At the northern edge of the field, McKinney's boys finished with the French artillerymen and never paused. They ran straight toward the French infantry, who were firing from behind logs that had been stacked to provide cover and camouflage their positions. The skirmishers hit the French Voltigeurs with shot and sharp steel, continuing the slaughter. Most of the horses that had pulled the French caissons into position broke harness during the fierce fighting and ran amok through the carnage as the 1st platoon fired point-blank into the backs of the surprised French. The battle was over in a matter of minutes, and men cried out for wives or girlfriends they would never see again. They cursed God, they cursed the English, and then they died.

When the rifles finally grew silent, McKinney slumped wearily against a small oak sapling and tried to catch his breath. He was nearly exhausted, and although it wasn't a very hot day, sweat poured from under his floppy hat, running down into his eyes, which caused his vision to blur. He blinked several times to clear it but failed, so he reluctantly propped his Baker rifle against his side and reached for his handkerchief. He was in the process of wiping the filthy cloth across his eyes and forehead when a savage growl penetrated his tired mind. He tried to focus on the figure that rushed at him out of the smoke of battle. Though his vision was still somewhat blurred, he could tell it was a very pissed-off French sergeant. The big man had blood all over his face from a head wound and his distinctive pig-tails, which hung lank under his helmet, dripped more. His thick mustache was covered with blood, and his teeth showed red when he snarled and lunged at McKinney. The only thing that McKinney had in his hand was the handkerchief, so in desperation, he threw it at the man and lunged sideways. He narrowly missed being skewered by the broken-tipped bayonet thrust at his chest. In his wild scramble to avoid being pinned to the tree, his Baker rifle fell to the ground with a thud. The Frenchman was a professional, and it showed. He recovered quickly from his missed lunge, stalking McKinney like a snake would a rabbit. McKinney stood with his back to the tree and waited. The big Frenchman smirked at his hapless target and started to lunge again when his whole body suddenly shook, his chest arched forward, and he rose up on his tiptoes as if trying to escape something. His bloodshot eyes looked down at the bloody tip of a bayonet that stuck out of his chest near the second button on his blue dragoon jacket. The big man coughed a couple of times and stared at McKinney with a sad, confused look. Then with a grunt, he fell forward at McKinney's feet. Sergeant Malone stepped up, put his foot on the Frenchman's back, and pulled. The steel bayonet made a wet scraping sound as it slipped out from between shattered ribs; Malone stood over the dead man and spat.

"It's all right, sir, I'll watch your back," he said, smiling at his wide-eyed friend. Both men turned slowly in a full circle, taking in the carnage of the battlefield. Finally, they flopped down on the ground and dropped their weary heads. The smell of gunpowder mixed with that of blood and sweat as the two men stared through the thick clouds of smoke that floated across the bloody field.

Minutes ticked by until, at last, Malone glanced over at McKinney whose face was filthy with black residue from the gunpowder, his eyes wide open. There was a small cut on his forehead that dripped blood down his dirty face.

"You look like hell, Mr. McKinney." Malone laughed just as he took a much-deserved drink from his canteen.

"Why, thank you, Sergeant Malone. You look like shit yourself," replied the weary McKinney with a laugh.

After taking another long drink from his canteen, Malone offered it to McKinney, who drank eagerly until water ran down his chin.

"Thank you, Sergeant," he managed to mumble as he wiped his chin with his shirtsleeve. Neither man had rested nearly enough, but they soon struggled back to their feet. Malone put his big arm on McKinney's shoulder:

"By god, sir, we did it." He practically shouted the remark because his ears still rang from all the firing. Both men stood atop the small knoll as their troops began to round up the few French who had survived the carnage. The survivors were shoved into a tight circle and placed under guard. McKinney rubbed his eyes and finally replied to Malone, "Yes, Mike, we bloody did it, didn't we?" Ensign McKinney had never called Malone by his Christian name, and Malone was glowing with pride. Smiling, the big Irishman went back to work. Resisting the urge to just shoot the bastards, he walked over to where the prisoners sat and chatted briefly with the guards. Then he went to check on his own wounded.

The job of being a skirmisher was not easy, and McKinney was used to all the dinks and bangs associated with it, but he couldn't, for the life of him, figure out why his hip was staring to hurt like hell. He hadn't fallen, at least that he could remember. He rubbed the sore spot, and his hand bumped against his pocket watch. Pulling it gingerly out of his pocket, he soon found the reason why he ached. A musket ball had obviously glanced off the watch cover because a shallow groove lay across its face. The watch still worked. It was three minutes past five according to the battered Hamilton.

"They're late," he announced to no one in particular as he looked out toward the southwest where the British artillery would be positioned. He couldn't see them for the forested ridges, but he could almost feel their presence.

The early dawn light had chased most of the shadows away, and McKinney watched as some of his exhausted men collapsed where they stood. In the distance, a rooster called his greetings to the new day, and a dog howled in protest. McKinney knew O'Shounessey's men would be set to start their attack, but not before the artillery barrage softened up the French lines. *So what was the holdup?* he wondered. *Was his watch wrong, by chance?*

The rooster, far down in the valley, was evidently satisfied with his waking call and had grown quite as had the dog. But another sound rode the winds that had suddenly picked up, chasing the cordite clouds away. A hawk's cry suddenly echoed eerily over the knoll, and to McKinney, it sounded almost like a warning, shrill and vivid. He glanced up to spot the hawk, but when he did, yet another sound screeched through the morning air. This sound turned his blood cold. It was the unmistakable whistle of artillery rounds.

"Incoming!" he cried at the top of his lungs. "Incoming. Get down! Get down!" he shouted again as his men began diving for cover.

The first airburst exploded over the edge of the field where several of the French horses were picketed. When the smoke had cleared, there were three horses down and a fourth that just stood shaking with glistening red blood dripping from its hind quarters.

Sergeant Malone ran hunched over through the flying debris and dove behind a tree that was far too small to give his considerable girth much protection. He landed not far from McKinney, who was lying behind a fallen log that provided similarly inadequate cover.

"Why the hell are the frogs firing on their own men?" Malone shouted the question toward McKinney, though a mere five feet separated the men.

"It's not the damn French!" shouted McKinney in reply. "It's our own artillery. It's that bloody Exler."

"Exler," parroted Malone as he watched another airburst explode, this time right over the top of the French prisoners, who were desperately clawing into the wet earth with their bare hands. One young Voltigeur had made the mistake of jumping up and running toward the wooded area; his head vanished in a red mist. All but one of the other prisoners lay screaming from shrapnel wounds.

There were more airbursts. And more and more of McKinney's men—good men, who only a few minutes before had risked their lives in an effort to help their friends—were dying.

Less than a mile away, the British regulars, splendid in their scarlet jackets, stood in long straight lines of battle formation and watched their artillery explode high on the ridge. They cheered and waved their shakos about their heads as the airbursts erupted in puffs of white and yellow. Little did they know that their friends were dying on that knoll from what, years later, would be called "friendly fire."

Thick smoke and dust hung in the air as McKinney glanced franticly across the shell-pocked knoll and assessed their situation. It was bad, bloody bad, as bad as he had ever seen; he knew he had to do something—and quick. Cursing under his breath, he began crawling over to where a young private by the name of Bumgarner lay hugging the ground. The young man was noted for his horsemanship to the extent that even some of the officers came to him for advice. McKinney, who was crawling so close to the earth that he could see bugs scurrying for safety in the dirt, reached Bumgarner just as the ground around them shook from a near miss. The boy had managed to curl up behind a mass of roots where a small tree had been blown over by one of the exploding shells. His eyes were squeezed shut, and his lips trembled as he recited a nearly forgotten prayer from his childhood.

"Bumgarner!" McKinney shouted his name, but the boy didn't move. "Damn it, Bumgarner. Look at me!" Slowly, his eyelids opened to reveal brown eyes so large they seemed to bulge from the sockets. Bumgarner blinked several times as if he were coming out of a dream.

"Listen to me, son." McKinney tried to soothe the boy's shattered nerves. "I want you to catch one of those damn horses," he said, pointing to several draft horses running about wildly just to their left, "and I want you to ride like hell was after you down to O'Shounessey's headquarters. Tell him to stop Exler from killing us. Tell him that we have the knoll secure and to stop the firing! Now go. Go!"

Bumgarner, still wide-eyed, grunted without hesitation, "Yes, sir." Then he sprang to his feet, leaving his rifle and pack where they lay. Tearing off across the field, he ran like a mad man. McKinney watched him sprint toward the frightened horses and, without much trouble, leap onto the back of a large bay mare. The boy was riding fast for the British lines before the next airburst exploded over his friends. Bumgarner had absolutely no desire to stay in the death trap on the knoll, and neither did the big Belgian.

The shells were coming rapidly, every thirty seconds, which meant the British gunners were working their deadly trade very well. *Very well indeed*, thought McKinney, hugging the ground as another shell exploded nearby. He peeked cautiously over the log he lay behind and saw two more men hit by shrapnel from the British guns. His men were dying, and all he could do was curse and pray.

"I can't lead from the damn front if I'm hiding behind this bloody log," he moaned loudly to the god of war as he summoned the courage to start developing a plan. McKinney, who hadn't prayed in a long time, doubted anybody was listening.

Private Timothy Bumgarner hugged the mare's neck and pushed her to the point of exhaustion. Each time he started to slow, the horse in order for her to rest, he saw another artillery shell arch over his head toward the knoll. The hilltop where his friends were dying was shrouded in smoke from the artillery rounds.

"Run hard, girl, run hard," he whispered, pressing his body to the mare's close-cropped mane. Bumgarner raced past the startled British sentries without slowing. They shouted for him to stop and even raised their rifles in frustration, but they didn't shoot. Fortunately, they could see his tattered uniform and green jacket, identifying him as one of their own.

Finally, feeling the horse at the brink of total exhaustion, Bumgarner spotted the tent flag marking O'Shounessey's headquarters blowing in the faint wind. He had no bridle to help stop the ton of charging horseflesh, so as he neared the tent, he simply jumped off the winded and much-lathered mare. The horse stumbled badly when her rider jumped off, but she managed to regain her footing and soon stood still—her head down and nostrils flared, drawing air into her great lungs. The boy hit the ground running, though with a slight limp from a previously unnoticed shrapnel wound, and headed straight for the colonel's tent. Bumgarner was immediately stopped by a mean-looking sergeant who stood guard in front of the headquarters tent.

"I ... I have to see the colonel," he stammered. "My friends are dying up there!" Bumgarner pointed toward the smoke-covered knoll. The sergeant was an old veteran from the Welsh Coldwater Guard, and it didn't take him but a second to understand what was happening.

Sergeant Phelps pushed the private through the tent door and called out, "Colonel, sir, you have to hear this," just as another volley belched from the British guns. Bumgarner hastily explained to O'Shounessey what was happening to the skirmishers. The colonel listened to the first few sentences of McKinney's message before jumping up and tearing out of the tent, shouting for his horse.

"Well done, Private," said Sergeant Phelps as he led the young man out of the tent. "Now go let the doctor have a look at that wounded leg." He patted Bumgarner on the back and showed the tired, battered young man the direction to the battalion hospital.

"Sergeant, shouldn't I go back up there?" Phelps looked toward the smoking knoll.

"You've done more than your share, son. Now go see the doc. I'm not sure what else we can do anyway." But he made the last statement to an empty space, as Bumgarner had already walked away.

Captain Queen was attending to his own horse nearby when he heard the colonel shout. Leaping onto the unsaddled gelding, he rode hard toward the voice, pulling the horse to a mudslinging stop when he spotted O'Shounessey waving his arms. The colonel was up on the horse's back as Queen literally fell off the other side, rolling in the mud to avoid the flying hooves. While O'Shounessey raced for the artillery park where Exler's battery was firing, Captain Queen quickly mounted another horse, which the harried stable hands brought to him, and tore off in the same direction. The remainder of O'Shounessey's staff scrambled to gather their mounts and figure out what the hell was going on.

When they were all mounted, they headed for the sounds of the big guns, which was the direction their boss had gone. O'Shounessey, mad as hell, rode straight for Exler, screaming: "Cease firing! For God's sake, cease firing!" Exler, who was standing beside his horse in a drunken daze, stared at the man who leaped off an unsaddled horse and ran straight at him with his sword drawn. O'Shounessey, nearly blind with rage, slammed the flat part of his sword down hard on top of Exler's head; and when the man fell to his knees, O'Shounessey kicked him viciously in the side. Then he spun on the gun crews. Luckily, the section chiefs, observing what was happening, had quickly extinguished the firing fuse on the howitzers. The big guns stood silent, smoke curling lazily up from the barrels. O'Shounessey stomped over to the gun crews with his sword held down at his side.

"You've been killing Englishmen on that damn hill!" he shouted. All heads turned toward the smoke-covered knoll. "That bloody fool …" He pointed at Exler, who was still kneeling in the mud. "He must have set the wrong elevation or distance. Hell, I don't know what he did," cursed O'Shounessey. The gun crews stood with their heads down as their colonel slowly pulled his pistol from its holster and walked back over to where Exler sat with his face buried in his hands. O'Shounessey pulled the hammer back and placed the tip of the barrel against the weeping man's head.

"Damn you to hell, man. You have been killing English soldiers. Far better soldiers than yourself."

Exler half rose as he mumbled something about wind and maps, things that O'Shounessey couldn't understand.

"You were firing long, damn you, and your barrage was fired late. McKinney and his men had already taken that bloody hill. They're on it now, what's left of them." O'Shounessey's hand shook, and the pistol was still pointed at Exler's head when Captain Queen gently placed his hand on top of O'Shounessey's wrist.

"He isn't worth killing, sir," said Queen, without taking his eyes off the pistol. O'Shounessey hesitated for a second as he looked from his aide, then to Exler, and back again. Several tense seconds passed before his thumb slowly lowered the hammer.

"Yes, Captain, I'm afraid you're right," he said, reholstering his pistol. Looking up at the smoking knoll, he whispered, "God forgive us," and walked back toward his headquarters.

* * * * *

Private Joseph Clark II stood near the south edge of the field and watched when the first shells arched up out of the valley toward them. Clark was a fairly old man for a private; he had actually made sergeant twice, but each time was busted back to private for being drunk and disorderly. Having endured shelling on many prior occasions, he quickly realized the shells were way too close to their position. Along with everyone else, he had bent over and ran like hell for cover, diving behind the same log where McKinney was hunkered down. Buchanan had been gone for several minutes when yet another airburst exploded near them; McKinney heard Clark scream and thrash around on the ground in pain. Keeping his head down as best he could, McKinney glanced over and saw a smoking piece of shrapnel sticking out of Clark's left shoulder.

"Stay down, Clark. I'm coming," he called and started crawling toward him. Shrapnel was flying everywhere, zinging through the treetops and slamming into wood and flesh. When McKinney finally reached the wounded man, he grabbed him by the arm and, as easily as possible, pulled him around.

"I'll try to pull the damn thing out!" he shouted, quickly looking around for something to protect his hand with. There was nothing within reach, so he tore a strip of cloth from the back of Clark's bloody shirt and wrapped it around his hand before grabbing the hot metal and pulling.

Clark had seen enough battlefield injuries to know what he needed to do. Placing the shoulder strap from his weapon between his teeth and biting down hard, he grunted for McKinney to pull. Big beads of sweat glistened on his forehead, and he groaned loudly as McKinney tugged on the jagged chunk of metal, but the shrapnel never budged.

"Damn," cursed McKinney, who pulled with all his might but to no avail. He knew he shouldn't stand up and expose himself above the tree trunk, but he had to get better leverage. Placing one knee on Clark's back, he rose up onto the other and put all his weight into it. The chunk of metal had just begun to move a little when McKinney heard the dreaded whistle of another incoming shell. It was going to be close, very close. The piece of shrapnel tore loose at the exact moment the airburst exploded, almost directly over their heads. The heated air and impossibly loud noise hit McKinney like a hammer, and he was sure that his good eardrum was busted. He thought this just before a blinding pain tore through his head and blackness consumed him.

Sergeant Malone, only a few yards away, saw the airburst explode right on top of them although, from where he lay, he couldn't identify the other man. Malone had seen too many airbursts in his day, and he knew McKinney was hurt; it was just too damn close. The big Irishman ignored the danger, jumped up, and ran over to his friend. What he saw made him sick. Desperately, he turned McKinney over and checked his pulse; there was none. He moaned as he looked over what the explosion had done to his friend's face and neck. Both were a terrible mess; blood ran from his nose and ears. The big man wept.

"God, why do we always lose the good ones?" he cried into the smoky sky.

Rocking back and forth, he unashamedly held McKinney's head cradled in his lap like a mother soothing her child. Several men slowly began to walk over to where their sergeant sat. They couldn't believe Ensign McKinney, who had been wounded so often, was actually dead. For some strange reason, Malone didn't want them to see McKinney so shot up, so he took off his green jacket and reverently placed it over McKinney's head and upper body. He managed to slide out from under McKinney's body and slowly, painfully stand up. He looked to the southeast toward the village of Leira; several skirmishers stood off to the side and hung their heads. From the volume of fire on the main battlefield, Malone could tell the fighting had intensified down there, but the shelling that had killed his friends and so many others had stopped. More cannon fire reverberated across the valley and more bugles sounded instructions. Malone's thoughts flashed to Exler: *That bloody drunk killed my friend!* his mind screamed as he walked slowly toward the center of the battered field. A simple plan began to form in his mind, but his first duty was to check the battlefield as best he could for more wounded and then get his boys off the knoll and back behind British lines.

The knoll had become eerily quiet. *Evidently Bumgarner had made it down the mountain to O'Shounessey's headquarters*, thought Malone as he wiped tears from his eyes. He began to assess the carnage around him; a lot of boys who should still be alive had been reduced to heaps of torn flesh. He shouted for the surviving skirmishers to form on him by platoon so he could get a proper head count. Slowly, they began to stagger into formation. He managed to keep his face stoic as the remnants of his company formed three ragged lines in front of him. The few men who had escaped injury helped the walking wounded, but some men were just too badly hurt to move. "We will come back and get these boys later," Malone said, looking at the bodies strewn across the ground.

Malone took a quick headcount and found that out of the original force of one hundred nineteen men and one officer, only fifty-five were now able to walk or at least hobble down the mountain. The

French had killed sixteen men, while twenty-one more were victims of Exler's misfired barrage. The French had wounded thirteen, and Exler had wounded another dozen; eight of those would die before help could arrive.

"A hell of a butcher's bill," growled Malone as he slowly led his tattered band of soldiers down toward the British lines. The few French prisoners who survived the fight and the bombardment trudged alone behind the skirmishers, forgotten for the moment. The skirmishers bypassed the fields they had crossed earlier because that was where the main battle still raged. From their vantage point along the edge of the woods, they could see that the French were slowly being driven back, but that brought them very little joy. Their hearts were cold from the price they had paid for taking the knoll. In the journals of the 1st Scottish Highlanders, the battle for Leira would be called the Battle of the Bloody Knoll.

The battered company was a pitiful sight as they limped toward the British picket lines, the sun sinking toward the western hills. It was a slow and painful journey, but as they drew near the sentries manning the picket lines, Malone straightened his back and shouted, "All right, you bloody bastards, I want you to straighten up and look sharp. We're skirmishers, by god." So the tired and bloody soldiers, who mostly hailed from the highlands of Scotland or the sewers of London, did their best to stand tall. As they passed through the picket lines, some leaning heavily on a buddy or a rifle, they held their heads high and marched into the battalion area with grim determination. The survivors of the bloody knoll, watched only by handful of camp followers, soon stood at attention in front of their top sergeant. Malone looked out at his men with their makeshift bandages, bloodshot eyes, and blackened faces. His heart, though pained, swelled with pride. Most of the men stared straight ahead as if seeing the battle all over again, and Malone knew he should to say something, something noble. But proper words would not come. All he could think of was killing Exler, so he simply told them what they already knew.

"You boys did damn fine today!" he shouted after the long pause. "Always remember that—always." He cleared his throat.

"Now, those of you who need to see the surgeon may go. Everybody else, try to get some rest. Colonel O'Shounessey will probably need us very soon. Company attention!" The men tried to straighten their tired shoulders as they waited for the next command.

"Dismissed!" Malone watched as his boys walked or, in some cases, hobbled away. Then he spun and headed straight for Colonel O'Shounessey's headquarters.

Just outside the main tent, he found O'Shounessey's aide seated in a camp chair and looking fairly glum, considering the ongoing victory against Soult's forces. He asked Queen if he would send some troops up to the knoll to get the wounded who were too badly hurt to walk out. Queen nodded and moved away briskly. Malone entered the tent to find O'Shounessey seated behind his desk pouring over his maps. Malone snapped painfully to attention and announced himself, "Sir, Sergeant Malone to report." Somewhat startled, O'Shounessey spun around and gasped.

"My god, man, please sit down." He gestured toward a chair. When Malone didn't move, O'Shounessey braced for the worst and simply stared at the wreck of a man in front of him.

"No, thank you, sir. I need to make my report and then get some … rest." O'Shounessey nodded.

"As you wish, Sergeant. Please make your report." Malone spoke quickly as he detailed their search for the French lines. He described how Ensign McKinney had found and proceeded to assault their artillery crews from the backside of the knoll while he led the other two platoons in attacking the front. After listening for a minute, O'Shounessey interrupted: "And just where is Ensign McKinney, Sergeant? With that young lady, I hope?" He tried to answer his own question.

"Ensign McKinney." Malone cleared his throat. "Ensign McKinney is dead, sir." Malone's eyes glistened slightly, but no tears fell. Stunned, O'Shounessey sat back; he stared at Malone as he tried to understand what he had just been told. Ensign McKinney was one of those men that seemed invincible. *Not McKinney*, he thought, *how could he be dead?* Malone's voice brought O'Shounessey back to the moment.

"I'm sorry, Sergeant. What did you say?"

"If you don't mind, sir, I'll be going," repeated Malone. O'Shounessey seemed not to hear him, so Malone assumed he was dismissed. He saluted and turned to leave.

"He's not worth killing, Sergeant," O'Shounessey said, shaking his head.

"Begging the colonel's pardon, sir, that drunken bastard killed a lot of good men on that hill today."

"I know, Mike. Those were my men, and Ensign McKinney was my friend also. I promise you that Exler will go before a court martial board. McKinney was a damn fine soldier and so were all the rest of those skirmishers, but throwing away your career by killing Exler won't bring them back."

Malone had returned to rigid attention and was staring at a spot just above the colonel's head. O'Shounessey was no fool; he knew his words were falling on deaf ears. He only hoped the court martial board wasn't going to be hearing a case against a sergeant instead of a lieutenant. O'Shounessey looked at his friend. *It's a hell of a war*, he thought to himself.

"Think about what I said, Sergeant. That is all." Malone saluted again and left. He headed straight for Exler's tent.

"Bloody hell," moaned O'Shounessey as he watched Malone leave. Then he turned back to his other reports; he still had a war to fight.

* * * * *

Elizabeth Feirra was franticly searching for Ensign McKinney. The word had spread quickly through the camp that the British artillery had mistakenly overshot their target on the knoll and that several men in the skirmishers' company had been killed. She ran from one tent to another, a feeling of dread growing in her stomach. All the returning soldiers refused to look her in the eye, and she knew that something was terribly wrong. As she made her way through the company area, she spotted Sergeant Malone leaving Colonel O'Shounessey's tent and ran after him, shouting, "Sergeant

Malone, Sergeant Malone, please wait!" The man walked on. *Surely, he heard me,* she thought, *so why* ... Then it hit her like a fist. *He knows.* "Sergeant!" she screamed at the top of her lungs this time, and Malone slowly turned around. His face told her everything.

"No, God, no," she moaned and sank to her knees. Malone walked over and grabbed her arm, easing her back up.

"Be strong, woman. He deserves that," he whispered.

"Where is he?" she managed to ask.

"We left them all on that damn knoll," said Malone, releasing her arm and stomping off toward the officers' area. He was looking for a reckoning!

Malone figured that Exler would have crawled back to his tent after the drumming that O'Shounessey had given him, and he was right. Malone walked up to the single guard who stood half asleep at the tent flap.

"Corporal, take a walk. Lieutenant Exler and I have something to discuss." The young soldier looked the battered, bloodstained sergeant up and down and decided that it was a good time to get some chow. Malone glanced around the officers' area and, not seeing another soul, stepped quietly into Exler's tent. Exler turned halfway around when he heard someone enter, but his attention was mainly focused on the last swallow of rum in the bottom of the bottle he held in his hand.

"Sergeant, did you come to beat me with your sword?" Malone didn't answer; he was busy inspecting the contents of the tent. Another bottle, this one empty, lay at the foot of Exler's cot, and a fancy-dueling pistol sat on a table next to him. Malone didn't hesitate; he walked over, grabbed the pistol, and placed the barrel against Exler's temple.

"I've come to kill you, you bastard," growled Malone. Exler dropped the bottle, and Malone pulled the trigger. Exler had started to look up, but the musket ball hit him just behind the right eye, and his head flew back hard, blood and gray matter splattering across the green army blankets stacked in the corner. Malone spat on the quivering corpse and quickly placed the smoking pistol in Exler's right hand before walking out into the fading light.

Elizabeth, still in shock, staggered around the company area looking for one of the soldiers' wives whom she hoped might watch her son while she went to retrieve her lover's body. In the back of her mind, she knew that if the burial crew beat her up the mountain, Ensign John McKinney's body would wind up in a mass grave with all the other poor souls.

Sure enough, an hour later, the burial crew was just in front of her as she worked her way toward the knoll. She couldn't let them find his body before she did; she just couldn't. Fighting back tears, she struggled desperately through the thick brush.

The stubby laurel bushes and green running briars tore at her dress and ripped the flesh of her legs, drawing blood. But she rushed on, racing the sun as it fell toward the mountain range that lay in the haze behind her. Just as the fiery red ball touched the dark ridge far to the west, she finally reached the field where the battle took place. Not all of the shells were airbursts, and the field looked like a giant's hand had stabbed the earth many times with a turning spade. *The burial crews will indeed be very busy,* she thought, observing the field covered with bodies, both British and French. The scene in front of her was surreal; nothing could have prepared her for the carnage in her path. *How will I ever be able to find John's body?* her mind screamed. Trees had become shattered hunks of burnt wood, and once-living human beings had suffered a similar fate. Gagging, she walked like a zombie in a widening circle, checking each body as she came to it.

"Oh lord, what horrors men are capable of!" Elizabeth shouted loudly to the whip-poor-wills that answered with a sad cry of agreement.

The sun slipped below the far ridge, and the light slowly faded along with her hopes of finding John McKinney's body. Stumbling from one body to the next, she was at the brink of exhaustion when suddenly she stopped. A strange sound drifted through the still, almost stagnant air. It lingered on the border of her recognition. It wasn't the sound of battle, for the battle of Leira was dying like the poor souls around her had done. It was the soft call of a dove that had caught her attention. *An odd sound to be heard on this eerily quiet knoll,* she thought, sitting down to listen.

Far below, where proud bugles had sounded charge after charge, the French had once more underestimated the outnumbered British—with their Baker rifles and steely resolve. Wellington himself had arrived on the battlefield; he and his commanders had cleverly maneuvered their smaller force onto the high ground and Soult, without his hidden artillery, had wasted his superior cavalry against the well-established British lines. The British artillery, including Exler's demoralized crew, had devastated the proud ranks of Napoleon's finest before they could even approach the outmanned redcoats. As the sun set on the ridges to the west, Marshal Soult's great army limped away from the fields they had paraded across only a few days before. Today they bled heavily on those fields, and now, as rain threatened to fall once again, they headed down the road away from the sleepy village of Leira.

From the outer edge of the field, with the smell of fresh-plowed dirt and gunpowder dense in the air, Elizabeth could see that the burial crews had broken out their lanterns as it became dark. They had finished digging the deep holes that would be the final resting place for the dead of both sides, and now the difficult part began: the sad, gruesome task of finding and then rolling the bodies, or in some cases tossing the body parts, into the cold, dark holes that waited like the jaws of hell. Elizabeth, who stood in the deepening shadows, shivered in the cool night air as she watched the burial crews work by lantern light.

The main battlefield lay below her, and it had become ghostly quiet, the silence broken occasionally by rifle shots ringing out in the night. *Probably some cavalryman putting his wounded horse out of its misery*, she thought to herself, hoping it wasn't something worse.

"God, if I don't find him soon, he will wind up in a ditch," she cried, resuming her frantic search once more. An evening mist had begun to drape itself over the field, and a dove—maybe the one she had heard before—called out from its perch nearby. Elizabeth walked in that direction and spoke to it. "Where is your hawk, little one," she whispered sadly, "and where is mine?" Her eyes were gradually becoming accustomed to the darkness, and she cautiously stepped over a large limb that had been ripped from a nearby tree by one of the exploding shells. She raised her leg high in order to clear the tangle of limbs, but the heel of her boot struck a hard knot, and she unceremoniously fell onto her hands and knees with a grunt. "Damn," she cursed lightly, brushing leaves and mud from her hands and knees.

She could no longer hear the dove and figured she had frightened it off. With a tired groan, she straightened up, brushed off a few more leaves, and stepped across another fallen limb. She was a little startled by the faint rustle of small wings just in front of her, but the sound guided her forward. Elizabeth took one more tentative step, and her foot found something—something soft—in the weeds.

"Oh, oh," she cried, cringing as she lifted her foot, afraid it was a dead body she had stepped on, or perhaps worse. But it wasn't a *dead* body. She heard a voice faintly croak in the still air.

"Did you come all the way up here to stomp on my hand, or did you come to help me?" Just then, the waning moon crested the near ridge, and through the semidarkness, Elizabeth could see a green jacket with a body moving ever so slightly underneath it. Sobbing, she knelt down, gently lifted the jacket, and gasped. John McKinney's blood-encrusted face appeared like a vision out of a nightmare. His head was completely covered with dried blood and dirt. One bloodshot eye looked up at her; the other was battered a deep purple and swollen shut. He looked like death, but she bent down and kissed his cracked lips anyway.

"Oh, John. Oh, John" was all she could say as her tears ran down onto his battered face. A hawk cried somewhere in the distance, and Elizabeth's heart sang. Her lover, her hawk, was alive.

* * * * *

"John, what can I do?" she whispered the question as if someone would overhear her and learn her secret, that John McKinney was alive!

"Stop crying and give me some water," he whispered hoarsely, reaching up to touch his parched lips. She was silent for a long moment, sniffing back tears. Glancing up at her with his good eye, he saw a panicked look spread across her face.

"You did bring some water, didn't you?" he finally asked.

"I … I … everyone thought you were dead. I came to retrieve your body and keep it from going into a mass grave." She broke down sobbing once more, and he reached up to weakly squeeze her arm.

"It's okay." He tried to reassure her, but his voice lacked conviction. Before he could brood too long on his predicament, though, a harsh Irish voice boomed from the shadows:

"I'll be damned. You're dead, and you're still making women cry." Sergeant Malone walked out of the mist like a big mean leprechaun, a mixture of relief and disbelief in his voice.

"I need water, not wisecracks," groaned McKinney, looking up at his friend with one bloodshot eye. "Did you bring any?" he pleaded.

"Yes, sir, I have water … but only for the living. You're supposed to be dead." He chuckled, almost in tears. Kneeling down, he gently placed the canteen to McKinney's mouth. "Not too much now, sir."

"Oh, bloody hell, that hurts," cried McKinney as water spilled from his swollen mouth, leaving a streak through the mud on his chin and neck as it ran down his face. Elizabeth reached up and gently wiped his cracked lips with a piece of cloth she had torn from her tattered cloak. He smiled at her as she fretted about his head.

"God help me, sir, I thought you were dead. There was blood everywhere, and you didn't seem to be breathing. Your whole damn head was split open. Hell, I couldn't find a pulse." Tears pooled in Malone's eyes as he spoke, and he unashamedly reached up to wipe them away with the sleeve of his shirt.

"So that's why my head hurts so badly," said McKinney. He tried to laugh but could only manage a pitiful cough, which made him flinch from the pain that ripped through his head.

Elizabeth didn't say a word; she just listened to the two soldiers talk as she fluttered around, brushing debris from McKinney's shirt and pants. After a few minutes, she smoothed out her crumpled dress and eased his head onto her lap. He started to rise in protest, but she gently placed her hand on his shoulder.

"I've got to ask Sergeant Malone some questions," he growled.

"Ask your questions, sir, but let her clean and bandage your head ... and any other place that you're wounded. I never checked anywhere else, but your head was bad enough." Malone wasn't sure if he should joke about his friend's injury, but he was so damn glad to see him alive that he couldn't help it. "I'll answer your questions while she tends to you," he continued as Elizabeth tore several long strips from her petticoat, which was the only relatively clean piece of material she had.

McKinney choked again on the water that Elizabeth was trying to give him, but he finally managed to clear his throat and ask Malone the question that was boiling under his skin.

"Was I right? Was it Exler?"

"Yeah ... I mean yes, sir. It was Exler all right. But, sir, you don't have to worry about him. It seems he shot himself. Distressed, I suppose." Malone stared straight ahead as if he were reading from a script held over McKinney's head.

"Exler shot himself?" McKinney questioned.

"That's right, sir. It seems he shot himself inside his own tent with that fancy pistol of his, or at least that is what the provost marshal said." Both men looked into the other's eyes, except McKinney had only one he could see through.

"Good riddance is what I say," said Elizabeth without looking up from her task.

Minutes passed as Elizabeth tried her best to clean McKinney's wounds without hurting him too badly; finally, with a long sigh, he laid his freshly bandaged head back into her lap and closed his eye. The small amount of water he was finally able to keep down had helped his parched throat, but his head still hurt like hell. Reaching over, he gently clutched Elizabeth's hand as he listened to Malone explain the chain of events that occurred after he was hit by the last airburst. None of them noticed the large red-tailed hawk that sat high atop a nearby pecan tree, its opalescent eyes taking in every detail of the surrounding area.

McKinney attempted a smile when Malone described how the bloodied skirmishers had straightened their ragged uniforms and stood tall as they marched through the battalion area. Malone never mentioned his part in Exler's death, and McKinney never asked. Some things were better left alone. *Malone will talk about it when he's ready*, thought McKinney, looking up at his friend.

"So I was actually hit with the last shot that bastard fired?" asked McKinney in painful recognition of the irony.

"It seems that way, sir," replied Malone, shaking his head in bitter disbelief. "Sergeant McClure said it was a sight to see, sir. Ol' Colonel O'Shounessey rode like a madman out to the artillery park, jumped off his horse, and slapped Exler hard on top of the head with the flat of his sword. It scared everybody, and it sure as hell stopped the firing." A sad laugh escaped Malone's lips, and both men stared off into the night. Elizabeth bit her lip.

After several long and silent minutes, McKinney tried once again to sit up; and this time, with Elizabeth's help, he managed to get it done. Sliding backward on his butt, he leaned back against the log that had been his first cover from the shelling. Malone watched his friend struggle in pain and decided to broach the subject that had been on his mind since finding McKinney alive.

"Sir, everyone, including Colonel O'Shounessey, thinks you are dead. Maybe you should stay that way." Malone paused for a second, hoping his words would somehow sink into his friend's thick, swollen head. When no harsh reply came, he continued, "You have been wounded more than any man in the entire regiment. You have paid your dues, sir." Malone sat with his big hands in his lap and waited. McKinney remained quiet for a moment before responding, "Actually, Sergeant, I thought about that while I lay here under your stinking jacket, after I came to that is," whispered McKinney with a hint of a smile. He spoke the words very low as if he were afraid that someone would hear. "I wasn't sure if the damn frogs would come back for their dead and finish me off or if the bloody crows would pick my eyes out."

Elizabeth shuddered at the thought and was, as usual, surprised by how casually they could speak of death and suffering. Death was a constant part of these men's lives, and she understood that perhaps they needed to use humor as a defense. For her, though, the gravity of it would never wane.

Without thinking, McKinney reached up and started to scratch his head, but he stopped just in time. He dropped his hand and fidgeted with his pant leg instead. "I was thinking it would be nice to just go back to Oban and grow old with Elizabeth and the boy. Maybe even make a few more boys." He smiled at the blushing Elizabeth.

"Or girls," she added. Her face, though hidden in the dark, grew even redder.

"Well, sir, this is your chance. This damn war is probably going to continue for a long time, and you've done your part for the king and country. Now do something for yourself, as well as for Elizabeth and the baby," said Malone.

"His name is Sterling," huffed Elizabeth.

Both men glanced over at her and then changed the subject. They went over the details of the battle and how the various men in their unit had performed. Elizabeth simply held McKinney in her arms and listened. None of them saw the wounded French sergeant, who throughout their entire conversation had lain silently under his greatcoat several yards away and who now slowly reached for his musket. But the hawk did. The big red-tailed hawks, which down through the ages had been called war hawks, were often seen sailing above battlefields—always vigilant. And now, this hawk turned its sharp eyes toward the Frenchman as his bloody hand curled around the muddy stock of the musket.

The hawk watched the ever-so-slight movement underneath the gray woolen coat, and glimpses of a dark-blue jacket appeared in the pale light. The jacket marked him as one of Napoleon's elite, a Dragoon chasseur. His waxed mustache and long pigtails set him apart from the artillerymen, as did his physical size. He was there for one reason: to prevent what had just happened, a rout of the much-needed artillery by the British. He had failed at his assigned task, but maybe not completely; he might still redeem himself to some extent.

Sergeant Joseph Dessel hated the British as much as the British hated him and his elite dragoons with their fur-trimmed shakos and handlebar mustaches.

"Viva la France," whispered the chasseur. With his teeth clenched to prevent a moan from escaping his parched lips, he crawled over to a small tree, trailing bright-red blood behind him. Propping his back against the sapling, he rested and listened. He couldn't understand much English, but he knew that the voices came from his enemy. That was enough to suppress the pain momentarily. He slowly raised the musket and braced it against his shoulder, grimacing as he took aim at the silhouettes dancing in and out of his blurred vision.

The hawk sat stoically on the thick tree limb as the Frenchman prepared his shot. Without warning, the hawk lifted its great wings as quietly as a falling feather and sprang from its perch. Sergeant Dessel's finger curled around the cold metal trigger, and he was slowly tightening his grip as the raptor sailed silently through the night air. Just before Dessel felt the gun slam into his shoulder, he heard a shrill cry directly above him. Raising his head from the well-worn walnut stock of his musket, he looked straight into eight sharp talons. They flared out just as they struck him—like the vengeance of the ancient gods.

The hawk's cry was mirrored by that of the Frenchman who instinctively pulled the trigger. The shot snapped a low-hanging branch from a gnarled pine tree several feet above where McKinney rested. The musket ball sped past and slammed into the tree where the hawk's attack had originated. The pine branch fell into Elizabeth's lap, right beside McKinney's head, while Malone's one good eye probed the deepening shadows for the source of the shot. He looked around like only an experienced warrior can and then quickly leaped up, throwing his body over McKinney and Elizabeth.

All three of them lay huddled together as dark storm clouds churned across the pale moon and a light mist filled the air. Barely forty yards away, blood poured from eight wounds in the big Frenchman's face and he collapsed onto the ground, moaning in pain. The hawk had flown into the night sky, its cry echoing across the field—a long sharp note that snaked through the fog, reverberating eerily like some lost soul. The great raptor soon sailed over the fields where the burial crews labored in their grisly task. They looked up and admired the hawk, wondering only briefly about the source of the gunshot before returning to their work.

"Did you see that?" asked a slightly startled Sergeant Malone.

"Not all of it," replied Elizabeth, her heart pounding in her chest. "But I saw enough to know that Ensign McKinney has a protector."

Malone cautiously rose from his prone position, brushing leaves and other debris from his pant legs. "Sorry, ma'am," he said as he reached out his hands to help her and McKinney sit up. They stared into the darkness, and then their eyes turned skyward.

"My grandmother would probably understand all of this business about the hawk," said McKinney, his eyes searching the night sky, "but I don't."

"The hawk and dove," whispered Elizabeth excitedly as she watched a small grayish dove join the hawk in its flight. They sailed together on the cold winds that were hurrying the rain clouds east into the mountains. After several minutes of silence, broken only occasionally by the faint moaning of the Frenchman across the way, Malone turned to look at his friend.

"Sir, you have to make a decision pretty soon. The burial crews will be over here in another couple of hours. They may even come sooner to see what that shot was about."

"I know, Mike," said McKinney with an air of acceptance in his voice. It was the second time in as many days he had used Malone's Christian name, and the big Irishman was just as pleasantly surprised as the first time it happened.

McKinney turned his gaze back toward Elizabeth, who sat propped against the log staring into the night sky. From between the clouds escaped silvery moonbeams, their reflection as bright as diamonds in her eyes. Her beauty took his breath away. Forcing his thoughts back to the problem at hand, McKinney looked over at his friend.

"I want you to tell Colonel O'Shounessey that you couldn't find my body. Use whatever excuse you can think of. If I decide to come back down, Elizabeth can help me. If not ..." He shrugged his tired shoulders before continuing, "Then it has been an honor to serve with you, Sergeant Malone." McKinney extended a large, calloused hand; Sergeant Malone reached out and gently shook it. Then Malone stood, saluted his friend, who returned the salute from his seated position, and started to leave.

"Before I go, I think I better check on our Frenchman. He sounds very unhappy," Malone whispered in disgust. He patted his knife and left, quietly disappearing into the mist.

As the dark clouds rushed by, a curious ring of vapor formed a shimmering circle around the pale moon. *A sure sign that foul weather is coming*, thought McKinney, remembering his sailing days. His father had taught him from an early age to watch closely for nature's signs of changes in the weather, like the red clouds that sailors hated to see boiling on the horizon in the early morning light. As his tired mind relived some of his early sailing days, McKinney thought he heard a muffled cry coming from the direction Malone had walked, but he couldn't be sure. His damned ears still rang form the explosion. Reaching up, he cupped a hand over his injured ear, but no audible sound escaped the night. Elizabeth hadn't seemed to notice the noise, so he didn't mention it.

McKinney tried to wipe the dried blood from his hands before he reached gently and turned her face toward him. He spoke softly: "Elizabeth, I'm not sure if you can, or will, or even if you want to wait for me, but I must go back. This is who I am." He held his arms out wide as if she had never seen his uniform.

They talked for over an hour. McKinney even managed to doze for a little while with Elizabeth's head on his shoulder, but the pain soon forced him awake. In the pit of her stomach, Elizabeth knew that this soldier, this hawk, would indeed have to go back. But she was so tired of war. She fought the idea of his returning with all her heart and soul, but nothing, no argument, no amount of pleading, could change his mind.

Strangely, there was a part of her that could understand his reasoning; another part, though, screamed in protest. She gazed into the night sky, the hawk and dove still soaring side by side. *So peaceful, yet so far from reality*, she thought. Closing her eyes, she decided to try, one more time, to persuade her lover to leave.

"John, like Sergeant Malone said, you have done enough, given enough; it's time for you to have a life—with me!" McKinney pulled her to him and held her as tightly as his battered body would allow. She wept softly while McKinney glanced toward where the burial crews were now tossing the French bodies into the common graves. He knew they would have to leave soon. The flickering light from the whale oil lanterns, lanterns whose globes were partly covered with black soot, cast an eerie yellow glow over the redcoats. The soldiers, who for disciplinary reasons had been assigned this unpleasant task, had stripped down to their white linen shirts, which hung loosely on their sweaty bodies and were covered with British as well as French blood. McKinney looked back at his woman.

"Elizabeth, I truly want to be with you and Sterling. I hope you know that. But ..."

"But what, John?" she tearfully interrupted.

"But ..." he searched for the words, "the job is not finished." He knew those weren't the words she needed to hear, but it was the truth as far as he could explain it. Elizabeth raised her head from his chest, where her tears had soaked his dirty officer's blouse.

"When will the damn job be finished, John? When you are dead and some Frenchman tosses your body into a stinking hole like those?" She pointed toward the burial crew. "You'll die on some god-forsaken battlefield, and I'll never see you again." Sobbing, she eased herself away from him. He watched her tears fall from her quivering chin.

"I'm not sure if I will know when it's finished," he said, looking far off into the night before he continued, "but I hope you will still be there for me when it is."

"Damn all wars to hell," she moaned with a sad tone of acceptance that caused her whole body to ache. A minute later, reluctantly, she went on, "John McKinney, I will take Sterling and go to Oban. We will wait for you if you think that your parents will accept us. But ..." This time, she turned his head to look at her. "I want"—she paused—"I need for you to come home to us as soon as you can." McKinney softly pressed his cracked lips against hers; the kiss was gentle but intimate. After a minute, their lips parted, and he gazed into her tear-streaked face.

"I love you," he whispered, just as the dove's mournful call descended from high overhead.

While they held each other, the hawk and dove sailed across the partially lit face of the moon as it sank slowly toward the dark sierras looming in the distance.

"John," she said, breaking a long silence, "I have had war take nearly everything that I have ever held dear. I couldn't bear losing you … again. Promise you will come back to me." She leaned her head onto his chest and sobbed. McKinney took her by the shoulders and held her away from him. With the back of his sleeve, he wiped away the tears that rolled down her cheeks.

"I love you, Elizabeth," he repeated as he looked deep into her beautiful hazel eyes. "It would be easy for me to promise you I will come back, but you know that promise would mean nothing. I can only tell you that I will try, and God knows I want to come back to you and Sterling. That I can promise!" He looked away as tears threatened to fall from his own eyes. "I have seen enough war, enough killing, and I have inflicted enough pain for two lifetimes. This war will end someday, and when it does, I will come home. I want peace, and I want you." Elizabeth laid her head against his chest once more.

"John, oh, John."

The moon had disappeared in its nightly journey to chase the sun from its hiding place as McKinney and Elizabeth walked and sometimes stumbled down through the fields. She did her best to help him as they struggled along, but his battered body demanded he sit often. His head was bleeding again, and the dizziness was awful, making him nauseous. But he kept going, though his breath was short, and he leaned heavily on his walking stick. They stopped to rest on a large rock near the edge of the gulley just above Leira. The burial crews still worked the main battlefield below. The sergeants who supervised the unlucky bastards stood beside the wagons and watched them labor. The big Henry wagons, with their oversized wheels and iron rims, held the shovels and picks that the burial crews used. The lanterns on the dropped tailgates glowed out into the night, illuminating the tired, dirty faces of the crew. They were called the damned, and their faces glowed an eerie yellow as they quietly went about their task, the lanterns dotting the battlefield like so many fireflies on a summer night.

"Let's go," grunted McKinney, having finally caught his breath. He pushed hard with his shaky legs and struggled to his feet. Although he was more than ready to lie down right there, he was afraid he would never get back up if he did. Elizabeth walked with her arm around his waist, McKinney's arm draped across her shoulder as they slowly approached the sentries.

"I bet we look bloody strange," whispered McKinney. And he was right, for the two young privates on guard stared questioningly at the ragged pair. She with a tattered dress half torn from her legs, and he with a bandage on his head that looked like a turban. Only McKinney's hard eyes and bloody green jacket kept the sentries from laughing out loud. It had been a difficult journey, but at last, they stood in the skirmishers' company area.

"John, I'll go get Sterling and meet you at our tent," said Elizabeth, kissing him lightly on the lips as she walked away. McKinney watched as she retrieved her son from Sergeant Hawkins's tent and carried him toward their own. The little trooper didn't seem to stir. With a hesitant sigh and a slight limp, McKinney turned and walked through the quiet camp toward Colonel O'Shounessey's headquarters. It was well past midnight when he finally stood in front of the tent of the battalion's headquarters, but he wasn't surprised to see O'Shounessey still at work. Two lamps burned on a table in the back corner of the tent, reminding McKinney of a jack-o'-lantern from his childhood. Tapping lightly on the flap of the stiff canvas tent, he waited for a call to enter. O'Shounessey, worn out from the day's fighting, assumed that at this late hour it must be Captain Queen, so he simply said, "Come."

O'Shounessey never looked up as McKinney limped in and stood shakily at attention. When the intruder never announced himself, O'Shounessey growled, "Well, Captain, what is it?"

"Sir," was all McKinney managed to say, but it was enough. O'Shounessey spun around and gasped as if seeing a ghost.

"My god, John," he groaned, rushing over and placing a camp chair behind the battered ensign.

"Here, sit down."

"Thank you, sir," moaned McKinney and promptly collapsed into it.

"Captain Queen!" shouted O'Shounessey. "Captain Queen!" he shouted again when he heard no answer.

After what seemed like a long time, for Queen was famous for his efficiency, a rustling sound stirred outside, and the captain's voice floated through the tent flap: "Sir." A second later, Queen stuck his head in and, after spotting McKinney, stood in the entrance staring.

"Captain Queen, get the battalion surgeon bloody quick." When Queen just stood there frozen, O'Shounessey shouted again, "Quickly, man!" McKinney nearly laughed as the tall lanky captain tore off in the direction of the hospital tent. O'Shounessey, confused but grateful that McKinney was back among the living, walked over and leaned against the main tent pole, watching his aide race through the battalion grounds. The old Irishman stood there, gathering his thoughts. When Queen disappeared into the mist creeping through the camp like one of the great plagues, O'Shounessey turned back to his supposedly dead friend.

"My God, John, everyone thought you were dead," he stammered, walking over to take a seat across from McKinney.

"Sergeant Malone was sure you were dead, although he did say he couldn't find your body when he went back up on the mountain."

"I'm not sure why he couldn't find me. Elizabeth did. But I can understand why he thought I was dead, sir. I must have looked pretty bad after that shell hit us," said McKinney staring down at his dirty boots.

O'Shounessey eased out of his chair, returned to his desk, and retrieved a half full bottle of rum from among the maps. He carefully poured two tumblers full of the smoky liquid and handed one to McKinney.

"John, it was Exler. He was drunk, and he ... he killed a lot of good men. I'm sorry." For a brief second, McKinney's eyes burned with an intense hate, but then it was gone. O'Shounessey saw the stare and knew he had to address it. "It seems that Exler shot himself, though," he added. "I assume out of remorse. I'll have to investigate it as a suicide." He waved his hand as if the task was an afterthought. "It seems pretty cut and dried." The two men looked at each other, and an unsaid acknowledgement passed between them. O'Shounessey looked away.

"John, what you did on that knoll saved a lot of English lives. We won the day down here, but only because you took out that part of their artillery we couldn't see. If you hadn't taken it out, well, let's just say we would surely be at the mercy of Marshal Soult right now." He shook his head. "Your actions will get you a medal and a promotion," he said, smiling before he finished with, "Lieutenant McKinney." McKinney's forehead wrinkled as he pondered the comment for a second.

"Sir, I thank you, but Sergeant Malone and the boys deserve the credit for taking that knoll. They were great, sir. You would have been proud." He tried to smile but could only grimace.

"I am proud of them, John. I have already put Sergeant Malone in for a medal and the skirmishers will get a unit citation." *Even if Exler's death is questionable*, thought O'Shounessey to himself.

The two weary soldiers drank deeply from their rum and sat in silence for a moment. Then as if noticing it for the first time, O'Shounessey looked at McKinney's bandaged head. "And who, may I ask, bandaged your head, John? It looks like a bloody turban." The rum gave O'Shounessey's demeanor a warm glow as he watched his friend's face blush despite the damage.

"It was Elizabeth, sir. She found me on the knoll before the burial crew could throw me into one of their holes." He laughed and then grimaced again.

"She cleaned my wounds," he said, touching his head, "and helped me down the mountain." *And Sergeant Malone couldn't find you?* O'Shounessey wondered to himself.

"She is quite a remarkable woman, your Elizabeth," said O'Shounessey with a smile. "Yes, sir, that she is ..." McKinney replied, looking down into his rum. "And more," he added. O'Shounessey poured the last of the rum into their glasses and offered a toast:

"To Elizabeth then."

"To Elizabeth," chimed McKinney. *And to the hawk and dove,* he added to himself with a painful smile.

* * * * *

A woman sought peace in the only way she knew and a warrior's fate rode on the wings of a hawk. Once more, the hawk and dove sail through the ages. This time they head west, across the gray Atlantic to another struggle.

CHAPTER 3

"☙"

The Grand Parade

Nobody knows the troubles I've seen. Nobody
knows the troubles I've been through.
—Old Negro hymnal

Red clay dust boils up from beneath bare feet black as indigo as twenty-five weary souls shuffle down a shady, tree-lined dirt road. Trudging along, no joy in their steps, they are driven by a dogged determination and the close presence of an eight-foot rawhide whip. The whip looks a lot like a blacksnake, and it is curled around the saddle horn of a man who knows how to use it. The sun, its rays gentle at this early hour, has barely begun to peek over the distant haze-covered hills to the east as the group of men, women, and children head toward two large tobacco fields that lay quietly in the early morning fog awaiting their arrival. The Negros sing an old hymnal, a mournful tune, as familiar to them as the very dirt they walk along. They are slaves, but they're allowed to sing their songs as long as they stay on the path, so near the master's house, with their heads down. The plantation foreman, a big rough-looking character from the hills of southeast Tennessee, sits atop his bay gelding, a shotgun cradled in his arms and a smirk on his ruddy face. The whip is never far from his hand.

One of the slaves, a young girl, barely sixteen, carries a small light-skinned child on her back, wrapped "Injun style." The girl's head is down like all the rest, but she sees the big house sitting off the road out of the corner of her eye. A huge black rod iron fence that appears to the girl to be ten feet tall, guards a well-manicured lawn just to her right. Young and a little foolish, she dares to glance up at the house that glimmers in the morning light like Camelot. Her eyes, the color of the fields, are drawn to the third floor of the mansion and a large corner window. There, another girl, about her age but white, looks down from what might as well be another planet. The young black girl is surprised to see the girl crying, tears running down her pale cheeks. *Lordy, why in the world would that child be so sad, she's the master's daughter?* wondered the young mother as she moves past flower beds ablaze with geraniums and irises. But she can't worry about the girl's tears for long; the foreman has seen her, and his shouts ring in her ears. She drops her eyes and scurries along. She doesn't want to get whipped, not with the baby.

* * * * *

The sweltering heat shimmers above the dirt road like an illusionist's image of some strange living thing, and the sun beats down hard on the weary men dressed in gray. It is early morning on an already hot summer day in late June. The year is 1863. It's the kind of day when young boys should be hiding from their chores. Hoeing corn and fetching stove wood could wait a little longer. They should be skinny dipping down in some familiar creek or watching a cork bobber slowly jump on the end of their fishing lines. Instead, the rumble of artillery reverberates through these ancient mountains, and a lot of the local boys march off to war.

Rugged mountains pierced by limestone outcroppings and bristling with stunted Virginia pines and twisted chestnut oaks tower above the soldiers as they march along. The high tops shelter several isolated farms scattered across the valley floor like pieces on a checkerboard. These mountains, untouched by the mighty glaciers, were old when the Himalayans were mere foothills, and the weathered peaks resemble old warriors battered down by time. The countryside looks very familiar to most of the boys as they march through the valley of the Clinch. For some, it is home, and for the others, it just reminds them of a place far away.

Another war rages, this one far removed from the remnants of the old groves. It rumbles in the distance and shakes people's lives. And once again, good men and women are called to task. This is a bitter war, as if all wars aren't, but this one pits brother against brother and friend against friend, and it is ripping a country apart. Young boys, barely men, hear the call, though, and march proudly toward the sound of battle. The fate of Joseph Walker's family is sadly typical. The Walkers live up near the Cumberland Gap, and they sent five boys off to fight in this damn war. Three went south; two went north. None came back alive. And the old gods, they simply watch from their hiding places and wonder.

The long gray line, the likes of which the old farmers who work the fields alongside the dusty road have never seen, march in columns of four. Some chat, but most just look down at the heels of the man in front of him. Oddly, many of the men are smiling; all but the hardest veterans are trying to inhale the sweet aromas filling the air despite the choking dust. It's late June and the time of year when the mountain laurels, which are in full bloom, carpet the hillsides with small pink blossoms. Wild flowers dot the fields, and well-pruned limbs seem to strain from the weight as the apple trees are loaded down with green orbs that, come September, will ripen into juicy red and yellow delights. The orchards, comprised mostly of McIntosh apples and sweet black cherries, are usually clustered near the big hay barns baking in the summer heat and awaiting the first cutting of the orchard grass.

A narrow dirt road winds up out of the Clinch River Valley and climbs steadily toward one of the few gaps in the long chain of ridges called the Cumberland Mountains. It twists around huge rock outcroppings, crosses bold steams, and tiptoes through quiet coves. This well-worn path the men trudge is an offshoot of the old wilderness trail that pioneers like Daniel Boone helped cut through this country a hundred years before. Native Indian tribes, mostly Cherokee and Iroquois, traveled through these same mountains and used the trail, before the white man's arrival, for thousands of years. The road now runs through several small towns before turning up steep to meet the mountains and the rocky tops that give birth to the Clinch.

The road is dry now, but it's deeply rutted from the heavy wagon traffic of an army on the move. From a distance or from high atop the granite cliffs towering above it, the road looks like a great red and brown snake crawling toward Big Stone Gap. Thick swirling dust boils up from behind the heavy wagons, and it covers every living thing within reach like a red blanket. Plants and trees along the side of the road are coated in red, the green of the leaves barely showing through for those who cared to look. Thousands upon thousands of soldiers, and nearly as many horses, trudge through the thick clouds of swirling Virginia clay. For now, the only price the men are paying for wearing the butternut and following the Stars and Bars is watery eyes, parched throats, and tired legs.

Sergeant Kenneth Nichols is one of those men who wear the gray, and he marches along with twenty thousand other sons of the south. His head is down, a damp handkerchief, tied behind his head, covers his nose and mouth. He, like almost all the men, daydreams of home. Nichols is marching with H Company of the 10th Battalion, one of several brigades under a fiery young general by the name of George Pickett. The entire 1st Corps of the army of Northern Virginia is stretched out along the snake of a road, racing northward in a mad dash to join General Robert E. Lee in his invasion of the north. Lee's old war horse, General James Longstreet, is the 1st Corps commander and is somewhere up ahead scouting the best route for his troops to join Lee.

Sergeant Nichols and the rest of the boys in gray are marching along this thoroughfare running from Knoxville, where they have been posted for the last several months, toward the upper Shenandoah Valley. Nichols has only been back with H Company for about four months ever since his escape from a Yankee hospital just north of Blountville back in November. He looks down at the stump of his left arm, and his mind immediately flashed back to that terrible day last September. *Only nine months ago, it seems longer,* he thought to himself as he trudged along.

The ambush that cost him his arm had occurred just a few miles further up this *very same road*, he realized. His company, H Company, had moved up the road way too fast. *Too damn big a hurry*, his mind screamed just before he was shot. His arm began to throb as he recalled that fateful day. Glancing around nervously, a little unsteadily on his feet, he began to recognize several features from their first trip, a rock wall here, an abandoned homestead there. A cold sweat broke out on his forehead as he plodded along, and his mood darkened like the clouds that crept across the ridge from the storm brewing behind the high peak.

Had Sergeant Nichols bothered to look up as he walked along, he would have seen a large hawk floating lazily on wind currents blowing up the west side of the Blue Ridge Mountains. The Easterly winds that where howling now due to the approaching storm blow in from across what the early settlers called the dark and bloody ground of ol' Kentuck. The hawk gave an occasional shrill cry that echoed off the high rocky tops as if it were lonesome for its mate, but Sergeant Nichols never looked up.

* * * * *

Kenneth Nichols was born one rainy spring morning twenty-one years earlier to a hard-working but poor Scots-Irish family. Two generations of Nichols had owned and worked on a small hardscrabble farm near Blacksburg, Virginia. They had never owned any slaves, and neither did most of the people in Pulaski County. What they did have though, like their neighbors, was a strong sense of loyalty to their land and to their state. They called it their home soil, even though their grandparents had been born far across the cold north Atlantic and lived for years under the oppressive thumb of English nobles. This land they now owned, and by god, they would fight to defend it.

So when the state of Virginia seceded from the Union, the Nichols family's loyalty went with her. There were many who filled the ranks of the Gray who owned no slaves, but what they did have was a steadfast belief in the rights of the state, not Washington, to tell them what to do. Their reasons varied as to why they picked up their muskets and marched off to war, but most felt that when Lincoln's Army invaded the south, it was time to fight. The Scots-Irish immigrants were a proud people, and they didn't take kindly to folks, especially government folks, lording over them or telling them what not to do. Kenneth, like many of his friends, had felt the same way, at least until he joined up.

"Yeah, right," he grumbled as he marched along. "I am being told to go back to the very place where I was nearly killed not long ago, and all I can do is grumble." The weary soldiers around Kenneth never bothered to look up at his mumbling. Most were used to it, although a few of the new guys eyed their one-armed sergeant suspiciously. Kenneth, like everyone else in H Company, was simply obeying orders from the higher-ups and following a young, easygoing lieutenant by the name of Roy Smith. Lieutenant Smith was another Virginia boy; as a matter of fact, he had been born in Dandridge, not far up the road from were Kenneth was raised.

* * * * *

Back in August of '62, Kenneth's brigade had been ordered to fast march up from Knoxville to the Big Stone Gap. H Company was then commanded by an over-eager graduate from VMI by the name of Mathew Stone. Actually, Lieutenant Stone had graduated in the last full class to finish from VMI before it was shut down because of the war. Shortly after Stone graduated, Thomas Jackson, the school's commandant, left the military college and joined General Robert E. Lee's army of Northern Virginia. Jackson would become famous at the battle of Fredericksburg in his heroic defense of a battered old stone wall, thus the nickname Stonewall Jackson.

Lieutenant Stone wanted very much to impress the brigade commander, General Lewis Armistead. Armistead was a graduate of West Point, class of '48, and even though the man finished dead last in his class, he was a good leader in the field. Stone admired Armistead and saw a chance to impress him by volunteering H Company to lead the forced march north. The Yankees had captured Big Stone Gap, a move that threatened to cut Lee's army in half. It was their job to prevent that from happening. This, thought Stone, was his chance to gain glory, so he drove his men quick time up the road without any flank or front pickets. The old veterans shook their heads and grumbled among themselves as they hustled along. They knew it was a stupid gamble that could get people killed. And so it did.

The lead column of H Company was hardly five hundred feet from the main gap when the first shots rang out, startling the young Lieutenant. He jerked his head around several times in an effort to figure out where the shots were coming from as more shots rang out and wounded men began to crumple to the ground. Lieutenant Stone, who was foolish but brave, stood in the middle of the road as musket balls swarmed through the air and looked around. Most of his men had dropped to the ground or dove to the roadside, but Stone stood, squinted his eyes, and peered into the sunlight in search of the enemy. Sweat dripped from his forehead and stung his eyes as the sunlight burst in mirror-like reflections off the granite boulders that carpeted the slope above him. Through blinking eyes, he could see several dozen white puffs of smoke drifting above the large rocks the Yankees hide behind.

"The bastards," growled Stone as his mind began racing through the hours of instructions he had received back at VMI. He had been an excellent student and remembered the textbook chapter on ambushes or at least part of it. The book said that, if at all possible, you charge an ambush; it was the "at all possible" that now confused the young lieutenant. He took a deep breath of courage and shouted, "Follow me!" And ten good men did follow him, straight into a hornet's nest of Yankee lead.

Kenneth was about fifty feet behind Stone when the lieutenant and several other men ran off the road and started climbing up through the boulders. Kenneth simply crouched down as the rounds whistled by his head. He was still in the center of the road, and he fought with himself over whether to follow the foolish lieutenant or not. He never saw the shot fired that slammed into his left forearm, but the force of the .51-caliber musket ball striking his arm was like being hit with a pole ax, and he went down hard. He was thrown backward and fell against one of his friends from back home, Gerald Ensley. Ensley took one look at Kenneth's arm and threw up near the side of the road. As he heaved up his meager breakfast, a musket ball blew the back half of his skull into tiny pieces, and his body fell forward into the vomit.

The fighting seemed to grind into slow motion as the world turned gray from the smoke swirling around him like flashes of a bad dream. He moaned out loud and rocked back and forth on his knees as he hugged his shattered arm to his side. The Yankee bullets filled the air and sounded like a swarm of angry bees except these bees made a sickening wet thud when they stung flesh. Sergeants shouted orders that few men even attempted to follow as the battle raged. The Yankees were dug in proper, and the road soon became a killing field, men quickly sought any cover they could find.

Even with the fog of battle, Kenneth knew he had to get off the road. Glancing around, he spotted a large boulder just to his left near the side of the road with a half-rotten white oak stump wedged into its lower side. Painfully, he cradled his shattered arm against his side, looped his rifle sling around his neck, and crawled slowly toward the rock. Using his good arm, he pulled his body along as his legs pushed. Finally, getting off the road, he pressed himself tightly between the stump and the warm granite as bullets ricocheted off the rock with piercing buzzes. Men were lying everywhere, some of the living called for their mothers. Some cursed God, but most lay where they had fallen and tried to make sense of what was happening.

The musket fire was deafening, amplified as it was by the bow-shaped hollow they were trapped in. Kenneth's face became a mask of pain as he looked down and watched his life blood run down his arm and drip onto the yellow clay. He quickly realized he had best stop the bleeding, or he would die right here in this hellhole. Bone from his forearm showed white as it stuck through the flesh in two places, and blood seemed to spurt from the hole made by the musket ball at every heartbeat. Struggling to stay hidden behind the big stump, he managed to take the sling off his rifle with his one good hand and wrap it, as carefully as he could, around his left bicep. Sweat poured down into his eyes, and he groaned in pain as he looked around for something to tighten the rifle sling with. Spotting a locust stick just within his reach, he leaned forward and grabbed it as musket balls kicked up clouds of dust all around him. One round ricocheted off the boulder and clipped the cuff of his sleeve as he pressed his back hard against the stump. Taking a deep breath, he twisted the tough little branch in the sling until it was tight enough to stop the bleeding. Exhausted from the loss of blood and the shock of being wounded, he laid his head back and closed his eyes.

Several hours later, the sun had gone down when Kenneth came to and attempted to open his eyes. Someone was hovering over him and trying to give him water from a canteen. Whoever it was looked like he had on the blue uniform of a damn Yankee. Kenneth tried hard to move away from the menacing figure, but all he managed to do was hurt his arm. He cried out in pain just before he passed out. In his semiconscious state, people floated in and out of his vision. Shades of blue were everywhere, but his tormented mind refused to accept the fact that he had become a prisoner. He accepted some more water, and his head was beginning to clear a little when someone raised his left arm. There is one good thing about pain; it's great for clearing your mind, and the pain that Kenneth felt cleared his mind and his lungs. He leaned up straight, screamed, and passed out once again.

* * * * *

A gut-churning jolt brought Kenneth out of the nightmare that had gripped his unconscious mind, and he moaned his disapproval. Through blurry eyes, he could tell he was in some sort of wagon. He heard the driver outside, obviously an experienced old mule skinner, slap the reins against the rumps of a matched pair of mules and shout.

"Pull Sally, pull Sarah." The wagon jerked again and finally rolled out of a deep rut. The skinner's eyes lit up like a boy in love. "Good girls," he clucked.

"Damn," cursed Kenneth as the pain shot through his arm again and he had to squeeze his eyes shut. But when he did, images of hawks and old warriors came crashing into his mind, so he forced them back open. He didn't like nor understand the strange dreams he had been having over the last few weeks. Cautiously glancing around the jostling wagon, he quickly saw he wasn't alone. A couple of other men rode in strapped-down cots next to him. It was obviously an ambulance wagon, not only because he and the other two men were wounded but the putrid smell of blood and urine was overpowering. The two men glared at him as he nervously glanced about. One of the first things he noticed was that they both wore the same damn blue uniforms. *Yankees!* his mind screamed. He continued to scan his new home, and his eyes locked onto the side of the wagon's canvas cover. The unmistakable "US ARMY" was printed on its side. He let out a mournful sigh and slowly lay his head back down.

"I'm a damn prisoner," he groaned as the reality hit him. "Where the blazes are they taking me?"

Evidently, he uttered the words out loud because one of the soldiers in the wagon, an older man who had sergeant stripes on what was left of his sleeves, leaned up on one elbow and answered.

"Well, Reb, you're right. You are a prisoner, and we're headed for the Union field hospital over near Blountville." The Yankee sergeant looked over at the other wounded man and winked.

"Oh god," Kenneth moaned again, "a den of Yankee sawbones." The other Yankee, who had a bloody bandage wrapped around his head, chuckled and winced from the effort.

"We could have just let you die with your buddies," he said in a deep harsh Irish accent before he laid his head gently back on a makeshift pillow of old rags and gripped the sides of the bouncing cot. After a pause, Kenneth grunted.

"Maybe you should have." He touched his left arm out of reflex. The pain in his arm kept him awake for a while, and he desperately tried to work through the fog surrounding the battle. So *the damn Yankees had ambushed and routed his company.* Everyone knew they were marching too fast, no flankers out, no picket lines. Stone had marched them straight into an ambush. *How many of his friends had been killed because of Stone's eagerness?* The image of his friend Ensley getting shot in the head flashed through his brain. The right front wheel of the wagon hit another hole in the road, and pain from his shattered arm shot up into his brain, blackness snapping his mind shut.

* * * * *

The pale bloody faces of his dead friends floated through his dreams, their screams and shouts filling his ears again. He jerked with a start as he came to and looked up.

"Oh god, I'm dead for sure," he managed to croak because leaning over him was the most beautiful woman he had ever seen. Although she had no wings, she had to be an angel, so he asked, "Is this heaven?" his voice dry and raspy. The pretty face moved back a little. The question had startled her, and besides, she thought this particular Reb would never wake up. With a stern look, she answered.

"No, soldier, this is an army hospital. It's closer to hell than heaven." Saddened by her own comment, she sat the water pail down she had been carrying and turned to go. Kenneth tried to reach out to her, wanting to ask her more questions, but he couldn't move his arm, which was strapped across his chest. But the arm on his chest couldn't be his; it was too short. Panic racked his conscious mind.

"What's wrong with my arm? This can't be my arm," he cried through clenched teeth. The realization hit him like a hammer.

"My god, you've cut my arm off. Oh, please help me. Help … me …" The blackness came crashing down again.

The mournful shout stopped Martha Anne as she was walking away. Reluctantly, she turned back toward the haggard and half-starved rebel soldier. *They all look as if they haven't eaten in a week,* she thought as she looked back and saw he had passed out. She knew she should leave him be, but something caused her to pick up the water bucket and grab a clean rag. She walked back to his bedside and began to press the damp cloth to his fevered forehead. After a minute, his eyes fluttered a few times and finally stayed open. Tears rolled slowly down his cheeks as he looked down at his stump of an arm.

"It was either your arm or your life," said Martha Anne, who spoke the words softly, not understanding why. Bright dots flashed in front of his eyes, and his breathing grew rapid as he glanced around the hospital ward as if seeing it for the first time.

"My arm, oh my god, my god," he babbled semicoherently as the fact slowly sank in that the damn Yankees had cut off his arm just below the elbow. Martha Anne had seen that dazed look before many, many times, as a matter of fact. Silently, she bent over, picked up her water bucket, and walked down the aisle to the next human tragedy, leaving the poor soul to his miseries.

As the shadows crept across the floor and evening approached, Kenneth woke from a fitful sleep and shouted mournfully.

"My arm hurts. Oh, my arm hurts, can somebody help me?" Sweat rolled down his forehead to pool in his eyebrows. His teeth chattered, and his body began to shake from the fever that soon racked his whole being. Hands shaking, he clung tightly with his one good arm to the thin army blanket that covered him.

The next morning, he lay quietly on his sweat-soaked cot and watched the butcher shop they called a field hospital do its dirty work. No anesthesia, no antiseptic—just guts, saws, and a little whiskey. Some men cried, most screamed, but all struggled in their own way with the loss of some part of their anatomy—an arm or leg or in some cases both. The stretcher bearers stayed busy hauling live men in and dead bodies out.

"God help us," he moaned as he tore his eyes away from the work of the bloody saws and stared up at a dingy white ceiling covered with spiderwebs. He watched intensely as one spider, big as a quarter, raced across its web and pounced on a fluttering moth that had picked the wrong place to land. *It's like this damn war*, thought Kenneth. *They pounce on us, and we pounce on them. What will we do when there are no more moths?* he wondered as sleep mercifully closed his eyes.

Days passed, and the healing painfully progressed. The only bright spot in the dark and ugly building was the sight of the young nurse. One minute, she was helping the surgeon with an operation, usually an amputation, and the next, she was holding the hand of some dying man. The strangest part of the healing process for Kenneth was the itching. His arm itched where there was no arm.

That part of my arm probably lays somewhere with a pile of other such parts, maybe in a ditch behind this damn hospital, thought Kenneth as he stared out the dirt-streaked window near his cot at nothingness.

The pitiful cries and mournful sobs of the wounded kept him awake most nights, and he lay anxiously in the dark, waiting for the sun to come up. When the fiery disk finally peeked over the eastern ridges, the nightmares that ruled this sad place in the dark of night would slowly fade back into their lair, and the young angel would appear with the sunlight.

One morning, as a cold rain beat steadily on the corrugated tin roof of the hotel turned hospital, Kenneth lay on his cot, waiting for the angel to walk by. He watched as she left the nurse's station and walked quietly down the aisle between the cots, looking at each man as she went. She moved slowly, truly like an angel, growing ever closer to him. Her eyes darted over each man from head to foot as she assessed their condition. Some begged for water, which she served from a tin pail she carried in her right hand. Some just cried while others simply looked up at the ceiling as if the answer to their problem was up there somewhere. She gave each man a gentle smile and a caring pat, which seemed to give peace to all but the most dreadfully wounded.

When she got to his side, he rose up on his good elbow. "Ma'am, water, please," he croaked. Martha Anne stopped and looked down at his young weathered face, and he looked up at her. The early morning light bounced off her reddish-brown hair, random wisps already escaping from the once tight bun that sat perched on her head like a small halo. Her green eyes darted from his face to his arm and back.

"I thought you would be dead by now," she announced almost matter-of-factly. "You lost so much blood before you got here. The doctor said you hardly bled at all when he took your arm."

"He didn't 'take' my arm. He cut the damn thing off," growled Kenneth as he lay despondent on his cot, his thirst forgotten for the moment and replaced by anger.

She stood beside his cot and looked at him for a long minute, her inquisitive green eyes taking in his ruggedly handsome features. She was trying to access the young rebel and maybe see inside him because, for some reason, she liked this man even though she knew she shouldn't.

"Like I said, soldier, you should be dead," she said softly, all the while glad he hadn't died. She blushed slightly from her thoughts, but at least her comment had broken the awkward silence that hung over them.

"I guess I'm just hard to kill, ma'am, but if you don't give me some water soon, I will die … from thirst!"

Martha Anne smiled despite herself and knelt down by his cot, cradled his head, and poured a small amount of water into his mouth. Kenneth's parched throat rejected the water at first, but Martha was careful and patient. Finally, he was able to keep a little bit down before he lay back, exhausted.

"Thank you, angel," he half-whispered with a smile, his first in many days. Martha Anne smiled back but quickly caught herself. She knew better than to allow herself to be emotionally involved with these soldiers. She had seen far too many, from both sides, die. God, she hated war—a man's game someone had called it—but she had held the hand of many dying men who would call her mother or some faraway girlfriend's name, as they struggled to get their last breath. *No, war was no game, and anybody that said it was had never been in one or seen the results!* her mind screamed the words. Martha Anne had to turn her back to this Reb with the amputated arm because tears had begun to run down her cheeks. *I will not get close, not again,* remembering a brief romance that had torn her heart apart a year earlier. Swearing to herself, she quickly walked down back the aisle between more broken men and out of sight. Kenneth wasn't sure if he had said something wrong or not, but he figured she just needed to be alone. Maybe, he did too, so he lay back and closed his eyes, though sleep was a long time coming.

* * * * *

Early the next morning, the angel returned to his bedside with some type of broth.

"What is this?" he asked as she handed him a well-used wooden spoon.

"The cook said it was chicken," answered Martha Anne as she looked into the badly chipped bowl she held in her lap, "but I can't be sure." Kenneth smiled at how she peered into the bowl, her forehead crinkled in concentration, as she tried to identify its content. Using his good arm, he leaned over and dipped the spoon down into the mystery contents of the bowl she held out for him. His hand shook ever so slightly, and broth dripped onto the floor as he attempted to feed himself. She moved closer to his side, her hip almost touching him, and for a brief second, they locked eyes. Suddenly, his arm didn't hurt quite as bad, and his anger, which was always just under the surface of his emotions, calmed. The early morning light struggled in an attempt to shine through the dirty, smudged glass of the window near his cot as they looked at each other. A mixture of alabaster hues managed to sneak through the grit and danced among the dark curls adorning his angel's head. His heart was racing as he lowered the spoon and simply sat staring at her, causing her face to glow red. She forced herself to look away from his penetrating blue eyes, but she didn't leave, which she knew she should have.

Wishing the bowl would somehow refill itself when the bottom came into view, Kenneth sought to prolong the moment with small talk. He tried a smile.

"If your name isn't Angel, then what is it?" Martha Anne didn't answer right away. Instead, she stared down into the nearly empty bowl. Kenneth began to wonder if she hadn't heard him or if she was going to ignore the question entirely, but finally, she looked at him as if she had been struggling to remember her name.

"My name is Martha Anne. Martha Anne Holmes," she answered a little formally; all the while her mind was screaming, *Don't, don't!* He smiled at her hesitation. Or was it reluctance? He wasn't sure which.

"Well, Martha Anne, I'm Kenneth Nichols, and I'm very pleased to meet you." Fighting the urge to extend his good arm in a handshake, he simply nodded.

He thought back to his few early courtships and wanted to laugh at their awkwardness but realized this situation wasn't much different. Besides, the look in her eyes said that nothing was funny around here. So instead, he coughed and dipped the well-worn spoon back into the last of the strange liquid. When he was finished with the chicken broth or whatever it was, Martha Anne took the spoon and bowl and prepared to leave. He stopped her with a question.

"Why does my arm itch where there is no arm?" His eyes scanned the bandaged stump.

Martha Anne thought for a minute and then shrugged her shoulders.

"I'm not really sure, but a lot of the men have the same complaint. The doctors say the itching will lessen in a few months, something to do with the nerves." With that said, she turned away and walked over to the next cot where she dipped a cloth into the water bucket and placed it over the man's forehead. Kenneth watched her work her way down the rows of cots until at last, she disappeared around the corner. Her leaving made him sad, and he felt a cold empty spot in his being as well as an empty place on his bunk. He reached his good arm out and lightly touched the spot where she had sat, then quickly drew it back. Slightly embarrassed, he glanced around, fearing someone had seen him and think him a pervert.

The wounded soldier in the cot next to Kenneth was a Yankee who spoke very little English. *Polish*, Kenneth thought to himself. The man had been shot through the shoulder, and Kenneth could smell the gangrene that had set up in the wound. *He'll not make it*, he thought and was somewhat amazed at how unconcerned he seemed. *I guess that's what war does to a man.* He sighed and closed his eyes. A few days later, he was proven right; the cot had a new occupant.

* * * * *

Several days passed, and Kenneth could feel his strength gradually increase until he was able to walk around the old two-story hotel that now functioned as a hospital. His first time out of bed was quite the struggle though. Martha Anne and an orderly helped him stand up beside his cot, but his head spun so badly he had to hold onto the big black orderly for support. Finally, the spinning slowed, and he was able to walk. But even with their help, his lightheadedness caused him to sit often. But being young helped, and after a few more days, he was walking and chatting with other patients. Most were Confederate prisoners, but not all. One afternoon, he was walking out the main door of the hospital when he noticed a group of men dressed in the familiar butternut, their uniforms soiled and tattered. He recognized one of the soldiers, a gruff and always angry sergeant from Richmond named Rathbone. The man was a pain, but Kenneth needed to talk to him. He walked over and stood off to the side, waiting for a private with a patch over his left eye and an empty sleeve where his left arm should have been to finish his tale. Everyone laughed except the crusty old sergeant who simply grunted.

Kenneth caught the man's eye and pulled him aside before he asked, "How you doing, Sarge?" Rathbone looked Kenneth up and down before he answered, "Not too well, or I'd be somewhere besides this damn place." He spat off the edge of the porch. Kenneth looked down at the spot where the tobacco juice had landed for a second before looking back at the sergeant.

"Sergeant Rathbone, do you have any idea what happened at the Gap?" Kenneth figured he would just get a snide remark, but he was wrong this time. The sergeant spat again and replied gruffly.

"I got hit early, just like you did, but what I did see was that dumb lieutenant and a few other poor souls charge that rock pile. Stone hadn't gone twenty feet up that slope before he took a musket ball to the head. He flopped like a fish out of water for a couple of seconds before finally lying still. Sadly, the other boys got cut down too." Tobacco juice drooled from the man's mouth as he headed down the steps. When he reached the bottom, he spat again before moving on, his crutches making a sucking sound as he pulled them out of the mud. His bandaged stump of a leg swung stiffly under him as he went down the path.

I hate it for those other boys, but God, I'm glad Stone got his, thought Kenneth to himself. *That bastard just as well killed a bunch of my friends.*

* * * * *

Fall was coming, and the days passed more slowly. The dog days of summer had lingered late into October, and every afternoon around three o'clock, a deep rumbling could be heard. The sound would grow in its fury until the ground shook and the old hotel trembled. Some of the men crawled under their cots while others just closed their eyes, trembled, and remembered. Within an hour, lightning would flash like cannon fire, and the torrents of rain would come. Nature could be violent in her own way, but at least the world would be cleansed for a short while.

The cold rains forced most everyone to stay inside. Weak from their wounds, they didn't want to get pneumonia, but many did anyway. A few of the men simply couldn't cope with their wounds either physical or mental, and standing in the rain was an easy way to commit suicide. The fever was a better way to die than what had happened to many of their friends. The long days inside proved difficult to Kenneth, so in order to pass the time in the bleak old building, he played mind games. He counted the number of beaded boards covering the wall near his cot; there were fifty-six. He knew how many steps it took for Martha Anne to get from her desk to his bed, thirty-four. And he knew each man's nightmare by his screams. He even knew how long it took for a man to bleed to death from a ruptured artery; most men took about twelve minutes. *It is odd what occupies a man's mind while his body tries to mend from a grievous wound,* thought Kenneth as the lay on his cot watching the spider overhead. He had named the spider Will, after his uncle who would get drunk and jump on people like the spider did the moths and flies that got caught in its web.

One rainy afternoon, as the thunder rolled past like an old locomotive, Kenneth sat under a large white oak tree, its trunk charred black by a long ago lightening blast.

"I'm sure glad I wasn't sitting here when you got struck, old boy." He spoke to the tree as he ran his hand across its scaly bark scarred very much like him. He leaned back against the cool trunk of the old silent giant, gazing out at the pasture that lay below him like a scene in some fancy painting. Colts ran about, and several horses rolled in the mud caused by the recent rains. *Most look like good saddle stock,* he thought as he watched them play. *Probably be Yankee Cavalry horses soon,* he spat after realizing who would be riding them. Bitterness over his lost arm ruined even this tranquil scene as hate boiled under the surface of his emotions. He looked down at the stump of his arm, and a tear swelled in the corner of his eye. He used the sleeve of his good arm to wipe it away.

A few minutes later, his mind had drifted back to his daddy's farm, and he didn't hear Martha Anne's long calico dress rubbing the wet grass until she was nearly beside him. He sat up straighter when she got close, but she was silent for a long time. Finally, she spoke without acknowledging him.

"I used to live on a horse farm very much like this place." She looked out across the pasture as if she could see all the way back to Kentucky. Kenneth sat there without saying a word. *Just let her talk.*

"My father raised thoroughbreds just outside of Louisville on land he had cleared himself. He raced some of them, or if they weren't fast enough, he sold them to the Army—the Confederate Army." She looked down at him to see his reaction, but he was looking out over the pasture. Gathering her dress, which was fairly easy since she never wore the fashionable hoop skirts, she sat down beside him. They both leaned back against the old tree and watched the horses frolic until finally Kenneth asked.

"Then why are you here in this hellhole? And why"—he shook his head as if he couldn't understand—"are you working for the damn Yankees?"

Martha Anne half smiled; she wasn't surprised by the question or by the contempt in his voice. She had been asked similar questions many times from other patients and even from her relatives, mostly in the form of letters. The question hung for a moment, like the damp fog that clutched the ridgetop across the valley.

"My father was a very successful man, but he started with nothing more than the clothes on his back. By the time I came along, he owned a thousand acres of fine farmland. He also owned as many as forty slaves to work it." She paused and seemed to reflect for a minute before she went on, "And even though he treated them better than most of the slave owners around us, they were still slaves. I could see the pain and the humiliation in their eyes every day. One morning—I think it was in June because the jasmine was blooming—a slave girl by the name of Sarah, who was about my age, came running up to me. She had given birth to a beautiful light-skinned baby boy a couple of months before, and that day the child was sick. He was far too sick to take to the fields with her. Sarah was crying and pleading. She told me the slave foreman had told her that he didn't give a damn if the baby was sick or even if it died. She had to work the fields. The tobacco crop was more important than any damn nigger baby. I think the child was his anyway, probably from a rape." She shook her head slowly and looked across the way. Lightning was flashing on the far ridge, and it was as if she could see the whole episode playing out on the dark angry clouds.

Kenneth chewed on a thin blade of grass and watched her until finally his gaze followed hers to the light show across the way. Like her, he became mesmerized by the powerful lightning display. After a minute or two, her gaze came down from the mountain and settled on her hands folded in her lap. Only then did she continue.

"I didn't bother with going to my daddy. I went straight to that foreman, Big Jake Parris. I was mad as hell, and I was probably crying. When I found him out by the fields, I talked to him loud enough for everyone in earshot to hear. I told him that Sarah and the baby were staying in that day, and if he had to have someone else to work the tobacco, then he and I both would take Sarah's place." She uttered a small laugh as she remembered the look on the foreman's face.

Kenneth spit out the blade of grass and laughed out loud. "Whoa, I bet that made your father and the foreman mad as a swarm of stepped-on yellow jackets." He shook his head, his dusty brown hair moving from side to side as he imagined the furor her actions probably caused.

"Daddy was terribly angry, and Mother was in tears. The good part was that Big Jake avoided me like the plague for the rest of the time I was home." She laughed slightly. "Daddy sat me down in the parlor that night, lectured me on economics, and then threatened to send me back east to a proper school for ladies if I ever did anything like that again."

After a minute, "Well, I've got to ask, did you?" quizzed Kenneth. He was pretty sure of the answer.

She smiled without looking at him. "Yes, I did, and yes, he sent me back east. A month later, the servants helped me pack my bags, and Daddy and Mother kissed me goodbye at the train station. They sent me to an all-women's college in New Jersey called Wellesley and Smith. It wasn't really that bad except for the fact I wanted to become a doctor and couldn't. The good professors, all males, looked down their noses at me and explained that a woman couldn't be a doctor because it was too demanding a job. When they saw my anger building, they quickly threw me a carrot by telling me I could become a nurse. I was mad and disappointed, but what could I do?" She asked the question without really expecting an answer. "I thought about running away, but instead I stayed, swallowed my pride, studied hard under a great lady by the name of Clara Barton, and became a nurse. And I'm a damn fine nurse, probably more qualified than most of these doctors here, but I'm still 'only' a nurse." The last remark delivered full of sarcasm as she continued to stare at the mountains. "I finished my schooling in three years and received my degree just after the war started. By the time I got back home, the war was raging, and all of Daddy's slaves had run away. And you know what?" She turned toward him like a child on a dare and looked him straight in the eye before she said, "I was glad."

The seconds ticked slowly by, and Kenneth's anger began to boil. Mainly because of the penetrating stare of those green eyes that challenged him but also because deep in his heart he knew she was partly right. That fact alone angered him until he couldn't help shouting.

"This damn war ain't about slavery! It's about states' rights." He glared back at her with a mixture of anger and defiance. She held his gaze for a heartbeat or two but finally realized no one could win this silly game, so she simply shook her head, huffed, and scooted across the damp grass away from him. Wrapping her arms around her knees, she pulled them up tight against her breasts, calico bunching up all about her as she rested her chin in the foils of cloth. Kenneth's face turned red as he waited for some kind of reply while her mind was racing like a runaway carriage until at last she turned back to him and half laughed.

"That business about states' rights may be what your friends say around the campfires at night or what some of these local preachers shout from their pulpit, but it's about slavery." She wanted and needed to see some kind of understanding from him, but all she saw was his jaw tighten and the veins in his neck pulse with his rapid heart rate. And for a brief second, she thought he might actually hit her. Realizing how upset he was caused her to pause for a minute and search for a way to change subjects, but all she could think of was, "Where are you from, anyway?"

He looked at her a little stunned. "Where am I from? Where am I from?" he parroted her words as he struggled with the change of topics.

"Yes, where did you grow up?" she asked as matter-of-factly as she could.

"I'm from just up the road in Virginia. I grew up not far from here in a little place called Blacksburg. And … and we never owned any slaves." What started out as a glare quickly softened into a look of confusion and hurt. The fire of a minute ago doused like a rained-on campfire. He glanced eastward when he heard, as well as smelled, the rain coming, the gray damp curtains blocking out the view of the far hills before he went on.

"We worked our own damn fields—most ever one around us did." He could feel the anger gradually running its course. "So this damn war is about the Yankees invading our state." He made the last statement without much conviction though. He looked down at his stump of an arm and shook his head.

When he had first joined up, two long years ago, he felt different than he did now, sitting here with this woman. *He sure the hell felt younger back then*, he thought to himself. He used his good arm and pushed himself up off the ground and dusted off his backside. Martha Anne looked up at the angry, broken young man, but didn't say anything. It wasn't because she wasn't as firm in her beliefs as he was. It was because she was tired, tired of fighting, any kind of fighting. And besides, she liked him. She badly needed a way to express her feeling without causing another wound, especially to someone she cared about, and despite all her efforts to the contrary, she cared about this Johnny Reb. This man who was as hard as nails on the outside but seemed tender deep inside, where she believed it counted the most. She just had to find a way to reach inside him, but she couldn't seem to find the right words.

"How can you defend the war when this"—she pointed to his bandaged stump of an arm—"is your reward?" She knew those where the wrong words when they left her mouth, but it was too late. Kenneth's jaw tightened again when she spoke of his arm, and his face turned deep crimson.

"The damn Yankees invaded my state, and we fought them, and by god, I will keep on fighting them until I lose more than my damn arm or they're whooped one." He pulled the old army blanket, which he had wrapped around his shoulders, tighter. He wanted to walk away, but his feet seemed to be frozen to the mud.

"Think about this, Kenneth," she went on despite her calmer part screaming for her to hush. "The Southern states seceded from the Union because they believed they had the right to own people— human beings—just like they own mules and horses. We 'damn Yankees,' as you call us, believe every man or woman, regardless of the color of their skin, has the right to live free. To live how and where they want. So by god, the north, under Mr. Lincoln, will fight to guarantee that freedom." Her face was red now, and she was ready to fight for what she knew was right if that was what he wanted. *So much for calm*, she thought as she managed to stand without asking for his help despite the light drizzle that had begun to fall. They stood glaring at each other, and she was surprised and a little disappointed when he simply turned and walked away. Taking a deep breath, she watched him go, her desire to be civil overridden by her anger as she shouted after him.

"We believe that every man and woman, regardless of the color of their skin, are created equal, and we will fight to our deaths to defend that idea."

Kenneth half-turned and looked back over his shoulder. He started to say something but didn't. Instead, he just lowered his head and walked on. He could almost agree with her; nobody had the right to own someone else, but his pride would never allow him to admit it, not to her, not right now anyway. So he walked up the slight incline toward the dark and foreboding hospital, his boots making a splashing sound in the mud. The light drizzle swept in from the east by the thunderstorm that had rolled through earlier dampened his spirits even further. His mind drifted back to the war and the many friends he had lost already. Friend after friend had died or been shot to hell, which was almost worse than dying, *and for what?*

The question hung in his weary mind as he trudged through the rain toward the old hotel that stood in the fog like a sentinel on the hill, his boots leaving small puddles in the red clay as he walked. Suddenly out of the mist, a mournful cry echoed through the evening sky like a sad whisper riding the winds, and it seemed to call him. He glanced skyward, the cold raindrops running off his forehead as he sought the source of the call.

Martha Anne stood with her arms folded across her breasts and watched him walk up the hill, his shoulders hunched forward against the chill.

"God, why can't I keep my big mouth shut?" she fumed at herself. Several damp curls escaped their confinement on top of her head as the rain became heavier and fell down into her eyes. Brushing the loose strands aside, she lifted her dress to keep it from dragging in the mud and ran after him. The desire for peace between her and Kenneth had overcome her feelings about the war for the moment, and her mind struggled to form an apology for she had hurt him, and that had not been her intent. Splashing though the mud with her skirts held high and the rain pelting her face, she called his name.

"Kenneth, Kenneth, please wait." Just as she caught up to him, her feet slipped in the mud, and she began to fall.

"Ugh" was the only sound that came out of her mouth as she started down. Kenneth, who continued to gaze up in the sky for what he knew was a hawk, reached out like magic with his good arm and caught her just before she hit the ground. He pulled her up tight against his side, her body warm to his touch despite the cold rain, but he was afraid to look her in the eye. The rain was mixing with his tears, and he refused to show her that.

The rustle of small wings and the soft call of a mourning dove caught their attention, and they watched as the small grayish bird flew from a nearby sourwood tree and joined the hawk as it circled in the rain. The hawk cried once more as both birds disappeared in and out of the mist. Martha Anne was fascinated, her gaze constantly shifting from Kenneth's face to the hawk and dove, whose flight path resembled a beautiful dance in the sky. They stood looking into the sky for several minutes as the rain poured from the heavens, their hips touching slightly and his hand burning a spot on her waist as he held her tightly, both secretly hoping the moment would last forever.

"Maybe if a hawk and dove can accept each other, then there is still hope even for you and me, Kenneth Nichols," said Martha Anne. Silence hung heavy and damp, like the air around them, until the birds flew over and settled on a crooked limb near the top of the scarred white oak that she and Kenneth had sat under. She smiled despite the tenseness of the moment when the dove rubbed its head against the much larger wing of the big raptor. Kenneth saw the dove's movement and turned his gaze from the darkening sky to Martha Anne's wet, upturned face.

"Maybe, there is," he said, "maybe there is." Releasing his grip on her warm waist, he turned reluctantly away and started walking up the hill, but his shoulders were a little straighter now, and there was a hint of a smile on his tired face. The steps of the hotel-turned-hospital creaked under his weight as he slid his hand up the well-worn handrail, which was in bad need of paint. The tall double doors of the entrance way yawned open in front of him like the mouth of some wild creature. He hesitated for a second before daring to enter as the smell of death and fear wafted his nostrils, but he steeled his resolve, stepped over the threshold, and headed toward his empty cot.

* * * * *

His nightmares were worse some nights more than others, and in the worst recurring one, the image of a Viking he had once seen in a drawing of barbarians of the North Sea would come at him with death on his face. The man would jump off a strange-looking ship wearing a leather helmet and carrying a sword half as long as he was tall. Kenneth, on the other hand, was always weaponless. With shirt and blanket soaked in sweat, he would wake up just before the sword struck him.

The stump of his arm was slowly healing, and Kenneth knew they would be sending him north to one of the Yankee prisons. *Probably Douglas, up in Chicago, very soon,* he fretted. All the prisoners had heard rumors of how bad it was in Douglas—very little food, no fresh water, and sickness everywhere.

Martha Anne was surprised at herself for constantly finding excuses to visit the tall, lanky rebel soldier. Their conversations had become less heated, and she always enjoyed his cutting wit and quick intellect. *So why not?* she convinced herself. She liked the way he smiled easily, and his teeth were white and straight, which was rare as hen's teeth, as the old-timers would say. She smiled at the image of his sandy-colored hair hugging his shirt collar and the way his blue eyes twinkled when he was full of merriment, which was not often enough, she sighed. She thought back, with a mixture of anger and sadness, to all the suitors her father had managed to press on her. Most were too old for her, in her unasked opinion, or simply too serious and stiff. The more her father had liked some of the boys or men, the more she had flirted with the ones she knew he would not approve of. He had hated her stubborn independence, and they quarreled often about it. She laughed at her early rebellious streak, and then realized that Kenneth was someone her father would probably have approved of.

"Hell, Daddy would most likely think Kenneth was grand," muttered Martha Anne out loud, but she smiled at the thought as she went about her duties.

A few days later, heavy fighting broke out over near Bristol, and the wounded of both sides began pouring into the already overflowing hospital.

"God, when will it ever end?" asked Martha Anne as she stepped away from the cot of a captured Confederate captain who had been shot in the left side of his head. One eye was gone, and the other was glazed over with a smoky film. He would never see again. The man knew it and was constantly crying for his wife, a woman named Martha. It chilled Martha Anne to the bone to hear her name called that way. "Martha, Martha, oh, Martha, help me, I can't see!" Her name echoed eerily down the rows of wounded men.

The three-stripe sergeant responsible for helping discharge the wounded prisoners and sending them north, Mroz Bergansky, walked up to Martha Anne one afternoon as she sat gazing out the dusty window behind her desk. Sergeant Bergansky, a big rough-looking fellow who had been born in Poland and drafted out of the slums of New York, was always trying to impress her with his supposed knowledge of the goings-on around the hospital. He was also deeply jealous of the skinny rebel soldier whom Martha Anne spent so much time with. He had been watching them together and was determined to ship the boy north as soon as he could.

"Well, Martha Anne, it seems as if the Johnny Rebs have been at it again." He looked around at all the new patients. "So we'll be sending a bunch of the better healed boys up north to the prison at Douglas. That'll hammer their damn pride a little." He laughed as he walked down the hall but stopped and turned back toward her just before rounding the corner. "That Reb I have seen you with so often, the one you seem so sweet on, well, we'll be sending him north on the next train. You had better tell him goodbye," he howled with laughter as he disappeared.

She had known the day was soon coming when the more mended patients would be sent north, but she had hoped it would be awhile yet. Sadly, she put her face in her hands and leaned over her desk.

"Oh, Lordy, I don't want him to leave," she cried and slapped one hand down hard onto the desk in frustration. Cold black coffee spilled from a small porcelain cup that had seen better days. The thick chicory-flavored liquid threatened to soak a stack of papers she had burnt a lot of midnight oil preparing, probably for some nosey bureaucrat in Washington.

"Damn this war, anyway," she groaned before grabbing a nearby rag and cleaning up the spilled coffee. Satisfied, she had saved her paperwork from an unsightly stain, she rose from her seat and ran down the steps in search of the young Rebel soldier.

Feeling restless and unable to sleep, Kenneth had decided to take a walk toward the area he and Martha Anne now called "their spot." He would have had to be blind not to notice the steady progression of ambulance wagons rolling into the hospital over the last couple of days. He figured Martha Anne would be busy as the dickens with the new patients, so he hadn't asked her to join him. He really wanted and needed to see her though and was pleasantly surprised as he neared the old scarred oak to find her sitting under its canopy. Most of the leaves that just a couple of weeks before had been a brilliant red with splashes of yellow and gold were gone.

"Winter is coming," he said as he walked up behind her. She never looked up when he spoke, but her hands were busy around her face. When she didn't acknowledge him, he coughed and asked, "May I sit down?" He was afraid she would simply want to be alone, and he so wanted to be with her.

"Yes, please. I need to talk to you," and she quickly hid the handkerchief she had been using to dab her eyes in a small side pocket.

Good, he thought to himself as he rushed to sit down, all the while being very careful not to sit too close. He found himself unsure of what to say to her now that she was just inches away, so he just kept quiet and looked out over the pasture. The horses, which had once filled the pasture, were nowhere in sight. That probably meant the cavalry had come through and pulled them into duty. *Some big fight fixing to happen*, he surmised and made a mental note of it for later when he got back to Confederate lines. Feeling a little uneasy, he glanced over at the young nurse, who sat about a foot away and had her hands folded in her lap. He could tell by her puffy eyes and the tear tracks on her cheeks that she had been crying, and he wondered why.

He longed to reach out and comfort her, but instead, he leaned forward a little and waited in silence for her to speak. The sun was fast losing its strength as it sneaked behind the dark gray mountains to the west, and he was glad he had once again brought his old army blanket. It was the only coat he had. The wind suddenly picked up and swirled brown leaves around in several small whirlwinds, a promise of cold weather blowing in their spinning circles.

Martha Anne shivered as the breeze tossed the leaves about, and he noticed she had forgotten the heavy wrap she usually carried, so he took his army blanket from around his shoulders and placed it around hers.

"You'll have to …" he started to say but was interrupted.

"They're going to ship you up north, tomorrow or the next day," she blurted out with a sob, her voice a high-pitched wail as tears flowed freely down her cheeks again. Kenneth's shoulders sagged as he struggled for a reply and finally he sighed.

"I figured it would be pretty soon but not this soon. I've been watching all the new wounded prisoners coming in, and I knew you didn't have room for us all here."

"I don't want you to leave, Kenneth," said Martha Anne as she turned full toward him, her hands reaching out to touch his hip gently.

"Ever," she added blushing. He looked down into the soft face of his angel.

"God, how beautiful you are." His boyish grin was making her heart race as he looked at her with those blue eyes. Her cheeks turned red again, but she managed to hold his gaze. She wasn't sure what she expected him to say, but the silence was painful, and her stomach churned as she waited for some sort of reply.

After a minute, she pulled the small handkerchief back out of her pocket and began twisting it around and around in her lap, waiting. Kenneth's eyes roamed over her soft features, the dimpled curve of her mouth, her misty green eyes, and her small button nose. *She could have been a nobleman's wife back in England,* he thought and suddenly realized that when he left this place, he would probably never see her again, and that saddened him.

He had to turn his eyes away from her loveliness, and his gaze settled on the far hills where he watched the last glimmer of daylight flutter through the skeletal branches of the trees that blanketed the far ridge.

"I'm going to try and escape tomorrow night then, me and a few other fellows," he announced, his voice sad and hollow. "We've been waiting for some word about when they would move us. We'll leave sometime after midnight," he added solemnly.

She looked at him as her heart slowly broke.

"Oh, Kenneth, please don't go, please don't," she pleaded. "I can get ol' Doc Rhinehart to write a letter keeping you here. He'll do anything for me. Oh please, oh—" She sobbed, her head burying into his shoulder as her arms clung desperately about him.

She felt rather than saw him move closer to her. He took her hands and kissed them, and then with his good arm, turned her face up to look at him.

"I have to go, Martha Anne, you know that. Sooner or later, they would send me up north to a prison, and prison would kill me just as dead as a Yankee bullet." He held her gaze until she lowered her eyes.

He leaned his face down to kiss her lips. Soft and red, her lips were laced with salt from her tears, and suddenly, the whole world seemed to stop. The pain and sorrow of his missing arm was replaced by a realization of what love really is. The damn war, that terrible instrument of destruction that maimed bodies and broke hearts, was pushed to the backs of their minds, at least for a little while. Martha Anne opened her mouth and accepted his probing tongue as a low sensual moan escaped her throat. She responded to his kiss with a fervor that surprised them both while the heat of passion boiled within her. Kenneth broke the kiss for a second as her swollen lips begged for more.

"I love you," he whispered, and they lay back on the green army blanket. They made love fast and urgent as if death, that stealer of hearts, would take one of them away even as they were in union.

Later, Martha Anne laid her head on his chest, and together, they watched the moon as it rose over the far ridge. The big oak and hickory trees scattered on the ridge were plastered on the face of the lady of the night, and she seemed in a struggle to escape from their grasp. Once free of the tree branches, though, she shined down on the young lovers like a torch.

"I'll never see you again, will I?" she whispered, trying hard not to cry.

"I don't think so, Martha Anne. I pray I will see you again, maybe even take you back to Kentucky. But in my heart, I know I will not survive this war." He glanced toward the hospital. It seemed empty except for the flickering dances of several candles perched on the sills of the dingy windows. It loomed above them as a constant reminder of why they were here.

"I have already lost so many friends, and the battles keep getting bigger and deadlier. We've become really good at killing ..." Kenneth's voice broke as he made a sad laugh. Martha Anne's eyes filled with tears as she watched him look back at the hospital. The image of his body lying on some battlefield, one of many bloody corpses strewn about, flashed in her mind like a vision of the future, and she shuddered. He reached over with his good arm and wiped a tear from her cheek then turned her to face him.

"I could go to whatever prison they assign you to and work there." She sobbed, blinking back tears as she looked up at him.

"I doubt seriously if there are any women at those prisons, Martha Anne. Besides, I would rather take my chances back with my old outfit. At least that way, I'll have a fighting chance."

"What about me?" she cried as he held her tight. "What about us?"

"Maybe God will see fit to spare me. If not, maybe we will meet again in the next life—when there are no more wars. Maybe as a hawk and a dove." He smiled weakly, as the mournful call of a dove echoed through the big oak tree that now seemed to stand guard over them. They made love again, this time more gently, and then the two lovers slept.

* * * * *

The night was black like pitch, the moon having hid its face behind a sky full of rumbling clouds. Kenneth and his three companions in the escape were struggling slowly through the rocky terrain about five miles from the hospital. The slope of the land had turned fairly steep, and the recent rains had made the ground slick as a greased pole. They had to hold on to the laurel bushes in several places to keep from falling as they made their way downhill toward a small creek they could hear in the distance. The laurel was thick, and the leaves wet as they stumbled along. The going was made more difficult by the many rock outcroppings, but it was the darkness that was their worst enemy. Being a country boy, Kenneth had foreseen some of the difficulties they would face and had asked Martha Anne to wrap extra padding around his stump of an arm before they sneaked away from the hospital. He figured the going would be rough and the stump of his arm was still tender. If he fell, which he probably would, and hit his arm ... Well, he didn't need any more pain. Leaving the girl was bad enough. He had figured right, because just then he slipped on a wet pine pole and fell. As he went down, a laurel branch slammed into his arm. He moaned and clutched his arm.

"God, that hurt," he growled as he rocked back and forth on his knees, hugging his left arm against his chest.

"Are you all right?" whispered Ronnie Stephens, a scrawny, tobacco-chewing man from the mountains of Western North Carolina. Stephens had walked over to where Kenneth knelt and was peering down at him like he was inspecting an insect.

"If I were all right, I wouldn't be here on my damn knees, rocking like an old woman," grunted Kenneth as he grabbed ahold of the laurel branch that had struck his arm and pulled himself to his feet. Peering down at the bandaged stump, he saw a dark wetness spreading across the cloth.

"Shit," he swore and pulled the stump close to his chest. He rubbed his left arm just above the elbow and glared down through the darkness of the woods.

"We've been walking for over two damn hours. How much longer before we reach our lines?" groaned Rick Smith, another North Carolina boy, as he rubbed his leg where a Yankee bullet had gone clear through the muscle without hitting bone. He had been lucky.

Stevens spat a wad of dark tobacco juice at something on the ground and growled in his Appalachian drawl. "I reckon we can rest and quench our thirst down at that creek I hear off yonder. The going will be a little easier after that. I'd say about three or four more miles. That should get us close to Ol' Colonel Travis's lines."

"Well, what if Ol' Colonel Travis has moved his lines?" questioned Kenneth in a mocking tone. He really didn't like Stevens very much.

"Colonel Travis is way too cautious to make a push without word from the higher-ups," said Stevens as he pulled on the strap of his left suspender that held up his filthy gray pants, an air of know-it-all in his voice. A few minutes later, Smith, who was walking in front of the small group, slipped on the wet ground and almost fell down the steep bank at the creek's edge. Holding on to a birch sapling, he growled.

"The damn night is so black a man could walk off a cliff and wouldn't know that he had until he hit the damn ground." He pulled himself to his feet and brushed dirt and leaves from his tattered pants before he carefully eased down the bank into the creek. The rest of the group slid down the muddy slope easier than Smith had. Once down, they dropped to their knees, submerged their sweaty faces in the cool waters, and drank their fill before crawling up the opposite bank. Stevens belched loudly as he stood up, smugly proud of his talent. They gathered around a couple of large boulders and plopped down in the shadows on the west bank of the creek to rest.

Kenneth's stomach growled, reminding him how long it had been since he had eaten, so he reached under his shirt and pulled out a large chunk of cornbread wrapped in a kitchen cloth. He carefully unwrapped the bundle that Martha Anne had sneaked out of the mess kitchen and began eating. The rest of the group just stared out at the edge of an old field as Kenneth took another bite, savoring the taste of the pork-flavored cornbread. His mind was on the girl back at the hospital when he realized that it had gotten very quiet, too quiet. Glancing around suspiciously, he saw three pairs of hungry eyes watching him. Looking down at his cornbread and then back at his obviously hungry companions, he growled.

"Ah, hell. Okay." He began breaking the cornbread into four not-quite-equal pieces. Stevens smiled a big bad-toothed grin. "Thank ya." Cornbread was falling from his mouth as he spoke. They were chewing on the last of the cornbread when Stevens began lamenting.

"We'uns were on another worthless patrol along the Clinch River up between Spear's Ferry and that little village of Piney Flats when them damn Yankees ambushed us." He spat again at an unwary bug that crawled near his boot, crushed the insect without a thought, and wiped tobacco juice from his chin before he went on.

"The sneaky bastards kilt Sergeant Bryson and five of our boys in the first volley. They hit me in the shoulder." He groaned as he rubbed his right shoulder and grimaced. "They crawled out of their hidey holes and took me and Smith and a few other boys prisoner. Me and Smith were both shot but not kilt."

"Obviously," huffed Kenneth as he watched Smith's bushy head, nodding in agreement off to the side. Stevens looked at him a little confused and wiped more tobacco juice from the corner of his mouth. How the man could manage to eat cornbread and chew tobacco at the same time, Kenneth had no idea.

When the pitiful meal was finished, they licked their fingers and tiredly stepped out into the old field where, true to Stevens' word, the going did get easier. They had finally broken out of the hellacious laurel thickets and were able to stand straight for the first time in hours. Cautiously, they walked along the edge of the old pasture whose chestnut rail fence lay in jumbled disarray in numerous spots. The cows and horses that had kept the grass and weeds eaten down had long ago disappeared, and the weeds were now waist-high. Blackberry briars tore at their legs and hands, but the plants couldn't offer their sweet juicy berries to the still hungry men as they walked along far too late in the season.

"I sure hope the sentries aren't real skittish when we draw near the picket lines," whispered Kenneth as he stumbled over a pole, catching himself on a small locust sapling whose thorns dug into his palms. "Shit," he cursed as he pulled a brown thorn from his hand and peered somewhat sheepishly into the shadows along the field in search of some reaction to his stumble. "I would hate to get killed after all this painful work."

His three companions laughed slightly at his jest, but their eyes started scanning the fields to their front, and they watched their footing even closer. The predawn light had created shadows that seemed to move about, forming shapes that the imagination could easily turn into Yankees, and it keep them on edge. The news that Ol' Stonewall himself had been shot by a jumpy picket line was enough to make even the veterans worry. By now, they were all bone-tired, their individual wounds having slowed them down some, but it was the constant worry of a sentry's quick trigger that reduced them to a snail's pace. Kenneth's arm hurt like hell, and having shared his food, he was still hungry, but they kept going. They had no choice. A sixth sense honed from too many battles told them that they were getting close to picket lines, hopefully their own, as they moved ever so cautiously along the edge of an old wagon road.

Suddenly out of the early morning fog, someone shouted, "Halt, who goes there?" Everyone crouched, frozen like statues. The command to halt had been shouted from a small clump of trees just off the north side of the road they had been walking. Kenneth looked at Stevens whose beady brown eyes were darting about like a deer caught in lantern light.

"Okay, Stevens. This is where you earn your keep."

Stevens spat a wad of tobacco near his boot and smiled as he wiped the juice from his mouth.

"I know that damn voice," he whispered.

"If you know who the sentry is, then why are you whispering?" asked Kenneth with a hint of sarcasm mixed with concern in his voice.

"Because the big son of a bitch don't like me very much."
Stevens stood up straight but didn't say anything for a minute while
he obviously pondered his survival chances.

"Well, it may get us all killed, but I've got to know. Why don't
the man like you, Stevens?" Kenneth growled the question as his
eyes bore into the night. Stevens hesitated for a second before finally
answering.

"Coz I beat him bad in a game of poker a few months back. He
thought I cheated him."

"Well, did you?" asked Kenneth without hesitating.

"Hell yeah, but he never figured out how." Stevens laughed as
he spat again.

Kenneth looked down and shook his head.

"Great. Now we get shot because you cheated some big mean
sergeant at cards," he moaned. The other two men looked at each
other nervously then back at Stevens and Kenneth. They weren't sure
where the kidding stopped and the serious stuff started.

"You damn well better say something or those sentries are going
to start shooting." It was the first words that the other member of
their little group had said. His name was Penland, and he was a nervous wreck. His shoved Stevens forward.

"Okay, okay, I'm going," Stevens grunted and stepped tentatively forward.

"Henson, you ugly bastard, it's me, Stevens. Don't shoot. We'uns
just escaped from a Yankee hospital up near Blountville."

There was a pause and the sound of low, hushed voices coming
from the clump of trees. After a couple of seconds, one spoke.

"If'un that be you, Stevens, step out to the edge of the road so I
can see your sorry ass," boomed the voice from the dark. No torches
were lit, but the early morning light was enough to tell friend from
foe or at least Kenneth hoped so.

"Okay!" shouted Stevens. "But don't shoot. There is four of us,
and we ain't armed."

Slowly Stevens led the small group over toward the clump of
trees on the far side of the road.

More hushed voices could be heard.

"I'll be damned, it is you," said the voice. "We all thought that you and Smith were dead, kilt at that ambush at Spears Ferry." After a few more seconds of uneasy silence, the voice shouted, "Damn you, Stevens. I ought to shoot you where you stand for cheating me at cards." A rustle of branches preceded the emergence of a big man also dressed in a tattered gray uniform, three stripes on what remained of his sleeve. The sergeant stepped out into the road with the business end of his musket pointed at Stevens's belly. Kenneth took a deep breath and quickly stepped between the two men.

"Sergeant, you can shoot Stevens for all I care, but make it later. I need to get this arm looked at real bad." Kenneth held up the stump of his arm showing where the red stain had spread over the entire bandage. The sergeant looked at Kenneth's arm then back at Stevens. The barrel of the musket wavered slightly for a second before slowly dropping down to point at the ground.

"Okay. The field hospital is about a half mile back down this road near the edge of a field. You can't miss it. The smell is terrible." He shook his head.

"The mess is set up nearby there, too. It looks like you boys are hungry." The big head swung back toward Stevens.

"Stevens, I'll deal with you later." He turned, and the sweaty gray back disappeared into the clump of trees.

"You're right, Stevens. That man don't like you," said Kenneth as he started walking down the road. The other tired, hungry men waited a second, their eyes darting from Stevens to Kenneth, who was fast disappearing down the road, and then back to their friend. A heartbeat later, they, too, were trudging toward the mess area.

Kenneth soon found the hospital. It consisted of two large tents roped together with several lanterns hanging from the high pole ceiling. At first glance, it seemed dirtier than the Yankee hospital they had just left. The sergeant had been right; the place smelled terrible. Kenneth was just about to turn around and leave when a fat, bald colonel walked up to him. The man had a tired, washed out look about his face, and a bloody apron tied around his neck. His hands weren't much cleaner. The doctor looked Kenneth up and down, his eyes finally settling on his arm.

"Somebody did a good job on your bandage, soldier," said the old sawbones as he reached for Kenneth's stump of an arm. The smell of blood, sweat, and other odors attacked Kenneth's nostrils to the point that the stench was overpowering. He wanted to run, but the sawbones was already unwrapping his bandage.

"Hm, not a bad job on the cut either." He reached for a yellow tin can that sat on a nearby table buzzing with flies and other insects. "I don't have many clean bandages, but the man that used to wear this shirt won't need it anymore." He began to tear the gray uniform shirt into long strips, then poured sulfur from the can onto Kenneth's stump while sweat ran down his forehead and dripped onto the new bandage.

"This should stop the bleeding," he said as he began rewrapping the stump of an arm. "That's all I can do for you, soldier. You can thank whoever wrapped this the first time." He waited a second before he added, "It probably kept your stump from bleeding you out."

"It was a Yankee nurse," answered Kenneth, as a vision of Martha Anne's pretty face crossed his mind. "A very pretty Yankee nurse," he added as he turned and walked out of the stench of the hospital. He missed her terribly already, but he knew he couldn't dwell on his leaving. There was a war going on, and he had to find his old outfit. The sawbones stood in the entrance to the tent and watched Kenneth walk away, his arm held tight against his waist.

"Huh, nurses. They're going to ruin the field of medicine if they keep letting women into it," he muttered. One of his orderlies glanced over at him strangely, but he was used to the old man talking to himself. The sun was coming up over the far ridge, and the old doctor from Richmond knew he had to wipe off his cutting instruments. There would be more fighting today. He spat as he walked back into his world.

* * * * *

It took more than two weeks and a lot of walking, but Kenneth finally located his old outfit camped along the Holston River, just a couple of miles southeast of Knoxville. For reasons that neither President Davis nor General Lee could understand, most of the people in Knoxville were sympathetic to the north, and Kenneth's company had become part of a rear guard under Pickett's division.

"No place for a fighting man," growled Roy Smith, the new company commander of H Company, as they marched through the outskirts of town. "We should be up in Virginia with Lee or at least helping keep Vicksburg out of Grant's hands." Kenneth only nodded. He was fine with staying right here along the quiet river.

Oddly enough, the fact that Kenneth had his arm amputated didn't bother the higher-ups one bit. He was even promoted to sergeant and handed a sword. The south truly needed every man it could muster.

"Just lead them from the front, Sergeant. Point that sword in the direction you want them to go and step out. Most of these boys will follow you through hell itself if need be," said Smith as they sat around a camp fire one night, listening to some mournful Irish tunes being sung. "They're good, boys," added Smith, a full minute later as he listened to the crooner with his eyes closed. Kenneth watched Smith. He liked their new lieutenant. *He takes care of his men as best as he can, unlike our last company commander.* Reaching down, he threw another small log on the dying embers.

One night in mid-May, the 10th Battalion was bivouacked at the junction of the Holston and French Broad Rivers. Kenneth, who was restless and couldn't sleep, walked forlornly among the rows of tents that housed what was left of H Company. *A lot of the old faces are gone*, he thought as he looked over the company area. The war was taking a heavy toll on all the units. The 29th Battalion that fought alongside them was down to half strength, and the 25th Battalion Virginia Regiment was worse than that. For weeks now, rumors had been flying that old General Lee and President Davis had cooked up a plan to invade the north again. Supposedly their thinking seemed to be that if they could threaten the Union Capitol—not necessarily take the Capitol but surround it—then the Yankees would sue for peace. Besides, most of the boys in gray were eager for a chance to pay the Yankees back for what they had done to the south, especially Virginia. The route north, if the rumors were true, would take them back through Big Stone Gap and then through the mountains of northwest Virginia, then east toward Maryland and on into Pennsylvania.

A few days later, that sad night on the river mostly forgotten, Kenneth sat trying to fold his shelter half with his one good arm while worrying about the possible trip back through the Cumberland Mountains. *I have always heard that Pennsylvania was a right pretty place, hayfields stretching as far as the eye could see, big barns and big orchards. Yeah, I'd like to see it*, thought Kenneth as he finished folding the shelter half and stuffed it into his rucksack. All around him, men were busy preparing to break camp and head north. Most of the boys in his outfit were happy about the pending invasion, but Kenneth wasn't. They were about to do the exact same thing that the damn Yankees had done—invade another country. That was the main reason he had joined up in the first place, to stop the damn invasion. *Wasn't it?* His mind spun trying to figure it all out, and the effort made his head hurt.

"Damn," he cursed as he stopped what he was doing and rubbed his temples. Flashes of tiny lights exploded in his vision, and they forced him to squeeze his eyes shut. The nagging headaches that hadn't been real bad when they first started a couple of weeks ago now were becoming worse. He blinked his eyes several times in an attempt to clear his vision, but it didn't help much. The bright spots were still there. He piddled with his rucksack as he thought through the things that Martha Anne had said to him that rainy day back at Blountville, and he had to shake his head. Try as he might, he just couldn't understand who was right and who was wrong in this damn war. Angrily, he grabbed a couple of cans of food and stuffed them into his pack, tied the cover straps down, and tossed the heavy thing off to the side. He didn't have to understand everything; he just had to do his job.

"I sure hope somebody understands," he growled as he rechecked his gear for the tenth time and finally leaned back against an old log near their small cooking fire.

It was suppertime, and several men were busy trying to stoke up the small fires that dotted the company area. Kenneth glanced up from a hickory stick he had been idly whittling on and watched as newly promoted 1st Lieutenant Smith sauntered up through the smoke to stand next to him and a few other NCOs of H Company. Kenneth's old buddy, Sam Fergusson, was trying to roast a pitifully small chicken over an open fire and having very little success. He stopped the makeshift rotisserie and looked at Smith as the lieutenant cleared his throat and announced, "General Armistead, our illustrious leader, says that the rumors have been right. Old Bobby Lee and Jefferson Davis have hatched a plan to force Lincoln to agree to a conditional surrender." He said it as if it were all news to them, which it wasn't. He looked over his men as he chewed on a piece of the tough old bird that Fergusson had handed him.

"All that we and General Lee have to do is invade the north, move above Washington somewhere, and draw the army of the Potomac out into the open. Then we destroy it. Simple enough." He laughed and walked away, picking chicken meat from between his teeth with a sharp birch twig. Kenneth and the other NCOs looked at each other and shook their heads. They figured their young lieutenant must have been drinking, because this damn war was never simple, and it sure as hell was never easy.

Kenneth's company was part of the 10th Battalion under General Armistead of Longstreet's 1st Corps. Longstreet's other brigades were scattered all over southwest Virginia and up around the Cumberland Gap. It would take several days to gather all the far-flung troops together. They started north forming a long gray snake along Kingston Pike in early June and crawled toward Johnson City on the dusty thoroughfare, which would later become Highway 11. General Armistead and his 10th Battalion brought up the tail end as they pushed north to join General Lee. *This invasion is going to be a big gamble for the south*, thought Kenneth as they marched through the little towns of Maynardville and Tazewell, even knowing how General Lee liked the offensive.

Some of the townspeople along the way cheered the troops as they marched by, but most just stared at them through tired, hungry eyes. The war was beginning to take a toll on everyone, especially the wives and children left behind. There was so little food to go around and no one but them to do the work. But even with the meager local support, Lee's telegram to Longstreet's headquarters about the move north was a happy one, and spirits were high.

"This is our chance to end the war, gentlemen, so trust in Almighty God and push your men," Lee told his Corps commanders in his daily telegrams. Longstreet, like everyone else wearing the gray, was eager to please the Old Man, so he drove his men hard in order to join forces with his boss somewhere northeast of Chambersburg in the state of Pennsylvania. Both the army of Northern Virginia and the army of the Potomac were on the move, although each was unaware of the other's exact position. Lee was moving his mighty gray army blindly through the mountains of western Virginia because his eyes and ears, General Jeb Stuart along with his Cavalry, were searching for their own glory north of Washington. Stuart, who liked reading about himself in the Yankee newspapers, even managed to give a few interviews to the curious newspaper men as he rode through the countryside. Miles away, the armies of the Blue and the armies of the Gray were converging on one another, groping through the fog of war in a date with destiny at a little crossroads town called Gettysburg.

* * * * *

Early on the morning of July 1, the sun, not having peeked over the near ridge yet, led elements of General Pettigrew's Confederate brigade trudging up the west side of McPherson's Ridge, a long finger of low hills that disappeared into the mist south of town. A drizzle cooled their heated bodies as the gray line crept forward while several dogs barked in protest in the distance. A fat gray squirrel sat on a low-hanging limb and angrily chattered as the southern boys moved forward. One young freckle-faced private pointed a finger at the squirrel and acted as if pulling a trigger. His buddies laughed, but the squirrel just sat and chattered as if mocking them. McPherson's Ridge overlooked the sleepy little town of Gettysburg from the west, a crossroad of unknowns and home to about five hundred people. Pettigrew and his boys were part of A. P. Hill's 3rd Corps, which was stretched back along the Chambersburg Road. General Buford, of the army of the Potomac, had wisely set up a hasty picket line on the east side of McPherson's Ridge near Willoughby Run just a mile out of Gettysburg facing west. Willoughby Run was a small creek that meandered due south just below the three-storied seminary that sat on the outskirts of town. There had been a hard drought all spring, and Willoughby Run was nearly dry. Buford wasn't exactly sure where the Rebs were, but being an old Indian fighter, he had a feeling, a hunch, that Lee's boys would use the Chambersburg Road as they crawled out of the Cumberland Mountains, which he knew they had been using as a screen for their advance. General Buford referred to his troops as mounted infantry rather than cavalry, and they manned the battle line like an infantry unit. The Yankee farm boys had learned well from Buford's great knowledge gained fighting the Indians out west and he was proud of them. Buford and his two overstrength brigades of dismounted cavalry were expecting the boys in gray, and they held the high ground.

Corporal Anthony Hodges, a large dark-skinned young man from Ohio, leaned against a hickory sapling and chewed nervously on a piece of cold hardtack, his Springfield musket just inches away. Hodges had been with the 1st Ohio, which was part of Buford's picket line, for less than a month. This would be his first real battle. He was so blamed hungry his stomach growled loud enough to wake the dead, but he knew, sadly, that the biscuit was all he was going to get for breakfast. His eyes blinked several times as he strained to see through the thick fog gripping the road. He thought he had heard something out in the fog, but he wasn't sure. *Blamed nerves*, he growled to himself as he sloshed what he knew would be warm water in his canteen to keep his shaking hand from being obvious to his friends. The thought of running down to the creek, which lay about seventy-five feet to his front, and filling his canteen with water, flashed through his mind, but he hesitated. The creek water would be cool and fresh, but he knew big Sergeant Delaney would probably see him and chew him out. So instead, he made a face and drank down the warm water, which tasted of metal and smelled of wet mud. He began taking a second gulp but nearly choked when, through the mist, he noticed several shadowy figures sneaking down the road toward the creek crossing. He couldn't tell if they were of the Blue variety, but he figured not and shouted a muffled warning to the big Sergeant he had been worrying about. Ten minutes later, Hodges's redheaded freckle-faced Lieutenant peered over his shoulder and told everyone in the picket line to get ready but hold their fire. The lieutenant, whose name was Stillwell, quickly scribbled out a note on a wrinkled piece of paper and sent it by messenger back to General Buford, who had made his headquarters on a small knoll a couple of hundred yards behind the picket lines. The note informed Buford that the Johnny Rebs were coming down the road, but he had no way of knowing exactly what strength they were probing with. Stillwell briefly watched the messenger run up the hill before he slowly turned back to his men.

"Okay, boys, choose your targets well, and remember to shoot low!" he shouted just before the first volley erupted in a cloud of smoke that hung in the air like the early morning fog.

The Battle of Gettysburg had begun, and the Yankees clung desperately to the high ground along Cemetery Ridge. Buford's dismounted cavalry bloodied Pettigrew's Georgia boys pretty bad as the sun rose over the eastern hills and managed to delay the Confederate advance for several hours in a series of slow withdraws until reinforcements arrived. Unfortunately, General Longstreet was late arriving on the battlefield that first morning, the road back toward Chambersburg being packed with troops and material. The sun was struggling toward its zenith when Longstreet and his nearly exhausted staff galloped down a narrow lane heading toward the sound of the big guns. They desperately sought a spot where they could see what was happening in the battle that seemed to rage just out of sight. Eventually, they reigned in their lathered mounts near the McPherson's House just past noon and were finally able to view the battle that was already unfolding southwest of town. After a few minutes of frantically glancing from his map to the ground in front of him and back to the map, Longstreet swung his field glasses east toward the two high knobs across the way. The round tops hung in the smoke and mist like watchtowers of some ancient castle, and it was immediately obvious to him that they dominated the entire area. He wondered who, if anyone, occupied them, but in his gut, he already knew.

"High ground, gentlemen. We need to take those two hills, or we will have hell to pay." He made the statement in a near whisper and to no one in particular as he gazed through his field glasses, but his entire staff heard him, and they in turn looked toward the knobs looming above the local cemetery like a bad omen.

The sound of many hooves pounding the ground filled the air and caused Longstreet to lower his glasses and turn toward the fast approaching group. He quickly saw that it was Lee and his staff entourage with their flags flying boldly. "General Hill and his boys will take those hills, rest assured," said Lee as he rode up beside Longstreet and his staff. Longstreet couldn't figure out if Lee had heard his comment or that the old man had read his mind.

"Morning, sir," said Longstreet as he saluted and handed Lee the map. Pleasantries where exchanged between the staff members as Lee and Longstreet moved their horses off to the side. "I sure hope you are right, General Lee. We need that high ground," cautioned Longstreet as he watched the old man view the twin knobs through his field glasses. Lee brought the glasses down and began rubbing his right arm unconsciously with a gloved hand, the hollow feeling in his chest never far from his mind.

"I have every confidence in General Hill and his Texas boys, he'll take them by noon tomorrow." Longstreet didn't say a word in response as he tore his gaze from the two hills and looked over the shallow valley that spread out in front of them. *We shouldn't be here, it's not good ground for us to fight on*, moaned Longstreet to himself as he took off his hat and brushed the sweat from his forehead with the back of a gloved hand. His hair was still thick, but streaks of gray had crept into the edges of his dark mat. A sign of wisdom, he had once mused, but he held his wisdom and his tongue as Lee switched to other matters of importance while their horses chomped on the short grass, oblivious to the battle raging around them. After a few minutes, Longstreet brought up their blindness and the absence of General Stuart, but Lee waved off his concern. A little dejected, Longstreet resigned himself to helping the old man plan their next move.

Kenneth and the rest of H Company were tired. They had marched all night and actually double-timed along the Chambersburg Road for nearly an hour in an effort to reach the battlefield. They were winded, but they were there; the battle they had heard all morning now raged along a ridge in front of them. Just off to the side, about fifty feet away, Lee and Longstreet sat on their mounts, talking. Some of the men removed their hats and simply gawked at Lee. Such was their reverence for the man. One of General Lee's aides, a young clean-shaven captain, rode up, handed the Old Man a map, and then eased off to the side as the two generals talked and pointed. All of H Company had been in enough battles to recognize the importance of the two knobs the generals pointed toward. At the moment though, the major fighting seemed to be centered near what looked like a new railroad cut off to the northwest of town. The fighting was extremely intense along two fronts that ran from the railroad cut through the peach orchard and along Cemetery Ridge, but General Pickett's brigades were being held in reserve. *Hell, some of our brigades haven't even arrived from Chambersburg yet,* thought Kenneth as he looked around and took note of the unit flags.

Somewhat in frustration but a little in relief, Smith had his boys drop in place while he went off in search of Armistead's headquarters. Kenneth, bone-tired as his men, shouted, "Get some rest boys, if you can. They will need us soon enough." Then he reached up and stiffly unshouldered his pack, leaned it against a large white oak, and plopped down. The long march north into Pennsylvania plus the quick time from Chambersburg had pushed them all to near exhaustion, but still, most of the men couldn't sleep, and Kenneth was no exception. He lay where he had dropped, sleep refusing to chase the pain in his arm away. He just closed his eyes and listened to the battle as it ebbed and flowed from one area to the next. Nightfall eventually came, and darkness crept over the battlefield as the moans and cries from the dying drifted on the light breezes, rustling leaves in the treetops. The pitiful moans must have even frightened the insects or maybe simply shamed them, but either way, they remained silent as if on a cold winter's night. It was the end of the first day of battle, and still no orders came for the men of H Company to double-time to the front.

Kenneth checked on his men for the tenth time that day and then flopped back down and leaned back against his pack once again. He had moved to a different spot, one that was under the shelter of a bushy topped pine tree in case the rain that had threatened all day finally came. He, like everyone else, lay and listened to the cannon duel between Colonel Anderson's artillery that lined the ridge out from the seminary and the Yankee guns that sat across the way on Cemetery Ridge. The big guns banged out their fire missions with volley after volley, but all that really occurred through the first long night was that both sides were deprived of much-needed sleep.

A thin mist of early morning fog covered the dead and dying in the valley south of the small town as a church bell tolled in the distance on the morning of the second day. It was a sad and lonely sound like the crying of the wounded, and it wasn't Sunday. Why it rang or who pulled the long bell rope, nobody knew. Kenneth roused his men from whatever shelter they had found during the night and told them to be ready.

"Check you gear!" he shouted above the roar of cannons off to the north.

"Again," came a lonely grumble from the back of his small company, and a few men laughed but most just rechecked their gear. Kenneth ignored the comment. *Hell, they have a right to bitch*, he grunted to himself as he rummaged through his rucksack for something to eat. Sadly, the only thing he found, the mess wagons, stuck somewhere west of them, was some hard tack and half-cooked bacon, which was difficult to wash down with warm water. And still they sat around and waited. Kenneth had just swallowed his last bite of biscuit when he looked south and saw Colonel Woodard, the XO of the 10th Virginia, riding up. Woodard had been unable to find Lieutenant Smith, so he rode up to the only NCO he could find, which was Sergeant Nichols.

He looks too young to even be in the Army, much less help command a regiment, thought Kenneth as he gave a half-hearted salute. Woodard's return salute was even sloppier than his own, noticed Kenneth as he walked up to the boyish-looking colonel who sat atop a prancing Bay gelding. Woodard was having a hard time controlling his jumpy mount, so Kenneth grabbed the horse's bridle and spoke softly to it, "Easy, boy, easy." The horse instantly seemed to calm down and, instead of jumping about, just pawed the ground as if eager to leave the battlefield. "I don't blame you, boy. I'd just as soon leave this place myself," whispered Kenneth low enough so that the boy colonel couldn't hear him.

"General Pickett has been placed in reserve," announced Woodard after his mount had come under control.

"Not again," growled Kenneth under his breath, but it came out a little too loudly, and he was rewarded with an angry and somewhat confused glare from the XO. After a pause, the man went on.

"General Lee plans to have General Hill's brigade drive to take those two round knobs over yonder," said Woodard as he pointed toward the rocky tops. They both looked over at the knobs that lay above the cemetery now swarming with Yankee artillery and what seemed like a thousand unit flags.

"I sure hope there aren't any Yankees on those rocky tops, sir, or General Hill's Texas boys will have some rough going," said Kenneth without taking his eyes off the two knobs.

The boy soldier looked at Kenneth, blinked a couple of times, and looked back at the two knobs. He shook his head as if discarding a reply and then jerked the reins out of Kenneth's hands. Glancing at the two knobs one more time, he spurred the lathered gelding toward the division's headquarters without saying anything more.

"What am I—" Kenneth never finished the question because Woodard had ridden out of hearing range. "Damn," he swore angrily and turned back toward the hundred expectant faces of H Company who stood watching him from the shade of the big oak trees of Spangler's Woods. Kenneth's eyes swept over the dwindling company of men as he walked back toward them. *So many are no longer with us,* he moaned as he struggled for words to explain their status. The old veterans of H Company weren't worried about their status, and Kenneth knew that as they simply leaned on their rifles and looked at the ground. They would take whatever the god of war threw at them. But the new people, the men with faces un-haggard by past battles, they eagerly watched him walk up.

Ragged, partly barefooted, the remaining cream of the south, silently waited. *What the hell do I tell them?* he groaned as he glanced down at his own dilapidated boots. Finally, he started.

"All right, boys, we have been put in reserve—again." He paused as some of the men breathed a sigh of relief, mostly the old-timers, while others grumbled to each other about their bad luck. "I want you to get as much rest and food as you can because I'm afraid those boys from Texas and Georgia, who are supposed to take those two hills"—he pointed across the valley toward the two hills—"are going to need our help real soon." That was all he could think of to say to them, and although some of the men wanted more, most just shuffled away, heads down, and waited … again. Kenneth watched them leave before he, too, dropped his head and walked over to where he had left his rucksack.

The fighting raged all through the second day. *It's a funny thing about being in reserve,* mused Kenneth as he sat swatting flies in the shade of the large pine tree. *There's a part of you that's glad it's not you getting your ass shot off or, even worse, taking a bayonet in the gut.* Kenneth feared that above all. *But there's also a part of you that wants to run to the sound of the fight to help your fellow soldiers. To stand in that line and blast the enemy to hell.* But still, they waited. A bayonet can only be sharpened so many times or a pack reshuffled or new letters written that are too similar to the previous ones you tore up a few minutes before. The big guns roared, and people died. Thousands of soldiers clothed in gray hunkered down in the shadows of Spangler's Woods and watched the couriers rush from general to colonel and back again. Even the lowest private could tell the Yankees were fighting better this time, and the Yankees still held the high ground—the two round knobs above Cemetery Ridge. Try as they might, General Hill's Texas boys, even with the help of those fighting demons from Georgia, couldn't take those knobs. They fought and bled for every rock in a valiant effort to claw their way up those bloody tops, but in the end, a courageous bayonet charge, led by a former professor of rhetoric, drove them back for the last time. And far below them lay a place called Devil's Den, named correctly for it looked like a butcher's shop with blue and gray piled atop one another. Still, Pickett's division waited.

Kenneth lay with his back against the big pine tree, hat pulled down over his eyes, dreaming about Martha Anne. They were walking hand in hand across a lush pasture filled with horses; a hawk and dove flew overhead. He was awakened from his revelry by the ground shaking under him. A group of riders raced along the wood's edge headed in his general direction. He pulled his hat up and rose to one knee as he watched General Lee, with his staff trailing along behind, ride up and confer with Longstreet who stood on the edge of the wooded area, in the open, his ever-present field glasses in his hand. It was early in the morning on the third day of fighting; the next day was Independence Day, July 4. Late the day before, Kenneth had watched the battle rage on both sides of a small valley that ran up toward a stone wall now lined with Yankee blue. Smoke had boiled from the many cannons aligned along the long, flat ridge where the cemetery sat, and off to the south, more men had died in a once-peaceful orchard that lay under the shadow of Little Round Top. A small clump of trees, ironically called a corpse, rose just above the stone wall that ran at an angle toward the ridge. That was the spot Lee was pointing toward. The whole area was enveloped with Union flags.

Somehow Kenneth knew in his gut that General Lee would want them to try, once again, to take that stone wall, but this time, by going straight up the valley. Straight up the belly of the beast, a beast with teeth of shot and shell. General Lee's confidence in his boys was untainted by the two days of hard fighting; he truly believed that his boys could take that hill—hell, any hill. Except this time, things seemed different. Even the least privates could tell it. This time, the Yankees were stronger. They fought harder, and they didn't run. They had held the two round knobs and had fought like crazy men against those Texas and Georgia boys.

As Kenneth watched the two generals confer, his gut turned over when he saw Longstreet's big head bow and start shaking from side to side. The grizzled old warrior, veteran of countless battles, was obviously against Lee's plan, a plan Kenneth figured amounted to a direct assault up the middle of the Union's line. He was right on both accounts, but what he didn't know, nor did anyone else at that time, was what Longstreet had just told General Lee. Longstreet, Lee's old workhorse and friend, had just told the Old Man, who many worshipped as a near god, that no fourteen thousand men ever assembled could take that hill, this day.

Longstreet stared stoically toward the valley his men would assault as Lee explained his plan further. A few minutes later, General Pickett, who had been summoned by Lee earlier, rode up to the two generals for his orders. Longstreet, in a rare show of emotion, had just offered to relinquish his command rather than order the assault. Lee refused the offer, and Longstreet, against his better judgment, slowly nodded. General George Pickett's division, which was now well rested, would lead the charge up the valley toward the stone wall.

"God help us," whispered Longstreet as a tear slowly rolled down a weathered cheek to disappear into his dusty beard. General Pickett, reddish blond curls aflutter, saluted, then in boyish exuberance, whooped loudly and headed back down the small knoll. He rode joyously toward Kenneth and the thousands of other cheering men standing in the shade of the dark woods. Kenneth's gut knotted up again as he looked out at the far ridge with the corpse of trees rising above the stone wall. It was covered in blue.

The final preparation for the assault was partly concealed by the large wooded area called Spangler's Woods, although it is extremely difficult to conceal fourteen thousand men being readied for battle.

Colonel John Anderson, who was in charge of the confederate artillery that day, stood off to the side of Battery A of the Mississippi 21st Artillery and watched as General Longstreet, absent his staff, rode up to him.

"Colonel Anderson," boomed Longstreet. "You must clear the Yankees off that ridge." He pointed across the way. "It's called

Cemetery Ridge. Apt name, don't you think?" mused the old warrior, more to himself than to Anderson.

"You must accomplish this before. Do you understand me? Before the assault can begin." Longstreet seemed a little confused to Anderson, but he finally went on. "And you must inform me personally when that task is complete. In essence, Colonel, you will be responsible for when the assault begins." The colonel had just looked at him, or maybe through him, and then over at the far ridge.

"I'll do my best, sir, but our supply of shells is getting short." It was all he could manage to say because Longstreet was already riding away.

The artillery duel between Blue and Gray commenced shortly after 1:00 PM and continued into afternoon. Kenneth and the remainder of H Company were hunkered down in the woods as shell after shell rained down around them. Shrapnel tore through the tree-tops, shredding leaves that fell like a young green snow. After about an hour of constant shelling, the duel gradually slowed down. The Yankees didn't know it, but Anderson's supply of shell was nearly exhausted. If the assault failed and a counter assault followed, they were in trouble. Howitzers and broken caissons lay scattered across the field by the dozens. Dead men and dead horses completed the horrific carnage. Kenneth searched desperately for Lieutenant Smith through the smoke of the bombardment. He figured the always smiling lieutenant was probably dead, but he needed to know for sure. As Kenneth's eyes scanned the battered wood line in search of Smith, a small drummer boy walked up to him out of the cordite haze. The boy looked to be about thirteen or maybe fourteen years old and wore a uniform that was much too large for his skinny frame. A battered old drum attached to a worn leather strap that crossed the boy's boney shoulders rested against his stomach. He looked at Kenneth's stump of an arm and then up at Kenneth's weathered face.

"Does it hurt to get shot?" he asked.

Kenneth looked down at the obviously frightened young boy and tried to think of something noble to say, but he simply couldn't find the words. So instead, he answered as truthfully as he could.

"Yeah, son, it hurts like hell, but only for a little while." Kenneth paused, struggling to make sense.

"But running away," he went on, "would hurt all the rest of your life." Kenneth watched the boy blink a couple of times and nervously fidget with his drum strap.

"I ain't going to run, Sergeant," replied the boy before taking a deep breath, turning and walking toward the front of the column.

Bugles were sounding and bands were playing as men scrambled out from under whatever cover they had found during the shelling. Brigade after brigade were forming in line at the edge of the woods and spirits were running high. They wanted one more chance to prove themselves to the Old Man. They could take that damn bloodstained hill.

Kenneth and a few of the NCOs were forming H Company into line since Lieutenant Smith was still nowhere to be found. They were aligning alongside B Company on the far right side of the lead column. Woodard had told them they would advance two companies abreast. The company had just finished the alignment as the bugles sounded "Prepare to Advance." Kenneth looked over near the tree line and spotted a very pale Lieutenant Smith slowly walking his way.

He took one close look at Smith and knew. *The trots*, he thought to himself. The old soldier's disease, generally gotten from eating green apples or cherries.

"Sir, you look like death warmed over." Kenneth tried to laugh but couldn't.

"Sergeant, I feel like hell. My stomach is killing me." And with that said, Lieutenant Smith groaned and ran behind a much too small of a tree to relieve his aching bowels once again.

A hell of a way to begin an assault, mused Kenneth as his stepped out in front of what was now his company.

H Company was formed, and Kenneth knew he should say something, but it was really far too late for high and mighty words. He looked down the long gray line—older men with gray in their beards, young boys not even shaving yet, all their anguished eyes on him.

"All right, boys. We need to keep the lines tight. You all know what to do." He did an awkward about-face and looked up the hill just as the bugles sounded again. He stepped out into the sun with fourteen thousand other boys of the south.

* * * * *

The sky was as clear and as blue as any that he had ever seen, the grass fields spreading out in front of them like a green welcome mat. It was a beautiful day as column after column of Pickett's division broke out from under the cover of the woods. They had traveled about a hundred yards in fine battle formation when Kenneth's eyes shot skyward for the source of a haunting cry echoing above what seemed like a parade ground. There, high to his left, a great hawk sailed majestically on the warm air currents, and he had to smile.

"It surely must be a glorious sight from where you are, big fellow, this grand parade." The shouts from fourteen thousand men brought him back to the work at hand.

Battle flags flew high, and a hundred drums rolled the advance as the pride of Virginia started up the belly of the beast. After hours of hellacious dueling, the artillery of both sides had gone silent, and even though they knew it wouldn't last, everyone prayed that the Yankee guns would remain that way. Generals Armistead and Kemper led Pickett's division forward on foot as Pickett himself rode his black sorrel just behind the mass of gray. General Garnett, who was ill, had decided to ride his horse instead of walking, knowing full well he would be the target of half the rifles on the stone wall. Armistead, not usually a showman, took off his hat and stuck it on the tip of his sword. He held it high for all his men to see. The Yankees, looking down the barrels of their rifles, saw it too.

General Lee's plan of a sharp wedge to drive into the middle of the Yankee's position moved forward. Everyone, even the Yankees, was in awe of fourteen thousand men, in perfect battle alignment, coming up the hill, marching straight for the wall. The lead companies topped the first small rise on their way toward the ridge walking proud and brave into the very jaws of death. The sound of the bands slowly faded into the background for it wasn't their job to assault the lines, but the young drummer boys marched on. Kenneth was surprised at how calm he felt, how unafraid of what lie ahead. The world moved in slow motion as the drums, the ever-present drums, rolled them forward. Kenneth glanced at the sky once again, a soft blue with a few cotton clouds floating by, then looked down at the grass still a deep green and somewhat damp from the night's rain. It truly was as if they were in a grand parade, marching down some Main Street. All he needed to do was simply lead his men through the town, and then they could stop, laugh, and maybe raise a few beers in celebration.

Just then, the air shook, and all hell broke loose. The massed array of Yankee guns erupted like the roar of a dragon, and over one hundred artillery pieces from General Hunt's Regiment ripped the heavens open. The distance between the two armies was still great enough that solid shot was all the Yankees were firing, but that would soon change. Several black cannonballs tore a crimson hole through H Company's line and exploded somewhere in the back ranks of gray. The young baby-faced colonel was swept from his horse with a shower of blood, the ten-pound ball that killed him rolling to a stop at Kenneth's feet. *The fool should never have been on a horse out here anyway*, thought Kenneth as he watched the horse scream in its death throes. Kenneth never looked down as he stepped over the pitiful lump of shredded flesh that lay very still in the afternoon sun.

"Keep those damn lines tight. Close up, boys, close up!" Kenneth shouted as he tried to remove the fence rails that paralleled the Emmetsburg Road. The well-built fence became a killing point, so rather than continue trying to remove them, he climbed up on and then over the four rails before falling to the other side. The great gray mass was shivering from the impact of the big guns and bodies were stacking up on the road. The mass of gray, what was left of it, headed for the angled wall.

"We have about five hundred feet to go, and we will be on that damn wall!" shouted Kenneth through parched lips. Their goal was to reach the rock wall that lay just below the crest of the hill. *God, would they ever make it? Too damn far*, he thought as he watched the Yankee artillery crews on the ridge. They were working like ants around the great guns that belched death every three minutes. Time slowed once again for Kenneth as the screams of the dying blended with the screams of the shells forming a violent symphony of death. The ten-pound balls were ripping great chunks out of the Gray lines, but still they pressed on forward. They were now at the half-trot. The inhuman cry called the Rebel Yell was being forced from ten thousand parched throats as they ran forward. Kenneth looked over to the side and saw the young drummer boy disemboweled with grape shot, his drum rolling back down the hill. The drum, its cover half torn off its frame and splattered with bright-red blood, made a strange rattling sound as it rolled.

General Armistead was still on his feet, his hat still held high as he ran for the rock wall that was only three hundred feet to their front. Kenneth couldn't believe the general hadn't been hit even though his hat was a tattered corpse of its former shape.

Men were falling all around him as he struggled forward. Sergeant Frank Crawford, H Company's big jovial color bearer, fell with a grunt, blood spewing from a large hole in his neck. Kenneth tossed his sword to the ground and grabbed the shredded battle flag from Crawford's dying grasp and ran on behind Armistead toward the angle in the stone wall straight in front of them. Suddenly, the whole right side of what remained of H Company disappeared in smoke and gore as a volley from Yankees rifles hastily positioned along their flank ripped into them from the area where Kemper's boys should have been. The fog of battle enveloped everyone, including Kemper. His boys, having failed to make an oblique turn, were now two hundred yards behind where they should have been. Some men were now fighting hand to hand as the lines merged in a few areas. Most throats were too dry to scream, yet the Rebel Yell could still be heard, the sound drifting above the cannon fire.

The Yankee fire had grown so fierce and intense that the men in gray had to literally lean into it as though a great wind was trying to blow them from the battlefield. All human emotions had left the men—except one. Hate. There was no fear, no mercy, only hatred—hatred for the men in blue who were trying to kill them. White puffs of smoke from a thousand rifles floated above the rock wall just to their front.

A musket ball tore through Kenneth's pant leg. Another one grazed the stump of his left arm. Still he ran for the wall. His eyes burned and watered from the smoke, but he could see General Armistead up ahead. The general was within ten feet of the wall. Then somehow the man was up on the damn wall, waving his sword, his hat finally gone. A hundred rifles were aimed only at him as he turned back to look at his men. The look on Armistead's face was a mixture of surprise and sadness. Then he was down, his body jerking from at least ten .51-calibre musket balls slamming into him. A Yankee officer ran up shouting, "No, no, not him. Don't shoot him." He ran forward crying, but it was too late. The Yankee officer was an old friend of Armistead in the days before this war, and he held the dying man in his arms. On the other side of the wall, Kenneth stopped running, knowing what Armistead had seen without looking back—the glorious division was gone; the grand parade had ended.

Pain was a dull slap as a musket ball tore into his shoulder. The impact of the lead projectile jerked him around and sucked the air from his lungs. He clung to the battle flag, which tilted heavily as he leaned on it for support. Kenneth squinted through eyes stinging with sweat and saw what General Armistead had seen. If there was a hell, then this was surely what it looked like. Thousands of dead scattered across a field that ran red with the blood of the south. Shattered bodies, men crawling with missing limbs trying to escape from the beast, other men simply staggering around as if undecided whether to run or surrender. A deafening explosion off to his right lifted him up like the hand of God, and a chunk of metal struck him just above the left knee, shattering his thigh bone, and he was down, down with the other dying.

Three hundred yards the other side of the stone wall, underneath a large blue hospital tent, a young dark-haired nurse cried out and dropped the bucket of water she carried. A bloody image of her man lying among hundreds of dead flashed through her mind, and she fell to the ground weeping.

Kenneth was on his back, his breaths coming in short rapid gasps as pain racked his body. Blinking back sweat and tears, he caught a glimpse of a hawk circling high overhead, its wings dipping ever so slightly as it sailed above the carnage. A small grayish-white dove soon joined the hawk, and Kenneth smiled as his life bled onto the clay ground. He could hear their calls echoing across the blood-stained field as the sound of the battle faded, realizing with his last conscious thought that they were mates.

"I will be with you soon," he whispered and closed his eyes. Martha Anne's face smiled at him through a great white light and then he was gone.

No one on the bloody field far below noticed as a second hawk appeared out of the cannon smoke, and its cry soon joined the others' call. Together, the trio sailed toward the southwest mountains, their shadows falling briefly across the hospital tent as rain clouds gathered on the nearby ridges. A misguided and unjust cause began fading into the mist as the heavens opened up and rain washed the world clean for a time.

CHAPTER 4

Pointe Du Hoc

Never, in the course of human endeavor, have so many owed so much to so few.
—Winston Churchill

Perched on an old rusty cross high atop an ancient cathedral, surrounded by snarling gargoyles and stern-faced angels, a large red-tailed hawk sits in a numbingly cold drizzle. Larger than any raptor born in a hundred years, its four-foot wingspan and razor-sharp talons make him, for it is indeed a male, a most fearsome predator. He turns his great head slowly from side to side as if taking in a play while droplets of rain shed off the sleek, downy feathers that are fluffed up against the chill of the evening and its persistent wetness. Opaque eyes peer down into a darkness that no human sight can penetrate. Suddenly, the head stops its rotation and turns slightly back to the west. A primal sound, not unlike a prehistoric creature calling for its mate, rips through the night air. A solitary train whistle screeches loudly into the darkness. The sharp, down-curved beak of the hawk opens to present a challenging cry.

Far below lies the old city of Dresden, a beautiful place mostly untouched by the ravages of the war. The city slumbers quietly as a thick blanket of fog swirls through its dark, narrow streets. The hated but necessary blackout is in effect, and not a single light is visible. It is as if the city were empty, abandoned to the gods of darkness.

Across most of Germany, the nights have been this way for months on end ever since the British and American bombers, with their small but deadly Mustang and Spitfire escorts, gained air superiority. Ironically, in the chancellery, Air Marshal Goring, who should stand in disgrace in the eyes of the führer for the Luftwaffe's inaptness, doesn't. Instead, he receives his second Iron Cross for services to the Fatherland. Naturally, he has blamed the Luftwaffe's problems on the new pilots' lack of courage, and many have been sent to the eastern front for punishment.

The chief engineer, an old and grizzled veteran of the rail, sits in the well-worn driver's seat of engine 571 and pulls a tarnished Merkle pocket watch from his vest pocket. Holding it a few inches from his face, he squints in an effort to see the time. The watch had been a gift from his father just before he left for the front during the last war. *Not that many years ago, actually, but it seems like a lifetime*, he muses to himself as he closes the watchcase. His mind automatically flashes back to the deadly no-man's-land and the filthy waterlogged trenches that had been his home for months on end in the spring of '17. An involuntary shudder racks his body. He blinks to clear his head of the still vivid images of the so-called Great War and forces his thoughts back to the present. Leaning closer to the firebox to observe the tiny hands of his watch, he reopens the case and sees that it is eleven fifty-five. Although extremely anxious to start this run, he knows he can't. Not yet. Punctuality had been engrained in him to his core, so he waits. For many years now, ever since his wife's death, the most important thing in life—the only thing really—is the train schedule. His beloved Ingrid had died soon after he came back from the last war, and sadly, she left him childless. His parents were both dead, so all that was left was his job. The current war, as useless and ill-fated as the last, had been grating hard on him, as well as everyone he knew. The awful blackouts, established during the long, cold winter of '43, certainly didn't help. Everyone was simply tired and scared. Tired of the deaths and the constant lies it took to cover them up, scared because once all the Jews were gone, who might be next? Sighing in a low breath, he reluctantly reaches for the whistle chain near his right shoulder, but he wants to reach for the throttle. Pulling hard on the chain, the five-minute warning for departure shook the night. The old man sighs again and stares off into the dark void.

The brick and granite train station, which had been built in the late 1890s under the reign of Kiser Wilhelm I, becomes eerily quiet after the lonesome whistle had shouted its warning. Only the sound of hissing steam, which escapes from beneath the huge boiler of the locomotive, can be heard. On the concrete station platform, several small clusters of soldiers stand under a large metal awning talking quietly. A few of the more fortunate soldiers have loved ones clutching their arms, but most stand alone staring into the night, smoking foul-tasting black-market cigarettes rolled with bitter Turkish tobacco. Rain drips off the rusty edges of the awning in a steady flow as the drizzle fights with the darkness over possession of their world.

The station, which stands near the heart of Dresden, had seen many such troop carriers pull out from her gates in the last eight years. Strangely, this one seemed a little less sad than most, probably because it was headed west. Everyone knew that to go east—especially now—was almost certain death. It didn't matter if you were a Jew going to the gas chambers of Auschwitz or a soldier going to the Eastern Front, where the Russian juggernaut was grinding up whole divisions as it rumbled through the steppes of the Ukraine, death awaited you. At least, on the Western Front, there was a chance of survival, and most of the battle-hardened Wehrmacht troops knew it.

Standing near the first Pullman car, a group of three men, their mud-splattered greatcoats hanging loose off their shoulders, chat quietly as steam hisses and swirls about their feet. Two of these grenadiers possess what the old veterans call "the stare," born from seeing and enduring things no one should ever have to see or endure. These men are only twenty-four years of age but look and act much older, having withstood six years of combat. The other soldier is still bright-eyed, barely eighteen, and fresh out of an abbreviated boot camp. The boy's name is Hermann Roehm, and he represents the führer's last-ditch efforts to save the Thousand Year Reich, sending the youth to die for the Fatherland.

The two veterans hold their cigarettes down by their sides in cupped hands, one of many survival tricks learned while serving with

Rommel in North Africa. Snipers could be anywhere. Both men had seen their work up close, many times. They kid the younger one for never having fired his weapon at the enemy or anyone else for that matter.

A few feet off to their right side stand three more grenadiers; the younger of these men wears the Knight's Cross of the Iron Cross around his neck. The führer himself had presented it to him months before. Most of the men preparing to board the train had noticed it but asked him no questions. Had they asked, he would have told them that the second battle of Kasserine Pass had been the instrument of passage for him into the world of warriordom. He had gone from being a naive eighteen-year-old boy to a hardened eighteen-year-old man in one long, bitterly painful night.

The old engineer looks anxiously into the dreary sky, his hand, which shakes slightly from too many dangerous night runs, reaches for the whistle chain again. The Merkle says it's twelve midnight and time to go. He pulls hard once again on the cold, worn chain, and the brass whistle screams its "All Aboard" call. The troops crush out their smokes and move like silent machines toward their appointed cars. The few remaining civilians wave a tearful goodbye and trudge off into the dark, rainy night.

High above, the hawk's cry echoes across the great dark void that lies below. Slowly, the wings lift, and with little noticeable effort, the hawk springs into the night air where it is quickly joined by a grayish dove, one fairly large for the species. Together they pass over the old city and turn toward the west, trailing after the locomotive.

* * * * *

When the copious illusions, which oftentimes accompany madness, are coupled with pure evil, it produces a sickness that has no cultural or ethnic boundaries. The year is 1943, and with men touched by this sickness ruling Germany, Japan, and Italy as well, the entire world suffers from another horrible war. Two mad men and a puppet called Il Duce walk together in lockstep. Blood is upon the ground where they walk. One of the madmen is a dejected Bavarian painter who never rose higher than corporal in the Great War. The other is a sad attempt at a Samurai, a little pouting brother whose troops chase the barefoot soldiers of Haile Selassie, trailing behind them.

The crueler of the Druids from the dark days would squeal with delight at the horrors that these three men have unleashed upon the world. Others from the sacred groves would turn pale with sorrow as a third plague devours huge chunks of mankind. False prophets declare "peace in our time," but the world still bleeds. And the spirits of warriors past, which are always present, sail forth once again.

* * * * *

The August heat beats down hard on weary soldiers running along a winding, dust-covered road flanked by tall green pine trees. These young men ran with M-1 rifles held across their heaving chests at Port Arms, while the red Georgia clay boiled as their combat boots struck the sunbaked earth. They sang, or at least attempted to, in a sharp discorded cadence as they moved.

One of the men running in the long green formation was from the mountains of Western North Carolina, two hundred miles to the north. His name was William Craig, and he was a big man, just over six feet tall, and broad at the shoulders. His grandfather had hoarded his pennies in order to leave his home country of Holland and finally moved to the high coves of the Appalachians to escape the religious persecution that had plagued the old land. His grandmother had come from Scotland, her people having braved the cold North Atlantic to reach America. Tiring of the hierarchy that had too long ruled their beloved highlands with pompous authority, they decided to go to America. They found the deep rich soil of the mountain hollows in North Carolina to their liking, where they could grow fat potatoes and keep the sheep with full bellies. Plus, the ancient fog shrouded coves reminded them so much of the rocky crags of their homeland.

William Craig was born and raised in a small town that lay nestled under the high peaks of the Great Smoky Mountains. Hillsboro was a sleepy little town that sat on the banks of a bold stream named for a Scot. It was a peaceful place, the kind of town where everyone knew each other and, in the fall, football was king. Craig was an average student in the classroom, but on the gridiron, he was a star, starting both ways for the Hillsboro Eagles' football team. On defense, he was a bruising linebacker who humbled many an opponent. On offense, all the quarterback had to do was give him the football, and his powerful legs would gain yardage like the "great galloping ghost." His athletic skills were enough to earn him a scholarship to the small college nearby in Cullowhee. There were many places around the mountains with Indian names, and Cullowhee was one of them. It meant "valley of the lilies," although no one in recent memory had seen any lilies in the Cullowhee valley except those brought by the Scots and Irish.

Craig played football for Western Carolina College for two years. He was a freshman in December of '41 when the war began, and by April of '43, he had decided that his country needed him far more than the Hilltoppers did. Across the big waters, the Old World was at war again, and by 1943 the United States was in the thick of it. Craig joined the Army in mid-April of that year and was quickly shipped off to Fort Benning, Georgia, for basic training. After finishing basic, William was sent to advanced infantry training at Camp Polk, Louisiana, where he volunteered for the new airborne training program back at Benning. As a result of raising his hand, here he was, trying hard to withstand the rigors of "jump school," as it was called, without throwing up. William Craig wanted to be a paratrooper, one of the fighting elite who brought what they called "death from above." Right now, though, all he wanted was to be done with this long ass run. Tired and hurting because of his brand-new jump boots, he sang, "I want to be an Airborne Ranger," through clenched teeth. His lungs burnt from the effort, and his quads were screaming for him to stop. But like in the song, "Can't stop, won't stop, Airborne," he drove on.

At that moment, had William Craig bothered to look up into the bright Georgia sky instead of at the heels of the man in front of him, he would have seen a fairly rare and beautiful sight. A rather large reddish-brown hawk was sailing on the soft wind currents that blew up out of the Gulf of Mexico, pushing the cotton-like clouds along their northeast journey across the Savannah plain. The hawk was about one hundred feet above the formation, and its cry echoed across the pine forest, as it seemed to float on the warm air that would, in a few days, hold the parachutes of these young men aloft. William, along with a couple of hundred other young men, would float above the parched fields along the Chattahoochee River that separated the lower part of Georgia from Alabama. Years later, those fields would take on names like Normandy and Bastogne; but for now, they were simply drop zone 1 and drop zone 2.

William's company had already run about three miles this particular day and still lacked another two before they were finished. Four long columns of green-clad warriors stretched over two hills as the 250 men of Airborne Class 21 suffered in the early morning heat. The drill instructors, with their Smokey the Bear hats, were running around the company formation like a swarm of angry bees darting in and screaming at any soldier they felt wasn't performing up to their standards, and their standards were high. These drill instructors were mainly three stripers; most had small potbellies from either too much 3.2 beer, too much army chow, or maybe both. But they were tough, tough as nails. The instructors were not only running in a circle around the entire formation, they were oftentimes running backward, screaming their heads off all the while. William and almost everyone else in the company were in awe of these seemingly inhuman machines.

The drill instructors, or DIs as they were called, wore tailor-fit and highly starched OD green fatigues. Their instructors' hats were pulled tightly in place by a leather chinstrap, and their haircuts were high and tight. These bulldogs dared anyone to fall out of formation as they ran along the dusty side roads. Some poor souls did indeed fall out, simply unable to withstand the difficult physical conditioning of the first week of training, which was called ground week. The exhausted soldiers who fell out were quickly pounced on by the angry instructors, told to quit, and sent to other non-airborne infantry units, which were called "leg units" by the paratroopers.

"I knew a girl named Skinny Minnie. Took her to the woods, but she wouldn't give me any." As they ran along, the DIs sang various cadence calls that could make a Phoenix City whore blush, and the men loved it. One particular DI, with a nametag sown into his starched fatigues that read "Moore," was the meanest of the mean. He was an older man, perhaps thirty-two or thirty-three, with a black tab on this left shoulder that said "Ranger." Moore threatened the entire company with a challenge: "If any of you damn people fall out of my formation, you damn well better fall out face first." Most of the recruits feared this man could crush them with his bare hands and maybe even walk on water!

Craig had been made squad leader of 1st squad, mainly because of his size but also because at twenty-one he was a few years older than the other men. As squad leader, he ran at the head of 1st Squad and was responsible for any slackers in his ten-man unit. After about three and a half miles on this particular run, Craig noticed that 2nd squad, which was to his right, was having a tough time keeping up with the brutal pace set by Sergeant Moore. One man in particular seemed to be hurting real bad and, in turn, was slowing down the entire squad. Before long, all of Second Squad was grumbling and falling behind. The tall lanky soldier who was having so much difficulty with the run was sweating profusely, his face as pale as clabbered milk as he staggered along. His fatigues were soaked and stained white in several spots from the salt loss. William moved closer to the soldier who was almost at his end. "Let me help you, buddy," he said in a low-enough voice that the instructors wouldn't hear. He reached for the man's carbine and was a little aggravated, but not surprised, when the guy became startled and reluctant, at least at first, to hand over his weapon. After all, it was a cardinal sin to leave your weapon unattended. But when the weary guy finally realized that help was right next to him, he managed a weak thank-you and released the weapon. Another soldier from Craig's own squad ran up and grabbed the struggling man under the arm and began running along, holding him up. Craig placed both his and the other guy's carbines on his left shoulder and then grabbed an arm. Slowly they increased their pace until they were back in line with everyone else.

As luck would have it, the chiseled-faced Sergeant Moore was making his rounds of the company formation about the time that Craig and the other two men regained their places. Moore ran up and started to scream something to his squad leader but then stopped and just stared—first at Craig, then at the soldier who was being helped. He started once again to say something but stopped himself, watching as the two men nearly carried the exhausted soldier along with very little visible effort. After a few seconds, Moore ran to the head of the column and shouted, "That's what I want to see. See and learn!" he shouted. "You have got to help your buddy if you want to stay alive in combat." With that announcement, other men stepped up to help the tired and now somewhat embarrassed soldier. Finally, the five-mile run was over, but it was still early morning. It would be a long, hard day for the paratrooper want-to-bes of class 32.

Many hours later, the sun was a fiery orb as it sank slowly below the dense wall of Longleaf pines that stood sentinel outside the newly constructed barracks. The ancient trees cast cool dark shadows across the company area and a light breeze rustled the needles high in the tops. The pungent odor of fresh-cut lumber and wet paint filled the air, and the buzz of mosquitoes, some seemingly the size of small birds, echoed among the wooden barracks. Two hundred fifty weary paratrooper trainees stood at attention in the fading evening light as Sergeant Moore's booming voice rang down the company street. "You people did real good today," he said as he looked at the line of tired young faces. Some smiled but most were just too damn exhausted to respond. "Today, you learned the first lesson of combat survival …" His voice rose to another level. "Today you learned to help your buddy. Company dismissed!"

Most of the men headed for the chow line, but some headed straight for their bunks—too tired to even eat. William found himself jogging (you never walked in the company area) alongside the soldier who had helped him carry the poor soul on the morning run.

"I'm William Craig," he said, extending his big hand in the direction of the broad-shouldered private.

"I'm Mike Bledsoe," came the reply, his southern accent hanging in the warm air like the smell of fresh molasses. Craig smiled when he heard the southern drawl.

"Where you from?" he asked, with only a hint of acknowledgment in his voice. The stocky blond-headed private hesitated, slightly suspicious for a second, before he answered.

"I'm from Knoxville," he said with a seriously straight face. "Knoxville, Tennessee," he added, as if the town needed a further explanation. Craig could tell the guy was a little defensive about the question, so he smiled again and said with a laugh, "I'll be damned. I live just across the Smokies from you, over near Cherokee, a little place called Hillsboro." Everybody seemed to know where Cherokee was, but very few people had ever heard of Hillsboro; it was just a small southern town hidden among the shadows of the great Plott Balsams. William watched as Bledsoe's stance loosened up a bit, and the big man smiled back.

"Hell, I've driven through Hillsboro before ... if I remember right, it sure didn't take long." He laughed and slapped Craig on the shoulder as they headed for the mess hall.

Both men stood in the long, winding chow line, talking about their mutual knowledge of the Smokies when the lanky, slightly stooped guy they had helped through the morning run jogged up. The newcomer cleared his throat with what sounded like either a half laugh or an "excuse me" cough.

"I really appreciate you guys helping me this morning. I don't think I could have finished the run without it." The Yankee accent stung their ears like fingernails scratching on a blackboard.

"That's all right," said Craig, resisting a shudder, while Bledsoe nodded in agreement. "Next time, it might be me that needs help."

"Well ..." The stoop-shouldered soldier looked Craig up and down before he went on. "You're too damn big for me to carry, but," he continued, "I'll make damn sure that you fall out face-first, if that helps." All three men laughed.

"What's your name, Yankee?" asked Craig, still laughing. *I like this guy*, he thought, as the line moved closer to the mess hall door.

Once inside, they would have to keep their mouths shut except to shovel in food.

"I'm Jerry Jamberdino," replied the Yankee as he extended his hand. "I'm from Buffalo," he stated proudly.

"Is that in the United States?" teased Bledsoe.

"Fuck you, Reb. It's in New York. That's one of the states that didn't secede." The three carried their laughter through the door and into the mess hall, an unforgivable sin according to the ever-watchful Sergeant Moore, whose big head now turned in the direction of the laughter while his eyes glared hard. The soon-to-be victims were moving innocently along the chow line, and Moore waited patiently until all three men had gotten their plates filled by the KP food shovelers. When they were about to sit down, he walked briskly to where they stood half-crouched in an attempt to sit. His green eyes were blazing as he looked down the brim of his hat.

"You scumbags seem to think that everything is pretty damn funny around here. Well, let's go outside and see if you think a hundred pushups are funny. Follow me." The three men looked at each other sheepishly as Moore stomped out of the mess hall. Setting their plates down, they hustled out of the building and ran until they caught up with Moore, then obediently followed him to the sandpit. The Smokey the Bear hat bobbed up and down on Moore's head as he led the three men, who now looked like scolded school children. When Moore spun around, the doomed men snapped to attention. Moore's expression grew even sterner as he looked down at their empty hands. "Where the hell are your plates?" he shouted. They looked at him, dumbfounded. "Your damn chow! Go get your plates of chow, now!" he screamed, and Craig tore off with Bledsoe and Jamberdino close behind. They grabbed their plates from the table and ran back out to stand in front of the irate Sergeant Moore. "That's better. Now put the plates down in the sand and give me a push up. Each time your face goes down, you had better take a bite of your food. We have to feed you pukes, so eat." Moore stood defiantly over them while they did their pushups. Down into the food, which was cold by now, and then back up, chewing. Jamberdino collapsed after seventy pushups, his face plowing down into what remained of his supper when his arms gave out. "God help us. And you want to be a paratrooper," said Moore disgustedly as he kicked sand into Jamberdino's face and walked off toward the mess hall.

When Sergeant Moore disappeared through the big double doors, all three men jumped up, grabbed their plates so as not to litter the company area, and ran toward their barracks as fast as they could go. It wasn't until they were safely inside that they dared to relax. But once there, they not only relaxed but began to laugh; they laughed so hard they were soon rolling around in the squad bay area. Tears poured from their eyes when Jamberdino actually blew a pea out of his nose. William's entire 1st Squad figured their squad leader had either gone nuts or all three guys wanted out on a section 8, a discharge for being crazy. Once the shock of the moment wore off and the laughing died down, they quickly realized they were probably high on Sergeant Moore's shit list. So hoping to prevent any further problems, they planned to look sharp in the morning. Dragging their footlockers out from under their bunks, they joined the other men in the squad bay area. It was time to make their jump boots shine, and after today's antics, they were badly in need of work.

The barracks that the want-to-be paratroopers were housed in were all two-story structures, and each level housed two squads. Double bunks lined the inner and outer walls with a common squad bay area in the center. This common area was where the sacred art of spit polishing was performed. Spit-shined boots were one of several things that separated the paratroopers from the nonairborne individuals, or legs. The tools required for a proper spit polishing were a can of Kiwi boot polish, a soft rag, elbow grease, and plenty of saliva. Mix these things properly, and you can get a mirror effect on the toe and heel of your jump boots. William and his two newfound friends chatted about their lives back home and told tales of past girlfriends as they worked the magic on their boots. Finally satisfied, they put away their gear and hit the sack just before lights out at 2300 hours. 0430 would come very early; it always did.

* * * * *

The first week of jump school is considered ground week. During that week, the drill instructors run your ass off. You run in the morning. You run to the training area. Hell, you even run to and from the latrine. You never wanted to be caught walking in the company area. Legs walked. Paratroopers ran. Thus was the unwritten rule that governed the entire training area.

The instructors also had to tighten your stomach. Tighten it to the point it was as hard as a washboard. Besides the running, squats and deep knee bends toughen your legs. Hard, strong legs were needed in order to withstand the parachute landing falls. The typical parachute landing was like jumping from a twelve-foot-tall building and landing on uneven ground. The term *parachute landing fall*, or PLF, was the name given to the proper form your body was supposed to obtain just before you hit the ground. Feet held together, knees slightly bent. You started your roll when your feet first hit the ground, then your calves hit, then your hip, and finally your shoulder. Four points of contact. You hit and roll, hit and roll. It's driven into your brain until you do it in your sleep. You were of no use to the Army or the war effort if you got hurt in combat from a bad PLF; therefore, you practiced, practiced, and practiced some more.

The constant running also gave you a unique feeling of invincibility, of being elite. A little swagger in your step and pride in your unit. That feeling would be sorely needed when you stepped out of a perfectly good aircraft flying at 120 miles an hour, 1,250 feet above the ground. Sometimes, during night jumps, you stepped out into a totally black void. Yeah, you need that swagger when the prop blast from a big Cummins engine nearly rips your clothes from your back as you exit the aircraft and the only protection you have is your faith in the twenty pounds of silk on your back, plus the small reserve chute that's attached on the front of your harness. You need to feel invincible. But even with your pride and newfound faith, you truly hope you don't have to pull the ripcord on your reserve chute. Horror stories abound about men falling from the sky with their reserve chutes wrapped around their bodies. Like the song says, "What a hell of a way to die."

William grew closer to his two friends as they sweated together through ground week and the second week, called tower week, which consisted of jumping from twelve-foot platforms and then moving up to a thirty-foot tower, always working on your PLF. On the last day of tower week, the troopers found themselves being pulled up to the top of, and then hanging from, the 250-foot towers. Once at the top, the apex of each man's chute was released from the huge hoop that had pulled him to the top of the tower, and he floated down with his chute fully deployed to land in deeply plowed dirt. That was the plan at least, and like most good plans, it worked most of the time—but sometimes not. There were many stories of chutes failing to release properly from the giant iron towers, and William's company witnessed one such mishap. The want-to-be's chute was late in releasing from the apex and the canopy skirt, having already released from the hoop, formed a perfect cigarette roll. The drill instructor shouted up at the anxious trooper, "What are you?" And he expected the traditional answer of, "Airborne, Sergeant," but what he got was a very shaky "I'm scared to death." Luckily, the plowed ground absorbed the shock of the soldier's landing, and he walked away fine, but it gave the troopers a small taste of things to come. The recruits had also heard but still found it hard to believe that these jump towers were used as an attraction at the '39 World's Fair held in Fleming Field, New York. *A damn tourist attraction*, thought William, as his scrotum tightened up just before he hit the ground on his jump or release, whatever the hell the proper name was. *Now we're training for war on the damn things. How ironic*, he thought as he hurried to S-fold his parachute.

The Saturday night before the start of what was called jump week, William sat sipping on a PBR someone had sneaked into the barracks. He was listening to Bledsoe talk about dropping out of high school because of a fight with his principal. Not just an argument but a real knock-down, drag-out fight. William was kind of amazed because his principal, old man Ernest Madison, had been a really nice guy and had even helped him get his football scholarship. *I guess I'm just lucky*, thought William, as Bledsoe talked about getting into fights in his neighborhood nearly every night. William wasn't quite sure why, but Bledsoe seemed to hold a lot of anger, and maybe a lot of pain, just below the surface of his skin. He figured Bledsoe's father had probably been pretty damn tough on him growing up, but he wasn't sure. Although William had no way of knowing it, he was right on the money about Bledsoe's father. The senior Bledsoe had been a rising star in the boxing circles around Knoxville in the early thirties, but the bottle had grabbed Carl Bledsoe hard and wouldn't let go. His dreams of becoming something more than a local wonder had been pissed away like the fiery liquid that flowed through his veins. When it became so bad that Carl couldn't even beat the no-talent bums that hung out at McClugg's gym, he began to beat his young son and then his wife.

A very bitter and very confused Mike Bledsoe took to roaming the back alleys of north Knoxville. A big, strong kid, Mike, refused to learn proper boxing techniques. Instead, he learned the street way: kick, punch, bite—whatever it took to hurt the other guy. And if you hurt him bad enough, he never bothered you again even if it was your principal. William and Jamberdino figured that since Bledsoe liked to fight, or at least said he did, then maybe the jump school boxing tournament would be a good way for him to release some of his pent-up anger. When another beer suddenly appeared out of nowhere, they handed it to Bledsoe and eagerly suggested he get into the tournament. Suggestions, much like plans, sometimes work out and sometimes don't. This particular suggestion turned out to be a huge mistake since the boxing committee threw Bledsoe out of the tournament during the first fight for kicking and biting. This wasn't Bledsoe's only opportunity to fight, though.

There was a small beer garden on post where the would-be troopers were allowed to go drink after the second week of training, and true to form, William and his two buddies bellied up for several beers whenever they got the chance. Late into one particular evening, William found himself standing alongside Bledsoe in one hell of a bar fight. There were several soldiers from a nearby artillery unit that had come to the beer garden that night, intending to strip some unwary paratrooper of his prized Cochran jump boots. One of them was a big, stocky buck sergeant from New Orleans with a nose that had long been crooked. When the fist swinging, chair throwing, and beer bottle tossing ended, Cajun blood ran freely from a nose that was broken yet again. Mike Bledsoe stood with his back against William's, sucking on a bloody knuckle, a smile on his unscratched face. Jamberdino had stood back and watched. "I'm a lover, not a fighter," he said, helping William drag the semiconscious buck sergeant into the dirt street and unceremoniously deposit him there.

By the third and final week of jump school, Bledsoe's own nose had been broken, not once but twice. William's nose was broken once, but Jamberdino's remained untouched. He did have a mysterious scratch on his left knuckle, of which he was very proud, although how he got the scratch wasn't exactly clear whether through fighting or perhaps loving in Jamberdino's case. The three men had become hard as nails and were finally ready to jump out of the damn C-47 even if the drill instructors told them they would hand them a chute on the way down.

The morning dawned clear and hot on the first jump day. There was palpable nervousness in the air as everyone went about their normal routine, the butterflies hidden from sight in jittery stomachs. This was the day they had trained so hard for, the day they would step out into the great unknown and fall at 120 miles per hour. The day when each soldier, try as he might, would squeeze his eyes shut as he exited the aircraft and perhaps not open them again until feeling the chute deploy—only then watching the ground sway far below his dangling feet. This is the time when training suddenly kicks in and the soldiers look up to make sure they don't have a cigarette roll or a Mae West, both serious malfunctions in the chute. If none appear, then and only then will they let out a sigh of relief. In the event that a chute doesn't open, you only have about eleven seconds before you hit the ground. Just like when they sang, "Glory, glory, what a hell of a way to die," the paratrooper version of "Glory, glory, hallelujah," it truly was a hell of a way to die. Kicking and screaming all the way down.

After two weeks, the five-mile morning runs had become less difficult. The men barely broke a sweat on the early morning run that first jump day. But by noon, with the sun beating down, the run from the training area to the airstrip was another story. The excitement and anticipation of their first jump caused their guts to churn as Airborne Class 21 neared the airfield. The heat from the asphalt runway rose in shimmering waves as the three friends stood alongside 247 other anxious men in a long line near the main hangar. Row after row of chutes were stacked on long black packing tables. The first-time jumpers moved along these tables, and a drill instructor handed each man his chutes, one main and one reserve. The T-7s had been prepacked by specially trained parachute riggers, and everyone hoped the chute they got was packed by a competent one. More instructors stood at the back of the huge hangar and made sure each man's parachute harness was fitted properly before he left the building. *Tight* was the key word, so tight in fact that the soldiers walked stooped over from the straps that wrapped around their groins and backs.

Once everyone was properly fitted with their chutes, the long line of want-to-be paratroopers headed for the waiting aircrafts. A dozen C-47s, the workhorses of the Army Air Corps, sat on the runway like ducks on a black pond. The gooney birds, as they were affectionately nicknamed, stood ready to take the men aloft. The aircrafts' rear loading ramps were down, and the men trudged toward them like condemned convicts headed to the gallows. The ramps led up into cavernous black holes that even the bright Georgia sun could not penetrate, and for a second, the forward movement of the paratroopers stopped, the lead soldiers hesitant to enter the black void. Only the shrill whistles and angry shouts of the instructors drove them forward. "Let's move it, people! The war is not going to wait for you to make up your mind! Let's go, go!" shouted Sergeant Moore as he stormed up and down the line. No one spoke except for the DIs, who screamed orders as the mass of humanity pressed on into the dark hole. Squeezed together like cattle in a slaughter pin, they sat and waited on the fold-down benches. The massive twin Cumming engines roared, spitting out blue smoke, while the large ramps were pulled up as if by an invisible hand. The ramps that allowed them to enter the aircraft now blocked their escape, and everyone felt the urge to run someplace, but it was too late.

A grizzled old jumpmaster walked down the aisle between out-stretched legs, and his shouting could be heard above the revving engines. "These are barf bags!" he shouted, holding up one of the bags for everyone to see. "If you need one, take one, but make damn sure you take it with you when you exit my aircraft." The jumpmas-ter was an E-6, three stripes up and one down, who walked with a slight limp. The limp came, courtesy of a round from a German machine gun in North Africa. He wore a Ranger tab on his left shoulder, just above the 101st Screaming Eagle patch. The sound of men puking filled the aircraft, and the smell of vomit floated on the hot air inside the plane, which shuddered along with its passen-gers. The big Cummins engines revved to the point that William was sure they would simply explode, but somehow, probably through the miracle of American engineering, they didn't. After several minutes of earsplitting noise, the pilot finally released the aircraft's brake, and the C-47 slowly rolled down the runway. Gradually, it gained speed until finally lurching into the warm Georgia air like a young mallard struggling to take flight for the first time.

William's mind raced through all the instructions that had led him to this point. He was about to jump out of a perfectly good air-craft, willingly. *God, let my chute open*, was the unspoken prayer that he and everyone else who would be truthful about the matter repeated in their minds. The flight to the drop zone at the Chattahoochee River was a short one, and before he or the others had too much time to worry, the jumpmaster shouted, "Outboard stick, stand up!" Men struggled to stand. "Inboard stick, stand up!" Everybody in the aircraft was now on their feet. Hearts were racing as barf bags were stuffed into shirt pockets or simply gripped tightly in damp sweaty hands. The next command echoed through the fuselage: "Equipment check!" And each man's eyes were on the chute of the man in front of him, checking to make sure all the lines and straps were in the right place. A few wise guys joked about problems on their friends' chutes, but for the most part, it was serious business. The jumpmaster stifled a laugh behind a wicked smile as he watched the nervous GIs await his next call. "Hook up!" he bellowed, and fifty static line hooks snapped shut on the main line that ran along both sides from the front of the aircraft to the back.

All eyes were on the jumpmaster as the want-to-bes held their collective breath for the next command; the old warrior smiled again and shouted, "Stand in the door!" A baby-faced second lieutenant shuffled into the door position, just two men in front of William, who could see the green canopy of the South Georgia pine forest flashing below the young lieutenant's feet. Most eyes were now on the jump light, which was mounted just above the jumpmaster's head. It still shone red. The jumpmaster had one hand on the lieutenant's shoulder, and the other braced against the fuselage. The lieutenant stared straight ahead, his mind on his wife and kids back in Richmond; his nametag read, "Stone." He was a recent graduate of VMI, a fine military school where his great-grandfather, who had been killed during the Civil War, had also graduated. The old veterans had told William and the others numerous times that their entire life would flash in front of their eyes just before their first jump. Good, bad, or indifferent, William's mind gravitated to a brief flash of Etta Jones's big titties. Etta had been his first love at the tender age of fourteen. Though a little heavy, she had been a very mature sixteen. But only that once had William gotten to see those big titties.

The jump light changed from red to green, and the jumpmaster shouted, "Go! Go!" He released his grip on the lieutenant's shoulder and gave him a slight push. Lieutenant Stone leaped from the door, and the next soldier stepped up to take his place. That soldier disappeared as well, and William was next in the door. His training kicked in, and he stood for a second, peering at the land that rushed by. Then he, too, was gone out the door. He tucked his body from reflex and began his count. "One thousand one, one thousand two ..." The wind roared in his ears as his body fell through the hot Georgia air. "One thousand three ..." His feet were slowly coming up even with his body. The ground was racing toward him fast as he said "One thousand four" and felt the slight tug of the chute as it slipped from the bag. He was a little surprised to find his hand already on the handle of his reserve chute. The shock of full deployment was brutal, but it came as a relief. The bone-jarring shock of the T-7 opening tested the straps that wrapped his legs, and he was glad they were tight.

A nervous laugh escaped from his throat when he realized his eyes were still squeezed shut; he forced them open and looked around. "Damn, what a sight," he exclaimed as he looked up and saw his chute billowing above him against the blue backdrop of the sky. He was floating high above the grassy field that served as drop zone 1, and he was awestruck by the sight of five more C-47s passing overhead. Each discharged its cargo of paratroopers out both sides of the aircraft like a duck birthing little ones on the fly. *I hope my form wasn't as bad as some of those guys*, thought William as he watched several bodies nearly tumble out of the planes. *Well, at least my chute opened okay. Now as long as I don't break a leg when I land, I will have survived my first jump.* He smiled at the thought.

William was floating on a warm air pocket that had slowed his descent to where it seemed he was barely dropping at all. It wasn't necessarily a bad thing, except that the warm air was forcing him toward the extreme western edge of the DZ. Beyond that stood the ancient longleaf pines that stretched toward the horizon for miles. These sentinels of the forest towered over a hundred feet in height and stood guard over the grassy fields. Their tight-limbed crowns swayed slightly in the light breeze as they watched dispassionately while the tiny humans made an attempt to live among their heights, however briefly.

It was that tremendous height, that hundred feet, that bothered William. *If I hang in one of those damn tops, I'm screwed*, he thought as he pulled hard on his risers just like he had been taught. To climb your risers, as the old-timers called it, was the only steering mechanism he had for his chute. If you pull down on one side of the chute, then air supposedly escapes from the other, and the chute moves in that direction. But not by much. The brass bracket at the top of his risers was only an inch from his hand when he decided to stop climbing for fear he might collapse his chute. *Wouldn't that be a hell of a way to die*, he thought, the tall pines growing ever closer. Even though the chute continued to drift west, it did turn—a little—from his efforts.

His body had twisted to face away from the big trees, and a low moan escaped his lips as he anticipated hitting their branches backward. He was looking over his shoulder as the pines rushed toward him when suddenly a large red-tailed hawk rose from an old lighting-scarred giant and flew straight at him. Fearing the bird might strike him for some unknown offense, William released his grip on the risers and threw his hands up in front of his face. The hawk cried out and shot by him, passing within a few inches, then circled his chute as if it were a Nazi aggressor. He cautiously eyed the hawk and then glanced down.

The wind hadn't changed direction, but somehow the chute's drift had slowed, and a small opening near the edge of the field appeared just below him. "Oh shit" was all he could say as he looked again at the hawk and then back at the rapidly approaching ground. *I guess the brushy edge of the drop zone is better than a tree landing*, he figured, and prepared for his first real PLF. He bent his knees slightly and pulled down on his risers just as he was about to hit the ground. Wham! "Ugh," he groaned loudly, pulling off an unconventional three-point landing, which wasn't exactly what the instructors had taught him. His feet, his ass, and then his head hit the ground hard, but he did manage to roll. Unfortunately, he hit a briar patch, making the roll painful and ugly. Still, he was on the ground and didn't feel as if anything was broken.

Slowly, he struggled to his feet and looked around sheepishly to see if anyone had been watching. To his relief, everybody seemed as busy as he was. So either they didn't see him or their own landings had been just as bad and they couldn't say anything. He tried to take a step toward the center of the DZ, the main gathering point for the jumpers, but was quickly jerked to a stop. Cursing himself, he realized he was still attached to his damn chute. Hitting the quick-release button on the front of his harness, he shrugged out of the web of straps, grabbed the chute, and was beginning to S-roll it when the roar of more aircrafts thundered overhead. He stood with a hundred other young men scattered across the field and watched as the last flight of Training Company 21 passed overhead. The sky filled once again with paratroopers, and it was truly an awe-inspiring sight. In a few short months, this scene would be repeated under very different circumstances.

The next four jumps were fairly uneventful except for William's first experience with what they call "walking off silk." He had just gone out the door for his third jump when he found himself floating over the top of another parachute. He was close, too damn close, and he knew it. In the blink of an eye, the other chute stole the air from his own, which partially collapsed. He dropped about twenty feet and landed almost dead center on top of the fully inflated chute below him. Sinking up to his knees on top of the OD green parachute, his mind raced as fast as his heart while he struggled to keep his balance. A high-pitched voice screamed at him beneath his feet, "Get off my damn chute, you bastard!" It was all the frightened paratrooper could do: curse, cling tightly to his risers, and watch as the two legs poking down into his canopy began to move. William remembered the drill his instructors had taught them, and he applied that knowledge quickly as he began walking through the silk toward the side of the parachute. Luckily, his chute stayed somewhat inflated while he struggled toward the edge of the chute he was on, and he was able to slide off the side of the canopy without getting tangled in the other chute's suspension lines. It was not an easy feat, but he soon found himself floating alongside a much-relieved trooper, who turned out to be Jamberdino. William smiled sheepishly at his friend and saluted. Jamberdino shouted, "Fuck you, Reb. We're even now." Then he smiled too.

Late that Friday afternoon, after the fifth and final jump of their training, William, Bledsoe, and Jamberdino stood in company formation as the jump school commander pinned the silver "blood" wings on their chest. The grim-faced captain, who had a small jagged scar running down his right cheek and looked tough enough to bite into 16-penny nails, walked down the line of paratroopers. The man's face was like a hatchet, his body tense and seemingly ready to explode. He too wore a Ranger tab on his left shoulder just above the Eighty-Second Airborne insignia. Making his way slowly and stiffly down the row of paratroopers, an obvious limp from some unknown wound hampering his progress, he finally walked up to William and pinned the wings on his chest. The captain's gravelly voice matched his demeanor as he grunted, "Congratulations, trooper," and moved to Jamberdino, who was the next man in line. He looked the lanky Italian up and down before he pinned the jump wings on him and growled, "Straighten your damn back, soldier." Jamberdino did his best to straighten his naturally stooped shoulders and answered, "Airborne, sir." The captain just shook his head, pinned the jump wings on Jamberdino's chest, and walked up to Bledsoe, the next paratrooper in line. Bledsoe was trying hard not to laugh, knowing full well the captain standing in front of him would put him on KP for life if he did. Despite the difficulty of the last three weeks, they were now officially United States Army Paratroopers. Airborne.

* * * * *

Most of the men of Airborne Class 21 were given two weeks' leave before they were to report to their next duty station, but some were shipped straight to their new units. The war machine was hungry, and the invasion of North Africa was close at hand. William and his two friends were assigned to Ranger School at Camp Foster, tucked somewhere in the Tennessee Hills, and they were eager to go. None of them knew exactly what Rangers were, except that Rangers received the toughest training of anyone in the world and were always the first to enter a combat zone. That was all these three needed to know. They wanted to be Airborne Rangers!

A couple of days after the jump school graduation ceremony, Jamberdino was saying goodbye to his two friends at the train station just outside of Columbus; he was headed for Buffalo. "I'll see you guys in two weeks," he said as he admired himself in the window of the ticket office. William and Bledsoe smiled at his antics as he puffed out his chest and strutted like a fighting rooster. They shook hands, and Jamberdino quickly boarded the train, which sat long and silver, hissing steam like some dragon in a knight's tale. Clouds of gray mist shrouded the sleek stainless steel Pullman cars as the two friends watched the train pull away. They watched until it passed out of sight, unaware that for some reason trains have that effect on most people—almost like watching your dreams float away into the night.

They left the train station on foot and walked the mile and a half to the bus station just outside of Fort Benning. Finding an empty bench inside the Greyhound terminal, they counted their money like a couple of kids in a candy store. Between them, they had enough to get to a little town in North Georgia called Dalton. "Hell, we can thumb from there," said Bledsoe, reassuringly patting his friend on the back. "It's not far from Knoxville." They walked up to the ticket counter and purchased the tickets. Normally, what Bledsoe said about being able to hitch a ride would have been true. Dalton was not that far from Knoxville, and most people would pick up soldiers who were thumbing. This time, however, the bus rolled into the town of Dalton at exactly 0200 hours, or for the unmilitary, 2:00 AM. There wasn't a car in sight.

The two paratroopers waited for all the other passengers, mostly soldiers, to offload before they exited the bus. William slowly looked around, then lowered his head and moaned, "Oh shit." Dalton, Georgia, was a sleepy little town nestled in the Blue Ridge Mountains, and at 2:00 AM, it was fast asleep. A small diner with bright stainless-steel siding and an awning not much bigger than the screen door it protected sat on the backside of a lightly graveled parking lot. The dimly lit diner, which also served as the bus station, was the only sign of life the men could see in either direction. A single street light stood at the intersection of Main Street and a narrow, no-name side street that was entirely dark. Light from the solitary globe struggled to shine through the mass of grit and spiderwebs that had attached itself over the years. Brightly colored moths circled the globe like yellow jackets around a half-empty Coke bottle. It was not exactly a beacon of hope.

The two GIs stood under the swarm of insects like bit actors from some Gene Kelly movie and counted their last bit of change. "God, Bledsoe," grumbled William as he reached into his pockets, "this damn town is dead, and with no cars on the road, we'll have to walk to Knoxville." He counted his meager change once more and was struggling to contain his mounting frustration when his eye caught the movement of a mangy black and tan hound that had appeared out of the darkness. The hound started to walk across the road on the outer edge of the light but changed its mind when it spotted the two soldiers standing beside the lamppost. It stopped, whimpered, and then tucked its tail under its scrawny belly before disappearing back into the bushes near the side of the road.

For some strange reason, William's attention was focused on the dog, and he watched it slink away into the night, wondering for a brief moment where it was headed before it decided to change course. *The damned dog is the least of my worries*, he thought to himself before finally turning back to Bledsoe.

"How much do you have?" he asked, fumbling deeper into his own pockets and trying to extract a reluctant dime, the dog forgotten for the moment.

"I've got one dollar and eighty-three cents," answered Bledsoe, turning his pockets inside out as if to show his friend he wasn't holding anything back.

"Well, I've got two dollars and fifty-one cents," added William as he unwadded the two-dollar bills. A frown crept over his face while he mentally added their funds. "Four dollars should get us another fifty or sixty miles. Maybe by that time it'll be daylight, and we can hitch a ride the rest of the way to Knoxville." With that small sliver of hope, which was somewhat brighter than the street lamp, William did a right face by reflex and headed toward the diner. Bledsoe shoved his hands into his pockets, leaned back against the lamppost, and wished for a cigarette. He hadn't had one since joining the Army, and even though he knew it was bad for his wind and that William would give him hell for smoking, he longed for just one drag from his favorite, Lucky Strikes.

William entered the smoke-filled building through a squeaky screen door and stood in the entrance like an old-time gunfighter, his eyes scanning the few locals and fellow bus travelers as he searched for the driver. He spotted the man, an older guy with salt-and-pepper hair cut short, sitting at the far corner of the counter, his driver's hat occupying the stool next to him. Hunched over a plate filled with apple pie and a cup of steaming black coffee in his right hand, he was scanning a crumpled newspaper for any topic of interest. Behind the counter, a pudgy middle-aged waitress, with a haggard look on her freckled face, was wiping crumbs off the countertop with a wet, dingy rag. She glanced up from her task when William approached, stuffed the rag into a hidden pocket in her apron, and quickly busied herself making another pot of coffee. The bus driver turned on his stool as the young paratrooper approached. He was used to soldiers riding his bus, most of them just boys on their first trip away from home. *Hell, they're a lot like I was in the last war, still wet behind the ears*; he almost laughed at the thought but caught himself as he looked the stern-faced young soldier up and down. William stood with his hat, or "cunt cap" as it was affectionately called, in his hand. It held the crumpled dollar bills and change like an offering to some minor god.

William couldn't help but noticed how the bus driver had looked at him as he walked up. Was it disapproval he had seen in the old man's eyes? His spit-shined boots were slightly scuffed from the ride, but otherwise, he thought he looked all right. *Oh well*, he thought as he cleared his throat.

"Sir, excuse me, but we need to know how far toward Knoxville four dollars would take us." The driver reached for his coffee cup and took a sip before looking down at William's boots and bloused Khakis, then back up at the shiny new jump wings on his chest. *Great*, thought William, *this man probably hates GIs*. The driver finally smiled and hope returned to William's heart.

"Well, son," he said, wiping apple pie crumbs from the corner of his mouth, "four dollars won't get you two boys very far." The old man saw disappointment cloud the young soldier's eyes. "But"—he smiled again—"if you both are asleep in my bus when I get back on, then I'll probably not see you. And the next scheduled stop is Knoxville." The driver swiveled around on his stool and returned to his neglected pie, a smile lingering on his weathered face. The waitress reached for the freshly made coffee and padded over to refill his cup.

William took the money out of his cap and tucked it into his trousers. He placed the cap, with its brand-new glider patch on the side, back on his head, and resisted the urge to salute. Instead, he did a very sharp about-face and ran, without thinking, back to the bus. Outside, he grabbed Bledsoe, who was still leaning against the lamppost, thinking about that cigarette, and said, "Let's go." His friend looked at him questioningly. "Don't ask. Just get in the back of the bus and go to sleep. I'll give you your money back when we get to Knoxville."

"Airborne," whispered Bledsoe as if he were afraid he would awaken the sleeping inhabitants of Dalton, and they, for some benign reason, wouldn't let him back on the bus. The two grateful but tired young soldiers tiptoed down the narrow aisle toward the back of the bus. Fifteen minutes later, when the bus driver crawled behind the wheel and headed up Highway 411 toward Knoxville, they were already fast asleep. Like a protector of the night, the scrawny old black-and-tan hound emerged from the shadows to watch the bus, which was belching black smoke, disappear into the night. Only then did he cross under the lamppost, stopping a moment to sniff the spot where the soldiers had stood before he too headed up the highway.

Three hours and near a hundred miles later, both William and Bledsoe shook hands with the driver, thanking him as they exited down the steps of the bus into a misty rain. The Greyhound station was situated just off Palmer Street in downtown Knoxville, and it was crowded with people. In addition to soldiers, there were merchants with samples of their wares and a handful of haggard mothers chasing small children. The two brand-new paratroopers grabbed their duffel bags and headed for the terminal. The driver watched them walk away through the drizzle and then looked around at the other soldiers. "I'm just trying to do my part, guys," he whispered before turning toward the office. He was tired from the overnight drive, but his shoulders were a little straighter as he walked away. There was a slight smile on his face as he rubbed his chin covered with gray stubble, realizing that he was badly in need of a shave.

Unbeknownst to all but a handful of people in the entire country, another war effort was in progress a mere twenty-five miles west of the bustling terminal. The Manhattan Project was in full swing in the area around Oak Ridge. The planners knew it would change mankind forever, but whether or not for the better was unclear.

The driver, whose name was Samuel York (no relation that he was aware of to the famous Sergeant Alvin York of nearby McMinnville), poured himself a cup of coffee from a steaming pot in the corner of the office. Gingerly sipping the hot brew, he walked over to the big window overlooking the terminal. He spotted his two paratroopers and watched as they shook hands before the big blond one walked out of the terminal and got into a taxi. The other one found a seat near the window and looked at the rain as it splattered on the street outside. "Good luck, you two. I'm afraid you are going to need it," he muttered softly, sipping his coffee and thinking back to his younger days, to the time of a different war. As part of Pershing's Expeditionary Force, the Rainbow Division, he stood tall and proud back then, just like these men. Without consciously thinking about it, he reached down and began rubbing an old scar on his right thigh, just above the knee. The jagged scar was from a German machine-gun bullet that had torn into his leg after killing his best friend. "God, what combat can do to you," he murmured as he began gathering his belongings from his battered grey locker, all the while rubbing his aching leg. *I need some shut-eye*, he moaned and walked out the door.

William patiently leafed through a tattered old edition of *Life* magazine, but the wooden bench he sat on became increasingly hard. He was waiting on his girlfriend from back home in Hillsboro, and he hoped she would arrive early. She was supposed to be there at 0700, and looking at his watch, he realized he still had thirty more minutes to kill. "Damn," he groaned and tossed the magazine aside, leaning his head back against the cool glass. The word *girlfriend* still seemed a little strange, but he knew she was the one he intended to marry. Her name was Beth Sellers, and although they were in love now, they barely knew each other in high school. He had been a big shot senior, and she had been a silly sophomore—way too skinny to catch his busy eye. But when he decided to cut his career short at Western Carolina and join the Army, he moved back home and found that she had grown up. *And how!* He smiled at the thought.

"Lord, girl, you're a woman now," he said one day while they were walking lazily down the main street of Hillsboro. Beth had blushed only slightly as she looked down at how her pink wool sweater clung tightly to her breasts.

Smiling she snapped, "Watch it, buster," and was rewarded for her comment by a tight, lusty squeeze as he pulled her toward him.

"I'll watch it, all right," he said as he bent to kiss her. She avoided his kiss but giggled merrily when he slapped her playfully on the butt before taking her hand and leading her into the local drug store for a soda.

Glancing at his Timex for the hundredth time, he stared sullenly through the big plate glass windows that lined the front of the terminal. He had to laugh despite the fact that he was tired and lonely for his Beth; the glass was heavily smudged with dozens of stick figures, probably drawn by some very bored child. Looking past the tiny dancing people, he realized the cold drizzle and fog reminded him of an old country song, the name of which stayed just on the fringe of his memory where he couldn't come up with it.

Noticing that the parking lot was half empty, which didn't really surprise him, considering how few people could afford the gas that was now being rationed because of the war, he worried about Beth being able to get enough gas to come get him. And what if there had been a rockslide on the mountain because of all this rain? *Oh shit*, he thought, his mind beginning to concoct all sorts of potential problems. Finally, after what seemed like hours but was actually just fifteen minutes, his worries were laid to rest. The battered '37 Chevy, which belonged to Beth's father, turned off Kingston Pike and pulled into one of the many empty spots in the parking lot. A small mist of steam rose from beneath the hood, a testament to the difficult climb across the Smokies. Smiling, he watched her check her makeup in the rearview mirror before getting out of the car and running through the rain toward the terminal. "You are so beautiful." He uttered the words aloud as he watched her dodge a few puddles and start to push open the terminal doors.

Her hand flew back in alarm when the doors suddenly sprang open as if by magic. Startled and a little embarrassed, she realized that several soldiers were fighting to see who could open the doors for her. She blushed, smiled, and said, "Thank you," shaking rain from her hair, her ample breasts bouncing invitingly beneath her blouse as she did so. The terminal was packed full of soldiers, sailors, and marines who also must have thought her beautiful, because they stepped back as if in awe and a way opened up for her like the parting of the Red Sea. She quickly walked up to where William stood smiling. The GIs where whistling like crazy when she finally reached him, her face turning a deep shade of crimson. He hesitated for a moment before taking her into his arms. He wanted to look at her forever. They stood awkwardly a couple of inches from each other until someone shouted, "Well, kiss her, paratrooper!" So William did just that. He grabbed her up in a big hug and spun her around, kissing her earnestly. Their audience cheered with approval.

Breathless, Beth broke the kiss, and tears began to streak the makeup she had just recently purchased at the new Sears and Roebuck store in Asheville. She dabbed at her eyes with a tissue that seemed to appear out of nowhere and looked up at him longingly. "Oh, William," she sighed.

After a few more heartbeats, he laughed and grabbed her hand. "Let's get out of here before this crowd gets any ideas," he said and led her through the cheering crowd of lonely GIs toward the Chevy. They looked back and waved at the many faces plastered against the bus station window and then drove out of Knoxville on Highway 441 toward Sevierville. They crossed the Holston River and newly formed Douglas Lake on the Tennessee River before starting up the mountain.

The old flathead six was struggling when it finally reached Newfound Gap, which sits at nearly five thousand feet on the North Carolina-Tennessee line. Highway 441 was now a very scenic road that snaked through the ancient forest of spruce and fir but just a few short years before it had been an old logging road. They pulled the car into a spot just beneath a plaque that was erected eight years prior for the dedication of the park—when a newly elected Franklin Roosevelt had stood on the elevated viewing area and declared the Great Smoky Mountains National Park a "jewel of the south."

A young doe stood deep in the shadows of the old growth timber, feeding on acorns and wiregrass as it stared down at the two lovers lying in the back seat of the Chevy. "Beth ...," whispered William. She lay with her head on his chest, her eyes closed, listening to the rhythm of his heartbeat in her ear. Holding her tight, he gazed down the cove toward Cherokee while a gray mist swirled about in the treetops. He had been thinking about this moment for weeks and knew it was not only the right thing to do but also the right moment to ask: "Will you marry me?" His breath blew warm air across her temple. She wasn't totally surprised by the question, but tears of joy rolled down her cheeks just the same. She had hoped and prayed for those very words for many months—ever since high school, in fact. And now that they had come, all she could do was bury her face in his chest and cry.

Several minutes drifted by, like the fog that rushed up out of the ancient cove, before she slowly lifted her head from his now damp shirt and sniffed. "Well, it's about damn time you asked," she said, the last of her makeup disappearing under a new flood of tears. William had to laugh because those were the same words he had said to her just before he left for the Army. They had taken a leisurely walk along the river outside of Hillsboro, and about ten minutes into the walk, Beth had spun him around and said, "I love you, William Craig." It was the first time she had ever told him exactly how she felt. His reply came a long minute later when he smiled and said, "It's about damn time," before grabbing her up in his arms.

She laughed, too, remembering that moment. Outside, the steam continued to escape from the old Chevy, and it quickly joined the mist that shrouded the fading sunlight. Through the dust-smeared windshield, they admired the multicolored sunset shimmering behind the dark peak of Clingman's Dome. William leaned up on one elbow and felt a slight tear in the fabric of the seat as he did so. Sheepishly, he changed positions before looking into her eyes. "I truly love you, Beth," he whispered again as he pulled her to him. First kissing her eyes, then her pert nose, and finally her lips that tasted of Juicy Fruit gum and a touch of salt from her tears. They made gentle love in the back seat of the old Chevy as the stars began to burn holes through the blackness of the indigo sky.

Later, Beth slept in his arms as he leaned against the back door and listened to the choir of night sounds. One particular voice rose above all the others. The soft melody drifted down from high atop a snarled beech tree that stood just above the viewing platform and seemed to gaze down the ancient cove. William identified the call of a mourning dove, and indeed, this one seemed to be mourning, maybe for a lost mate. She was persistent in her lonesome call, but as far as he could tell, it was never answered by another dove. After some time though, another voice did fill the night sky, riding ghostlike on the cool, clean air. A hawk's cry echoed from far down in the cove, and the shrill call sounded as lonesome as the dove's. It floated through the mist as if it were searching for something, though William had no idea exactly what. Relishing the moment, he laid with his head against the armrest and listened to Beth's soft breathing. The sound mixed well with the serenade of the night creatures that stirred in the depths of the forest.

* * * * *

William's two-week leave flew by in a blur of activity—mainly due to the rushed wedding plans and short honeymoon. When you are in the military though, it seems as if any time off is fleeting. The night before he was due to ship out to Ranger School, the two newlyweds were walking along the sandy shores of Lake Thorpe, a man-made lake that sat high in the mountains near the Eastern Continental Divide. The late September harvest moon bathed the lake in sparkling jewels of light. Small ripples, like miniature waves, rode on the water's surface and danced with the moonbeams. The water nymphs hid in the depths had diamonds in their hair that night.

William took Beth's hand and held it tightly as they stood listening to the waves gently lap the sandy beach. A small fishing boat puttering along in the center of the lake, its lights sparkling on the water, created a wake that spread out behind it, eventually ending at their feet. They looked back along the beach where they had walked and saw their paired footprints etched in the damp sand. William turned, took his new wife in his arms, and kissed her, her body eagerly pressing against his. Their lips had barely touched when the cooing of a nearby dove interrupted their amorous efforts. William's head cocked to the side, and he listened with a smile. *You're being watched,* he joked to himself.

After a minute or two, he looked down at his wife's beautiful face and whispered as if the dove might object to the interruption: "When I was a little boy, Grandma Conner would tell me stories about our ancestors. She was born in Scotland, somewhere in the Highlands if I remember right, and like most Celtic folks, her people were extremely superstitious. Grandma Conner was about thirteen when her family decided to move to America. Fresh off the boat as a young girl on Ellis Island, she quickly fell in love with America, yet often, especially late at night, she yearned for her homeland. The stories she had been told by her own grandparents became the tales of my childhood. She often talked about her ancestors and how some of them were Vikings. Having a lot of Norsemen in the family tree is typical of the mountain people, but the next part isn't. She believed, even on her deathbed, that they were protected by a dove. Now get this, not just any dove, but a dove that had a hawk as a mate."

As soon as William said the word *hawk,* a large dark shadow floated across the sand in front of them, and the chilly night air was pierced by a shrill cry.

"William," whispered Beth, her voice full of awe. "Do you understand what we're hearing?" She grabbed his arm excitedly and looked up. "And seeing?" she added quickly as they spotted the hawk sailing over the trees near the edge of the lake.

"Well …" He paused to choose his words. "In Grandma Conner's tale, the hawk and dove were mates, but that big hawk up there"—he nodded toward the hawk as it glided on the autumn breeze—"will probably eat that dove we hear." They stood with their hips touching ever so slightly and looked into the night sky.

"I'm not so sure," exclaimed Beth, who gasped as the cooing dove suddenly broke from its cover in a young hemlock just in front of them and sailed up to join the hawk. The dove's grayish wings shone in the moonlight, and the two birds began a slow-winged dance across the night sky.

The young couple stood transfixed as the pair of shadows slid across the diamond-tipped waves, the fierce cry of the hawk harmonizing with the mournful cooing of the dove. Together, their calls created an odd but ancient melody that stirred a deep, forgotten part of William's mind. He could almost—but not quite—remember something. *But what?*

"Maybe your ancestors' spirits are looking after you, William," Beth said in a voice full of wonder as well as concern. As she stood there, she couldn't deny the presence of a distinct fear that suddenly crept into the back of her mind. It made her shudder with an unknown dread. Maybe the ancestors weren't so much watching over him, but actually calling to her new husband—perhaps with a message that his time was near. *No, not my William!* Her mind screamed with the thought.

A strong sense of urgency in his voice pulled her from her dark thoughts. "Remember that night last week when the big owl landed on a tree limb just above our heads while we were sitting on the deck?" He nearly whispered the question.

"Yeah," answered Beth, eager to get her mind on happier thoughts. "I was a little frightened at first, mainly because the owl was so big and so very close, but you seemed utterly amazed, and I figured it had to be okay." He smiled at the memory of the hoot owl with its big saucer eyes.

"Well, that owl wasn't fifteen feet from us, yet it showed no fear, none at all. It just sat there and watched us." Turning fully toward her, he put both hands on her shoulders and looked into her expectant eyes. "That was a once-in-a-lifetime experience to be that close to an owl, I mean. Well, I think the way this hawk and dove are acting like mates is even more rare than that." He shook his head and looked down. "I have no way to really explain it," he stammered, frustrated with his inability to find the right words.

"Maybe you don't need to," said Beth, putting her finger to his lips. "Just enjoy the moment like they seem to be doing." She nodded toward the hawk and dove that circled overhead.

"You're right," he said, pulling her tightly into his arms once more. Together, they gazed up at a sight few people had ever seen, at least not in the last eighty years or so. Despite the serene comfort of the moment, Beth felt the dread resurface, and it spread through her conscious mind like a dark storm. Finally, she broke from his arms in anguish and demanded, "Tell me everything your grandmother told you about your ancestors, William. Everything." To her, the fear in her voice seemed obvious, but if he noticed the slight quiver there or the urgency in her request, he never acknowledged it. He closed his eyes in deep thought for a minute and then answered.

"She told me that the Vikings among our ancestors believed that if a warrior dies a good death—I suppose she meant a brave death in battle—then his spirit would come back as a Great War hawk." He opened his eyes and looked up at the birds.

"What about the dove?" asked Beth excitedly, glancing from her husband to the dove and back again.

"Well, she said the dove was a seeker of peace and a sign that even if you were a warrior you could still want peace. After all, who knows the pain and horror of war better than a warrior?"

When she didn't immediately respond to his last comment, he tore his gaze away from the hawk and glanced at her inquisitively. He couldn't help smiling at the serious look on her face, nor could he resist the urge to kiss her just then. He was somewhat hurt and a little surprised when she dodged his lips.

"What?" he growled, stepping away and staring back up into the night sky, not quite sure why she was upset.

Ignoring his tone, she answered his half-forgotten question. "Well, I think maybe a wife or girlfriend knows pain and suffering just as well as the warrior, only in a different way." She hesitated and turned her head as a tear swelled in the corner of her eye. "Maybe she knows the need for peace better too," she added, her mind struggling with what he had just said.

He thought for a minute before responding: "Well, I can't argue with that." This seemed to curb her anxiety. Casting aside his own hurt feelings, he pulled her closer, and this time, her lips were ready for his. A few minutes later, they walked toward the waiting Chevy that sat like a valiant steed in the gravel parking lot. The dove's cooing drifted over the lake while the hawk sailing by her side held his cry for another time.

* * * * *

Most of the three-week Ranger course was scheduled to take place at a makeshift training area called Camp Foster, located just north of Chattanooga in the southeastern hills of Tennessee. It was smack dab in the middle of nowhere, and that was exactly where the Army wanted it. The Ranger School instructors were even less friendly than the jump school cadre. All of them were hardened combat veterans who had been bloodied at Kasserine Pass in North Africa and other no-name places where the 1st Ranger Battalion had fought. The instructors' motto and training creed was "Rangers are always the first ones in." They drove the recruits accordingly.

The instructors were hard to a fault; they used live ammo in all the training exercises in order to simulate actual combat conditions, and their hand-to-hand combat training would simply kick your ass. The old Rangers believed this type of intense preparation could save lives when the big invasion of Europe took place, which they knew couldn't be far off.

William figured he and Bledsoe could handle the tougher training that was fixing to start, but they worried about their friend Jamberdino; they weren't sure he could take it. The little five-mile runs at jump school were nothing compared to the ten-mile runs in full combat gear that Ranger School required, not to mention the twenty-five-mile forced marches they would have to endure. These had broken many a good man. But Jamberdino took everything they threw at him, fooling everyone, including his friends. Gerald Jamberdino, whom they called Jerry, was the first child born in America to his Italian parents. Raised a good Catholic, he went to confessional almost every week until he joined the Army. Thus began his decline into girls and alcohol, and he was so very glad.

In training, Jamberdino might be struggling at the back of the pack, but he never quit, never complained. He never dropped any of his gear, and he finished every run under his own power. Some of the guys in the training company would try to lighten their loads during the long runs by tossing part of their mandatory gear into the bushes. Sometimes the instructors wouldn't catch the slackers, but when they did, they sent them packing. The embarrassed troopers would be sent back to their old units with a letter in their records declaring that they needed to be watched. It sure wasn't very good for your career.

The intensive training became a little easier after a couple of weeks, and the men's bodies became even harder. They learned that their bodies would and could do whatever their minds told them to do, no matter how tired they were. The rappelling, which was part of their mountain training, was easy enough even under a heavy load with live rounds going off all around. But it was the climbing—the god-awful ropes courses—that tired even William and Bledsoe's strong arms. William had to drag his 220 pounds of body weight, plus 75 pounds of combat gear, up the limestone cliffs around Camp Foster. The first sergeant of the training company made William a fire team leader during the first week. A fire team was made up of ten men—a little less than a squad—and William soon found out that all his men were good at their job.

One fairly chilly morning, William was wrestling his way up a long, difficult climb when the group encountered boulders the size of small cars blocking their way up the limestone cliffs. Bledsoe was right behind him and carrying the detonators while Jamberdino was two men back carrying the primer cord. Everyone else just carried their regular gear plus extra rope. William had ten pounds of C-2 in his pack. C-2 was the new plastic explosive that had been invented primarily for the US military, but they actually got the idea from the British, who at that time always seemed to be one step ahead. The pliable dough-like substance wasn't as touchy as dynamite or nitro, and it could be shaped if need be. A shaped charge could be concentrated in a smaller, more specific spot and create more damage.

A thick gray fog swept up through the jagged cliffs, a strong, cold wind pushing it along. As the fog lifted, more rock outcroppings appeared ahead. William had just dragged his bruised chest and stomach over a rocky ledge and was hoping he could soon rest his shaking arms. "Damn, what a climb," moaned Bledsoe, who was ten feet below William and ready for this exercise to be over. William was crawling up a sloped boulder that sat precariously on the lip of a larger ledge when he stopped to catch his breath for a second. Looking around, he could see for miles when the fog reluctantly opened a gap. *If I weren't so damn tired, I might enjoy the view,* he admitted to himself just before he raised his head up past the flat edge of the big rock.

His right hand was already gripping the rock's edge. As he pulled up, a sudden motion drew his eyes to the side—about three feet to the left of his hand. He inhaled sharply as he stared into the beady eyes of the largest rattlesnake he had ever seen. The thing was huge; its mass of coiled muscle probably would have measured six feet if it had been stretched out. But it wasn't; it was coiled in a deadly pose. The snake's rattling tail beat a steady rhythm in the packed clay.

"Oh god," was all he could say. *What now, what now?* his mind screamed. The black-and-yellow timber rattler seemed to be weighing his options as well, its tongue flicking in and out as if licking its lips in anticipation. Man and snake, a confrontation as old as the mountains, stared into each other's eyes. "What's the damn hold up?" shouted Bledsoe from just below the last ledge, his arms burning from the exertion. He was clueless about the life-and-death chess match occurring ten feet above him.

If the damn snake strikes you in the face, you'll never make it back to the Camp hospital, William reasoned matter-of-factly. *And if you move, he will strike.* His eyes remained solemnly locked with the rattler's as he looked for some movement or small sign that the snake might back off. Back when he was a young boy, he had seen a man die from a rattlesnake bite. The man was a timber cutter who worked for his father on several occasions. They had been logging up in the high Balsams, and the man was making a back cut on a big red oak when the snake struck him. The man's leg had swollen up to twice its normal size, turning an ugly bluish black. He had lain in agony for hours and finally died a few days later. When you're twelve years old, you don't forget things like that. *No, sirree, I don't want any part of being bitten by a damn rattlesnake*, he said to himself.

William knew if he released his grip on the rock ledge, he would fall backward onto Bledsoe, and there was a slight chance he might be able to regain a grip after the short fall. He might also knock Bledsoe loose from his hold on the cliff, causing them both to fall. "Damn," he cursed as he reluctantly made the decision to release his grip. Anything was better than getting a snake bite.

William made his choice at the exact instant the snake made his, figuring that the thing in front of it was a danger and needed to be struck. The snake's big, broad head slowly pulled back, and the tail began to beat even faster. Suddenly a shrill cry sounded from above William's head; it pierced the silence that had wrapped around the cliff like a knife driving into a heart. A huge hawk with its talons flared dove past William's right shoulder. It slammed into the flat head of the snake just as it struck forward, the hawk's beak tearing at the neck of the reptile as the great wings beat the ground in a struggle to lift the thrashing serpent. The hawk cried loudly as it finally rose with its prey and flew out over the cliffs, the snake dangling from the razor-sharp talons, its head flopped to one side. William's head dropped onto the rock ledge as the hawk's cry echoed over the Tennessee Mountains.

"Did you see that?" William stammered excitedly when he was finally able to speak.

"See what?" asked Bledsoe. "All I see is your big ass, and I'm getting real tired of looking at it. Let's finish the damn exercise and get off this mountain."

"Okay, okay," said William, taking one last look at the spot where only a few seconds before the snake had lain coiled and ready to strike. William could see where it had wallowed out a place in the dirt, just like an old bear would prepare its bed in a pile of leaves. The dust was slightly disturbed where the hawk had dragged the snake skyward. "God, how could they not have seen that hawk?" whispered William as he stared out in the direction the hawk had flown. Jamberdino's voice snapped William out of his trance.

"I can't hold here much longer. What's the problem up there?"

"We're moving," shouted William as he stood up and prepared to step where the snake had been. His boot hovered just above the dust, not quite touching it, until suddenly he stomped down hard. He shuddered as the dust drifted up to his nostrils, the odor of the snake heavy and pungent.

The last thirty feet of the climb were easier than what they had crawled over up to this point, and the men were actually able to climb faster. Finally, William topped the last ledge and shrugged out of his sweat-soaked pack. He reached down and offered his hand to Bledsoe, who gave him a strange look and climbed over the edge by himself. The next three men took his hand, though, and finally the whole fire team was up on the cliff. Jamberdino collapsed into a sweating heap, his head resting on his pack, his eyes closed. William looked at the exhausted men; no one mentioned the hawk, so he thought it best not to say anything either. There was something surreal about the whole episode anyway.

After a few minutes' rest, William and Bledsoe shouldered their packs and started walking up the ridge without saying a word. The rest of the fire team soon followed. At least now the men could walk instead of climb, but the terrain was still steep. The mountain laurel and green running briars were thick on Firescald Ridge. The assigned target was a simulated coastal defense gun, which was actually an old lightning-scarred chestnut oak whose blackened trunk was partly hollowed out by the many forest fires that had swept over the ridge through the years. The old sentinel of the Chilhowie had seen hundreds of vicious storms through the years but nothing that could compare to what the Ranger want-to-bes were fixing to do.

The fire team found the supposed gun that was marked with a red X on their map as well as on the tree itself. William carefully placed the entire ten pounds of C-2 explosive around the base of the old monarch of the forest. Bledsoe attached the blasting caps to the C-2, and Jamberdino unrolled the detonator wire. Cipriani and Lazcano, two Italian boys from Brooklyn, walked behind Jamberdino to make sure nothing hindered the cord. Bledsoe looked around for a safe spot from which to work the plunger, the device that sent an electric current through the cord to detonate the caps and thus the C-2. The only tree that the cord could reach, which was also big enough to hide behind, was another chestnut oak. This tree, however, was barely two feet in diameter, just big enough to protect two men. But Jamberdino hugged up close behind Bledsoe and William anyway. The rest of the fire team ran much further down the ridge. "God, you two stink." Jamberdino laughed. Bledsoe, looking at him with a smile, shook his head before kneeling down and hooking up the detonator cord to the plunger. He took one last look around to make sure the rest of the team was a safe distance away and then shouted, "Fire in the hole!" After waiting five seconds for any shout of alarm, he pushed down the handle of the plunger.

The earth gave a mighty shudder, and dust and debris filled the morning air. Chunks of wood flew everywhere; the lower part of old chestnut oak disintegrated while the upper part lifted into the air and then fell sideways with a crash. One large piece of wood about three feet long was torn loose from the base of the oak and slammed like a cannonball into the tree the three men crouched behind. The three Ranger want-to-bes hugged up to each other and tried hard to be small.

"Oh hell." Bledsoe coughed as he swatted at the dust that threatened to choke them. "You used too much damn C-2 ... again." The three men coughed and laughed as tree limbs and leaves fell all about them like a green snow.

"Well, maybe I did put a little too much of the explosive around this gun, but at least I won't have to carry the damn stuff back to camp," admitted William. A couple minutes later, the other fire team members cautiously walked up through the dust and stared in wonder at the spot where the tree used to stand and the three men rolling around on the ground laughing.

Within five minutes of the blast that felled the mighty oak, a large mean-looking buck sergeant walked up to where Bledsoe and Jamberdino sat, leaning back against what remained of the target.

The rest of the fire team sat off to the side eating K-rations and smoking.

"If I were a damn Kraut, you guys would be dead by now. Just because you blew up the coastal gun doesn't mean the damn war—" He stopped when he felt the barrel of someone's carbine tapping him in the back.

"You were saying, Sergeant?" asked William as Bledsoe, and the rest of the fire team erupted with laughter. William had figured that one of the instructors might try to sneak up on them after the blast, so he hid in the brush and waited. He and his team were ready, by god!

"Well, soldier, you used a little too much C-2," said the buck sergeant, now red-faced as he turned toward William, who lowered the barrel of his M-1 and smiled back. The big sergeant pulled out a crumpled notepad before he went on: "But your team was the fastest in the whole company, so congratulations. You are now Airborne Rangers." The fire team stood and shouted like crazy. William, just as excited, walked over and shook each man's hand while they patted each other on the back. The new Rangers headed down the mountain, followed by the buck sergeant, who was writing furiously on his pad. The sun, finishing its day's traverse, sank into the autumn-colored forest far to the west.

* * * * *

Uncle Sam, in his infinite wisdom, gave the three buddies another two weeks of leave after graduation from Ranger School, and the time flew by as it always does during leaves. After making the rounds visiting friends and family, William took his young bride down to the small seaside resort of Myrtle Beach, South Carolina. It was a quaint little town with a newly constructed boardwalk, numerous bars, and a handful of glitzy motels. In twenty more years, it would become a serious tourist hub filled with young tanned bodies covered in oil, but for now, it was a fairly quiet place where you could walk miles of beaches without seeing too many people, especially in the winter. The newlyweds strolled the clean sandy beaches during the day, and when the sun went down, danced the night away at the new Myrtle Beach Pavilion near downtown. It was December, and the sea breezes were stiff and constant, but they were still much warmer than the cold mountain air back home. For the moment, the lovers were content.

Mike Bledsoe drove down from Knoxville and hung out with William and his bride for a few days, but his real reason for coming was the hope that some lonely beach maiden would feel inclined to help him ease the pain of going off to war. Unfortunately, his batting average with the girls on the beach was lower than DiMaggio's that year. All the big blond-headed guy from Knoxville found were a few seashells—and no female sympathy. Jamberdino called to check in once, saying it was just too damn far from Buffalo for him to drive down. Besides, he said he had a girlfriend now, some gal named Dinah who he had met at a USO canteen. William and Bledsoe figured she must be a dog, but they wished him the best anyway.

Early into the fourth day of their little getaway, Beth watched as her husband and Bledsoe sat on the boardwalk benches and chatted aimlessly about their training. She sensed they needed a boy's night out before their vacation came to a close, so she decided to stay at the motel, pack for home, and give the guys their chance to hang out.

The two men met up in the parking lot of the motel about 5:00 PM and quickly headed for a small bar that the locals said was a great place to get cold beer and good, cheap food. It was called the Bowery and sat right across a side street from the Pavilion. Their specialties were foot-long hotdogs and thirty-two-ounce mugs of Pabst Blue Ribbon. The two Rangers walked through the big double doors and immediately bellied up to the bar. They ordered the house special and sat listening to the jukebox wail its mournful tunes. Soon after ordering a second round, they walked out on the small boardwalk, food in hand, and watched the waves wash up on the beach. The sandpipers were dancing along the surf's edge, looking for their supper while chatty seagulls flew overhead in the stiff breeze.

Neither man spoke for a few minutes until Bledsoe finally looked at his friend and asked, "Have you told Beth that we are shipping out for England in a few weeks?" His mouth was half-full of hotdog, making his question muffled.

William looked at his beer, as if something was floating in it, before he answered. "No …" He paused. "I think she knows already, but I wanted to wait until we got back to Hillsboro to tell her for sure. If I had told her sooner, it might have ruined this little getaway." After taking a long drink from his big mug of Pabst, he continued, "It's going to be hard on her, I know. She is so hoping that the war will end, or we will somehow find a way to stop the fighting and just talk it out." William shook his head and laughed lightly.

"It wouldn't hurt my feelings a damn bit if we just talked them to death," Bledsoe chimed in with an unusual hint of seriousness in his voice.

"Well, we do have a secret weapon in this war." William chuckled as he thought about his next comment. Bledsoe looked at him questioningly. "Jamberdino," William said.

"How so?" asked Bledsoe, smiling as he thought about their tall, lanky friend.

"If anyone could talk the Germans to death, it would be our buddy Jamberdino." William laughed at his own jest to the point that beer spewed out of his nose and tears flowed from his eyes. Bledsoe howled and then began a sloppy attempt to mimic their friend. "Please, Mister Airborne Ranger, we Germans give up. Just make that man stop talking." Both men doubled over and held their stomachs from laughing so hard.

The other patrons of the Bowery became wary and watched the two big soldiers with a cautious eye as they drank and told stories throughout the evening. By midnight though, all but a few of the patrons had left. It was a Thursday night, and most people had to work the next day. A couple of serious drinkers sat at one end of the tiki-style bar, each caressing a gin and tonic. There was also a young couple who didn't seem to be getting along very well, sitting near the door. They and the two GIs were the only ones left from the earlier crowd. The couple—she no older than twenty and he perhaps five years older—sat at a dimly lit table where several empty beer bottles were stacked near an overflowing ashtray. The man was drunk. He kept slapping the top of the table with the flat of his hand, making the beer bottles rattle. *That asshole seems to like watching the girl jump,* thought Bledsoe, who kept an eye on him, hoping for an excuse to break his jaw. Each time the guy hit the table, the girl would look over at Bledsoe as if in search of help or at least some sympathy. Bledsoe figured maybe she was used to being hit, but he was still pissed at the drunk for disturbing their evening.

After another beer, he and William decided to step down off the boardwalk and make their way out onto the beach. They stopped short of where the waves crawled up the sandy shore and then retreated into the black foamy surf. Staring eastward as if they could see England, their beers grew warm in their hands, and a strange silence crept over them. At last, Bledsoe asked, "How far is it to England anyway?" His voice was unusually stern.

"I think it's about 1,800 miles northeast of here," answered William as he watched his friend staring out into the Atlantic.

"It's a long way to go to die," said Bledsoe, his voice carrying a sad, reflective tone that William had never heard from his friend before.

"Our job is to make those bastards die for their country," William quoted gruffly from General Patton's famous speech at Camp Polk during the great Louisiana Maneuvers. It was a weak attempt to lighten the mood, and Bledsoe didn't bother to respond to the humor.

Angry shouts suddenly erupted from the bar area, and both men jerked their heads around. Although they were too far away to make sense of the argument, they could tell it was the young couple, or at least the male half. Bledsoe took a couple of tentative steps toward the bar as the angry voice of the drunk drifted out to them. His eyes burned with disgust, and from deep within the recesses of his memory, images of his drunken father intermingled with the present commotion. After a long minute, he simply shook his head, turned around, and walked further up the beach. He stopped to pick up a half-buried seashell and examined it closely before tossing it back into the sea. Then he stood staring out across the ocean again, the drunk seemingly forgotten for the moment.

Standing three or four feet behind his friend, William watched Bledsoe pour his warm beer into the wet sand, the empty mug dangling from his fingertips. After taking one last sip of the now tepid PBR, William dumped the remaining contents of his own mug. "Let's go get another beer," he grunted, his words slurred following several hours of drinking. William was somewhat surprised, though, when after a couple of minutes Bledsoe continued to stare out to sea. For his friend not to respond to the mention of more beer was an unusual thing, but not knowing exactly what to do, William simply shrugged and headed back to the bar alone.

He was climbing a little unsteadily up onto the deck of the Bowery just as the quarreling couple stormed out. The guy bumped into William, who just said, "Excuse me," and went on inside, not thinking much of it. The guy's mistake was bumping into Bledsoe, who had decided to follow his buddy back to the bar after all and was walking up the steps when the drunk staggered down them. The man's shoulder struck Bledsoe a glancing blow, and the man turned with anger flashing in his eyes.

"Watch where you're going, asshole!" he shouted, wet saliva spraying from his lips. Bledsoe turned calmly and looked at the man, then at the girl who stood behind him and slightly to the side; her face revealed a red puffy bruise just below the left eye. *Probably from a slap*, thought Bledsoe. He turned his gaze back to the drunk, who had stepped closer, narrowing the gap between the two men.

"I'm talking to you, soldier!" he nearly shouted. Bledsoe just smiled.

"Sure you are, buddy," Bledsoe replied as his big right fist slammed hard into the man's nose. Bledsoe felt the nose break, and the drunk's head flew backward in a shower of blood. He landed flat on his ass in the sand at the foot of the steps, out cold. Bledsoe looked down at the unconscious drunk and then over at the young woman.

"I'm sorry, ma'am, but he asked for it," he explained. Then noticing the woman was smiling at him, Bledsoe smiled back.

"He's a jerk," she said, "and my name is Susan by the way." She extended her soft warm hand.

"I'm Mike," said Bledsoe, taking her hand. "Do you need a ride somewhere?" he asked, after observing that she wasn't wearing a ring.

"I don't now," she said, still smiling. Stepping over the unconscious drunk, she put her arm around Bledsoe's waist, and together they walked back into the Bowery.

William stood at the bar, drinking a long-neck Budweiser and marveling at the painting above the bar. It depicted a slightly chubby and totally naked young woman lounging on a red velvet couch; she seemed to be staring out at the patrons. When Bledsoe and the girl came back inside, the bartender was busy setting chairs onto tabletops in the back corner. Everyone was gone except William, and they walked up to the bar to stand beside him.

"I don't want any trouble in here," the barkeep said as he placed another chair onto a table and then wiped sweat from his face.

"There won't be any. Not now anyway," answered Bledsoe, turning toward the woman.

"Susan, this is my good friend, Ranger William Craig. William, this is Susan." Bledsoe winked at his buddy and ordered three more beers. The bartender looked at his watch but didn't say anything; he just walked over to the cooler, reached inside, and pulled out three Budweisers. Setting them on the bar in front of Bledsoe, he went back to stacking chairs.

"Susan, it's a pleasure to meet you," said William as he looked over her shoulder and watched the drunk stand up with help from the deck railing. Pressing a handkerchief to his nose, the man glanced inside the bar. William could detect a sense of fear in his eyes and was relieved to see the drunk stagger on toward the parking lot.

The three sipped their beers and made small talk for a few minutes until it became obvious to William that his friend and the girl needed some space. Her hands lingered on Bledsoe's shoulders and back as their eyes remained locked on each other. William finished his beer, bowed somewhat drunkenly to the girl, and said goodnight. Smiling to himself, he staggered out of the Bowery and headed toward his motel. *Good for you, Mike Bledsoe*, he thought to himself as he looked back and saw his friend, with the girl on his arm, heading toward his parked car. The drunk was sitting in his own vehicle, nursing his broken nose as well as his broken pride when Bledsoe and the girl walked up. Seeing Bledsoe's hard glare and bulging biceps, the man quickly realized that the best thing for him to do was to take his broken nose and go home. So forgetting the pain in his nose and his pride, he cranked the car, burnt rubber pulling out onto the road, and disappeared down Main Street without a look back. *The guy's damn lucky Bledsoe didn't hurt him worse*, thought William, who began fumbling in his pants pockets for the room key. Finally, he remembered putting it in his wallet, and he was slightly embarrassed but relieved when he pulled the key from its hiding place. Then he proceeded to drop the damn thing twice as he walked toward the motel. That's when he realized that he was quite drunk—so drunk, in fact, that when he finally made it to the Low Country Inn he had to lean his head against the door as he attempted to put the key into the keyhole, which kept moving. Suddenly and without warning, the door opened, causing William to stagger forward, almost falling onto Beth, who stood smiling at him in a short black negligee. Finally getting his balance, all he could do was grin like a possum at his beautiful wife. "Hi, big boy" was all she said before dragging him through the door and kicking it shut behind her.

* * * * *

The next day dawned gray and rainy. Bledsoe honked his horn as he and his newfound friend pulled out of the parking lot and headed toward her place up near Summerville. William stood in the drizzle and waved while they drove away. Then he went back to loading the car.

"God, I'll never drink again if you make this hangover go away," he whined, the most frequent lie in the annals of military drinking. He looked up into the dreary sky and said, "I mean it, honest." The cold rain only poured harder from the heavens. "This rain sure isn't helping my aching head any, Lord," he groaned as he packed the last of their belongings into the Chevy. Despite his headache, it made him smile to watch his wife race through the deluge toward the car after she paid the bill at the motel office. When she neared the Chevy, he whistled and gallantly opened the door for her as if she were royalty. She grinned and quickly jumped in, her skirt riding high up on her tan, shapely legs. Sliding across the bench seat, she struggled briefly with her umbrella before finally throwing the wet, dripping thing into the back seat.

"Thank you, kind sir." She laughed as he bowed deeply.

"My head hurts, madam, when I bend over."

"Poor baby. I'm so sorry that I have a drunk for a butler." She laughed and attempted to spread her damp skirt down over her legs, which her husband was staring at.

"Begging the madam's pardon, but I'm your chauffer, not your damn butler. Butlers have no class." They both laughed as she pulled him across the seat and forced his head down onto her breasts.

"You're whatever I say you are." She giggled, pulling his hand out from under her skirt and shoving him over behind the wheel. "Drive, chauffer," she urged in mock gruffness.

"Don't make me laugh any more. That makes my head hurt too," he moaned as he pulled out onto the highway and headed west.

The incessant rain grew heavier as they neared Columbia, and the remainder of the trip home was slow and nerve-racking. Beth seemed lost in her own thoughts, and William had to force his mind to concentrate on the road. He strained to see the white lines as the wipers fought a losing battle with the sheets of rain that attacked the windshield. Finally, just outside of Spartanburg, the deluge slackened, and William could relax his grip on the steering wheel. After a minute or two of flexing his fingers, he called her name, "Beth ..." He took a long breath and exhaled. "I think you may already know this, but we're shipping out for England in a few weeks. I'm not exactly sure where in England we're going, but we're definitely going ... soon." He placed the emphasis on *soon*, the wipers still pounding out their rhythm on the slightly smudged windshield. She didn't say a word in reply, and he thought maybe she was asleep, so he dared a glance over at her. She was not only wide awake but was staring at him with green eyes as big as saucers. A tear was slowly making its way down her lightly sunburned cheek. She had heard him all right, but she couldn't bring herself to reply just yet. Other tears followed the first, and they began streaking her makeup the way a summer shower can streak a windowpane.

"I'm pregnant," she finally managed to whisper, fighting back a sob. William's head flew sideways, and the Chevy swerved on the rain-soaked road. He straightened the car just before it hit the shoulder. He drove another quarter of a mile before finding a solid pullover, and only then did he ease the Chevy to the side of the road. They sat looking at each other, both a little dumbfounded. After a minute or so had passed, he asked in a small voice, "Are you sure?" Her face turned red, and she nodded.

"Why do men always seem to ask that stupid question?" she huffed and reached for a tissue in the glove compartment. "Yes, I'm sure. I think it happened that night on the Smokies. I haven't had my period since then." She waited for some sort of reply as she blew her nose on the Kleenex. When none came, she went on, "I don't know whether to be happy or sad or scared, but I'm really all three." William's mind was into a mode of semi-shock; he hadn't thought about a baby so soon. He couldn't come up with the right words, so the only thing he thought to do was pull her into his arms and gently kiss the tears from her eyes.

"I'm happy you are carrying our baby. I really am," he finally managed to say, although a little too formally. "And I'm scared, too, especially because I will probably be gone when the baby arrives. Hell, I'll be gone until the end of the war, and who knows when that will be." He reached down and took her hands, then brought them to his mouth and kissed them.

"Just come back to me ..." She caught herself, then continued, "To us. Just come back to us, William." She laid her head on his shoulder, carefully placing his hand on her stomach. "I hope it's a girl. Maybe the two of us together can keep you in line, soldier." With a smile, she snuggled into his arms. After a few minutes, the rain finally stopped, and the sun peeked through the fast-moving clouds. A shimmering rainbow arched across the highway with one end disappearing into a clump of pine trees off to their right. *That's a good hiding place for a leprechaun's gold*, thought William as he looked toward the cluster of tall, stately shortleaf pines where the end of the rainbow appeared to lead. Smiling, he pulled the Chevy into first gear and eased back onto the road.

"A good sign." They both spoke the words at the same time and laughed. Then Beth snuggled up to his arm and closed her eyes. The rest of the way home was a blur as William contemplated the somewhat scary idea of being a father. It was dark by the time they hit Waynesville, and he listened to the soft breathing of his young wife as they crested Balsam Gap and headed down into the valley of Scott's Creek.

* * * * *

The last couple of days of his leave were spent in hectic motion and a flurry of activity. On his second-to-last night in town, William's mother and Beth's mother joined forces to throw a going-away party. Most of the town showed up, including a bunch of William's old college football buddies who ogled Beth until she was blushing and William was beaming with pride.

William spent his final day at home in seclusion with Beth. They slept late, puttered around at his father's home through the afternoon, and then late in the evening walked slowly around Buchanan Loop hand in hand. The air was chilly, and a winter's breeze that spoke of snow caused Beth to shiver despite her heavy jacket and thick gloves. She pulled the fur collar of her coat up around her neck and tried to lose herself inside it. A full moon crept over the Balsam Mountains to the east and shone down bright on the young lovers, their breath like vapor above a boiling teapot. A silver frost glistened on the short fescue grass of the pasture that ran alongside the road, and Black Angus cattle lay nearby, huddled together on the edge of a small pond. William pulled Beth closer when he saw her shiver.

Despite a valiant effort to the contrary, Beth had spent considerable time during the last several days worrying about her husband, her mind aching with the knowledge that he had a bad habit of taking far too many chances. She just couldn't figure out how to talk to him about his total disregard for his own well-being, and she questioned whether she should even say anything at all. He always took care of his men but not necessarily himself. The constant worrying had begun to show on her pretty young face and was reflected in the somber mood that gripped her like a cold hand on this, their last day together before he shipped out. *Who knows how long he will be gone*, she grumbled to herself as they walked up the steep hill toward the old hall house. After watching his wife's face grow ever gloomier by the minute, William finally turned her toward him, lifted her chin, and looked into her beautiful eyes. He seemed to have read her mind when he whispered, "I promise I won't take any more chances than I absolutely have to in order to get the job done. I promise," he repeated as he watched her eyes. She started to say something but stopped when she noticed a small rabbit race out of the pasture and scurry across the road in front of them. The rabbit stopped, its long ears laid back and its nose twitching as it listened. Then in a flash of soft grayish fur, it rushed forward and disappeared under a large brush pile on the bank of the road, seemingly content to bed there for the night. Beth started to move on, but William stopped her. "Watch," he whispered. After a couple of minutes, a pair of small brown-and-white beagles came trailing out of the pasture, their high-pitched voices echoing in the cold air. With their noses close to the frost-covered ground, they barked excitedly around the pile of old pine limbs, their tails wagging. The rabbit, fairly safe under the brush, must have gone into a deep cozy hole because the dogs soon tired of the chase and plodded off into the night.

William smiled as he watched the disgruntled dogs disappear into the woods; it reminded him of his younger days and hunting with his old beagle named Poochie. His father had called the dog Pooch until he found out she was a female. Then reluctantly, he changed her name to Poochie. William laughed at the memory and absentmindedly walked a few steps further along the loop road before he realized that Beth wasn't following him. Turning, he waited as she walked toward him, slowly shaking her head. "Don't you know that Bledsoe and Jamberdino talk to me about what a driven person you are?"

"What?" He had briefly forgotten what they were talking about. She went on as if she didn't hear him.

"William, I know you will take chances. That's your job. That's who you are. I ..." She paused and touched her stomach, which was barely showing under the heavy coat: "We just want you to come home to us. I want you to help me raise our child."

He leaned down to kiss her upturned lips just as the unmistakable sound of the hawk's cry echoed down from the mountain, which loomed over them in the moonlight. Beth's eyes rushed to scan the sky, for the creature she feared was calling her husband.

"I now truly believe that hawk is one of your ancestors, William. And even if he is supposed to be your protector, this whole business still frightens me," she added.

The young father-to-be looked up at the hawk and reflected for a moment before responding. "Maybe more than you think," he replied hesitantly. "The protector part, I mean."

Beth's eyes bore into him. "What ... what do you mean?" she asked, half afraid of what the answer would be. He stared skyward and tried to figure out a way to explain what had happened back at Camp Foster. Forcing his eyes from the hawk, he turned toward his woman.

"Well," he swallowed like some sinner at a confessional. "I haven't told anyone about this, not even Bledsoe," he said, his voice rising from a near whisper as he spoke. "But a hawk may have saved my life down in Ranger school."

"What? How?" she stammered, confusion and anxiety gripping her stomach as she waited for an explanation. Struggling to stay calm, she listened to her husband tell the story of the hawk and the snake back at Camp Foster. When he was finished, all that she could say was, "My god, William."

Her head spun as she shifted her gaze from her husband's face to the hawk that sailed through the treetops just overhead, its shrill cry piercing the night air. Suddenly, she grabbed her stomach. The baby had kicked hard in unison with the hawk's cry. *At the same instant!* her mind screamed. William rushed to her side, and the baby kicked again. "I'm scared, William. Something very strange is going on here. The baby kicks every time the hawk cries." She looked down at her stomach as if the unborn child could explain its actions.

"Surely, it's a coincidence," he said, only half believing it himself. Then he, too, looked down at the small bulge in his wife's coat.

"Or some kind of sign." She shuddered at the thought.

As frightened as she was about the whole situation, when the hawk flew up and joined the dove that now sailed above them, she began to feel better almost immediately. *And that's strange too*, she thought, unconsciously rubbing her stomach. Nevertheless, she was comforted by the small gray dove's appearance alongside the great raptor, and the baby had stopped its kicking.

The feathered pair dipped their wings almost simultaneously as they sailed in large circles, feathers ruffled against the cold wind. But their cries had stopped. As Beth and her husband came up around the circle behind the old courthouse, they could see the lights of the houses glowing warm and inviting in the cold night.

"Maybe I should just go with you and be by your side," she whispered as they approached William's father's house, her head leaning against his shoulder. He looked down at her beautiful face, so serious in her thoughts, and he had to resist a laugh. To keep from being punched, he just smiled.

"I'll have enough to worry about without worrying about you too."

"Huh, the hawk doesn't seem to mind that its mate is with him," Beth replied as they stood at the steps leading into the house. William thought for a minute about a reply, but he didn't want to say that the hawk wasn't being shot at like he would be. Instead, he said what the instructors always told them when they didn't have an answer: "Take it up with the chaplain." He got hit anyway. Beth punched him on the shoulder as they took the last few steps into the house. The shadows of the hawk and dove floated across the frosty lawns in the moonlight.

* * * * *

Two days later, after a lot of hurry-up-and-wait followed by a long train ride, William, Bledsoe, and Jamberdino met up in New York City, where they would board the troop ship bound for England.

Jamberdino was excited about showing his southern friends around the Big Apple and couldn't wait to get started. Having been to the city several times, he was looking forward to the tour with great enthusiasm. Several hours and much neck-straining later, neither of the southern boys were overly impressed by the hustle and bustle of the big city, except for the sight of the Empire State Building. Rising into the fog like a bizarre version of *Jack and the Beanstalk*, it got the attention of the two mountain boys. William, ever the training master, thought it would be a good exercise to run up the 120 flights of steps and then back down. "Let's run to the top of that damn thing," he said excitedly as he gazed up into the sky where the peak of the building disappeared into the clouds. Bledsoe and Jamberdino laughed heartily until they looked at him and saw that he was indeed serious.

"You're crazy as hell if you think I'd run to the top of that building," growled Jamberdino, leaning his head back in an effort to see the top of the skyscraper.

"I wouldn't run up all those stairs if Dorothy Lamour was going to screw me when I got to the top," added Bledsoe as he too looked skyward.

"Oh, hell yes, you would," kidded Jamberdino when the three finally turned their backs to the concrete giant. "But you would probably be too tired to do anything after that damn run, and that's when I would step up." They glanced back once more at the tall building then continued walking down Fifth Avenue.

"Well, I seriously doubt Miss Lamour would be willing to screw either ones of you jerks anyway." William chuckled as they turned off the sidewalk and stepped into a busy tavern called the Shamrock Pub and Grill.

"You just never know," quipped Bledsoe. "You just never know." He brushed back what remained of his close-cropped hair and threw out his chest, laughing. "After all, I am an Airborne Ranger, you know."

* * * * *

Except for the constant fear of the German U-boats, the boring lifeboat drills, and the crowded living conditions, the boat trip across the North Atlantic was fairly uneventful. There were two thousand troops, plus the crew, living on a ship designed to handle half that many passengers. The bulky Mae Wests, the affectionate name given to the life preservers, were a pain in the ass and the all-civilian crew of the SS *Thomas Paine* wasn't very friendly, but it was the seasickness that was the worst. A third of the troops on board were affected to some degree, but Jamberdino felt sure he was going to die. He became nauseous on the very first day out, and he stayed in sick bay most of the trip. William and Bledsoe went down to check on him each day, and each day he looked worse.

Early on the third day, a cold misty morning greeted the two men as they walked along the upper promenade deck checking out the possible living situation there. Having made a joint decision to rescue their friend from the jaws of death, or at least from the sick bay, they went below with grim determination. They found Jamberdino, pale as a ghost, swaying in his hammock. The makeshift bed was strung between two bulkheads along with thirty others, making them look like giant cocoons lined up along the wall. Jamberdino lay in his skivvies moaning, a tin barf bucket hugged to his chest.

"You look like shit, buddy." Bledsoe laughed. He and William pulled up two folding chairs and sat down beside the bulkhead.

"Don't you dare puke on me, you damn Yankee," cursed William as Jamberdino gagged and heaved into the bucket.

"I've thrown up all my digestive juices. There's simply nothing left down there," cried Jamberdino as yet another heave racked his body nonetheless. William glanced around the stuffy sick bay, sniffed the air, and looked over at Jamberdino. He and Bledsoe had already made the decision to get their buddy topside.

"This place is a shithole. It's no damn wonder you can't get better. Get your gear, soldier. We're going topside." Bledsoe helped his friend negotiate the maze of ladders while William carried his gear. Together, they made their way out onto the breezy deck of the once fancy cruise liner. The air was cold, but it was clean. The foul smell of sickness left far below.

The constant rolling of the big ship seemed much less dramatic up topside, and Jamberdino's stomach settled down a little before they even hung his hammock. A few other brave souls had strung their hammocks on the top deck, and bunched together, they looked like a small hobo town. The clean air worked though, and the next day, Jamberdino wasn't nearly as sick.

The ocean liner had finally rounded the coast of Ireland, and as a result, the seas became much calmer there. The SS *Thomas Paine* had made this trip dozens of times in the past, before she was pressed into military service, and she seemed to know her way along the rocky coastline like an old mariner. But her job now was ferrying soldiers, instead of tourists, across the cold waters of the Atlantic, and the constant threat of German U-boats was never far from the minds of the crew members. The mighty Atlantic current, which had pushed and battered them all the way across the frigid ocean, was slamming into the west coast of Ireland while the SS *Thomas Paine* made her way leeward of the island toward Liverpool and the calmer waters of the Irish Bay. Her cargo of two thousand GIs, stuffed into every nook and cranny on the ship, was more than ready to feel land under their feet once again.

Early on the last day, the three friends stood in the damp morning air and leaned on the guardrail with a thousand other soldiers. They watched the tugboats, black smoke billowing from their stacks, strain to guide the big boat into her berth on the partially covered pier—a pier that had seen thousands of warships come and go through the ages. The bustling port city of Liverpool lay sprawled in the mist like an image out of some Dickens novel. Soot-covered smokestacks punched up through the gray fog, belching coal smoke that rose black into the sky only to fall back to earth as a sooty rain. Liverpool, the heart of the Lake District, had barely been touched by the mighty Luftwaffe, at least compared to London. But her time would come.

The GIs made their way down the shaky gangplank toward land. "Give me an airplane ride anytime over this damn boat," cried Jamberdino as he dropped his duffel bag, knelt down, and kissed the soot-covered dock.

"Give me a cold beer and a hot English woman," Bledsoe chimed in, stepping around his kneeling friend.

"Just give me a little room away from you two stinking guys." William laughed as they struggled across the wharf toward the waiting deuce-and-a-halves.

"Praise the Lord! The Americans have landed!" shouted someone in the back ranks.

His remark instantly drew a salty "Shut the hell up and form on your units!" from one of the sergeants who was running around, trying to make order out of the mass chaos. The Rangers' First Sergeant was a huge bear of a man by the name of Roy Baker, and today he was not very happy. He stood on a slightly raised platform, shouting at the top of his considerable lungs, "H Company of the 2nd Rangers! Form on me!" His cold blue eyes darted from one soldier to another as the men rushed to form lines.

Finally, after much jostling, H Company, minus one lost soul who was counted AWOL, was unceremoniously loaded up on ten olive-drab deuce-and-a-halves that lurched into the flow of traffic. The convoy headed into town on a street teeming with people who had grown very accustomed to seeing soldiers. Most of the good folks of Liverpool never even bothered to look up at the trucks loaded with Americans as they passed. But the young GIs wanted to be noticed. After all, they had come to save the world, or at least that's what they thought. They couldn't resist leaning out the backs of the big trucks and whistling at anyone who wore a skirt. A few of the more curious women did glance up and smile at the attention they were receiving, but most simply looked down and kept walking.

The city's main train station, where the trucks were headed, was nearly a hundred years old, and its domed stained-glass roof made it look sinister in the swirling fog. It took the convoy almost an hour to fight their way through the snarling traffic, but they were helped along by the sharp whistles from the English Bobbies lining their route. The whistles blended in with the noise of a hustling humanity as the trucks finally pulled up in front of the station. First Sergeant Baker stepped briskly out of the lead truck and bellowed for H Company to form on him. "You will load by platoon, starting with

1ˢᵗ Platoon," his booming voice informed the soldiers and anyone else within a half a mile.

"What a concept." Jamberdino laughed until he saw the big head of Sergeant Baker rotate in his direction. Baker's hard eyes bored into him intently. "How could he have possibly heard me?" moaned Jamberdino as he shuffled meekly into formation.

"Sergeant Baker hears all and knows all," William replied in a very low whisper. "He makes Sergeant Moore look like a boy scout."

The coal burning locomotive sounded its brass whistle, and the old train slowly pulled out of the station, heading north with its cargo of Rangers. Black smoke billowed from the stack, and the iron pistons pushed hard to drive the big wheels. The train gradually gained speed until the bustling city faded into the dirty fog. The scuttlebutt had it that H Company was headed for Scotland to train in the rugged highlands with their cliffs and caves. The Glasgow Special reached its cruising speed of forty miles per hour as she rumbled north into the night.

Darkness came quickly in the high latitudes of Scotland, and most of the Rangers slept where they could. But a few couldn't sleep at all, and these either just looked out the windows at nothing or they talked. Newly promoted Corporal William Craig sat talking with Sergeant Baker, who watched William's pitiful attempt to sew the new double stripes onto his fatigue jacket.

"Corporal Craig, you can sew those damn stripes on after we get to Oban," growled Baker, who was tired of watching the man stick himself with the needle. William reluctantly put the needle and thread away in his old AWOL bag and leaned back in the stiff seat.

"I want to thank you again for the promotion, Sergeant," beamed William with obvious pride.

"Don't be so damn quick to thank me, Craig. There is a hell of a lot of responsibility that comes with those stripes," growled Baker. "You may get your ass shot off trying to take care of your fire team, or at least those two bozos." Baker nodded toward Bledsoe and Jamberdino, who pretended to be asleep. William thought for a minute as he looked at his two friends.

"Well, at least I'll have a little more money in my pockets when they shoot me," he replied with a halfhearted smile. Out of the back of the semi-dark Pullman car came Bledsoe's southern drawl: "Yeah, me and Jamberdino can fight over your recently acquired wealth." Newly promoted Corporal William Craig just smiled at the quip, but Sergeant Baker shook his big head in disgust, then leaned back and closed his eyes in hopes of catching a little sleep.

Daylight was struggling to push aside the dark shadows when the little port town of Oban came into view through the mist. The train lurched slightly as the engineer slowed down in an effort to negotiate a fairly sharp curve just outside of the sleepy little hamlet. Sitting high above the tracks on a stone-covered ridge, the ruins of an old castle looked forlornly down on the windswept bay. William, who had changed seats with Sergeant Baker, wiped the moisture off the dingy windowpane and glanced out at the ruins as they passed by. *They look vaguely familiar for some reason*, he thought before the ruins were devoured by the fog once more.

Oban was a small fishing village with a beautiful harbor, a Scotch distillery, and an old monastery that overlooked the bay. The train pulled up to the tiny station that sat just above the harbor, where a small white-haired stationmaster stood under a leaky awning and waved his lantern. A light drizzle greeted the Rangers as they stepped off the platform into the narrow street while an early-morning fog floated in among them like one of the plagues that fell on the Egyptians in biblical times. Puddles of water filled the many potholes in the road, a road that eventually meandered toward the mountains and the town of Inverness.

Baker formed the company without having to shout, and they marched silently through the quiet streets. Their destination was the old monastery, where they would be housed for the duration of their training. A few early risers from the village stood on the roadside and watched unconcerned as the so-called Yanks trudged through the mist. The old monastery was made almost entirely of stone, and it rose up out of the fog like a bad dream as H Company reached its destination.

The Rangers sullenly stood at attention, the steady drizzle dripping off their ponchos. The cold dampness seemed to shout a warning to them of things to come, but the ancient stone structure looked down with indifference as Sergeant Baker explained their billeting. With no questions, except the one that nobody asked about when they could get out of the damn rain, he dismissed them, and two hundred rain-soaked GIs trudged through the huge double doors that hinged on squeaky flat iron straps. William led his team up a stairwell of worn limestone, dimly lit by several oil lamps mounted on the stone walls. Their shadows crawled along behind them as they walked up the steps. The air was damp and chilly, but no fire burned in the great fireplace that dominated the main floor.

"This place is damn creepy," moaned Jamberdino, rubbing his rosary, a gift from his very devout mother, as they climbed the steps toward their rooms. The hair stood up on the back of William's neck, and deep inner senses stirred as the scent of burnt wood from long ago assaulted his nostrils.

"This place is not just creepy. It's old, real old," growled McClure in a hushed whisper. McClure was one of William's fire team members, another southern boy from South Carolina.

"Why in the hell is everyone whispering?" shouted Bledsoe, throwing his arms into the air and running around like a ghost. "And you call yourselves Rangers," he lambasted the fire team who looked around sheepishly at each other. His shouting had the desired effect on the men though, and it lightened the mood a little. Everyone was soon laughing about Bledsoe's antics and bitching about their accommodations.

"Okay, people, this is going to be our home until the Army tells us to leave or until the good people of Oban throw us out because Bledsoe tried to screw all the young women," announced William after he had stored his gear.

"Hell, he'll try to screw the old ones too." Someone laughed from the back of the room as they all settled down to eat cold K-rations.

After a long run in the rain and more cold chow, darkness spread down from the high peaks, and the Rangers crawled into their racks, anticipating a long day to come. An ancient harbor bell sitting atop a buoy off the Isle of Kerrera tolled mournfully throughout the long night, the thick fog only slightly muffling the sound.

Early the next morning, having slept fitfully, William woke with a gasp. "God, what a dream," he cried in a low breath, looking around a little confused as to where he was. When he finally got oriented, he swung his feet off his cot, gingerly put them on the cold floor, and stared at the damp stone walls, images of Norsemen sailing on a windswept sea floating through his mind. Glancing at his watch, which read 0400, he groaned. *Lord, the CQ will be through in a few minutes. I might as well get my ass up.* He continued bitching to himself as he reached for his boots. Dressing in the predawn light, the oil lanterns having been snuffed out hours ago, he laced his Cochran jump boots in the airborne fashion and silently walked out onto the small balcony that faced the harbor.

Leaning lightly on the masonry wall, he peered out into the bay and took a deep breath of the salty air. Warily, he glanced around at the empty balcony before his eyes drifted farther to the left, where the town of Oban lay sleeping. The streets were empty and the buildings dark, except for a few lamps along the sidewalks. An eerie silence hung in the damp air, the only sound the distant tolling of the harbor buoy. His most recent dream flashed through his mind again. He had been on some kind of landing craft with his squad, but as they stormed ashore, the man next to him suddenly turned into a Viking with a leather helmet, iron straps gleaming in the sunlight. The man's eyes were like fire, and his long blond hair dangled from under his helmet. The Norseman, dressed in leather britches, had carried a large sword in one hand and a shield in the other. That image he could have pulled from many stories, but the strangest part was the hawk. A war hawk flew at the man's shoulder. "A hell of an imagination," growled William out loud, and he shook his head to dispel the image.

He heard his fire team begin to stir behind him, and his mind quickly snapped back to the present. The CQ had evidently already passed through and awakened them. He needed to go in and talk to his men about the upcoming day, but for some reason, he couldn't seem to take his eyes off the harbor. Finally, he forced himself to look away; it was not unlike pulling a piece of metal away from a magnet. As he turned to go back inside though, he stopped and watched Oban's small fishing fleet heading out to sea. Three large trawlers and several smaller ones were headed toward the reef just below the cliffs of Crag Bharrain to see if Neptune, the old man of the sea, would be kind to them today. He smiled as the little armada chugged past their running lights soon lost in the fog. Only when the trawlers were out of sight was he able to walk back inside.

* * * * *

The training schedule was heavy, and it started that very day. Constant and difficult, it punished them to the extreme. The cadre was mostly made up of British commandos, men who had been hardened in North Africa and India. They were all business, and their RSM, a hard-as-nails Sergeant Major by the name of Clerk, told the young Yanks that his people weren't there to make friends. Their job was to make Kraut killers out of them, and that was exactly what they intended to do. William listened to every word the commandos had to say, and he drove his team accordingly. After a month, his team was the best in the company.

"We will work harder, and we will train smarter than anyone else. And we will work together. Each man will know not only his job, but his buddy's job too. If someone gets killed, the mission will go on!" shouted William one snowy day at the firing range. They became more familiar with the American weapons as well as the British and German ones. William found that if he drove himself hard, his team would follow, and they could all hear Sergeant Baker bellowing incessantly in the background: "Go hard, go hard!"

Weeks turned into months, and their minds became as hard as their bodies. The long Scottish winter gave way to a rainy spring, and still they trained. The cliffs around Oban became as familiar as the local pubs. One pub in particular welcomed the brash young Yanks with their shiny boots. The Hawk & Dove was a lively place on most Saturday nights, Celtic music exciting the locals as well as the Rangers, especially the southern boys. The pub got its name from a local legend about a young Viking warrior who married a village girl. A healer, the girl supposedly persuaded the Norseman to seek peace instead of war. His grandmother's tales echoed this same legend.

The odd-shaped structure that housed the pub had seen several fires down through the years, the dry-stacked stone walls showing signs of the damage. A recent addition extended outward from the main building at an unusual angle for about thirty feet, and its back wall was constructed of rough-cut pine boards. This enclosed area, just off the side door, had become a small courtyard patio, where down through the years many a pint had been raised in toast.

On one unusually clear spring night, William, Bledsoe, and Jamberdino sat around an old iron table that had seen better days. It wobbled badly and was in dire need of a piece of wood or something to steady one leg. "If this old table could only talk ..." Bledsoe mused in a solemn tone as he admired the iron table. "I would like to have heard the tales that have been told around it." Running his finger along the inlaid swirls, he noticed the rust-covered initials "JMc+EF 1815" scratched into the cast iron on the tabletop. *Probably with a knife or bayonet,* he thought. *Were they really that old, and if so, who were these people?* His nostalgic comment surprised both of his friends, and their faces showed it. It wasn't like Bledsoe to be concerned about the past, or anything else for that matter.

The crowd around them, mostly Rangers, was quickly becoming boisterous. The rest of their fire team was sitting at the next table over getting quite drunk, but the three friends stayed somber. "I think I would like to bring Beth back here after the war," said William with a hint of melancholy in his tone as he gazed up at the surrounding hills. "It's almost like coming home," he continued.

"Not me," Jamberdino chimed in, clueless to his buddy's comment. "I'm sick of this place and all of its damn rain."

"Yeah, I don't ever want to leave Knoxville again," exclaimed Bledsoe. "That is if I even make it out of this damn war alive," he added solemnly.

"Well, I'll come back," said William staring down into his beer. "Somehow." Bledsoe glanced over at his friend and then at Jamberdino. William never saw the shared look of worry on their faces. Far to the west, the sun burnt an orange hole in the sea as it slowly sank out of sight. A chubby redheaded waitress shuffled over and lit the well-used candles that were stuffed into the necks of two dark-burgundy wine bottles. The three Rangers finished their beers while the tiny lights flickered in the breeze.

It was the middle of May, and the last training session on the schedule was to be as close to the actual D-day landing as possible. After this final exercise, they were to head back to Liverpool and wait. This last leg would require William's team to scale a high cliff that sprang up from a narrow rocky beach about two miles up the coast from Oban. The waters of the bay were extremely choppy as the amphibious landing craft chugged toward its objective in a driving rain, but the craft was in excellent hands. As tough as the pounding surf was, the landing was completed without a hitch, except for one sprained ankle. Private Lazcano, who was clumsy as hell anyway, hit the deck hard when he exited the landing craft, and his ankle twisted on a large rock. Swelling up like a goose egg, it quickly forced him out of the exercise.

The British coxswains who piloted the landing crafts were veterans of many tough landings, and they handled the LSTs like experts, which they were. You would have thought they were on the Thames with their sweethearts instead of the churning waters of Oban Bay. The Brits shook their heads in mock amazement, laughing at Lazcano hobbling back to them after his fall. Despite their merriment, they carefully loaded him back on the craft and took him away. "In a real landing, you would be dead, mate" were the last words the team heard as the boats roared back out into the sea.

The Rangers struggled through the waist-deep surf, approaching the base of the cliff with William in the lead as usual. Bledsoe was right behind him. The handholds cut out in the rock were easy for the first fifty feet of the climb, but after that, it got tougher. At about ninety feet up the ascent, William heard the familiar sound of a cooing dove. Oban was noted for its many doves that nested in the cliffs, but this sound came from a solitary bird somewhere above him, and he craned his neck in an attempt to spot it. *There you are*, he thought to himself when he finally picked out the grayish bird sitting near what looked like a small opening about twenty feet above him and to his right. Something in a deep forgotten part of his brain called out *the cave.* He looked up at the dove and then down at Bledsoe. Shouting loudly so that he could be heard over the roar of the surf, William's voice reached Bledsoe's ears: "Mike, I've found a cave up here. I'm going to take a quick peek inside." With that said, he carefully worked his way up and over to the opening.

"That's not on our schedule, and we're running behind already!" shouted Bledsoe, knowing his words of warning were lost in the gale-force winds that had suddenly swept across the cliff. "Damn," he growled, "we can't pull off an exercise just to look in a fucking cave." He shook his head in anger as Jamberdino hugged the cliff next to him, and together, they watched their friend's body disappear into the dark hole that reminded them of their first jump day. "Hellfire," cursed Bledsoe again, deciding to scramble after his friend, the rest of the team following him like sheep.

William climbed up to the cave's entrance and stared into the dark hole. Glancing around at the disheveled rock, he could tell the cave had once been much larger. Without really thinking about why he was going into the hole, he began crawling forward on his hands and knees. Five feet in his pack caught on a jagged rock, and he rolled on his side in order to shed the straps off his shoulders. Dragging his pack full of C-2 alongside him, he crawled deeper into the blackness. After about twenty feet, the light became so dim it took a few minutes for his eyes to adjust. When they finally did, he crawled forward for another fifteen feet or so to a point where the opening rose to a height of about seventeen or eighteen feet, and he was able to stand up.

A primal part of his brain screamed caution, and the hair stood up on the back of his neck as his eyes scanned the area in front of him. All the while, the wind howled through the cave's mouth like some wild beast caught in a trap. *What the hell am I doing in here?* he thought, but that didn't stop him from taking a tentative step forward. The small amount of light that made its way into the cave danced along the limestone ledges like the reflection of a long ago fire. Bats squealed and fluttered about in protest as he invaded their domain. Holding his eyes extra wide open (a trick his British instructors had taught them), he gradually became more accustomed to the low light and eased toward the back of the cave.

A faint flutter of wings told him the dove was probably roosting on one of the ledges just above his head. He was straining his eyes, peering into the dark corners when suddenly he blinked and took a step back. Rubbing his eyes in astonishment, he stared at a white shimmering form slowly taking on the appearance of a dark-haired woman dressed in a homespun woolen dress. *This can't be a real woman*, his mind told him, but his eyes said, *Oh, yes, it is!*

The figure of the woman stood near where he had last heard the dove's call. The dark-haired beauty floated in and out of focus like a mirage shimmering above an empty lakebed. Captivated by the peaceful aura given off by the image, William took a deep breath and stepped in her direction. Another step and he was within ten feet of her, where he instinctively dropped into a crouch with his carbine at the ready. "What the hell is going on?" The question escaped from his raspy throat as sweat rolled down his forehead to sting his eyes, which he blinked in a steady motion, trying to make sense of what was happening. The carbine muzzle never wavered.

A haunting voice that faintly resembled the cooing of a dove echoed across the cave floor. "You are of my blood, William Craig, and you must become a warrior for peace. Help stop this mindless killing," the voice pleaded.

William rubbed his eyes with shaky hands, hoping he would snap out of the crazy dream—or nightmare, whatever it was that he was in. He glanced at the cave entrance and then back to the image, which was quickly fading into the rock.

"Wait, please. I don't understand. No, wait." He lowered the carbine and moved forward. "What do you mean be a warrior for peace? What the hell do you want from me?" Now he was shouting.

"Be a warrior for peace," the voice repeated. "When the time comes, you will understand." The voice drifted away just like the image, and William found himself standing alone, with his head down and the carbine pointing aimlessly at the ground. His mind replayed the words and the scenes from his dreams, now racing across his memory, clouding his vision.

He wasn't sure how long he had stood there, but his trance was broken by noise coming from the front of the cave. Turning slowly toward the opening, he watched two shadows spread across the floor of the cavernous hole like cave bears coming back to their dens. Hands shaking, he gripped his rifle hard and waited. The blackened faces of Bledsoe and Jamberdino came into view as they crept forward with their carbines at the ready, and William let out an audible sigh of relief.

"What the hell are you trying to …?" Bledsoe broke off his query when he saw the dazed look in his friend's eyes. Cautiously, he eased up beside his obviously bewildered team leader. Bledsoe grabbed William by the arm in hopes of keeping him from firing his weapon. "Damn, buddy, you look like you just saw a ghost."

"I … I think maybe I just did," whispered William, reaching down to grab his pack. Then without another word, he headed for the cave opening on unsteady feet.

He stumbled toward the entrance just as the rest of the fire team appeared one by one at the opening. Staring wide-eyed and unsure of what to do, they ducked when a flutter of wings announced the passage of not just one but two birds escaping from the cave. The utterly savage cry of the hawk caused everyone to tense.

"I need to know if you are okay, really okay," Bledsoe asked his friend as they stood beside at the mouth of the cave. William blinked his eyes several times before he answered, "I'm not sure, Mike." He whispered the words and then shook his head from side to side in an effort to clear the strange images from his mind.

Bledsoe looked him over from head to foot. "Well, you have all twenty pounds of the C-2. If you aren't sure, maybe me or Jamberdino should carry the damn stuff."

"No!" William shouted in frustration but with a little more clarity. "You already have the blasting caps, and Jamberdino has the primer cord. We can't chance putting them together." He rubbed his eyes and stretched before continuing: "I'll be all right. Just give me a minute."

Bledsoe looked around in a hurried attempt to sort out what the hell had happened in this cave to get his buddy so off-kilter. "Tell me what the hell happened in here," he said, the rest of the fire team standing a short distance away, staring at them in anticipation.

"I'll tell you guys everything," answered William, glancing toward the back corner of the cave as he spoke. "But first, we have to finish this damn exercise. Sergeant Baker will have our asses if we screw up."

William and Bledsoe, followed closely by Jamberdino, walked up to the rest of the fire team, who appeared anxious as the trio approached. If they were expecting an immediate explanation, they were sorely disappointed. "Okay, people, let's go finish this damn training session" was all William said to the men. Then he led the team on up the mountain. As if the episode at the cave was a bad omen, the remainder of the training leg was total misery. Besides the usual cuts and bruises, their troubles truly began shortly after midnight when a vicious late spring storm blew in off the Hebrides. The team was struggling to get up and over, yet another very steep and rocky ridge when Jamberdino slipped and fell back into the man behind him, a tall, lanky kid from Concrete, Washington, named James Cloer. If it hadn't been for the quick reaction of Bledsoe and Private Frady, both men would have fallen into a boulder-strewn ravine raging with storm water. As it turned out, Cloer was the only one hurt beyond a few scratches. His arm was cut deep by Jamberdino's combat knife, which he had been using to dig out handholds on the limestone slope, inadvertently slashed Cloer's arm during the fall.

"Damn, that was close," growled William, inspecting the bloody gash on Cloer's arm.

"Yeah, but it could have been worse," said Bledsoe as he slapped a bandage on the cut and helped Cloer to his feet. "If Frady hadn't been there to help me grab that damn Yankee, both these assholes would be floating toward the sea." Jamberdino sheepishly slid his knife back into its sheath and shrugged his shoulders.

William patted his friend on the back before continuing up the mountain. "Okay, people, let's be very careful out here. We've got a long, hard trek ahead of us." No proclamations or extra precautions could placate Mother Nature though, for the storm's fury pounded them unmercifully throughout the night. It was near first light before the storm finally let up a little.

The high winds and pouring rain made even simple tasks, like rolling out the detonator wire, more dangerous than normal. After stumbling around in the dark for hours with only one working flashlight, they managed to find their objective and blow the thing to smithereens. Worn out and demoralized from the difficulty of the training, the team trudged through what had become a steady drizzle—their moods as somber as the dark rain clouds—heading back toward Oban. The slackening of the rain wasn't much consolation to the weary Rangers; neither was the sight of the old monastery that slowly came into view, emerging from the mist. William quickly dismissed his team and was making a beeline for the big double doors when he glanced toward the hill above the gray stone building. Sergeant Baker stood on a large rock with no rain gear, unlit cigar stub clenched between his white teeth, hands clasped behind him at the small of his back. The big man was staring out into the bay as rain ran down his face like heavy tears. He almost looked as if he were searching for something. William wiped the rain out of his eyes and stomped through the doors, leaving Baker to his own thoughts.

The next night was cool and rainy, as usual. The entire company had been given a weekend pass to celebrate the completion of training, and the three friends found themselves sitting around the same old table they had occupied several nights earlier. Rain dripped steadily off the edge of an olive drab tarp that had been stretched over several of the tables, "US ARMY" stamped boldly on its corners. For a Saturday night, it was fairly quiet in the little pub, and several tables sat empty. Bledsoe, tired of staring into his beer, looked up at his friend across three half-eaten meals that had been pushed to the center of the table.

"William, I'm not at all sure what happened in that damn cave yesterday, but you are scaring the hell out of me with this silence crap."

"Yeah, talk to us, buddy," echoed Jamberdino, taking a long drink from his beer and then dropping the empty mug with a thud on the wobbly table.

"Huh," grunted William as he shook his head. "How do I start?" After a few long minutes, though, he finally began.

"Okay, I'll try to explain this shit the best I can, but bear with me. It's going to sound weird." He looked up from his beer mug and stared at the two men across the table from him. "Do you remember the last exercise we had back in Ranger School?"

"Yeah," replied Bledsoe. "You stopped short of the top on a rocky ledge. It had been a long, hard pull, and we were all killed. After a few minutes, you hollered down and asked if we had seen anything." Jamberdino nodded in agreement.

There was a pause in the conversation, and William's eyes drifted back down to stare into his beer. But something in Bledsoe's voice suggested more was coming. The big guy from Tennessee thought hard for a minute as if replaying the scene over in his mind, wanting to get it right. "Well, I never said anything then, but I did see something." He paused, wondering if he should continue with the story.

"I'll be damned." William sighed. "I knew I wasn't crazy! You saw the damn hawk, too, didn't you?" His hands gripped the table's edge as he waited for an answer.

"I think—hell, that's not right. I *know* what I saw. I saw a big hawk swoop out of the mist behind us and strike something just about level with your head," growled Bledsoe, all the while shaking his head as if he were mad for having revealed a dark secret.

"What else did you see?" probed William. "Tell me. It's important." He urged his friend on. Beer spilled from the recently filled mugs, the table rocking under the force of William's grip, and the foamy liquid dripping onto the moss-covered limestone tiles. Bledsoe hesitated again, and William began telling his story: "That damn hawk saved my life that day. I had come upon the biggest rattlesnake I have ever seen, and it was just about to strike me when the hawk flew by my shoulder, grabbed that damn snake, and flew off again." William released his grip on the table, sat back, and looked at his hands. His fingers had turned white from the worrisome pressure.

In unison, he and Bledsoe turned up their beer mugs and drained them. Jamberdino remained somewhat clueless and simply watched. All this was sure the hell news to him!

Now seemingly eager to finish his story, Bledsoe looked his friend in the eye and whispered, "That's not all I saw." Jamberdino's chair squeaked as he leaned forward, but William remained slouched frozen in position. "When that hawk sailed off with the big snake twisting in its talons …" He paused to swallow the tangy bile that had suddenly formed in his throat, the images now fresh in his mind once more. Taking another long drink from yet another beer that had appeared like magic from the hand of their waitress, he continued, "It must have been the light playing tricks on my eyes or something because it seemed like the damn hawk turned into a large Viking creature. Whatever it was tore that snake to pieces." Bledsoe's shoulders sagged, and he sat back as if the tale had worn him out. William just stared into his beer, not saying a word.

The same chubby, red-cheeked waitress who had brought them their beers took away the half-empty plates and didn't bother to ask if they wanted anything else. Sarah was her name, and she was truly hoping to get home early for a change. Her little boy, Timmy, was sick with a cold, and she felt one coming on herself.

Jamberdino turned toward William and asked in a low whisper, "Just what did you see in that cave?" William appeared to ignore the question, simply staring into space for a long time. Jamberdino started to ask again, thinking his friend hadn't heard, but at the last second caught Bledsoe's hand motion and an almost unnoticeable shake of his head. Another minute passed before, at last, William cleared his throat and raised his head.

"I saw, or think I saw, a woman. A ghostlike woman." He waited for some sort of rebuke or laugh from his friends, but when none came, he went on. "She spoke to me, or maybe more accurately, *at* me." Pausing to finish his beer, he quickly waved for the waitress to bring three more. She frowned, shook her head, and reluctantly went inside. William laughed sadly as he looked up into the green tarp. "It gets better," William said. "I'm pretty sure that woman is the mate of the big Viking." He glanced sheepishly around the nearly empty tavern as if he were afraid someone would hear.

"What the hell did this ... this spirit say?" asked Bledsoe, who for some reason seemed to be slightly angry about the whole thing.

"The woman told me that I was of her blood and that I was supposed to be a warrior for peace. What the Sam Hill does that mean?" he growled.

"Boy, I miss all the good stuff," joked Jamberdino.

"Go to hell," William shot back, and Bledsoe gave his Yankee friend a hard look. Jamberdino hung his head like a small boy who had just been reprimanded by his father.

"Listen, we're all tired and a little confused. Let's change the subject. I don't like it when my squad leader is all freaked out," Bledsoe said, draining the last remnants from his fourth mug.

"I'll be all right. Just give me another beer," William replied sullenly as he sat his empty beer down on the wobbly table and reached for the new mug.

"I know you will." Bledsoe smiled. "And it's your time to buy, Corporal." That brought a smile to William's face, and Jamberdino slapped him on the back.

"Yeah, Corporal, you got the big pay raise," he parroted.

* * * * *

The train ride back to Liverpool began early the next morning and lasted most of the day, but the fog was so thick you couldn't see anything of the countryside. Not that the Rangers necessarily wanted to—most had seen enough of Scotland. The fog may have slowed the train a little, but the rumor mill was running wide open. Everyone was preoccupied with the pending invasion and what they thought they knew about it. The rumor mill seemed to have an answer to every question: when, where, you name it. William sat dejectedly near the window and tried to ignore the gossip. Even with the help of his friends, he couldn't shake the gloomy mood that gripped him. He simply stared out the window into the gray fog, and his reflection stared back.

The Liverpool train station was just as crowded as when they had left to go north nearly three months before. Soldiers and sailors from dozens of countries could be seen on the sidewalks as the Rangers silently loaded onto the big trucks. The same OD-colored trucks that had delivered them to the station rumbled back through the crowded streets, but instead of heading toward the dock, they turned due east on a narrow, winding by-road and disappeared into the night. H Company was headed to an abandoned RAF base at an undisclosed location on the eastern coast of England. The same thick, soupy fog they had ridden through from Oban seemed to follow them. Seven hours later, they offloaded from the trucks and headed toward a large blacked-out hangar that would be their new home, at least for now.

Sergeant Baker, always watchful, noticed how quiet Craig and his fire team had become. He just figured they were nervous about the upcoming invasion, and he knew exactly how to fix that. Sergeant Baker's answer to gloomy moods, or anything else for that matter, was to run and run some more. So he ran the entire company twice a day. He ran them until they were too tired to worry about anything except sleep. It was fairly unusual for a first sergeant to run with the company formation, but Sergeant Baker was an unusual man. He ran at the front of his Rangers.

"Damn," moaned Jamberdino about halfway through a rainy ten-mile run. "Ol' Sergeant Baker is going to kill us before the Krauts get a chance."

"Oh, I think the Krauts will have plenty of chances to shoot your slow ass." Bledsoe laughed as they jogged along, water splashing out from under their boots, drenching their already soaked fatigues. Bledsoe was leading their fire team on this particular day. William had broken the sacred rule of formation running and sprinted way out front, trying to use the run as a chance to clear his mind. He was running hard and alone, several hundred feet in front of the company. Sergeant Baker, generally very strict on running formation, just let him go. He knew Craig had something troubling him; he just wasn't sure of what it was. Maybe running alone would help.

As he ran, William's mind kept pondering the woman's remarks: "Be a warrior for peace." *What the hell does that mean?* he asked himself for the hundredth time. *And why me?* His grandmother's tale of a Viking in his ancestry kept running through his mind also. Plus, there was the hawk and dove. Could all this be somehow connected? His mind ran as fast as his feet until at last he fell to the ground, exhausted. He was on his hands and knees, throwing up as Baker led the company past. "Fall in at the rear of the column, Corporal. Now!" Baker's voice boomed, and William struggled to his feet to chase after the formation.

Everyone knew the date for the invasion was getting close. All passes had been cancelled, and everyone, even the top brass, was confined to their base area. The weather had suddenly turned real shitty on the first of June, and there was no letup in sight. Heavy rain and high winds wreaked havoc with any training except for Baker's runs. Nothing stopped that! A few landing exercises were attempted, but they were soon called off because the sea was way too rough. Everybody just sat around and played poker, wrote home, or prayed.

"If I take this damn weapon apart one more time, I think I'll scream," moaned Jamberdino as he sat on an old footlocker he had found discarded in the back corner of the hangar, reassembling his M1.

"I promise you one thing, Yankee. If you do scream, I'll move my cot over to the other side of the damn hangar," growled Bledsoe as he finished reassembling his newly issued Thompson machine gun. Holding the weapon up, he peered down the oil-slicked barrel and grunted his satisfaction. William smiled at their banter, but his spirits were still as low as the dark clouds pressing down on this place, which, like the rain, seemed to have no end. 3rd platoon had their squad bay area in the far right corner of the huge hangar. Cots and duffel bags were lined up four feet apart along the wall; the weapons rack sat to the side of the bay area. Several pin-up posters of Rita Haywood in her swimsuit decorated the walls, but the tension was high and tempers were quick to flare; several fights broke out between the restless men. The endless waiting was getting to all of them, even the veterans.

William was sharpening his bowie knife for the umpteenth time when he felt, rather than saw, everyone's head turn in the direction of the front door. Sergeant Baker had shoved the wood and metal doors aside and was walking briskly toward the corner where H Company, 2nd Battalion, 75th Rangers waited. All eyes were on their first sergeant as he walked up, his stern face a mask.

He stopped in the center of the company area, and his voice boomed: "Listen up, men." His shadow swayed across their faces as the lights moved with the breeze overhead. Baker, who as a young buck sergeant in Hawaii back in the early thirties had given PT to a battalion of men without the use of a bullhorn, did not have to shout. A thousand men spread out over two acres had heard him then, and these Rangers heard him now!

Nobody spoke while they waited for him to go on. "The weather prophets say this storm is going to blow out of here in the next couple of hours," Baker continued. Pulses raced in anticipation of the next words. "Therefore, the cloud cover should lift, and the invasion will start." No one said a word; silence hung heavy in the dim light. He looked out at the anxious young men, some of whom were already blackening their faces. "And who will lead this damn invasion, men?" Baker shouted the question expecting a reply.

"The Rangers!" shouted two hundred voices as one.

"That's right! The Rangers will lead. You will lead! So get your shit together and try to get some rest. We board the aircrafts at 0100 hours. I want all squad leaders to meet me in front of the main hangar doors in ten minutes. That is all." And with that, Sergeant Baker did a perfect about-face and marched off toward the front of the hangar.

The long, agonizing wait was over; the terribly hard months of training were all past. Now was the solitary gut check time for each man. Everybody tried to sound cool and act like it was no sweat, but inside each man fought the twin demons of doubt and fear.

Exactly ten minutes later, Sergeant Baker stood at parade rest under the small light at the main door, looking even larger than normal in his combat gear. He had his signature unlit stub of a cigar chomped between his teeth. Fourteen squad leaders and four platoon sergeants stood facing him, and he slowly looked each man in the eye. He peered deep into their souls and knew that most were ready.

"Gentlemen, we have trained as hard as humanly possible for this day. I have pushed you as hard as anyone can be pushed, and you have exceeded my expectations. We have gone over and over all your objectives. You are as ready as I can make you. Now it is up to you to lead your people and get the job done!"

Baker's voice echoed through the metal building. "Are there any questions?" No one had any that they were willing to ask just now, so they swallowed their fears and took courage from their first sergeant. Stomachs turned flips while the demon of self-doubt lurked about the edges of every man's consciousness. Most knew, or at least felt, that they were ready for the task assigned. It was the unknown, the horror of combat, the fog of battle that no one can really be ready for. The curse of the unknown would change many of their lives forever.

"Okay, people." Baker's voice had come down several notches. "You have two hours. I suggest you double-check your gear and your squad's gear. We will chute up at 0000 hours, and we will load the aircrafts at 0100 hours. Understood?"

All the voices shouted, "Airborne, First Sergeant!"

Sergeant Baker did an about-face and slowly walked away, his shadow following him like an old friend. Baker had to fight his own demons, demons that inevitably attach to any man who has to lead others into battle. Baker worried mostly about how many bad decisions he would make in the next few hours and how many of these young men he had just looked in the eye would die from those mistakes. The weight of command was just one of Sergeant Baker's demons. He shook his head as he walked outside and looked up into the night sky. The clouds were racing east. *Good*, he thought, *the damn Krauts can get rained on for a while.*

William, deep in thought, walked with his head down, his mind rushing back to Hillsboro and his young pregnant wife—the image of her smiling face warming his soul. Then he brought his head up and saw his men watching his every move. Glancing around in a near panic, he struggled to gather his thoughts. Should he speak to them, say something grand and reassuring like Sergeant Baker? If so, what?

His mind ran in a thousand different directions, the silence of the hangar bearing down on him.

He raised his eyes toward the upper reaches of the building in a futile search for wisdom, but all he found were cobwebs and blackened windows that the Brits had wisely taken care of years before. *At least somebody has their shit together*, he moaned. The dingy light of several large fixtures hanging from the ceiling on long chains danced to a stiff breeze, unfelt by people on the floor. Suddenly, the girl and the hawk flashed across his mind as he looked at his men. *Not now*, his mind screamed, but he was unable to shove the images back into their hiding place. He stood in the middle of the small squad bay area, seemingly alone. Thankfully, most of his men had quit watching him and had busied themselves, preparing their combat gear. As he watched them, he knew, or at least felt, that they were ready. He had checked and rechecked each man's gear from his combat boots up to his steel pot and back down again. They were ready! "God, I just hope I'm ready," he whispered to the shadows, then walked up to Lazcano to ask him again about his strained ankle.

"I'm okay, boss," replied the nervous kid from the Bronx. Then he dove back into his duffel bag, searching for God-knows-what.

William turned slowly in a half circle, his eyes scanning the preparation for war: faces being blackened, knives sharpened for the last time, and the all-important good-luck pieces placed nearby. He smiled as he watched Jamberdino wrestling with his weapons bag; his friend always had trouble arranging his gear. After watching him struggle for a minute or two, William walked over to give him a much-needed hand. He moved around like a mother hen helping the other members of his team.

He was keeping his hands busy, but his mind was quickly clouding over with doubt. A second lieutenant from the 101st had trained with them toward the end of May and was supposed to have led this mission, but he had broken his leg in a freak jeep accident the week before and was out of action. *If Lieutenant Kreuger hadn't broken his damn leg in that stupid jeep wreck last week, he would be in charge here and not me*, William cursed for at least the tenth time. Captain Derby, their CO, had simply told him there wasn't time to train a replacement, "You're the man in charge now, Craig," and that was it. Besides, the rest of the battalion had trained for the beach cliff assault of Point de Hoc. The ugly fears clawed their way to the surface of his brain like something dark and evil from a Lon Chaney movie. What would he forget? Would he freeze at the sight of one of his men blown to pieces? Would he hug the ground and refuse to move when the big rounds began to fall? Would his decisions get some of these men killed? William had no way of knowing what he would do, nor did any of the others who stood or sat around him. These same doubts, these worrisome questions, had plagued warriors from the beginning of time. The truth is that no one knows for sure how they will act until they are thrust into the situation. Even then, a man's reaction can vary with each fight. It is said that combat tests men's souls. Sherman was right: "War is hell!"

* * * * *

At 0045 hours, William's squad trudged along behind him, moving toward their assigned C-47. It's powerful Cummins engines were roaring like a chained beast as it sat on the runway with hundreds of other aircrafts belching blue smoke out of their exhaust pipes and waiting for their paratroopers. The entire airfield was alive with the men and machinery of war. *All this in preparation for the largest invasion in history*, thought William. For some reason, his mind shot back to a world history class he had taken in college long ago. Professor Hubel's course had been pretty interesting, and at some point, they had studied the attempted Mongol invasions of Japan, undertaken by Kublai Khan in the late thirteenth century. Despite the fact that the combined forces of the Mongol and Chinese invaders greatly outnumbered the Japanese, the ill-fated invasions had failed. "Huh," he grunted when he remembered that more than half of the invading Mongol ships were lost at sea in a great storm. "That's a hell of a thing to be thinking about right now," he murmured to himself as Bledsoe walked up beside him.

"Did you say something?" Bledsoe shouted the question over the roar of the big engines.

"No, nothing important," growled William as he tugged on his groin strap and trudged on toward their aircraft.

The particular aircraft designated for their mission was sixth in line and had "Kraut Killer" painted along the side of the fuselage in bold red letters. William stepped out of line to admire the painting skill of the unknown artist while Bledsoe kept moving and led the squad into the belly of the aircraft. The olive-drab plane towered above William, and while his men shuffled past, his gaze turned toward the riveted seams that held it together. Glancing up at the cockpit, he was amazed by the frenzy of activity inside and pleasantly surprised to see a grim-faced pilot look down and give him the thumbs-up. William, equally grim-faced, returned the gesture before turning back to watch his men finish loading.

The red emergency lights cast an eerie glow whose reflection danced like fire in the eyes of the men, who reluctantly trudged deeper into the gut of the aircraft. The young warriors with their faces blackened took on the appearance of strange creatures of the night, which wasn't far from the truth, for that's what they were, these Rangers—creatures trained to kill, especially at night. No one talked as they walked up the steep ramp into the Gooney Bird. Every man was struggling a little with his weapon and the heavy equipment bag attached at his waist. The equipment bag would remain attached until just before they hit the ground, and only then would they release the snaps to let the bags dangle below them on ten-foot cords. William stepped back in line after the last man in his squad walked past; it was Lazcano, and the little Italian was trying hard not to limp as he headed up the ramp. *Gutsy*, thought William. *Hell, they all are!* He tugged on his shoulder strap where it cut into the flesh, but he didn't complain. The tightness was oddly reassuring to him.

William nodded to the jumpmaster as he shuffled past. The old warrior who stood off to the side turned and walked over to the ramp controls, where he prepared to raise the ramp. William's oversized squad had been assigned this aircraft solely for their mission; fifteen men were all he would have to complete the task. He cursed his luck for the hundredth time. Why they hadn't sent another officer or at least a staff sergeant to replace Lieutenant Kreuger, William wasn't sure; he didn't buy the explanation that there wasn't time to train a replacement. Whatever the reason, he was in charge. *God, I hope fifteen is enough*, he fretted as he watched Bledsoe shuffle forward until he was in position to take a seat nearest the jump door. Bledsoe was in the position called "in the door," and when it came time to go, he would be the first to see the hell they were about to jump into.

The jumpmaster pressed the red knob that caused the giant ramp door to begin to close. Just like back in jump school, a moment of panic shot through the minds of several of the men as the ramp clamped shut like a giant bear trap. The only way out now was through the jump door! The Rangers, after months of training, were used to the tremendous vibration of the Cummins engines, but when the pilots revved them up, testing and retesting all the equipment, the screaming noise still bothered them. After what seemed like hours but was only ten minutes or so, the words "Clear to take off" and "Godspeed" came over the pilots' headphones and fifteen C-47s taxied into line. This group of aircrafts carried Bravo Company of the 504th 101st, two companies of the 2nd Battalion 75th Rangers, and William's oversized squad aloft and into history.

Somewhere across the English Channel, a channel now filled with thousands of allied ships of every description, a young resistance fighter waited. And so did two divisions of German soldiers. William leaned back against the aircraft's bulkhead and closed his eyes as he ran their objective through his mind for the ten thousandth time. Why his small group had been assigned the task of taking out a battery of sixteen-inch shore guns hidden in a man-made cave high above Utah Beach in Section Orange from the top while the rest of the battalion would have to come ashore and storm up the one-hundred-foot cliffs that lined the beach below Pointe Du Hoc, he didn't know, and it wasn't his job to ask. The tiny village of St. Eglish, which sat just under the rocky point called Pointe Du Hoc, meaning "point of the hawk," would be their kickoff spot. "The damn hawk again," growled William.

"What did you say?" asked Jamberdino, who sat next to him, fiddling with the sights on his M-1.

"Nothing, Jerry, just talking to myself," he answered, staring at the aerial map that trembled ever so slightly in his hands.

They had been supplied with recon photos that were just twelve hours old, and these showed the guns atop a cliff that was most approachable along a steep, narrow trail, which came up the backside of the cliff. His squad was supposed to meet up with a French resistance fighter near the village of St. Eglish, and the man was to show them the hidden path up to the guns.

"A damn Frenchie. I sure hope he shows up," William grumbled under his breath. He glanced over at Jamberdino to see if his friend had heard him muttering, but Jamberdino was busy with his equipment bag and must not have heard him.

Butterflies of worry were going crazy in the pit of his stomach as the pilot, a recently promoted major from Chicago named Jim Kell, released the brakes and the cumbersome C-47 inched down the runway. Every man in William's squad was loaded to the gills with equipment, and even though there were fewer bodies, the aircraft was heavy with extra fuel for the return trip. It struggled in its effort to separate from the earth. "Not enough runway," cried someone as they all strained to look out the small windows. Up front, Kell's knuckles were white as he pressed forward on the throttle with all his might. Finally, the heavily loaded bird took to the air as asphalt turned to grass and then woods under the wheels. Major Kell and his copilot exchanged quick glances, and the wheels retracted into the belly of the aircraft with a dull thud. Both men let out a deep sigh of relief, for they, even better than their astute passengers, knew they had used the entire runway and then some in order to get the aircraft aloft. Kell, cold sweat glistening on his brow, turned the big yoke toward ninety-six degrees east by southeast and settled back in his seat. The copilot/navigator busied himself plotting the route to Pointe du Hoc, while the other forty-nine Gooney birds followed their leader into the night sky. One hundred fifty more aircraft sat idling on the runway. Some were attached to gliders loaded with the 504th of the 101st Screaming Eagle, while others carried the 82nd aloft.

Thirty minutes later, the lead aircraft caught the tail end of the storm that had hammered the British Isles and delayed the invasion.

The yoke shook in Kell's hands as the winds tossed the aircraft about. But as bad as the storm's turbulent winds were, they were nothing compared to the man-made storm brewing on the horizon.

William had managed to drift off into a troubled sleep but was now awakened by the bouncing of the aircraft. Some say a combat nap is your body's attempt to escape, but all combat veterans know there is no escape from the reality of war—none at all. William could have sworn he had just closed his eyes for a few minutes, but when he looked out the small porthole window behind him, he knew it had been longer. They were nearly across the channel. The AA flak, just to their front and about a mile out, was like a solid red curtain. Fire so thick and tracers so continuous, William couldn't imagine being able to fly through it without being hit. He turned in his seat, looked slightly to the left, and saw dozens of C-47s flying in tight formation, a mere hundred feet separating their wingtips. He jumped slightly and watched horrified as one aircraft flew through what looked like a solid wall of tracers. The plane shuddered; then the cockpit burst into flames as the aircraft's right engine exploded, riddling the fuselage with more shrapnel. Following another burst of AA flak, William watched the plane nosedive with its load of troopers and plunged into the sea. "God help us," he moaned, turning his back to the window.

"I'm afraid God may have stayed back in Oban," said Jamberdino. "Hid in that monastery someplace. That's exactly where I should be too." A crooked little smile spread across his worried face, and he nervously fiddled with some rosary beads.

The jumpmaster, who was just as pale as the rest of his human cargo, struggled down the aisle, stepping over and around combat gear as well as paratroopers. The plane was shaking violently—as if an angry god wasn't back in Oban at all but right there in the middle of this mess, shaking the aircraft in his big hand. Suddenly, the aircraft seemed to moan and red-hot flak tore through the floor, cutting electrical wires as it shot through the roof. Sparks flew everywhere, and smoke began to fill the cargo bay full of worried young men who looked at William for some sort of reassurance.

He saw the looks and shouted, "All right, people, stay calm! We'll exit this tub in a couple minutes!" His words didn't do much to stop the worrying, but what else was he supposed to say? The smoke was getting thicker, and several men started for the jump door. "Sit down, damn it," said William, and he glanced at the jumpmaster in desperation. The man was struggling to hear through his headset. "It's almost time to go!" William shouted at Jamberdino, but it was more an effort to encourage himself than his buddy. Luckily, his men heard him, too, and it helped calm their rattled nerves.

"Two minutes!" shouted the jumpmaster as he staggered toward the front of the aircraft. "Two minutes!" He finally reached the jump door, grabbed the side of the fuselage, and turned around, shouting the all-familiar: "Stand up, hook up, equipment check." Then finally, there was the gut-churning call, "Stand in the door." Mike Bledsoe looked back at his two buddies, gave them a thumbs-up, and shuffled toward the door. The door, now a gaping portal into hell, stared back at him. He bent his knees slightly, held on tight to the sides of the exit door, and peered out. The plane was shaking violently. The jumpmaster spoke into his ear, "Good luck, trooper," and squeezed his shoulder. The gesture was supposed to be comforting, but it wasn't, for Bledsoe was looking out into a world like none he had ever seen, a world filled with green and red tracers crisscrossing the black void of night just in front of him. His fingers were white from gripping the door jamb, and he tried in vain to stare straight ahead. He was praying for the light to change to green before they were shot out of the sky when the night suddenly exploded again in orange and red. Just a hundred yards to their left and slightly behind them, another aircraft had been hit by flak and burst into flames, coughing up its load of humanity. He squeezed his eyes shut and tried to block out the horror, just like he had done as a child when his father would come home drunk and beat his mother.

Sparks flew again, and Jamberdino jerked his head back as blood splattered in his face. The trooper standing beside him, Sam McClure, screamed as a piece of red-hot shrapnel tore through his foot and severed his left arm just below his elbow. Blood was flying everywhere. William and Jamberdino worked desperately to get the wounded man unhooked and out of his harness. They couldn't afford a delay now; if the jump light turned green and they didn't move quickly, they would be miles from their objective in a matter of seconds. Private Bruce Singleton, the medic assigned to them for this mission, quickly unhooked his static line and stumbled across several men in an effort to help. Dropping to his knees, he pulled a large bandage out of his medic bag and handed it to Jamberdino, who was busy trying to apply a tourniquet to the severed arm. William took the bandage and tied it around the stub of McClure's arms while several men held him down.

Some people say that Murphy sits at the right hand of the god of war, and so it was at this desperate moment the all-too-powerful Mr. Murphy decided it was a good time to change the jump light from red to green. The light flashed angrily above the head of the jumpmaster, and chaos mounted. William fought to get his men headed toward the jump door and then get his own equipment bag hooked back up after having loosened it to help Singleton. He looked up just as the jumpmaster shouted, "Go! Go! Go!" Bledsoe, who had been watching his friends and the medic struggle with McClure, locked eyes with William for just a second. He nodded, and Bledsoe was out the door into the man-made hell.

"Singleton!" shouted William as he approached the door. "We need you on the ground. Let the jumpmaster finish with McClure." The tourniquet had stopped the severed arm from bleeding, but the mangled foot still poured bright-red blood forming a puddle on the floor. William patted McClure's shoulder and then turned to follow Jamberdino out the door into the damnedest fireworks display he had ever seen. Singleton hesitated for a second while the jumpmaster bent over to wrap McClure's foot; then he jumped up and sprinted out the door behind the others.

William forced his eyes open and looked down as his chute fully unfurled. He could see most of his squad floating below him—the canopies of their chutes transparent enough that he could see the muzzle flashes from the Germans' weapons being fired in the direction of the suspended targets. Suddenly, there was a flash just behind him; he saw it out of the corner of his eye, and for a heartbeat, William thought it was the damn hawk again. Whatever it was, though, never came back. He strained his eyes, peering into the dark night, and could make out two of his men hanging lifeless in their harnesses as tracers tore through their canopies. He couldn't tell who the dead Rangers were; he just prayed to whatever god looked after men like them that it wasn't Jamberdino or Bledsoe.

Through the smoky haze, William could see a tiny village about a half mile away shrouded in the early morning mist. It was to their west, though, and if it was St. Eglish, it should be to their east; he could only hope that there hadn't been some mistake. Looking around in an effort to get his bearings and trying to remember the map, he pondered the situation. "Damn it, we must be east of our LZ," he moaned, realizing they had been dropped at least a mile from where they should be. He flinched as several tracer rounds tore through his canopy and small arms fire began to pepper the air around him. Trying hard to become smaller, he prayed for the ground to hurry.

Just to the south of where they floated earthward, the German AA batteries concentrated on the aircrafts that filled the night sky, and the Wehrmacht ground units lit up the sky with huge spotlights. The problem for his Rangers was that the damn spotlights, which were designed to expose night-flying aircrafts, were reflecting off the nylon canopies, making them perfect targets. William ducked again as several more red tracers arched up and tore through his canopy, which was beginning to look like Swiss cheese. He could feel the heat from the rounds, which passed within inches of his sweating face. Fifty more feet, and he would be down.

The enemy fire had finally turned toward the other troopers that were just now exiting their aircrafts high above, and William tore his gaze away from the horrific scene above to look back down. The ground was rushing at him, and he barely had time to prepare for his PLF. He had just released his equipment bag and bent his legs when suddenly the sky erupted in orange as yet another C-47 took a flak burst near the fuel tank and exploded. The night was filled with airplane parts and dead paratroopers.

William pulled hard on his risers just before he collided with the ground. Luckily, the recent storms had softened the earth, and all he got was a large dose of humility as he tumbled in the muddy field. Struggling out of his chute, he jumped when an unexpected voice drifted on the damp air like a leprechaun's jest: "That was the worst damn PLF I have ever been witness to."

"Fuck you, Bledsoe. I'm alive, and that's what counts." William coughed, looking around for a place to hide his chute. Bledsoe strolled through the darkness as if he were out for a morning walk, his Thompson strapped across his chest. He and William stood watching the tracers streak toward the Rangers who had just exited their aircrafts and not yet reached the ground. They stood mesmerized for a few seconds, and then Bledsoe helped his squad leader gather his gear.

"That's more than I can say for our medic," said Bledsoe as he kicked dirt over William's chute, which had been thrust in a quickly dug hole.

"What the hell is that supposed to mean?" asked William, having totally forgotten what he had just said. *Surely Singleton followed me out of the aircraft*, he thought to himself.

"Evidently, Singleton was in such a hurry to get out of the plane he forgot to hook back up," said Bledsoe as he and William walked over toward the rest of the squad. "His chute was still in the pack. He never even tried to open his reserve," continued Bledsoe. William shook his head when he realized it had been Singleton who fell past him without making a sound.

"Damn. You can bet we'll need a medic before we get out of this shit," he cursed, kicking the muddy earth.

"We already do," deadpanned Bledsoe as they neared the huddled group of Rangers.

The remainder of the squad was kneeling near a wounded Ranger when they walked up. "Who else got hit?" asked William as he watched Jamberdino work on the wounded man, whom he recognized as Brooks. The always-joking Brooks had been hit by a couple of rounds: one in the left knee and one in the left buttocks.

"Moody was hit on the way down, and so was Menickelli. They're both dead. Brooks was hit after he landed," added Bledsoe, kneeling down beside the wounded soldier, who was in a hell of a lot of pain and moaning loudly. He whispered something in Brooks's ear, and the man's eyes grew large as saucers, but he quickly quieted down. Bledsoe grabbed a stick from the ground, put it between Brooks's teeth, and turned back to his squad leader. Brooks gagged, but he didn't dare spit it out. William thought briefly about asking his friend what he had said to Brooks but decided not to. It really didn't matter. Instead, he unfolded his map, dug out his penlight, and got down to business.

"Mike, the best I can figure, we're about a mile east of where we should be, which is here." He pointed to a marked spot on the wrinkled map. "The rendezvous point is a dilapidated barn just outside of St. Eglish, supposedly to the west." He touched the map again. Both men jerked around in response to another loud moan from Brooks. "Mike, have Murdock stay here with Brooks. Tell him to do his best to keep him quiet. If the Krauts get them, they're screwed, and so are we," growled William as he folded his map and stowed it in his pack.

"Roger that," said Bledsoe, who walked over and took Private Gerald Murdock by the arm. He led him off to the side about twenty feet. "You have got to keep Brooks quiet. If the Germans catch you, our mission is dead, and so are you. Plus, a lot of other good men," he added. "Do you understand me?" Murdock looked into Bledsoe's eyes and saw the truth.

"Yeah, yeah, I understand," he said gravely.

"Good, just keep him quiet—whatever it takes." After repeating the warning, Bledsoe walked back to where the rest of the squad waited. Without saying a word, everyone shouldered their packs, and the squad—minus five men—headed west.

The Army had issued each man a small clicker device designed specifically for the invasion to allow individuals and small units to engage in nonverbal communication when they approached each other. One click meant "We are friendly" while two clicks in response meant "We understand." During their push west, William's squad was approached several times by individuals or whole units of soldiers who had been dropped miles from their intended targets. The clickers saved many lives, and by the time the Germans figured them out, most units were at least close to where they were supposed to be, making the clickers less important.

Entire companies were on the move through the countryside, looking for their objectives. Rangers and 101st Screaming Eagles were mixed with troopers from the 82nd. William's group was one of the few squad-sized units that had been assigned a mission. The powers that be, in their infinite wisdom, had figured that a small unit could better navigate the tough climb up to where the coastal guns were hidden while the main assault attacked up the sheer cliff face of Pointe du Hoc. *There was wisdom in there someplace*, thought William, *but it was deep*. His squad was the best preforming in the battalion, so they got the "golden fleece." That it was now being led by a corporal didn't matter.

Bledsoe was walking point, about twenty feet out, as they trudged west; William was next in line, keeping a close eye on his compass. The rest of the squad was spaced about ten feet apart, with Jamberdino bringing up the rear of the column. William's RTO man was right behind him, a young American Indian named Geronimo C. Valencia. He was a full-blooded Comanche from Arizona, and he swore that the *C* stood for Cochise. No one knew for sure, but it did make one hell of a good drinking story!

They had managed to travel about a mile, back to where they should have been dropped in the first place, without making any contact with the Germans. But they could see and hear small fire-fights breaking out all around them. Suddenly, without any prior warning, Bledsoe held up his hand with his fist clenched, a signal to stop. He slowly knelt down on one knee and motioned for William to come forward. William eased toward his friend at a low crouch, his M-1 held at the ready, his eyes sweeping everything to his front. When he got within a couple feet of Bledsoe, he, too, dropped to one knee and whispered, "What's the problem?" Without speaking, Bledsoe pointed to a spot about fifty yards to their east where a glider lay crumpled around a rock. It had skidded through a small field and then crashed hard into a large rock outcropping. Bodies and jeep parts were strewn everywhere. It took William a few seconds to comprehend what had happened.

"Can you tell if there are any survivors?" he asked solemnly.

"I haven't seen any movement, and I don't hear anything, so I doubt it. It's pretty torn up," answered Bledsoe as he glanced down at his watch and then back up at the wreckage. They had no medic, and time was short.

"I don't see any sign of the Krauts having been here yet either," whispered William, peering into the shadows. "We've got to get to that damn gun battery, or there will be a lot more dead bodies around here."

"Maybe the Krauts ran for the hills when they found out the Rangers were coming," grunted Bledsoe.

Glancing over at his friend, William growled, "How the hell can you joke about this shit?"

"Fuck you, William. It's how I keep focused," cursed Bledsoe. Then both men grew silent, simply staring into the dark void in front of them.

Several seconds ticked by while they stood rooted in place; smoke continued to curl up from the carnage at the glider. William's head spun in circles as he struggled with what to do, the demon of self-doubt emerging from its hiding place.

Both men jumped slightly when Jamberdino's voice screeched out of the blue, "That's a fubarred glider."

His mood sour and his patience thin, William spun around angrily. "What the hell are you doing up here, Jerry? You're supposed to be watching our backs," he snapped. His retort was harsh, and Jamberdino's frown vanished in a heartbeat. His head hanging like a scolded dog, he turned to go back to the rear of the column. *Why the hell did I come up here?* Jamberdino scolded himself. *It's sure as hell no time for being slack.* William watched his friend walk away, and he cursed too. *Calm down, Corporal, and get a damn grip on this situation.*

"Jerry," he called. But Jamberdino kept walking. "Jerry, damn it, you're already up here. Stay for a while. Cloer can take rear guard. Besides, we may need you." William watched, a smile spread over his friend's face as he headed back toward them.

They made the joint decision to press on and not spend time at the wreckage, but they all eyed the glider as they moved quietly past it and into the night, wondering if it was the right decision. The wreckage soon faded into the damp mist, and their training took over. While their eyes darted from one side of the road to the other, every tree limb and piece of brush crowding the narrow path become the enemy. "The map says it's a road, but hell, it's only a damn pig trail," grunted William after he tripped and nearly fell over a rock.

"White men," Valencia retorted under his breath, picking up the rock. *How the hell did they win the west?* he fumed to himself before tossing the fist-sized stone into the bushes and trudging after his squad leader.

"Stay alert and stay alive" was the golden rule of the night fighters, and William sure needed to stay alert. His mind was constantly going over his many challenges, top among them being the reduced size of his unit. He simply did not have enough men. They were down to ten already and hadn't even reached the damn climb yet. He cursed the powers that be for their frugal use of manpower. His mind snapped back to the situation at hand, though, when Bledsoe swung the column toward a clump of trees about a hundred yards to their left and up a small rise.

A well-worn footpath led past a copse of trees in the direction of a fairly large opening in the hedgerow. Bledsoe's big hand went up, and he signaled for everyone to stop. Another hand sign followed, telling William to come forward slowly. Crawling forward with Jamberdino in tow, William rose up on one knee by Bledsoe's side.

"I don't like the looks of that opening," whispered Bledsoe.

"I don't like it either, Mike, but we don't have any other choice. We have to go in that direction," said William, pointing past the opening. "We've got to rendezvous with that damn Frenchie, and he's on the other side of that hedgerow. Without him, we will probably never find that trail up the cliff, especially in the dark," he went on as if talking to himself, all the while staring at the dark opening.

"I'll bet a month's pay the damn Krauts have a machine gun nest, or maybe two, covering that opening," moaned Jamberdino as they crouched behind a small tree.

"Yeah, I know. That's a fine place for an ambush, but that's still the damn direction we have to go in," said William, thinking back to Sergeant Baker's word on his promotion. *Don't be so quick to thank me. You may get your ass shot off, or worse, you may get your friends killed.* He shook his head to clear his mind and then turned to look at Jamberdino. "Jerry, I want you to go back and stay with the squad. Mike and I are going to have a closer look at that opening." Jamberdino didn't say a word; he simply nodded as his two friends began low crawling forward. Actually, he was okay not going forward with his buddies, and that realization surprised him a little. On the other hand, he was still sort of proud of his own calmness out here in this hellhole, and he smiled to himself as he eased back to where the others knelt.

William, with Bledsoe right beside him, crept forward for another fifty yards before stopping. He took a deep breath and began to rise up on one knee for a better look at the opening, but Bledsoe's big hand grabbed his shoulder, and he froze. Unable to see a damn thing, he was about to say something but changed his mind. He trusted his buddy and knew better than to question his actions, so he eased back down into a low-crawl position. Bledsoe was staring into the dark like a shaman but finally gave the hand signal for "I hear something," and William understood. They both tried to slow their breathing and listen despite the night sounds that were erupting around them. Suddenly, the faint glow of a cigarette could be seen in the hedgerow about thirty feet from the right corner of the opening. After a few seconds, the sound of German voices drifted toward the two Rangers' ears. They listened for a minute and then looked at each other; William motioned with his head back to the squad.

They began to crawl ever so slowly back the way they had come. As they got closer to the rest of the squad, they crawled faster and faster until finally they were nearly running on their hands and knees. When they reached the safety of the trees and the company of the other Rangers, the two men rolled over onto their backs and sucked huge breaths of air into their lungs. "That was too damn close," moaned Bledsoe. Jamberdino and the others watched in curious fascination as their squad leader finally rolled back over and struggled to sit up. "Okay, people," he announced, having caught his breath enough to speak. "There are Krauts covering that opening in the damn hedgerow. We don't know how many troops or how many machine guns, but we can't afford a long firefight, so we have got to find another way through that hedge." The other Rangers just looked at each other.

Huddled in the damp grass near the small clump of trees, they fidgeted with their weapons; nobody seemed to know exactly what to do. "Corporal Craig," a voice called from the back of the group. It was the other Italian boy from the Bronx, Cipriani, and all heads turned in his direction. "I remember seeing an old farmhouse on the map." William waited, a little confused, for him to go on.

"So ..." Bledsoe finally grunted from his prone position.

"What's that got to do with our current problem?" William asked patiently as he studied the map he had just pulled out of his pack again.

"Well, it's marked as ruins on the map, right?" Cipriani asked, while William stared at the map.

"Yeah," answered William. Everyone else just responded to the dark-haired Italian with confused looks.

"Go on," urged Bledsoe, rising to one knee, already guessing Cipriani's point.

"Well, if there is an old house there, then maybe there is an opening—maybe one the Germans haven't found."

"Maybe. Hell, Cipriani, I bet you're right. If there is an old house, then there has to be some kind of an opening," said Bledsoe excitedly. He got up and looked over William's shoulder at the map.

"I hope you two are right," grunted William, "because it's a little out of our way. But it seems to be the best shot we've got." He rolled up the map and was fixing to stow it in his pack when a Hershey's bar fell out of a side pocket.

Bledsoe snatched it up, broke it in half, and mumbled, "Thank you," before shouldering his pack.

"You're welcome, asshole," growled William as he munched on his half while sliding his pack onto his shoulders. Jamberdino walked over and patted Cipriani on the back, and the little man smiled proudly.

In less than a minute, they were moving in search of a safe passage through the impenetrable hedgerow that blocked their route to the shore battery. The battery, if not destroyed, would rain death and destruction down on the boys trying to come ashore at Utah Beach as well as the big destroyers that were to soften up the landing area.

Bledsoe was walking point, as usual, as they moved slowly in the direction of the old farmhouse, a little northwest of their original path. The heavy cloud cover was breaking up, and the moon was peeking out for a look-see every now and then, much to the chagrin of the men who crept along the trail. The path led toward the ruins and ran parallel to the hedgerow that loomed large and foreboding a hundred yards to their west. Their detour around the machine gun nests took fifteen minutes of valuable time, but they had no other choice. William remained about ten paces behind Bledsoe, with Valencia, his RTO, close at hand.

The constant firing from the AA batteries kept everyone on edge, and each shadow took the shape of a German. The extreme closeness of the small arms fire told them that the Krauts were out there in the dark somewhere. William was staring at what resembled a 105 howitzer over near the hedgerow but was actually a large dead snag sticking out of the brush when he noticed Bledsoe go into a quick crouch and then stop. William halted the squad in another clump of trees before he went forward to where Bledsoe was kneeling. He had learned Bledsoe's method of scouting, and neither of them spoke as they stared at the old farm ruins.

"I don't like the looks of this either, William. I'll bet ten bucks the Krauts are in that damn building," whispered Bledsoe as cold sweat rolled down into his eyes. The old farmhouse, marked as ruins on the map, stood fifty yards east of the hedgerow at the top of a small rise. Bledsoe wiped the back of his hand across his brow and fought the urge to sling the sweat from his hand. Sudden movement like that could attract unwanted attention, and you could end up getting yourself shot.

"You could be right," replied William as they both strained their eyes in an attempt to see any telltale sign of the Germans. "But I don't see anything."

"Do you want me to check it out?" asked Bledsoe with a nervous edge in his voice. He glanced several times from the ruins back to his squad leader as he waited for an answer. William stared at the ruins, too, and hesitated for a second without answering. Then he looked back toward where the rest of the squad waited.

His mind shouted, *No!* But he knew it was the right thing to do. "No, Mike. I need you here. I'll send Jerry," he finally answered. "Besides, he's more rested." Bledsoe looked at his friend, then back toward where Jamberdino sat talking to Frady. He and William briefly exchanged glances before William eased back to where Jamberdino knelt. He looked his friend in the eye. "Jerry, I need you to scout that hedgerow." He nodded toward the mass of tangled hedge. "I want you to ease up against it, be watchful around that old building, and see if you can find any sort of opening in that mess. And remember, we don't have much time." William watched his friend stare at the hedgerow. "Jerry, you with me?"

"Yeah, I got you," replied Jamberdino.

"Okay," grunted William. "If you find any kind of passable opening, use your clicker … twice. Do you understand?" He asked the question with a hint of worry in his voice because his friend was just staring at him as if he wasn't sure what was going on. After a second, Jamberdino simply nodded because his heart was beating way too fast to trust a reply. Turning slowly toward the hedge, he started to leave when William grabbed his arm. "Be careful, you damn Yankee. We need you with us!"

"Airborne," said Jamberdino with a sheepish smile, and he moved off into the night.

"I hope to God he's careful," whispered Bledsoe as he and William watched their friend walk in a crouch toward the hedgerow.

"He'll do what he needs to do," answered William. Baker's words, "Don't thank me," echoed again in his brain.

"Geronimo, get on the horn and try to raise Lieutenant Ellis or Sergeant Baker. Tell them where we're at and find out what the hell's going on." Valencia took the radio from his back and cranked on the handle.

"Blackhawk One, this is Night Eyes, over." Static crackled in the night air. He waited a second and cranked on the handset once again, repeating the call: "Blackhawk One, this is Night Eyes, do you copy? Over." Nothing. "Damn radios," growled the young Indian. "Might as well use smoke signals."

"Try again," whispered William. "We need to talk to them." Valencia shook his head but tried once more to raise either Ellis or Baker. He failed. Angrily, he slipped the radio onto his back and knelt with his carbine across his knee.

A hundred yards away, Jamberdino was having troubles of his own. First, he was wondering why William had picked him for this damn recon. Second, why he had so easily agreed. "I can't see a damn thing," he moaned to the darkness. *But guess what, you wop, maybe the Germans can't see any better than you can,* he quarreled at himself as he crept along. Moving forward in the traditional half crouch, he made his way quietly alongside the dark mass of the hedgerow. A stiff breeze out of the west rustled the leaves in the treetops near the dilapidated building, and like an invisible hand, it began to chase the early morning mist—just as Jamberdino's hopes began fading. He blinked several times as the mist swirled around him in a last-ditch effort to see what obviously wasn't there. As the night began to clear, he spotted what looked like some kind of black hole. Was it an opening? He looked again. *Yes!* his mind screamed. It was small and overgrown, but as he got closer, he realized it was definitely some kind of entrance into the otherwise-impenetrable wall of vegetation. "I'll be damned. Cipriani was right," he cursed and immediately crossed himself, like a good Catholic, for invoking damnation. *Now isn't a good time to piss off God,* he surmised as he contemplated how to approach the opening.

Remembering his training, he dropped onto his belly and low crawled the last few feet to the opening. "Hell yeah," he whispered as he looked into the hole and then reached for his clicker. A pitiful cry rose in his throat as his fingertips searched for the small piece of metal but found only lint. Panic and uncertainty began to spread up his empty fingers to his mind. "Damn it. I know I had it in my pocket," he groaned as he searched his pockets once more for the clicker—and found nothing. He sank slowly down to his haunches and looked back across the now-sinister-looking field toward where his friends anxiously waited for his signal. "God, if I cross that field one more time, I may push my luck too damn far," he moaned, his hands desperately searching the ground around him for the lost clicker. But again, he came up empty. After a couple more minutes of frantic but fruitless searching along his approach path, a realization finally sank in. He would have to cross the field again. "I was only kidding about you being back in Oban, Lord." He prayed a small prayer, rubbed his rosary, which was around his neck, and rose reluctantly back into a half crouch. He took one tentative step toward his buddies, then another and another, until at last he had reached the top of a small rise in the old pasture. It was at this exact moment that the quarter moon decided to make an appearance from behind the scattered clouds and its muted light spread across the field like a stage light on a Shakespearian actor.

Jamberdino froze. Without looking around, he knew he had become silhouetted against the skyline like a chimneysweep from an old Dickens novel he had once read. At the bottom of the field, William, Bledsoe, and the rest of the squad could only watch. Sadly, they weren't the only ones to see Jamberdino plastered on the skyline. A young German gunner on the other side of the field saw him also. Bledsoe started to run forward, but William grabbed his arm. "We can't" was all he said, and Bledsoe banged his head in the dirt in frustration. "Get down, damn it, or run," he cried softly, and they watched helplessly.

Jamberdino's brain screamed, *Run!* And he did finally start to run, but it was a little late. Seconds later, his heart nearly stopped when he heard the unmistakable sound of a round being chambered in a weapon. He remembered the sound from his training at Oban and knew it was probably a Messerschmitt air-cooled machine gun being readied. And it was close. The modern advancements in weapons of war had far outpaced the human ability for flight, and because of that, a deadly race began. Jamberdino ran as fast and as low as his lanky frame would allow, his legs pounding the earth as fear drove him forward. The Messerschmitt MG 34 is a very reliable weapon, capable of firing 360 rounds of .45-caliber bullets in one minute. The weapon was being sighted by a young but combat-hardened veteran of the Afrika Corps. An Iron Cross pin adorned his field uniform. The Wehrmacht grenadier looked down the barrel and placed the sights slightly ahead of the crouched figure running on top of the ridge. Why the American was in plain sight on the ridgetop, the young German neither knew nor cared. The moon was being fickle, playing hide-and-seek with the clouds, and Jamberdino's silhouette faded in and out of sight as a result. But the firepower of the Messerschmitt MG was in experienced hands. A calloused finger tightened on the trigger just as the moon goddess peeked down on the mortals once again, and the muzzle of the machine gun exploded red.

The first six-round burst streaked just in front of Jamberdino's chest, missing him by mere inches, but for some unknown reason, he never changed course. His eyes were glued on the clump of trees that hid his friends, and he ran straight for them. The Messerschmitt belched again, and this time it didn't miss. The burst struck Jamberdino across the right thigh. The .45-caliber rounds hit bone, and he straightened up in pain as his stride faltered. He ran straight into the next three rounds that stitched across his stomach and severed his spine. Private Jerry Jamberdino from Buffalo, New York, never felt the impact of the ground as his limp body slammed hard into the damp earth of the pasture. The remaining rounds flew harmlessly over his head and reflected red and green in his dead eyes.

"Get down!" Bledsoe screamed in a hushed whisper as he watched his friend race for his life. But he was racing against .45-caliber bullets, and there could be only one winner. William closed his eyes and then dropped his head when Jamberdino's body jerked from the impact of the rounds. "He's hit," cried someone needlessly as Bledsoe led everyone forward. They sprinted toward Jamberdino's body, using a slight depression in the pasture as cover for their approach.

They reached the limp and bloody form just as the moon, whose light had revealed Jamberdino's position, snuck back behind the rushing clouds, as if trying to separate itself from the tragedy that just occurred. William helped Bledsoe drag the lifeless body off the ridge and down out of sight of the Germans. Bledsoe cradled Jamberdino's head in his lap and cried, "Oh god, oh god," over and over. He first shook the lifeless body in some futile attempt to revive him, and when that failed, he simply held his friend tenderly in his arms; tears mixed with blood ran down Jamberdino's pale cheeks.

The remainder of the squad circled their fallen comrade as Bledsoe continued to rock the lifeless body. William sat off to the side with his head buried in his hands. After several uneasy minutes, Lazcano crept forward and called, "Corporal Craig, Corporal Craig, what do we do now?" The question hung in the air like the tracers that were constantly arching skyward. In William's mind, he heard Sergeant Baker's word once again: "Don't thank me. Those stripes come with a hell of a lot of responsibility."

A dark and sad part of his brain screamed, *Leave me alone! Just leave me the hell alone.* But another part soon challenged, *No, we have to go on.* And that voice grew louder. William looked up at the expectant faces of the men, blinked a couple of times, and then squeezed his eyes shut. After a second, he opened them, shook his head as if coming out of a daze, and growled, "Okay, people, listen up. We're Rangers, by God, and we have a job to do." Everyone nodded. "Then let's finish it." Standing up, he turned and looked over at his two friends, one dead and one still alive. Sighing, he reached out to Bledsoe and gently touched him on the shoulder. "Mike, we have to move. We're out in the open. We have to get through that damn hedgerow." Bledsoe didn't say a word. He just rocked his dead friend. After another minute, William called out again: "Mike, Mike, damn it. We've got to move now!" Mike Bledsoe finally looked up at William as if he were a stranger, and then gently laid his buddy's head down on the wet ground and stood up. William took one last look at Jamberdino's body before leading his squad toward the dark and sinister-looking hedgerow that seemed to stare back at them with malevolence.

Working their way cautiously across the lower edge of the field, they crept up against the hedgerow and walked in its shadow. Unknowingly, they traveled in Jamberdino's footsteps for about twenty-five or thirty feet until they spotted the opening that he had found. The black hole glared back at them; it had already taken one life and seemed hungry for more. William was about ten feet out from the hedge and about that same distance from the opening when he stepped on something metallic; he froze, thinking it might be a land mine. His right foot felt like lead, and the weight of it caused a muffled metallic click; he knew instantly what it was. He bent down—his pounding heart gradually slowing—and his fingers found the clicker Jamberdino must have inadvertently dropped. He picked it up reverently and looked at it as if the small shiny piece of metal could tell him what had happened to their buddy.

"I'll bet Jerry somehow dropped the damn thing, and that's why he was coming back to us, to tell us about the opening." He closed his eyes to thank his friend and then carefully put the clicker in his pocket. Bledsoe, who stood a couple of feet away, just looked at him. *His eyes seem to be boring straight through me*, thought William, the coldness of the metal clicker burning his leg. The big blond-headed kid from Knoxville said nothing. William shrugged off his pack, dug out his map again, and carefully marked the location of Jamberdino's body so that the grave registration team could find it later.

Rechecking the location of the farmhouse ruins, he restowed the map, grabbed his pack, which was loaded with C-2, and slung it back on. Then he led the way into the vine-covered hole. Slowly, reluctantly, the men followed. With their eyes darting from side to side, they nervously filed through the tunnel of vegetation like insects sneaking into a spider's web. Everybody except Bledsoe trudged through the opening. Mike Bledsoe didn't follow the others; he had only one thing on his mind, and it wasn't going through that damn opening. It was ... revenge. He turned back toward the field and low crawled over the wet grass toward the old farmhouse where he had seen the fire that cut down Jamberdino had come from. The damn Krauts killed his friend, and now he was hunting them. As he crawled along, he smelled harsh Turkish cigarette smoke well before he actually spotted the machine gun nest. Cautiously, he moved ever closer until he heard whispering, German whispering, "Das Amerika, Amerika kaput," and then laughter. Bledsoe's blood boiled as he crawled within ten yards of where the three Germans Wehrmacht troopers manned the machine gun. But unlike his friend, he was coming up from behind the gun crew. Without thinking or even caring, Mike Bledsoe stood up and walked up to the three German soldiers. He stopped when he was about five feet behind them and patiently waited for their reaction.

The fickle moon decided once again to come out of hiding, and its appearance cast an eerie glow on the surprised Germans, who spun around and stared down the barrel of Bledsoe's Thompson submachine gun. The moon seemed to work for the Americans this time as Bledsoe fired three well-controlled bursts into the chest of each German as they struggled to fire their own weapons. The Afrika Korps veteran who had killed Jamberdino and joked about it just a moment before was still alive. Bledsoe stared down at him in a rage. "Bitte, bitte," pleaded the young gunner, shifting his gaze from his bleeding stomach and painfully looking up into the hate-filled eyes of the American. There was no mercy in the dark orbs that stared back at him. Tears of pain and regret streamed from the eyes of the young German as the commando knife came toward his throat. Death is never easy, but helplessly watching it approach is the worst.

Bledsoe finished the task and then raced away from the gun position, but only after having wiped the blood from his knife on the uniforms of the three dead Wehrmacht grenadiers, especially the one with the Iron Cross whose throat he had cut. The guttural sound of excited German voices could be heard on the dead men's radio as Bledsoe sprinted into the hole. Hurriedly, he caught up with the tail end of the squad about half a mile on the other side of the deadly barrier. He didn't bother using his clicker to signal his approach; he simply stepped out of the shadows behind Sam Frady. Frady, on edge like everyone else, spun around with his carbine at the ready, his finger roughly caressing the trigger. Bledsoe grabbed the cold steel of the barrel as it swung toward his stomach and pushed it aside.

"It's me," he said, holding the weapon out away from him.

"Damn you, Bledsoe. I thought you were a Kraut," cursed Frady, who angrily jerked his weapon from Bledsoe's grasp.

He glanced nervously from Bledsoe's blood-splattered face to the last man in line, who just had disappeared around a bend in the trail. Frustrated, Frady shouldered his carbine and turned to head after his friends. "If I had been a damn German, you would be dead right now," whispered Bledsoe as he brushed by Frady and quickly moved to the front of the squad. He started to resume his position at point but was jerked to a stop by Corporal Craig.

"Where the hell have you been?" he asked, releasing his grip on Bledsoe's arm and moving in close so that he could look his friend in the eye. Bledsoe stared back with an almost vacant look, and William's eyes traveled down to the bloody handle of his commando knife. He shook his head as he looked back up. "Mike, I need you with me to finish this damn mission." He paused. "We can't afford to lose another man."

"You should have thought of that before you sent Jamberdino to find that damn opening," growled Bledsoe under his breath.

As he looked his friend in the eye, tension mixed with anger poured from the big squad leader. The silence was palpable until at last Bledsoe spoke, "I'm back. Okay, I'm with you now, so let's go." The two men stood toe-to-toe looking at each other for a long time as the remainder of the squad stood back and watched. Finally, William shed his pack and reached for his map.

With penlight in hand, he knelt and spread the map on the damp grass. "Tell me what you think," he managed to say to Bledsoe, who knelt down stiffly and peered at the spot on the map. "We're supposed to meet the Frenchie at an abandoned farm just outside of St. Eglish, about here." He pointed to an X on the map. "The barn is supposed to have the remnants of a red tile roof. The walls are probably pretty well torn down, and according to the boys in S-2, the Germans won't be using it."

"I guess we'll find out soon enough," grunted Bledsoe. William shook the moisture from the map and put it away. He stood up and re-shouldered the canvas pack, which seemed to get heavier by the minute.

"The Frenchie is supposed to be aware of our clickers," said William offhandedly as he looked at his squad.

"Then maybe he won't shoot us like those French bastards who shot up part of the 2nd Rangers near the Libyan capital," said Bledsoe without any humor in his dull voice. William glanced at his friend and then turned to the squad. "Okay, people, let's move out slowly and keep your damn eyes and ears open."

After about fifteen minutes of anxious walking, William stopped the group of tired, demoralized Rangers and again motioned for Bledsoe to kneel beside him. Jamberdino's death had cast a veil of gloom over everybody, and it showed in their nervous body language. *I hope to hell we're on target*, thought William as he broke out his well-worn map for the hundredth time and looked toward the west. "That looks like the old barn over there." He pointed toward a dilapidated barn that stood in the mist off in the distance. The barn, which they could see at the edge of an old field, had a few red tiles still intact on its roof—a roof that had partially caved in years before.

Everyone's eyes were on the barn when Bledsoe asked, "Do you want me to go check it out?"

William never hesitated as he shot back. "No. I'll go, Mike. I need you here, and I need you to have a clear head. If I'm not back in fifteen minutes or if you hear shots, I want you to try to find that trail up the cliff by yourself. I'll leave you the map, but remember, we only have two hours before the ships will appear on the horizon." He looked at his watch, as did everyone else. "We have got to stop those guns."

"I'm clearheaded," Bledsoe retorted, a hint of anger in his voice. "Very clearheaded. We'll get those damn guns," he added. William looked at his friend, and Bledsoe's eyes never wavered. *Good*, he thought, *maybe he is back*. Then William moved out in search of the Frenchman.

It was a difficult few minutes of walking; William skirted the edge of the field so that he could approach the barn through a clump of small trees and long green running briars. He crouched down behind a pile of half-rotten logs and scanned the area around the barn from about fifty feet away. Seeing nothing out of the ordinary, he crept forward until he was beside an outer wall that was connected to what remained of a corral. He unfastened the chinstrap of his steel pot and carefully removed the helmet before raising his head to inspect the barnyard. "Shit!" he cried out, startled by the black eyes of a dove staring straight into his own. The bird sat there calmly as if it had been expecting him. "Damn, not again, not now," he cursed as he dropped back down and leaned against the wall to gather his thoughts.

He closed his eyes and took a deep breath, steeling his resolve. He stood up slowly, hoping it was all an illusion from battle stress. No such luck, though; the dove was still there. "Just leave me the hell alone," he growled, shooing at the bird in an effort to scare it away. But the dove just walked along the rock wall like any normal dove would. Its feathers were slightly ruffled as if annoyed by the presence of the human, but after a minute, it seemed to tire of the game and flew into the dark loft of the barn ruins, its gray wings beating the air fiercely. "Hellfire. Why me?" cursed William as he inched his way along the outer wall of an adjacent shed until, at last, he could see into the main part of the barn. He pulled out Jamberdino's clicker and looked at it for a second before mashing it twice. Nothing, not a sound in reply. He waited two minutes and depressed the clicker twice more.

More silence. He stood with his head cocked to the side—straining to hear something, anything—when he was startled yet again, but this time by a soft female voice behind him.

"You could wake the dead with that thing, monsieur. Or worse, wake the Germans," the voice added. He spun around quickly, knuckles white from bearing down on the stock of his carbine, his finger tightened on the trigger. When he saw who spoke to him, he managed to keep from pulling the trigger. Unfortunately, his feet slipped in the wet grass, and he lost his balance in the turn. He fell unceremoniously at the feet of a darkly clad woman, who scoffed at him in English laced with a strong French accent: "And you Americans expect to defeat the Germans, huh?" William pulled himself up from the muddy ground and sheepishly brushed the dirt from his trousers and the stock of his weapon, which had dug into the damp earth. He didn't make eye contact with the Frenchie for a minute, but he finally looked down at the figure standing in the shadows in front of him.

Blinking a couple of times, he looked closely at the partly obscured face that stared back at him from underneath a dark hood and gasped, "Oh my god, not you." He rubbed his eyes in disbelief.

"I beg your pardon, monsieur." She waited for a reply while William growled to himself, *Not now, not here!* The woman had the hood of her cloak pulled around her face, but it only partially hid her features. And William could see her eyes clearly. This woman was a spitting image of the ghost lady from the cave back in Oban.

"You ... you look so much like someone I met back in Scotland," he stammered, glancing around, half expecting the big Norseman to step out of the shadows. The combat-ready Ranger with his face blackened and the darkly clad lady stood staring at each other; neither moved nor said a word. William had to resist the urge to reach out and touch her to see if she was real or not.

"Are you the French partisan we are supposed to meet?" William asked the question grudgingly as he slowly regained his composure. "And if you are, what's the damn password?" He was angry with himself for letting her sneak up on him and was trying hard to regain a little dignity, but he couldn't resist putting a little indignation in his voice.

"Monsieur, it is a little late for the use of a password. If I were a German spy, you would be dead by now, as well as the eight men hiding back on the ridge," replied the young woman calmly, nodding in the direction William had come from.

"Okay, okay, but just humor me and tell me the damn password," he said as he raised the muzzle of his carbine ever so slightly.

The woman looked at William's M-1, then up at him, and smiled.

"The password is *firefly*, monsieur, and it seems very appropriate indeed for a night like tonight." She glanced around at the sky that was filled with tracers—red, green, and white. In some bizarre way, they did resemble fireflies.

"Okay, that's better. Now I'm Corporal Craig of the 2nd Rangers, and—"

She interrupted him, "I know who you are, William. I know all about you."

He glared at her for a second. "Well, well, so you guessed my name. Maybe you were with a circus before the war, I don't know, but what I do know is we can't stand here all night, chatting. I'll go get my men. You wait here." He shouldered his weapon and headed off toward where the squad sat waiting. As he walked away from the barn, he kept looking back over his shoulder. *At least she didn't disappear ... this time*, he said to himself, finally turning fully away from the barn and the woman.

In a few minutes, he returned with his small band of warriors to the bar. They were within ten yards of the partisan when the unmistakable whistle of incoming artillery shattered the silence of the night. Everybody hit the dirt as several rounds screeched overhead and exploded near the back of the dilapidated old barn. A loud clatter from falling lumber erupted somewhere inside the dark interior as the whole structure shook from the impact of the shells. William couldn't tell if it was American or German artillery, but it really didn't matter. It was too damn close, and either one could kill you.

"That was German artillery, monsieur," said the woman matter-of-factly as if reading his mind. The other Rangers stood and brushed mud and grass from their trousers. "They are still somewhat confused about who you are and what you are trying to do," she added.

"Well, if that's the case, let's hope they stay confused just a little while longer," said William as he fell in several steps behind the woman, who was already headed up the trail.

"They won't," she replied without looking back, her dark silhouette merging with the shadows along the trail.

The Rangers had to quicken their pace as they followed her through the brush toward the high bluff that towered in front of them like some medieval castle. Pointe du Hoc waited for them in the early morning fog.

William's left knee was hurting, and he walked with a slight limp about ten paces behind her as they trudged through the brush. His mind flashed back to his last game against Swain County and the jarring tackle that had twisted his knee: *That hurt like hell!* He groaned from the vivid memory. Meanwhile, this mysterious woman had disappeared around a slight bend in the trail, and William cursed himself as he increased his pace. *How could she ease along the trail without making a damn sound? Like a ghost,* his mind told him. She seemed to float in and out of sight in the thick underbrush of the so-called trail. They had walked about a mile when the girl suddenly stopped. William held up his hand with his fist clenched, and the well-trained members of his squad quickly dropped to a one-knee defensive position and waited. He crept forward until he stood beside the dark figure, almost invisible in the shadows.

"The trail starts up the cliff here. The Germans will have sentries on the ledge just below the big guns. How many, I'm not sure. At least three," she continued as she turned her gaze from the dark trail to look him in the eyes.

"The sentries will be good soldiers, monsieur. Probably hardened in North Africa or the Eastern front. They will be alert, have no doubt." A few feet away, Frady nudged his buddy Lazcano, who knelt beside him.

"I sure like the way she talks," he whispered, staring at her like a moonstruck teenager. William glanced over and shot him a dirty look, but he said nothing, concentrating on what she was telling him.

"What will you do while we go up the cliff?" asked Bledsoe, who stood off to the side, staring up the cliff like everyone else.

"I'm going with you," she answered calmly and turned to head up the trail.

William's head snapped around. "The hell you are," he grunted in a strained whisper, reaching for her shoulder. Her skin felt hot under his grip, and she turned to face him with an angry stare.

"I'm going, William. You will need me," she stated flatly, their eyes locked in a mental struggle. The young partisan and hardened Ranger stood glaring at each other as a hawk's shrill cry echoed eerily over the cliffs. All eyes shot skyward again.

A swirling mist, pale and dirty, rushed in from the sea, its tentacles wrapping around boulders and trees alike. The hawk's mournful cry seemed to radiate from the rough granite face of Pointe du Hoc.

"He calls us, William," she whispered in a voice so low that no one heard but him.

"Huh," he scoffed, tearing his eyes from the steep crag. He started to say more—actually needed to say more—but she was already gone up the steep trail. He held onto the straps of his pack and watched her disappear into the night.

"I don't even know your damn name." He groaned to the vacant space in front of him and shook his head. Sullenly repositioning his pack, he headed up the trail after her. Bledsoe, lost in the shadows, watched William move up the trail and out of sight before he looked skyward again. He could barely make out the hawk as it circled high overhead, its dark shadow passing just in front of him. "Let's go, people," he growled, grabbing his pack. *This damn thing weighs a ton*, he whined to himself and then almost laughed at his complaining. He grunted as he struggled into the pack straps. He chanced one last glimpse at the hawk, and as he looked skyward, its shadow fell across his face. A strange chill passed through him like a sharp knife, and he almost stopped in his tracks. Frady, who was walking with his head down just behind him, nearly ran into the big Tennessean.

"You all right, Bledsoe?" he asked, taking a step back. Bledsoe turned slowly and looked at him.

"Yeah," he answered weakly and started up the trail. *It's just a damn night chill*, he told his worried mind, but it conjured up images of the big Viking from Ranger School just the same. Refusing to look up again, he somewhat reluctantly led the rest of the squad up the steep incline.

The climb was steeper and more difficult than they thought it would be, but it was nothing like the hard going their fellow Rangers were having on the cliffs near the beach. The long days of disciplined training they received from the British commandos served them well as they made the ascent in complete silence without a single injury. Not one displaced rock tumbled down the mountain, and no loose equipment clanged to warn the Germans of their approach. This female partisan, who never seemed out of breath, was still slightly in front of William as they neared the ledge where the Germans patrolled. He glanced at his watch, which read 0329. They had to blow the guns by 0400!

William, stopping to catch his breath, signaled for Bledsoe to come up beside him. "Mike, take two men and eliminate the sentries," he said stoically, looking his friend in the eyes. Bledsoe never said a word; he simply nodded, moved back down the trail, and tapped Frady's shoulder, then Cloer's. Together, they started up the trail, which was extremely narrow in places. The three men had to squeeze by William and the Frenchie, who hugged the edge of a rock outcropping in order to let them pass. As Bledsoe eased by, he reached out his hand to rub her ass, but instead of tender flesh, he felt the tip of a small dagger prick his hand. "Damn," he gasped and brought his hand up to his mouth to suck the blood. Her white teeth shone in a smile as she sheathed the small knife and moved tight up against the rock. "Go do your job, monsieur," she whispered in his ear as he passed.

A few minutes later, Bledsoe crouched in the dark shadows cast by several conifers and timed the sentries as they walked the rocky path, the cut on his hand forgotten. One sentry passed by every six minutes. *That's good*, he thought, closing the cover on his watch. It would give them time to hide each body before the next soldier had a chance to see it. And as best he could tell there were only three of them, just like she said. The only problem that flashed through his mind was that there was no way of telling how long the sentries' watch was, but on second thought, he realized it really didn't matter.

He slid his knife, its handle encrusted with dry blood from its damp sheath and signaled to the other two Rangers that he was going to use a standard rear takedown of the next guard who passed. Bledsoe was extremely good at the rear takedown; his big hands gave him strength, and he had an uncanny feel for where the blade should go. The left hand would clamp firmly over the mouth to prevent a scream, while the right hand drove the blade between the seventh and eighth rib deep into the kidney. When the blade was in, he then pulled up toward the heart and twisted. If the knife wasn't placed correctly, then the next move was to extract it and try to cut the throat. This method was messier but very effective.

The first grenadier who approached the kill zone happened not to be a veteran as the Frenchie had said. He was, in fact, a new recruit, fresh out of his basic training. But his two buddies, the other sentries, were veterans. They had served with Rommel in the deserts of Africa and had often given the boy—as they liked to call him—hell for never having seen combat in North Africa or the Eastern front. The young grenadier walked the rocky path with his rifle slung over his right shoulder; a cigarette hung from lips, shadowed by a peach fuzz mustache. He was a small-framed kid from a village just outside of Cologne; he was a little frightened and significantly awed by the firefights that raged far below him. The sound of hundreds of planes passing overhead shook the mountain. The sheer height of Pointe du Hoc gave a false sense of security to all of the guards, and tonight it allowed for a fine view of the aerial battle—a battle that lit up the night sky, especially to the southeast, where red and green tracers, plus the brilliant AA flak, bursts painted a bizarre tapestry of death.

The young grenadier's mind was on the firefights that were erupting below him, which proved to be a fatal mistake. Bledsoe's powerful arms reached out and jerked the kid's head back as his hand covered the young German's mouth. The cold steel of the commando knife slammed between the seventh and eighth rib on its way toward the kidney. The blade struck with such force that air burst from the boy's lungs with a gushing sound. Seconds later, Bledsoe laid the dead German on the ground—his eyes, still wide open, saw nothing. Frady and Cloer dragged the body off the trail and hid it in the bushes, then carefully eased back and waited for the other two guards.

* * * * *

A gray mist swirled ghostlike through the windswept oak trees as William crouched in the shadows of the high rocky point and allowed his mind to race through the events back at the cave above Oban. He was still confused, not to mention unsettled, by the host of strange events that had transpired, including his apparent connection to the hawk and dove. The bizarre scene was floating through his memory when the high-pitched, haunting cry of the hawk shot into his consciousness. William jumped slightly and cursed under his breath. Cocking his head to the side, he listened to the raptor's call as it eerily drifted across the cliff; then he turned toward the supposed Frenchie, who stood looking up into the night as if she could see what no one else could.

He watched her out of the corner of his eye. Her slight athletic frame exuded a great deal of grace and power, and she reminded him of his wife. He wondered if they, too, were kindred spirits. After several minutes, William finally asked, "Do I know you from someplace?" He asked the question even though he was slightly afraid of the answer he might receive. While obviously contemplating the answer, the young French woman reached up and slowly removed the hood that hid her pretty face. Her hair, dark and unruly, blew about her face, and she had to fight with the curls that attempted to cover her pale but flawless complexion. He almost smiled at her struggle as he waited for an answer.

She hesitated, bringing her hair under control with a narrow strip of ribbon. Then finally she turned toward him and replied, "You know me from many places, William." Her eyes locked onto his as she spoke.

Breaking the eye contact, which unnerved him, he shook his head in disgust. "That's not a damn answer," he snorted and turned to walk away.

She didn't follow him but called in a low voice, "Your destiny is tied to mine, as well as our friend," explained the girl as she looked again into the night, the hawk's lonely cry echoing off the high cliffs as if in answer to the assertion.

William turned around and walked back to the girl. "How the hell can a hawk be part of my destiny?" he growled, nervously glancing from her, to his watch, and then back. She didn't answer for a minute, so he grunted, "That's what I figured," and turned his back to her before checking his watch one more time.

"Time will show you, William." Her voice sounded faraway.

"Time, huh? I'll tell you about time. It's time that Bledsoe was back. That's all I know about time." Just then, Bledsoe stepped out of the dark shadows that lay along the trail like some spirit of the night.

He looked first at his squad leader and then at the girl before he spoke: "I left Frady and Cloer back on the ledge in case anyone comes looking for the three sentries," he whispered to William, but he was looking over his shoulder and watching this woman. William simply nodded as he motioned for everybody to gather around him.

"Okay, people. You know your jobs, so let's go to work." This time, he led the way toward the high ledge. Luckily, the trail was easier to follow here. Their mystifying guide walked several paces back. The pungent odor of fresh blood and soiled uniforms hung in the damp morning air as they retrieved Frady and Cloer and headed for the shore guns.

When they reached the cave entrance, William quickly signaled for his small band to begin securing the perimeter. He watched proudly as they spread out silently just like clockwork. Then he and Bledsoe went about the job of setting the charges on the guns. The three motley-colored shore guns protruded from the cave opening like huge gray thorns that had been thrust into the side of the granite mountain. The two men hurried at their task, knowing full well that the gun crews could exit their underground bunker any minute. It was 0347.

The bombardment from the Navy's battleships and destroyers was set to commence at 0415, and when it began, the ships would be visible on the horizon like so many sitting ducks. After placing a pack of C-2 inside the breach of the first sixteen-inch gun, William glanced up briefly and watched as Lazcano and Cloer positioned themselves near the exit of the bunker, which obviously served as the Germans' sleeping quarters. Their M-1s pointed at the opening that was roughly five feet wide by seven feet high.

"Damn, these guns are huge," groaned Bledsoe, who was working hard to keep up with his squad leader. His job was to shove the blasting caps into the packs of C-2 that had been placed inside and around the battery of guns.

"I've never seen real sixteen-inch guns before," said William as he shoved more C-2 under the turret that aligned the barrel. "I hope we brought enough of this shit." He carefully patted a pack of the bluish, cellophane-wrapped C-2.

Though it seemed longer, within five minutes, the pair had placed all the C-2 around the guns, a total of forty pounds of highly explosive ordinance. They were now ready to roll out the detonator wire and do the final hook up. William motioned for everyone except Cloer and Lazcano, who were guarding the bunker, to form on Bledsoe and him. As they gathered around, William glanced at this lone female and asked, "What's your name, anyway?" She looked at him and smiled.

"I was once called Morea," she answered, her accent now sounding a little Scottish to his ears. The image of a Viking ship flashed through his mind when she spoke, and he quickly rubbed his eyes to dispel it. He looked from her to the tired and dirty faces of his Rangers; they, in turn, stared back at him with anxious looks.

"Okay, people. Morea here will lead you guys back down the trail. Bledsoe and I will follow as soon as we blow these guns to hell." No sooner had he said *hell* than the entire bunker entrance suddenly filled with Germans. Both groups stared at each other for a long second until Bledsoe's Thompson began its song of death. He fired full automatic bursts at the closest German while Cloer and Lazcano's M-1s banged relentlessly against their shoulders. Cloer grunted and staggered sideways against the wall of the cave, clutching his stomach in pain. With his back to the cold granite, he cradled the M-1 against his hip and tried to keep firing, but after a couple short bursts, the pain intensified to the point that he dropped his weapon and clutched his bloody stomach. Sinking slowly to his knees, he leaned his head back on the irregular-shaped wall of the cave and closed his eyes. His mind was already back in the hills of North Carolina when another burst from a German grease gun sent him down in a pile of bleeding flesh.

Everyone was firing and shouting at the same time—English and German becoming indistinguishable. Battle discipline, as it often does, flew out the window. Bullets flew, and men on both sides fell.

Valencia, who had shed his radio back at the ledge, was standing just two feet from William and firing his M-1. Suddenly, William's face was showered with blood and gray matter as Valencia's head exploded in a red flash. Blinded temporarily, William fell to one knee and tried to clear his eyes. Bledsoe, Frady, and Hall dove into prone positions and slowly began to establish a little firing discipline.

Five Germans had fallen in the first few seconds of the firefight, as well as Cloer, Valencia, and a quiet kid from South Dakota named Crawford. Hall had taken a ricochet round in the thigh and was struggling to stop the bleeding with a makeshift tourniquet. The time was 0405, and the situation, if not desperate, was very close to a Mexican standoff. They couldn't blow the guns, and the Germans, who had fled back inside the bunker, couldn't escape. William's mind spun in a near panic as he looked around and tried to evaluate their situation. A crazy idea began to creep into his skull. He shouted to the girl who sat calmly behind a large boulder where she had been throughout the brief firefight.

"Do you speak German?"

She looked over at him, a little confused, before shouting back, "Yes, monsieur, but I'm not fluent."

"Well, you will just have to do the best you can." She waited for an explanation, but he seemed to hesitate. His great idea now sounded absurd as he played it over in his mind. *What the hell, I've got to do something*, he thought, taking a deep breath.

"Ask them to surrender!" he shouted a little too loudly. His ears were still ringing from all the firing, and he couldn't hear shit. She whispered something under her breath before she asked him to repeat the request. "You heard me, damn it. I want you to ask them to surrender!" he shouted again. There was about twenty-five feet between them, but her eyes bore into his as if she was right next to him.

"And if they won't surrender?" she asked.

"Then tell them we will blow them to hell, along with the guns," he called back matter-of-factly. She held his gaze for a second before finally turning toward the bunker entrance, which sat like a giant spider's lair. In German, she shouted the request for surrender and explained what would happen if they refused.

Cordite smoke floated around in thick swirls as the seconds ticked by. William scanned the room and did a quick head count. Of the nine who started up the cliff with him, three had been killed, and a fourth was down. Although Hall had managed to stop the bleeding in his leg, he had lost so much blood that he was nearly unconscious. That left Bledsoe, Frady, Lazcano, Cipriani, and the woman. "God, I hope the Krauts don't know how few people we have left." He made the statement to her, who had crawled over behind another boulder a little closer to him. She made no reply. He looked at his watch, shook his wrist, and looked again. If the damn thing was right, they had five minutes. He had no choice now; there just wasn't any time left. She was on the move again, repositioning herself closer to the bunker, and William called out to her. "Tell them their time is up." He grabbed the detonator wire and began to hook it up. Just as she prepared to shout the warning, a sharply dressed German officer emerged from the bunker with a white handkerchief tied on a pole. An Iron Cross hung around his neck, its silk strap dyed a brilliant blue. "Don't shoot, don't shoot, we're coming out!" shouted the Hauptsturmführer in perfect English.

William, along with the other surviving Rangers, was shocked when sixteen German soldiers filed out of the bunker with their empty hands held high. Cautiously, the Rangers stood up, and William motioned for the Krauts to line up against the wall. "Beeil dich, beeil dich!" William repeated the command to hurry. Bledsoe, with his Thompson pointed menacingly at the Germans, walked over to stand beside William.

"Mike, you and Frady keep them covered while I finish the hook up." William glanced over at his friend, who had not said a word since the firefight died down. "Mike ..." He waited a second. "Mike, damn it, look at me!" Ever so slowly, Bledsoe's head turned toward his squad leader, but his eyes said his mind was somewhere else. Emotionless, vacant orbs stared back. William's mind screamed, *Oh god, he's not with us.* William placed his hand gently on his friend's shoulder. "Mike, they're our prisoners. Treat them that way. Do you hear me?"

The mouth spoke, but the eyes never changed. "Yeah, I hear you, William. I'll treat them just like they treated Jerry." Venom dripped from every word he uttered.

William's eyes bore into his friend. "Just keep your shit together for a few more minutes. A few more minutes, that's all I ask." He watched the big man from Tennessee turn back toward the Germans, Bledsoe's knuckles white from gripping his Thompson. *Is my friend losing it?* William wasn't sure. But he did know that his talk had bought him and the Germans, who were lined up against the wall just to the left of the number-one gun, a little more time.

He worked quickly, double-checking the detonator wires and then connecting the blasting caps to the plunger. As he hurried about the task, his eyes darting between the detonator wire and the C-2 pack, a bad feeling began creeping over him. It grew worse when the hawk's cry shook the cave like a blast from a bullhorn. Bledsoe's state of mind, coupled with the fact that the Navy ships, would begin their bombardment in less than four minutes, scared him. William's hands shook despite his best efforts to remain calm. He had to get his people as well as his prisoners down the cliff, but he also had to finish the damn job.

He jumped when a hand touched his shoulder. "God, you scared me," he swore as he fumbled with the detonator cord and glanced at up as the woman leaned close to his ear.

"Your big friend is going to kill the prisoners," she whispered as if reading from a script.

He looked at her for a second, not fully understanding her words; then he glanced over where Bledsoe stood staring at the Germans. "I'm almost finished," he grunted and looked toward the horizon, which was starting to glow a pale orange. It was time. He sat the plunger in the safe position and walked up to his friend. "Mike ..." The name had hardly left his mouth when Bledsoe spun around faster than William thought humanly possible. He had to step back to keep the muzzle of the Thompson from slamming into his stomach. William looked at his friend, and his heart sank. The man looking back at him wasn't Mike Bledsoe; it was his body, all right. The same bushy blond hair and broad chest, but the man inside was gone. Some dark part of Bledsoe's mind had taken control.

"Are you okay?" William asked the question, stalling for time, but already knew the answer. He watched his friend's breathing become shallow and rapid, his eyes darting about.

"They have to die, William—all of them—for what they did to Jamberdino. They have to die." He repeated the phrase with a voice William barely recognized. Sweat ran down Bledsoe's forehead as he shook his head from side to side. William closed his eyes and thought for a second. *Two minutes, that's all I need. Two minutes.* He looked back up and softly pleaded with his friend. "Mike, listen to me. We have to get off this cliff—all of us! That includes the prisoners," he added.

"No!" Bledsoe screamed as he swung the Thompson around and pointed it at William's stomach.

They say the eyes are the gateway to the soul, and if they are, then William could easily see that Mike Bledsoe's soul had already left his body. What remained was an empty hull with a fully loaded Thompson submachine gun. And it was staring at him—hard.

William heard the hawk's cry before he actually saw the raptor. The sound pierced the early morning air like a siren in the dark of night. Some almost forgotten part of Bledsoe's mind recognized the sound too, and he glanced skyward. When he did, the great hawk dove toward him, bearing its talons. Seizing the moment, William grabbed the still-warm barrel of the Thompson and tried to pull it away from the mesmerized Bledsoe. The barrel moved only slightly to the side as Bledsoe's finger tightened on the trigger. The roar of the Thompson thundered inside the gun emplacement as the two friends looked at each other wide-eyed. For a second, both men just stood there, unable to figure out what had just happened, but William slowly released his grip on the barrel and sank moaning to his knees.

The German Wehrmacht troops dared not move. They had seen this hate before, and they knew that the crazed American would turn on them in a heartbeat. Frady exchanged nervous glances with Lazcano, but he managed to keep his eyes on the prisoners, who seemed as shocked as everyone else.

"Oh god," cried Bledsoe, and he started to kneel beside his friend. William was holding his stomach and looking at blood pouring between his fingers. The sound of flapping wings mixed with the moans from the wounded William Craig, but another sound shook the air. A cry filled the cave as death once again rode the talons of the great war hawk. Bledsoe was on one knee when the hawk struck him on the side of his face. "No, God! Not me, not me!" he shouted and staggered to his feet, screaming as he moved closer to the edge of the cliff called Pointe du Hoc, all the while fighting to escape the hawk's fury. The hawk's talons ripped at his face until the sudden call of a mourning dove brought the attack to a halt. The hawk screeched its defiant call one final time and then flew out of the cave into the early dawn light.

Stunned and on the edge of shock, William faded in and out of consciousness as visions of Vikings and other soldiers floated through his mind. The pain was excruciating, but the haunting call of the dove brought him back to a state of clearheadedness. The call seemed to wrap itself around him, and the pain somehow began to ease off, floating just out of his consciousness. He was able to look quickly around and attempt to analyze the situation they found themselves in. It was obviously desperate. He glanced over at Frady, who simply stared back ashen-faced. The slightly built Latino kid's hand shook, as did the M-1 that he held tightly against his shoulder, but it remained pointed at the Germans who wisely hadn't moved.

"Frady." William coughed up blood as he called out. "We have to blow these guns now! I'll do that, but you have to get these people down the trail! Lazcano, help me over to the detonator and then help Frady get that girl and the Krauts down the trail." He was repeating himself, but that was okay. Struggling to stay conscious, he groaned as Lazcano helped him over to where the detonator sat, but he managed to kneel down and place his hands on the plunger. The little Italian's eyes were as big as saucers, watching the blood pour from his squad leader's stomach and soak the ground.

"Corporal Craig, you can't blow the guns from here. You'll …" He didn't finish the thought, already understanding what would happen. William responded with half a smile as more blood trickled down his chin.

"Private, just get these people out of here. Bledsoe and I will follow you in a few minutes."

"She's gone," Cipriani shouted from the cave's entrance.

William closed his eyes. He was surprised she would run off, but evidently, she had disappeared. "Oh well," he said, spitting out a mouthful of blood. "You just can't trust a woman to stay for the fun part." He nearly fell over, and blood mixed with tiny air bubbles gathered at the corner of his mouth. "Go! Go! Get the hell out of here!" William shouted. The surviving Rangers herded the German prisoners out of the cave and headed down the trail, but one German stopped. The English-speaking officer turned back toward William and raised his arm in a salute—not a Nazi salute but a military salute of respect.

"I thank you, Corporal. You saved our lives," said the German, holding the salute for a long second before turning to follow the others down the trail.

William sat alone, looking around the cavernous hole in the side of the mountain, the detonator plunger under his hands. A smile suddenly spread across his blood-splattered face. *A warrior for peace.* Her words rang in his ears. *I stopped senseless killings.*

A few feet away, near the cave's entrance, Bledsoe sat clutching his tattered face. He had grown silent, except for an occasional sob. While William waited for the Rangers to get farther down the trail, the loud boom of the battleships' guns shook the cave. The ships sat just over the horizon. "All this may have been for nothing," he said to the guns as his vision faded in and out. "But I can't take any chances." He glanced once more at his friend, still hunched over, and he started to say something but didn't. What was there to say? He looked down at the plunger and then closed his eyes as he conjured up an image of Beth in his mind. The words of the woman named Morea flashed alongside her: *Our friend waits for us.* Then he pushed down the handle.

* * * * *

Two thousand miles away a young wife struggled in the pains of childbirth. Beth Craig's eyes closed as she tried to push the baby out. Suddenly, the image of two hawks and a grayish-white dove flashed across her mind. She screamed. The image was so clear, so vivid. The face of a young warrior blended with one of the hawks; it was her husband. The shock of recognition forced the baby out in a gush of blood.

The blast of C-2 was so strong that the guns were thrown into the air and ripped open. "Too much damn C-2." Bledsoe chuckled through tattered lips, just before the blast hit him. William closed his eyes and smiled as the image of a baby girl passed through his mind as the mighty explosion hit him, tossing both men's shattered bodies over the cliff's edge of Pointe du Hoc.

A hundred yards down the trail, Private Scott Frady and the others, including the German prisoners, were hiding under a rock ledge as the debris from the blast rained down around them. Frady carefully peeked out from the rock while the thick cloud of dust settled over the area. He blinked several times and rubbed his eyes. He thought—no, he definitely *saw*—something strange was sailing on the early morning air. Sunlight reflected off the wings of not one, but two great hawks and a dove. Together, they soared high above the point of the hawk.

* * * * *

The pair of hawks and the dove circled Pointe du Hoc a few more times as the guns of the battleships belched their reply to the führer and the 75th Rangers swarmed over the cliffs. Then the trio dipped their wings to the troops storming ashore and flew south-by-southeast toward a land where the spirits of old still whispered, calling them home.

CHAPTER 5

A Warrior for Peace

There was never a good war, or a bad peace.
—Benjamin Franklin

A young mother, her black cotton dress long and simply cut, sits rigidly in a hard steel chair gazing through a black mourner's veil while her infant daughter somehow manages to sleep, although fitfully, cradled in her arms. Both mother and child jump slightly as a series of three shots ring out across a hillside dotted with white crosses. A dirty-gray cloud of cordite drifts slowly across the small knoll where the three riflemen stand with their weapons tucked alongside their pant legs. The acrid stench of gun smoke stings everyone's nostrils as the haunting notes, like a call to arms that can't be answered, echo through the valley. The lonesome, mournful sound of taps ends and the teary-eyed mother, far too young to be a widow, solemnly watches the bugler remove the bugle from his lips and stand at attention. A stone-faced captain steps up, hands her the neatly folded flag that was draped across her husband's casket, and says something about a grateful nation. He steps back and salutes, does an about-face, and walks away. The child stirs and has to be shifted in her arms.

The young widow has handled the ceremonial funeral well but when she watches the dull-colored casket being lowered into the dark hole, she sobs. She will be expected to watch as dirt is thrown onto her beloved William and she is not sure she can handle it. Tears flow down her cheeks. "Your father would kiss these tears away," she whispers to her sleeping daughter. Someone offers her a handkerchief but she shakes her head in refusal. *I need the feel of the tears*, she thinks to herself, and then a shudder runs through her as the call, she somehow knew was coming, echoed over the valley. She dared not look up at the hawk.

* * * * *

Down through the ages, great warriors have never been gender bound, and although unnoted by their critics, the warrior's cry for peace has rung as loudly as others cry for war. So it is, in a land ravaged by hatred and blood oaths, that a woman, guided by warrior spirits, finds herself carrying the fate of an entire land on her weary shoulders. She is a woman born into war, but fate has placed her alongside UN peacekeepers in an effort to prevent the spread of genocide in this lush land. This woman, who is a warrior for peace, is as courageous and strong as any man who ever stood in a shield wall or charged up a valley that spewed canister. And the old gods—they look out from their hiding places and take notice of her. For this land, this dark continent is a place where the ancient voices, although mere whispers can still be heard—and they summon the spirits.

* * * * *

The sweltering summer heat beats down with a vengeance in this East African country of Rwanda. The year is 1994, and the stench of death hangs heavily in the air, a stench so vile that it seems to seep into every pore of the men and women who live and work in this former paradise. There is an old saying in this region that warns if the smell of death lingers in your nostrils overnight, it will enter your body and kill your soul. There are those among the Interahamwe that have inhaled this stench their entire lives and their souls have turned black. Only the insects, especially the flies, seem to thrive in the heat and decay. Every other living thing suffers. There is no escape from the heat, not even deep in the shade where the birds, so beautiful in their multicolored feathers, refuse to leave their roosts. Here, they sit and watch the pitiful drama unfold below them.

There is a deep and strange silence that seems to hang over the land like an invisible shroud. It is as if the dark mysterious jungle holds its breath, knowing its terrible secrets are about to be uncovered. Just back from the jungle's edge, a pair of sightless eyes peer out of the shadows at a solitary vehicle bouncing along a deeply rutted road. The SUV is enveloped in dust as it rolls to a stop on the outskirts of this small town near the southeast corner of Rwanda. Three people exit the battered old Land Rover that has faded UN insignias on its doors. A single bullet hole adorns the dust-covered windshield just above the driver's-side wiper blade. Sweat drips steadily into their eyes as they unload several bags of equipment.

One of the three is a female, the recently appointed director of the Department of Peace and Stability, a newly created entity of the United Nations. The other two are her cameraman and his assistant. They are from the neighboring country of Ghana and speak with a clipped British accented English when they do speak, which is seldom. The director is American. Above the American's slightly gray eyebrows, sweat puddles and slowly trickles over the edges of her eyelids. It runs down into her soft blue eyes, causing them to blink in a constant motion. She knows the routine, having been in similar situations before, and her hand reaches down, almost by reflect, into an old AWOL bag and pulls out a neatly folded handkerchief. Pouring water from her canteen, she soaks the cloth and ties it like a bandit behind her head. She gags despite her feeble attempt to prevent the stench from making her sick.

Walking tentatively, she heads down a narrow street littered with all matter of trash, her cameraman in tow. Several small mangy dogs scurry out of her way. They're in search of food, and except for a timid growl, they pay her no attention. She puts her hand up to shade her eyes from the blazing sun as she moves through the street, her sunglasses having been forgotten back at the UN headquarters in her rush to get here. The scene in front of her appears to float in the still air, shimmering in and out of focus like a mirage above a dry lake bed. "If it were indeed only a mirage," groans Faith Lee who wears the title of director on her name tag. The damp handkerchief doesn't help much as the stench wafts in the stagnant air on the edge of the little town square and stings her nostrils. She fights back the urge to gag as she cautiously trudges forward.

The town—or more accurately, village—is as quiet as some long forgotten tomb on a lonely windswept ridge. A few frightened villagers peek out from mud and thatch huts as she walks by, small children standing close behind them in the doorways. As the woman and her crew move along the deserted street, an old man emerges from the jungle that looms on the outskirts of the town like a reminder of the past. He stands, a solitary figure, on the edge of the dirt street and watches them. Village elders often whisper about this old man in their council hut. Some among them say that he is a spirit; others say that he is as old as the village itself. Nobody seems to know for sure.

Man or spirit, his weathered skin is the color of sunbaked asphalt, and his sightless eyes stare straight ahead yet seem to follow the crew's every move, especially the woman's. He is naked except for a feathered ankle bracelet and a tattered old loincloth the color of spilled milk. No shoes adorn his leathery feet as he limps along, a well-worn ironwood staff clutched tightly in his right hand. The twisted and slightly bent staff is decorated with bones from an unknown animal and more ancient than the man himself. The old shaman cocks his head slightly to the side as his glazed eyes follow the woman, and an ancient chant soon fills the air around him. The sound coming from his dry throat is much like that of the bones that rattle against the ironwood. His chant grows in volume as the woman walks toward the dead. She steps over a broken plastic table and rounds the corner of a dilapidated colonial-era building, its once brightly colored walls a fainted memory, and she stops.

The cameraman and his assistant almost walk into her as she stands there with tears instead of sweat in her eyes. They peer around her and then quickly reach into their hip pockets for handkerchiefs that they press to their mouths and noses. The camera, a black-bodied Nokia, continues to swirl as they slowly move forward among the bloated fly-covered bodies of at least three dozen dead children. The children lay in poodles of dried blood, and their numbers fill the dusty courtyard. Their tiny bodies, already swollen to twice their normal size under the brutal assault of the sun, show signs of mutilation. Death by machete is always horrible. Several adults lie among the dead—adults who thought (or had at least hoped) that they were safe in this village. The UN, in its countless statements to the world, had called this village a safe haven, but Umkuba, in the southwest corner of Rwanda, was not safe.

Since the middle seventies, Umkuba had been home to a small Catholic orphanage run by an old priest named Father Turlington and three middle-aged nuns from Belgium. All four of them lay butchered beside the children they had served. The nuns' long black habits were shamefully pulled up over their heads, revealing their bloody torsos to an uncaring world. The priest had died in a similar manner, his body draped over a small child he had tried to protect. Ironically, the nuns and priest were from the Order of Mercy, though they had obviously received none here. "It's always the children, always the little ones who suffer so horribly," mumbles faith as she walked through the macabre scene. The dead children ranged in age from about four to maybe twelve, the upper age limit for stay in the orphanage. The front courtyard of the orphanage is eerily quiet, only the buzzing of the flies as they feast on the bloodied corpses can be heard. One slow step at a time, they walk across the courtyard and stare at the two-story building as if it could offer an explanation for what had happened at its entrance.

Hesitantly, Faith Lee and the cameraman's assistant enter the charred but mostly intact main dormitory of the brick and stucco orphanage. The cameraman stays outside, his camera absorbing the horrific crime that had occurred here. Faith's eyes scan the sparse, utilitarian nature of the living quarters, and as they sweep across the room, they stop on one sad and pitiful detail. Most of the children, especially the smaller ones, had removed their tiny shoes and placed them neatly under their bunks before being led outside to be slaughtered. Shoes of any type were a luxury to these poor children, and the gesture was heart-wrenching.

"Oh god," she moans, "Is there a god?" Her question, unanswered, rises up to float among the rafters like the pigeons that flutter about there.

When the woman disappears inside the building, the old shaman stomps his feet twice in the hard clay, and small clouds of red dust trail him as he shuffles off into the jungle. He disappears down a scarcely noticed but well-worn path leading into the dark foliage. A hawk's cry echoes eerily down the trail as the old man fades into the shadows.

* * * * *

The director of the Department of Peace and Stability is a serious woman who was born and raised in the mountains of Western North Carolina. Her name is Faith Lee, and she is pretty by most standards with shoulder-length brown hair, slightly peppered with gray now that she usually wears tied back in a ponytail. Her khaki-tan blouse and shorts, soaked with sweat, cling to her still trim body. *The mountains*, she sighs thinking about home for some strange reason—a place of peace and tranquility as far removed from the terrible scene that surrounds her as to be on another planet. She moves laboriously through the building. The horror of what happened here virtually sucks the energy from her body, yet her mind wanders to the many places her career has taken her through the years. First as an Army nurse and then later, after more schooling, working with the United Nations, she had served in many war torn areas, places very similar to here in Rwanda. Nicaragua, Bosnia, and her first experience with the sight and smell of death … Vietnam.

Suddenly, without warning, her throat constricts as tiny lights dance in front of her eyes, and she can't seem to get enough air. Her deep breaths draw no oxygen, and the walls of the building close in on her. She franticly looks around for a way out. *A door, where is the damned door?* her mind screams, and she rushes over to a battered old door she hopes will lead outside. Yanking it open, she bursts through the opening as the hinges squeak noisily in protest. In her desperation to get outside, she has completely disregarded the rules for her safety and that of her crew, but she doesn't care. She has to get outside. Gasping for breath, she staggers over and sits down on a hard wooden bench in the shade of a snarled old fig tree and tries to calm herself. Unlike the courtyard out front, this one is surprisingly serene, and her heart rate gradually begins to slow. Wiping the ever-present sweat from her eyes, she looks out into the heat that envelops the countryside. *Vietnam, so damn long ago*, she groans as her body finally begins to relax and her mind drifts back to that part of her life.

Faith Craig, Lee being her married name, graduated from the same small college her father, William Craig, had attended. He had played football for Western Carolina College a couple of years before the Second World War pulled him into its grip. Faith's degree had been in nursing, and like her father, she had joined the Army. Another war raged, and she felt she was needed. She was commissioned a second lieutenant upon enlistment and, after very little actual field training, shipped off to the war. Faith Craig arrived in country just in time to celebrate the Vietnamese Tet holiday in early February of 1968.

Faith had been raised by her widowed mother, Faith's father having been an Army Ranger who was killed on D-day high above the cliffs on Utah Beach. He died the same day—her mother had always told her the exact moment—that Faith was born. Beth Craig, Faith's mother, often told her daughter tales of how her father had been watched over by a great hawk. Not only a hawk but also the hawk's mate, which was, of all things, a dove. As a little girl, Faith loved listening to her mother's tales, but as she grew older, she scoffed at the absurd idea of a hawk and a dove as mates. Years later, she learned that sometimes it's better to view the world through the eyes of a child.

No amount of schooling, lectures, or operating room experience can truly prepare a person for the horrors of war; and Faith was no exception. Within days of her arrival in country, she was overwhelmed by the mangled flesh brought into the field hospital at Tay Ninh. Day after day, she saw firsthand what modern weapons could do to the human body. She soon became hardened against all wars but particularly this war in Vietnam. *There has to be a better way to resolve regional conflicts*, she kept telling herself and anyone else that would listen. *And by god, I'm going to make that my life's mission—not simply this piecing back together of mangled bodies.*

During the months of February and March, the medivac choppers flew in daily, sometimes hourly, to the hospital, and Faith got to know most of the pilots and their crews. One medivac pilot who seemed to fly in the most often was a 1st Lieutenant from Sacramento, California, who flew for the 1st Cavalry. David Lee was a veteran pilot; this was his second tour in Nam, and he was good at his job. He was a few years older than Faith and, like most of the other pilots, had a huge crush on the cute nurse from Tar Hill. Oddly enough, in what little time they had off, they loved to talk politics. Faith often wondered if having lost a father to war had prompted her interest in the politics of war. Whatever the reason, she was a worthy adversary in the sometimes heated debates. David was a staunch Republican, while she was an open-minded fairly liberal Democrat. Having minored in political science, Faith was always eager to confront her friend and his views on the war.

It seemed as if no matter how good his points were, the domino effect "if we don't stop communism" was his best. She could always gain the upper hand, though, by repeating her favorite line from Arthur Wellesley, the duke of Wellington from the British Army of the early 1800s. "Remember, David," she would explain, "99.9 percent of all wars are caused by failed or, in some cases, the total lack of diplomacy." Then she would continue in her lecture fashion while David Lee would simply stare at her starstruck. Her intent was never to hurt his feelings or to make him mad. So when she came close, she would always soothe his ruffled feathers with a smile and finish with "Had we listened more or perhaps tried a different approach, then this"—and she would point to the row after row of aluminum caskets stacked in the hangers ready to be loaded with bodies and shipped back to the US—"might never have occurred." Smiling, she would shake her head, causing her ponytail to sway from side to side and whisper, "Checkmate," before walking away. She often wondered, though, as she would walk toward her hooch, what it would really take to make him understand. But David Lee did understand, maybe better than most. He just couldn't make her understand him. Usually, he would just watch her walk into the night before he himself would rise up off the sandbag wall and trudge past the caskets on his way to his bunk. There was always another medivac flight, and it was never a long wait. That was what he understood.

David Lee was infatuated with the young nurse from North Carolina and had offered many times to take her for a ride in his chopper, but each time, she had refused. It wasn't that she was afraid of flying. On the contrary, she loved to fly. It was because—and she didn't dare tell him—she didn't trust herself alone with him. Hell, he was a handsome pilot with surfer boy looks and a quick smile. That was dangerous territory. She kept telling herself she didn't need a love affair—not now, not here. He thought she just didn't like him very much; nothing was farther from the truth.

One especially hot and humid night in late April, they sat on the sandbagged wall surrounding the nurse's hooch, talking, the buzzing of insects occasionally interrupted by the distant firing of artillery in support of some poor infantry unit that were always getting hit at night. When someone was wounded in these firefights, it was David's job to fly off into the dark sky like airborne cavalry, which was what they were, and get them. Not always but oftentimes, they flew into the hell of a hot LZ. Faith's olive drab utilities were soaked with sweat as she, David, and another nurse friend by the name of Liz Connolly sat on the sandbags; and as usual, the conversation turned to politics.

"The Democrats are lost without Johnson, and you two know it." The boyish looking pilot laughed. David was kidding them about the Democrats running McGovern against Nixon.

"Well, the damn Republicans were lost when they selected tricky Dick as their man," interjected Faith with a laugh. He smiled and scratched his head, which he usually did just before he told a joke, but stopped when he heard footsteps crunching in the sand. Glancing up, all three friends watched suspiciously as the officer on duty hurriedly walked up. The OD nodded at the nurses and then addressed David.

"Lieutenant, an urgent call just came in from that Special Forces compound over near the Fishhook area," said the out-of-breath duty officer. "Their CO has been hit bad and needs medivac ASAP." He paused for a second before he went on. "I've looked all over, but I can't find a medic to fly with you, though. They're all out on flights or down at the damn vill," he explained. He stood there with his arms down by his side as if half expecting a refusal.

"I know their company commander. His name is Mickler, and he's a good man," said David as he dusted sand off his backside and moved toward his chopper. He stopped after a few steps and looked back at Faith.

"You want to be my medic tonight?" He paused and changed the request. "Will you? I'll probably need you," he pleaded when she seemed hesitant. Faith looked over at her friend Liz for support, but Liz just shrugged.

"I ... I ..." she sputtered as she looked from David to his chopper. Finally, she nodded. "Okay, okay. I'll go, but I need to get a few things first."

"I'll help you," pitched in Liz as she and Faith ran toward the medical supplies hooch.

"Good, I'll fire up the chariot," said David as he turned and ran the rest of the way to the Huey already being prepped by the door gunner.

A few heartbeats later, Faith came running from the med tent with Liz close on her heels. The chopper sat spinning in full throttle as the nurses ran toward it. Faith carried an old AWOL bag stuffed with what she thought she might need, and Liz carried a steel pot with a peace sign painted on the cover. They had found it lying on the floor off in the corner, probably a piece of lost gear from some grunt who had been brought in for surgery. The door gunner, a buck sergeant by the name of Baker, helped Faith into the center fold-down seat and handed her a flak jacket that was much too big for her. The blades swirled as Faith muttered to herself, doubts of her sanity flooding her mind. David talked briefly to the small control tower that stood off to the side of the runway, and then he swung the Huey out of its revetment and headed northeast.

Faith sat ashen-faced as the chopper sped out into the dark night. David flew the Huey at nap-of-the-earth, which was at treetop level in hopes of confusing any VC spotters who might be stationed along the way. Surprisingly, to Faith, he brought the chopper up a few hundred feet every time they neared a village, no matter how small. Faith wondered why until she suddenly saw tracers streak up toward them from the next village.

"Doesn't anybody like us?" quizzed Faith as she spoke into the headset the door gunner had given her. To her surprise, Baker, not David, replied.

"Most of these people just want to be left alone, ma'am, and work their rice fields. They've been at war here for over thirty years. First the Japanese, then the French, and now us. They're tired of war." He paused for a second, and she thought maybe he was finished, but his southern drawl came back off the headset.

"They also know that where we—the 1st Cavalry, I mean—go, death is always on our heels." With that said, Baker grew quiet and leaned out the chopper door, his M60 cradled in his lap. Baker's 60 hung from the inside roof of the chopper by an elastic bungee cord and rested on his knee. It was the preferred method of most gunners of the 1/9, no pussy poles for them. The box of ammo was slid up beside his seat.

Faith sat back and watched her friend fly the chopper. She was amazed at how he could fly treetop level at over a hundred knots, all the while talking to the radio operator at the SF compound. As they drew closer to the firebase, she could tell by the tone of the conservation between David and the radio operator at the compound that the situation was obviously getting desperate. The gooks weren't inside the walls yet, but they were close to breaching one on the southeast corner of the old French fort. "Hurry" was the urgent request that crackled over the radio.

"Oh my god," gasped Faith minutes later as she looked out the left side of the chopper while David circled the compound. *It's like a sick and very bizarre fireworks show*, thought Faith as she stared mesmerized. The constant firing seemed to create a solid wall of red and green tracers running into and out of the compound. The young pilot, well aware of the fact that many choppers had been shot down by friendly fire, took a deep breath and pulled the cyclic hard to the left; the chopper responded like a well-trained horse. He did one more fly-over and headed in. Faith could see RPGs slamming into the compound walls, especially to the south, and there were literally hundreds of ghostly shadows running toward the tightly packed pole walls. Several illumination flares popped in the ink black sky and floated eerily back to earth.

Faith heard the words *red smoke* over the headset, and suddenly the chopper dove out of the sky, barely missing the compound wall as Baker fired up the running shadows that swarmed toward the camp. Ejected shell casings rained down all around the interior of the chopper as Baker did his work. Faith ignored the hot casings that burned her arms and threatened to roll down her collar as she strained to see the red smoke through the clouds of cordite that enveloped the whole area. David could hear the occasional ping as a round punched into the magnesium alloy shell of the Huey. His eyes searched the compound desperately until finally he saw the red smoke swirling near the main bunker and dropped the Huey hard onto the old helipad nearby. The H model Huey groaned as the skids nearly collapsed from the impact. It bounced once and then settled while he kept the throttle wide open.

Two ghostlike figures ran out of the swirling smoke and dust, both wearing the Vietnamese Tiger fatigues and had their faces blackened. They raced with a stretcher held between them, their M16s strapped across their backs. The two SF sergeants quickly slid the stretcher holding their company commander into the chopper and then handed Faith the IV bag that was attached to the unconscious soldier. The larger of the two men, a black E-6 with a hooked nose, tried to shout over the noise of the firefight, but all Faith heard was something about morphine.

The two turned and sprinted away, but no sooner had they gotten out from under the Huey's twirling blades then dove into the dirt. An RPG round had struck the far corner of their bunker, narrowly missing them. Groggily they managed to regain footing and scramble on toward safety. David began to lift the cyclic in order to get the hell out of dodge but stopped when Faith suddenly shouted over her headset.

"David, don't go yet! I didn't understand what that sergeant said about the morphine. I don't want to kill this man after all he has been through." Before he could protest, Faith was out of the chopper and running after the two crouched figures. She didn't have to run far because both men were stopped about forty feet from the chopper. A group of six very scared and very angry South Vietnamese soldiers milled about in front of them, their weapons pointed at the ground, for now. Faith nervously eased up beside the big SF sergeant who, like his buddy, held his M16 pointed at the ARVNs.

"I thought they were on our side," she hissed into the sergeant's ear.

"They're on their own side, and they want to leave this hell-hole—on your chopper," grunted the big man while his finger roamed around on the trigger of his M16. Horrified, she watched the ARVN's defiantly lock and load their weapons and moved toward the chopper. The other SF sergeant, a Latino-looking kid, fired his M16 at the feet of the advancing ARVNs, and they reluctantly stopped.

"Didi mau, didi mau!" he shouted and waved his weapon back toward the fighting position they had left. The Vietnamese soldiers looked from the chopper back to the weapons pointed at them, their singsong language exploding as their fingers fidgeted on their weapons. The black E-6 knew they were weighing their chances he wouldn't shoot them. It would be a bad bet, for he would, in a heart-beat. He hated cowards. Both sides faced each other in an odd sort of Mexican stand-off as the firefight for firebase Oscar swirled around them.

Back on the chopper, David was weighing his own options, which weren't many, when he suddenly ducked down because the whole right side of the Huey's windshield shattered from several rounds of very close AK fire.

"Damn," he cursed as he brushed Plexiglas from his lap and scanned the area in front of him. He had to do something quick, or they would never make it out of the damn compound.

"Hold on, Tom, I've got an idea!" he shouted to the gunner over the intercom. He quickly spun the chopper around and maneuvered it until the door gunner was able to point his M60 directly at the startled ARVNs. Baker stared down the barrel of his weapon and waited. His pale blue eyes were unreadable orbs.

The obvious shift of firepower gave the Vietnamese pause, and it was all the time that Faith needed to extract the information from the now grinning SF sergeant. When she found out what had been given to their CO, she spun on her heels, ran back to the chopper, and unceremoniously dove in alongside the still unconscious Mickler. David dared a last glance at the two SF NCOs and nodded in response to the "Get out of here!" mouthed by the sergeant. He pulled power on the cyclic, and the Huey leaped into the air. It shuddered like a wounded duck as several more rounds found their mark, but the chopper cleared the wall and quickly disappeared into the night. The barrel of Baker's M60 glowed red as he poured a steady finger of fire at anything he could see below him, for the area outside the compound was a free-kill zone. Within a couple of seconds, only the blackened forest lay under the chopper as they darted behind a small hill and gained altitude.

Faith's hands began to shake as the adrenaline rush from the firefight slowly wore off and she leaned her head back in the jump seat and closed her eyes. Her mind raced as fast as the chopper. She looked down at her hands and knew she had to steady herself. *Do your damn job!* her mind screamed. She leaned up, unhooked her safety belt, knelt down beside the wounded man, and went to work. The sergeant back at the compound had told her that he had been hit with shrapnel from a mortar in the back and head, but a quick check revealed his heart rate was good considering the loss of blood and the morphine. The IV bag hung from a hook that Baker had attached to the ceiling for just that purpose. The bag swung slightly while plasma slowly dripped down the clear tube. The morphine the SF medics had given their CO seemed to be doing its job because Mickler remained unconscious. Faith checked and rechecked his vital signs, which were weak from blood loss but otherwise stable. She was a little amazed at the great patchwork the soldier medics had done on their wounded captain, considering the circumstances they were under. Lucky for him, all the SF soldiers were cross-trained as medics. That fact alone had saved many lives in Nam and other places that the shadowy units went. Despite the damage to his body, Faith felt Mickler would make it—that is if the chopper didn't crash. Just as that thought crossed her tired mind, the battered chopper shuddered and slipped sideways as David fought the cyclic for control. At least one, maybe two, hydraulic lines had been hit, and it was all he could do to keep the chopper aloft. When it shuddered again, violently this time, the wounded SF captain groaned in response. All Faith could do was hold his hand and try to pray.

Despite her name, Faith hadn't prayed since she was a little girl, and now, in this dire situation, she didn't know who or what to pray to. Maybe her father's spirit would look after her. She laughed slightly at her silliness and thought about the father she never knew as she squeezed Mickler's hand. Minutes later, the door gunner tapped her on the shoulder and pointed toward lights on the distant horizon. "Tay Ninh?" she asked hopefully, and he nodded. She relaxed a little and took a deep breath. *Okay, okay. He—and we—will live*, her mind told her.

"But just how okay can you be when your mind and body have gone through this shit?" she cried aloud into the night. The few stars that shone down from the dark heavens didn't seem to have an answer.

David didn't bother to circle the medivac helipad. He just sat the wounded chopper down as gently as he could, but even the soft landing was enough of a jolt to finish breaking one of the already damaged skids. The smoking chopper listed heavy to the side as the nurses and orderlies offloaded the SF captain and rushed him toward the operating room. Baker helped Faith offload and then opened the pilot's door to help a shaken David Lee out of the Huey.

"Thank you, Tom," said the young pilot as he patted his door gunner on the back.

"Airborne, sir," replied Baker, who liked to remind people that he was the only airborne-qualified door gunner in the outfit.

Faith walked a little unsteadily toward the sandbag wall that surrounded her hooch. The eight-inch self-propelled gun battery sitting a couple of hundred yards away began firing a mission, and Faith jumped when the big guns belched out their fury.

"I wonder if they're firing in support of that SF camp we just came from," Faith asked the otherwise still night. She stood there silently listening to the far-off rumbling of more artillery before she answered herself.

"Hell, who knows?" Grumpily, she plopped down on the sandbags and soon collapsed into a prone position, looking up into the night.

A few minutes later, David Lee trudged up and sat down on the warm bags beside her as an apology for getting her into such a terrible situation formed in his mind. After a few minutes of awkward silence, Faith mumbled tiredly, "God, is it always like this?" David, who had been watching his door gunner secure the crippled aircraft, looked over at his pretty friend.

"Sometimes it's worse," he groaned as the sound of choppers shattered the still night. He looked up at the cobra gunships circling overhead. "At least we weren't shot down and we were able to give Mickler a chance to live," he added as he shook his head. His hands shook ever so slightly, and he stared at them as if he had never seen them before. Stripping off his Nomex gloves, he quickly ran the trembling digits through his hair, which was a little longer than regulation called for. *And why the hell not?* he grumbled, his mind swirling in all directions as the stress eased off. The 1/9 generally wasn't very picky about such matters with their flight crews. Hell, his door gunner, Baker, wore a Fu Manchu. He looked down at his now wet hands, and the shakes had eased off.

"It's the dead ones, the ones we can't save, that are the worst, though." He nearly whispered the words without taking his eyes off his hands. "They come back." He paused. "They come back to visit me sometimes." Faith looked at him. "In my dreams," he finished in a somber tone, wiping his hands on his trousers.

No words came for several minutes as they both stared into the night and watched the lightning fire up the mountains on the far horizon. Thunder soon rumbled in and shook the air slightly just like the eight-inchers that now sat silently within the sandbagged perimeter across the way.

"Faith," David finally broke the uneasy silence. "I'm sorry I got you into such a shitty situation. But you handled it very well." His words hung in the air like the night insects. Faith's head turned slowly in his direction, but she could only stare as her mind raced. The fear of a few minutes ago was gone, replaced by a growing anger, anger at the war, anger at her damn government—hell, anger at men, all men. Tears ran down her cheeks as she shouted at the startled pilot.

"Did well? Did well? What the hell does that mean? I—no, no, we—had a job to do that no one should ever be asked to do, and you dare say that I did well?" David was stunned; all he could do was sit and listen as the angry young woman ranted on.

"Damn our government. It did not do well, or we wouldn't be here in the first place. And why are we fighting these people any-way? We should be talking, not killing. You don't see those bastards in Washington over here. Hell no, and ... oh, what's the use." She jumped up and stormed off toward the door of her hooch. David shook his head sadly. Nearing the door, she reached up and angrily removed the steel pot from her head, fighting with the damp locks of matted hair. The door banged loudly behind her as she stormed inside. David looked over at his crippled chopper, still emitting oily smoke, and then jumped slightly when the 105s next door began firing another support mission.

"God, I'm tired," he moaned as he painfully rose from the sand-bags and headed toward his bunk.

Early the next morning, Faith crawled stiffly from her cot and stretched like an old cat. She still wore the same fatigues she had worn the night before and as a consequence could detect a foul odor about herself. She crinkled her nose when she sniffed the sleeve of her uniform as she staggered blurry-eyed out the door of her hooch. The air was warm and damp as she closed her eyes and inhaled deeply, stretching her sore back one more time. A multitude of insects sang their mating calls into the morning stillness, and she listened to the rare quiet. She hadn't slept well the night before, with visions of hawks and doves floating through her dreams and a big Viking ran through one dream. Where the hell that had come from, she had no idea. She looked forlornly out into the still dark night; her Timex said that it was four forty-five. Dawn was still nearly an hour away.

Quietly, she eased back inside, shed the odorous fatigues, and slid into clean underwear. She had asked her mom to send her some nicer underthings, but they hadn't arrived yet, so the OD green panties and bra would have to do for now. A shower would just have to wait. *That's why God made Right Guard.* She laughed slightly at her jest, grabbed a pair of clean but wrinkled fatigues, and struggled into them.

"Damn, I need to eat more," she growled as the pants nearly fell from her hips. She tightened the belt another notch and marched out the door. Needing a cup of coffee really bad, she headed for the officers' mess, hoping to find both caffeine and David Lee. She wanted to apologize for her outburst last night, knowing full well he didn't deserve to be screamed at like that.

The night duty officer, Lt. Steve Adams, sat by himself near the back of the mess hall, stuffing greenish scrambled eggs into his mouth. He seemed to be in a hurry as he gulped down forkful after forkful. It was as if he thought they were going to run out of food, but he really wasn't in any hurry. It was just his nature to eat fast. He had grown up in a big family with six brothers and two sisters. If you didn't eat fast, someone else would eat it for you. Adams took another bite and quickly washed it down with hot coffee before reloading his fork. He heard the footsteps coming through the empty mess hall and begrudgingly looked up as Faith walked toward him. They both stared at each other for a second as she stood in front of his table, the loaded fork halfway to his mouth. She cleared her throat.

"Lieutenant Adams, have you seen Lieutenant Lee?" she asked with a nervous smile. Adams looked down at his plate as if he were afraid it might go someplace and then looked back up at the young nurse. He sat the fork down and wiped crumbs from the corner of his mouth.

"Ma'am, Lieutenant Lee got another medivac call around 0400. The call came in from that damn American Battalion that supports the 1/9 over near My Lai. Evidently, one of their companies shot up a bunch of gook civilians in what was supposed to be a simple sweep of the village."

He paused to let his words sink in because the young nurse seemed somewhat shocked, or either she didn't understand him, so he explained further. "That Americal bunch is a pretty shitty, undisciplined outfit anyway. They usually have more KIA than the damn gooks." The tired and obviously hungry duty officer waited for some kind of reply, but when none came, he went back to his green eggs. Faith stared down at Adams while she pondered what she had just been told. A minute later, she turned and moaned, "Oh god," before leaving the mess hall in a slight daze.

Walking out into the predawn light, her mind spun in a thousand directions. Somewhat confused, she headed toward the post-surgery recovery area to check on the wounded SF captain. Walking along in deep thought, she was oblivious to the beauty of the far hills as the sun's first light began to peep over them, its golden rays washing out over the deep green countryside, a beautiful but deadly country. She was about halfway across the small compound area when she moaned softly, "Oh god, I'm so sorry, David." But David wasn't around, so her apology was heard only by the coming dawn.

Trudging along, her boots kicking up small clouds of red dust, an all-too-familiar sound reached her ears. She could almost feel the *pop-pop-pop* of the inbound Huey as the sound filled the air. Usually, another inbound chopper was no big deal, but this one seemed to be in trouble. She turned in the direction of the approaching chopper and waited for it to come into view, holding her hand up to shield her eyes. The crippled chopper rode the glaring rays directly from the east. Black smoke was the first sign of trouble, and it poured from the engine cover. When the chopper limped closer, Faith could see the windshield was partly blown out on the copilot's side. The pilot was struggling to keep enough altitude to clear the few buildings near the helipad, and the rear rotor had obviously been damaged as the chopper slipped sideways toward her. She figured the controls must have been shot up and the pilot probably wounded when the Huey simply dropped out of the sky from about twenty feet. The forced landing missed the helipad completely and the chopper's skids slammed into the sandbag wall of the revetment. The hard landing caused the chopper to bounce four or five feet into the air and then come crashing down on the left skid, which quickly collapsed under the pressure with a loud bang. Faith held her breath as the blades of the chopper, designed to flex only a few inches, flexed a foot or more and briefly clipped the sandbags. The battered Huey finally settled back down onto the one good skid like a wounded animal while smoke poured from the engine area.

Several nurses and a couple of orderlies anxiously stood back as the chopper blades, which groaned loudly, gradually slowed their spin after the pilot managed to shut off the engine. The blades finally ground to a halt, and everyone quickly rushed forward, including Faith, who had been holding her breath through the whole episode. They converged on the chopper. The door gunner had jumped down and was carefully unloading six small Vietnamese children and one older girl, maybe ten or so, when Faith and Liz reach the aircraft. The older child was screaming in pain as they lowered her as gently as possible onto an awaiting stretcher.

"My god," whispered Faith as she tried to comfort the girl who looked as if she had been burned with a torch.

"Napalm," said Liz under her breath as the orderlies rushed off with the young girl. The girl's pitiful screams echoed throughout the compound until they disappeared inside the OR. Finally, utter exhaustion overcame her, and she was only able to whimper when the orderlies placed her stretcher beside the operating table. Perhaps mercifully, when they attempted to shift her over, she passed out from the pain, and the frail body at last relaxed.

The orderlies finished transferring the girl onto the OR table while the doctor tried desperately to insert a needle into the small arm of the now-unconscious child. His hand seemed huge as he gently grasped her wrist. Dr. Stuart's daughter back at Fort Benning was about the same age as the girl who lay in front of him. "God, help us," he said as he finally managed to start the IV, tears running down his cheeks until one of the nurses wiped them away with a cloth.

The last child, a small boy of about five, was gently offloaded onto a stretcher, his whimpers trailing after the orderlies as they again rushed toward the OR. He and all the others had been shot or hit with shrapnel or in some cases both. Faith watched as the little boy was rushed away, and only then did she turn to the pilot's door. A dark dread suddenly came over her. She hesitated for a second but finally managed to jerk the door open.

"Oh, David," she gasped as her dread became reality. David Lee was slumped forward onto the control panel. Blood, pooled in the floor of the chopper, ran slowly over the side panel and dripped onto Faith's boots. With shaking hands, she grasped the shoulder harness and was attempting to drag him out when the door gunner moved beside her.

"Excuse me, ma'am, let me get him out of his harness." Baker quickly unfastened the straps as Faith stood off to the side. When Baker had the pilot free, Faith reached in and helped him lower her friend onto another waiting stretcher. Covering her mouth with her hand, she looked fretfully down at the unconscious David Lee and fought back tears. Her feet seemed stuck to the ground as she watched the orderlies rush him away from her toward the OR.

Snap out of it, her mind shouted, and she hurriedly turned to the gunner.

"Sergeant, go help the copilot, I'll go with Lieutenant Lee." Baker looked at her sort of blurry-eyed and then looked over at the copilot's seat.

"Ma'am," he said softly, "Warrant Officer Clark is dead but"— he had to gather himself—"if it's okay, I'll get him out."

Stunned, Faith looked over at the body slumped over against the bulletproof door panel. She immediately saw what she hadn't noticed before. Clark had been shot through the head, blood still oozing from a large hole in the front of his flight helmet. Her heart sank as she watched Baker ease the dead pilot out of the Huey and lay him gently on the ground. A thousand questions ran through her mind but now wasn't the time to ask them, nor could she think of anything to say, so she shook her head sadly, spun, and raced after the stretcher. Catching up with the orderlies, she reached down and grasped David Lee's hand and was rewarded with a weak but notice-able squeeze. She looked down and watched his blue eyes flutter a few times before they stayed open, and a smile spread across his pain-racked face. When they reached the door to the OR, she looked back at the dead copilot. *It could have been David,* her mind screamed.

The OR was a madhouse of activity as they rushed the wounded pilot through the door. Nurses and doctors raced about while the generator-powered lights flickered slightly in their attempt to shed light on the chaos below. The children had been placed on all the available operating tables, so David Lee's stretcher was quickly sat on a stack of sandbags they had thrown in the corner of the canvas and wood hooch. The overworked nurses cut off his flight suit, and the surgeon began working on his shattered leg. Faith, by now a mental wreck, decided she would just be in the way and staggered back out into the morning air. The sun beat its way through the early morning mist, and the heat was already suffocating everything that dared to move. The distant artillery thundered its reminder that the war raged on.

With her head down, she shuffled off toward her favorite spot and collapsed onto the sandbagged wall of her hooch. Luckily, the shade hadn't disappeared yet as she wearily put her head in her hands and waited. Even in the shade though, sweat soon dripped from her forehead, and she watched it dampen the sand that slowly leaked from a shrapnel hole in the bag. The spilling sand slowly began to create a small mound, and she watched it grow with a strange fascination. As she watched, a soft somewhat soothing sound began to enter her foggy mind while images of David's ashened face floated across her semi-consciousness. The sound gradually grew louder as it worked its way into her psyche. Suddenly she recognized the sound. "A dove," she whispered to the pile of sand growing at her feet. Smiling, she raised her head and listened. She hadn't even known there were doves in Nam. The little girl in Faith caused her to strain her eyes in an effort to locate the bird. A small clump of banyan trees stood just off the east corner of the nurse's hooch, and that was where the calling seemed to come from, but the dove was invisible in the dark-green foliage.

The words of her mother gently echoed through her mind as she listened to the soft mourning call of the dove. *Maybe my mom's story wasn't so dumb after all,* she thought as she cocked her head to hear better. Faith had always felt a calming effect from the call of doves, and today, right now, she sure needed to be calm. Standing up, she brushed the sand off the seat of her pants and walked toward the trees that hid the dove as if drawn by its call. Two hooches down, Liz came out of the OR and looked around for her friend. She finally spotted her and walked, very tiredly, to where Faith stood listening to the soft cooing. Faith was so engrossed in listening to the dove that she didn't hear Liz walk up, and she jumped nervously when Liz called her name.

"Faith."

"W-what?" stammered Faith as she spun and looked at Liz's concerned face. Liz, who was obviously worried about her friend, felt the news about David Lee would cheer her up, so she smiled and announced.

"David will be okay. The round went clear through the leg, breaking the tibia but missing the artery."

"Thank God," cried Faith and wrapped her arms around her friend.

They hugged and laughed and cried all at the same time, tears flowing from their happy eyes. Walking alongside her friend toward the Banyan trees, Liz explained further.

"Dr. Stuart said they would ship him to Japan for a few weeks, but he should be fine and could soon be able to return to this paradise and all its fun." Faith grunted a short laugh.

"This damn war needs to end real soon before we are all dead," moaned Faith.

"Amen," added Liz as they walked along. They reached the clump of tall slender trees and looked up just as the dove broke from her cover and rose into the bright sky. The two women shielded their eyes to watch the dove fly away, but instead of flying away, the dove flew over to another tree that stood nearby and settled next to a large brownish bird that Faith had not seen before.

"My god, Liz, do you see that?" cried Faith.

"Yeah, it's a hawk, and maybe your mother wasn't as crazy as you thought," answered Liz as they both stared at the two birds side by side. After a few minutes, the feathered friends, tired of being watched, flew toward a nearby rice patty while Faith and Liz walked back to their hooch. When they neared the screen door, Liz turned to Faith.

"Did you hear what happened during David's medivac run?" asked Liz.

"No," replied Faith anxiously, "tell me, please. I was afraid to ask anyone!"

"Well, let's get out of this damn sun, and I'll tell you all I know," said Liz as she reached for the door. They went inside and plopped down on their bunks, music from *The Graduate* softly playing from someone's reel-to-reel toward the back of the hooch. Liz reached into her small fridge and pulled out two PBRs; she handed one to Faith and quickly opened the other drinking deeply.

"Well," she started after wiping the back of her hand across her mouth, "the NVA had moved into a village over near the Parrots Beak and, along with some local VC cadre, had taken it over. My Lai, I think it's called. That's northwest of here." She looked northwest as if to confirm her directions. "Anyway, the big brass sent in a company from that American Battalion assigned to the cav, and they started clearing the village. The poor villagers, as usual, got caught up in the middle of the fight. Sadly, the grunt company got shot up pretty bad before the NVA, and their pals had had enough and took off."

"With no bad guys to take revenge on, the grunts turned on the villagers. The young company commander, Calley—with a *C*, I think—lost all control of his men. The grunts went crazy and started shooting up the villagers—old men, women, hell, even children, as we just saw. David's medivac call came in for several grunts shot by the NVA early in the sweep through the village. But when he got there, he saw what was happening and landed his chopper between a group of villagers huddled together around the local well and the kill-crazy grunts. For a minute or two, nothing happened, and David though maybe it was over, so they loaded two of the wounded soldiers onto the chopper and prepared to leave. For some crazy reason, just before they took off, one of the grunts fired into the chopper and hit David in the leg. Another burst killed Clark and almost hit the wounded GIs that had been loaded in for evac. Luckily, the door gunner wasn't hit, and he fired a burst from his M60 at the feet of the damn grunts, and that seemed to snap them back to their senses." Liz took another long drink from her PBR.

"David, although he had to have been in a lot of pain, had the medic load as many of the wounded children they could carry, which weren't many since the wounded GIs were still on board. Well, get this, the two wounded grunts ask to be offloaded so that more of the children could be medivaced."

Tears rolled down Liz's cheek. "Ain't that crazy or sweet or brave or something?" She cried and blew her nose on a handkerchief Faith handed her.

Liz's voice trailed off into a sob, and Faith reached out and hugged her friend as she continued. "Somehow, David remained conscious and was able to fly the chopper in." They both turned their heads at the same time and looked out the screen window at the chopper that still sat against the sandbagged wall like a battered old warrior. Faith stared out past the crippled Huey for a long time, her mind racing through a thousand thoughts. Finally, she turned toward her friend.

"I'm going to marry that man." They laughed and tapped their empty PBRs together in a toast.

"Well"—Liz smiled—"you had better do it in Japan because they're shipping him over there in a couple of days." The two teary-eyed friends hugged again and made another toast with full beers as the war continued to rage around them. Later the *pop-pop-pop* of a Huey bringing in more wounded brought them out of their revelry. They were nurses, and they had work to do.

Faith was able to secure a five-day R & R to Japan the next week. When she arrived in Osaka at the Army base, David had already had his additional surgery. Two days after proposing to him, Faith Craig and David Lee were married in a small chapel on base. The honeymoon was short but filled with love, peace, and sex. The war was pushed aside, and except for the need for some very careful lovemaking positions, it was a normal honeymoon. Although one very drunken night, after far too many Mai Tais at the Officers' Club, they attempted lovemaking on the beach, and David burst a few stitches in his eagerness. Faith had to slow down long enough to administer first aid, and by then, there were people on the beach wondering if by chance he had been shark-bitten. After a glorious week, Faith returned to Tay Ninh, and several weeks later, David returned to the war, but this time he got a new assignment flying VIPs out of Saigon.

All went fairly well until they both had about three weeks left in country. The entire 1st Cavalry was low on pilots and David Lee, a warrior, volunteered to fly a resupply mission to a besieged firebase at the foot of Dui Ba Din Mountain. The Black Virgin Mountain lay just southeast of Phoc Vinh, home of the 1/9 1st Cavalry. A 1st Cavalry observation compound on top of the mountain had been overrun during the night, and the VC were lobbing mortars down on the firebase below. Both David and his door gunner were short, very short. Ironically, the gunner was his old friend from the medivac company, Buck Sergeant Tom Baker. After the business at My Lai, Baker had asked for a transfer out of medivacs. The copilot was an FNG by the name of Breese, fresh out of flight school and twenty days in-country.

There were ten resupply choppers circling the firebase in a stacked traffic pattern; David's chopper was going to be the sixth one down. His gut told him this was bad business as they watched help-lessly while the mortars slammed into the area where they were to touch down and unload their cargo of food, water, and ammunition.

"I'm too damn short for this shit," growled Baker as he fidgeted with his 60; he had three days left in country. His stomach churned as he watched the mortars walking toward the chopper, waiting to get offloaded. The red dust swirled under the rotor blades as the grunts rushed about, trying to get the cargo that was literally being thrown out of the chopper. The shock and concussion from the near misses of the mortars was shaking the earth under their feet as they labored. Ten short minutes later, it was their turn to go in. David dropped the chopper down quickly onto the spot where the grunts pointed and left the engine wide open. Baker locked eyes for a brief second with the first grunt to reach their chopper, a young black kid who shouted, "Don't mean nothing," as he grabbed an ammo box and tore off toward the bunker. Sweat rolled out from under Baker's helmet as he tossed out another ammo box, all the while repeating the often used phrase "Don't mean nothing." After all the ammo was offloaded, he turned to food and water. Food was a luxury, but they would need the water. Thirty seconds later, Baker shouted, "Go, go, go!" and threw the last box of C rations onto the pile before collapsing back into the center fold-down seat, his M60 tangling from its cord. David shoved the cyclic forward and pulled all the power the Huey could provide as mortars thumped and walked their way. The chopper had just responded to the cyclic shift when one of the 4.2 mortar rounds hit five feet in front of the charging Huey. David Lee saw the flash, felt the concussion and searing pain, and then nothing.

The mangled chopper rolled twice, breaking off the main rotors in the tumble, which saved the door gunner's life, but both pilots were dead. The veteran with three weeks left in country on his second tour and the cherry with a lifetime to go lay slumped over in their harnesses, their shrapnel-riddled bodies already turning pale. Luckily, Faith never saw her husband's body, but she did see his battered chopper being flown over her hospital on its way to the helicopter graveyard near Saigon. The door gunner lived but never went up in a chopper again. Seldom does the brain completely lose the terrible images that the eyes sometime send it. For Faith, the exact image of her husband's young face had faded through the years. She often gave herself grief for that, but there were just so few pictures.

* * * * *

The muffled sound of booted feet approaching snapped Faith out of her flashback. Groggily, she looked around, unable to tell exactly where she was. Her sense of awareness began to clear as she focused on a very worried-looking military figure and a three-person entourage that marched her way. From his uniform and the insignia on his shoulder, Faith determined that he was an airborne captain in the Belgium army. He wore the blue beret of the UN peacekeeping force also. She rose from the bench as he walked up and started to extend her hand but stopped when, in a voice that failed to hide his anger, he demanded.

"Who are you, madam, and what the hell do you think you are doing here?" Faith straightened her shoulders and looked the man eyeball-to-eyeball. Her five-ten height helped along with the fact that she was in no mood for strutting peacocks today. Trying to stay calm, she took a deep breath and looked at his name tag before she spoke. "Captain Brunei, my name is Faith Lee, and I'm trying very hard to do my job, and"—she looked around him at his staff—"I highly suggest that you go somewhere and do yours."

His eyes blinked a couple of times as he took in her comment and formulated a reply.

"Ma'am, my job is to get all non-Rwandan personnel"—he looked over at Faith's cameraman and his assistant before he went on—"out of this village." The two Ghanaian glanced from Faith to the captain and then back to Faith again with big worried eyes.

"That, madam, includes you and your"—he paused again as he looked at her helpers once more—"staff" he finished. The relief was evident on the smiling faces of Faith's camera crew when the Ranger included them. But Faith wasn't finished.

"Captain"—she almost spat the words—"I work for the same people that you do." She cut her sentence short but added, "Surely, you have seen the slaughter that has occurred here. My job is to document it." Although she was used to seeing the pale blue berets that the UN troops wore, she still struggled to reconcile the rifles slung across their chests with name tags that said "Peacekeepers."

"Ms. Lee," the Captain began again, having noticed the woman's name tag that rose and fell on her ample breast. "I have seen the butchery, but the Indians, as your cowboys would say, are about to attack again, and we must get out of Dallas." He almost smiled at his attempt at American slang.

"It's Dodge," she corrected as he looked at her puzzled. "Get out of Dodge, not Dallas. Anyway, the Indians of the Old West never treated children the way these little ones have been treated by the damn Interahamwe, and I damn well intend to finish documenting this … this tragedy. My report, if I can get it finished, will go to the highest levels of international diplomacy to help us stop any more slaughter of innocents." She realized she had been practically shouting as she spoke the last few words, so she slowly exhaled and fought back tears of anger.

Any sign of a smile quickly left Captain Geoff Brunei's face. He looked straight into the eyes of the American woman. *So this is the resolve, the determination that has made her country great. I like it,* he thought. Forcing back a smile, he asked, "How long, madam, will it take you to finish your work here?" She looked around at what was left to be filmed and thought for a minute.

"Twenty minutes. If you can give me twenty minutes, I believe we will have gathered all the ..." Her voice cracked as she searched for a better word than *facts.* But none came. "All the facts necessary," she concluded with a slight nod. *Facts, facts, the only damn word I can come up with to describe all this savagery is* facts? *God, help us,* she moaned to herself.

"Ms. Lee, I will do all I can to give you your twenty minutes, but remember, I have only one understrength company of very inexperienced soldiers here." Exhaling deeply, he turned and walked away, leaving Faith alone with her two helpers. They were alone in a sea of death and stench, but as she looked around, she noticed the sky was a beautiful emerald blue stretching horizon to horizon with a few cotton-like clouds floating by. The tranquil scene stood in stark contrast to the horror that lay all around her. She closed her eyes for a second, and a primal instinct stirred deep within her. Opening her eyes, she turned toward the edge of the jungle. Although she could not see them, she could feel the eyes of the Interahamwe watching. "I am not afraid of you." The words were coming out automatically and intentionally. Turning her back to the jungle, she continued recording the handiwork of the Hutu rebels.

The day gradually grew hotter, and the rebels of the Hutu tribe, known as the Interahamwe, grew bolder as they drank their local beer from large tin buckets. Within thirty minutes of Brunei's departure, they emerged from the depths of the forest in groups of twos and threes. Strutting about in a drunken state, they half hid and half lounged at the edge of the dark-green forest. No more than three hundred yards separated them from where Faith and her crew were finishing up their work. The rebels, mostly young, uneducated men and boys from the isolated villages, glared malevolently through bloodshot eyes at the inhabitants of Umkuba.

Many of the rebels carried bloodstained machetes in their hands or else simply hung across their backs with crude straps of rough rope. They waited much like vultures would wait for a calf to die before beginning their feast. They waited for the Belgium soldiers to leave so they could kill the remaining cockroaches that inhabited the village of Umkuba.

Faith was helping her cameraman roll up the last of the cords when Captain Brunei returned, red dust swirling behind the pale-blue vehicle as it sped across the field. A "peacekeepers" flag flew at the tip of the radio antennae, it too covered with the ever-present dust. The commander of the Belgian paratroopers jumped out before his driver had fully stopped and almost tripped. Regaining his balance, he briefly fumbled with his clipboard before marching up to the woman he had been ordered to remove. Faith could tell that he was more angry than before, and she braced herself for his onslaught.

"I simply cannot believe how stupid and heartless the fools back at headquarters can be," fumed Brunei as stood in the boiling sun with her hands of her hips. "They must be aware," he continued as he shook his head and tapped the clipboard against his hip, "what will happen if and when we pull out of this village." Faith stared at the man for a second before she realized what he was saying.

"Wait, back up. What do you mean *pull out*? What are you talking about?" Fear grew in the pit of her stomach as she asked the question. "Your orders were to get us out of here, not abandon the village." He stiffly handed her his clipboard, which she stared at for a second before throwing it onto the ground. Brunei looked down at the clipboard, and then back up at Faith but made no attempt to pick it up.

He took a deep breath. "We were supposed to get you and your staff and any other non-Rwandan personnel out of this village. We were to load you onto our two deuce-and-a-halves and escort you to

Kilgula. We were also supposed to keep a substantial force here to protect the village."

"I understand that," answered Faith impatiently. "So what has changed?"

"Well ..." He knelt down and retrieved the clipboard, wiping dust from his notes as he did. "Well," he began again, "Battalion has ordered my company to leave Umkuba. They say the village is too dangerous for us to remain. That its security is an internal matter." Geoff Brunei's eyes scanned the village, whose inhabitants were mostly women, children, and a few old men all nervously huddled at the entrances of their homes. Brunei's steel-gray eyes then turned toward the jungle's edge, where the rebels stared back sensing their moment was drawing near again.

Faith stared at the flustered Brunei in disbelief. "What about these poor people that have stayed?" she shouted. "You can't just leave," she repeated, "you simply cannot," her voice trailing off into a whisper. Brunei turned in a complete circle as the woman pleaded with him.

"You can't let those"—she pointed to a group of rebels lounging under a large banana tree drinking from a small bucket—"those butchers." She struggled for a more descriptive word, "Those murderers into this village." Captain Brunei straightened his shoulders and turned his eyes toward her.

"Ma'am, I have my orders," he snapped.

"Orders," she parroted. "The hell with your orders, and don't call me ma'am. You can't simply leave and let these people die."

Tears swelled in her eyes as she looked at Brunei and then at the villagers who had stepped into the street and were watching the two UN officials argue. They had been abandoned by white men before, and they sensed the struggle here involved them. The children began to cry. They could feel the tension in their mothers as they anxiously eyed the Interahamwe. Suddenly, Faith's ears caught a sound that surprised her, and she cocked her head to listen.

"What? What is it?" asked Brunei as he watched the American strain to hear the sound above the shouting of the rebels. The drunken mob had grown louder as a large middle-aged man angrily waved a machete over his head and sang an age old chant. Hatred dripped from his lips as his words helped drive the mob into a frenzy. He was a big man, and his battered army boots, blue jeans, and South African Army shirt with sleeves cut off at the shoulders made him look even bigger.

Faith listened to the dove's call echo over the area where she and Brunei stood, and a part of her wanted to escape this nightmare and fly away. But the bird didn't fly away, and neither did she. In fact, the dove flew from its perch and sailed just above her and the Belgian officer before heading for the banana tree that shaded the rebels. Faith watched the dove fly toward the rebels and unashamedly asked, "So where is your hawk, little one?" Brunei was about to ask what she was talking about when another sound filled the air, this one a loud piercing sound that seemed to shake the sky. The sound seemed too large for its source, which appeared to be a big red-tailed hawk. The winged predator flew out of the dense jungle and circled the two figures that stood alone in the big field. The hawk's fierce cry actually seemed in defiance to the shouting of the Interahamwe as it flew overhead.

"Little one, you do have help," whispered Faith in awe of what she was witnessing.

"What or who or … what's going on?" asked a very confused Captain Brunei. He glanced from the woman to the hawk and back again to the woman. His question was ignored by Faith, who was formulating a simple plan that she didn't want to call an attack plan though it was of sorts. A minute later, a smile briefly crossed her face.

"I have a plan" was all she said in explanation. *A plan that might save these people, but it might also get us all killed,* her mind shouted.

"Captain Brunei," she called his name with a new steadfastness as she looked toward the group of rebels jumping and shouting while passing around yet another jug of the local brew.

"I want to have a meeting with those rebels." Having made her request, she turned back toward him.

"I … I …" he stammered as he stared at her in disbelief. While he was trying to formulate a reply, Faith caught movement out of the corner of her eye. Her gaze turned toward the edge of the jungle just behind the orphanage's main building. Someone was watching her. She blinked from the glare of the sun but for a moment, and the smiling face of a young pilot returned her gaze. She rubbed her eyes and looked again only to see an old shaman standing under a stooping mahogany tree. The old man stared straight at her as he stomped the dusty ground and shook his crooked staff. She could see several clumps of weathered bones tied to the upper portion of the staff.

She looked back at Captain Brunei, who had given up on a proper answer to her absurd request and was busy watching the rebels. When she glanced back for the old man, he was gone. All that remained was his ironwood staff leaning against a snarled tree, which was as black as the old man himself. Brunei's voice brought her back around.

"That's impossible," he stammered. For a minute, she thought he was talking about seeing David, but she sadly realized he was referring to her request to talk to the rebels. Brunei was still shaking his head at such a nonsensical idea when he saw her start walking away toward the rebels!

"I didn't mean for you to send someone, Captain. I meant that I want to meet with them, me alone." With that said, Faith resumed what could be her last walk ever.

"Now hold on there," shouted Brunei as he began running after her. "Ms. Lee, have you gone mad? Those men will gang-rape you and then cut you up into small pieces for dog food." Faith stopped and turned to face him as he caught up to her. She never blinked as she looked him in the eye.

"I'm not so sure, Captain. I'm not sure if anyone has ever tried to talk to them. Hell, I'm not sure of anything, except the fact I must try. For the sake of these villagers, I must try something, and talking to them—with them—seems the right thing to do." She paused and looked over where the old man had stood. "I must try for the ones who have already died." Tears ran down her dusty cheeks. Her voice trembled, but her composure and resolve were steady. "And for the ones who still live. Besides"—she looked at him and shrugged—"you're leaving with your troops, and with these *facts*." She handed him the tapes she had almost forgotten she was carrying. "These must get back to the UN immediately." She put the tapes in his hand, and he looked down at them as if the blood of the dead children would run out onto the ground.

They stood in an awkward silence until Faith took a deep breath. "Isn't it strange how you can see everything more clearly when you think the end may be near?" She whispered the words as she gazed at the jungle foliage a deep green against a sky so blue and endless. Long-horned cattle grazed in the shade of several slender trees near the outskirts of the village, and a rooster crowed in the back of a nearby hut. She saw and heard all these things as she restarted her journey toward what might be a certain and very ugly death.

Geoff Brunei stood as if his feet were planted in the earth. His brain screamed, *Go after her!* at the exact moment his radio operator raced up to him.

"Captain Brunei, Captain Brunei!" the young soldier shouted as he slowed his pace to a fast walk as he neared.

"What is it, Corporal?" growled Brunei as he watched Faith walk away. "Captain, it's the colonel, and … and he's mad as hell!" The corporal whispered the last words as if his voice might carry over the airwaves even with the mike off. The nervous radio operator handed Brunei the headset, and both men could hear Colonel Mike Kanumbo's voice booming over the earpiece. Brunei stared at the mike for a second before sliding the headset over his head.

"Sir, this is Captain Brunei," announced the Belgian. He pulled the earpiece away from his ear when Kanumbo thundered.

"It's about damn time you answered my call, Captain." His harsh tone was never changing. "You, Captain, must get your people out of that village. Now, right now, do you understand me?" he shouted over the mike.

"But, sir," pleaded Brunei as he watched the American woman continue to walk toward the rebels. There was silence on Kanumbo's end for a second, so Brunei went on.

"Sir, you know the Interahamwe will move into this village the moment we leave, and we just can't allow that to happen." Brunei's head snapped back when Kanumbo's voice shouted into his ear.

"Captain, I don't have time to argue with you. I want you, your men, and that damn American woman out of that village in thirty minutes. That, Captain"—Kanumbo nearly spat the words—"is an order!"

Brunei held the headset away from his ear and looked at it again as if it were an alien thing. His head spun as he turned and watched the American draw closer to what he knew was a certain death.

With his hands down by his side, he looked around and saw that many of the villagers had huddled in small groups near the center of town. Several small children cried in their mother's arms as the old men squatted in a resolved position in front of them, stoically waiting. They knew what would happen when the soldiers left; it had happened all over their country many times. The Belgium soldiers milled around their trucks and looked expectedly over at their commander. Brunei and his First Sergeant locked eyes for a moment, and then Brunei sadly closed his.

He shook his head, took off the headset, and spoke into the mike. "Sir, I respectfully refuse that order. I will not stand down and allow these people to die without at least trying to help them. They're human beings, sir, and it's the least that we can do." He paused for a heartbeat before he went on. "That, sir, is called principle." Kanumbo was screaming now.

"Your career is over, soldier. Do you hear me? It's over if you do not ..." *Click*. Captain Geoff Brunei, with twelve years in the military and a bright future ahead of him, clicked off the radio as the colonel's angry threat hovered in the air. The young radio operator took the headset from his captain and saluted.

"Sir, the men are all with you on this. We have to help these people."

Brunei looked at his corporal a little confused, then turned and looked at the American. He snapped out of his confusion, though, when he saw how close she was to the rebels. Brunei turned back to his radio operator.

"Corporal, tell Sergeant Fowlkes to gather all the villagers into what remains of the orphanage. He can establish good perimeter there and then wait until I get back."

"Yes, sir," snapped the corporal, who started running toward the trucks. But after just a few strides, the young man stopped in his dash back to the waiting troops. Turning, he shouted to Brunei, who was running hard toward the woman.

"Sir"—he paused an uncomfortable second—"what if ..." Brunei smiled at the unasked question. "These people need your help, soldier. If I don't return, just do your best to stop any more slaughter." The two exchanged salutes and ran in different directions.

"Ms. Lee, please wait. We must talk!" Brunei shouted breathlessly as he ran after the woman. "Ms. Lee, please stop." Faith heard Brunei shouting, but she didn't want to stop. To stop now might be construed as fear by the hate-filled leadership of the group that sang their chant mostly for her benefit. Soon she heard the shrill cry of the hawk echoed over the chant, so she gradually slowed her pace to locate it. Only then did she look back at Brunei. The hawk cried again, and Faith shaded her eyes, looking up.

"No!" she shouted. "We will do this another way. This time, a peaceful way." She attempted a smile but was cut short by a new and more eerie chant that suddenly erupted from a small group of the rebels. Brunei caught up with her, and they both stood watching the Interahamwe.

"That is a different chant, Captain Brunei. The rhythm is strange. More harsh. Do you know its meaning?" Brunei struggled to catch his breath as he listened.

"It's an ancient ritual chant intended to invoke the help of the old gods in killing one's enemies," he answered with a frown.

The dove, which had been silent for a while, began its call, seemingly as a counter to the ancient chant. It remained perched on a limb just above the heads of the rebels while Faith and the Belgian captain, about fifty feet away, watched them dance and shout. A few seconds later, Brunei announced matter-of-factly, "Ms. Lee, we're not leaving." Faith closed her eyes and took a deep breath before turning to look at him, forcing a smile.

"Captain, it's about damn time somebody around here listened to me." Brunei's eyes blinked several times as he tried to understand her humor; finally, he gave up and asked nervously.

"So tell me about your plan."

Faith looked at the rebels as even more men and boys emerged from the dark shadows of the jungle.

"Um, well, I'm simply going to talk to them," answered Faith. "I'm going to ask them why they are killing these innocent people. I'm also going to ask them what we can do to help them all live together in peace. I need to know what the UN can do for them in order to help prevent more slaughter." Brunei stood with his eyes on the rebels as he waited for more information to come from the American. After a few seconds, when none came, he slowly turned his gaze toward the determined but obviously clueless woman.

"That's it, that's your plan?" he asked, his face a little pale. Faith simply nodded and looked a bit sheepishly at the Belgian. "Oh, great!" he shouted in a voice full of sarcasm and despair. "I'm sure that will work, and maybe they will just kill us for being stupid instead of simply being white." His hand eased down to feel the reassurance of the .45-caliber pistol at his side. As Brunei finished his rant, the dove perched above the chanting rebels flew to where Faith stood. The bird seemed to hover near her shoulder for several seconds before flying back toward the rebels and circling just above the banana tree. Then the hawk appeared and circled alongside the dove just above the astonished rebels.

Brunei and Faith, their hips almost but not quite touching, watched with fascination the rebels' reaction to the birds.

"I have heard that the Hutu are an extremely superstitious lot," whispered Brunei. "Maybe these birds will help your plan."

"I hope so," answered Faith as she and Brunei took the last few strides toward the rebels.

They walked up to the closest group of about twenty young fighters as a commotion in the back of the crowd caused heads to turn. A beat-up old three-quarter-ton Dodge truck rolled to a stop in a cloud of dust, and suddenly, the rebels began stepping aside, making way for a small group of men. Their leader was a huge man, about thirty years of age, and he walked straight toward Faith while totally ignoring Brunei. A bottle of foul-smelling beer was clutched in one calloused hand; and a machete, dried blood caked on its blade, was in the other. The machete looked small in the left hand of Nguma Isiahlukotuma as he stood with his legs spread wide, his bloodshot eyes boring hard into Faith's. His head was close-shaven, as was his face, and an old jagged knife scar ran across his thick neck and down his left shoulder. No emotion showed on the man's face, and Faith could see only emptiness in his eyes. She stood with her hands on her hips and tried to appear courageous while a single question kept thundering from the depths of her being. The words escaped her mouth as if on their own.

"Why?" she asked. "Why are you killing these people?"

Brunei's hand went down to grasp the butt of his .45 as the hardened leader of the Interahamwe looked down at the American as if she were a pestering insect. His eyes registered hate, but for a brief second, Faith also saw shock. Most people trembled with fear when they first encountered Isiahlukotuma but not this woman, at least not yet. As his mind spun and his anger grew, he quickly realized he would have to do more to scare her in order to gain the upper hand in this senseless meeting. He drew himself up to appear as big and menacing as possible, which was not difficult, and then looked around at his followers, who were as equally shocked at her defiance. Then he begun to laugh, a laugh that was deep and long, and soon his followers laughed with him. That was what he wanted, what he needed. Some people would call it support, but Isiahlukotuma would call it control, control of not only the situation but, most importantly, his people. After a minute, he stopped laughing and announced in a deep, well-practiced command voice.

"My name is Nguma Isiahlukotuma"—he paused and laughed again—"but everyone calls me Ike." A smile spread across his hard face, but it never entered his eyes. Then as quickly as it appeared, the smile was gone.

"And what is your name, madam?" he asked in a deep rumbling British accent, still totally ignoring Brunei's presence.

Faith was a bit taken aback by the big man's laughter and his cordial introduction, but it was his eyes that told the true story. She managed to stand her ground and even masked her fear as she spoke to what felt like an evil spirit.

"Ike, my name is Faith Lee, and I am a director with the United Nations." She watched him turn his gaze from her to Captain Brunei and then back to her.

"I need to know why you are killing all these people. Have they done you some kind of harm?" She waited for an answer, but when none came, she pressed on. "Surely, there is something we can do to help you, to aid you, and in return, we would ask for your help in stopping this senseless slaughter." He just stared down at her as she spoke.

"The peoples of this region once lived in peace with one another, did they not?" Ike scowled at her last remark as he watched her eyes. He wanted to see fear, but what he saw unsettled him. He saw courage, an almost natural but ancient courage that flowed within her veins. *This woman is dangerous*, he thought to himself as he devised a plan to gain the upper hand before he killed her.

A flutter of small wings announced the dove's return. It landed on a low-hanging branch of a banana tree and began its mournful call. Distracted and irritated, Ike scowled again.

"Kill that damn bird," he bellowed in his native Hutu, never taking his eyes off Faith. A grizzled old rebel with tattered Nike tennis shoes on his feet and an ancient shotgun in his hand, nervously stepped beside Ike and pointed the weapon skyward. The dove never moved, and the old man's finger slowly began to press against the trigger. Everyone waited for the blast, but the trigger wouldn't move. He squeezed harder and still nothing. His eyes quickly shifted from the bird to the side of the old weapon. It was then he realized the safety was on. A slight shrug of his shoulders preceded as he brought back down the shotgun, the old man not daring to look at the withering stare coming from Ike. He flipped off the safety and started to shoulder the weapon again when a primal cry pierced the air. Eight sharp talons dove out of the blue sky and raked deep into the weathered face of the unlucky rebel. The shotgun clattered to the ground as the rebel clutched his bleeding face and fell to his knees.

Blue veins bulged from the neck of the rebel leader as his glare shifted from the wounded man to the hawk that flew to settle calmly beside the dove on the limb above his head.

"Trained birds are a cruel trick for a peacemaker," spat Isiahlukotuma. His voice was loud, but he couldn't quite hide the slight quiver of ... what? *Fear*, thought Faith, *he's a little frightened.*

"Those aren't my birds, Ike," she answered, struggling to keep a smile from forming on her lips. "Maybe they are the spirits of all these innocent children you have murdered." She spoke the words softly. Ike's eyes burned with fire, but he didn't move a muscle.

"We have been run over by these cockroaches all our lives." He spat and took a long drink from his beer, throwing the empty bottle into the bushes with disgust. "It's these innocent people, as you so ignorantly call them, who have done us wrong." Many of the rebels around him, the ones who understood English, nodded in agreement, but not all.

"Tell me, Ike, you're a strong man. How did these young orphaned children wrong you?" asked Faith calmly. Sinew bulged in Ike's arms as he squeezed his machete.

"They would have grown up to be big cockroaches," he hissed, looking toward the village. The Belgian troops were quietly moving the villagers into the main building of the orphanage. He scowled. Meanwhile, Faith's mind raced in desperate search of words that could possibly reach through the hatred in Ike's heart and touch some small hidden trace of humanity still buried there.

The dove continued its calling from the banana tree, but the hawk had sprung into the air and flown deep into the forest, where the echo of its cry lingered in the shadow-draped cove. The eyes of the Interahamwe turned from the dove to Ike and then back in a nervous shift, while images of warriors and women, hawks and doves, intermingled in Faith's mind. And from somewhere deep in her soul, a female voice spoke to her, and the ancient words poured forth.

"The killing has to stop, Ike. These people want only to live in peace, just like I believe you want to live in peace. Let the killing stop now, right here in this village. You're their leader, Ike. You can make it happen. Let it be a new beginning." Her voice grew in urgency. "The people—all the people of your country—will sing your name in praises for a hundred years. Just think, Ike. You have the ability to make peace happen." She could sense that at least some of the younger rebels, especially the ones closely surrounding her and Ike, were listening. *Hope, oh, dare hope!* her soul screamed. "I, too, have the ability to help all of your country's people. I know we haven't done it right in the past, but with your help, Ike, we can get it right this time. I give you my word that I and others"—she looked over at Brunei, who was listening to her intensely as he kept an eye on the crowd—"can help create a better place for your children, for the young and old men who stand with you right now." She watched the faces of the younger Interahamwe. *God, they're only children themselves. Maybe thirteen, no more than fourteen, and they are listening.* "I know it won't be easy, Ike, but if you help me, and I help you, together we can change things." She looked the big man in the eye; the air became still, even the birds quiet, and then it came in a deep angry voice.

"Will you help us like the damn Belgians have helped us for a hundred years?" He glared at Brunei as he spoke through clenched teeth. "Will you help us like the Christian missionaries helped by destroying our old ways, laughing at our gods?" He glared at Faith for a long time; finally, as if some kind of inner decision had been made, he looked away. Glancing around, he watched as the last of the villagers were herded into the orphanage. Then he looked back at his ragged band of young warriors and slowly began to raise his hand. The bloodstained machete gleamed in the sun just as a lone ebony-skinned figure emerged from the jungle. The old shaman stood as still as the air for a moment and then began chanting an ancient song while shaking his bone-laden ironwood staff high in the air. He looked directly at Nguma Isiahlukotuma, and Ike shuddered. But the dye was already cast.

Seconds ticked by until at last Ike spoke. "Enough of this talk, woman. We don't need your damn help. We will cleanse the world of all these cockroaches and the Belgian scum along the way." His muscles grew taut as his arm drew back, intent on striking the woman who was impeding his efforts to rule his old homeland. Time seemed to slow as Faith watched, mesmerized as Ike's machete rose above her head. Out of the corner of her eye, she could see Brunei struggling to draw his pistol from a reluctant holster. She looked skyward and saw the hawk diving toward the rebel leader. She saw all this pass in a split second, and she knew that they would all be too late. Sadly, this job would go unfinished, these people's suffering unabated.

The shaman stomped his feet and shouted a chant not heard in several lifetimes when suddenly a sharp crack split the silence. The calloused hand that held the machete aloft wavered a little and the hate-filled eyes of Nguma Isiahlukotuma blinked and bulged from their sockets. After a long second, the machete slipped from his hand, and dust boiled up from where the weapon hit the ground with a thud. Ike's body contorted as he half-turned to look at the shaman, whose staff was pointed at him. The man staggered slightly but managed to turn back to look at Faith Lee. Their eyes met as the hawk and dove called from above. Ike almost smiled as he looked once again at the ancient shaman, who stared back briefly before turning and disappearing into the jungle. Ike Isiahlukotuma was dead when his face struck the ground, and the African dust settled slowly about him.

A young Interahamwe rebel approached the somewhat stunned American and Belgian. He wore only sandals and the dirty remains of a Michael Jordan T-shirt around his skinny shoulders. Cut-off blue jeans completed his uniform. A hard boyish grin briefly crossed his face before he spoke.

"Many of us believe you are right, woman. The killing must stop. It should have stopped a long time ago," he said as he glanced down at Ike's fly-covered face. "Maybe now, it can." He redirected his eyes and his words to Faith. "Thank you for your courage and your promises. We will meet with our people and the old one." He looked where the shaman had stood and then back at Faith. "If you can do what you say you can do"—he paused while he surveyed the beautiful landscape around them—"maybe this land can be peaceful again like the old one says it used to be." He paused again as a tear ran down his dark dusty cheek. "I ..." He glanced around at his band of boy warriors. "We are ready to go home." The fourteen-year-old, obvious new leader of the Interahamwe, turned toward his fellow rebels, took a half-empty bucket of beer from one older man, and poured the contents onto the ground. Tossing the bucket into the brush, he soon faded into the jungle, and slowly the others turned and followed him.

Director Faith Lee and Captain Geoff Brunei stood alone together at the edge of the field. The hawk and dove had settled beside each other on a nearby limb. The hawk was silent, but the dove cooed softly.

"Who do you think fired that shot?" asked Brunei as he fiddled with his pistol. "Was it a rifle shot, or did the old shaman take Ike down?"

"We'll probably never know," answered Faith.

Brunei thought to check his pistol again, still unsure of why it had not released moments earlier. It came out easily. He worked it in and out of the holster several times, baffled why it seemed to be stuck just a minute ago. "Well, I'll be damned," grunted Brunei.

Faith turned in a circle finally facing west and watched the sun's orange ball sink below the dark-green canopy of the jungle. She smiled at the Belgian officer and whispered, "I doubt that very much, Captain."

Tired but together, they walked back toward the village as the hawk and dove circled overhead. A light cleansing rain, unusual for this time of year, began to fall. The echo of the hawk and dove's joint cry drifted deep into the forest to settle in a small glen where an old ironwood staff leaned against a dark rock near a partly hidden path deep in an old grove.

About the Author

Tom Baker is a US Army combat veteran from the Vietnam War. He was a grunt with the 101st in Nam and a parachute rigger, and he spent most of 1968 as a door gunner with the 1/9 1st Cavalry. An Army brat, he was raised by an old brown-boot sergeant major from one of General Patton's units in the 8th Armored Division. He lives in Sylva, North Carolina, with his wife, a retired rhetoric and writing professor, whom he refers to as his chief editor and whose Air Force father flew C-130 gunships in Nam. Tom has been a forester and logger in Western North Carolina for over forty years.

CPSIA information can be obtained
at www.ICGtesting.com
Printed in the USA
FFHW021733210619
53140822-58804FF